**Also available from
Linda Lael Miller
and HQN Books**

The Carsons of Mustang Creek

Once a Rancher
Always a Cowboy

The Brides of Bliss County

Christmas in Mustang Creek
The Marriage Season
The Marriage Charm
The Marriage Pact

McKettricks of Texas

An Outlaw's Christmas
A Lawman's Christmas
McKettricks of Texas: Austin
McKettricks of Texas: Garrett
McKettricks of Texas: Tate

The Creed Cowboys

The Creed Legacy
Creed's Honor
A Creed in Stone Creek

Mojo Sheepshanks

Arizona Wild (previously
published as
Deadly Gamble)
Arizona Heat (previously
published as
Deadly Deceptions)

**And don't miss more
Carsons of Mustang Creek**
Forever a Hero

**And from
B.J. Daniels**

The Montana Hamiltons

Wild Horses
Lone Rider
Lucky Shot
Hard Rain
Into Dust
Honor Bound

Beartooth, Montana

Mercy
Atonement
Forsaken
Redemption
Unforgiven

Look for
Renegade's Pride
A Cahill Ranch Novel

LINDA LAEL MILLER

B.J. DANIELS

Heart of a
COWBOY

HQN™

HQN™

Recycling programs for this product may not exist in your area.

ISBN-13: 978-0-373-80188-6

Heart of a Cowboy

Copyright © 2017 by Harlequin Books S.A.

The publisher acknowledges the copyright holders of the individual works as follows:

Creed's Honor
Copyright © 2011 by Linda Lael Miller

Unforgiven
Copyright © 2012 by Barbara Heinlein

CONTENTS

CREED'S HONOR   7
Linda Lael Miller

UNFORGIVEN   367
B.J. Daniels

CREED'S HONOR

Linda Lael Miller

To some of my favorite Laels:
Mike and Sara and Courtney and Chandler

CHAPTER ONE

Lonesome Bend, Colorado

TRICIA McCALL WAS not the type to see apparitions, but there *were* times—especially when lonely, tired or both—that she caught just the merest flicker of a glimpse of her dog, Rusty, out of the corner of one eye. Each time that happened, she hoped for the impossible; her heartbeat quickened with joy and excitement, and her breath rushed up into the back of her throat. But when she turned, no matter how *quickly,* the shepherd-Lab-setter mix was never there.

Of course, he wasn't. Rusty had died in his sleep only six months before, contented and gray-muzzled and full of years, and his absence was still an ache that throbbed in the back of Tricia's heart whenever she thought of him. Which was often.

After all, Rusty had been her best friend for nearly half her life. She was almost thirty now, and she'd been fifteen when she and her dad had found the reddish-brown pup hiding under a picnic table at the campground, nearly starved, flea-bitten and shivering.

She and Joe McCall had debugged him as best they could, fed him and taken him straight to Dr. Benchley's office for shots and a checkup. From then on, Rusty was a member of the family.

"Meow," interrupted a feline voice coming from the general vicinity of Tricia's right ankle.

Still wearing her ratty blue chenille robe and the pink fluffy slippers her best friend, Diana, had given her for Christmas many moons ago as a joke, Tricia looked down to see Winston, a black tom with a splash of white between his ears. He was a frequent visitor to her apartment, since he lived just downstairs, with his mistress, Tricia's great-grandmother, Natty. The separate residences were connected by an inside stairway, but Winston still managed to startle her on a regular basis.

"Meow," the former stray repeated, this time with more emphasis, looking earnestly up at Tricia. Translation: *It's cat abuse. Natty McCall may* look *like a harmless old woman, but I'm being starved, I tell you. You've got to* do *something.*

"A likely story, sardine-breath," Tricia replied, out loud. "I was there when the groceries were delivered last Friday, remember? You wouldn't go hungry if we were snowed in till spring."

Winston twitched his sleek tail in a jaunty, oh-well-I-tried sort of way and crossed the small kitchen to leap up onto Tricia's desk and curl up on a tidy stack of printer paper next to the keyboard. He watched Tricia with half-closed amber eyes as she poured herself a cup of coffee and meandered over to boot up the PC. Maybe there would be an email from Hunter; that would definitely lift her spirits.

Not that she was down, exactly. No, she felt more like someone living in suspended animation, a sort of limbo between major life events. She was marking time, marching in place. And that bothered her.

At the push of a button, the monitor flared to life and there it was: the screensaver photo of her and Hunter, beaming in front of a ski lodge in Idaho and looking like—well—*a couple*. Two happy and reasonably attractive people who belonged together, outfitted for a day on the slopes.

With the tip of one finger, Tricia touched Hunter's square-jawed, classically handsome face. Pixels scattered, like a miniature universe expanding after a tiny, silent big bang. She set her cup on the little bit of desk space Winston wasn't already occupying and plunked into the chair she'd dragged away from the dinette set.

She sat very still for a moment or so, the cup of coffee she'd craved from the instant she'd opened her eyes that morning cooling nearby, her gaze fixed on the cheerfully snowy scene. Big smiles. Bright eyes.

Maybe she ought to change the picture, she thought. Put the slide show of Rusty back up. Trouble was, the loss was still too fresh for that.

So she left the ski-lodge shot where it was. She and Hunter had had a good thing going, back in Seattle, in what seemed like a previous lifetime now even though it had only been a year and a half since the passion they'd been so sure they could sustain had begun to fizzle.

As soon as she sold the failing businesses she'd inherited when her dad died—the River's Bend Campground and RV Park and the decrepit Bluebird Drive-in theater at the edge of town—she could go back to her *real* life in the art world of Seattle. Open a little gallery in the Pike Place Market, maybe, or somewhere in Pioneer Square.

Beside her, Winston unfurled his tail so the end of it brushed the back of Tricia's hand, rolled it back up again

and then repeated the whole process. Gently jolted out
of her reverie, she watched as wisps of black fur drifted
across her line of vision and then settled, with exquisite
accuracy, onto the surface of her coffee.

Tricia shoved back her chair, the legs of it making a
loud, screeching sound on the scuffed linoleum floor,
and she winced before remembering that Natty was
out of town this week, visiting her eighty-nine-year-
old sister in Denver, and therefore could not have been
disturbed by the noise.

Muttering good-naturedly, she crossed to the old-
fashioned sink under the narrow window that looked
out over the outside landing, dumped the coffee, rinsed
the cup out thoroughly and poured herself a refill.

Winston jumped down from the desktop, making
a solid thump when he landed, as he was a somewhat
rotund fellow.

Leaning back against the counter, Tricia fortified
herself with a couple of sips of the hot, strong coffee
she knew—even without Natty's subtle reminders—she
drank too often, and in excessive quantities.

Winston had been right to put in his order for breakfast, she reflected; it was her job to feed him and empty
his litter box while her great-grandmother was away.

"Come on," she said, coffee in hand, heading toward
the doorway that led down the dark, narrow stairs to
Natty's part of the house. "I wouldn't want you keeling
over from hunger."

You're not even thirty, commented a voice in her
head, *and you're talking to cats. You seriously need
a life.*

With a sigh, Tricia flipped on the single light in
the sloping ceiling above the stairs and started down,

careful because of Winston's tendency to wind himself around her ankles and the bulky slippers, which were a tripping hazard even on a flat surface.

Natty's rooms smelled pleasantly of recent wood fires blazing on the stone hearth, some lushly scented mix of potpourri and the lavender talcum powder so many old ladies seemed to favor.

Crossing the living room, which was stuffed with well-crafted antique furniture, every surface sporting at least one intricately crocheted doily and most of them adorned with a small army of ornately framed photographs as well, Tricia smiled. At ninety-one, Natty was still busy, with friends of all ages, and she was pretty active in the community, too. Until the year before, she'd been in charge of the annual rummage sale and chili feed, a popular event held the last weekend of October. Members of the Ladies' Auxiliary—the organization they'd been auxiliary *to* was long defunct—donated the money they raised to the local school system, to be used for extras like art supplies, musical instruments and uniforms for the marching band. And while Natty had stepped down as the group's chairperson, she attended every meeting.

Natty's kitchen was as delightfully old-fashioned as the rest of the house—although there was an electric stove, the original wood-burning contraption still dominated one corner of the long, narrow room. And Natty still used it, when the spirit moved her to bake.

Without the usual fire crackling away, the kitchen seemed a little on the chilly side, and Tricia shivered once as she headed toward the pantry, setting her coffee mug aside on the counter. She took a can of Winston's regular food—he was only allowed sardines on Sundays, as a special treat—from one of the shelves in the pantry, popped the top and dumped the contents into one of several chipped but still beautiful soup bowls reserved for his use.

Frosty-cold air seemed to emanate from the floor as she bent to put the bowl in front of him. Tricia felt it even through the soles of those ridiculous slippers.

While Winston chowed down, she ran some fresh drinking water and placed the bowl within easy reach. Then, hugging herself against the cold, she glanced at the bay windows surrounding Natty's heirloom oak table, half expecting to see snowflakes drifting past the glass.

A storm certainly wouldn't be unusual in that part of Colorado, even though it was only mid-October, but Tricia was holding out for good weather just the same. The summer and early fall had been unusually slow over at the campground and RV park, but folks came from all over that part of the state to attend the rummage sale/ chili feed, and a lot of them brought tents and travel trailers, and set up for one last stay along the banks of the river. The modest fees Tricia charged for camping spots and the use of electrical hookups, as well as her cut of the profits from the vending machines, would carry her through a couple of months.

Some benevolent soul could still happen along and buy the properties Joe had left her, but so far all the For Sale signs hadn't produced so much as a nibble.

Tricia sighed, watched Winston eat for a few moments, then started for the stairs. Yes, it was early, but she had a full workday ahead over at River's Bend. She'd already let the seasonal crew go, which meant she manned the registration desk by herself, answering the phone on the rare occasions when it rang and slipping away for short intervals to clean the public showers and the restrooms. After the big weekend at the end of the month, she would shut everything down for the winter.

A lump of sadness formed in Tricia's throat as she climbed the stairs, leaving the door at the bottom open for Winston as she would the one at the top. As a child, she'd loved coming to River's Bend for the summers, "helping" her dad run the outdoor theater and the campground, the two of them boarding with Natty and a series of pampered cats named for historical and/or political figures the older woman admired.

One had been Abraham; another, General Washington. Next came a redoubtable tabby, Laurel Roosevelt, and now there was Winston, for the cigar-smoking prime minister who had shepherded England through the darkest hours of World War II.

Tricia was smiling again by the time she reached her own kitchen, which was warmer. She was about to sit down at the computer again to check her email, as she'd intended to do earlier, when she heard the pounding at the back door downstairs.

Startled, Winston yowled and shot through the inside doorway like a black, furry bullet, his trajectory indicating that he intended to hide out in Tricia's bedroom, under the four-poster, maybe, or on the high shelf in her closet.

Once, when something scared him, he'd climbed straight up her living room draperies, and it had taken both her *and* Natty to coax him down again.

The pounding came again, louder this time.

"Oh, for pity's sake," Tricia grumbled, employing a phrase she'd picked up from Natty, tightening the belt of her bathrobe and moving, once more, in the direction of the stairs. She followed the first cliché up with a second, also one of Natty's favorites. "Hold your horses!"

Again, the impatient visitor knocked. Hard enough, in fact, to rattle every window on the first floor of the house.

A too-brief silence fell.

Tricia was halfway down the stairs, steam-powered by early-morning annoyance, when the sound shifted. Now whoever it was had moved to *her* door, the one that opened onto the outside landing.

Murmuring a word she definitely *hadn't* picked up from her great-grandmother, Tricia turned and huffed her way back up to her own quarters.

Winston yowled again, the sound muffled.

"I'm coming!" she yelled, spotting a vaguely familiar and distinctly masculine form through the frosted glass oval in her door. Lonesome Bend was a town of less than five thousand people, most of whom had lived there all their lives, as had their parents, grandparents and *great*-grandparents, so Tricia had long since gotten out of the habit of looking to see who was there before opening the door.

Conner Creed stood in front of her, one fist raised to knock again, a sheepish smile curving his lips. His blond hair, though a little long, was neatly trimmed, and he wore a blue denim jacket over a white shirt, along with jeans and boots that had seen a lot of hard use.

"Sorry," he said, with a shrug of his broad shoulders, when he came face-to-face with Tricia.

"Do you know what time it is?" Tricia demanded.

His blue eyes moved over her hair, which was probably sticking out in all directions since she hadn't yet brushed and then tamed it into a customary long, dark braid, her coiffure of choice, then the rag-bag bathrobe and comical slippers. That he could take a liberty like that without coming off as rude struck Tricia as— well—it just *struck* her, that's all.

"Seven-thirty," he answered, after checking his watch. "I brought Miss Natty a load of firewood, as she wanted, but she didn't answer her door. And that worried me. Is she all right?"

"She's in Denver," Tricia said stiffly.

His smile practically knocked her back on her heels. "Well, then, that explains why she didn't come to the door. I was afraid she might have fallen or something." A pause. "Is the coffee on?"

Though Tricia was acquainted with Conner, as she was with virtually everybody else in town, she didn't know him well—they didn't move in the same social circles. She was an outsider raised in Seattle, except for those golden summers with her dad, while the Creeds had been ranching in the area since the town was settled, way back in the late 1800s. Being ninety-nine percent certain that the man wasn't a homicidal maniac or a serial rapist—Natty was very fond of him, after all, which said *something* about his character—she stepped back, blushing, and said, "Yes. There's coffee—help yourself."

"Thanks," he said, in a cowboy drawl, ambling past her in the loose-limbed way of a man who was at ease wherever he happened to find himself, whether on the back of a bucking bronco or with both feet planted firmly on the ground. The scent of fresh country air clung to him, along with a woodsy aftershave, hay and something minty—probably toothpaste or mouthwash.

Tricia pushed the door shut and then stood with her back to it, watching as Conner opened one cupboard, then another, found a cup and helped himself at the coffeemaker.

Torn between mortification at being caught in her robe with her hair going wild, and stunned by his easy audacity, Tricia didn't smile. On some level, she was tallying the few things she knew about Conner Creed—that he lived on the family ranch, that he had an identical twin brother called Cody or Brody or some other cowboy-type name, that he'd never been married and, according to Natty, didn't seem in any hurry to change that.

"I'm sure my great-grandmother will be glad you brought that wood," she said finally, striving for a neutral conversational tone but sounding downright insipid instead. "Natty loves a good fire, especially when the temperature starts dropping."

Conner regarded Tricia from a distance that fell a shade short of far enough away to suit her, and raised one eyebrow. Indulged himself in a second leisurely sip from his mug before bothering to reply. "When's she coming back?" he asked. "Miss Natty, I mean."

"Probably next week," Tricia answered, surprised to find herself having this conversation. It wasn't every day, after all, that a good-looking if decidedly cocky cattle rancher tried to beat down a person's door at practically the crack of dawn and then stood in her kitchen swilling coffee as if he owned the place. "Or the week after, if she's having an especially good time."

"Miss Natty didn't mention that she was planning on taking a trip," Conner observed thoughtfully, after another swallow of coffee.

The statement irritated Tricia—since when was Conner Creed her great-grandmother's keeper? All of a sudden, she wanted him *gone,* from her kitchen, from her house. He didn't seem to be in any more of a hurry to leave than he was to get married, though.

And he was using up all the oxygen in the room.

Did he think she'd bound and gagged Natty with duct tape, maybe stuck her in a closet?

She gestured toward the inside stairway. "Feel free to see for yourself if it will ease your mind as far as Natty is concerned. And, by the way, you scared the cat."

He flashed that wickedly innocent grin again; it lighted his eyes, and Tricia noticed that there was a rim of gray around the blue irises. He had good teeth, too—white and straight.

Stop, Tricia told her racing brain. Her thoughts flew, clicking like the beads on an abacus.

"I believe you," he said. "If you say Miss Natty is in Denver, kicking up her heels with her sister, then I reckon it's true."

"Gee, that's a relief," Tricia said dryly, folding her arms. Then, after a pause, "If that's everything…?"

"Sorry about scaring the cat," Conner told her affably, putting his mug in the sink and pushing off from the counter, starting for the door. "Truth is, the critter's never liked me much. Must have figured out that I'm more of a dog-and-horse person."

Tricia opened her mouth, shut it again. What did a person say to that?

Conner curved a hand around the doorknob, looked back at her over one of those fine, denim-covered shoulders of his. Mischief danced in his eyes, quirked up one corner of his mouth. "If you wouldn't mind letting me in downstairs," he said, "I could fill up the wood boxes. There's room in the shed for the rest of the load, I guess."

Tricia nodded. She had an odd sense of disorientation, as if she'd suddenly been thrust underwater and held there, and on top of that had to translate everything this man said from some language other than her own before his meaning penetrated the gray matter between her ears.

"I'll meet you at Natty's back door," she said, still feeling muddled, as he went out.

She stood rooted to the spot, listening as the heels of Conner's boots made a rapid thunking sound on the outside steps.

Winston crept out of the short hallway leading to the apartment's one bedroom and slinked over to Tricia, purring companionably while he turned figure eights around her ankles.

Wishing she had time to pull on some clothes, fix her hair and maybe even slap on a little makeup, Tricia went back down to Natty's place, bustled through to the kitchen, turned the key in the lock and undid the chain, and wrenched open the door.

Conner was already there, standing on the porch, grinning at her. After looking her over once more in that offhand way that so disconcerted her, he shook his head slightly and rubbed the back of his neck with one hand.

"Thanks," he said, his tone husky with amusement. "I'll take it from here."

Tricia felt heat surge into her cheeks, spark in her eyes. He knew she was uncomfortable and not a little embarrassed, damn him, and he was *enjoying* it.

"I'll come back in a few minutes to lock up behind

you," she replied, ratcheting her chin up a notch in hopes of letting Conner know he wasn't getting to her.

Well, maybe he was, a little, she admitted to herself, terminally honest. But it wasn't because of the invisible charge buzzing around them. She wasn't used to standing around in her bathrobe talking to strange men, that was all.

"Fine with me," Conner answered, lifting the collar of his jacket against a gust of wind as he turned to descend the steps of Natty's back porch. His truck, large and red, with mud-splattered tires and doors, was parked alongside the woodshed.

Possessed of a peculiar and completely unreasonable urge to slam the door behind him, hard, Tricia instead shut it politely, turned on one heel and fled back upstairs to her apartment.

There, in her small bedroom, she hastily exchanged her robe and pajamas for jeans and a navy blue hooded sweatshirt, replaced the slippers with sneakers. Advancing to the bathroom—she'd had larger *closets,* she thought, flustered—Tricia washed her face, brushed her teeth and whipped her renegade hair into a tidy plait.

Intermittently, she heard the homey sound of wood clunking into the boxes beside Natty's fireplace and the old stove in the kitchen.

She nearly tripped over Winston, who was lounging in the hallway, just over the bedroom threshold.

"That," Tricia sputtered, righting herself, "is a *great* place to stretch out."

"Meow," Winston observed casually, flicking his tail and giving no indication that he planned on moving anytime soon. He was quite comfortable where he was, thank you very much.

Tricia took a moment to collect her wits—why *was* she rushing around as though the place were on fire, anyway?—smoothing her hands down the thighs of her jeans and drawing in a deep, slow breath.

Consuming a carton of low-fat yogurt for breakfast, she stood on tiptoe to look out the window over her kitchen sink, which afforded her a clear view of the backyard.

And she forgot all about reading her email.

AFTER HE'D FILLED Miss Natty's wood boxes, making sure she had plenty of kindling, Conner unloaded the pitch-scented pine—a full cord—stacking it neatly in the shed. With that done, he could check the delivery off his mental to-do list and move on to the next project— stopping by the feed store for a dozen fifty-pound bags of the special mix of oats and alfalfa he gave the horses. When he finished that errand, he'd head for Doc Benchley's office to pick up the special serum for the crop of calves born that spring. Doc had served as the town's one and only veterinarian since way back.

Unlike a lot of people in his profession, Hugh Benchley didn't specialize. He treated every animal from prize Hereford bulls to Yorkshire terriers small enough to fit in a teacup, and had no evident intention of retiring in the foreseeable future, even though he was well past the age when his fellow senior citizens preferred to spend their days fishing or patronizing the flashy new casino out on the reservation.

"I won't last six months from the day I close my prac- tice," Doc had told Conner more than once.

Conner understood, since he thrived on work him- self—the more physically demanding, the better. That way, he didn't have time to think about things he wished were different—like his relationship, if you could call it that, with his twin brother, Brody.

Dusting his leather-gloved hands together, the last of the wood safely stowed for Miss Natty's use, he started for the driver's-side door of his truck. Something made him look up at the second-story window, a feeling of prickly sweetness, utterly strange to him, and he thought he saw Tricia McCall peering through the glass.

Wishful thinking, he told himself, climbing into the rig.

He'd seen Tricia lots of times, usually at a distance, but close-up once or twice, too.

How was it that he'd never noticed how appealing Natty's great-granddaughter was, with her fresh skin and her dark, serious eyes? She had a trim little body—he'd figured that out right away, her sorry bathrobe notwithstanding—and just standing in the same room with her had put him in mind of an experience when he and Brody were kids. Nine or ten and virtually fearless, they'd dared each other to touch the band of electric fence separating the main pasture from the county road that ran past the ranch.

It had been raining until a few minutes earlier, and they were both standing in wet grass. The jolt had knocked them both on their backsides, and once they'd caught their breath, they'd lain there laughing, like the pair of fools they were.

Because any memory involving Brody tended to be painful, the good ones included, Conner avoided them when he could. Now, as he shifted the truck into gear and eased out of Miss Natty's gravel driveway, his thoughts strayed right back to Tricia like deer to a salt lick.

He signaled a right turn at the corner, heading for Main Street, and the feed store.

As a kid, he recalled, Tricia had spent summers in Lonesome Bend with her dad. Shy, she'd kept to herself, sticking to Joe's heels as he went happily about his business. Even then, the run-down drive-in theater, with its bent screen, had been a losing proposition, and the campground hadn't been much better.

Like all his friends, Conner had gone swimming at River's Bend every chance he got, but he didn't remember ever seeing Tricia so much as dip a big toe into the water. She'd sit cross-legged and solemn on the dock, always wearing a hand-me-down swimsuit, with a towel rolled up under one arm, and watch the rest of them, though, as they splashed and showed off for each other.

At the time, it was generally agreed that Tricia McCall was a little weird—probably because her parents were divorced and lived in different states, an unusual situation in those days, in Lonesome Bend if not in the rest of the country.

Since his older cousin, Steven, split his time between the ranch and a mansion back in Boston, neither Tricia nor her situation had struck Conner as strange—she was just quiet, liked to keep to herself. He'd been mildly curious about her, but nothing more. After all, she always left town at the end of August, the way Steven did, turning up again sometime in June.

Drawing up to the feed store, Conner pulled into the parking lot and backed the truck up to one of two loading docks. He shut off the engine, got out of the rig and vaulted up onto the platform to help with the bags, stacked and waiting to be collected.

And still Tricia lingered in his mind.

As a teenager, Tricia continued to visit her dad every summer, and she went right on marching to her own private drumbeat, too. The popular girls had declared her a snob, a snooty city girl who thought she was too good for a bunch of country kids. But she was wearing some guy's class ring on a chain around her neck, Conner recollected, and he'd steered clear because he figured she was going steady.

And because he'd been bone-headed crazy about Joleen Williams, the platinum blonde wild child with the body that wouldn't quit.

Somebody elbowed Conner, and that brought him back to the here and now, pronto. Malcolm, Joleen's half brother and a classmate of Conner's since kindergarten, grinned as he pushed past with a bag of horse feed under each arm. "Clear the way, Creed," Malcolm teased, his round face red and sweaty with effort and a penchant for triple cheeseburgers and more beer than even Brody could put away. "People are trying to *work* here."

Conner grinned and slapped his friend on the back in greeting. The day was cool and crisp, but the sun was climbing higher into a sky blue enough to make a man's heart catch, and the aspen trees, lining the streets of Lonesome Bend and crowding the foothills all around it, were changing color. Splashes of bright crimson and gold, pale yellow and rust, and a million shades in between, blazed like fire everywhere he looked.

"How've you been, Malcolm?" he asked, because in small towns people always asked each other how they were, even if they'd seen each other an hour before at the post office or the courthouse or the grocery store. Moreover, they cared about the answer.

"I was fine until you showed up," Malcolm answered, tossing the feed bags into the bed of the pickup and turning to go back for more. "What kind of fancy horses are you keeping out on that ranch these days, anyhow? Thoroughbreds, maybe? This stuff costs double what the generic brand runs, and I swear it's heavier, too."

Conner laughed and hoisted a bag. "Maybe you ought to sit down and rest," he joked. "It would suck if you had a heart attack right here on the loading dock."

"It would suck if I had a heart attack *anyplace*," Malcolm countered, continuing to load the truck. "Hell, I'm only thirty-three."

Conner, sobered by the picture the conversation had brought to mind, didn't answer.

"You heard about Joleen?" Malcolm asked, when they'd finished piling the bags in the back of the truck.

Conner jumped down to level ground and put up the tailgate on his rig with more of a bang than the task probably called for. He'd been over Malcolm's sister for years, but any mention of her always stuck in his craw. "What about her?" he asked, looking up at Malcolm, who stood rimmed in dazzling sunlight on the loading dock like some overweight archangel.

"She's coming back to Lonesome Bend," Malcolm answered. His tone was strange. Almost cautious.

"No offense, Malcolm," Conner replied, "but I couldn't care less."

Malcolm was quiet for a moment. Then, in a rush of words, he added, "You want this feed put on your bill, as usual?"

"That'll be fine," Conner said, opening the door of

his truck and setting one booted foot on the running board, about to climb behind the wheel. "Thanks, Malcolm."

"Conner?"

Halfway into the rig, Conner ducked out again. Malcolm had shifted his position, and his features were clearly visible now. He wasn't smiling.

"What?" Conner asked.

Malcolm sighed heavily, swept off his billed cap and dried the back of his neck on one shirtsleeve. "She's with Brody," he said, as though it pained him. "I guess they've been—seeing each other."

Everything inside Conner went still. It was as if the whole universe had ground to a halt all around him.

Finally, he found his voice. "I guess that's their business," he said, flatly dismissive, "not mine."

CHAPTER TWO

THE WIND RUFFLED the surface of the river, placid enough where it nestled in the tree-sheltered bend, the stony beach curving easy around it, like a cowboy's arm around his girl's shoulders, but wilder out in the middle. There, the currents were swift and, a mile downriver, there were rapids, leading straight to the falls.

Every so often, some hapless soul would be swept away in a canoe or even an inner tube, and find himself rushing at top speed toward a seventy-five-foot drop over the waterfall and onto the jagged boulders below.

It was a miracle nobody had been killed, Tricia thought, pulling her jacket more tightly around her and surveying the rocky shore in front of her. The area was littered with crushed beer cans, cigarette butts and fast food wrappers—kids had been partying there again.

Sighing, Tricia pulled a pair of plastic gloves from her pocket and snapped them on, then unfolded the large trash bag she'd tucked into the waistband of her jeans. There were No Trespassing signs posted, of course, but they seemed to have no more effect that the ones that read For Sale.

She picked up all the aluminum cans first—those were destined for the recycling bin—then collected the rest of the trash, using a smaller bag.

Tricia liked being outside, chilly as it was, under

that blue, blue sky, breathing in the singular scents of autumn, though cleaning up after thoughtless people wasn't her favorite chore. It would be a nice day for a bonfire, she reflected, bending to retrieve a potato chip bag that looked as though it had been chewed up right along with its contents.

It was then that she made eye contact with the dog.

Nestled beneath the very same picnic table where she and Joe had found Rusty all those years ago was a painfully thin mutt with burrs and twigs caught in its coat and sorrow in its liquid brown eyes.

"Hey," Tricia said, dropping to her knees.

The dog whimpered, tried to scoot out of her reach when she moved to touch him.

"It's okay," she murmured. She tried to harden her heart a little, but it remained tender. "I won't hurt you, buddy."

Resting on her haunches, her hands on her thighs, Tricia studied the animal carefully. He was probably yellow under all that dirt, she concluded, though there would be no way to know for sure until he'd been cleaned up a little. Since he wasn't wearing a collar, let alone ID tags, Tricia never seriously entertained the idea that some anxious pet owner was out there somewhere, searching frantically for the family dog.

She extended one hand cautiously, still wearing the plastic gloves, though they wouldn't protect her from a bite. The poor creature snarled feebly in warning.

Tricia drew back. "No worries," she said gently. "Wait here, and I'll bring you something to eat."

She got to her feet and headed for the log building that housed the office and a couple of vending machines, tossing the trash bags into a Dumpster as she passed it, the gloves following quickly behind.

Inside the tiny space, measuring no more than twelve by twelve in its entirety, a fire burned in the Franklin stove, exuding pleasant warmth, and the varnish on the front of the big rustic reception counter bisecting the room reflected the dancing flames.

For just a moment, Tricia paused, feeling a pang of regret at the prospect of moving away. This place had seen a lot of happy times in days gone by—families eager to camp out in a tent, cook their meals under the sky, swim in the calm inlet of the river. As eager as she was to sell everything and return to Seattle for good, letting go would be hard.

Shaking off the spell, she rounded the counter, took her purse from one of the shelves underneath it and scrabbled around in the bottom of the bag for the change she continually tossed in. Maybe she'd get one of those little plastic coin holders, the kind that gaped open like a grin when you squeezed either end. For now, though, the slapdash method had to do.

When she had a palm full of quarters, dimes and nickels, Tricia approached the vending machine. Chester, the man who ran the route, dropping sandwiches and candy bars and snack-size bags of chips into the slots, hadn't been around recently. It was the end of the season, and the pickings were slim.

She finally decided on a ham sandwich, sealed inside a carton with a see-through top—the edges of the bread were curling up—dropped the appropriate number of quarters into the slot and pushed the button. The sandwich clunked into the tray.

Tricia studied it with distaste, then sighed and

marched herself toward the door. Outside, she peeled back the top of the container, and walked back to the picnic table.

A part of her had been hoping the dog would be gone when she got back, she realized as she knelt again, but of course he was right there where she'd left him. He raised his head off his outstretched forelegs and sniffed tentatively at the air.

Tricia smiled, broke half the sandwich in two and held out a portion to the dog.

He hesitated, as though expecting some cruel trick—the world clearly hadn't been kind to him—then decided to chance it. He literally wolfed down the food, and Tricia gave him more, and then more, in small, carefully presented chunks, until there was nothing left.

"Come out of there," Tricia coaxed, fallen leaves wetting the knees of her jeans through and through, "and I'll buy you another sandwich."

The dog appeared to consider his—or her—options.

Tricia stood up again, backed off a few feet and called for a second time.

A frigid wind blew in off the river and seeped into her bones like a death chill. She longed for hot coffee and the radiant coziness of the fire in the Franklin stove, but she wasn't going to leave the dog out here alone.

It took a lot of patience and a lot of persuasion, but the poor little critter finally low-crawled out from under the picnic table and stood up.

Definitely a male, Tricia thought. Probably not neutered.

"This way," she said, very softly, turning and leading the way toward the structure her dad had euphemistically referred to as "the lodge." The dog limped along behind her, head down, hip bones and ribs poking out as he moved.

Tricia's heart turned over. Was he a lost pet or had someone turned him out? Dropped him off along the highway, thinking he'd be able to fend for himself? That happened way too often.

The dog crossed the threshold cautiously, but the heat of the stove attracted him right away. He teetered over on his spindly legs and collapsed in front of it with a deep sigh, as though he'd come to the end of a long and very difficult journey.

Tears stung Tricia's eyes. There was no animal shelter in Lonesome Bend, though Hugh Benchley, the veterinarian, kept stray dogs and cats whenever he had room in the kennels behind his clinic. His three daughters, who all worked for him, made every effort to find homes for the creatures, and often succeeded.

But not always.

Those who didn't find homes ended up living on the Benchleys' small farm or, when they ran out of room, in one of the shelters in nearby Denver.

This little guy might be one of the lucky ones, Tricia consoled herself, and wind up as part of a loving household. In the meantime, she'd give him another vending machine sandwich and some water. Most likely, he'd been drinking out of the river for a while.

While the dog ate the second course, Tricia called Dr. Benchley's office to say she was bringing in a stray later, for shots and a checkup. It went without saying that a permanent home would be nice, too.

Becky, Doc's eldest daughter, who kept the books for her father's practice and did the billing at the end of the month, picked up. Fortyish, plump and happily married to the dairy farmer on the land adjoining the Benchleys', Becky had a heart the size of Colorado itself, but she sighed after Tricia finished telling her what little she knew about the dog's condition.

"It never stops," Becky said sadly. "We're bulging at the seams around here as it is, and at Dad's place, too, and Frank says if I bring home one more stray, he's going to leave me."

Frank Garson adored his wife, and was unlikely to leave her for any reason, and everybody knew it, but Becky had made her point. Bottom line: there was no room at the inn.

"Maybe I could keep him for a little while," Tricia said hesitantly. Then she blushed. "The dog, I mean. Not Frank."

Becky laughed, sounding more like her old self, but still tired. Maybe even a little depressed. "That would be good."

"But not forever," Tricia added quickly.

"Still not over losing Rusty?" Becky asked, very gently. As a veterinarian's daughter, she was used to the particular grief that comes with losing a cherished pet. "How long's it been, Tricia?"

Tricia swallowed, watching as the stray got to his feet and stuck his muzzle into the coffee can full of water, lapping noisily. "Six months," she said, in a small voice.

"Maybe it's time—"

Tricia squeezed her eyes shut, but a tear spilled down her right cheek anyway. "Don't, Becky. Please. I'm not ready to choose another dog."

"We don't choose animals," Becky said kindly. "They choose us."

She couldn't possibly be expected to understand, of

course. As soon as a real-estate miracle happened—and Tricia had to believe one *would* or she'd go crazy—she'd be moving away from Lonesome Bend, probably living in some condo in downtown Seattle, where only very small dogs were allowed.

She swallowed again. Dashed at her cheek with the back of her free hand. The canine visitor knocked over the coffee can, spilling what remained of his water all over the bare wooden floor. "Be that as it may—"

"How's eleven-thirty?" Becky broke in, brightening. "For the appointment, I mean?"

Tricia guessed that would be fine, and said so.

She hung up and hurried into the storage room for a mop, and the dog cowered as she approached.

Tricia's heart, already pulverized by Rusty's passing, did a pinchy, skittery thing. "Nobody's mad at you, buddy," she said softly. "It's all okay."

She swabbed up the spilled water and made a mental note to stop off at the discount store for kibble and bowls and maybe a pet bed, preferably on sale, since the trip to the vet was bound to cost a lot of money. The dog—he needed a name, but since giving him one implied a commitment she wasn't willing to make, *the dog* would have to do—could live right here at the office until other arrangements could be made.

Taking him home, like naming him, would only make things harder later on. Besides, Winston would probably take a dim view of such a move, and then there was the matter of seeing another dog in all the places where Rusty used to be.

She did wish she hadn't been in such a hurry to give Rusty's gear away, though. She could have used that stuff right about now.

The dog looked up at her with an expression so hopeful that the sight of him wrenched at something deep inside Tricia. Then he meandered, moving more steadily now that he'd eaten, over to the vending machine. Pressed his wet nose to the glass.

Tricia chuckled in spite of herself. "Sorry," she said. "No more stale sandwiches for you."

He really seemed to understand what she was saying, which was crazy. The similarities between finding Rusty and finding—well, *the dog*—were getting to her, that was all, and it was her own fault; she was letting it happen.

She brought him more water, and this time, he didn't tip the coffee can over.

Gradually, they became friends, a three steps forward, two steps back kind of thing, and while Tricia doubted he'd tolerate being scrubbed down under one of the public showers, he did let her remove the twigs and thistles from his coat.

At 11:15, she hoisted him into the backseat of her secondhand blue Pathfinder without being bitten in the process. A good omen, she decided. Things were looking up.

Maybe.

Doc Benchley's clinic was housed in a converted Quonset hut left over from the last big war, with an add-on built of cinder blocks. As buildings went, it was plug-ugly, maybe even a blight on the landscape, but nobody seemed to mind. Folks around Lonesome Bend appreciated Doc because he'd come right away if a cow fell sick, or a horse, whether it was high noon or the middle of the night. He'd saved dozens, if not hundreds, of dogs and cats, too, along with a few parrots and exotic lizards.

He drove his ancient green pickup truck through snowstorms that would daunt a lesser man and a much better vehicle, and once or twice, in a pinch, he'd treated a human being.

Distracted, Tricia didn't notice the other rigs in the clinic's unpaved parking lot; she wanted to borrow a leash and a collar before she brought the dog inside, in case something spooked him and he took off. And she was totally focused on that.

She fairly collided with Conner Creed in the big double doorway; his arms were full of small boxes and he was wearing a battered brown hat that cast shadows over his facial features.

"Sorry," she said, after gulping her heart back down into its normal place. Nearly, anyway.

He said something in reply—maybe "Excuse me"— but Tricia had already started to go around him, unaccountably anxious to get away.

Becky stood behind the counter, wearing colorful scrubs with pink cartoon kittens frolicking all over the fabric, holding out the leash and collar without being asked. Her eyes sparkled as she looked at Tricia, then past her, to Conner.

"Thanks," Tricia said.

She turned around, and Conner had disappeared. Her relief was exceeded only by her disappointment.

All for the best, she told herself firmly. *It's not as if you're in the market for a man. You've got Hunter, remember?* Never mind that she hadn't seen or even spoken to Hunter lately.

Outside, Conner was just turning away from his

truck, where he'd stowed the boxes he'd been carrying before. He adjusted his hat, giving her another of those frank assessments he seemed to be so good at.

"Need help?" he asked, at his leisure.

Tricia realized that she'd stopped in her tracks and made herself move again, but color thumped in her cheeks. "I can manage," she said.

Conner approached, nonetheless, and when she opened one of the Pathfinder's rear doors, he eased her aside. "Let me," he said, taking the leash and collar from her hand. He lifted the panting dog out of the vehicle and set him down, offering the leash to Tricia. "What's his name?"

"I call him *the dog*," Tricia said.

"Imaginative," Conner replied, with another of those tilted grins.

Tricia bristled. "He's a stray. I found him hiding under one of the picnic tables at River's Bend, just this morning."

What all this had to do with naming or not naming the animal Tricia could not have said. The words just tumbled out of her mouth, as though they'd formed themselves with no input at all from her brain.

"So you're leaving him here?" Conner asked. His grin lingered, but it wasn't as dazzling as before, and his voice had a slight edge.

"No," Tricia said. She'd just gotten her feathers smoothed down, and now they were ruffled again. "He'll be staying at the office until I can find him somewhere to live."

She'd hoped that would satisfy Conner and he'd go away, but he didn't. He dropped to his haunches in front of the dog and stroked its floppy ears.

"A name doesn't seem like too much to ask," the rancher said mildly.

Tricia tugged at the leash, to no real avail. "We'll be late," she fretted. As if she had anything to do for the rest of the day except clean restrooms at the campground. "Come on—dog."

Conner stood up again. He towered over Tricia, so her neck popped when she tilted her head back to look into his face.

She liked shorter men, she reflected, apropos of nothing. Hunter, at five-eight, was tall enough. *Perfect,* in fact. He was the perfect man.

If you didn't mind being ignored most of the time.

Or if you set aside the fact that he didn't want children. Or that he didn't like animals much.

"He'll be here at the clinic awhile," Conner said, ostensibly referring to the dog. "Have lunch with me."

Tricia blinked. She didn't know what she'd expected, if indeed she'd expected anything at all, but it hadn't been an invitation to lunch. Was this a date? The thought sent a small, shameful thrill through her.

"Natty's a good friend of mine," Conner went on, adjusting his hat again. "And since you and I seem to have started off on the wrong foot, I thought—"

"We haven't," Tricia argued, without knowing why. The strange tension between them must have made her snappish. "Started off on the wrong foot, I mean."

Again, that slow grin that settled over her insides like warm honey. Agitated, she tugged at the leash again and this time, the dog was willing to follow her lead. Relieved, she made her way to the doors.

But Conner came right along with her. He was a persistent cuss—she'd say that for him.

"My, my," Becky said, rounding the desk to take the leash from Tricia but looking all the while at the dog. "I see a bath in your future," she told him. Then, meeting Tricia's gaze, she added, "We're looking at an hour and a half at the least. More likely, two. Dad's schedule is packed."

The dog whined imploringly, his limpid gaze moving between Tricia and Conner, as though making some silent appeal. *Please don't leave me.*

She'd better toughen up, Tricia thought. And now was the time to start.

"Mr. Creed and I are going to lunch," she heard herself say, in a perfectly ordinary tone of voice, and was amazed. "I'll check back with you later on."

"Good idea," Becky agreed, with a little twinkle.

Just as Conner had done earlier, the woman crouched to look into the dog's eyes. "Don't you be scared, now," she said. "We're going to take good care of you, I promise."

He licked her face, and she laughed.

"Hey, Valentino," Becky said. "You're quite the lover."

Valentino, Tricia thought.

Oh, God, he had a name now.

But as Becky rose and started to lead the dog away, into the back, he made a sound so forlorn that Tricia's eyes filled.

"We have your cell number on file, don't we?" Becky turned to ask Tricia, who was still standing in the same place, feeling stricken. "You haven't changed it or anything?"

"You have it," Tricia managed to croak. She felt Conner take a light hold on her elbow. He sort of steered her toward the doors, through them and out into the parking lot.

"Lunch," he reminded her quietly.

Her cell phone chirped in her purse, and she took it out, looked at the screen, and smiled, though barely. There was a text from Diana's ten-year-old daughter, Sasha. "Hi," it read. "Mom let me use her phone so I could tell you that we're on a field trip at the Seattle Aquarium and it's awesome!"

Tricia replied with a single word. "Great!"

"No sense in taking two rigs," Conner commented.

The next thing Tricia knew, she was in the passenger seat of his big truck, the cell phone in her pocket.

It's just lunch, she told herself, as they headed toward the diner in the middle of town. Except for the upscale steakhouse on the highway to Denver, Elmer's Café was the only sit-down eating establishment in Lonesome Bend.

All the ranchers gathered there for lunch or for coffee and pie, and the people who lived in town liked the place, too. It was continually crowded, but the food was good and the prices were reasonable. Tricia occasionally stopped in for a soup-and-sandwich special, sitting at one of the stools at the counter, since she was always alone and the tables were generally full.

Today, there was a booth open, a rare phenomenon at lunchtime.

Tricia wondered dryly if the universe *always* accommodated Conner Creed and, after that, she wondered where in the heck *that* thought had come from.

Conner took off his hat and hung it on the rack next to the door, as at home as he might have been in his own kitchen. He nodded to Elmer's wife, Mabel, who was the only waitress in sight.

Mabel, a benign gossip, sized up the situation with a

good, hard look at Tricia and Conner. A radiant smile broke over her face, orangish in color because of her foundation, and she sang out, "Be right with you, folks."

Conner waited until Tricia slid into the booth before sitting down across from her and reaching for a menu. She set her cell phone on the table, in case there was another communiqué from Sasha, or a call from Doc Benchley's office about Valentino. Then she extracted a bottle of hand sanitizer from her bag and squirted some into her palm.

Conner raised an eyebrow, grinning that grin again.

"You can't be too careful," Tricia said, sounding defensive even to herself.

"Sure you can," Conner replied easily, reaching for a menu.

Tricia pushed the bottle an inch or so in his direction. He ignored it.

"There are germs on everything," she said, lowering her voice lest Mabel or Elmer overhear and think she was criticizing their hygiene practices.

"Yes," Conner agreed lightly, without looking up from the menu. "Too much of that stuff can compromise a person's immune system."

Tricia felt foolish. Conner was a grown man. If he wanted to risk contracting some terrible disease, that was certainly his prerogative. As long as he wasn't cooking the food, what did she care?

She dropped the bottle back into her purse.

Mabel bustled over, with a stub of a pencil and a little pad, grinning broadly as she waited to take their orders.

Tricia asked what kind of soup they were serving that day, and Mabel replied that it was cream of broccoli with roasted garlic. Her own special recipe.

Women in and around Lonesome Bend were recipe-proud, Tricia knew. Natty guarded the secret formula for her chili, a concoction that drew people in droves every year when the rummage sale rolled around, claiming it had been in the family for a hundred years.

Tricia ordered the soup. Conner ordered a burger and fries, with coffee.

Then, as soon as Mabel hurried away to put in the order, he excused himself, his eyes merry with amusement, and went to wash his hands.

Tricia actually considered making a quick exit while he was gone, but in the end, she couldn't get around the silliness of the idea. Besides, her SUV was still over at the veterinary clinic, a good mile from Elmer's Café.

So she sat. And she waited, twiddling her thumbs.

Damn, Conner said silently, addressing his own reflection in the men's-room mirror. It was no big deal having a friendly lunch with a woman—it was broad daylight, in his hometown, for God's sake—so why did he feel as though he were riding a Clydesdale across a frozen river?

Sure, he'd been a little rattled when Malcolm told him Brody and Joleen were on their way back to Lonesome Bend, but once the adrenaline rush subsided, he'd been fine.

Now, he drew a deep breath, rolled up the sleeves of his shirt and hit the soap dispenser a couple of times. He lathered up, rinsed, lathered up again. Smiled as he recalled the little bottle of disinfectant gel Tricia was carrying around.

Of course there was nothing wrong with cleanliness, but it seemed to Conner that more and more people were phobic about a few germs. He dried his hands and left the restroom, headed for the table.

Tricia sat looking down at the screen on her cell phone, and the light from the window next to the booth rimmed her, caught in the tiny hairs escaping that long, prim braid of hers, turning a reddish gold.

Conner, not generally a fanciful man, stopped in midstride, feeling as though something had slammed into him, hard. Like a gut punch, maybe, but not unpleasant.

Get a grip, he told himself. Out of the corner of his eye, he saw Mabel and everybody at the counter looking at him.

Pride broke the strange paralysis. He slid into the booth on his side, and was immediately struck again, this time by the translucent smile on her face. He'd never seen anybody light up that way—Tricia's eyes shone, and her skin glowed, too.

"Good news?" he asked.

She didn't look at him, but he had a sinking feeling the text was from a guy.

"Very good news," she said. Her gaze lingered on the phone for a few more moments—long ones, for Conner—and then, with a soft sigh, she put the device down again.

Conner waited for her to tell him what the good news was, but she didn't say anything about it.

"Do you have a dog?" she asked Conner.

Momentarily tripped up by the question, he had to think before he could answer. "Not at the moment," he said.

"Maybe you'd like one?"

Mabel arrived with their food, and Conner flirted

with the older woman for a few seconds. "Maybe," he said, very carefully, when they were alone again. "Sometime."

"Sometime?"

"We're pretty busy out on the ranch these days," he told her, picking up a French fry and dunking it into a cup of catsup on the side of his plate. "A dog's like a child in some ways. They need a lot of attention, right along."

Belatedly, Tricia took up her spoon, dipped it into her soup and sipped. He could almost *see* the gears turning in her head.

"Dogs are probably happier in the country than anywhere else," she ventured, and her eyes were big and soulful when she looked at him. He felt an odd sensation, as if he were shooting down a steep slope on a runaway toboggan.

"Plenty of townspeople have dogs," he said, once he'd caught his breath. He knew damn well what she was up to—she wanted him to take Valentino off her hands—but he played it cool. "Even in big cities, you see every size and breed walking their owners in the parks and on the sidewalks."

Some of the color in her cheeks drained away, and he could pinpoint the change in her to the millisecond—it had happened when he said "big cities."

"I wouldn't want to keep a dog shut up in an apartment or a condo all day, while I was working," she said. Even though she spoke casually, there was a slight tremor in her voice. "Not a big one, anyway."

He thought of that morning, when he'd poured himself a cup of coffee in her kitchen above Miss Natty's place. Her apartment *had* looked small, but he didn't think she'd been referring to her present living quarters.

Suddenly Conner remembered all those For Sale signs. Of course—Tricia was planning to leave town when she finally sold the campground and the RV park and that albatross of a drive-in theater. These days, when folks wanted to see a movie, they downloaded one off the net, or rented a DVD out of a vending machine. Or drove to Denver to one of the multiscreen "cina-plexes."

Conner cut his burger in half and picked up one side. He'd been hungry—breakfast time rolled around early on a ranch, and he hadn't eaten for hours—but now his appetite was a little on the iffy side.

"You planning on leaving Lonesome Bend one of these days?" he asked, when he thought he could manage a normal tone of voice. As far as he knew, the properties she'd inherited from her dad weren't exactly attracting interest from investors—in town or out of it.

She glanced at her phone again, lying there next to the salt and pepper shakers and the napkin holder, and a fond expression softened her all over. A little smile crooked one side of her mouth. "Yes," she answered, and this time she looked straight into his eyes.

"When?" he asked, putting down his burger.

"As soon as something sells," she said, her gaze still steady. "The campground, the RV park, the drive-in— whichever. Of course, I'd like to get rid of all three at once, but even one would make it possible."

"I see," Conner said. Why should it matter to him that this woman he barely knew was ready to get out of Dodge? He couldn't answer that, yet it did matter.

Then she smiled in a way that turned his brain soft. "Now, about the dog…"

CHAPTER THREE

TRICIA WAS GETTING nowhere with Conner Creed and she knew it. The dog wasn't going to have a home on the range—not the *Creed* range, anyway.

"I'd better get back to the clinic and pick up my car," she said, watching as Mabel removed their plates and silverware from the table and hurried away at top speed as though she thought she was interrupting something. "I have things to do while Doc Benchley is treating Valentino."

It was dangerous, saying the name, actually giving voice to it. She might start caring for the dog now, and where would that lead? To another fracture of the heart, that's where.

Conner paid for their lunches, shaking his head in the negative when Tricia offered to chip in, and they left the diner, headed for the parking lot where his truck was parked. He held the door for her while she climbed in, like the gentleman he probably wasn't.

He was quiet during the drive back to the clinic, even a little cool.

"Thanks for lunch," she told him when they drew up alongside her Pathfinder, getting her keys out of her purse and unsnapping her seat belt.

Conner was wearing his hat again; he simply tugged at the brim and said, "You're welcome," the way he might have said it to the meter reader from the electric company or a panhandler expressing gratitude for a cash donation.

Tricia got out of the truck, shut the door.

Conner nodded at her and waited until she was behind the wheel of her own rig, with the engine running. Then he backed up, turned around and drove away.

Why did she feel sad all of a sudden? To cheer herself up, Tricia pulled her phone from its special pocket in her purse and pressed one of the buttons. Hunter's smiling face appeared on the screen, along with the message he'd texted earlier.

I miss you. Let's get together—soon.

Tricia waited to be overtaken by delight and excitement—hadn't she been missing Hunter for a year and a half, yearning to "get together" with him?—but all she felt was a strange letdown that seemed to have more to do with Conner Creed than the man she believed she loved. Weird.

There was no figuring it out, she decided with a sigh. She put the phone away and went over her mental shopping list as she headed for the big discount store where a person could buy pretty much anything.

The dog beds weren't on sale, but she found a nice, fluffy one for a decent price and wadded it into her cart. On top she piled a small bag of kibble, two large plastic bowls, a collar and a leash and, because she didn't want Valentino to feel lonely when she left him at the office for the night, she sprang for a toy—a blue chicken with a squeaker but no stuffing—to keep him company.

There were a few other things Tricia needed to pick up, but none of them were urgent and her cart was full, so she wheeled her way up to the long row of checkout counters and got in line.

Twenty minutes later—a woman ahead of her paid for a can of soup with a credit card—she drove back to the campground office with her purchases, arranging the bed in front of the woodstove and hauling the kibble to the storeroom, where she opened it and filled the bowls—one with food and one with water.

She set them carefully within reach of the dog bed, adjusted everything and was finally satisfied that the arrangement looked welcoming. As the finishing touch, Tricia removed the price tag from the blue chicken and laid the toy tenderly on the bed, the way she might have set out a teddy bear for a child.

"There," she said aloud, though there was nobody around to hear. Talking to herself—she had definitely been alone too much lately, she decided ruefully, especially since Natty had left to visit her sister.

Conner popped into her mind, but Tricia blocked him out—with limited success—and told herself to think about Hunter instead. In the end, she had to bring up the phone picture again just to remember what Hunter looked like.

And even then the image didn't stick in her mind when she looked away.

NOT GOOD, CONNER thought when he pulled in at the ranch and saw Davis, his uncle, waiting in the grassy stretch between the ranch house and the barn. Davis's expression would have said it all, even if he hadn't been pacing back and forth like he was waiting for a prize calf to be born.

"What?" Conner asked, once he'd stopped the truck, shut it down and stepped out onto the running board.

Davis was an older version of his son, Steven, with the same dark blond hair and blue eyes. He was a little heavier than Steven, and his clothes, like Conner's, weren't fancy. He was dressed for work.

Steven had a ranch of his own now, down in Stone Creek, Arizona, not to mention a beautiful wife, Melissa, a six-year-old son named Matt and another of those intermittent sets of twins, both boys, that ran in the Creed family.

In fact, if Conner hadn't loved Steven like a brother—had the same strong bond with his cousin that he'd once shared with Brody—it would have been easy to hate him for having more than his share of luck.

"Did you get the serum?" Davis asked, as though Conner were on an urgent mission from the CDC, carrying the only known antidote to some virus fixing to go global.

Conner gave his uncle—essentially the only father he'd ever known, since his own, Davis's older brother, Blue, had died in an accident when Conner and Brody were just babies—a level look. "Yeah," he answered, "I got the serum. Didn't know it was a rush job, though."

Davis sighed, rummaged up a sheepish smile. "We've still got plenty of daylight left," he said. "Kim and I had words a little while ago, that's all. She put my favorite boots in the box of stuff she's been gathering up to donate to the rummage sale. I took issue with that—they're good boots. Just got 'em broken in right a few years ago—"

Conner laughed. Kim, Davis's wife, was a force of nature in her own right. And she'd been a mother figure to her husband's orphaned twin nephews, never once acting put upon. It was a shame, Conner had always thought, that Kim and Davis had never had any children together. They were born parents.

"I reckon it would be easier to buy those boots back at the rummage sale than argue with Kim," Conner remarked, amused. The woman could be bone-stubborn; she'd had to be to hold her own in that family.

"We won't be here then," Davis complained. "I've got half a dozen saddles ready, and we'll be on the road for two weeks or better."

"I remember," Conner said, opening a rear door and reaching into the extended-cab pickup for the boxes of serum he'd picked up at Doc Benchley's clinic. There were still a few hours of daylight left; if they saddled up and headed out right away, they could get at least *some* of the calves inoculated.

So Conner thrust an armload of boxes at Davis, who had to juggle a little to hold on to them.

"You'll be here, though," Davis went on innocently. "You could buy those boots back for me, Conner, and hide them in the barn or someplace—"

Conner chuckled and shook his head. "And bring the wrath of the mom-unit down on my hapless head? No way, Unc. You're on your own with this one."

"But they're lucky boots," Davis persisted. "One time, in Reno, I won $20,000 playing poker. *And I was wearing those boots at the time.*"

"We're doomed," Conner joked.

"That isn't funny," his uncle said.

Davis and Kim lived up on the ridge, in a split-level rancher they'd built and moved into the year Brody and Conner came of age. Because Blue had been the elder of the two, the firstborn son and therefore destined to inherit the spread, the ranch belonged to them.

Conner occupied the main ranch house now, and since Brody was never around, he lived by himself.

He hated living alone, eating alone and all the rest. He frowned. There he went, thinking again.

"Everything all right?" Davis asked, looking at him closely.

"Fine," Conner lied.

Davis was obviously skeptical, but he didn't push for more information, as Kim would have done. "Let's get out there on the range and tend to those calves," he said. "As many as we can before sunset, anyhow."

"You ever think about getting a dog?" Conner asked his uncle, as they walked toward the barn. "Old Blacky's been gone a long time."

Davis sighed. "Kim wants to get a pair of those little ankle biters—Yorkies, I guess they are. She's got dibs on two pups from a litter born back in June—we're supposed to pick the critters up on this trip, when we swing through Cheyenne."

It made Conner grin—and feel a whole lot better— to imagine his ultramasculine cowboy uncle followed around by a couple of yappers with bows in their hair. Davis would be ribbed from one end of the rodeo circuit to the other, and he'd grouse a little, probably, but deep down, he'd be a fool for those dogs.

Reaching the barn, they took the prefilled syringes Conner had gotten from Doc Benchley out of their boxes and stashed them in saddlebags. They chose their horses, tacked them up, fetched their ropes and mounted.

Once they were through the last of the gates and on the open range, Davis let out a yee-haw, nudged his gelding's sides with the heels of his boots, and the race was on.

VALENTINO LOOKED LIKE a different dog when Becky brought him out into the waiting area, all spiffy. His coat was a lovely, dark honey shade, and when he spotted Tricia, he immediately started wagging his tail. She'd have sworn he was smiling at her, too.

"See?" Becky bent to tell him. "I told you she'd come back."

Tricia felt a stab at those words—she was only looking after this dog temporarily, not adopting him—but when she handed over her ATM card to pay the bill, she got over the guilt in short order.

Good heavens, what had Doc done? Performed a kidney transplant?

Taking Valentino's new collar and leash from her bag, Tricia got him ready to leave. While she was bending over him, he gave her a big, wet kiss.

"Eeeew," she fussed, but she was smiling.

"Looks like we're due for a change in the weather," Becky commented, nodding her head toward the big picture window looking out over the parking lot and the street beyond. She sighed. "I guess it's typical for this time of year. Winter will be on us before we know it."

Tricia had noticed the dark clouds rolling in to cover the blue, but she hadn't really registered that there was a storm approaching. She'd been thinking about Valentino, and Hunter's text message—and Conner Creed.

"Let's hope the snow holds off until after the big rummage sale and the chili feed," Tricia said, her tone deceptively breezy. If the weather was bad, the campers and RVers wouldn't show up for that all-important final weekend of the season, and if *that* happened, she was going to have to dip into her savings to pay the bills.

"Amen to that," Becky said, but her old smile was back. She leaned down to pat Valentino's shiny head.

"Aren't you the handsome fella, now that you've had a bath?" she murmured.

A light sprinkle of rain dappled the dry gravel in the parking lot, raising an acrid scent of dust, as Tricia and Valentino hurried toward the Pathfinder. She opened the rear hatch and was about to hoist the dog inside when he leaped up there on his own, nimble as could be.

"You *are* pretty handsome," Tricia told him, once she'd gotten behind the wheel and turned the key in the ignition. She'd just buckled her seat belt when the drizzle suddenly turned into a downpour so intense that the windshield wipers couldn't keep up, even on their fastest setting.

Thunder boomed, directly over their heads, it seemed, and Valentino gave a frightened yelp.

"We're safe, buddy," Tricia said gently, looking back over one shoulder.

The dog stood with his muzzle resting on the top of the backseat, looking bravely pathetic.

"Now, now," she murmured, in her most soothing voice, "you're going to be fine, I promise. We're just going to sit right here in the parking lot until the storm lets up a little, and then we'll go back to the office and you can eat and drink out of your new bowls and sleep on your new bed and play with your new blue chicken—"

Tricia McCall, said the voice of reason, *you are definitely losing it.*

Another crash of thunder seemed to roll down out of the foothills like a giant ball, and that was it for Valentino. He sprang over the backseat, squirmed over the console and landed squarely in Tricia's lap, whining and trembling and trying to lick her face again.

That was the bad news. The good news was that even though there was more thunder, and a few flashes of lightning to add a touch of Old Testament drama, the rain stopped coming down so hard.

After gently shifting Valentino off her thighs and onto the passenger seat, Tricia put the SUV in gear and went slowly, carefully on her way.

Valentino, panicked before, sat stalwartly now, probably glad to be up front with Tricia instead of all alone in the back.

"You're not going to make this easy, are you?" she asked the dog, as they crept along the rainy streets with the other traffic.

Valentino made that whining sound again, low in his throat.

"I'll take that as a no," Tricia said.

They got back to River's Bend in about twice the time it would normally have taken to make the drive, and by then, the rain was pounding down again. Tricia parked as close to the office door as she could, but she and Valentino both got wet before they made it inside.

Shivering and shedding her jacket as she went, Tricia headed straight for the stove and added wood to the dwindling fire inside.

Valentino sniffed his kibble bowl and drank some water, then went back to the kibble again. There was more thunder, loud enough to raise the roof this time, and flashes of lightning illuminated the angry river out past the safety ropes that were supposed to keep swimmers within bounds.

Tricia wondered how Winston was faring, back at the house; he didn't like loud noises any more than Valentino did, and the poor cat was all alone at home, probably terrified and hiding under a bed. He'd want his supper pretty soon, too, she thought, biting her lip as she stood looking out at the storm. Winston liked his routine.

She turned from the window and smiled as Valentino gulped the last of his kibble ration, washing it down with the rest of the water. Then he inspected the bed, sniffed the blue chicken, and turned three circles before giving a big yawn and curling up for a snooze.

Tricia refilled his water dish at the restroom sink and put it back in place, then checked the office voice mail, hoping for a few reservations for the last weekend of the month, but there had been no calls.

Resigned, she fired up the outdated computer she used at work, and waited impatiently while it booted up. The black Bakelite office phone with a rotary dial rang while she was waiting.

Over by the fire, Valentino began to snore.

Smiling a little, Tricia checked the screen on her phone, saw Diana's number and answered with a happy "Hello!"

"You'll never guess," said Diana. A smashing redhead, Diana had been the most popular girl in high school and probably college, too. She was smart and outgoing, then as now, and she was the best friend Tricia had ever had.

"What?" Tricia asked, leaning on the back of the counter and grinning. "You won the lottery? Paul's been elected president by secret ballot? Sasha is bored with fifth grade and signing up for law school?" Paul was Diana's husband; the two had been happily married since they were nineteen.

"Better," Diana replied, laughing. "Paul got that promotion, Tricia. We'll be moving to Paris for *at least two years*—Sasha will *love* it, and we've already found the perfect private school for her." Diana, a teacher, home-schooled Sasha, not to keep her out of the mainstream but because the child had a positively ravenous capacity for absorbing information. "The French school is famously progressive. Of course, we have to go over there as soon as possible, to look for an apartment…"

It was a dream come true, and Tricia was happy for her friend, and happy for Paul and Sasha—she truly was. But Paris was so far away. She could hardly get to Seattle these days. How was she supposed to visit France?

"That's…great…." she managed.

"You'll come over often," Diana said quickly. She was perceptive; that was one of the countless reasons she and Tricia were so close.

"Right," Tricia said doubtfully.

Valentino's snores reached an epic crescendo and then started to ebb.

Diana went on. "Paul and I were hoping—well—that Sasha could stay with you while we're away, check-ing out real estate. Paul's folks would look after her, but they're traveling in Australia, and mine—well, you know about my parents."

Diana's mother had a drinking problem, and her dad went through life on autopilot. Letting them babysit Sasha was out of the question.

Tricia closed her eyes. She loved Sasha but, frankly, the responsibility scared her to death. What if the ad-venturous ten-year-old got hurt or sick or, God forbid, *disappeared?* It happened; you couldn't turn on the TV or the radio without hearing an Amber alert. "Okay," she said. "Sure."

"Don't be too quick to agree," Diana said, with a smile in her voice. "We'll be gone for two weeks."

Tricia swallowed. "Two weeks?" The words came out sounding squeaky. "What about her schoolwork? Won't she get behind?"

"Sasha is way ahead on her lessons," Diana assured her. "Two weeks will be a nice break for her, actually."

"You don't want to take her to Paris?"

Diana chuckled. "It's a long flight, especially from the West Coast. We'd rather she didn't have to make that round-trip twice. Besides, we don't get that many opportunities for a romantic, just-the-two-of-us getaway."

"Two weeks," Tricia mused aloud, then blushed because she'd only meant to think the words, not *say* them.

This time Diana laughed. "Feel free to say no," she said sincerely. "I know you're busy with whatever it is you do down there in Colorado. Paul can go to Paris alone—he's perfectly capable of choosing an apartment that will suit us—and I'll stay here in Seattle with Sasha."

Affection for her friend, and for Sasha, warmed Tricia from the inside. Made her forget about the driving rainstorm she had to drive through to get home, for the moment at least. "Nonsense," she said. "Paul is real-estate challenged and you know it. Remember the time he almost bought that mansion with the rotting floors and only half a roof? I'll be *glad* to have my goddaughter visit for two weeks." She paused. "Unless you'd rather I came over there."

"Sasha's never been to Colorado," Diana said gently. "She'll love it. You do have room for her, don't you?"

The apartment had one bedroom, but the living room couch folded out. "Of course I do," Tricia responded.

"It's settled, then," Diana said.

"It's settled," Tricia agreed, already starting to look forward to Sasha's visit. The child was delightful and Tricia adored her.

"So what do you hear from the biggest loser these days?" Diana asked.

Tricia sighed. That was Diana's nickname for Hunter, whom she had never liked, though, to her credit, she'd always been polite to him. "I had a text from him today, as a matter of fact," she replied lightly. "He misses me."

"I'll just bet he does," Diana said dryly.

"Diana," Tricia replied, good-naturedly but with the slightest edge of warning.

"When were you planning to rendezvous?" Diana asked, with genuine concern. "Are Paul and I messing up your love life by dumping our brilliant, well-behaved and incomparably beautiful child on you, Trish?"

What love life? Tricia wanted to ask, but she didn't.

"Hunter and I have waited this long," she said practically. "A few more weeks won't matter. And I can't wait to see Sasha."

"You're a good friend," Diana said.

"So are you," Tricia replied. Okay, so Diana wasn't Hunter's greatest fan. She didn't really know him, that was all. She was protective of all her friends, especially the ones who had been painfully shy in high school, like Tricia.

"Trish—"

Tricia tensed, sensing that Diana was about to say something she didn't want to hear. "Yes?"

Diana sighed. "Nothing," she said. When she went

on, the usual sparkle was back in her voice. "Listen, I'll make Sasha's flight arrangements and email her itinerary to you. I suppose she'll fly into Denver. Is that going to be a problem for you? Getting to the airport, I mean?"

Tricia smiled. "No, Mother Hen," she said. "It will *not* be a problem."

Diana really *was* a mother hen, but not in an unhealthy way. She liked taking care of people, but she knew when to back off, too. She'd learned that the hard way, she'd once confided in Tricia, courtesy of her profoundly dysfunctional parents. "All right, then," Diana said. There was another pause. "By the way, do you have plans for Thanksgiving? Paul doesn't have to start his new job until after New Year's, so you could join us in Seattle—"

Valentino stretched, got to his feet and went to press his nose against the door, indicating that he wanted to go out.

Point in his favor, Tricia thought. *He's house-trained.*

"Thanksgiving is Natty's favorite holiday," she reminded Diana, crossing to open the door for Valentino. "We always spend it together."

Standing on the threshold, Tricia noted that the rain had slowed again, but the sky looked ready to pitch a fit.

Valentino went out, showing no signs of his previous phobia.

Tricia remained in the doorway, keeping an eye on him, the phone still pressed to her ear.

"I knew you'd say that," Diana said.

Tricia laughed. It was still midafternoon, but thanks to the overcast sky and the drizzle, she had to squint to see Valentino. "It's always good to be invited," she said.

The dog lifted his leg against one end of a picnic table and let fly.

The conversation wound down then, to be continued online, with email and instant messaging.

Tricia said goodbye to her friend and put down the phone before going back to the open door and squinting into the grayish gloom.

There was no sign of the dog.

"Valentino!" she called, surprised by the note of panic in her voice.

Just then, he rounded the row of trash receptacles, trotting merrily toward her and wearing a big-dog grin.

By the time Tricia left for home an hour later, Valentino was sound asleep on his new bed. She carefully banked the fire, made sure he had plenty of water and an extra scoop of kibble in case he needed a midnight snack. She'd been dreading the moment she had to leave him, but he didn't seem concerned.

She promised she'd be back first thing in the morning and, apparently convinced, Valentino stretched on his cozy bed and closed his eyes.

DAVIS AND CONNER rode back toward home with a hard rain beating at their backs and soaking their clothes. They'd managed to rope and tie at least a dozen calves, injecting each of them with serum before letting them up again.

In the barn, they unsaddled their horses and brushed the animals down in companionable silence.

"You sure you won't buy those boots back for me?" Davis asked, with a tilted grin that reminded Conner of Steven and made him feel unaccountably lonesome.

"At the rummage sale, I mean? You're not really all that scared of a little bitty thing like Kim—"

Conner rustled up a grin. "Nope," he admitted. "I'm not scared of Kim. But I *do* have some pride. You think I want the whole town of Lonesome Bend knowing I bought your broken-down old boots?"

Davis chuckled, sweeping off his hat and running a wet shirtsleeve over his wet face. "Since when do you give a damn what the 'whole town' thinks about anything?"

Conner rested a hand briefly on his uncle's shoulder. "You go on home," he said. "Change your clothes before you come down with pneumonia or something. I'll finish up here."

"Kim thought you might want to come over for supper tonight," Davis ventured. He and Kim worried about him almost as much as they did Brody. "She's making fried chicken, mashed potatoes and gravy—"

Conner's mouth watered, but the idea of cadging a meal from the people who'd raised him, though it was an offer he would have gladly accepted most times—especially when his favorite foods were being served—didn't sit so well on that rainy night. "No, thanks," he said.

He wanted a hot shower, a fire in the wood-burning stove that dated back to homestead days, and something to eat, the quicker and easier to cook, the better.

Those things, he could manage. It was the *rest* of what he wanted that always seemed just out of reach: a woman there to welcome him home at night, the way Kim welcomed Davis. Not that he'd mind if she had a career—that would probably make her more interesting— as long as she wanted a family eventually, as he did…

"Conner?" Davis said.

He realized he'd been woolgathering and blinked. "Yeah?"

"You sure you don't want to have supper with us?"

"I'm sure," Conner said, turning away from Davis, silently reminding himself that he had horses to feed. "Go on and get out of here."

Davis sighed, hesitated for a long moment and then left.

Moments later, Conner heard his uncle's truck start up out front. He went back to thinking about his non-existent wife while he worked—and damn if she didn't look a little like Tricia McCall.

WINSTON SAT ON a windowsill in the kitchen, looking out at the rain. The wind howled around the corners of Natty's old house, but the cat didn't react; it took thunder and lightning to scare him.

And there hadn't been any since Tricia had arrived home, taken a quick shower to ease the chill in her bones and donned sweatpants and an old T-shirt of Hunter's. Every light in the room was blazing, and she'd even turned on the small countertop TV—something she rarely did. That night, she felt a need for human voices, even if they did belong to newscasters.

Tricia couldn't help thinking about Valentino, alone at the office, and when she managed to turn off the flow of *that* guilt-inducing scenario, Conner Creed sneaked into her mind and wouldn't leave.

"I know what you're thinking," she told Winston, opening the oven door to peer in and check on her dinner, a frozen chicken potpie with enough fat grams for three days. "That I should be eating sensibly. But tonight, I want comfort food."

Winston made a small, snarly sound, and his tail bushed out. He pressed his face against the steamy glass of the window and repeated insistently, *"Reowww—"*

Tricia frowned as she shut the oven door. And that was when she heard the scratching.

Winston began to pace the wide windowsill like a jungle cat in a cage. His tail was huge now, and his hackles were up.

Again, the scratching sound.

Tricia went to the door, squinting as she approached, but there was no one on the other side of the glass oval.

"What on earth—?" She opened the door and looked down.

Valentino sat on the welcome mat, drenched, gazing hopefully up at her.

"How did you get here?" Tricia asked, stepping back and, to her private relief, not expecting an answer.

Valentino's coat was muddy, and so were his paws. He walked delicately into Tricia's kitchen, as though he were worried about intruding.

Winston, to her surprise, didn't leap on the poor dog with his claws bared, despite all that previous pacing and tail fluffing. He simply sat on his sleek haunches as Tricia closed the door and began grooming himself.

Valentino plunked down in the middle of the floor, dripping and apologetic.

Tricia's throat tightened, and her eyes burned. Somehow, he'd gotten out of the office, and then found his way through town and straight to her door.

She bent to pat his head. "I'll be right back with a towel," she told him. "In the meantime, don't move a muscle."

CHAPTER FOUR

WITHIN THREE SHORT DAYS, during which the rainstorms dwindled and finally passed, leaving the scrubbed-clean sky a polished, heartrending shade of blue, Valentino charmed his way into Tricia's affections and even won Winston over.

Of course she was still telling herself the Valentino arrangement was temporary that Saturday morning, and she wrote her festive mood off to her lifelong love of autumn and the fact that she would be meeting Sasha's plane in a couple of hours. She'd been in regular contact with Hunter, though mostly by email, because he was so busy getting ready for a big show at a new gallery on Bainbridge Island. Also, it didn't hurt that virtually every camping spot and RV space was booked for the following weekend—*plus* a big group had reserved the whole campground for a Sunday barbecue.

The deposits had fattened Tricia's bank account considerably, and thus it was with figurative change jingling in her jeans that Tricia loaded Valentino into the back of the Pathfinder a few minutes after 10:00 a.m. and set out for the Denver airport.

She put on a Kenny Chesney CD as soon as she cleared the city limits—this was the only context in which Lonesome Bend, population 5,000, was ever referred to as a "city"—so she and Valentino could rock out during the drive.

Kenny's voice made her think of Conner Creed, though, and she switched it off after the third track, annoyed. Shouldn't it be *Hunter* she had on her mind? Hunter she imagined herself dancing with slow and close to the jukebox in some cowboy bar? After all, she hadn't seen Conner since their lunch date.

Hunter, on the other hand, had invited her to join him on a cruise to Mexico the week between Christmas and New Year's, going so far as to buy the tickets and forward them to her as an attachment to one of his brief, manic emails.

Remembering that, she frowned. She was—thrilled. Who wouldn't be? It was just that he hadn't consulted her first, had just assumed she'd be willing to drop everything—or worse yet, that she didn't have any holiday plans in the first place—meet him at LAX on Christmas night, and board the ship the next morning.

She knew a sunny, weeklong respite from a Colorado winter would be welcome when the time came and, besides, all that merry-merry, jing-jing-jingling stuff always gave her a low-grade case of the blues. Sure, she had Natty to celebrate with, but the music and the decorations and the lights and the rest of it made her miss her dad so keenly that her throat closed up, achy-tight. Joe McCall had loved Christmas.

To her mother, Laurel, December 25 was a nonevent at best and an orgy of capitalistic conspicuous consumption at worst. A skilled trauma nurse, too-busy-for-her-own-daughter Mom was always in the thick of some international disaster these days—floods in Pakistan, earthquakes in China, tsunamis in the Pacific, mudslides in South American countries whose names and borders changed with every political coup.

Suffice it to say, Laurel and Tricia weren't all that close, especially now that Tricia was a grown-up. To be fair, though, except for her parents' quiet divorce when she was seven, and all the subsequent schlepping back and forth between Colorado and Washington state, her childhood had been a fairly secure one. Until Tricia started college, Laurel had stayed right there in Seattle, working at a major hospital, making the mortgage payments on their small condo without complaint, and showing up for most of her only child's parent-teacher conferences, dance recitals and reluctant performances in school plays.

If there had been a coolness, a certain distance in Laurel's interactions with Tricia, well, there were plenty of people who would have traded places with her, too, weren't there? So what if she'd been a little lonely when she wasn't staying with Joe and Natty in Lonesome Bend?

She'd had a home, food, decent clothes, a college education.

Not that Laurel considered a BA degree in art history even remotely useful. She'd recommended nursing school, at least until one of those Bring Your Kid to Work things rolled around when Tricia was thirteen. Laurel had been in charge of Emergency Services then, and it was a full moon, and Tricia was so shaken by the E.R. experience, with all its blood and screaming and throwing up, that she'd nearly been admitted herself.

Even now, though, on the rare occasions when they Skyped or spoke on the phone, Laurel was prone to distracted little laments like, "It would be different if you were an *artist*—your degree would make some kind of *sense* then—" or "You *do* realize, don't you, that this Hunter person is just using you?"

Tightening her hands on the steering wheel, Tricia shook off these reflections, determined not to ruin a happy day by dwelling on things that couldn't be changed. Better to concentrate on the road to Denver, and Sasha's much-anticipated visit.

Valentino, meanwhile, sat quietly in the back, watching with apparent interest as mile after flat mile rolled past the Pathfinder's windows. He was good company, that dog. No trouble at all.

When they reached the airport, and she rolled a window down partway and promised she'd be back before he knew she'd even been gone, he settled himself in for a midmorning nap.

Tricia locked the rig and headed for the nearest bank of elevators, checking her watch as the doors slid open and she stepped inside. Sasha was scheduled to land in less than half an hour.

So far, so good.

THE BIG TOUR BUS rolled up the dusty road to the Creed ranch house just before noon, and the sight of it made Conner smile. The monstrosity belonged to Steven's wife Melissa's famous brother, the country-western singer Brad O'Ballivan, and there was an oversize silhouette of his head painted on one side, along with the singer's name splashed in letters that probably could have been read from a mile away, or farther.

Davis and Kim had postponed their own road trip as soon as they learned that the Stone Creek branch of the family had decided on a spur-of-the-moment visit, and they were standing right next to Conner, grinning from ear to ear at the prospect of seeing their three grandchildren.

Conner, just as pleased as his aunt and uncle were, had nevertheless been waiting for the proverbial other shoe to drop ever since he'd learned that Brody was headed home, with Joleen Williams in tow. Several days had gone by since Malcolm had broken the news on the loading dock at the feed store, and there'd been no sign of David and Bathsheba in the interim, but Conner remained on his guard just the same. Brody *would* show up in Lonesome Bend, if not on the ranch, that was a given; it was only a question of when.

The Bradmobile came to a squeaky-braked stop in between the main ranch house and the barn, and the main door opened with a hydraulic *whoosh*. Six-year-old Matt and his faithful companion, a dog named Zeke, if Conner recalled correctly, burst through the opening.

Sparing a grin for his "Uncle Conner" as he dashed straight past him, the little boy hurtled off the ground like a living rocket, and Davis, laughing, caught the child in his arms.

"Hey, boy," he said.

Steven got out of the bus next, turning to extend a hand to his spirited wife, Melissa, a pretty thing with a great figure, a dazzling smile and a law degree.

"Where are those babies?" Kim demanded good-naturedly.

Smiling, Melissa put a finger to her lips and mouthed the word *Napping*.

Steven approached, shaking his father's hand and then turning to look at Conner. "Any word from Brody?" Steven asked.

Conner stiffened, a move that would have been imperceptible to most people, but Steven knew him too well to miss any nuances, however subtle. "Now, why would you ask me that, cousin?" Conner retorted.

Steven's nonchalant shrug didn't fool Conner, because the nuance thing worked two ways. "He told Melissa and me he might be headed this way," he said. "That was a week ago, at least. I figured he'd be here by now."

"He might be in town someplace," Conner allowed, his tone casual. "Staying under the radar."

Steven gave a snortlike chuckle at that. "As if Brody Creed has *ever* stayed under the radar," he replied. His eyes were watchful, and gentle in a way that made Conner wary of what would come next. "You know he and Joleen hooked up somewhere along the line, right?"

Conner cleared his throat, watching as Kim and Melissa crept into the tour bus for a glimpse of the six-month-old twins, Samuel Davis, called Sam, and Blue, named for Conner and Brody's dad. Davis, Matt and the dog were headed for the barn, because Matt had a serious addiction to horses.

"Yeah," Conner said belatedly, and his voice came out sounding huskier than he'd meant it to. "I heard." He displaced his hat, shoved splayed fingers through his hair and sighed. "Why does everybody seem to think I'm going to have to be talked in off some ledge because Brody and Joleen are up to their old tricks?"

Steven rested a hand on Conner's shoulder and squeezed. "'Everybody' doesn't think any such thing," he said quietly. "It's a long way in the past, what happened. Maybe far enough that you and Brody could lay the whole thing to rest and get on with it."

Conner made a derisive sound. "I'm sure that's what he wants, all right," he said sarcastically. "Why else would he be bringing Joleen with him?"

Steven sighed. Dropped his hand from Conner's shoulder. "This is Brody we're talking about," he reminded his cousin. "My guess would be, he figures bygones are bygones after all this time."

Kim and Melissa emerged from the bus, each of them carrying a bundled-up baby and beaming. Conner wondered if Kim had "accidentally" awakened the twins from their naps.

"That is some bus," he said, shaking his head. "If I didn't know better, I'd think you wanted to attract as much attention as possible, cousin."

Steven laughed. "We've stirred up some interest at gas stations and rest stops between here and Stone Creek," he admitted. "But as soon as folks realize Brad O'Ballivan isn't going to pop out and strum a few tunes on his guitar, they leave us alone."

Kim and Melissa went on by, headed for the house with the babies, and Steven ducked into the bus, returning moments later with a fold-up gizmo that might have been either a portable crib or a playpen.

The sight gave Conner a pang, and he wasn't very proud of himself, knowing that what he was feeling was plain old envy.

Steven had a ranch and a wife and, now, kids. Pretty much everything Conner had ever hoped to have himself.

Steven read Conner's expression as he passed. "Let's get inside," he said easily. "It's colder than a well-digger's ass out here and, besides, we've got a lot to catch up on."

A FEMALE FLIGHT attendant escorted Sasha out into the arrivals area.

"That's her!" Sasha whooped, pointing at Tricia and practically jumping up and down. "That's my Aunt Tricia!"

Beaming, Tricia opened her arms. The flight attendant smiled, watching as the child, bespectacled and pigtailed, clad in a pink nylon jacket, a sweater and little jeans with the flannel lining showing at the cuffs, left her carry-on bag and ran into Tricia's hug at top speed.

"I got to sit in first class!" Sasha announced, when Tricia and the flight attendant had had a brief exchange, the purpose of which was to verify Tricia's identity. "I was next to a man who kept clearing his sinuses!"

Tricia chuckled. "Yuck," she commented.

Sasha grasped the handle of the carry-on and jabbed at her smudged glasses where the wire rims arched across her tiny, freckled nose. "We don't even have to stop at baggage claim," she informed Tricia proudly. "All my stuff is right here in this suitcase. Mom said I didn't need to bring my whole wardrobe since you probably have a washer and dryer."

"There's a set downstairs, in my great-grandmother's section of the house," Tricia said, taking Sasha's free hand and leading her toward the first of several moving walkways. "Do you need to use the restroom or anything?"

Sasha shook her head, making her light brown pigtails fly again. "I did that on the plane," she said. "There wasn't even a line in first class."

"Wow," Tricia said. "What about food? Are you hungry?"

Sasha grinned up at her. Her permanent teeth were coming in, too big for her face. She'd be a beauty when she got older, Tricia knew, just like Diana, but right now, she was headed into an awkward stage. "Aunt Tricia," she said patiently, "I was in *first class*."

Tricia laughed again. "So you mentioned," she teased.

On the way to the parking garage, Sasha chattered on about the upcoming move to Paris, and how she'd be attending a *real* school over there, with other kids and different teachers for different classes and everything, because her mom and dad had been able to find one that could provide "the necessary academic challenges." Homeschooling was okay, she stressed to Tricia, but it would be fun to ride buses and have a school song and all that stuff.

Tricia listened in delight, though a part of her was already missing Sasha and Diana and Paul, which was silly, when they hadn't actually moved yet.

When they reached the Pathfinder, Valentino was standing with his nose pressed to the window on the rear hatch, steaming up the glass.

"You *have a dog!*" Sasha crowed, obviously thrilled by the discovery. "You actually got another dog!"

"Not exactly," Tricia said, but Sasha didn't hear her. She was totally focused on Valentino.

Tricia unlocked the doors and lifted the hatch, fielding Valentino with one hand, so he wouldn't jump out of the vehicle and hurt himself, and hefting up Sasha's surprisingly heavy bag with the other.

Sasha tried to scramble into the back with Valentino, and Tricia stopped her. It was only then that she realized she didn't have a booster seat for the child to ride in. Feeling incredibly guilty, she helped Sasha onto the backseat and waited while she buckled up.

"In Washington," Sasha informed her cheerfully, "I have to use a booster seat. It's against the law not to."

It's against the law here, too, Tricia thought ruefully, rummaging up a smile. "We'll stop and buy one first thing," she said.

"What's the dog's name?" Sasha asked, straining to pat his head, when Tricia was behind the wheel, belted in, and ready to head out.

"Valentino," Tricia answered, wondering if she ought to explain that she was just keeping him until she could find him a good home and deciding against the idea in the next instant. Sasha wouldn't understand.

When the time came, Tricia thought sadly, neither would Valentino.

"Doesn't he need to get out of the car before we go?" Sasha inquired, ever practical. She got that from her dad; Diana was smart, but impulsive.

"We'll hit the first rest stop," Tricia promised.

"What if he can't wait?" Sasha fretted.

"He's a good boy," Tricia said, driving slowly along the aisle leading to the nearest exit. "He'll wait."

"Not if he *can't*," Sasha said.

"Sash," Tricia said gently. "He'll be okay."

"He doesn't look anything like Rusty," the little girl observed, after a short silence, while Tricia was stopped at the pay window, handing over her ticket and the price of parking.

The remark gave Tricia a bittersweet feeling, a combination of affection for the child and grief for Rusty. "No," she said softly, as they pulled away. "He's not Rusty."

"That's okay," Sasha said earnestly, evidently addressing Valentino. "Rusty was a *really nice dog,* but you're nice, too."

Tricia smiled, though her eyes stung a little.

They stopped at the first shopping center they passed and took Valentino on a little tour of the grassy dividers in the parking lot before settling him in the Pathfinder again and dashing into a chain store, hand in hand, to buy a proper booster seat.

Though Tricia was at a loss, Sasha knew the layout of the store from visiting the branch nearest her home in Seattle, and she went straight to the section with car seats. Once the purchase was made and they were back at the car again, they wrestled the bulky seat out of its box, laughing the whole time, and it was Sasha who showed Tricia how the various straps and buckles worked.

She had a booster seat just like it, she said.

A store employee, rounding up red plastic shopping carts, took charge of the empty box, and they were good to go.

"Now we're legal," Sasha said. "Valentino and I would be stranded if you got arrested."

Tricia drove out of the lot and onto the highway. "The most important thing is that you're safer now," she told her goddaughter. "But even if something did happen, you wouldn't be left to manage on your own."

"But who's going to use this seat when I'm in Paris?" Sasha asked. "It cost a lot of money."

There it was again—her practical side. How many kids troubled their heads about such things?

"Not to worry," Tricia answered, wanting to reassure the child. "It'll come in handy now, and when you visit again."

Sasha sighed. "But it might be a long time before that happens," she said. "I might be too big to even *need* a booster seat next time I come to Colorado. I might even be a *teenager* by then." From her tone, she didn't find the idea of being a teen completely unappealing.

"It'll be a while," Tricia said, though she knew Sasha would be grown-up long before anybody else—Diana and Paul included—was the least bit ready for that to happen.

Mercifully, Sasha moved between subjects like a firefly flitting from branch to bough, and her concern over the expense of the booster seat was apparently forgotten. "Are we going to do fun stuff while I'm staying with you?" she asked.

Tricia reached up and adjusted the rearview mirror just far enough, and just long enough, to catch a glimpse of Sasha's face. Valentino, living up to his name, rested his muzzle against the little girl's cheek.

"Yes," she said. "We are going to do fun stuff."

"Like what?"

"Well, we could go out for pizza. And rent some DVDs at the supermarket—"

Tricia couldn't help thinking how ordinary those activities must sound to an urban child, and she stumbled a little. "And there's a barbecue at River's Bend tomorrow afternoon. We're invited."

The mysterious Sunday reservation had been made under the name "Stone Creek Cattle Company," and Tricia had regarded the invitation as a formality, never intending to attend as a guest. Now that she had a child to entertain, it sounded like a good idea after all—the sort of Western shindig one might expect to see in Lonesome Bend, Colorado.

"Will it be like a party?" Sasha piped up, clearly intrigued. "With music and sack races and games of horseshoes and stuff?"

"I don't know," Tricia confessed, mildly deflated. Good heavens, she was really batting a thousand here.

"You're invited, but you don't know what kind of party it's going to be?"

Sasha, Tricia thought wryly, would probably grow up to be a lawyer.

"The people are from out of town," she said. "I had the impression that it's a pretty big gathering."

"They're strangers?"

"I guess so, but—"

"A barbecue might be fun. They have them in people's backyards sometimes, in Seattle, but I'll bet cookouts are pretty unusual in France."

Tricia smiled. "Probably," she agreed. "But the French are very good cooks."

"My friend Jessie," Sasha remarked, "says the French don't like Americans."

"Jessie?" Tricia countered, stalling so she could think for a few moments.

"Jessie's mom homeschools her and her brother, the same way my mom does me," Sasha said. "She's ten, just like me—Jessie, I mean—but she doesn't have to sit in a booster seat anymore because she's taller than I am. A *lot* taller." She paused, drew a breath. "What if I don't grow any bigger? What if I'm as old as you and Mom and I still have to ride in a stupid booster seat, like a baby, because I'm *short?* Jessie says it could happen."

"Jessie sounds—precocious," Tricia said. "You aren't through growing, kiddo—take it from me. Your dad is six-two, and your mom is five-seven. What are the genetic chances that you'll be short?"

"Grandma is short," Sasha reasoned.

"I've met your grandmother," Tricia responded. "And you don't take after her at all."

"But she is short," Sasha insisted.

"I guess," Tricia allowed, picturing Paul's sweet mother, who was indeed vertically challenged. "Care to make a wager?"

"What kind of wager?" Sasha asked, sounding eager.

"I'll bet that when you come home from France, you'll be at least five-five."

"What if I win? I mean, suppose I'm still four-six-and-a-half?"

"I'll buy you a whole season, on DVD, of whatever shows your mom will let you watch."

"Mom *hates* TV," Sasha said. "But I get to watch an hour a day when we live in Paris, if I have all my homework done, because that will help me learn the language."

Tricia barely kept from rolling her eyes. Sometimes Diana, who had been adventurous in the extreme before Sasha came along, overdid the whole responsible-parenting thing. "Okay," she said. "What would work for you?"

"The *Twilight* series," Sasha answered, with a marked lack of hesitation. "*All* the books in it."

"Deal," Tricia said, hoping she wouldn't have to pay up before Sasha was old enough to read about teenage vampires in love.

"What do you get if I lose?" Sasha wanted to know.

Tricia considered carefully before she replied. "Well, you could draw me a picture."

"I'd be willing to do that anyway," Sasha said, sweet thing that she was. "Your prize has to be something better than *that*."

"Let's think about it," Tricia suggested.

"Pizza for supper tonight?" Sasha asked.

"Pizza for supper tonight," Tricia confirmed.

"Yes!" Sasha shouted, punching the air with one small fist. "Mom *never* lets me eat real pizza, but Dad and I sneak it sometimes."

Valentino, caught up in the excitement of the moment, barked in happy agreement.

THE STONE CREEK Cattle Company, Tricia discovered the next day, when she and Sasha arrived at the campground to attend the barbecue, was owned by none other than Steven Creed.

There were Creeds everywhere—Davis and Kim, whom Tricia liked very much, were in attendance, each of them carrying a duplicate baby, dressed up warm. Conner was there, too, looking better than good, hazy in the heat mirage rising from the big central bonfire.

"Hello, Tricia," Steven said, when she stopped in her tracks. Suddenly, all her youthful shyness was back; she might actually have fled the scene if Sasha hadn't been with her, all primed for a Wild West experience she could brag about when she started school in Paris.

"Steven," she said, with a polite nod. "How are you?"

"Fantastic," Steven replied. "Married, with children." His blue gaze shifted to Sasha, who was staring at him in apparent fascination, probably thinking, as a lot of people did, that he looked like Brad Pitt. "Is this lovely young lady your daughter?"

Sasha gave a peal of laughter at that, as if it was

totally inconceivable that her honorary aunt could be somebody's mother.

"No," she answered. "Aunt Tricia is my mom's best friend. I'm visiting for *two whole weeks* because we're moving to Paris in a couple of months—"

"Nice to see you again, Steven," Tricia said, after laying a hand lightly on Sasha's small shoulder to stem the flow.

He looked around, probably for his wife, and when his eyes landed on the friendly woman bouncing one of the matching babies on one hip while she chatted with some other guests, they softened in a way that moved Tricia deeply and unexpectedly.

Had Hunter ever looked at *her* that way? If he had, she hadn't noticed.

"Looks like Melissa is caught up in conversation," Steven mused, smiling. "Don't take off before I get a chance to introduce you two."

"Sure," Tricia answered, blushing. "I'd like that."

Steven nodded, excused himself and walked away. Sasha had wandered off to play with some of the other kids, but Tricia wasn't alone for long. She followed him with her gaze, and when she looked back at the space he'd occupied before, Conner was there.

"Hi," he said.

She smiled up at him, even though she felt incredibly nervous. The dancing-to-a-jukebox fantasy from the day before, when she'd had to turn off Kenny Chesney, filled her mind.

"Hi," she replied. Oh, she was a sparkling conversationalist, all right.

"I'm glad you're here," Conner said. She wouldn't have known that by his expression; he wasn't smiling.

In fact, he looked as though he were trying to work out some complex equation in his head. "How's the dog?"

"Valentino's fine," she answered. She'd thought she was over her childhood shyness, but here it was, back again. "He's at home, with Natty's cat."

Could she sound any more inane?

Conner finally grinned, a spare, slanted motion of his mouth. "He's going to be big when he's full grown, you know," he remarked.

Was it possible that Conner Creed was shy, too? Nah, she decided.

"That's why I'm hoping to find him a home in the country someplace," she said. "Where he can run."

Conner merely nodded at that.

Tricia blushed, wishing the tension would subside. It didn't, of course, and she couldn't stand the brief silence that had settled between them, at once a bond and a barrier, so she burst out with, "He was supposed to live here, in the office, but he wouldn't stay put. He managed to escape somehow, and showed up on my doorstep in the middle of that last big rainstorm—"

Stop babbling, she ordered herself silently.

Conner frowned. "How could he have gotten out?" he asked, and when he walked over to examine the office door, Tricia followed right along. The rest of the world seemed to fall away, forgotten. "You locked up, right?"

"I forget sometimes," Tricia said, enjoying his apparent concern for her personal security more than she probably should have. "And the lock is old, like the rest of this place, and it doesn't always catch. A gust of wind could have blown it open."

"Or somebody could have broken in," Conner said,

taking the dark view evidently. "Did you call Jim Young and report what happened?"

"No," Tricia said. "I drove over here and checked things out myself, after I got Valentino dried off and settled at the apartment. Nothing was missing, or anything like that."

Just then, Steven's attractive wife joined them, baby tugging happily at a lock of her bright hair.

"I'm Melissa Creed," she said, smiling at Tricia, putting out her free hand.

Tricia took the other woman's hand and smiled back. "Tricia McCall," she said.

Melissa slanted a mischievous glance at Conner, who was just standing there, contributing nothing at all. "Of course I might have expected you to introduce me," she told him.

He shoved a hand through his hair, sighed. He looked mildly uncomfortable now, as though he might bolt. "Clearly," he said, "that wasn't necessary."

Melissa laughed at that, and her eyes shone as she turned her attention back to Tricia. "The food is almost ready," she said. "Women and children get to be first in line."

By tacit agreement, they started toward the picnic area, where the huge grill was emitting delicious aromas, savory-sweet.

Tricia called to Sasha, who came reluctantly. She'd already made friends with some of the other kids, though they'd only been there a few minutes.

Melissa stayed at Tricia's side while they waited their turns.

"What's the occasion?" Tricia asked, taking in the

crowds of people. She recognized most of them, but there were some strangers, too. "For the party, I mean?"

Melissa smiled. "My husband likes to bring people together," she said. "The more, the merrier, as far as Steven's concerned."

"Oh," Tricia said, at a loss again.

Just then, Melissa spotted some new arrival and waved, smiling. "Excuse me," she said. "I might have to referee."

With that, she hurried away.

Tricia turned her head, and there was Brody Creed in the distance, looking so much like his brother that it made her breath catch.

CHAPTER FIVE

BRODY.

Conner couldn't have claimed he was surprised to see his brother; he'd been warned well ahead of time, after all. But he still felt as though he'd stepped through an upstairs doorway and found himself with no floor to stand on, falling fast.

Careful as Conner was to keep a low profile, Brody's gaze swept over the crowd and found him with the inevitability of a heat-seeking missile. It was, Conner supposed, the twin thing. He'd nearly forgotten that weird connection between him and Brody, they'd been apart for so long. As kids, they'd been a little spooked by the phenomenon sometimes, though mostly it was fun, like scaring the hell out of each other with stories about escaped convicts with hooks for hands, or swapping identities and maintaining the deception for days before anyone caught on.

Brody narrowed his eyes. His hair was longer than Conner's, he hadn't shaved in a day or two, and his clothes were scruffy, but for all that, seeing him was, for Conner, disturbingly like looking into a mirror.

Where was Joleen? Conner wondered, subtly scanning Brody's immediate orbit. There was no sign of her—which didn't mean she wasn't around somewhere, of course. Like Brody, Joleen had a talent for turning up unexpectedly, in his thoughts if not in the flesh; she probably enjoyed the drama of it all. Joleen had always been big on drama.

Now Brody made his way through the clusters of people, smiling and speaking a word of greeting here and there, but he was headed straight for Conner. Pride made Conner dig in his boot heels and stay put, though he didn't feel ready to deal with Brody just then. He folded his arms, tilted his head to one side, and waited. If he bolted, Brody and whoever else was looking might think Conner was afraid of his brother—and he wasn't. It was just that there was so damn much going on under the surface of things, and Conner had trouble maintaining his perspective, at least as far as Brody was concerned.

"Hello, little brother," Brody drawled, when the two of them were standing face-to-face. He'd been born four minutes ahead of Conner, as the story went, and he'd always enjoyed bringing it up.

Like it gave him some advantage or something.

Conner gave a curt little nod, realized his arms were still folded across his chest, and let them fall to his sides. "Brody," he said, in gruff acknowledgment that the other man existed, if nothing else.

Brody indulged in a cocky grin, his mouth tilting up at one corner, his blue eyes mischievous, but watchful, too. Despite all his folksy affability, Brody was on high alert, just as Conner was. Maybe it had slipped his mind that they'd always been able to read each other like bold print on a billboard, but Conner definitely remembered.

"I'm just passing through," Brody said, and while his voice was easy, his eyes gave the lie to the impression he was doing his best to give. Whatever his reasons for returning to Lonesome Bend might be, they were important to him. "So there's no need for you to get all bent out of shape or anything."

"Who says I'm bent out of shape?" Conner asked, sensing that he had the upper hand. Since they'd always been so evenly matched that all either of them ever gained from a fistfight, for instance, was a lot of cuts and bruises but no clear victory, the insight came as something of a revelation.

"Just going by past history," Brody replied, raising both eyebrows. "Last time we ran into each other, at that rodeo in Stone Creek, you landed on me before I could get so much as a *howdy* out of my mouth."

Conner felt a twinge of shame, recalling that incident, though he wasn't about to concede that he'd started the row—it had been a mutual, and instantaneous, decision. And, as usual, it had ended in a standoff.

"What do you want, Brody?" he asked now. His arms were folded again. When had that happened?

"Just a place to hang my hat for a while," Brody replied, sounding sadly aggrieved.

"How about on Joleen's bedpost?" Conner asked, and then could have kicked himself, hard. Not because the remark had been unkind, but because of the way Brody might interpret it.

That slow, Brody-patented grin spread across his brother's beard-stubbled face. "So *that's* the way it is," he said, hooking his thumbs in the belt loops of his jeans, like some old-time cowpuncher surveying the herd. Next, he'd probably turn his head to one side and spit. "I don't mind telling you, little brother—I didn't figure you'd give a damn what Joleen and I might do together, after all this time."

The old rage seethed inside Conner, but glancing past Brody, he caught a momentary glimpse of Tricia McCall, sitting at one of the picnic tables, in the midst of a crowd of other diners, and something shifted inside him, just like that.

It hurt, like having a disjointed bone yanked back into its socket, but there was an element of relief, too. What the hell?

"You're right," Conner told his brother stiffly, finally paying attention to the conversation again. "The two of you can join the circus and swing from trapezes for all I care."

Brody put one hand to his chest, his fingers splayed wide, and feigned emotional injury. "Then you shouldn't have a problem with me bunking out at the ranch for a couple of weeks," he said. "Especially since the place is half mine anyhow."

By that time, Davis had worked his way over to them, probably dispatched by Kim. She wouldn't want any fights breaking out, with all those kids and women around, and if anything happened, the gossip wouldn't die down for years.

"You two are bristling like a couple of porcupines," Davis observed dryly, his Creed-blue eyes swinging from one brother to the other. "I don't need to tell you, do I, that this is neither the time nor the place for trouble of the sort you're probably cooking up right about now?"

Conner let out his breath, rolled his shoulders again.

Brody grinned at their uncle. "Just saying hello to my brother," he said, sounding guileless, but unable to resist adding, "and meeting with the usual hostile response, of course."

"Where's Joleen?" Davis asked quietly, watching Brody.

Brody rolled his eyes and flung his hands out from his sides. "Why the hell does everybody keep asking me that?" he wanted to know. Fortunately, he didn't raise his voice; that would have been like dropping a lighted match into a puddle of spilled kerosene. "I'm not the woman's keeper, for God's sake."

Just her lover, Conner thought, automatically, and waited for the rush of testosterone-laced adrenaline. It didn't come. And that threw him a little.

Brody thrust out a dramatic sigh, looking like a man who'd bravely fought the good fight, heroic in the face of great tragedy, won the battle but lost the war. "Look," he said, still careful to speak quietly, since half the town was present and watching out of the corners of their eyes. "Joleen and I met up by accident, at a rodeo in Lubbock, that's all. She'd just split the sheets with some yahoo, and she was too broke to even buy a bus ticket back home, so I brought her, since I happened to be headed in this general direction anyway. End of story."

Conner leaned in until his nose and Brody's were almost touching. "You've obviously mistaken me," he growled, "for somebody who gives a rat's ass why you and Jolene came back to Lonesome Bend."

"That's enough," Davis said sternly, as in days of old, when Brody and Conner had been even more hotheaded than they were now. "*That will be enough.* This is a party, not some dive of a bar in Juarez. If you want to beat the hell out of each other, be my guests, but do it at home, behind the barn. Not here."

A brief and highly incendiary silence fell.

"Sorry," Conner finally ground out, insincerely.

"Me, too," Brody added, lying through his teeth. "Fact is, I've lost my appetite anyhow, so I'll just be heading home to the ranch—if nobody minds."

Like he cared whether or not anybody minded anything, ever. Brody had always done whatever he damn well pleased, and people who got in his way were just expected to deal.

"Kim and I will be hitting the trail right after Steven and Melissa and the kids leave tomorrow," Davis said, watching Brody. "I'd offer to let you stay at our place and look after things while we're gone, but Kim's already made other arrangements."

Brody raised both hands, palms out, like the not-too-worried victim of a stick-up. "No problem," he said, after a pointed look at Conner. "I've got a yen to sleep in my own bed, in my own room, anyway. 'Course I'll have to sleep with one eye open, since I'll be about as welcome as an unrepentant whore in church."

Davis leveled a glance at Conner, put an arm around Brody's shoulders and steered him away, toward the barbecue area, where the grill was smoking and food was being handed out. "Don't say anything to Kim," the older man began, his voice carrying back to Conner, "but there's this pair of boots she donated to the rummage sale—"

In spite of everything, Conner chuckled. If Davis Creed was anything, he was persistent—some would say stubborn—just like the rest of their kin.

After giving himself a few moments to cool off, Conner made his way to Kim's side. She immediately turned to face him.

"Thanks for not making a scene," she said, not unkindly but with the quiet directness they'd all come to expect from her. "This get-together means a lot to Steven. It's his way of showing off his wife and kids to the hometown folks, and I'd hate to see that get ruined."

"I hear you, Kim," Conner replied. Brody and Davis were in line for grub by then, each of them holding a throwaway plate and jawing with folks around them. "But if anybody ruins this shindig, it won't be me."

Real pain flickered in Kim's eyes. Conner's biological mother had died soon after giving birth to him and Brody, leaving Blue alone and grief-stricken, with no clue as to how to look after two squalling, premature newborns, and this woman had stepped up, loved them like her own. She'd been firm, even strict sometimes, Kim had, but there had never been a single moment when Conner had doubted her devotion, and he was pretty sure Brody would have said the same.

They'd been lucky to have Kim in their lives, and even luckier to have Davis, because their uncle had run the ranch for them after Blue's death, and guarded their interests with absolute integrity. On top of that, he'd been a father to them.

"If only you and Brody could get along," Kim said sadly.

"That requires trust," Conner replied, his voice quiet. "And Brody and I don't have that anymore." Without conscious effort, he sought Tricia again, with his eyes, found her, and he was heartened by the mere sight of her.

Why was that?

Kim, typically, had followed Conner's gaze, registered that he was watching Tricia, even though he would have preferred to keep that particular tidbit of information to himself. "Tricia McCall?" Kim asked, her voice very soft, pitched to go no further than Conner's ears. "My faith in your judgment is restored, Conner Creed. Frankly, it's a mystery to me why a woman like that is still single."

"Maybe she likes being single," Conner suggested.

"The way *you* like being single, Conner?" Kim immediately retorted.

His hackles didn't exactly rise, but they twitched a little. "What is that supposed to mean?"

"You know perfectly well what it means," she answered, but she rested a hand on his forearm and squeezed. "Even without these two eyes in my head, I would still have known how much you want somebody to share your life. Whenever you so much as look at Steven, or Melissa, or any of those kids—even the dog, for heaven's sake—it's right there in that handsome mug of yours. A sort of lonely hunger."

"'Lonely hunger'?" Conner asked, with a lightness he didn't feel. "You read too many of those romance novels."

"It wouldn't hurt you or Brody or, for that matter, Davis, to read a few romances," Kim said, undaunted. "That way, you might know how a woman likes to be treated."

Conner let out a huff. "My point," he said, "is this— don't get carried away—Tricia's involved with some guy in Seattle. Keeps his picture on her computer monitor as a screen saver."

Kim smiled. "You've been to Tricia's place?"

Conner felt his neck go warm. "Yes," he answered. "I took Natty a load of firewood, as I do every fall and right on through the winter, and since the old gal was away, I needed somebody to let me in so I could fill the wood boxes. Tricia lives upstairs, above Natty's."

Kim was musing now. Thoughtful, but still amused. "Maybe the guy in that picture is her brother or just a good friend. He might even be gay."

"Right," Conner said dryly. "And Santa Claus might come down my chimney on Christmas Eve and stuff a Playboy bunny into my stocking."

Kim arched an eyebrow, but she was smiling again, full-out. "Bitter," she said. "Conner Creed, you are a bitter man. And in the prime of your life, too."

"I'm not bitter," Conner retorted, knowing that what his stand-in mom said was true. He *was* bitter, over what he perceived as Brody's betrayal of his trust, over the way he'd never met the right woman, as so many of the guys he knew had—Steven in particular.

"Don't try to B.S. me, Conner," Kim said. "I know you better than you know yourself. You're taken with Tricia, and there's not a darn thing wrong with that. Man up, why don't you, and ask her out?"

"To do what?" Conner scuffed, strangely unsettled by the idea of making a move on Tricia. What if she said no? What if she said *yes?* "Go to a hoedown? Or maybe that rummage sale slash chili feed? Anyway, she has company, a little girl."

"Sasha," Kim clarified knowledgeably. "She's Tricia's best friend's daughter, and she's ten years old. Also, she's horse crazy, like most girls her age."

"Meaning?"

"Meaning, you thick-headed cowboy," Kim replied, with exaggerated patience and wry affection, "that if you invite Sasha to go riding on the ranch, Tricia will automatically come with her. That's how Davis and I fell in love, you know. We were on a trail ride together, with a bunch of friends, and the first night, we got to talking by the campfire, and it was happy trails from then on. We've been traveling side by side ever since."

"In that case," Conner answered, his tone dry, "I'll take care to avoid trail rides."

Kim quirked a smile. "Don't give up your day job," she whispered, before turning to walk away. "You'd never make it as a comedian."

Conner watched her go. And he steered clear of the chow line, since his stomach felt all tensed up, as if it were closed for business. If Steven and Melissa's visit hadn't been such a short one, he would have gotten into his truck and gone home.

Maybe saddled a horse and headed up into the green-and-gold-and-crimson foothills, where the aspens whispered, where the streams tumbled over rocks and, except for the occasional call of a bird, those were pretty much the only sounds.

Up there, in the spectacular hills, a man could hear himself think. Get some kind of handle on the stuff that was—or wasn't—happening in his life.

But he was stuck, for now anyway.

Might as well make the best of it, and join the party.

TRICIA HELPED WITH the cleanup, telling herself that she ought to leave the barbecue now that she'd put in a cordial appearance, but the bonfire was nice and people were having fun, especially the children, and somebody was tuning up a banjo. The thought of going home, even though Sasha would be with her, was an intensely lonely prospect.

Carolyn Simmons, perhaps the only person in Lonesome Bend who was even more rootless than Tricia, helped, too. A gypsy with no apparent home, Carolyn joined in with the other women and a few men, gathering paper plates and cups and plastic flatware from the ground and the tops of the picnic tables, stuffing the detritus into garbage bags.

"Are you volunteering at the rummage sale again this year?" Carolyn asked Tricia, her tone and manner at once casual and friendly.

"Natty's been trying to pin me down for kitchen duty," Tricia said, smiling in response. "I think she only wants me to guard the family chili recipe, though." Like just about everyone in Lonesome Bend, Tricia was curious about Carolyn, who was always ready with a cheerful hello or a helping hand, but extremely private, too. She kept a roof over her head by housesitting, mainly for the reclusive movie stars, corporate execs and other famous types who bought or built enormous homes outside town but rarely used them. Besides that, her only known income was from the original clothes she designed and sold online or through consignment boutiques.

Carolyn chuckled at Tricia's answer. She had shoulder-length hair, streaked blond but somehow very natural-looking, and her eyes were wide and green, surrounded by thick lashes. "I don't blame Natty one bit," she said warmly. "That chili is so good it ought to be patented."

"Amen," Tricia agreed. The chili recipe was closely guarded indeed; only Natty and her sister, the one she was visiting in Denver, knew how to make it. The single written copy in existence was brought out of some secret hiding place every October, on the Thursday pre-

ceding the rummage sale, and carefully protected from
prying eyes.

Even Tricia, a true McCall, had merely managed
glimpses of that tattered old recipe card over the years,
with its bent corners and its spidery handwriting slanting hard to the right, though Natty had intimated that
it might be time to think about "passing the torch."
That remark never failed to alarm Tricia, who adored
her great-grandmother, and couldn't imagine a world
without her in it.

"How is Natty, anyway?" Carolyn asked, dropping
a full garbage bag into one of the trash containers and
dusting off her hands against the thighs of her black
jeans. "I usually run into her at the grocery store or the
library, but I haven't seen her around lately."

Tricia explained about the Denver trip, and quickly
realized that Carolyn wasn't listening. Her gaze had
snagged on Brody Creed, laughing with friends on the
other side of the campground, and she seemed power-
less to jerk it away again.

Intrigued herself, Tricia watched Brody for a few
moments, too, thinking in a detached way that while
he and Conner *did* resemble each other closely, there
were obvious differences, too.

Conner moved with quiet purpose, for example,
while Brody was loose-limbed, ready to change directions at any given moment, if it suited him to do so.
There were other qualities, too—some of them so in-
tuitive in nature that Tricia would have had a hard time
putting names to them. She knew, somehow, that even
if the Creed brothers *tried* to look as alike as possible,
she would still know Conner from Brody in an instant.
And that was puzzling indeed.

Carolyn snapped out of her own reverie a bit before Tricia did, and when their eyes met, a sort of understanding passed between them—empathy, perhaps. Or maybe just the silent admission that some questions didn't have answers. Not obvious ones, at least.

And then Carolyn surprised Tricia by saying calmly, "What a fool I was, way back when."

This time, it was Hunter who popped into Tricia's mind. She shook off the image and smiled reassuringly. "Weren't we all?"

Carolyn's gaze strayed back to Brody, but didn't linger. When she looked at Tricia again, it was clear that a door had closed inside Carolyn. It reminded Tricia of the way people board up a house when they know there's a category 4 hurricane on its way. "Some of us," she said sadly, with one more glance at Brody, "knew *exactly* what they were doing."

Carolyn had a history with Brody Creed?

Whoa, Tricia thought, hoping Carolyn hadn't noticed the way her eyes had widened for a second or two there. She'd lived part of every year in this small, close-knit community, starting with that first summer after second grade, when Joe and Laurel had called it quits and filed for a divorce, and for the better part of a year and a half since her dad's death.

None of which meant that she was any kind of insider when it came to the locals and their secrets, but, still, she usually had a *glimmer* of what was going on, if only because of things Natty and her friends said in passing, when they got together to sip tea around the old woman's kitchen table. In many ways, Lonesome Bend was like a soap opera come to life, and everybody kept up with the story line—except her, evidently.

Carolyn gave an awkward little laugh. "I'm sorry," she said, embarrassed. "That came out sounding pretty bitchy."

Tricia decided not to comment. Then she remembered that she was still holding her own bag of after-barbecue trash and tossed it into the bin.

"I'm going to be staying on the Creed ranch for a while," Carolyn said, as she and Tricia walked away from the line of garbage cans. "Looking after things for Davis and Kim, I mean. It's a great house, and they have horses, too. I have permission to ride the gentler ones, and I was wondering—"

Her voice fell away, perhaps because she'd seen something in Tricia's face.

Tricia *had* felt a hard jab to her middle when Carolyn announced her next housesitting assignment, given that, living on the ranch, the other woman would be in close proximity to Conner, and, recognizing the emotion for what it was, she was ashamed. Yes, Carolyn was an attractive woman, presumably available. But she, Tricia, certainly had no business being jealous and, anyway, if Carolyn *was* interested in one of the Creed men, it was Brody, not Conner.

Her relief was undeniable.

"What?" she asked belatedly. "What were you wondering?"

"Well, if you and your niece might like to go trail riding sometime," Carolyn said, almost shyly.

"I've never been on a horse in my life," Tricia replied. It wasn't that she didn't *like* horses, just that they were so big, and so unpredictable.

Diana was an accomplished equestrian, and because

of that, Sasha was comfortable around the huge creatures.

"Well, then," Carolyn said, spreading her hands for emphasis and grinning a wide, Julia Roberts grin, "it's time you learned, isn't it?"

"I don't know—"

Just then, Sasha rushed over. Sometimes Tricia thought the child had superpowers—particularly as far as her hearing was concerned. Just moments before, she'd been on the other side of the campground, playing chasing games with other kids and several dogs. Let the word *horse* be spoken, though, and she was Johnny-on-the-spot.

"I want to go riding," Sasha crowed. "Please, please, *please*—"

"Do you read lips or something?" Tricia asked.

"Matt's uncle Conner is going to ask us to go riding, with a bunch of other people. Matt heard him talking about it, and he told me, and *you've got to say yes,* because I honestly don't know how I'll go on if you don't!"

Tricia chuckled and gave one of Sasha's pigtails a gentle tug. "When is this big ride supposed to take place?" she asked, hoping nobody would guess that she was stalling.

"Next Sunday, after the chili feed and the rummage sale are over," Sasha expounded, breathless with excitement. "It'll be the last of the good weather, before the snow comes."

"We'll see," Tricia said.

Carolyn was still standing there, smiling.

"Please!" Sasha implored, clasping her hands together as if in prayer and looking up at Tricia with luminous hope in her eyes.

"I have to ask your mom and dad first," Tricia told her, laying a calming hand on the little girl's shoulder. "I'll send them a text, and when they land in Paris, they'll read it and we'll probably have our answer right away."

"They'll say yes," Sasha said confidently, beaming now. "I ride with Mom *all the time*." The smile faded. "We mostly just ride in arenas and stuff, because Seattle's such a big city. In France, we probably won't get to do it at all. But this is *real* riding, on a *real* ranch, just like in that movie, *City Slickers*."

Tricia and Carolyn exchanged looks, both of them smiling now.

Somehow, they'd gone from being acquaintances to being friends.

"Not *too* much like it, I hope," Tricia said. "And that's what we are, isn't it? A pair of city slickers?"

"Speak for yourself," Sasha joked, folding her arms decisively in front of her little chest and jutting out her chin. "I might *live* in a city, but I know how to ride a horse."

"Yes, you do," Tricia conceded. "Now, what do you say we head for home? Valentino probably needs to go out for a walk, and Winston likes to have his supper early."

"Can we give Winston sardines?" Sasha asked. "It's Sunday, and he always gets sardines on Sunday. That's what you said."

"It is indeed what I said," Tricia answered, nodding to Carolyn as the other woman waved goodbye and walked off. "And I am a woman of my word."

"Good," Sasha said, in a tone of generous approval. Tricia took the little girl's hand. "Let's go thank

Matt's dad and mom for inviting us to the barbecue," she said. "Then we'll go home and walk Valentino and give Winston his sardines."

Sasha yawned widely and against her will, politely putting a hand over her mouth. It was still fairly early in the day, but she'd been running around in the fresh air for a couple of hours now, laughing and playing with a horde of energetic country kids, and she probably wasn't over the jet-lag of the trip from Seattle.

By the time Sasha had had a warm bath and watched part of a Disney movie on DVD, she'd be asleep on her feet.

"Can I send the text to Mom and Dad?" she asked, when goodbyes and thank-yous had been said, and the two of them were back in Tricia's Pathfinder, headed toward home. "I know how to do it."

Tricia smiled, remembering the message she'd received from Sasha before, from the aquarium in Seattle. "Sure," she said. She pulled over to one side of the road, just long enough to extract the cell from her purse and hand it to Sasha. "Remember, your mom and dad's plane didn't leave Sea-Tac until this morning, so they're still in transit."

Sasha sighed in contented resignation. "And that means they won't get the message until they land. I *know* that already."

"I did mention it before, didn't I?" Tricia admitted, in cheerful chagrin.

"That's okay, Aunt Tricia," Sasha said, already pushing buttons on the phone like a pro. "You're probably tired, like me."

Love for this child welled up in Tricia, threatening

to overflow. "Probably," she agreed, her voice a little husky.

By the time they pulled into the driveway along-side Natty's venerable old Victorian, Sasha had finished transmitting a fairly long text message to her parents and put the phone aside.

They could hear Valentino barking a welcome-home from the bottom of the outside stairway, and he was all over Sasha with kisses the moment Tricia unlocked the door.

She was about to reprimand the dog when Sasha's delighted giggles registered.

They were having fun.

"I'll get the leash," Tricia said, stepping around the reunion on the threshold. She set her purse and phone on the counter and glanced at her computer monitor, across the room, wondering if Hunter had sent her any emails. There would be plenty of time to check later, she decided, collecting Valentino's sturdy nylon lead from the hook on the inside of the pantry door.

Sasha and Tricia took the dog for his much-needed walk, bringing along the necessary plastic bag for cleanup, and Winston was waiting when they got back, prowling back and forth on his favorite windowsill and meowing loudly for his dinner.

Sasha fed the cat an entire tin of sardines from Natty's supply downstairs, while Tricia gave Valentino his kibble and freshened his bowl of water.

Since both Sasha and Tricia were still stuffed from all they'd eaten at the barbecue, supper would be con-tingent on whether or not they got hungry and, if they did, it would consist of either leftover pizza from the night before or cold cereal, sugary-sweet.

They watched a movie together, then Sasha went into the bathroom to bathe, don her pajamas and dutifully brush her teeth, all of these enterprises closely supervised by Valentino. In the meantime, Tricia folded out the living room couch, retrieved the extra bed pillows from the coat closet and fluffed them up so Sasha would be as comfortable as possible.

The little girl insisted on checking Tricia's cell phone, just in case there had miraculously been an answer from Diana and Paul, and seemed mildly disappointed when there wasn't. "Missing your mom and dad?" Tricia asked softly, sitting down on the hide-a-bed mattress while Sasha squirmed and stretched, a settling-in ritual she'd been performing since she was a toddler.

"A little bit," Sasha admitted wisely. "But I like being here with you and Valentino and Winston, too."

Tricia kissed her forehead. "And we like having you here," she said. "In fact, we love it."

Sasha snuggled down in her covers, while Valentino took up his post nearby, eschewing his dog bed for a hooked rug in front of the nonworking fireplace. "And you love *me,* too, right?"

Tricia's throat tightened again, and she had to swallow a couple of times before she replied, "Right. I love you very much."

Sasha's eyes closed, and she sighed and wriggled a little more. "Love—you—" she murmured.

And then she was sound asleep.

CHAPTER SIX

BRODY AND CONNER stood in the side yard of the main ranch house that blue-skied morning, keeping the length of a pitchfork handle between them, watching as two shiny RVs pulled out onto the county road, one after the other. Both horns tooted in cheery farewell and that was it. Melissa and Steven and the kids were on their way back to Stone Creek, Arizona, in the Bradmobile, while Davis and Kim were heading for Cheyenne, where they intended to pick up their just-weaned Yorkie pups.

And Conner was alone on the place with his brother, which was the only thing worse than being alone on the place *period*. Brody served as a reminder of better times, when they'd been twin-close, and instead of assuaging Conner's loneliness, it only made him feel worse, missing what was gone.

Since country folks believe it's bad luck to watch people out of sight when they leave a place, especially home, Conner turned away before the vehicles disappeared around the first bend in the road and made for the barn. He'd saddle up, ride out to check some fence lines and make sure the small range crew moving the cattle to the other side of the river, where there was more grass, was on the job.

The crossing was narrow, through fairly shallow water, and the task would be easily accomplished by a few experienced cowpunchers on horseback, but Conner liked to keep his eye on things, anyhow. Some of the beeves were bound to balk on the bank of that river, calves in particular, and stampedes were always a possibility.

Conner was surprised—and *not* surprised—when Brody fell into step beside him, adjusting his beat-up old rodeo hat as he walked.

"So now that the family is out of here," Brody said mildly, "you're just going to pretend I'm invisible?"

Conner stopped cold, turning in the big double doorway of the barn to meet Brody's gaze. "This is a working cattle ranch," he reminded his brother. "Maybe you'd like to sit around and swap lies, but *I* have things to do."

Brody shook his head, and even though he gave a spare grin, his eyes were full of sadness and secrets. "Thought I'd saddle up and give you a hand," he said, in that gruff drawl he'd always used when he wanted to sound down-home earnest. He came off as an affable saddle bum, folksy and badly educated, without two nickels to rub together, and that was all bullshit. No one knew that better than Conner did, but maybe Brody was so used to conning people into underestimating him, so he could take advantage of them when they least expected it, that he figured he could fool his identical twin brother, too.

Fat chance, since they had duplicate DNA, and at one time they'd been so in sync that they could not only finish each other's sentences, they'd had whole conversations and realized a lot later that neither of them had spoken a single word out loud.

"Thanks," Conner said, without conviction, when

the silence became protracted and he knew Brody was going to wait him out, try to bluff his way through as he'd do with a bad poker hand, "but it's nothing I can't handle on my own." *Like I've been doing all these years, while you were off playing the outlaw.*

Of course, Conner had had plenty of help from Davis along the way, but that wasn't the point. The ranch was their birthright—his and Brody's—and Brody had taken off, leaving him holding the proverbial bag, making the major decisions, doing the work. And that, Conner figured, was a big part of the reason why he didn't have what he wanted most.

Brody sighed heavily, tilted his head to one side, as though trying to work a kink out of his neck, and looked at Conner with a mix of anger, amusement and pity in his eyes. Then he rubbed his stubbly chin with one hand. "This place," he said again, and with feigned reluctance, "is half mine. So are the cattle and the horses. While I'm here, I mean to make myself useful, little brother, whether you like it or not."

Conner unclamped his back molars. "Oh, I remember that the ranch is as much yours as it is mine," he responded grimly, forcing the words past tightened lips. "Trust me. I'm reminded of that every time I send you a fat check for doing nothing but staying out of my way. That last part, I did truly appreciate."

Brody chuckled at that, but his eyes weren't laughing. "God damn, but you can hold a grudge like nobody else I ever knew," he observed, folding his arms. "And considering my history with women, that's saying something." He paused, taking verbal aim. "You want Joleen back? Go for it. I'm not standing in your way."

Conner spat, though his mouth was cotton-dry.

"Hell," he snapped. "I wouldn't touch Joleen with *your* pecker."

Brody lifted both eyebrows, looking skeptical. "You know what's really the matter with you, little brother? You're *jealous*. And it's got nothing to do with Joleen or any other female on the face of this earth. It's because I went out there and *lived,* did everything you wanted to do, while you stayed right here, like that guy in the Bible, proving you were the Good Son."

Conner's temper flared—Brody's words struck so close to the bone that they nicked his marrow—but he wasn't going to give his brother the satisfaction of losing it. Not this time. "You're full of shit," he said, turning away from Brody again and proceeding into the barn, where he chose a horse and led it out of its stall and into the wide breezeway. Brody followed, selected a cayuse of his own, and the two of them saddled up in prickly silence that made the horses nervous.

As usual, it was Brody who broke the impasse. He swung up into the saddle, pulled down his hat yet another time, which meant he was either rattled or annoyed or both, and ducked to ride through the doorway into the bright October sunshine.

"What would you say if I told you I'd been thinking about retiring from the rodeo and settling down for good?" he asked, when they were both outside.

"I guess it would depend on where you planned on settling down," Conner said.

"Where else but right here?" Brody asked, with a gesture that took in the thousands of acres surrounding them. The Creed land stretched all the way to the side of the river directly opposite Tricia McCall's campground. "I respect Steven's decision to buy a place with no history to it, make his own mark in the world instead of sharing this spread with us, but I'm nowhere near as noble as our cousin from Boston, as you already know."

Conner made a low, contemptuous sound in his throat and nudged his horse into motion, riding toward the open gate leading into the first pasture. The range lay beyond, beckoning, making him want to lean over that gelding's neck and race the wind, but he didn't indulge the notion.

He didn't want Brody thinking he'd gotten his "little brother" on the run, literally or figuratively. "You're right about this much, anyway," he said, his voice stony-quiet. "You're nothing like Steven."

Brody eased his gelding into a gallop just then, but he didn't speak again. He just smiled to himself, like he was privy to some joke Conner didn't have the mental wherewithal to comprehend, and kept going.

The smug look on Brody's face pissed Conner off like few other things could have, but he wouldn't allow himself to be provoked. He just rode, tight-jawed, and so did Brody, both of them thinking their own thoughts.

About the only thing he and Brody agreed on, Conner reflected glumly, was that Steven, as much a Creed as either of them, should have had a third of the ranch and the considerable financial assets that came along with it. Steven had refused—hardheaded pride ran in the family, after all—and set up an outfit of his own outside Stone Creek.

He'd met and married Melissa O'Ballivan there, Steven had, and he seemed happy, so Conner figured things had worked out in the long run. Still, he could have used his cousin's company *and* his help on the ranch, since Brody was about three degrees past any damn use at all.

It might have been different if Steven had ever wanted for money, but his mother's people were well-fixed, high-priced Eastern lawyers, all of them. Steven, whom Brody invariably called "Boston," had grown up in a Back Bay mansion, with servants and a trust fund and all the rest of it. Summers, though, Steven had come west, to stay on the ranch, as his parents had agreed. And he'd been cowboy enough to win everybody's respect.

Even though he could have had an equal share of the Colorado holdings, which included the ranch itself, some ten thousand acres, a sizable herd of cattle, and a copper-mining fortune handed down through three generations, multiplying even during hard times, Steven had wanted two things: a family and to build an enterprise that was his alone.

And he was succeeding at both those objectives.

Conner, by comparison, was just walking in place, biding his time, watching life go right on past him without so much as a nod in his direction.

Brody had accused him of jealousy, back there at the barn, claiming that Conner had played the stay-at-home son to Brody's prodigal, and was resentful of his return. The implications burned their way through Conner's veins all over again, like a jolt of snake venom.

Conner had to give Brody this much: it was true enough that he'd gotten over Joleen with no trouble at all. What he *hadn't* gotten over, what he couldn't shake, no matter how he tried to reason with himself, was being betrayed by the person he'd been closest to, from conception on.

The idea that Brody, so much a part of him that they were like one person, the one he'd been so sure always had his back, would sell him out like that, with no particular concern about the consequences and no apology, either, well, *that* stuck in Conner's gut like a wad of thorns and nettles and rusted barbed wire. It chewed at him, on an unconscious level most of the time, but on occasion woke him out of a sound sleep, or sneaked up from behind and tapped him on the shoulder.

Brody's presence wasn't just a frustration to Conner— it was a bruise to the soul.

Reaching the herd, the brothers kept to opposite sides, helping the four ranch hands Conner and Davis employed year-round—there had been three times that many at roundup—drive nearly three hundred bawling, balking, rolling-eyed cattle across the ford in the river.

The work itself was bone-jarringly hard, not to mention dusty and hot, even though summer had passed. It took all morning to get it done, because cattle, which, unlike dogs and horses, are not particularly intelligent, can scatter in all directions like the down from a dandelion gone to seed. They get stuck in the mud and sometimes trample each other, and many a seasoned cowboy has fallen beneath their hooves, thrown from the saddle. Once in a while, the man's horse fared even worse, breaking a leg or being gored by a horn.

Brody proved to be as good a hand as ever, considering that he probably did most of his riding for show now that he was a big rodeo star, but what did that prove? Good horsemen weren't hard to come by in that part of the country—lots of people were practically born in the saddle.

Good brothers, though? Now, there was a rare commodity.

Once all the cattle were finally across the river, en-

joying fresh acres of untrampled grass, their bawls of
complaint settling down to a dull roar, Conner spoke
briefly with the foreman of the crew and then reined
his horse toward home. He wanted a shower, clothes he
hadn't sweated through and a sandwich thick enough
to cut with a chain saw. For all his lonesomeness, an
emotion endemic to bachelor ranchers, he wanted some
time alone, too, so he could sort through his thoughts
at his own pace, make what sense he could of recent
developments.

No such luck.

Brody caught up to him as he was crossing the river,
their horses side by side, drops of water splashing up to
soak the legs of their jeans.

It felt good to cool off, Conner thought. At least,
on the outside. On the inside, he was still smoldering.

"That old house sure has seen a lot of livin'," Brody
remarked, once they'd ridden up the opposite bank onto
dry land, standing in his stirrups for a moment to stretch
his legs. The ranch house, though still a good quarter
of a mile away, was clearly visible, a two-story structure, white with dark green shutters and a wraparound
porch, looked out of place on that land, venerable as it
was. A saltbox, more at home in some seaside town in
New England than in the high country of Colorado, it
was genteel instead of rustic, as it might have been expected to be.

In the beginning, it had been nothing but a cabin—
that part of the house was a storage room now, with the
original log walls still in place—but as the years passed,
a succession of Creed brides had persuaded their husbands to add on a kitchen here and a parlor there and
more and more bedrooms right along, to accommodate

the ever-increasing broods of children. Now, the place amounted to some seven thousand square feet, could sleep at least twelve people comfortably and was filled with antique furniture.

Conner, spending a lot of time there by himself, would have sworn it was haunted, that he heard, if not actual voices, the echoed *vibrations* of human conversation, or of children's laughter or, very rarely, the faint plucking of one of the strings on his great-great-grandmother Alice's gold-gilt harp.

Spacious and sturdily built, the roof solid and the walls strong enough to keep out blizzard winds in the winter, the house didn't feel right without a woman in it. Not that Conner would have said so out loud. Especially not to Brody.

"I guess the old place has seen some living, all right," he allowed, after letting Brody's comment hang unanswered for a good while.

"Don't you get lonely in that big old house, now that Kim and Davis are living in the new one?"

Conner didn't want to chat, so he gave an abrupt reply to let Brody know that. "No," he lied, urging his tired horse to walk a little faster.

"You remember how we used to scare the hell out of each other with stories about the ghosts of dead Creeds?" Brody asked, a musing grin visible in spite of the shadow cast over his face by the brim of his hat.

"I remember," Conner answered.

They were nearing the barn by then. It was considerably newer than the house, built by the grandfather they'd never known, after he came home from the Vietnam War, full of shrapnel and silence.

He'd died young, Davis and Blue's father, and their

mother hadn't lasted long after his passing. Now and then, in an unguarded moment, Conner caught himself wondering if he'd stayed single because so many members of the family had gone on before their time.

"You ever smile anymore?" Brody asked casually, as they dismounted in front of the barn. "Or say more than one or two words at a time?"

"I was thinking, that's all," Conner said.

"All the way up to *five* words," Brody grinned. "I'm impressed, little brother. At this rate, you're apt to talk a leg right off somebody."

Conner led his horse inside, into a stall. There, he removed the gear and proceeded to rub the animal down with one of many old towels kept on hand for that purpose. "I don't run on just to hear my head rattle," he said, knowing Brody was in the stall across the aisle, tending to his own horse. "Unlike some people I could name."

Brody laughed at that, a scraped-raw sound that caused the horse he was tending to startle briefly and toss its head. "You need a woman," he proclaimed, as if a man could just order one online and have her delivered by UPS. "You're turning into one of those salty old loners who talk to themselves, paper the cabin walls with pages ripped from some catalog, grow out their beards for the mice to nest in and use the same calendar over and over, figuring it's never more than seven or eight days off."

A grin twitched at Conner's mouth at the images that came to mind—there were a few such hermits around Lonesome Bend—but he quelled it on general principle. "That was colorful," he said, putting aside the towel and picking up a brush.

When Conner looked away from the horse he was grooming, he was a little startled to find Brody standing just on the other side of the stall door, watching him like he had a million things to say and couldn't figure out how to phrase one of them.

Sadness shifted against Conner's heart, but he was quick to dispense with that emotion, just as he had the grin.

"Sooner or later," Brody said, sounding not just solemn, but almost mournful, "we've got to talk about what happened."

"I vote 'later,'" Conner replied, looking away.

"I'm not going anywhere, little brother," Brody pressed quietly. "Not for any length of time, anyway. And that means you're going to have to deal with me."

"Here's an idea," Conner retorted briskly. "*You* stay here and manage the ranch for a decade, as I did, and *I'll* follow the rodeo circuit and bed down with a different woman every night."

Brody laughed, but it was a hoarse sound, a little raspy around the edges. "I hate to tell you this, cowboy, but you're too damn *old* for the rodeo. *That* stagecoach already pulled out, sorry to say."

The brothers were only thirty-three, but there was some truth in what Brody said. With the possible exceptions of team and calf roping, rodeo was a young man's game. A *very* young man's game, best given up, as Davis often said, before the bones got too brittle to mend after a spill.

Again, Conner felt that faint and familiar twinge of sorrow. He was careful not to glance in Brody's direction as he made a pretense of checking the automatic waterer in that stall. The devices often got clogged with bits of grass, hay or even manure, and making sure they were clear was second nature.

"What now, Brody?" he asked, when a few beats had passed.

"I told you," Brody answered, evidently in no hurry to move his carcass from in front of the stall door so Conner could get past him and go on into the house for that shower, the triple-decker sandwich and some beer. "I'm fixing to settle down right here on the ranch. Maybe build a house and a barn somewhere along the river one of these days."

"There's a big difference," Conner said, facing Brody at long last, over that stall door, "between what you say you're going to do and what you follow through on— *big brother.* So if it's all the same to you, I won't hold my breath while I'm waiting."

Brody finally stepped back so Conner could get by him, and they both fell into the old routine of doing the usual barn chores, feeding the horses, switching some of the animals to other stalls so the empty ones could be mucked out.

"I meant it, Conner," Brody said gruffly, and after a long time. "This place is home, and it's time for me to buckle down and make something of the rest of my life."

Surprised by the sincerity in his brother's voice, Conner, in the process of pushing a wheelbarrow full of horse manure out to the pile in back of the barn, a fact that would strike him as ironic in a few moments, stopped and looked at the other man with narrowed eyes.

Brody's gaze was clear, and he wasn't smirking.

Conner almost got suckered in.

But then he reminded himself that this was *Brody*

he was dealing with, a man who'd rather climb a tall tree to tell a lie than stand flat-footed on the ground and tell the truth.

"Brody?" he said.

"What?" Brody asked, a wary note in his voice.

"Go to hell," Conner answered, wheeling away with the load of manure.

"YES!" SASHA CRIED, glowing and fairly jamming Tricia's cell phone under her nose as she searched the commercial real-estate listings on the internet in her kitchen, hoping to discover that places like River's Bend and the derelict drive-in theater were finally starting to sell again. "Mom and Dad landed in Paris without a problem, and they think it would be *wonderful* if you and I went horseback riding on the Creed ranch next Sunday!"

Discouraged—there *were* no properties like hers for sale online, it seemed—Tricia smiled nonetheless. Above their heads, a light rain began to patter softly against the roof, and twilight, it seemed to Tricia, was falling a little ahead of schedule. Valentino and Winston were curled up together on Valentino's dog bed over in the corner, like the best of friends, snoozing away.

"Yep," Tricia said, accepting the phone and reading the text message for herself. "That's what it says, all right." She felt resignation—she'd been hoping Diana would refuse to grant Sasha permission to ride strange horses—but there was also a little thrill of illicit anticipation at the prospect of spending time with Conner Creed.

Of course, it would have helped if she'd known the first thing about horses, and if the very thought of perching high off the rocky ground in some hard saddle didn't scare her half to death. Sasha, perceptive beyond her tender years, rested a hand on Tricia's arm and looked at her with knowing compassion. "You can *do* this, Aunt Tricia," she said earnestly. "And I'll be right there to take care of you, the whole time."

Tricia's heart turned over. The child was only ten, but she meant what she said—she'd do her best to keep Tricia safe. And that was way too much responsibility for one little girl to carry.

"I'll be just fine," Tricia assured Sasha, giving her a quick, one-armed hug.

Sasha's attention had shifted to the computer monitor. "How are things in the real-estate business?" she asked, again sounding much older than she was.

Tricia sighed. "Not terrific, I'm afraid," she replied.

"Dad says the economy is coming back, no thanks to the politicians," Sasha told her. "He says he's nonpartisan, but *Mom* says he doesn't trust *any* elected official."

Tricia smiled and pushed back her chair, being careful not to bump Sasha. Ten years old, and the kid was using words liked *nonpartisan*. There was no question that homeschooling worked in her case, but was she growing up too fast? Childhood was fleeting and, sure, knowledge was power and all that, but Tricia couldn't help considering the possible trade-offs.

None of your business, she reminded herself silently, and turned up the wattage on her smile a little as she touched Sasha's nose. "Let's walk Valentino once more and then start supper."

Sasha glanced at the window and gave a little shiver. "But it's starting to rain," she protested, not quite whining, but close.

"You're from Seattle," Tricia pointed out. "You won't melt in a little rain."

"But Valentino is *sleeping,*" Sasha reasoned, widening her eyes. "Maybe we shouldn't disturb him. And if we go out, Winston will be all alone in the apartment."

Tricia crossed to the kitchen door, took her jacket off one of the pegs and held Sasha's out to her. "Winston," she said, "will find ways to amuse himself while we're gone." Valentino awakened, apparently sensing that there was a walk in the offing, and stretched luxuriously. He went to Tricia, waited patiently for her to fasten the leash to his collar.

Sasha resigned herself to the task ahead and pulled on her coat. Her mind was like quicksilver, and she immediately backtracked to the Seattle reference Tricia had made earlier. "You're from Seattle, too," she said. "Are you *ever* coming back?"

"Yes," Tricia answered, though there were times when she wondered if she'd ever get out of Lonesome Bend. It wasn't just the properties her dad had left her— she'd made a lot of friends in town and, besides, the thought of leaving Natty alone in that big house bothered her.

They stepped out onto the landing and found themselves in a misty drizzle and a crisp breeze. It wasn't quite dark, but the streetlights had already come on, and a car splashed by, the driver tooting the horn in jaunty greeting.

Busy descending the outside stairs, Tricia and Sasha both took a moment to wave in response.

"Who was that?" Sasha inquired, taking Valentino's leash from Tricia when they reached the bottom.

Tricia laughed. "I have no idea."

"When, though?" Sasha asked.

Tricia blinked. The child did not do segues. "Huh?"

"*When* are you moving back to Seattle?" Sasha sounded mildly impatient now, as they crossed the lawn to step onto the sidewalk.

"When I sell the campground and the drive-in theater," Tricia answered, putting herself between the little girl and the dog and the rain-washed street. "And, of course, I'll have to make sure my great-grandmother will be looked after."

"Oh," Sasha said, her expression serious as she weighed Tricia's reply. "Then are you going to marry Hunter?"

Tricia sighed. For all their "carrying on," as Natty referred to it, she and Hunter had never actually talked about marriage. "Do you want me to?" she asked, stalling.

To her surprise, Sasha made a face. "No. I just want you to live close to us again, so we can do things together, the way we used to."

Tricia didn't pursue her goddaughter's obvious distaste for Hunter, though she felt a slight sting of resentment toward Diana for passing her unfair antipathy toward him on to the child. "You're going to be living in Paris for a few years, remember? So we won't be seeing each other as often anyway."

Sasha looked up at her with big, worried eyes. "I miss you when we're not together, Aunt Tricia," she said. "You *are* coming to visit us in Paris, aren't you? We could go to the top of the Eiffel Tower and visit the Louvre—"

"I'll do my best," Tricia promised quietly, hoping Sasha would cheer up a little. "France is a long way from here, though, and the airline ticket would cost a lot of money."

"I'll bet you could get a ticket with Dad's frequent-flier miles. He's got a million of them."

"We'll see," Tricia hedged, as they all stopped to wait for Valentino to sniff the base of a streetlight.

Sasha changed the subject again, this time to the horseback ride on the Creed ranch, scheduled for the following Sunday afternoon. She was practically skipping along the sidewalk, she was so excited.

Tricia listened and smiled, gently taking Valentino's leash from Sasha, but behind that smile, she was wishing for a gracious way to get out of the whole thing.

With Natty away, she really should help run the rummage sale and chili feed, and she'd already be super busy at the campground and RV park, with so many customers reserving spots. The biggest job—cleaning up—would come after everyone had gone home, but Murphy's Law would be in full operation throughout the weekend, too. Things invariably went wrong with this electrical hookup or that part of the antiquated plumbing. Such situations made for unhappy campers, and Tricia had to be on call to make sure the repairs were done promptly.

Where, she wondered now, had she thought she would get the *time* to go riding on the Creed ranch? And what if she got hurt?

Valentino made good use of his walk, and Tricia, carrying her trusty plastic bag, picked up after him.

Back at the apartment, Valentino and Winston greeted each other as joyfully as if they'd expected to be apart forever, touching their noses and then retiring to the dog bed again.

Tricia washed up and started supper—a simple meat loaf made from canned soup—and Sasha, having been granted permission, sat down in front of the computer and went online to check her email.

It seemed to Tricia that kids today came into the world already hard-wired for all forms of technology. When *she* was Sasha's age, she reflected, personal computers were just coming into common use, and things like digital cameras and MP3 players hadn't even been *invented* yet. She'd listened to CDs and watched movies on VHS and wondered how her parents, not to mention her great-grandmother, had gotten by with vinyl records and analog TV.

She was considering all this, and keeping one eye on Sasha and the display on the computer monitor, *plus* chopping vegetables for a salad to go with the already-baking meat loaf, when the wall phone jangled.

"Hello?"

"It's you, dear," Natty's quavery voice responded, with relief. Whom, Tricia wondered, had her great-grandmother *expected* to answer?

Natty promptly answered that unspoken question, as it happened. "I meant to call Conner Creed," she said. "I must have dialed your number out of habit. How are you, dear? How is Winston?"

Tricia barely registered the words that came after *I meant to call Conner Creed,* but she managed to get the gist of them. "Winston and I are both doing fine. How are you?"

Natty sighed. "I'm afraid I've developed a little hitch in my get-along," she said. Then, almost too quickly, she added, "Not that it's anything serious, of course. I planned to be back in Lonesome Bend before the weekend, so I could oversee the chili making, but it seems my heartbeat is a tiny bit irregular and the doctors don't want me traveling just yet."

Tricia was so alarmed that she forgot to ask why Natty wanted to call Conner. "Your heartbeat is irregular? I don't like the sound of that—"

"I'll be fine," Natty broke in, chirpy as a bird. "Don't you dare waste a moment worrying about me."

Tricia closed her eyes, opened them again. Forced a smile that she hoped would be audible in her voice. "I have a visitor," she said, and proceeded to tell her great-grandmother all about Sasha and the move to Paris. "Oh," honor compelled her to add, at the tail end of the conversation, "and I'm fostering a dog. I hope you don't mind. He's really very well behaved and Winston seems to like him a lot."

"I didn't object to Rusty," Natty said, sounding less shaky-voiced than before and thereby lifting Tricia's spirits, "and I certainly won't object to this one. You're alone too much. A dog is at least *some* company."

Sasha, eavesdropping shamelessly, frowned.

When Natty and Tricia finally said goodbye, Sasha planked herself in front of Tricia, hands on her hips. "You're just *fostering* Valentino?" Sasha demanded. "He doesn't get to stay with you?"

CHAPTER SEVEN

CONNER, WHO HAD taken his sandwich and his can of beer out onto the porch so he could watch the rain fall while he ate—and, in the process, ignore Brody—fumbled for his ringing cell phone, juggled it and finally rasped a gruff "Hello?" into the speaker.

His favorite elderly lady announced herself in a perky tone. "Natty McCall here," she said brightly. "I *am* speaking to Conner, aren't I?"

He chuckled. "You are," he said. Seated in the wooden swing some ancestor had added, Conner shifted to set the beer and his sandwich plate aside on a small wicker table. "Are you back in town, Natty, or do we have to get by without you for a little while longer?"

"You always were a charmer," Natty said, all aflutter. "Alas, I've been detained in Denver for a little longer, and I have a favor to ask."

Conner smiled at her terminology—the word *detained* made it sound as if she'd been arrested. "Have you been carousing around the Mile High City again, Natty?" he teased. "Riding mechanical bulls in honky-tonks and the like?"

She tittered at that, well aware that he was joking, but probably a little bit flattered to be thought *capable* of walking on the wild side, too. "I do declare," she said, and he could actually hear a blush in her voice.

That was when the screen door creaked on its hinges, and out of the corner of his eye, he saw Brody step out onto the porch. "You know you're my best girl," he told her. "What's the favor?"

Natty was warming to her subject; there was a sense of revving up in the way she spoke—it reminded him of the toy cars and trucks he and Brody had as kids, the kind a kid winds up by rolling them fast and hard on the floor before letting them speed away. "Nothing big," she said. "I'd like you to check on my house now and then, that's all. Just to make sure everything's all right with—well—with the *plumbing* and things of that sort."

Conner raised his brows slightly, avoiding Brody's gaze, though he could see out of the corner of his eye that his brother was leaning idly against the porch rail, rain dripping from the eaves in a gray curtain behind him, his arms loosely folded. He wasn't even trying to pretend he wasn't listening in.

"The plumbing?" Conner echoed, searching his memory for any occasion when Natty had expressed concern about the pipes in her house, to him, anyway.

It crossed his mind that the old woman might be up to some matchmaking between him and Tricia, but he quickly dismissed the thought as unworthy of Natty.

"Pipes can freeze, you know," Natty fretted, her voice still picking up speed. "And I would hate to come home and find that there had been a flood in my kitchen or something like that. Those floors are original to the house, and it would be a pity if they were ruined, being irreplaceable and all—"

"Natty," Conner interrupted gently.

She paused, drew an audible breath and let it out again. "What?"

"I'll be happy to check on the plumbing at your place," he said.

Brody grinned at that. Shook his head slightly, as if he was at once bemused and disgusted.

"It's mainly the pipes under the house that I'm concerned about," Natty went on. "I couldn't ask Tricia to crawl around under the house. There might be spiders."

"I'm on it," Conner reiterated, "but I do have one question." He'd never known Natty to miss the annual rummage sale/chili feed. She was, after all, the Keeper of the Secret Recipe. "Are you all right?"

"I'm fine," Natty said briskly.

He suspected that she was fibbing, but challenging an old lady's statement hadn't been part of his upbringing. Elders, be they friends, like Natty, acquaintances or total strangers, were to be treated with respect—particularly if they happened to be female.

"You're sure?" he ventured just the same, slanting a glare at Brody then. *Go away.*

Brody, being Brody, didn't budge an inch. He just broadened his grin by a notch.

"I'm *absolutely* sure, Conner," Natty replied. Then she gave a trilling little laugh that sounded almost bell-like. Years fell away, and Conner could easily picture her as a young woman, and a pretty one, not unlike her great-granddaughter. "I'm perfectly fine. Fit as a fiddle."

"It's just that the rummage sale is coming up," Conner pressed, still concerned.

Brody frowned comically at this.

"I've stepped down from chairing the committee," Natty told him. "I am getting on a little, you know."

She'd been ninety-one on her last birthday, Conner

knew, though he'd missed the party because he was down in Stone Creek at the time, helping Steven paint the nursery before the twins were delivered.

"You're younger than springtime," Conner said, recalling the line from one of the old songs Natty liked to play on her stereo.

"And you're full of beans," Natty shot back, always ready with another cliché. She was getting tired, though; he could hear that in her voice.

The chat ended soon after that and, for all Natty's insistence that she was "just fine," Conner was still worried. He sat there frowning for a few moments, then decided he'd head for Natty's house as soon as the chores were done the next morning. Take along some insulation and some duct tape to wrap around the pipes under the house.

Tricia probably wouldn't be around, of course. She'd be over at the campground, working, or maybe at the drive-in theater—a spooky place, closed down long before the multiplex movie houses in Denver came along—doing whatever might need doing.

He'd track her down, ask her if she'd spoken to Natty recently.

Brody, still lounging against the porch railing, shifted his weight from one side to the other, distracting Conner from his thoughts. "For a minute there," Brody said, in a low drawl, "I had high hopes that you were lining up a hot date."

Conner realized that he was still holding his phone and dropped it back into the pocket of the clean but worn flannel shirt he'd put on, along with a pair of jeans, after his shower. Then he reached for his beer and took a long draw of the stuff before answering, "There

are other things in life besides getting laid, you know."
The statement sounded prissy-assed even to him, and
Conner immediately wished he could take it back.

"Like what?" Brody joked.

Conner didn't reply, but simply sat there, holding
his beer and wishing Brody would go away. To another
state, say. If not another planet.

"Once upon a time," Brody said easily, determined
to push, "you had a sense of humor."

"I still do," Conner said, staring past Brody, into
the gray drizzle. "When something's funny, I laugh."

Brody heaved a sigh. Pushed away from the porch
rail, finally, to stand up straight. His arms fell to his
sides. "It's hard to imagine that," he said, very quietly,
and then he went back inside the house. The screen door
shut behind him with barely a sound.

And Conner felt guilty. How crazy was that? If
Brody had expected to just pick up where they'd left
off—before their knock-down-drag-out over Joleen—
he'd been kidding himself. Conner swore under his
breath and used the heels of his boots to thrust the ancient porch swing into slow, squeaky motion.

Brody wouldn't stay long, he thought, trying to console himself. His brother was bound to get bored with
Lonesome Bend and the ranch, sooner rather than later,
and hit the road again, following the rodeo. Or some
woman.

The rain picked up, and the wind blew it in under
the roof of the porch, and Conner finally had to give up
and go inside. He climbed the front staircase, noticing
that the crystal chandelier was dusty, and headed for
the master bedroom. The suite had belonged to Kim
and Davis before they moved into the new house, and

it didn't lack for comfort. There was a big-screen TV on one wall, and the private bath was the size of an NFL locker room, with slate-tile floors, a big shower with multiple sprayers and a tub made for soaking the ache out of sore muscles.

While all that space might have made sense for his aunt and uncle, it felt cavernous to Conner. He probably would have moved back into the room at the other end of the corridor—the one he'd shared with Brody and, in the summertime, Steven, too, when they were all growing up—but he knew Brody had stowed his gear in there.

Conner switched on the TV, then switched it off again, in the next moment. In his opinion, TV sucked, for the most part. He did enjoy watching athletic women in bikinis "surviving" in some hostile environment, but that was about all.

He hauled his shirt off over his head, to save himself the trouble of unbuttoning it, and tossed the garment to one side. Then he sat down on the edge of the bed, which was way too big for one person, and got out of his boots and socks. Standing up again, he dispensed with his jeans, too, and stood there, in the altogether, thinking Brody wasn't so far wrong, implying that he didn't have a life.

In the end, he tossed back the covers, crawled between them and reached for the thick biography of Thomas Jefferson sitting on the nightstand. He sighed. Another night with nobody but a dead president for company.

Yee-freakin'-haw.

TRICIA OPENED ONE EYE—how could it possibly be morning already?—and slowly tuned in to her surroundings, glimmer by glimmer, sound by sound, scent by scent.

The sun was shining. Rain dripped from the eaves, but no longer pelted the roof. The timer on the coffeepot beeped, and the tantalizing aroma of fresh brew teased her nose.

Valentino approached, laid his muzzle on her pillow, inches from her face, and whined almost inaudibly.

Something, somewhere, was clanging.

Tricia sat up, glanced at her alarm clock, which she'd forgotten to set the night before, and sucked in a breath. She'd overslept. And that wasn't like her at all.

Clang, clang, clang.

Since she was wearing a sweat suit, and she figured that was the next best thing to being fully dressed, Tricia didn't bother with a robe. Nor did she pause to put on the ugly pink slippers. Sasha, still clad in pink pajamas, joined her in the kitchen.

The child's eyes were big. "What *is* that?" she asked, nearly in a whisper.

"I'll find out," Tricia said, annoyed but not alarmed. She went to the sink and, wadding up a dish towel, wiped a circle into the steam covering the window so she could peer out at the backyard.

The driveway was empty.

"Is something going to blow up?" Sasha fretted, probably imagining an antiquated furnace, or even a steam boiler with a pressure gauge, chugging cartoonishly away in Natty's basement, building up to a roof-raising blast.

"No, sweetie," Tricia said, offering what she hoped was a reassuring smile. "I'm sure nothing is going to explode. This is an old house, and sometimes the pipes make odd noises. So do the floorboards."

"Oh," Sasha said, clearly unconvinced.

Valentino, meanwhile, was standing very close to Sasha, actually leaning into her side. Clearly, he was no guard dog.

"Wait here, while I go downstairs and have a look around," Tricia told them both.

Sasha swallowed visibly, looking small and vulnerable, and then nodded.

The clanging resumed, intermittent and muffled.

Tricia descended the inside stairway and followed the sound through Natty's chilly rooms to the kitchen.

Silence.

Then the clang came again, this time from directly under her feet.

Tricia started slightly, then after gathering her resolve, marched over to Natty's basement door. She barely registered the rapid rush of footsteps on the wooden stairs beyond—she hadn't had coffee yet—and she'd turned the knob and pulled before it occurred to her that the idea might not have been a good one.

A squeak scratched its way up her windpipe and past her vocal cords when she found herself staring directly into Conner Creed's smiling face. Because he was still on the basement stairs, they were at eye level.

And that alone was disconcerting.

"Sorry," he said, clearly delighted by her expression. "I didn't mean to scare you."

"What are you doing here?" The squeak had turned to a squawk, but at least she could speak coherently now. Tricia's heart seemed to be trying to crash through her rib cage.

Conner held up a roll of gray duct tape in one hand and a wrench—no doubt the source of the clanging sounds—in the other. "Plumbing?" he asked, as though he wasn't entirely sure what he'd been doing and wanted Tricia to affirm it for him.

She folded her arms, foolishly barring his way into the kitchen. "You could have knocked," she said.

Conner lifted one shoulder, lowered it again. His grin didn't falter. "Natty called me last night and asked me to wrap the pipes. I crawled around under the house with a flashlight for a while, making sure there weren't any obvious leaks, and then I checked the situation in the basement." He paused, ran his eyes lightly over Tricia's rumpled hair, coming loose from its braid, before letting his gaze rest on her lips for one tingly moment. "The padlock on the cellar door probably rusted through years ago. I didn't need the key Natty told me about."

At last, Tricia found the presence of mind to back up so Conner could step into the kitchen. Now he stood a head taller.

"I'll be happy to replace it," he added. His eyes narrowed a little as he watched her, as if he'd suddenly noticed something new and disturbing about her.

"Replace what?" she asked.

The grin returned, faintly insolent and, at the same time, affable. Even friendly.

"The padlock?" he prompted, in the same guessing-game tone he'd used moments before.

It was the most ordinary conversation—about padlocks and plumbing, for Pete's sake. So why did she feel like a shy debutante about to step onto the dance floor at her coming-out ball?

"Oh," she finally managed. "Right. The padlock."

Natty's kitchen was frigidly cold, and yet, because they were standing within a few feet of each other, the hard heat coming off Conner's body made Tricia feel as though she were standing in front of a blazing bonfire.

Or was *she* the source of it?

Conner set the duct tape and the wrench aside on a countertop, rested his hands on his hips. "Will you be joining us for the trail ride on Sunday?" he asked.

Not for the first time, Tricia had a strange sense of needing to translate the things this man said from some other language before she could grasp their meaning. "I—guess," she said, recalling in the next instant that she'd promised Sasha the outing, and backing out wasn't an option.

"But—?" he asked, watching her.

She finally rustled up a smile, but it felt flimsy on her mouth and wouldn't stick. "It's just that I've never been on a horse before," she admitted.

His eyes lit at that, blue fire framed by a narrow rim of steely gray, and his mouth crooked up in that way Tricia couldn't seem to get used to. "No problem," he told her, his tone faintly gruff.

No problem.

Easy enough for *him* to say, she thought, just as Valentino and Sasha clomped down the stairs from her apartment. Conner Creed had probably been born in the saddle, growing up on a ranch the way he had. She, on the other hand, had never ridden anything more dangerous than a carousel.

"We'll put you on one of the mares," Conner went on, when she didn't speak. "Sunflower would be a good choice—she's three years older than dirt and you'd be more likely to get hurt riding a stick horse."

Tricia was relieved and, at the same time, a little indignant. Before she could come up with a fitting response, however, Sasha and Valentino made their appearance.

Seeing Conner, Sasha beamed. "Hello, Mr. Creed," she said.

He nodded to the child, smiled back. "It's okay to call me Conner," he told her.

Pleased, Sasha barely glanced at Tricia, stroking Valentino's head as the two of them stood just inside the kitchen doorway. "I'm Sasha," she announced.

"I remember," Conner said easily. "My nephew, Matt, introduced us at the barbecue last weekend, didn't he?"

Sasha nodded eagerly. "He's pretty nice, for a little kid," she said.

Conner chuckled and looked briefly in Tricia's direction—just in time to catch her sneaking a step back. She felt magnetized, like a passing asteroid being pulled into the orbit of some enormous planet.

He smiled, dashing all hope that he hadn't noticed.

Tricia's cheeks flamed. She'd worked hard, ever since high school, to overcome her natural shyness, but when it came to this man, all that effort seemed to be for nothing. A look from him, a word, and every cell in her body suddenly leaped to electrified attention.

It was ridiculous.

"Do you think Natty's all right?" he asked, his expression serious now. His face could change in an instant, it seemed, and that made him hard to read.

Tricia didn't like it when people were hard to read.

"Why do you ask?" she inquired, a little jolt of alarm trembling in the pit of her stomach.

Conner wasn't wearing a hat, being indoors, though she could tell that he'd had one on earlier. He ran the fingers of his left hand through his hair, watched with a smile in his eyes as Sasha excused herself and left the room, Valentino trotting alongside.

"I guess it bothers me a little that she's staying on in Denver," Conner sighed, when he and Tricia were alone in the big kitchen again. "It's not like your great-grandmother to miss out on the big weekend, even if she has stepped down as head chili commando."

Though quiet, his tone was so genuine that it touched something deep and private inside Tricia, stirred a soft but still-bruising sweetness where he shouldn't have been able to reach. They were basically strangers, she and Conner—they certainly hadn't been more than summer acquaintances growing up—and yet it was as if they'd known each other well, once upon a time and somewhere far, far away.

When she thought she could trust herself to speak, Tricia found another smile, and managed to hold on to it a little longer this time. In truth, she was worried, too. Should she mention that Natty was staying in Denver at the suggestion of her doctor?

No, she decided, in the next second. If Natty had wanted Conner to know why she'd postponed her return to Lonesome Bend, she would have told him herself.

"I'm sure she's fine," she said at last, though of course she wasn't sure at all. Natty *had* said her heart had been racing.

Conner studied her for a few moments, looking like he wanted to say something but wouldn't, and then he flashed that dazzling grin at her again. It was like stepping into the glare of a searchlight on a moonless night, and Tricia blinked once.

"You might want to keep it a little warmer in here," he said, in another of those hairpin conversational turns of his. "Even wrapped, some of the pipes might freeze if you don't turn on the heat."

Tricia nodded, feeling stupid because no response came to mind.

Conner grinned, gave his head an almost impercep- tible shake. "Sorry if I scared you a little while ago, banging on the plumbing with my wrench. I got here a little earlier than I expected and, though it seems ironic now, I was pretty sure you'd already gone out."

Again she felt that sugary sting, inexplicably pleas- ant, but highly discomforting, too. "Natty asked you to come over," she said, with a verbal shrug, "and I'm sure she appreciates your help."

His grin was rueful now, but it tugged at her, none- theless. "I'd do just about anything for Natty," he said, moving to retrieve the duct tape and the wrench from the nearby counter and then stopping to look back over one shoulder. "Turn up the heat," he added.

Tricia almost said, "I beg your pardon?" but she stopped herself in time. Nodded again.

"Sixty-eight degrees ought to do it," Conner said. He took another long, slow look at her. "See you around," he told her, heading for the back door.

See you around.

That was all he'd said. And it was a perfectly nor- mal remark, too.

Just the same, Tricia stood as still as if her feet were glued to the floor until several seconds after he'd closed the door behind him.

The first thing she did, once she could move again, was turn the lock. The second was to find and adjust the downstairs thermostat.

Now, she thought, making the climb back up to her

own space, if she could just turn down the heat inside *herself.*

Upstairs, she found Sasha eating cold cereal at the table, while Winston and Valentino enjoyed their separate bowls of dry food.

After pouring a cup of much-needed coffee, Tricia booted up her computer. The screen saver loomed up automatically, filling the monitor and taking Tricia a little aback, even though she'd seen that picture of herself and Hunter, in front of the ski lodge, at least a jillion times.

"Mom says you can do a lot better than Hunter," Sasha remarked casually, no doubt prompted by the photograph.

A little of Tricia's coffee splashed over the rim of her cup and burned her fingers, but beyond that, she showed no outward reaction. "Does she, now?" she asked, amused but mildly resentful toward Diana, too. Surely her very best friend in the world hadn't meant to make such an observation within her daughter's earshot.

"That's what she told my dad," Sasha said, and resumed her cereal crunching.

Tricia kept her back to the little girl, focusing on the computer's keyboard instead, going online and clicking on the mailbox icon at the top of the screen.

Normally, she would have felt a little thrill to find no less than three messages from Hunter in among the usual sales pitches for miracle vitamins, quick riches and sexual-enhancement products. This morning, in the wake of another encounter with Conner Creed, all Tricia could work up was a dull sense of futility. Seattle seemed very far away, and so did Hunter.

Sasha, apparently, was determined to keep the verbal ball rolling. "I think Conner is *really* handsome," she observed.

"Hmm," Tricia responded noncommittally, without turning around. She'd opened the first of Hunter's emails.

Hi, babe, he'd written.

Much to her own surprise, Tricia bristled a little. *Babe?* Mexican cruise or not, where did Hunter get off calling her *babe?* After all, the man virtually ignored her for weeks—if not *months*—at a time. Wasn't that term a touch on the intimate side, considering how they'd drifted apart?

Tricia felt a twinge then; when her conscience spoke, it was usually in Diana's voice. *You* did *accept the invitation, Miss Hot-to-trot,* came the brisk and typically no-nonsense reminder. *Did you think Hunter was suggesting a platonic getaway?*

Tricia's spine straightened. Why—oh, *why*—had she blithely sidestepped what should have been obvious to anyone?—*that she and Hunter would be sharing a cabin on the ship. And that meant sex.*

"Oh, Lord," she said aloud.

"Huh?" Sasha asked, from the table.

"Never mind," Tricia said, focusing in on the rest of Hunter's email.

It amounted to online foreplay, essentially, and she closed it with a self-conscious click of the mouse. Then she deleted it entirely. And felt even more foolish than before.

In that moment, she would have given just about anything to exchange some girl talk with Diana, despite the sure and certain knowledge that her best friend would tell her to kick Hunter to the curb and get on with her life.

With her friend in another time zone, though, and Sasha right there in the same room, a chat simply wasn't feasible.

"Don't you have to work today?" Sasha asked. Tricia hadn't heard her push back her chair to rise, but the little girl was standing at her elbow now, studying her thoughtfully.

Tricia couldn't find a smile. Maybe, she thought, with rueful whimsy, she could pick one up at the rummage sale.

"There isn't much to do, with the camping season coming to an end," she said. "We're all ready for the weekend, so I thought we'd go over to the community center and help set up for the rummage sale."

Sasha, who had probably never rummaged for anything in her admittedly short life, lit up at the prospect. "Awesome!" she enthused. "Can Valentino come, too?"

"I don't think he'd enjoy that," Tricia answered diplomatically. "What do you say we get ourselves dressed and take a certain dog out for a quick walk?"

CHAPTER EIGHT

BRODY WAS DEFINITELY up to something, though damned if Conner could figure out what it was. He'd helped himself to a pair of Conner's own jeans, Brody had, and one of his best shirts, too, and he'd shaved for the first time since his return to Lonesome Bend. If his hair hadn't been longer than Conner's, and way shaggier, they'd have been mirror images of each other.

And if all that wasn't bothersome enough, Brody not only had the coffee on by the time Conner wandered into the kitchen, after making the run into town to check on Natty McCall's pipes, he was cooking up some bacon and eggs at the old wood-burning stove.

Conner meandered over to the counter, took the carafe from its burner and poured himself a dose of java. He'd been thinking about Tricia ever since he'd scared the hell out of her at the top of Natty's basement steps that morning, and irritation with his brother provided some relief.

"Mornin'," Brody sang out, as if he were just noticing Conner's presence.

Conner squinted, studying his brother suspiciously. He'd gotten used to living his life as a separate individual since Brody left home, and it was a jolt to look up and see *himself* standing on the other side of the room. Gave him a familiar but still weird sense of being in two places at once.

"Since when do you cook?" he asked, after shaking off the sensation and taking a sip from his mug. Only then did he take off his coat and hang it from its peg by the back door.

Brody laughed at that. "I picked up the habit after I left home," he replied easily. "Believe it or not, I find myself between women now and then."

Conner rolled his eyes. "So then you just knock some hapless female over the head with a club and drag her back to your cave by the hair? Tell her to put a pot of beans on the fire?"

Brody slanted a look at him, and there was a certain sadness in his expression, Conner thought, unsettled. "I didn't mean it like that," Brody said, his voice quiet.

"Right," Conner said, his voice gone gruff, all of a sudden, with an emotion he couldn't name. He looked his brother up and down. "So what's up with the clothes?"

Again, the grin flashed, quick and cocky. Brody speared a slice of bacon with a fork and turned it over in the skillet before looking down at Conner's duds. "All my stuff is in the laundry," he said. "Hope you don't mind."

Conner scowled and swung a leg over the long bench lining one side of the kitchen table, taking more coffee on board and trying to figure out what the hell was going on.

"Would you give a damn if I *did* mind?"

Brody didn't say anything; he just went right on rustling up grub at the stove, though he did pause once to refill his own coffee cup, whistling low through his teeth as he concentrated on the task at hand. That tuneless drone had always bugged Conner, but now it *really* got on his last nerve.

"If you insist on staying," he told Brody's back, "why don't you bunk in over at Kim and Davis's place?"

Brody took his sweet time answering, scraping eggs onto a waiting platter and piling about a dozen strips of limp bacon into a crooked heap on top.

"I might have done just that," Brody finally replied, crossing to set the platter down on the table with a thump before going back to the cupboard for plates and flatware, "except that they've already got a housesitter, and she happens not to be one of my biggest fans."

Conner stifled an unexpected chuckle, made his face steely when Brody headed back toward the table and took one of the chairs opposite. They ate in silence for a while.

Kim *had* mentioned hiring somebody to stay in their house while she and Davis were on the road, Conner recalled. Most likely, it was Carolyn Simmons; she was always housesitting for one person or another.

"Carolyn," Conner said, out loud.

Across the table, Brody looked up from his food and grinned. "What about her?"

Conner felt his neck heat up a little, realizing that there had been a considerable gap between Brody's remark and his response. "I was just wondering how you managed to make her hate you already," he said, somewhat defensively, stabbing at the last bite of his fried eggs with his fork.

"I didn't say Carolyn hated me," Brody explained, the grin lingering in his eyes, though there was no vestige of it on his mouth. "I said she isn't one of my biggest fans."

He paused, finished off a slice of bacon, and finally went on. "We have a—history, Carolyn and I."

To Conner's knowledge, Brody hadn't been anywhere near Lonesome Bend in better than a decade, and Carolyn hadn't moved to town until a few years ago. Which begged the question, "What kind of history?"

Brody sighed deeply, crossed his fork and knife in the middle of his plate and propped his elbows on the table's edge, his expression thoughtful. Maybe even a little grim. His gaze was fixed on something in the next county.

"The usual kind," he said, at some length.

"How do you know her?"

Why, Conner wondered, did he want to know? He liked Carolyn, but things had never gone beyond that, attraction-wise.

Brody met his eyes with a directness that took Conner by surprise. "It's a small world," he said. After a beat, he added, "You interested in her? Carolyn, I mean?"

Conner made a snortlike sound, pushed his own plate away. "No," he said.

"Then why all the questions?"

"What questions?"

"'What kind of history?'" Brody repeated, with exaggerated patience. "'How do you know her?' *Those* questions."

"Maybe I was just trying to make conversation," Conner hedged. "Did you ever think of that?"

"Like hell you were," Brody scoffed, with a false chuckle. "You can't wait to see the back of me and we both know it. But here's the problem, little brother— I'm not going anywhere."

Something tightened in Conner's throat. He might have said he was sorry to hear that Brody was staying, but he couldn't get the words out.

Brody shoved back his chair and stood, picking up his empty plate to put it in the sink, the way Kim had trained all three of "her boys" to do after a meal, from the time they could reach that high. "I could tell you a few things, Conner," he said hoarsely, "if I thought there was a snowball's chance in hell that you'd listen."

With that, Brody turned and walked away.

He set his plate in the sink and banked the fire in the cookstove and slammed out the back door—after shrugging into Conner's flannel-lined denim jacket.

FOLKS WERE LINED up all the way to the corner that next Saturday morning when Tricia and Sasha drove past the community center and circled around back to park in one of a half-dozen spots reserved for volunteers. They'd already stopped by River's Bend, where every camping spot and RV hookup was in profitable use by the annual influx of visitors, just to make sure everything was in order.

Although they'd spent much of the previous day helping to set up for the big sale, and were therefore in the much-envied position of having seen the plethora of merchandise ahead of time, Sasha was impressed by the size of the crowd.

"There must be a lot of hoarders in this town," she said. "Why do they want to buy the stuff other people gave away?"

Tricia chuckled, then squeezed the Pathfinder into the last parking space and checked her watch. "It must be the thrill of the hunt," she answered. "Or it could be the chili. Natty's been offered a small fortune for the recipe."

Sasha considered the reply, still fastened into her booster seat, then observed, "It was funny, how you made all those other ladies turn their backs while you put in the secret ingredients."

After consulting Natty by telephone the day before, Tricia had run the family chili recipe to ground and memorized the unique combination of spices some ancestor had dreamed up. She had indeed insisted that all present look away while she extracted various metal boxes and sprinkle jars from a plain paper bag and added them to the massive kettles of beans already simmering on the burners of the community center's commercial-size stove.

Her great-grandmother's cronies, tight-lipped at all the "folderol" involved in keeping the formula a secret, had agreed only because the event just wouldn't be the same without Natty's chili. Indeed, Minerva Snyder had allowed, there might even be a riot if they failed to deliver.

Chuckling at the memory, Tricia got out of the rig and went to help Sasha release the snaps and buckles holding her in the booster seat.

Sasha's eyes twinkled with excitement. She'd sneaked a peek at the mysterious items while Tricia was doctoring the chili the day before and, given the child's IQ, Tricia had no doubt that she could have recited the recipe from memory. "Remember," Tricia said, putting a finger to her lips, "Natty doesn't want anybody to know what's in that chili."

After jumping to the ground, Sasha nodded importantly. "Well, there are beans and some hamburger. Everybody knows that part."

"Yes," Tricia agreed, going around behind the Pathfinder to raise the hatch. "Everybody knows that part." They'd left Valentino at home, contentedly sharing his dog bed with Winston while they both snoozed, but Tricia, feeling inspired, had scrounged up a few more donations the night before, including the pink furry slippers Diana had given her, tossing them into a cardboard box with some other stuff. She'd put the slippers at the bottom, hoping Sasha wouldn't spot them and report the incident to her mother the next time they talked or texted.

Just as Tricia turned around, having hoisted the somewhat unwieldy box into both arms, juggling it awkwardly while she shut the hatch again, Conner Creed walked up to her. Her breath caught, and the box wobbled in her arms.

Conner took it from her just before she would have spilled its contents into the dusty gravel of the parking lot.

How did he manage to startle her the way he did? Tricia wondered, bedazzled, as always, by his ready grin. It was an unfair advantage, that grin.

"Hello," she said stupidly.

"Howdy," he replied, holding the cumbersome box easily in his two muscular arms. He looked down at Sasha and winked. "Hey," he greeted the enthralled little girl. "Are we still on for the trail ride tomorrow afternoon?"

Sasha nodded eagerly and then blurted out a happy "Yes!" for good measure.

"Good," Conner said, heading toward the back door of the community center, which was propped open with a big chunk of wood that had probably served as somebody's chopping block, sometime way back. People in Lonesome Bend liked to put things to use, no matter how ordinary.

Tricia locked the Pathfinder with the button on her key fob and followed Conner and Sasha, who was practically skipping alongside the man, toward the rear entrance.

"More stuff?" one of the women in the kitchen

chimed. Several volunteers had stayed through the night, keeping an eye on the simmering pots of chili. "That Kim. She always donates twice as much rummage as anybody else in town!"

Conner, his back still turned to Tricia, chuckled at that. "True," he said. "But Tricia brought these things."

Tricia peeked around him, waggled her fingers in greeting. Some of Natty's friends, like a flock of old hens, still had ruffled feathers from yesterday's intrigue involving the spices for the chili.

One or two straightened their apron strings, and another harrumphed, but these were small-town women, basically sociable, and they wouldn't hold a grudge— not against Natty McCall's great-granddaughter, anyway.

Conner seemed to know where to set the box down— there were plenty of last-minute donations, it appeared, even though the door was about to open to the anxious public.

"Thanks," Tricia said, as Conner passed her, doubling back toward the kitchen.

"You're welcome," he told her, with a nod of farewell.

She hadn't really expected Conner to hang around the rummage sale all day—it was a rare man who did— but Tricia felt oddly bereft when he'd left, and when Sasha tugged at her hand to get her attention, she realized she'd been staring after the man like some moonstruck teenager.

Carolyn Simmons turned up just then, greeting Tricia with a smile and a gesture toward the front of the building, where the waiting customers were already pressing their faces to the windows, ogling the chicken-shaped egg timer, the row of ratty prom dresses, the chipped teapots, and the dusty books and the jumbles of old shoes piled on the table marked, "Everything 50 Cents!"

"Looks like we're in for another big year!" Carolyn said. Her attractively highlighted blond hair was pulled up into a ponytail and, like Tricia, she wore jeans, a long-sleeved T-shirt and sneakers.

"Looks that way," Tricia agreed, while Sasha sat down on the lid of a donated cedar chest, which had been découpaged at some point in the distant past with what looked like pages torn from vintage movie magazines, and folded her hands to wait for the onslaught.

The whole thing probably seemed pretty exotic to a little girl raised in Seattle, Tricia thought, with that familiar rush of tenderness. What a gift it was, this visit from Sasha, and how quickly it would be over.

Evelyn Moore, one of the women from the kitchen, bustled to the foreground, holding a stopwatch in her plump hand, and a great production was made of the countdown.

"Three—two—one—"

New Year's Eve in Times Square had nothing on Lonesome Bend, Colorado, Tricia thought, amused, when it came to ratcheting up the suspense.

At precisely nine o'clock, Evelyn turned the lock and took some quick steps backwards, in order to avoid being trampled by eager shoppers.

The next hour, naturally, was hectic indeed—at one point, when two women wanted the same wafflemaker and seemed about to come to blows, Tricia and Carolyn had to intervene.

"It probably doesn't even work anymore," Sasha observed, with a nod at the small appliance. She'd been helping to bag people's purchases, and when Tricia's pink slippers went for a nickel, she hadn't so much as batted an eye. "And, besides, the cord is frayed."

"The hunter/gatherer phenomenon," Carolyn explained, though she looked as mystified as Sasha did.

Tricia gave one of Sasha's pigtails a gentle tug. "Let me know when you're ready to try the chili," she said.

"We just had *breakfast,*" Sasha reminded her, casually horrified.

Tricia laughed and then there was a rush on the prom dresses and they both went back to work.

"Look," Sasha said, when the rush had subsided a little, sometime later, "Conner's back." Her forehead creased into a frown. "Who is that woman with him?"

Tricia, feeling that annoying tension Conner Creed always aroused in her, turned to see a couple just coming through the main door. She blinked. The tension ebbed away.

The man smiling down at the beautiful red-haired woman, his hand pressed solicitously to the small of her back, *wasn't* Conner. It was Brody.

Tricia couldn't have said how she knew that, because the resemblance was stunning; Brody was a perfect reflection of Conner, right down to his clothes and a very recent haircut.

Back in the day, the Creed brothers had been infamous for impersonating each other and, not knowing them well, Tricia had been fooled, like almost everyone else.

Now, he approached her, the lovely Joleen Williams trailing behind him, bestowing her breathtaking smile on all and sundry. "Tricia," he said, with a little nod.

Her hand tightening slightly on Sasha's shoulder, to keep the child from blurting out something *Tricia* would regret, she replied, "Hello, Brody." She looked past him, nodded. "Hi, Joleen. It's been a long time."

"Yes," Joleen said thoughtfully, sizing Tricia up with a slow sweep of her emerald-green eyes. "So long that I can't remember, for the life of me, who you are."

"Tricia McCall," Tricia offered, amused. Of course, being one of the most popular girls in town, Joleen wouldn't remember her, the summer visitor who rarely said more than two words running.

Brody gave Joleen a mildly exasperated glance.

"You're Conner's *twin*," Sasha said, with the air of one having a revelation. "You were at the barbecue by the river."

"Yep," Brody said.

"You didn't look so much like him then," Sasha went on, nonplussed. "Your hair was longer and your clothes were different. Now, you look *exactly* like Conner. I thought you *were* Conner."

"Sasha," Tricia said, squeezing again.

Joleen, evidently bored, wandered off.

"How are people supposed to tell you apart?" Sasha demanded, as though confronting an imposter.

Brody chuckled. "I'm the good-looking one," he said.

Sasha wasn't amused, though Tricia, knowing her well, saw that she was softening a little.

"Most kids like me," Brody said, with a twinkle in his eyes, as his gaze connected with Tricia's again. "But I seem to be zero-for-zero with this one."

Sasha, Tricia noticed, was watching Joleen. "Is she your girlfriend?"

"Sasha!" Tricia said.

But Brody didn't seem to be bothered by the question. He crouched, so he could look directly into Sasha's face. "Nope," he said seriously. "Is that a good thing or a bad one?"

"Depends," Sasha answered, sliding another glance in Joleen's direction and neatly slipping out of shoulder-squeezing distance from Tricia. "Does Conner like her?"

Tricia's mouth fell open.

Brody chuckled, shook his head. "I don't think so," he said. As he straightened up again, he was looking at Tricia's overheated face. Something shifted in his eyes, with a distinct but soundless click. "Guess I'd better get in line if I want any of that famous chili," he finished, before walking away.

Tricia looked around for Sasha, found her behind the book table, looking very busy as she restacked the volumes into tidy piles. If Carolyn hadn't been standing right next to Sasha, Tricia probably wouldn't have noticed the way the other woman followed Brody's progress through the crowd.

She recalled something Carolyn had said the week before, when they were cleaning up after the barbecue at River's Bend. *What a fool I was, way back when.*

As though she'd felt Tricia watching her, Carolyn swung her gaze away from Brody and back to her friend's face. She made a funny little grimace and shrugged.

Tricia's curiosity was piqued, but she was a great believer in her late father's folksy philosophy: everybody's business was *nobody's* business. She didn't know Carolyn well enough to grill her about her fascination with Brody, though a part of her wished she did. Because then she would have had someone to confide in about *Conner.*

It was all so confusing, and Diana was so far away.

You, Tricia McCall, she thought glumly, *are flirting with slut-dom. You're going on a romantic cruise with one man, and getting all hot and bothered over another. Not becoming. Not becoming at all.*

Fortunately, there was a new run on the community center when the chili was finally served, and Tricia was so busy helping to ring up the sales—if making change from a cigar box could be called "ringing up"—that she didn't have a chance to think about Brody *or* Conner again until early afternoon.

There was a lull, so she and Sasha grabbed the opportunity to go home, take Valentino out for a walk and measure more of the top-secret spices into plastic bags, to be added to tomorrow's batch of chili as soon as the door closed on the last of the rummagers at six that evening.

They were about to head back, in fact, when a hired sedan drew up at the curb in front of the house and who should get out of the back, with the driver's careful assistance, but Natty McCall herself.

Tiny, with a cloud of silver hair pinned into a billowing Gibson-girl style, Natty reminded Tricia of the late stage actress Helen Hayes. She had beautiful skin, virtually wrinkle-free and glowing with good health, and blue eyes that snapped with intelligence, energy and, occasionally, mischief.

"Natty!" Tricia cried, descending on her great-grandmother with open arms. "You're home!"

"I couldn't stand being away any longer," Natty admitted, fanning herself with one hand. "Worrying about the chili recipe, I mean. Surely *that* wasn't good for my heart or my blood pressure."

Smiling, the balding, middle-aged driver left Natty in Tricia's care and went to collect her suitcases from the trunk of the Town Car.

"And who is this lovely person?" Natty asked, her gaze falling, benevolent but unusually weary, on Sasha.

Tricia made the introductions.

"And this is Valentino," Sasha chirped, indicating the dog, who seemed on the verge of genuflecting to Natty. She had that effect on people, as well as animals, with her queenly countenance. "He lives with Aunt Tricia, but she says she's not going to keep him."

"Famous last words," Natty commented wryly, allowing Tricia to take her arm and escort her toward the front steps, while Sasha and Valentino and the driver followed. "I *have* missed Winston sorely," the older woman confided, handing the key to Tricia, who unlocked the front door.

Winston was right there, waiting to greet his elderly mistress with a plaintive meow that might have translated as, *Thank heaven you're home. Another day, and I would have starved.*

Delighted, Natty scooped the cat up into her arms and held him while Tricia squired her to her customary chair in the old-fashioned parlor.

"You should have called," Tricia fretted, glad Conner had persuaded her to turn up the heat that morning, when he stopped by to bang on the pipes with a wrench. "I would have had a nice fire going, and prepared a meal—"

"Don't be silly, dear," Natty scolded, in her sweet way, once she was settled in her chair, Winston purring and turning happy circles in her lap. She handed her small, beaded purse to Tricia. "Pay the nice man, won't you?" she asked, indicating the driver.

Tricia settled up with the fellow from the car service, and he left. Natty's baggage stood in the entryway.

Both Sasha and Valentino seemed fascinated by the old woman. They stared at her, as though spellbound by her many charms.

"Would you mind building a fire now, sweetheart, and putting on a pot of tea?" Natty asked Tricia, stroking Winston with a motion of one delicate hand. The cat purred like an outboard motor.

"Of course I wouldn't mind," Tricia said, grateful, now, that Conner had laid a fire on the hearth and all she had to do was open the damper and light a match to the crumpled newspaper balled up under the kindling.

Soon, cheery flames danced on the hearth.

Tricia tucked a knitted shawl around Natty's shoulders before hurrying into the kitchen. While she was making the requested tea, she listened to the rise and fall of voices as her great-grandmother and her goddaughter chatted companionably, getting to know each other.

"And I think Aunt Tricia really *likes* Conner," Sasha was saying, as Tricia entered the parlor carrying a tea tray. "He likes her, too. You can tell by the way he looks at her. It's the same way my dad looks at a cheeseburger."

Natty smiled at that, and her wise, china-blue eyes shifted to Tricia with a knowing expression. "How is the rummage sale going?" she asked.

Tricia set the tray down, poured hot, fresh tea into a delicate china cup for her favorite elderly lady. "It's an enormous success, as always," she answered.

"You'd better get back there," Natty said, after taking a sip of tea. "I wouldn't put it past Evelyn to sneak a sample of that chili out of the community center and have it analyzed by some lab, just so she could find out what makes it so special."

Tricia smiled, sat down on the chair nearest Natty's. There were blue shadows under the old woman's lively eyes, and she looked thinner than she had before she left for Denver. "I'll guard that recipe with my life," she vowed, making the cross-my-heart-and-hope-to-die sign. "But right now, I'm more concerned about you."

Sasha, by that time, was busy entertaining Valentino on the rug in front of the fire, so Tricia felt free to express her concern.

"I'll be perfectly all right," Natty said, looking down at Winston with a fond expression and continuing to stroke his sleek back. "Now that I'm home, where I belong."

"Just the same—"

Natty yawned and patted her mouth. "Winston and I," she said, "would love a nap." She sighed, a gentle, joyous sound, full of homecoming. "Right here, in our very own chair. Do hand me the lap robe, Tricia dear."

Tricia obeyed.

"I could stay here and look after Natty," Sasha said, in a loud whisper, when Natty had closed her eyes and, apparently, nodded off. "Valentino, too."

Tricia was reluctant to agree. After all, Sasha was only ten.

"Please?" Sasha prompted. "It's so nice here, with the fire and everything."

"You know my cell number," Tricia said, relenting. She nodded to indicate Natty's old-fashioned rotary phone, in its customary place on the secretary, over by the bay windows.

Sasha seemed to read her mind. "I know how to use one of those, Aunt Tricia," she said patiently. "Dad bought one on eBay last year, and he showed me how it works."

Tricia chuckled. "Okay," she said, with a fond glance at Natty, who was snoring delicately now, obviously happy to be home. In a day or two, she'd probably be her old self again. "I won't be long, in any case. I just have to make sure tomorrow's chili is underway."

"Valentino and I will take care of Natty," Sasha promised solemnly.

Overcoming her paranoia, Tricia went into Natty's kitchen, measured out the spices and peeked into the parlor once more as she passed.

Natty was unquestionably sound asleep. So was Valentino.

But Sasha sat on the ottoman at Natty's feet, watching her intently, as though poised to leap into action at the first sign of any emergency.

Touched, Tricia left the house again, with the chili ingredients safely stashed in her purse.

The rummage sale/chili feed was going at full tilt when Tricia arrived back at the community center, so she pushed up her sleeves and got busy helping, careful to keep her cell phone in the pocket of her jeans in case Sasha called.

After an hour, Tricia took a break and dialed Natty's number, just in case.

Natty answered, sounding quite chipper. Evidently, the nap had restored her considerably. "We're doing just fine, dear," the old woman said, in reply to Tricia's inquiry. "Sasha and I are about to play Chinese checkers, right here by the fire, where it's cozy." A girlish giggle followed. "The child swears by all that's holy that she's never played this game before, but I suspect she'll trounce me thoroughly at it, just the same."

Tricia smiled, impatient to join Natty and Sasha at home. She'd missed her great-grandmother sorely while she was away and, with the move to Paris looming, she wanted to spend as much time with Sasha as she could.

"No one ever beats you at Chinese checkers," Tricia said.

Again, Natty giggled. "I used to be pretty wicked at Ping-Pong, too, if you'll recall," she replied sweetly. "But I'm not as quick with a paddle as I used to be."

Tricia smiled again, recalling some lively Ping-Pong tournaments she and her dad and Natty had competed in, after stringing a net across the middle of the formal table in Natty's dining room.

Her great-grandmother had indeed been formidable in those days. Neither Tricia nor Joe had been able to beat her, except when she decided to throw a game so they wouldn't lose interest and stop playing.

"Shall I bring some chili home for supper?" Tricia asked, feeling an achy warmth in her heart that was partly love for the spirited old woman and partly nostalgia for those long-ago summers, when her dad was still around. "I'm sure there are some plastic containers I could borrow."

"Yes," Natty decided immediately. "And bring home some of Evelyn's cornbread, too, if the supply hasn't been exhausted already."

Tricia promised to head home with supper as soon as possible.

Along with Carolyn and several other volunteers, she waited on the steady stream of customers—it never ceased to amaze her how many people showed up for the event. Many of them, of course, were out-of-towners, staying at River's Bend, but the locals came in waves, often for both lunch *and* supper.

At six the last few stragglers wandered out, and Evelyn promptly locked up behind them.

By then, the huge kettles had been emptied, scrubbed and filled with fresh salted water and bags full of dried beans, and while the others sat at the public tables in the front of the community center, relaxing and enjoying a well-earned meal of their own, Tricia stirred spices into the cooking pots.

A few minutes later, Tricia left by the back door, carrying two bulky plastic-lidded bowls full of food, and spotted Carolyn, just getting into her aging compact car.

She made an oddly lonely figure, in the twilight-shadowed parking lot and, on impulse, Tricia called out to her. There was a kind of brave sadness about Carolyn that she hadn't noticed before.

Smiling, Carolyn turned from her open car door. "I should have thought of that," she said, with a nod to Tricia's takeout.

"There's plenty," Tricia said. "Why don't you join Natty and Sasha and me for supper?"

Carolyn hesitated—she looked tired—but then she gave a little nod. "I'd like that," she said.

"Good," Tricia said. "Follow me."

CHAPTER NINE

THE FOUR OF THEM—Natty, Sasha, Carolyn and Tricia—
had enjoyed a lively supper of chili and cornbread, seasoned with plenty of laughter, sitting around Natty's
kitchen table, and Carolyn had stayed to help clear away
after the meal.

Natty, explaining that the effects of her afternoon nap
had worn off, excused herself from the kitchen and made
her way to her bedroom, Winston soft-footing it along behind her, his tail curved like a question mark. Valentino
looked almost sad as he watched his feline friend disappear
into the hallway without so much as a backward glance.

Sasha, alternately giggling and yawning, asked if she
could use the computer upstairs; her parents had taken
their laptop to France with them, and though they'd had
some problems accessing wireless services in their hotel
room, the little girl was certain they must have resolved the
trouble by now. She was eager to send an instant message
and, hopefully, receive an immediate response, and Tricia didn't have the heart to point out that since it was after
2:00 a.m. in Paris, Paul and Diana were probably sleeping.

Although she did fine in the daytime, when there was
plenty going on to engage her interest, Sasha missed her
mom and dad more poignantly after sunset. Tricia well remembered being her goddaughter's age, how she'd felt for
several weeks every September, when she was back in Se-

attle to start the new school year. With her mother working nights at the hospital, and Mrs. Crosby from downstairs as a babysitter, Tricia had lain in her childhood bed and silently *ached* for her life in Lonesome Bend, for her dad's easy companionship, and for Natty's, and for the fleeting magic of little-girl summers in a small town.

"This is a terrific old house," Carolyn commented, effectively bringing Tricia back from her mental meanderings. "It has so much character." She spoke with sincere appreciation, her blue eyes taking in the bay windows, with their lace curtains, the lovely hand-pegged floors, the fine cabinetry, the antique break-front full of translucent china, every piece an heirloom.

"On Natty's behalf," Tricia smiled, "thank you. The house was one of the first to be built, when the town was just getting settled." Tricia pulled on her jacket, which she'd left draped over the back of her chair earlier, when she and Carolyn had first arrived with their rummage-sale supper, and took Valentino's leash from the pocket.

The dog's ears perked up at the sight of it, and he came to Tricia, waiting patiently while she fastened the hook to the loop on his collar.

"I wonder what it would be like," Carolyn mused, "to have such deep roots in a community." She spoke in a light tone, but there was some other quality in her voice, something forlorn that made Tricia think of the way Valentino had watched Winston follow Natty out of the room—as if he'd lost his last friend in the world.

What could she say to that? Tricia liked Carolyn tremendously, but even after working with her at the community center all day and then sharing a meal, they were still essentially strangers.

Tricia was quite shy, though she'd made a real effort

to overcome the tendency, especially since she'd returned to Lonesome Bend to sell off her dad's properties and make sure Natty really *would* be okay on her own, as she claimed. Carolyn, on the other hand, didn't seem shy at all, but merely—well—*private*. She was a person with secrets, Tricia was sure, though not necessarily dark ones.

Valentino was anxious to get outside, so Tricia opened the back door, instead of heading for the front, and Carolyn followed. Both women were silent as they walked around the side of the hulking old house, Tricia juggling the leash, Carolyn with her hands thrust into the pockets of her blue nylon jacket.

Carolyn's car was parked out front, in a pool of light from a streetlamp, and her keys made a jingling sound as she took them from her pocket. "Thanks for inviting me over tonight," she told Tricia, who was gently restraining Valentino. He wanted to head off down the sidewalk, make the most of his final walk of the day.

"I enjoyed having you here," Tricia said truthfully. "So did Sasha and Natty."

Carolyn flashed her warm, wide smile. "I was too tired to stay and eat with the other volunteers after the sale closed for the day, but the prospect of dining alone wasn't doing much for me, either."

Valentino began to tug harder at the leash. He needed a little training, Tricia thought. Maybe, when she found a permanent home for him, he could learn to heel instead of crisscrossing in front of her, nearly making her trip.

Tricia chuckled ruefully and shook her head, and Carolyn gave a little laugh, too. "I'll see you at the community center tomorrow?" Carolyn asked, stepping off the sidewalk and going around to open the driver's-side door of her car.

"Yes," Tricia said, as Valentino yanked her into motion. "See you there."

"And you'll be going on the trail ride, too?" Carolyn persisted. "The one at the Creeds'?"

Looking back over a shoulder, Tricia nodded. Carolyn had seemed uncomfortable around Brody Creed earlier, but evidently she was over that now. Possibly, she didn't expect to see him on the ranch the next day.

"I'm afraid I can't get out of that," Tricia responded. "Sasha's counting on some time in the saddle."

Carolyn's face, like her hair, was lit with moonlight. She had, Tricia noticed, the bone structure of a model; she was one of those women who, like Natty, remained beautiful as they aged.

"It'll be *fun,*" Carolyn insisted. "You'll see."

With that, she got into her car, shut the door and started the engine. The headlights were bright enough to make Tricia blink as the rig drew up alongside her and Valentino. Carolyn gave the horn a little toot and drove away.

It'll be fun. You'll see.

Tricia still wasn't entirely convinced of that. Horses were foreign creatures to her, huge and disturbingly unpredictable, and not only did they shed, they'd been known to bite. *Plus,* it was a very long fall from their backs to the hard ground and what if she—or worse, Sasha—was not only thrown, but stepped on? Or what if something spooked the horses, and they ran away? She'd seen it happen a hundred times in the vintage Western movies her dad had loved.

Conner Creed's face rose in her mind in that moment and, somehow, Tricia knew—*just knew*—that he wouldn't let anything happen to Sasha, or to her, or to anyone else who might be joining them on the trail ride the next day. She knew less than nothing about horses, it was true, but *Conner* was an expert. For that matter, so was Sasha, though, of course, she wasn't as experienced as he was, being only a child.

It didn't take long to traverse Lonesome Bend from one end to the other, even on foot, and Tricia and Valentino got all the way to the old drive-in theater before Tricia decided they'd walked far enough. Farther on, the road curved dark along the edge of the river, and there was only the glow of the moon to light the way.

While Valentino was occupied in the high grass alongside the collapsing fence, Tricia looked up at the big, ghostly remnant of the outdoor movie screen. It was faced with corrugated metal, the white paint chipping and peeling, and time had bent one rusted corner inward, like a page marked in a book.

The projection house/concession stand was dark, naturally, and the rows of steel poles supporting the individual speakers tilted this way and that, resembling pickets in a broken fence. Or tombstones in a forgotten graveyard.

A shiver went up Tricia's back, then tripped back down. A *graveyard?* That, she decided, was an unfair analogy—the Bluebird Drive-in Movie-o-rama had been a happening place in its heyday. The sad old screen had been lit up with light and color and pure Hollywood glamour five nights a week in summer. Her dad must have told her a dozen stories about how thrilling it was to sprawl on the roof or the hood of somebody's car, or in the bed of a truck, the sky a dark canopy overhead, liberally dappled with stars, while John Wayne headed up a cattle drive, or the Empire struck back, or Rock

Hudson and Doris Day fell in love, or James Dean rebelled without a cause—

A lump formed in Tricia's throat. Her own memories of the drive-in were scented with buttery popcorn from the big machine on the concession counter; she recalled the scratchy sounds of music and dialogue crackling from the cumbersome speakers, designed to hook onto the car windows, and the delicious frustration of waiting for darkness to fall, so the movie could be shown to advantage.

Still, business had already dropped off dramatically by the time Tricia began tagging along to the theater with her dad on those sultry, star-spattered summer nights, and the films were the sort that go straight to DVD or cable now, without ever hitting the big screen in the first place.

"It's the end of an era," she remembered Joe McCall saying sadly, one late-August night, when the credits were rolling on the last offering of what would turn out to be the Bluebird's final season, though Tricia hadn't known that then. She'd been twelve at the time, not even a teenager, and scheduled to board a flight from Denver to Seattle first thing the next morning.

"The end of an era," Tricia repeated softly.

Now Valentino was on the move again, making for the bright lights of town, and he pulled her right along with him.

Tricia's eyes burned, and she had to wipe her cheek once, with the back of one hand. Later, when she was older, and she had her dog, Rusty, and the drive-in was starting to look downright decrepit, she'd been a little ashamed of the place. "Why don't you sell it?" she'd asked her dad once, when they'd spent a hot afternoon picking up litter, the drive-in being a popular spot for illicit parties, and mowing the grass.

He'd laughed and said times were hard because the Republicans—or had it been the Democrats?—were in office, so nobody was spending much money, particularly when it came to commercial real estate. Then, more seriously, that sadness back in his eyes, Joe had said, "Someday, it'll be yours—the drive-in, the campground and the rest of it. This is all riverfront property, Tricia—that's Creed ranch land over on the other side—and when the time is right, you'll sell it for a good price, and you'll be glad I held on to it for you."

Hauled along by Valentino, now determined to go home, it would seem, Tricia glanced back over one shoulder, took in the shadowy form of the big For Sale sign nailed to the front gate next to the rickety ticket booth—the whole scene awash in the orangish shimmer of a harvest moon, partially obscured by clouds now—and sighed. Her dad had been so certain that he was leaving her something of value. If Joe had lived, though, he'd have been very disappointed in the state of his legacy, and maybe in her, too.

Another tug from Valentino's end of the leash alerted Tricia to the fact that she'd stopped walking again—it was as though the past had somehow reached out, with invisible hands, and held her in place.

"Sorry," she told the dog, getting into step.

When they got back to the house, the downstairs lights were off, except for the one on the porch, and, Valentino at her side, Tricia climbed the front steps instead of taking the outside stairway, as she would normally have done. She wasn't sure the door was properly locked; Natty had been overtired and she'd most likely forgotten, and Tricia and Carolyn had left the house by the back way.

Sure enough, the knob turned easily.

Suppressing a sigh, Tricia stepped over the threshold, as did Valentino. She took off his leash, wound it into a loose coil and stuffed it back into her jacket pocket. Valentino looked up at her questioningly and she smiled, turning to engage the lock on the front door.

She flipped a nearby switch and the chandelier came on, spilling crystalline light into the entryway. Tricia proceeded toward the kitchen, intending to secure the back door, which she'd left unlocked on her way out, but Valentino took a detour as they passed the stairs and trotted up to the apartment, perhaps looking for Sasha, though he might just as well have been hoping for Winston's return. He'd become attached to that cat.

Natty was sitting at the round table when Tricia reached the kitchen, sipping herbal tea from one of her prized china cups. She wore a cozy blue chenille bathrobe, the front zipped to her chin, and her lovely silver hair, held back at the sides by graceful little combs, trimmed in mother-of-pearl, fell nearly to her waist, still curly and thick even after nine decades of life.

Seeing Tricia, the old woman smiled sweetly, and her cup made a delicate clinking sound as she set it in the matching saucer.

"I think Carolyn needs a friend," Natty said, with a gentle smile.

I know I *could use one,* Tricia thought wearily. Diana was and would always be her closest confidante, but they lived in separate states as it was, and soon they'd be on separate *continents.*

"I agree," Tricia replied, after securing the lock on the back door. She glanced toward the ceiling, and Natty read the gesture with an astuteness that was typical of her.

"Sasha is just fine," she said. "She got through to her

parents, via the computer, and she was so excited that she came downstairs to tell me all about it."

"And that's why you're still awake?" Tricia asked, with an effort at a smile. She'd put in a long day at the community center, and she couldn't wait to soak in a hot bath and tumble into bed for eight hours of semicomatose slumber.

"Heavens, no," Natty replied. "I watched some television in my room—you know, to unwind a little—and I do like a cup of raspberry tea before I turn in."

"You'd tell me," Tricia said, "if you didn't feel well?"

"I'd tell you," Natty said, eyes twinkling. "You worry too much, young lady."

Still wearing her jacket, Tricia went to stand beside her great-grandmother's chair, and laid a gentle hand on one of the woman's fragile shoulders. "Of course I worry," she responded. "I love you."

Natty reached to pat Tricia's hand lightly. "And I love you, dear," she said. Then she gave a small, philosophical kind of sigh. Her cornflower-blue eyes caught Tricia's gaze and held it. "If anything *did* happen to me, you'd make sure Winston was looked after, wouldn't you?"

Tricia crouched next to the old woman's chair, her vision blurred by hot, sudden tears. Despite Natty's advanced age, and her recent health issues, the thought of her passing away was almost inconceivable. "No matter what," Tricia said, her throat thick with the same tears that were stinging in her eyes, "Winston will be fine. I promise you that."

Natty rested one cool, papery palm against Tricia's cheek. "I believe you," she said tenderly. "But can you promise me that *you* will be fine as well? I'd feel so much better if you were married—"

Tricia gave a small, strangled giggle as she stood

up straight again. She felt torn between going upstairs to Sasha—it was past the girl's bedtime—and keeping Natty company in the dearly familiar kitchen. "I can take care of myself," she reminded her beloved great-grandmother softly. "Isn't that better than being married just for the sake of—well—*being married?*"

Natty chuckled fondly. Shook her head once. "I know you think I'm old-fashioned," she said, "and you're at least partially right. But it's a *natural thing,* Tricia, for a man and a woman to love and depend on each other. Certain members of your mother's generation—and yours, too—seem to see men as—what's the word I want?—*dispensable.* I think that's sad." As tired as Natty looked, the twinkle was back in her eyes. "There's nothing worse than a bad man, I'll grant you that," she summed up, waggling an index finger at Tricia, "but there is also nothing *better* than a *good* one."

Tricia laughed. "Duly noted," she said. "Shall I help you back to bed?"

"I can get *myself* back to bed," Natty informed her. "Besides, I haven't finished my tea. I may even have a second cup."

Tricia was moving away by then, though her pace was reluctant, shrugging out of her coat as she started for the hallway and the staircase beyond, "If you need anything—"

"I'll be fine," Natty said, making a shooing motion with one hand. "You just think about what I said, Tricia McCall. Fact is, I'm not sure you'd know a good man if he was standing right in front of you."

Tricia stopped, turned around in the doorway to the hall, narrowing her eyes a little. Like Diana, Natty wasn't keen on Hunter. *Un*like Diana, she'd never met him.

"If that was a reference to—"

"It was a reference," Natty interrupted succinctly, "to Conner Creed."

"I barely know the man," Tricia pointed out, lingering when she knew it would be better—and wiser—to go upstairs.

"Well," Natty said, rising from her chair and picking up her saucer and empty cup, apparently having decided against a second helping of tea, "perhaps you ought to make an effort, dear. To get to know him, I mean. He comes from very sturdy stock, you know. Granted, Conner's dad was something of a renegade, and it looks as though Brody takes after Blue, but Conner's more like Davis, and a finer man never drew breath. Unless it was my Henry, of course."

The corner of Tricia's mouth twitched. "Of course," she said.

Her great-grandfather, Henry McCall, had been dead for decades, but thanks to Natty, his legend as a man and as a husband lived on. Their only child, Walter, Tricia's grandfather, had died in a car accident, along with his wife, when Joe was still in high school.

Tricia's dad had gone away to college the following year, then served a stint in the Army. Having met and married Tricia's mother soon after his discharge, he'd gone to Seattle and tried hard to make a life there, while a still-spry Natty ran the drive-in and the campground for him. After the divorce, Joe had returned to his hometown and, at his grandmother's urging, converted the second story of the old house into an apartment. He'd lived there until his own death, from a heart ailment, only two years before.

"Good night, Tricia," Natty said, setting the cup and

saucer carefully on the countertop, next to the sink. "Sleep tight."

"Good night," Tricia said, feeling as though she and her great-grandmother had just engaged in some sort of gentle contest, and Natty had come out the winner.

Which was just silly.

THE ATMOSPHERE IN the community center's kitchen was redolent with the delicious aromas of spicy chili and fresh coffee the next morning, when Tricia, Sasha and special guest star Natty McCall entered through the propped-open back door.

The night shift—three women who had remained at the center to oversee the kettles of fresh chili simmering on the stove—reacted with delight when they spotted Natty. She didn't even get a chance to take off her tailored black coat before they were hugging her and telling her how much they'd missed her, all of them talking at once. So far, one of the women reported, the profits from the event were even higher than last year's had been. People had come from miles around to sample Natty's famous chili, and sales of the donated goods were up, too. Those fancy new uniforms for the high school marching band were as good as ordered.

"See?" Natty told her friends, her cheeks flushed, her eyes bright, as Tricia helped her out of her coat. "I *told* you the sky wouldn't fall if I retired as head of the committee, didn't I?"

Sasha took Natty's coat from Tricia and went to hang it up on the portable closet in the storage room. "There must be fifty million people lined up out front," she said, when she returned. "*Again.* I can't figure out where they're all coming from."

"Everywhere," Natty told the child, after winking at Tricia. "Henry McCall's secret chili recipe attracts foodies from all over the United States and Canada."

That, Tricia thought wryly, might have been something of an exaggeration, but it *was* true that Natty had had several opportunities to sell the recipe over the years, not only to two different manufacturing firms, but to a well-known chain of restaurants, too. Tricia had seen the letters herself.

Someone brought Natty a cup of coffee, once she was settled at the long table in the kitchen. Evelyn barely opened the door separating them from the main part of the building and peered through the crack, clucking her tongue at the size of the crowd waiting on the sidewalk out front.

"Just imagine how many there would be if *church* services weren't in session all over town," she said. "We'd need the riot squad, or even the National Guard."

Natty and her friends chortled merrily at that. All of them were faithful members of their various churches, but every year when the rummage sale/chili feed weekend rolled around, they threw themselves upon God's patient understanding and skipped a week.

"I say it's a good thing today's a half day," one of the other women remarked, after stifling a yawn with one hand. "We're not getting any younger, ladies."

Carolyn hurried in through the back door just then, pulling off her jacket as she walked. "*Who's* not getting any younger?" she teased happily.

"Well," Evelyn conceded, smiling, "you and Tricia *might* be. Maybe it's time for you to take over the biggest event of the year so all us old ladies can follow Natty's lead and put our feet up."

"You'd miss it too much," Carolyn replied.

Natty checked the wall clock above the giant coffee percolator on the nearby counter. "It's almost time to admit the eager hordes," she said.

Evelyn huffed at that. "It won't kill those people to wait a few more minutes, Natty. They bought everything they really wanted yesterday, you can bet on that, and today they're just here to inhale every last chili bean and buy back the stuff they wish they hadn't given up when we held our big donation drive back in August."

Tricia and Carolyn exchanged amused glances.

Sasha, standing close to Natty's chair, rubbed her small hands together. "I wouldn't mind opening the door," she allowed diplomatically, "if no one else wants to do it."

Evelyn chuckled and handed over the keys. "Wait five more minutes," she told a beaming Sasha. "Our kitchen reinforcements haven't arrived, and Carolyn and Tricia can't be expected to wrangle that mob without help, either."

Sasha's eyes were wide with solemn excitement. "But *I'd* be there to help them," she said.

Evelyn patted the girl's head. "Of course you would," she agreed. "Mind, you stay behind the door when you open it. Junk collectors are a dangerous breed—they might just run right over a little bitty thing like you."

About that time, the day crew arrived to monitor the sales of chili and hot coffee, and Evelyn and her bunch put on their coats, picked up their large patent-leather purses, said goodbye and left.

Two other women turned up to help Carolyn and Tricia out front, and Sasha raced to unlock the door.

Time, as Natty had always maintained, had wings.

The morning flew by, the chili was consumed, along with two giant urns of coffee and all the canned soda that was left from the day before, and the last of the rummage was boxed up for charity.

"Now we can go riding!" Sasha cried, all but jumping up and down in the kitchen.

Tricia had taken Natty home some time before and the day crew was busy scrubbing out the huge soup kettles, sweeping up and putting the third load of dirty coffee cups into the dishwasher.

"Yippee," Tricia said mildly, putting on her jacket.

Since they'd dressed casually for rummage sale duty, and she'd taken Valentino out for a quick walk when she drove Natty back to the house earlier, there was no reason to go home.

Tricia and Carolyn left the center together, Sasha skipping along behind them, unable to contain her joy. "It's still an hour before the trail ride starts," Carolyn said, after looking at her watch. "Why don't you and Sasha follow me back to Kim and Davis's place, and we'll head over to the main house when the time comes?"

Tricia recalled that Carolyn was housesitting for Davis and Kim, who were away on one of their frequent road trips. She considered both of them friends, but she'd never actually visited their home, and she was a little curious, so she agreed.

Once Sasha was safely ensconced in her booster seat, Tricia got behind the wheel of the Pathfinder and followed Carolyn out of the parking lot, into the alley behind the community center and then onto a paved street.

The drive out into the countryside was spectacular, the hillsides practically on fire with changing leaves in every shade of orange and crimson, yellow and rust, the sky so blue that just looking at it made Tricia's throat constrict a little.

Carolyn led them past the colonial-style ranch house that had stood even longer than Natty's house in town. Like Natty's property, it was well-maintained, with grass and a picket fence and venerable old rosebushes everywhere. The barn, though it looked sturdy enough to last another century, showed its age. The reddish paint, fading and peeling away in places, lent it a distinctly rural charm.

The rambling one-story log house Kim and Davis Creed called home stood high on a ridge, overlooking much of the ranch, and was considerably newer than its counterpart, though it had a rustic appeal all its own. The driveway was paved, and there was a huge metal outbuilding, which most likely housed the couple's RV.

The Creeds had a barn, too, smaller than the one down the hill, but surrounded by a large, fenced-in pasture. Three horses grazed the plentiful remains of that year's grass crop.

"Are they the ones we're going to ride?" Sasha piped up, before she was even out of the booster seat. She was pointing toward the buckskin, Appaloosa and bay in the field.

Carolyn, having parked her car and waited for Tricia and Sasha to get out of the Pathfinder, smiled and shook her head. She looked every inch the country woman, Tricia thought, standing there in her jeans and boots and Western-cut blouse, with her hands in the pockets of her coat.

"Nope," Carolyn answered. "These guys are all retired. They're basically pets. The horses we'll be riding are down at the other place."

Sasha frowned. "I didn't see any horses there," she said.

Carolyn chuckled. "Trust me, they're around," she promised. "Let's go inside."

They entered through a side door, stepping into a spacious modern kitchen. Everything gleamed—the windows, the floors, the appliances and the countertops.

"Kim's a housekeeping demon," Carolyn explained, evidently reading Tricia's mind. "It's intimidating, isn't it?"

Tricia laughed. "I'd be dusting twice a day."

Carolyn nodded, hanging her shoulder bag from a peg on the wall next to the door and then placing her jacket on top of it. "If Kim wasn't such a nice person," she agreed, "I'd probably be so paranoid about messing something up that I couldn't housesit."

Sasha, a city child, was taking in the wide-open spaces of a Colorado ranch house. "Is it scary, staying here all alone?" she asked.

"No," Carolyn answered, with a smile. "I like it a lot."

"Can we look around?" Sasha asked, barely noticing as Tricia helped her extract herself from her coat.

"Sure," Carolyn said. "Let's take the tour."

The living room and dining area were one huge room, and the table, surrounded by more than a dozen charmingly mismatched chairs, must have been twenty feet long. The natural-rock fireplace was so big that Sasha could have stood upright in the cavity, and there were floor-to-ceiling windows on all sides.

The view was quite literally stunning.

"Wow," Tricia said.

"Yeah," Carolyn agreed wryly. "*Wow* is definitely the word."

By tacit agreement, they didn't go into the master

suite, but the other bedrooms, one of which Carolyn was using, were all impressive. Each boasted its own bath and, like the ones in the living/dining room, the windows offered a grand tableau of the mountains and the vast expanse of rangeland.

A well-stocked library with a baby grand piano and a spacious, leather-scented studio, where Davis did his saddle making, completed the house.

"Where do you live when you're not here?" Sasha asked Carolyn, when they were back in the kitchen.

Something flickered in Carolyn's eyes—the briefest flash of sorrow, Tricia thought—but her smile didn't waver.

"All over," Carolyn answered. "That's my job. I take care of people's houses for them when they're away."

"But where's *your* house?" Sasha persisted.

"Sasha," Tricia protested quietly.

Carolyn swallowed, went to shove her hands into her jacket pockets before remembering that she wasn't wearing the garment. Still, her smile held. "I don't really need a house," she told the child, after tossing an *It's okay* sort of glance at Tricia.

"*Everybody* needs a house," Sasha maintained. She could be stubborn, when she took a notion.

"Sasha," Tricia repeated, this time more forcefully. "That's enough, honey."

Sasha looked up at her then, and Tricia was startled to see tears shining in the little girl's eyes. "But what if people stop going on trips?" she fretted. "If everybody stays home, all at once, Carolyn will be *homeless*."

Tricia felt that familiar pang of love for this amazing child, but she was a little embarrassed by the outburst, too. "I'm sure Carolyn earns a very good living," she said, in an awkward rush. The words were out of her mouth before she realized how lame they sounded.

Carolyn smiled and gave Sasha a sideways hug. "As the cowboys say, don't you worry your pretty little head, missy. I enjoy being a gypsy."

Sasha looked only partly mollified by the claim. In her world, people without homes slept on sidewalks and panhandled for change in downtown Seattle. "But, you don't *look* like a gypsy—"

"Figure of speech, kiddo," Carolyn said, the soul of kindness. Then she held up one arm and tapped at the face of her watch. "Look at the time," she went on, her smile mega-bright. "We'd better get ourselves down to the main barn if we want first pick of the horses."

That was all it took to distract Sasha from the plight of the homeless. For the moment, at least.

The ten-year-old let out a whoop of sheer pleasure and dashed for the door, grabbing her coat from the peg where Tricia had hung it earlier, along with her own.

Within moments, they were back in their vehicles, on their way to one of the last places Tricia wanted to go. And it wasn't just because she was timid around horses.

Tricia would have liked more time to brace herself for another encounter with Conner Creed, but, alas, it wasn't to be. He was standing in front of the barn when they pulled in, and he looked wicked good.

CHAPTER TEN

IF BRODY CREED was around, there was no sign of him, which probably accounted, at least in part, for Carolyn's good spirits. Not that Tricia was really paying that much attention; even before she'd parked the Pathfinder beside her friend's car and turned off the ignition, she was feeling it again, that sense of being *magnetized* to Conner.

The vulnerability of that made her want to drive right on past, back to town. Forget the whole crazy idea of going on a trail ride, of all things, with a guy who affected her like a turn on a runaway roller coaster.

As if escape were even possible, with Sasha along and excited enough to jump out of her skin.

Although she didn't notice until after the fact, there *were* other people around, and other vehicles, mostly trucks and large SUVs, with horse trailers hitched behind them. Friends and neighbors began unloading various mounts and saddling up.

"This is Buttercup," Conner said, as Sasha hurried up to him, Tricia lagging a pace or two behind the child.

Tricia blinked. The docile-looking mare might have materialized beside Conner by magic, so thoroughly had the creature evaded her notice.

Conner's smile was slow and easy, and fetchingly crooked in that way that made Tricia's nerves skitter wildly out of control. Holding Buttercup's reins loosely in his left hand, he stroked the horse's neck with the other.

"Is that the horse I get to ride?" Sasha asked, almost breathless.

"Nope," Conner replied, never looking away from Tricia's face. "Buttercup is more suited to a greenhorn." At last, his gaze slanted to Sasha. "You'll be on the one we call Show Pony. She's gentle, too, but old Buttercup, here, she's practically a rocking horse."

Tricia tensed ever so slightly, her pride nettled by the term *greenhorn*. Okay, so she wasn't an experienced rider. She wasn't a coward, either. She was *there,* wasn't she, in spite of all her very sensible trepidation, willing to try something new?

A blue spark ignited in Conner's eyes, there for an instant and then gone again, and Tricia knew he'd been joshing her a little. "Ready?" he asked, watching her in a way that made her feel electrified.

Everyone except for the two of them and Buttercup seemed to have slipped into some kind of dimly visible parallel universe. There was an indefinable charge, a silent buzz, in the crisply cool air, too, and Tricia was startled to recognize it as anticipation, not fear.

"Ready," she confirmed.

Carolyn came out of the barn, leading a pinto mare she must have saddled herself, and a smaller horse that was probably Show Pony. Sasha needed no urging at all to scramble up into the waiting saddle.

Tricia, meanwhile, tried to follow Conner's quiet instructions. Approaching Buttercup's side, she put her left foot into the stirrup, as he told her to do, and reached up to clasp the saddle horn in both hands, praying she could make it without needing a boost.

And then she was up, sitting astride Buttercup's narrow back, and she'd gotten there under her own power, too, without the humiliation of being goosed in the backside. Exhilaration filled Tricia, straightening her spine, raising her chin a notch or two. Buttercup stood still as stone, bless her equine heart.

Conner smiled. "You're doing fine," he said. Then, with a twinkle in his eyes, he added, "It's okay to let go of the saddle horn now." He reached up, placing the reins in Tricia's hands. Although their fingers barely brushed against each other, the contact sent a hot jolt racing through Tricia's entire body. "That's it," he said. "Just let the reins rest easy in your grasp, and whatever you do, don't wrap them around your hands."

Tricia nodded, one step from terror and, at the same time, thrilled through and through.

She was on a real horse.

Of course, it wasn't *moving* yet, but so far, so good.

Sasha rode up, buckling on the riding helmet Carolyn must have brought from the barn. The little girl's smile stretched from ear to ear.

"You're a natural!" Sasha said, beaming at Tricia.

Carolyn, riding up beside Sasha, held out a second helmet to Tricia. "Put this on," she said, with an encouraging smile. Tricia knew, even without looking around, that she and Sasha were the only riders present who'd be wearing headgear, but she didn't care. She *did* have a moment of panic, however, when she looked around for Conner and realized that he was gone.

Buttercup didn't so much as flick her tail, but Carolyn leaned from the saddle to take a light but firm grip on the mare's bridle strap, probably so the animal wouldn't spook while Tricia was putting on the helmet.

Conner reappeared a moment later, ducking with magnificent grace as he rode out through the wide doorway of the barn, mounted on a black gelding with three white boots and a matching blaze on its face.

The sight of him, so at ease riding that powerful horse, literally took Tricia's breath away. Her heart started to pound as Conner adjusted his hat with a second-nature motion of one hand, grinning at the other riders as he passed through their midst to rein in beside Tricia.

Even then, Buttercup didn't move a single muscle. She might have been stuffed, that mare, for all the animation she seemed to possess. And that was just fine with Tricia.

The problem was that everybody else was on the move—even Sasha and Carolyn were riding away, like all the others, toward the gate opening onto the rangeland beyond the corral and the pasture.

Conner waited, shifting in his saddle once, adjusting his hat in what must have been an attempt—a vain one—to hide his grin in the shadow of the brim.

Buttercup stood still as a statue.

"Should I—well—nudge her with my heels or something?" Tricia asked.

A few of the other riders were looking back at her and Conner, and some of them were smiling. Exchanging little comments Tricia was glad she couldn't hear.

"You could do that," Conner answered affably, and in his own good time. "But Buttercup won't go anywhere until Lakota heads out."

Lakota, Tricia deduced, was the gelding Conner rode. "Oh," she said, at something of a loss. Now what?

This time, Conner made no attempt to hide his

amusement. Tricia could have hit him if she weren't
afraid to let go of the reins. She felt silly, sitting there
like a child waiting for the carousel to start turning, the
only grown-up wearing a helmet.

"Buttercup is Lakota's mama," Conner explained,
in that same slow drawl he'd used before. "She likes to
keep him in sight when they're out of the corral."

"I see," Tricia said, though she *didn't,* actually. All
she could think of was a special she'd seen on TV once,
and it had been about elephants, not horses. It seemed
that baby elephants would follow their mother for their
entire lives, unless, of course, they were separated.

"If you're ready," Conner went on, "we'll start."

Tricia swallowed hard. Sasha and Carolyn and the
other participants in the trail ride—over a dozen of
them—were way ahead. A few of the more experienced
people were even racing each other.

"I'm ready," Tricia lied.

Conner nodded, clicked his tongue once, and Lakota
started to walk away.

Buttercup didn't actually bolt, but she moved forward
so quickly that Tricia was nearly unseated.

"You're doing fine," Conner told Tricia, riding
alongside and obviously controlling the gelding, which
wanted to run. Tricia could tell that by the way the muscles bunched in its haunches.

And then, they were trotting. Tricia bounced unceremoniously in the saddle. Conner and the others, by
contrast, Sasha included, moved *with* their horses, almost as though they were part of them.

"It takes practice," Conner said.

Tricia didn't dare answer, bouncing like that. She'd
sound like someone driving a springless wagon over

a washboard trail, and maybe even bite her tongue in the process.

Practice? she thought, skeptical. She would probably have bruises after this, along with back spasms and, as for her thigh muscles, forget about it. She was doomed.

Conner's mouth kicked up at one corner again as he slowed Lakota to a walk, which prompted Buttercup to stop trotting, too, of course. Once again, he resettled his hat, the gesture so innately masculine that, for a moment, Tricia's immediate predicament went right out of her head. She even allowed herself to imagine— very briefly—what it would be like to make love with Conner Creed.

Her cheeks burned as if the scene had been flashed onto the screen at the Bluebird, on a very dark night, instead of on the back of her forehead.

"You must want to ride with the others," she said, in a tone of bright misery, nodding across the widening breach between her and Conner and the rest of the party. "We haven't gone far. I could walk back."

Conner tilted his head to one side, looked at her from under the brim of his hat. It was an ordinary thing to do, especially for a cowboy on horseback, but it had the same impact as before, practically knocking the breath out of her. Like a hard fall.

"You'd probably never live that down," he teased. "Walking back to the house, I mean."

Never mind living anything down, Tricia thought, with bleak resignation. She had to keep Sasha in sight, the way Buttercup did Lakota. Even though the child was perfectly safe riding with Carolyn.

"Probably not," she replied, just so Conner wouldn't think she'd been struck dumb in the interval.

"As I said, learning to ride takes time and some practice, same as anything else," Conner told her.

"That's easy for you to say," Tricia responded, though she was smiling. Even starting to relax a little. "You've probably been riding horses since you were a baby."

He chuckled. Made that hat move again. "Before that," he said. "According to Davis, Brody's and my mother was a champion barrel racer. She competed until about a month before we were born, and wouldn't have quit then if the rodeo people hadn't banned her from the event."

While it wasn't a particularly intimate thing to talk about, Tricia still felt moved, as though she'd received some kind of rare gift. She didn't know a lot about Conner Creed, beyond the fact that he was dangerously attractive, but she *was* aware that he was the quiet type, not exactly an introvert, but not an extrovert, like Brody, either.

"I don't think I ever met your mother," she said, mostly to be saying something. Otherwise, his words might have just hung there, between them, fragile as icicles in a spring thaw.

Conner wasn't looking at her now, but straight ahead, at the other riders. "Nobody around here ever did," he said quietly, and after some time had gone by. "She wasn't a very big woman, and carrying twins was hard on her. She fell sick right after Brody and I were born, and never got better. After the funeral, our dad brought us home to the ranch, and we were still pretty little when he died, too."

Tricia's heart found its way into her voice. "I'm sorry," she said.

Conner's smile came as a surprise, given the psychological weight of what he'd just told her. "We were lucky," he said. "Davis and Kim raised us like we were their own. Gave us a good life."

A rush of emotion, partly admiration for Conner's uncle and aunt and partly something considerably harder to identify, surged through Tricia like the first hopeful breeze of a hard-won spring. Conner was stubborn, and he could be taciturn, she knew, but he was also rock-solid, to the very core—a grown *man,* not a boy, like so many other guys his age.

The realization shook Tricia up, and left her with a lot to think about.

The ride went on, Buttercup and Lakota moving at a snail's pace. That didn't seem to bother Conner, though Tricia could tell that he was keeping a close eye on the goings-on up ahead.

This was his ranch, and because of that, he probably felt a responsibility for every person and every animal on that trail ride.

"Your turn," he said presently, and it took Tricia a moment or two to pick up on his meaning. "I knew your dad—he and Davis were good friends—but nobody ever said much about your mother, Natty included."

Tricia was getting used to the slow rhythm of Buttercup's plodding stride. She was still going to be sore, she knew that for certain, but at least she had some inkling of why people liked to ride horses. There was a sort of freedom in it, a kind of quiet power, and she could see a long way into the distance.

"Mom's a trauma nurse," Tricia said. "She and Dad were divorced when I was seven, which is why I split my time between Seattle and Lonesome Bend while I was growing up. She's out of the country now, working for one of the emergency relief agencies."

"It was like that for Steven," he said. "The going back and forth between his folks, I mean. His mom and Davis were married for about five minutes before they realized they'd made a terrible mistake—they might as well have come from different universes—and went their separate ways. Davis wanted to be part of his son's life, though—he insisted Steven had to grow up as a Creed, and spend his summers here in Colorado until he was old enough to decide things for himself, and he paid child support right along, even when Steven's mother said it wasn't necessary because she didn't need his money."

There it was, Tricia thought. That quiet integrity, that steadiness she'd recognized in Conner a few minutes before. Maybe he'd inherited the trait, though not from his dad, to hear Natty tell it. Just the night before, she'd described Blue Creed as a "renegade," said Brody took after him, but not Conner.

In this case, Tricia figured it was more a case of nurture than nature. Conner was the way he was because, despite losing both parents, he'd been raised in a loving household. It had mattered to Davis and Kim Creed how their infant nephews turned out.

Brody's famous wild streak, on the other hand, was harder to figure out. Maybe, in his case, the reverse had been true, and nature had prevailed over nurture. The whole thing was beginning to tangle Tricia's brain.

The two of them rode in companionable silence for a while and, eventually, the riders up ahead stopped along a quiet inlet in the river, to dismount and stretch their two legs, and let their four-legged companions drink.

Even from so far back, Tricia could see that Sasha was having a good time—maybe the best since she'd arrived in Lonesome Bend for a visit that was already halfway over—and that touched her heart.

Her feelings must have shown in her face, because Conner commented, "That little girl means a lot to you."

"Yes," Tricia agreed, after swallowing. "Sasha's mother, Diana, and I are close friends." She sighed, and then added, without meaning to at all, "Seattle won't be the same without them." A pause. "They're moving to France, because of Paul's job. That's Sasha's dad."

Conner absorbed that. Nodded. "You're planning on going back there?" he asked presently. "To Seattle?" His voice was quiet, and if he cared about the answer, one way or the other, there was nothing in his tone to indicate it.

"If I ever manage to sell the drive-in and River's Bend," she said, "I'll definitely go back. I loved living there."

"Why?" Conner asked.

The simplicity and directness of that question caught Tricia off guard. "I guess I'm a city girl at heart," she finally replied. "And Seattle is a great town."

"I hear it rains a lot." His tone was noncommittal and a little flat.

Tricia grinned. "Not as much as the hype would lead a person to believe," she replied. "When the weather is good, Seattle is unbelievably beautiful. It's so green, and the Olympic Mountains are white with snow year-round. The seafood is excellent, and you can buy the loveliest fresh flowers at the Pike Place Market—"

Conner didn't comment.

Tricia watched him out of the corner of her eye for a

few moments, then went on talking. She wasn't one of those women who couldn't stand silence, but today, for some reason, it made her uncomfortable. "I guess it's all a matter of perspective," she said tentatively, standing up in the stirrups because her thighs ached.

After this, she was going to be bow-legged.

"I guess so," Conner agreed. "I can't imagine living anyplace but here."

They'd almost reached the river's edge by then, where the other riders and their horses were taking a break, and she could see the campground on the opposite side of the water, and beyond that, a glimpse of the top of the peeling screen at the Bluebird Drive-in, since the two properties adjoined each other.

Over the years, Diana had accused Tricia of not knowing when to cut her losses and run—referring to Hunter, in most instances—and this was evidently one of those times. She knew she should shut up, but the words just kept spilling out of her. "You've never even thought about living anywhere but Lonesome Bend?" she asked, finding that hard to believe.

"I went to college in Denver," Conner said, tugging his hat brim down lower over his eyes and keeping his face in profile. "Couldn't wait to graduate and get back here."

To Joleen, Tricia thought, with a bruising sting in the center of her heart, and then wondered where in the heck *that* had come from.

"What about Brody?"

Conner spared her a sidelong glance, but it didn't last more than a moment. "What about him?" he asked, and there was a tautness in his voice now. The Conner who'd told her about his mother, the pregnant barrel racer, was gone.

Tricia closed her eyes for a moment, realized how tightly she was gripping the reins and eased up a little. "I just meant—well—he left Lonesome Bend—"

"That he did," Conner bit out.

Tricia sighed, watching him out of the corner of her eye. *Shut up, shut up,* said the voice of common sense.

"And now he's back," she went on, against her own advice.

"Yeah," Conner said. "Until he starts itching to follow the rodeo again, anyhow." His tone was entirely civil, but it was also cold. Even dismissive. He was telling her, as surely as if he'd said it in so many words, that he didn't want to talk anymore.

Not to her. And not about Brody.

Before, they'd been enjoying an easy, open exchange, a friendly chat. When, Tricia wondered, saddened, had things taken this unhappy turn? When she'd told him that she planned on leaving Lonesome Bend, once she'd sold her land, she thought. But, no, that couldn't be it. Why would Conner Creed care whether she stayed or moved away?

By then, they'd caught up with the others, and Sasha rushed over on foot, bright-eyed from the fresh air and an afternoon spent doing something she clearly loved. She gripped Buttercup's bridle expertly and smiled up at Tricia.

"Get down and walk around," the little girl said. "That way, you won't be as sore later on."

Conner swung down off Lakota's back and left the horse to graze. He waited, probably intending to help

Tricia down from the saddle, but she, smarting at the way he'd suddenly shut down, had something to prove.

And that something was that she didn't need Conner Creed's help to get down off a horse.

She dismounted, glad her back was turned to him when her feet struck the ground, because pain raced up her legs on impact, so intense that she caught her breath and squeezed her eyes shut for a few seconds.

"You shouldn't jump down like that," Sasha counseled solemnly, and very much after the fact. "It usually hurts a lot, landing on the balls of your feet. Has to do with the circulation."

Tricia lifted her chin. Then turned, smiling, from Buttercup's side.

"No worries," she said, too quickly to be really credible, even to a child.

Conner sliced one unreadable look at her and then walked away, engaging Carolyn and some of the other riders in conversation. In its own way, that hurt as much as making contact with the ground had.

"You're doing really well," one of the rancher's wives told Tricia. Her name, Tricia recalled, was Marissa Rogers. In the old days, she'd been part of Joleen Williams's crowd, with no time for the likes of Tricia.

Now, though, the look in Marissa's clear eyes was kind and friendly.

"Thanks," Tricia said, managing a little smile. It wasn't as though Marissa had shunned her when they were kids, or bullied her in any way. She'd simply ignored her, and it had all happened a long, long time ago.

"I hear Natty's back from Denver," Marissa went on. "I'd love to stop by the house and say hello, but I don't want to intrude if she's not feeling well."

"Natty's a little tired," Tricia replied carefully. Her great-grandmother was a sociable person, and she enjoyed company, but she wasn't a hundred percent by any means. "I'm sure she'd be glad to see you, though."

"I'll give it a few days," Marissa said, with a smile. But then she was looking past Tricia, her eyes narrowing a little. "Uh-oh," she murmured, so quietly that Tricia nearly didn't hear her. Automatically, Tricia turned to follow Marissa's gaze.

Brody and Joleen were riding toward them, at top speed, both of them laughing, though the sound didn't carry above the sound of their horses' hooves. They were racing, and it was neck-and-neck, a dead heat.

Tricia looked around for Conner, and this was an automatic response, too, but her glance snagged on Carolyn first. Her friend's face was full of pain.

Tricia started toward her, but before she could make her way to Carolyn's side, the other woman was back on her horse and riding along the riverbank, her head held high, her spine rigid.

"Poor Carolyn," Marissa said, in a tone of genuine sympathy, standing at Tricia's elbow.

Tricia didn't ask what Marissa had meant by that, though she wanted to. To do so would have been a little too much like gossiping behind Carolyn's back.

Sasha had Show Pony by the reins again, and she looked as though she might mount up and chase after Carolyn herself.

"Let her go," Tricia said, very gently, putting a hand on Sasha's shoulder.

After that, though it was a while before everybody headed back, the party was essentially over. If Brody and Joleen cared, they gave no sign of it; they didn't even slow their horses as they shot past, both of them leaning low over the animals' necks and shedding happy laughter behind them like a dog shaking off water.

When the time came to get back in the saddle, Tricia hauled herself up onto Buttercup with a difficulty she hoped no one else noticed. Conner had left Lakota standing nearby, and he mounted up with barely a glance at Tricia.

He stayed close beside her all the way back to the barn, dutiful but silent, the small muscles along his jawline bunched tight. And for all that Tricia could have reached over and touched him, she knew by the set of his shoulders and the way he held his head that his thoughts were far away.

ON THE WAY HOME, Conner was careful to hold Lakota in check—the horse wanted with everything in him to bolt for home at a dead run, and it wasn't going to happen. Buttercup, despite her age, would go from zero-to-sixty in hardly more than a heartbeat, causing Tricia to either fall off or be scared half to death.

You're a damn fool, Conner Creed, he told himself grimly. By his reckoning, any half-wit should have known a woman like Tricia wouldn't be content to spend the rest of her life in a backwater place like Lonesome Bend. Why, she'd fairly shimmered before, telling him about Seattle, with its seafood and its cut flowers and its snow-covered mountains.

Hell. *Colorado* had snow-covered mountains aplenty, and fields *full* of wildflowers three seasons of the year. As for seafood—who needed it, when the river and the creeks and a dozen lakes were all right there, handy and practically brimming with fish?

Conscious of Tricia beside him, Conner went right on ignoring her. He knew she wasn't going back to Seattle at the first opportunity because of that city's many charms. The real draw was the guy he'd glimpsed on her computer monitor that first morning, when he'd dropped by with Natty's firewood.

Conner unclamped his back molars, to ease the growing ache in the hinges of his jaws. He supposed the yahoo in that screen-saver picture was good-looking enough to suit most women, but Conner figured him for an idiot, if only because he'd let Tricia McCall out of his sight for what—a year and a half? In the other guy's place, he would have visited often, at the very least, and probably made sure there was an engagement ring on her finger, too. One with plenty of sparkle, so any man with eyeballs would know she was spoken for.

He was thinking like a cave dweller, thinking like *Brody*—Conner knew that. But he couldn't seem to get a handle on his attitude. Being around Tricia made him feel as though all the known laws of physics had been suspended—up was sideways and down was someplace beyond the clouds.

Conner swept off his hat with one hand, ran the other through his hair and sighed. And if all that wasn't enough to chap his hide, there was that little show Brody and Joleen had put on, out there on the range.

What the hell was *that* about?

And why had Brody helped himself to Conner's clothes and gotten his hair cut shorter? It gave Conner a schizophrenic start just to look at his twin, since he'd gone to the barbershop the other day as Brody and come out as a more-than-reasonable facsimile of Conner.

Yep, Brody was definitely up to something. But what?

"Conner?" Tricia said, out of the blue.

They'd almost reached the far side of the inner pasture by then, moving, as they were, at the breathtaking speed of rocks trying to roll uphill, and the rest of the trail riding party was already at the barn. Folks were unsaddling their horses, leading them into their trailers. Hell, some of them were already on the road home.

"What?" he asked, sounding more abrupt that he'd intended. Out of the corner of his eye, he saw her bite her lower lip.

When she'd formulated her reply, she said, "Thank you."

He turned his head to look straight at her then. "For—?"

She blushed. Her eyes dodged his, widened when she forced herself to face him again. "Inviting Sasha and me on the trail ride," she told him shyly.

He felt like a jerk. "You're welcome," he bit out.

CHAPTER ELEVEN

"DON'T ASK ABOUT the trail ride," Tricia told Natty early the next morning, when she and Valentino got back from their walk. "It was an absolute disaster."

Still in her robe and slippers, though she had pinned her silver-white hair up into its customary Gibson-girl style, Natty sat at her kitchen table, Winston perched on the chair next to hers while she fed him little morsels of sardine.

"Did I ask about the trail ride?" Natty inquired sweetly.

Sasha was out of bed, Tricia thought, with a glance up at the ceiling. She could hear the shower running upstairs.

"You were *about* to ask," she said, unfastening Valentino's leash so he could walk over and rub noses with Winston.

Natty waited a beat. "Why was the trail ride a disaster, dear?"

Tricia sighed, shoved the leash into the pocket of her jacket, and helped herself to a cup from Natty's cupboard and coffee from her old-fashioned plug-in percolator. "Let me count the ways," she said, after a few sips.

Valentino lost interest in Winston and focused on the little plate of sardines instead. Natty fed him the last smidgen, much to her cat's consternation, and rose to set the dish in the sink and wash her hands.

"Sasha had a *marvelous* time," Natty observed, drying her fingers on a small embroidered towel with a fussy crocheted edge and returning to her seat at the table.

Winston, disgruntled, leaped down from his chair and pranced into the hallway. Valentino was right behind him.

"Sasha," Tricia said patiently, "knows how to ride a horse. She didn't need babysitting the whole time, the way I did."

Natty arched one snowy eyebrow. "'Babysitting'?" she repeated. Her tone was innocent, but her eyes danced with amused interest.

"Conner gave me a horse reserved for greenhorns, and rode beside me the entire time," Tricia said.

"Why, that awful man," Natty teased.

Tricia frowned. When it came to the list of things she wanted to talk about, Conner Creed ranked dead last. "It was embarrassing," she said, somewhat lamely.

Natty sighed deeply. "How I miss that particular brand of embarrassment," she said. "In my day, we women *liked* being protected by a handsome cowboy."

Tricia huffed out a breath.

And Natty chuckled. "From what you've told me so far," she said cheerfully, "I'd hesitate to describe the experience as a 'disaster.' But that's just me."

Tricia thought of Carolyn then, and the way she'd vanished after Brody and Joleen showed up out there on the range, racing their horses and laughing into the wind. She'd looked for her friend after she and Conner got back to the barn area, but Carolyn had already put her horse away, gotten into her car and left.

"All right," she conceded, "maybe *disaster* is too strong a word."

Just then, there was an exuberant clatter of small feet on the inside stairway and, moments later, Sasha burst into Natty's kitchen, fully dressed, her hair still damp from the shower. "Mom and Dad sent me an email!" she announced. "They're coming back early!"

While this was obviously good news to Sasha, who had missed her parents a lot, it further dampened Tricia's already low spirits. "Oh," she said, aware of the understanding glance Natty sent her way.

"They found the *perfect* house for us to live in," Sasha said, bubbling with enthusiasm, "and they're lonesome for me, so they're catching an earlier flight. Mom said she'll call you later today, on your cell phone, so the two of you can decide what to do next."

Tricia managed a smile—if Sasha was happy, *she* was happy—and went to hug the child. "I'm going to miss you something fierce," she said.

"You could live in Paris, too," Sasha suggested. "Then we could all be together, you and me and Mom and Dad, whenever we wanted."

Tricia held on to her smile, though it felt shaky on her mouth, as if it might fall away at any moment. "I'll visit if I can," she said, very quietly. "In the meantime, let's make the most of our together-time. I'll fix us all some breakfast, and then, while Natty's resting, you and I will go over to the campground and make sure it's still standing."

Sasha nodded, pleased by the simple prospect of food and an outing. Of course, her excitement might wane a little when she realized they were going to pick up litter and sweep ashes out of the fire pits.

Breakfast was a speedy matter of cold cereal, sliced

bananas and milk, as it happened. Natty declined the meal and went into the "parlor" to watch her favorite morning news show on television. She was a big fan of Robin Roberts.

By the time Tricia, Sasha and Valentino reached River's Bend in the Pathfinder, the campers were all gone, though it looked as if they'd left the place in unusually tidy condition. Without the tents and the RVs, not to mention the people, the campground had the lonely feel of a ghost town, not only deserted, but forgotten as well.

"Why are you so sad?" Sasha asked, tugging at the sleeve of Tricia's jacket to get her attention. Her eyes were huge and somber in her little face.

Tricia swallowed. "I'm not sad," she said, and her voice came out sounding hoarse. "I'm just feeling a little nostalgic at the moment, that's all."

"Isn't nostalgia the same thing as sadness?"

Tricia smiled and tugged lightly at one of Sasha's pigtails. "A perceptive question if I've ever heard one," she replied. "But there is a subtle difference. Nostalgia is a way of remembering people and places and things, and wishing things hadn't changed. It has a sweetness to it. Sadness is just—well—*being sad.*"

"Okay," Sasha said, drawing the word out and looking benignly skeptical.

Tricia laughed, though her eyes were stinging.

"I'm glad I came to Lonesome Bend," Sasha said, when they'd both been quiet for a while. Valentino had wandered down to the swimming beach, and he was sniffing at some invisible trail running along the edge of the river. "Now, when I think about you, I'll be able to put houses and people around you in my head."

Tricia bent, kissed her goddaughter on top of the head. "I'm glad you came to Lonesome Bend, too," she said. "Let's go inside and get a fire started. I have some paperwork to do, and I want to check the voice mail one last time before I shut this place down for the winter."

Sasha nodded, but her arm was still around Tricia's waist, and her face was pressed into her side. It took Tricia a moment to realize that the little girl was crying.

"What is it, honey?" she asked, leading Sasha to the nearest picnic table, so they could sit down side by side on the bench.

Sasha sniffled and rested her head against Tricia's upper arm. "I know you love your great-grandma Natty and Valentino," she replied, "but it makes me have nostalgia when I think about you being here and Mom and Dad and me being all the way over a whole ocean, in Paris, France."

Touched, Tricia held the child close for a long moment. "You're going to have a wonderful time in Paris," she said, when she could trust herself to speak. "But you won't be in Europe forever. Your mom is pretty sure your dad will be transferred back to Seattle in a couple of years, and I'll be right there waiting for you when you get home."

"But I'll be a different me then," Sasha protested, "and you'll be a different *you*."

"And we'll still be the very best of friends," Tricia promised gently. Then she gave a little shiver—the wind blowing in off the river had a bite.

Valentino came when Tricia summoned him, and settled himself in front of the fire inside the office as soon as she'd gotten it going.

Sasha, though still a bit subdued, explored the tiny lodge while Tricia booted up her computer to enter the weekend's receipts from River's Bend into her accounting program. Joe had taken a number of black-and-white photographs of the place over the years, and he'd framed a lot of them.

"Is that you, with the fishing pole?" Sasha asked once.

"Um-hmm," Tricia replied, concentrating on debits and credits. Once she'd made her entries, she would write up a bank deposit slip.

"That must be your dad," Sasha said, a little later. "The guy standing on the swimming dock with the kayak?"

"Yup," Tricia said. "That's him."

Soon, the little girl got bored, since there was only so much to see in a place that small. She curled up on the rug next to Valentino, wrapping both arms around him, and drifted off to sleep.

The sight brought tears to Tricia's eyes again, but she blinked them away. Parting would be difficult, but that was life for you. There was always someone to say good-bye to, always someone to miss when they were gone.

Determined to keep it together, Tricia added up checks, cash and credit card slips from the weekend just past, and filled out the deposit slip.

Then, reluctant to disturb Sasha and Valentino—why trifle with a perfect moment before it was absolutely necessary?—she dialed the number and access code for her voice mail. She was pretty much going through the motions, given that the season was over and people wouldn't be asking for reservations at the campground or looking for a place to park travel trailers and RVs until early spring, at least.

Tricia wondered if she'd still be in Lonesome Bend then, marking time, waiting for somebody to buy River's

Bend and the Bluebird Drive-in and getting older by the minute. It was a dismal thought.

"You have two messages," a robotic female voice reported from inside the ancient telephone receiver.

Tricia frowned slightly and settled back in her uncomfortable desk chair to wait.

"This is Carla, with Lonesome Bend Real Estate," said another voice, this one fully human. "It's Monday morning, early. Call me. I have big news."

Tricia's heart shinnied up into the back of her throat.

The second message came on. "It's Carla again. I forgot to leave my cell number, and since you might not have it handy—" A pause, during which Carla drew in an audible breath. "It's 555-7242. *Call me.*"

Tricia hung up the handset, picked it up again and worked the rotary dial with an unsteady index finger.

Carla didn't even say hello when she answered her cell, she simply blurted out, "Two offers! Tricia, we have *two offers* on your properties, and they're good ones!"

Tricia put a hand to her heart, temporarily speechless. Nearly two years without a single showing, and now, all of a sudden, they had *offers?*

"One came in this morning, and one was waiting in my fax machine when I got home last night," Carla rushed on. "It was late, or I would have called you then. I was so excited, I didn't even *think* about leaving a message on your cell."

"But how, who—?"

Carla laughed. "Well, that's the mystery," she said merrily.

"The mystery?"

"It's corporate," Carla said, almost whispering, like

she was confiding a secret. "That's how these big companies operate. They buy real estate through their attorneys—most often as tax write-offs, but sometimes as investments."

Tricia wondered why she wasn't happier. After all, she'd been waiting for this news. Hoping for it. Constructing her whole future around it.

Now here it was—her problems, the financial ones, at least—were over. And she felt hollow, rather than jubilant.

"Okay," she managed. "What happens now?"

"Well," Carla nearly sang, "we're in the enviable position of choosing between two excellent offers. They're very similar, both a little over the asking price, if you can believe it, and all cash." She paused, clearly savoring what she was going to say next. "There might even be a bidding war, Tricia."

Tricia's head was spinning by then, and Valentino and Sasha were both awake, and watching her. *A bidding war?* Was this really happening? It was all too much to take in.

"Tricia?" A giggle from Carla. "Are you still there? You didn't faint, did you?"

"I'm here," Tricia said woodenly. "These corporations—which ones are they?"

"Why should we care?" Carla reasoned. "We're going to be laughing all the way to the bank, as the old saying goes." She was quiet for a moment. "Tricia, this *is* what you want, isn't it?"

Tricia imagined leaving Lonesome Bend. Leaving Natty. Leaving her apartment. Maybe never seeing Conner again.

"I—yes—yes, *of course* this is what I want."

She'd set the asking price high, in the beginning, to leave room for negotiation. Even after settling debts and paying taxes, *and* opening her own art gallery in Seattle, she would be very well off indeed. In fact, working would be optional—so maybe she'd take that trip to France after all. She'd set herself up in a modest hotel, refusing to impose on Diana and Paul, and get to know Paris. She might even purchase a train pass and explore the Continent—

But what about Natty?

Her great-grandmother might be seriously ill—after all, she was over ninety—and Tricia had made certain promises. Just that morning, in fact, she'd assured Natty that Winston would be looked after, no matter what.

And then there was Valentino. She couldn't— *wouldn't*—abandon him just because she suddenly had the means to live anywhere she chose. No, she would have to find the dog a home—and just the right one, too—before she could even consider leaving town for good.

"Tricia?" Carla prompted again.

"Still here," Tricia said weakly.

"Forgive me," Carla said, gentle now. "I guess I got a little carried away for a minute there. I know River's Bend and the Bluebird have been in your family for a long time, and you *must* have a sentimental attachment to them. Letting go won't be easy, and we don't have to decide this second."

Realistically, Tricia couldn't afford to miss out on this opportunity, and she knew it. What if both buyers changed their minds, and she never got another chance to sell the businesses? River's Bend barely brought in enough to cover local taxes and a very modest living allowance for her. The Bluebird, going unused, was probably *costing* her money.

"Get the best deal you can," she told Carla.

"Leave it to me," Carla said. Very briefly, she outlined her plan to contact both buyers' representatives and explain the situation. "I'll get back to you as soon as I know anything more."

When the conversation was over, Tricia was slow to hang up.

"I guess that wasn't my mom calling," Sasha said, approaching Tricia to perch on the arm of her chair and slip an arm around her shoulders.

"No," Tricia said. "It wasn't your mom."

"Is something wrong?" Sasha asked, in a small voice, looking worried. "You'd tell me if something happened to my mom and dad, wouldn't you? If their plane went down or they got into a really bad car crash, like Princess Diana did?"

"They're *fine,*" Tricia told the child, pulling her onto her lap and hugging her tightly. "That call was from my real-estate agent, Carla Perkins. The news is good, kiddo. Somebody—*two somebodies*, actually—wants to buy the properties my dad left me."

"Then how come you look like you're going to cry?" Sasha asked. "Are you nostalgic, or sad?"

Tricia smiled, kissed the little girl's forehead. "Nostalgic," she said.

"Good," Sasha said.

"Tell you what," Tricia began. "We'll run by the bank, you and me and Valentino, so I can make a deposit to my account, and then we'll go home and make lunch. By then, I'll bet we'll have heard from your mom."

Sasha smiled, slid off Tricia's lap. "Grilled cheese

sandwiches?" she asked. "They're my favorite thing to have for lunch, and Natty likes them, too. She told me so."

"Well, that settles it, then," Tricia said. "Grilled cheese it is."

CONNER HELD THE cordless phone away from his head for a moment, glared at it, and then pressed it to his ear again. "What do you mean, there's another offer? Those properties have been for sale since Joe McCall died and now, all of a sudden, there's a land rush?"

Conner's lawyer, Mike Summerville, chuckled. "Somebody else wants the Bluebird Drive-in Movie-o-rama and that sorry, run-down excuse for a camp-ground. Go figure."

"Who?" Conner demanded.

"How should I know?" Mike retorted good-naturedly. "According to Ms. McCall's real-estate agent, the other offer is solid, all cash, ready to go into escrow."

Brody ambled into the kitchen, having slept in late enough to miss helping out with the chores. Some things just never changed.

Conner glared at his shirtless brother, who yawned, took a mug from a shelf and headed for the coffeemaker, paying him no mind at all.

Mike waited.

Conner glowered at Brody.

Brody grinned and raised his coffee mug in a smart-ass toast. "Cheers," he said.

Mike cleared his throat. "Business is business, Con-ner," he said. "Do you want to raise the offer you made, or let it ride?"

"I want you to find out who the competition is and

what they plan on doing with that land, Mike," Conner responded.

"What are *you* planning to do with it?" Mike countered. He was a friend of the family, having gone through law school with Steven, so he could ask questions like that and get away with it.

"Add it to the ranch, I guess," Conner said. He'd made the offer for one reason and one reason only—so Tricia could leave town, if that was what she wanted, and go back to Seattle and the guy in the ski gear.

"For as long as I can remember," Mike said, "the party line has been that the ranch is big enough already. Why make it bigger?"

"I just want to, that's all," Conner replied, still peevish.

Brody snickered, shook his head once, and took a slurp from his coffee mug. It would be nice if he'd at least *pretend* he wasn't eavesdropping, Conner thought, but that was probably too much to ask.

"All right, all right," Mike sighed. "I'll try to find out who else is interested, and get back to you."

"Fine," Conner said. Then he bit out a testy "Goodbye" and hung up.

"Still mad because Joleen and I crashed the trail ride yesterday?" Brody asked, with that damnable tilted grin of his.

"I never gave a rat's ass in the first place," Conner replied. "I believe I've already told you that."

"Right," Brody drawled.

"If you want to get under my hide, brother," Conner challenged grimly, "you're going to have to do a little better than that."

Brody laughed. Nodded in the general direction of

the phone. "You in the market for some real estate?" he asked, with a casualness that should have alerted Conner to what was coming, but didn't.

"Maybe," Conner said.

"I'll outbid you," Brody told him.

Conner, about to open the fridge and see if there was anything in there that could possibly be construed as lunch, froze in his tracks.

"What?" he asked.

"I want that land," Brody said easily. "And I'm willing to pay for it."

Conner narrowed his eyes. He could barely believe what he was hearing. "*You're* the competition?"

Brody raised one hand to shoulder level, like he was swearing an oath. "That's me," he said.

"Now why the *hell* would a saddle bum like you want that land?"

Brody made a shruglike movement, all but imperceptible. "Maybe I'm tired of being a saddle bum," he said. He was using that quiet voice again, the one that didn't sound like it was really him talking. "I mean to bulldoze the whole thing—except for the trees, of course—and build myself a house overlooking the river. A barn, too."

Conner gave a raspy laugh, without a trace of amusement in it. "Half of this place is legally yours," he reminded his twin. "Remember?"

"And I feel about as welcome here as a case of whooping cough on a transatlantic flight," Brody replied. He set his coffee aside and leaned back against the counter, folding his arms. "We'll share the rangeland—if I'm going to run cattle, I'll have to put them someplace. Otherwise, you can keep to your side of the river and I'll keep to mine and that'll be that."

Conner opened his mouth. Closed it again. Shoved a hand through his hair. "You're crazy," he said, at length.

Again, Brody chuckled. "So I'm told," he said. "But the prodigal son is home for good, little brother, and you'd better start getting used to the idea."

"I'll believe it when I see it," Conner snapped. He didn't dare hope Brody meant to stay—it would hurt too damn bad when he changed his mind and took off again.

"Start believing," Brody said. "Unless you slow things down by making a pissing match out of this, I'm going to buy that land, Conner. I'll live in that chicken coop Joe McCall called a lodge until spring, and then I'll start on the house and barn. I want something to leave to my kids when I die. A legacy, you might say."

For a long moment, Conner just stared at his brother, at this confounding version of himself, and then he said, "*You* have kids?"

Brody laughed. "Not that I know of," he replied. "But I'm capable of making some, when the time and the woman are right."

"With Joleen?" Conner asked. In the next instant, he wished he'd bitten off his tongue first.

"I've already told you," Brody said, serious again. "Joleen is just a friend. And frankly, I'm a little surprised at the way you keep bringing up her name. I would have sworn you were taken with Tricia McCall."

Conner swallowed hard. Felt his neck go red and the blood pound under his cheekbones. "If that's what you think," he seethed, "why haven't you made a move on her?"

Brody sighed. It was a heavy sound, and bleak.

Conner was almost convinced.

"You think I'd do a thing like that?" Brody asked.

"I *know* you would," Conner shot back, grabbing his jacket off the hook beside the back door. "From experience."

"Conner—"

"Buy the land," Conner broke in furiously. "Build your house and your barn and run all the cattle you want to, but, for once in your life, Brody, keep your word. Stay on your own side of the river."

Brody raised both hands, palms out. The look in his eyes might have been pain. More likely, it was just good acting.

"Have it your way," he said.

And Conner slammed out, got into his truck. His stomach rumbled, almost as loudly as the motor.

He'd get lunch in town, he decided.

"DIANA?" TRICIA SAID, smiling into the mouthpiece of her cell phone. She was standing in front of her kitchen stove in the apartment, making grilled cheese sandwiches for Sasha, Natty and herself.

"Hello!" Diana chimed. "How is my lovely child?"

"Lovely," Tricia answered, with a fond glance at Sasha. She and Valentino were playing nearby, with the blue chicken Tricia had bought for the dog just after she got him.

"Did she tell you we found the perfect house—not a flat, mind you, but a *house?* It's a five-minute walk from the nearest Metro stop, and the neighborhood is simply wonderful. There's even a park across the street."

"It sounds great," Tricia said.

Diana was quiet for a few moments. "So much for wild enthusiasm on your part," she said, sadly but gently.

CHAPTER TWELVE

TRICIA REMINDED HERSELF that Conner Creed was a guest in her home, albeit an uninvited one, and hadn't she just told Diana over the telephone that she would fly over to Seattle on Wednesday if she could be sure both Valentino and Natty would be all right during her absence?

Her great-grandmother's care remained a problem, but Tricia knew in her very bones that Valentino would be fine in Conner's care. Half the dilemma solved.

"Sit down," she told him, her tone clipped. Then, addressing Sasha, Tricia forced a wobbly smile and said, "Do you suppose Natty is ready to have some lunch now? Would you mind checking with her, please?"

Sasha was flushed, and there was a rebellion brewing in her normally clear eyes.

Valentino, having skulked under the table by then, let out a worried little whimper.

Conner sat down, after shooting an unreadable glance at Tricia, and bent to peer under the tabletop and speak quietly to the dog. "There, now, buddy," he said. "Don't be scared. Nobody's gonna hurt anybody."

As tough and masculine as he was, Conner's voice sounded almost fatherly, comforting Valentino like that.

"Go," Tricia told Sasha.

Sasha got to her feet, but she was none too happy about obeying, that much was plain to see. "Mom *said* you could bring Valentino to Seattle!" she reminded Tricia, but she was on her way toward the inside stairs.

"Seattle is a city," Tricia told the little girl quietly, and very gently. This outburst, she knew, wasn't entirely about the dog. Sasha was realizing a lot of things, like how far away Paris actually was, and how different her life would be there. The move, probably just an abstraction to her before, was taking on substance now. "Valentino will be happier on a ranch."

"No, he *won't!*" Sasha cried. "He'll know you went off and *left him!*" With that, she bolted, clattering down the inside staircase.

Tricia closed her eyes, praying the child wouldn't fall and hurt herself.

"Well," Conner said, after clearing his throat, "now I wish I'd kept my mouth shut about the dog."

"Me, too," Tricia said, with icy sweetness. A part of her still wanted to wring the man's neck but, fortunately, good sense and civility prevailed. "Valentino needs another place to live," she said carefully, moving to stand behind the chair opposite Conner's and gripping its back so hard that her knuckles ached. "If you promise he'll be *loved,* not just tolerated—that you won't make him live outside or in the barn or anything like that—he's yours."

Tricia had to turn her head then, since she felt as though the words had been coated with hot wax, pressed into her flesh and then ripped away. Merely *saying* them had left a raw sting in her throat.

She heard Conner's chair slide back and then he was in front of her, taking a firm but gentle hold on her shoulders, the blue of his eyes practically burning into her face.

"Dammit," he rasped, on a single hoarse breath. And then, just like that, Conner *kissed* Tricia—hard and deep and with a thoroughness that left her gasping when he drew back.

Even after the fact, lightning continued to bolt through Tricia, fairly fusing her feet to the floor. She stared at him, amazed by what he made her feel. By what he made her *want.*

"No," she heard herself say. And she had no earthly idea what she was talking about, or who she was talking *to,* exactly. It might have been Conner, it might have been herself, it might have been the universe as a whole. *"No."*

Conner's gaze softened unexpectedly and a smile kicked up at the corner of his mouth as he brushed her cheek with a touch so light and so fleeting that it might have been a soft summer breeze instead of a caress.

He was smiling. He'd just rocked her world, and he was *smiling.*

A passionate rage rose up inside Tricia, fierce and delicious, and there was no telling what she might have said to that man if Natty hadn't appeared at the top of the stairs at that exact moment, her breathing rapid and a little shallow, one beringed hand pressed to her chest.

"Good heavens," Natty said, when she could speak. "What's the matter with Sasha? Why, the child is practically hysterical!"

Stricken with alarm, Tricia started toward Natty, meaning to take her arm and help her to a chair, but Conner got there first. He sat the old woman down and went straight to the sink to run a glass of water for her.

Even in that fractured moment, Tricia had to admire his presence of mind. He was so *calm.*

Natty sat fluttering one hand in front of her face. "I'm *fine*," she insisted. "It's *Sasha* who needs tending."

Tricia's gaze collided with Conner's, over Natty's head, then ricocheted away, like a bullet.

"I'll see to Sasha," she said quietly.

Conner gave a nod, his face grim, and brought Natty the glass of water.

Tricia found her goddaughter in Natty's pantry, sitting on the floor between the built-in flour bin and a ten-pound sack of potatoes, her face buried in her hands.

"Sweetheart," Tricia said softly, crouching. Reaching out to touch the child.

But Sasha must have been peeking between her fingers, because she knew the touch was coming and jerked away to avoid contact. Sobs racked the little girl, causing her shoulders to shake, and she was making an awful wailing sound, woven through with threads of pure, childlike despair.

"Go away!" she almost shrieked.

Tricia shifted to her knees, facing her best friend's daughter. "Sasha, honey—please listen to me—"

"No! I don't *want* to listen, I want to *cry! Leave me alone!*"

Tricia wasn't going anywhere. The hard floor made her knees ache, so she sat cross-legged on the pantry floor, facing Sasha, prepared to wait the child out, no matter how long that might take.

Having already expended considerable energy, Sasha soon began to wind down. The sobs became sniffles, and then hiccups, and finally, after what seemed like a very long time, she lowered her hands and looked at Tricia with red-rimmed, swollen eyes.

"Everything is changing," Sasha said, her voice so

small that Tricia barely heard her, even in that small space. "I'm *tired* of things changing!"

Tricia spotted a roll of paper towels within easy reach on a low shelf and picked it up. Tore away the plastic wrapper and handed Sasha a sheet.

"I know," she said tenderly. "Same here. Blow."

Sasha wadded up the paper towel and blew her nose into it.

"Sometimes it's really hard when things change," Tricia said. She drew a deep breath, let it out. "You're going to love Paris, Sasha," she went on. "You'll make new friends and see wonderful things and learn more than you can even imagine right now. Best of all, your mom and dad will be right there with you, the whole time, loving you and keeping you safe."

Sasha pondered all that. Crumpled the used paper towel in one hand. At considerable length, she asked, "What if Valentino doesn't *like* being a ranch dog?"

Tricia moved to sit beside her. Slipped an arm around the child, but loosely, because the moment was fragile and so was this beloved child. "He will," she said. "Valentino's going to be a very big dog one of these days, Sasha. And big dogs need space to run. Plus, he'll enjoy riding around in Conner's truck and all the rest of it."

"There are dog parks in Seattle," Sasha wasted no time in reminding her. "And lots of people have big dogs. It's not as if they're *illegal* or anything."

"Valentino would be alone in some condo all day, honey, while I worked. He'd be lonesome and bored and he wouldn't get enough exercise." Tricia paused, surprised at how attached she'd become to that silly dog in such a short time. "Trust me, if I could offer him a choice, he'd take the ranch life, any day."

Sasha drew up her knees and rested her forearms on them. "Don't you want to keep him, even the littlest bit?"

"I'd *love* to keep Valentino," Tricia replied. "But we're not talking about what I want, here, Sasha. We're talking about what's best for a growing dog."

Sasha turned to her, looked up at her with tired eyes, and dropped a bombshell. "You could marry Conner, and then you and Valentino would *both* live on the Creed ranch. That would be the perfect solution."

Tricia laughed, hugged Sasha close and rested her chin on top of the little girl's head. "It's not that simple, honey," she said, but just the same, she couldn't help imagining what it would be like to live under the same roof with Conner. Her body did a déjà vu thing, reliving that kiss they'd shared earlier.

Sasha gave a big sigh. "I'm sorry, Aunt Tricia. For acting like a baby and everything."

Tricia squeezed her again. "Don't worry about it," she said. "You're allowed to have feelings, you know."

"I'm going to miss Valentino," Sasha admitted.

By some unspoken agreement, they both stood up.

"So will I," Tricia said.

"And I'll miss *you*," the child replied. "I thought I'd gotten used to it, you've been away from Seattle for so long, but being here with you, and doing fun stuff—" Sasha fell silent, and Tricia was afraid she'd start to cry again. Afraid both of them would.

So Tricia paused, when they were out of the pantry and standing in Natty's quiet, fragrant kitchen. She cupped a hand under Sasha's chin, and gently lifted. "I'll miss you, too. But we can email, write each other letters, talk on the phone once in a while, and maybe—"

she tried to look stern, but a smile broke through "—*just maybe*—no promises, now—I'll come to visit."

Sasha threw both her arms around Tricia's waist and hugged her hard, clinging a little.

A bittersweet ache filled Tricia, made up of love for this child, for Natty and her lost father and her dog, Rusty. Love for Seattle *and* for Lonesome Bend, for life itself, so fleeting and so very precious.

Love hurts, she thought, as the wispy strains of an old song drifted up from her memory. That was the paradox—love *did* hurt, though not always, of course. Yet, just as the poet said, it was surely better to have loved and lost than never to have loved at all.

"Let's go upstairs and see how Natty's doing," Tricia said. "She needs to know you're all right, for one thing."

Sasha nodded and led the way, her small hand clasping Tricia's. They arrived to find Natty looking much restored, her color good and her eyes shining, chatting happily away while Conner stood at the stove, listening and tending a whole new batch of grilled cheese sandwiches.

Sasha went straight to Natty, and the old woman gathered the child into an embrace. Tricia had to look away—if she hadn't, she would have burst out crying for sure—but as luck or fate would have it, her gaze landed on Conner's face and stuck there.

Something silent and powerful passed between them; for Tricia, it was as if their two souls had met and joined, in a way their bodies never had, sealing some sacred bargain. Or *renewing* one that was older than the stars.

Tricia might have thought she was going crazy if she hadn't seen a flicker of confounded shock ignite in

Conner's eyes. Within half a heartbeat, the look was gone, but it had been there, all right—proof that he'd felt something, too.

Deftly, Conner picked up a spatula and scooped one of the golden-crisp sandwiches he'd made onto a plate, and then carried it over to Natty.

Natty looked up at Tricia, who was still trying to recover her inner equilibrium, and winked. "He even cooks," she said, as though Conner wasn't standing right there, hearing every word. "If I were sixty years younger, Tricia McCall, I'd give you a run for your money."

Tricia's cheeks blazed.

Conner gave her one of those tilted grins, probably to let her know he was enjoying her obvious discomfort, and Sasha sank into the chair nearest Natty's and chimed, "That sandwich smells a lot better than the ones *Tricia* made. Hers were burnt offerings."

Conner laughed at that, breaking the spell he'd cast over Tricia. "Want one, shortstop?" he asked the child.

"Yes, please," Sasha said. Like Natty, she appeared to have recovered completely—Tricia was the only one still traumatized.

Conner's glance slanted to Tricia. "Hungry?" he asked. He had a puzzled expression in his eyes now, and his voice was husky.

Oh, she was *hungry,* all right—but not for grilled cheese sandwiches.

The air seemed to collapse and then withdraw, leaving a vacuum behind.

"N-no, thanks," she said.

He dished up a second sandwich and set it before

Sasha, who would have dug in immediately if Tricia hadn't warned, "Wash your hands."

Sasha sighed dramatically and headed for the bathroom.

"Yes, indeed," Natty went on, as though there had been no interruption in her observations, "a man who cooks is a rare commodity."

"Oh, for Pete's sake," Tricia muttered, mortified all over again.

"You can't blame a girl for trying," Natty remarked, singsong.

Tricia set her hands on her hips, wondering which "girl" Natty was referring to—herself or her great-granddaughter. "Oh, yes, you can," she replied.

Conner interceded skillfully, retrieving his jacket from the back of the chair, shrugging it on with a gesture that could only be described as masculine grace. "I'll come back for Valentino another time," he told Tricia, just as Sasha bounded back into the room.

"Good idea," Tricia said, her voice taut. She was careful not to look directly at Conner.

He *still* didn't leave. *When* was the man planning to *leave?*

All his attention was on Sasha now, and she was about to inhale her grilled cheese. Apparently, the major emotional storm over Valentino's impending change of address hadn't done her appetite any harm.

"If I don't see you again for a while," Conner told the little girl, "it's been good to have you around. You be sure to come back and see us as soon as you can."

To Tricia's surprise, Sasha suddenly sprang out of her chair, the much-anticipated sandwich temporarily forgotten, it would seem, and propelled herself across the room and into Conner's arms.

He picked her up, hugged her once and set her down again.

"Goodbye, Conner," Sasha said solemnly, sounding very grown-up.

He tugged lightly at one of her pigtails. "See you around, kid," he said.

Sasha went back to her chair and her sandwich.

Natty waggled her fingers at Conner in farewell, a little smile lurking around her mouth but not quite coming in for a landing.

Conner headed for the door and, interestingly, Valentino followed him that far. Conner leaned down to pat the dog's head once, and say something Tricia didn't hear, and then he was gone.

"You should marry him, Aunt Tricia," Sasha announced, talking with her mouth full.

Tricia didn't reprimand her, either for the breach in table manners or the outrageous statement she'd just made.

"Amen," Natty agreed. She'd finished her sandwich by then—eaten everything but the crusts, in fact—and now she waved one hand in front of her face as though she were overheated. "Phew," she said. "It's *tense* in here."

"Thanks to you," Tricia said dryly, but with a little smile, as she started water running in the sink.

"Oh, quit puttering and sit down," Natty commanded, when Tricia began washing cereal bowls left over from breakfast. By then, Sasha had finished eating and she and Valentino were in the living room, playing the kinds of games kids and dogs play when they're indoors.

Tricia sighed, rinsed the suds off her hands, and dried them on a towel. With the big rummage sale over and River's Bend not only closed for the season, but almost certainly sold, she didn't exactly have a full agenda for the day. So she sat.

"I've been thinking," Natty began, with soft portent, and she wasn't smiling now.

Instinctively alarmed, Tricia leaned forward in her chair. Waited.

Few things the old woman could have said would have caught Tricia so off guard as what came out next.

"This drafty old house is getting to be too much for me," Natty told her, her expression solemn, regarding her levelly. "And I've come to the conclusion that Winston and I might be better off in Denver, living with Doris. My sister is getting on in years, you know, and she has only those two little toothless Pomeranians for company."

Doris was indeed "getting on," though she was younger than Natty, but Tricia didn't remark on that, because she was too stunned by her great-grandmother's calm decision to skip town. For good.

Natty had lived in that house literally all her life. She'd been born in the upstairs bedroom that was now Tricia's, and, when she married Henry, the two of them had taken up residence there immediately after the honeymoon. Both Natty's mother and grandmother were still living then, and she'd looked after them until they died.

If she'd said she planned on dying in the same place she was born one time, she'd said it a *hundred* times.

Now, suddenly, she'd decided to take Winston and move to Denver?

Tricia supposed she should have been relieved—just as she should have been happy to sell the Bluebird and River's Bend. After all, with Valentino slated to be Conner's dog, and Natty safe and sound in Denver, with her beloved sister, she herself was free to leave Lonesome Bend and resume her old life in Seattle.

Instead, the whole thing gave her a sinking feeling, as though she couldn't trust her own footing, needed to reach out and grab hold of something to stay upright.

When Tricia didn't speak right away—she was too busy blinking and swallowing—Natty took her hand, gave it a gentle squeeze. "I was happy in Denver," she confided quietly. "Doris and I get along very well. We like the same books and the same television programs and, more importantly, we have the same *memories*." As Natty went on, her voice grew even quieter, and yet there was conviction in it. "No one else remembers my Henry as well as Doris does, or your grandfather, my son, Walter, or the kind of boy your dad was. When we talk about old times, Tricia, it's as though we're back there for a little while, with all our loved ones still around us."

Tricia's throat ached. She turned her hand over in Natty's and held on.

Sasha was right, she thought. Too many things were changing.

"I understand," she managed, after a hard swallow. She didn't try to hide the tears standing in her eyes. Natty wouldn't have missed them, or even have pretended she did. "It's just—I mean—I didn't see this coming, that's all."

"As you know," Natty continued, tossing one hasty glance over her shoulder to make sure Sasha was still busy in the living room with Valentino, "Doris and her Albert never had any children. She's leaving her estate to various charities. But my sister and I both agree that you ought to have the chili recipe, along with this house and my savings, such as they are."

Tricia didn't say anything. She *couldn't*.

Natty, it seemed, had no such problem. She picked up conversational speed, wanting, apparently, to get everything said as quickly as possible. "This house and the chili recipe," she confided, "are *family* holdings. That's why they're going to you."

Tricia could only nod. The thought of Natty leaving this house forever, whether for Denver or for the Great Beyond, was painful even to contemplate.

Natty patted Tricia's hand. "Now, I know you planned on going back to Seattle once you'd sold your father's businesses, and I wouldn't *think* of persuading you otherwise, but I do hope you'll keep the house until precisely the right buyers come along."

"H-how will I know?" Tricia choked out, lest Natty start worrying that she'd lost her voice forever. "That the buyers are the right ones, I mean?"

Natty smiled fondly. Looked around her, seeing memories everywhere, it seemed. Good ones. "You'll know," she promised. "You'll just know."

For a long time, the two kinswomen sat in silence, Natty's thoughtful and reflective, Tricia's stricken and forlorn.

Sasha and Valentino popped into the kitchen.

"It's snowing!" Sasha announced. "It's actually *snowing!*"

CONNER SHIVERED ONCE as the first flakes of snow drifted past the windshield of his truck. Winter was a challenge in the high country, where blizzards had been known to bury entire stretches of rangeland, along with houses and barns and whole herds of cattle. Since he'd never taken much interest in skiing or racing around on snow-mobiles, Conner hated to see cold weather coming on.

It made every aspect of ranch life just that much harder.

Generators failed. Truck and car motors wouldn't even turn over, let alone start, well pumps froze and roofs gave way. Even with county snowplows working around the clock, the roads were sometimes impassable for days at a time.

Two years back, Conner had been stuck in a dark, cold house for a full week, while a record-setting storm raged all over that part of Colorado. Fortunately, the tractor still ran, and he'd scraped out a path between the house and the barn, and managed to keep it plowed so he could feed the horses. During that ordeal, Kim and Davis had been coping at their place in pretty much the same way.

The Creeds had sacrificed some twenty head of cattle to that one storm, and they'd have lost more if the Bureau of Land Management hadn't sent up helicopters to drop bales of hay over a few hundred square miles, so the livestock and the wildlife wouldn't starve.

Even with all that, though, it wasn't the cold or the snow that worried Conner most. It was the loneliness, the shrill ache of enforced solitude so deep and so lasting that there were times when a man needed the sound of another human voice almost as desperately as he needed his next breath. It wasn't the kind of thing people talked about, of course. Not men, anyhow.

Davis and Kim had each other, and most of the folks on surrounding farms and ranches were married, with kids. The year of the big snow, Conner would have been glad even to have *Brody* around, and that was no small thing.

They'd have argued, for sure, especially shut in by a blizzard, but even butting heads would have been better than that snow-muffled silence.

The flurries increased as he drove out of Lonesome Bend proper and into the countryside. The heater was going, and so was his CD player, but Conner couldn't seem to shake the blue chill that had settled on him after he left Tricia's apartment.

He doubled up one fist and struck the steering wheel with the fleshy side, just hard enough for emphasis.

Tricia.

If only he hadn't kissed her, things might not seem so bleak and hopeless now. But he *had* kissed her and in the process, he'd stumbled and then fallen headlong, right down the proverbial rabbit hole.

And he was still falling.

It was an internal thing, of course, but Conner had no more control over it than he would have if he plunged into a mile-deep mine shaft. End over end, in slow motion, he fell and fell and fell.

When he reached the ranch road, he was irritated to find the gate standing wide open and dust billowing from under the rear tires of a double-decker semi loaded with impatient cattle. Brody's old pickup was parked in front of the barn, and he'd saddled a horse and left it to graze on snow-dappled grass, but he was nowhere in sight.

Conner stopped his own truck, got out and shut the gate, swearing under his breath and secretly glad to have something to be pissed off about, because that gave him a respite, however brief, from thinking about winter coming on and Tricia leaving Lonesome Bend forever.

When he noticed that two *other* semis had arrived ahead of the first one, Conner swore and scrambled behind the wheel again, laid rubber on that dirt driveway getting where he wanted to go.

Brody and the few cowboys who'd be wintering over on the ranch in distant house trailers were herding horses, a great many cows and several Brahma bulls through the gate opening between the corral and the open range.

"What the hell—?" Conner snarled, to nobody in particular, as he sprang out of his truck again and strode toward his brother.

Brody looked a sight, standing there in the swirling snow, covered from his hat brim to his boot soles in good Colorado dirt, and grinning like a fool.

"I told you I was serious!" he called, over the bawling of the cows, the snorting of the bulls and the whinnying of the horses.

Conner strode over to him, full of a strange and hopeful fury.

Critters streamed past, raising more dust and carrying on like the devil was chasing them with a whip. Only Brody would have unloaded broncos and bulls in the same place at the same time. The man had no patience, no apparent need to do things *right,* dammit.

In the midst of all that ruckus, Conner didn't fail to

notice that the horses, like the bulls, were big and sturdy and just plain wild. He dragged off his hat, slapped it against his right thigh in a burst of frustration, and then jammed it back onto his head.

"This is a historic moment, little brother," Brody shouted affably, above the unholy din. "You are witnessing the birth of the Creed Stock Company!"

Conner was torn between chewing the bark off the nearest tree and grabbing Brody by the shirt and slamming him against the nearest hard surface. Since there were no trees handy, he went for the latter choice.

Brody flew back against the weathered gatepost, while his hat went rolling into the path of the controlled stampede. He looked surprised at first, but when he came off that post again, he'd made the switch to pissed off.

He threw a punch at Conner, who ducked it and offered an uppercut as a response. Before it could make contact, though, two of the ranch hands stepped in to drag the brothers apart.

"Now you know that won't do either one of you any good," drawled old Clint, who'd worked for their grandfather even before Davis took over the operation. Despite his age, Clint's hold on Conner was steely, and Brody, restrained by Juan Manuelo, another long-time employee, was in the same fix.

"Just like the old days!" Juan crowed, delighted. "Eh, Clint? Remind you of Davis and Blue, when they were kids?"

"Sure does," Clint agreed, with a husky chuckle. Then, closer to Conner's ear and much more quietly, he said, "You promise me you won't go after Brody, and I'll let you go."

Conner's neck and face were hot; he was aware of the truck drivers and the other cowboys looking on, and he felt like he was sixteen again, and stupid in the bargain.

A few feet away, Juan and Brody seemed to be having the same kind of exchange.

"All right," Conner finally said, rolling his shoulders when Clint released his hold. "But if he comes at me—"

Brody neither advanced nor retreated. He looked around for his hat, spotted it lying flat in the dirt and shook his head in disgust.

The noise had abated a little, anyway, since the first two trucks had been unloaded and the third one hadn't been maneuvered into position yet.

"What the hell do you think you're doing?" Conner finally ground out.

"Easy," Clint counseled, from just behind him.

"I'm unloading *my* livestock on *my* rangeland," Brody retorted, peevish. "And that was a damn good hat. You *owe* me, little brother."

Conner shifted his weight, doubled up one fist.

"Don't even think about it," Clint said easily.

Conner wrenched off his own hat and flung it at Brody, who caught it in both hands and pulled it on so hard that it was a wonder he didn't lower his ears a notch or two.

"If you're not going to lend a hand," Brody growled, "then get out of the way, Conner. I've got *work* to do!"

"Have at it," Conner said generously, grinning because he knew that would get under Brody's hide, and quick.

It did just that. If Juan hadn't been so fast on his feet, and gotten Brody by the bends in his elbows before he could take a second step, the fight would have been on. And this time, there would have been no breaking it up.

After that, Brody got on with it, while Conner watched from alongside the fence as that crazy mix of bulls and broncos and thick-legged cows spread out over the range in all directions. He gave an affable nod as Brody passed by, on horseback now, to do some herding.

Clint and Juan got on their horses, too, and rode out, and for a while the whole thing was like a scene out of a modern-day *Lonesome Dove*. The truckers unloaded the third rig—just cattle in that one—and once the last cow was through the gate, Conner secured the gatepost with the customary barbed-wire loops.

Rodeo stock.

Trust Brody to come up with a fool idea like raising bad broncos and even badder bulls, on the same range with beef cattle.

Conner splayed the fingers of one hand and shoved them through his hair, now damp with snowflakes and matted with dirt, and pointed himself toward the barn, where the usual chores awaited.

If Brody thought for a New York nanosecond that he was going to stick his "little brother" with the responsibility for any or all of that extra livestock when the urge to roam came over him again, as it inevitably would, he was sadly mistaken.

Conner walked around the three semis, feeling the cold bite into the back of his neck, and he was clear inside, out of the weather, before he realized that he was grinning fit to split his face in half.

CHAPTER THIRTEEN

"I'VE MADE LISTS for the movers," Natty said, bright and early on Tuesday morning, standing in the middle of her coffee-scented kitchen and holding up a clipboard. The sky was blue and the ground was bare of snow, but there was a wintry nip in the air, too, one that made Tricia shiver in her jeans and wooly sweater.

Once Natty had announced her intention to move herself and Winston in with Doris and the Pomeranians in Denver, things started happening at a breakneck pace, it seemed to Tricia.

Except for a few personal belongings—clothing, books, photographs and special pieces of jewelry, mostly—Natty wasn't taking much along with her. Tricia was to have her pick of the furniture, dishes, quilts and a myriad of other items, and the rest would be boxed up by moving men and hauled to a storage unit, there to await donation to next year's rummage sale/chili feed.

Sasha was scheduled to fly home to Seattle the next day, and Tricia was going with her. For no reason she could pinpoint, she hadn't called, texted or emailed Hunter. She'd gone so far as to change her screen saver for a shot of herself and Rusty, posing in front of a long-ago Christmas tree, both of them smiling amid stacks of wrapped packages.

Seeing Rusty's image flash onto her computer monitor still threw her a little, especially when she was thinking of the million and one things on her to-do list, but underneath was a sense of healing. The grief was beginning to subside at last, leaving a sweet, quiet joy behind.

Now, confronted with Natty's clipboard, not to mention the outfit, a tiny red running suit with white racing stripes down the pant legs, topping off a matching pair of high-top sneakers, Tricia wedged her hands into the pockets of her hooded sweatshirt and grumbled, "Okay."

"You'll have to keep an eye on them," Natty warned, shaking an index finger at Tricia. "The moving men, I mean. Make sure they put things in the right boxes and label everything properly—"

"I'll see that they do the job right," Tricia promised glumly.

"I'm counting on that. When Esme Smithers went into assisted living, her children hired movers, and her entire teapot collection went missing—she swore she saw her grandmother's Wedgwood on eBay!"

Tricia sighed, bent distractedly to pat Valentino's head. He seemed to sense change coming on, and he stayed close to her when he wasn't following Sasha around.

"You don't think you're, maybe, *rushing into things,* just a little?" Tricia asked diplomatically.

Natty drew on her apparently inexhaustible supply of timeworn clichés for a reply. "Make hay while the sun shines, that's what I always say," she chirped, pursing her lips as she studied the papers on her clipboard. "Last week, I felt terrible. *This* week, I'm just *full* of energy. Heaven only knows why that is, but I'm taking advantage of a good thing while it lasts."

"Right," Tricia said. There was no use in urging Natty to take it easy. If she wasn't bedridden, she was bustling from project to project.

Natty looked up from the clipboard and narrowed her twinkly blue eyes. "Are you coming down with something, dear?" she asked. "You aren't your old self."

No, I'm not *my old self,* Tricia thought crankily. *And I'm not at all sure who the* new *self is, either.*

"I'm just tired, I guess," she said, in belated response to Natty's question.

"Where's Sasha?" Natty asked, checking off an item on her list.

"She's upstairs, in my kitchen, sitting in front of the computer and exchanging instant messages with her dad," Tricia answered, crossing to the table and plunking down in a chair.

"There's coffee," Natty said. "Or would you rather have a nice cup of tea?"

"Nothing for me, thanks," Tricia replied, as Valentino, still at her side, laid his muzzle on her knee and gave a shuddery canine sigh.

Natty took a chair opposite Tricia's, setting the clipboard aside with a matter-of-fact motion of one hand. "I never thought I'd say this," the older woman began, "but I think a trip to Seattle might be just what you need right now. You could use a change of scene, a fresh perspective."

Tricia stroked Valentino's head. He liked Conner, and she suspected he would adapt to the change of households quickly, but she dreaded saying goodbye to the dog. It made her throat tighten painfully every time she considered the prospect.

"You may be right," she agreed halfheartedly. She *was* looking forward to spending time with Diana and Paul, though of course they'd be busy making preparations for their upcoming move, and she planned on checking out some potential gallery spaces and condominiums, too. She wanted to do some shopping as well—her wardrobe had dwindled to jeans and casual tops since she'd moved to Lonesome Bend. She hoped to reconnect with some of her friends and possibly hit a favorite restaurant or two.

"Tell me what's the matter, then," Natty insisted quietly. "You're *moping,* Tricia. Does this mood of yours have something to do with that—that man you were seeing, before you left Seattle?"

Tricia frowned. "Hunter?"

"Yes," Natty said. Her tone wasn't exactly disdainful, but it was crisp. "That's it—*Hunter.*"

Tricia nodded. "Have you ever been very, very sure of something," she began, "or of *somebody,* only to find out, when push came to shove, that you're not sure after all?"

Natty giggled, and that broke the tension. "No," she said, "I haven't. I was sure of my Henry from the day I first set eyes on him to the day we laid him to rest, God keep his fine and honorable soul. But we're not discussing me, are we, dear? We're talking about *you* and—Trooper."

"Hunter," Tricia corrected wryly.

"Whoever," Natty retorted, with a wave of one hand.

Tricia couldn't help smiling a little, sad sack that she was these days. "Stop it," she said. "You know perfectly well what Hunter's name is. There's nothing wrong with your hearing or your memory."

"All right," Natty conceded sweetly, with another wave of her hand. The huge diamonds in her wedding and engagement rings caught a flash of sunlight through the window. "Hunter, then. I take it he's the 'thing' you were 'very, very sure' about and now—not so much?"

"Not so much," Tricia confessed, with regret. While she wasn't sure how she felt about Hunter, she knew now that she *should* be sure, or at least have some idea. The only certainty here, as far as she could say, was *un*-certainty, but she had figured out this much: she wasn't going on a romantic cruise with one man when she'd so enjoyed being kissed by another. Even if that kiss was bound to lead nowhere.

Deep down, she knew she had to make a clean break with Hunter—and soon. "I think," she went on softly, and at some length, "that I've been in love with love all this time. I didn't want to let go of the *concept,* even though the reality might never have existed at all."

Natty smiled and got out of her chair, very spry for a woman getting ready to downsize practically every area of her life. "I'm making that tea," she said firmly, "and don't try to talk me out of it."

Tricia chuckled, feeling better. Valentino stretched out at her feet, let out a sigh and went to sleep. "I know better than to try to talk Natty McCall out of *anything,* once she's made up her mind. Or *into* anything, either, for that matter."

Natty busied herself with the process of brewing tea from scratch, something she could probably have done in a catatonic state, she'd had so much practice over the years. While the loose-leaf orange pekoe steeped in a china pot, Natty got out cups and saucers to match, and brought them to the table.

Once the teapot had been transported, too, Natty sat down with a happy sigh. "Now," she said. "Where were we? Oh, yes. You were telling me that you only *thought* you were in love with this Hunter person, but now you realize that you're meant to spend your life with Conner Creed instead."

Color flared in Tricia's cheeks. "I don't realize anything of the sort," she replied, not unkindly, but in a rather terse tone that she instantly regretted. She drew a deep breath and let it out very slowly. "I'm willing to admit that I'm attracted to Conner," she said, changing her approach. The kiss replayed itself in her mind yet again—it was on a loop, evidently—and the reverberations spread into every cell of her body, causing her to blush even harder.

She held up a palm when Natty's eyes began to dance with joyful mischief. "I said I was *attracted* to the man, not madly in love with him. And, anyway, we're moving in different directions—Conner and I. He'll get old and die on that ranch of his, content to live out his days within a stone's throw of his hometown. I, on the other hand, want a city bustling around me, 24/7. I want sidewalks and bright lights and malls and bookstores and *people*. I want to go to operas and symphonies and get season tickets to the theater—"

"Denver has all those things, and it's only an hour's drive from here, when the roads are clear," Natty was quick to point out. "And while I certainly wouldn't describe you as antisocial or anything, you aren't at all fond of crowds. They wear you down, remember? Sap your energy. I know you're young, and you've probably felt pretty isolated here in Lonesome Bend over the last couple of years, but—"

Tricia raised an eyebrow. Poured tea for her great-grandmother and then for herself. "But?" she prompted.

"It wouldn't be wise to do anything drastic," Natty said, her brow knitted with concern. "For heaven's sake, Tricia, give yourself a chance to *think* before you go rushing off to things you've *already left behind*."

"You're a fine one to talk," Tricia pointed out, thinking that she'd never loved her spunky great-grandmother more than she did right at that moment. She huffed out a breath. "You were *born* in this house, Natty. You were married here, you raised your son and your grandson here. Now, all of a sudden, you're moving to Denver— and that isn't *drastic?*"

"It's not sudden," Natty said, though she didn't deny the "drastic" part, Tricia noticed. "Doris and I have been talking about sharing her house for years. It's smaller and more modern—much more manageable, for two old women especially—than this one. For a long time, I couldn't face the idea of living anywhere but here. Now, well, there's just too much to worry about— plumbing that might freeze, heating bills that are higher with every passing year and then, when spring comes around, there's the yard, and the flowerbeds—" Natty stopped, and her beautiful blue eyes filled with tears. "I'm *tired,* Tricia—tired of being weighed down by *things,* and commitments and responsibilities."

Tricia nodded, took a sip of tea. It gave her an almost instant lift, and she wondered, very briefly, if the sweet old lady sitting across from her in a red running suit might have laced it with some kind of fast-acting antidepressant.

"I just want you to be happy, Natty. That's all."

"I want the same thing for you, dear," Natty pointed out. Her gaze dropped to Valentino, sleeping peacefully on the floor. "What's the plan for the dog?" she added, in a whisper.

Before Tricia could reply that Conner would stop by the house and pick Valentino up in the morning, after she and Sasha left for the airport, Sasha strolled into the kitchen, all smiles.

"Dad had to go offline," she told Natty and Tricia. "He and Mom are checking out of the hotel in a little while, then they're going to have dinner, and *then*—" Her eyes sparkled with excitement and anticipation. "And *then* it will be time for them to leave for the airport so they can board their flight back to Seattle—where you and I will be waiting!"

Tricia smiled at Sasha's happiness—it was catching—and slipped an arm around the child's waist, holding her close.

But Sasha pulled free, and reached into the deep pocket of her pink sweater to bring out Tricia's cell phone. "You left this on the counter upstairs," she said. "And it rang a couple of times."

Tricia thanked her, took the phone from her hand and checked for messages.

Carla, her real-estate agent, had called twice, clicking off the first time but leaving a message the second. "Tricia? I'm assuming you're at home, even though you didn't answer your phone, and I'm on the way over there in a few minutes. I know who the competing buyers are, and you are never going to believe it—I have to see your face when I tell you."

Tricia didn't bother to call Carla back; it was already

too late. She saw the woman's big car bounce past Natty's kitchen window as she sped up the driveway.

"Land sakes," Natty said, alarmed. "If you could see your expression. What on *earth* is going on?"

Tricia didn't answer; she just went to the back door and opened it.

Valentino roused himself to give a couple of lackluster barks before settling down again.

Carla, a small woman with a short pixie haircut and big sunglasses, was just getting out of her car. Her teetery high heels sank into the soft ground, and she carried a smart leather portfolio under one arm. "I have the papers and a check for the earnest money right here!" she sang out, beaming.

Although strangely nonplussed herself, Tricia certainly understood Carla's delight in making a deal. Besides the reclusive movie stars and upper-echelon executives who occasionally bought or sold ridiculously large houses hidden away in copses of aspen trees, at the ends of long, long driveways, she didn't have all that many clients. In Lonesome Bend, properties tended to be passed down from one generation to the next, without ever sporting a single For Sale sign.

To Tricia, and most of the other people in town, those VIP mansions were hardly more real than the village of Brigadoon. The owners evidently came and went under cover of darkness; no one ever saw them walking along the streets of Lonesome Bend, like the locals, and they certainly didn't socialize.

"Aren't you going to ask about the buyers?" Carla trilled, coming up the steps of the back porch.

Tricia stepped back to let her in, nearly tripping over Sasha as she did so.

She didn't get a chance to say anything, though, because Carla entered talking.

"Both Brody and Conner Creed put in bids," she said, nodding to Natty and eyeing Valentino with a degree of trepidation. Given that he was sleeping, the trepidation was brief. "Conner withdrew his offer this morning, but Brody is prepared to close the deal at any time. *And* he's willing to pay your asking price, if you recall."

Tricia just stood there, not knowing *what* to think.

Conner had wanted to buy the campground, the RV park and the Bluebird Drive-in? Why?

Carla laughed merrily at Tricia's look of consternation. "Who would have thought Brody Creed would ever show his face in Lonesome Bend again after—" She looked at Natty, then at Sasha. "After what happened," she finished.

"What happened?" Sasha asked.

"Never you mind," said Natty, watching Carla but speaking to the child. Then, for Carla's benefit, she added, "Besides, all of that was a long time ago, wasn't it?"

Carla gave another of her tinkly, music-box giggles, but it sounded tinny this time around. "Yes," she said. "What's done is done. Water under the bridge, and all that."

"Precisely," Natty said. Then she turned a warm smile on Sasha. "Dear, would you mind carrying in some of that nice firewood Conner brought by while I was in Denver? I think a cozy blaze would be just the thing, on a cold day like this."

Sasha hesitated, clearly aware that she was getting the bum's rush so the adults could talk freely, but in the end she was too well-mannered to object. She gave an

eloquent sigh and pounded upstairs to get her jacket.
Carrying wood in from the shed out back would be
chilly, splintery work.

"All you have to do is sign on the dotted line, accepting Brody's very generous terms, and we can get this
thing rolling," Carla said, slapping her portfolio down
on Natty's tablecloth and slipping out of her stylish coat.

"Why were they so secretive in the beginning?" Tricia
asked, barely scratching the surface of what she wanted
to know. "Brody and Conner, I mean. You said the offers came through corporate attorneys."

"They did," Carla said, taking a chair and briskly unzipping the portfolio, taking out a sheaf of documents.
Again, Tricia had that disturbing sense of everything
speeding up, reeling out of control, like some carnival
ride gone berserk. "But each of them was trying to keep
the other out of the loop—they weren't out to deceive
us in any way."

"But—"

Sasha reappeared, wearing her coat, and headed outside to get the requested firewood, closing the door
hard behind her.

Both Natty and Tricia smiled.

Carla merely started slightly and shook her head.
Her expression said, *Kids.*

"Did Brody happen to say why he wants River's
Bend and the drive-in?" Natty asked mildly.

Carla smiled an oh-happy-day kind of smile, tapping the already tidy stack of papers against the table.
"Does it matter?"

Tricia thought about her dad, cutting the grass out
at the drive-in for years after it closed, picking up litter

over at the campground, teaching her to fish at the edge of the river. "Yes," she said, very quietly. "It matters."

Carla reddened slightly. Hesitated.

From the woman's expression, a person would have thought Brody Creed intended to turn River's Bend into a dumping ground for toxic waste.

Carla held out the pen.

Tricia ignored it.

Outside, chunks of firewood could be heard striking the back porch.

Carla sighed. "Brody wants to make the properties part of the Creed ranch," she said, her eyes darting between Natty and Tricia. "That's all."

Tricia kind of liked that idea. She'd always known, of course, that the old movie screen would have to come down; it was an eyesore. It was nice to imagine cattle and horses grazing there, meandering down to the riverside to drink.

"Why did Conner try to buy it?" Natty asked.

"You know how those two are," Carla said, with another anxious little smile. "They—compete. It goes all the way back to—well—that scuffle over Joleen."

"Ancient history," Natty said.

"I guess so," Carla agreed, uncertainly.

"Joleen used to come here for piano lessons," Natty recalled fondly. "Every Tuesday, after school. She was a spirited girl, there was no denying that, and she enjoyed playing games, too, always pushing the envelope when it came to flirting and boys. But she wasn't cut out to marry Conner Creed, or live in Lonesome Bend for the rest of her life, and everybody knew it."

Everybody except, maybe, Conner, Tricia thought, with rising despair. Had Conner wanted to buy her land because he knew she meant to leave town as soon as the ink was dry on the contracts?

"And we're talking about seven figures, here," Carla reminded everyone.

Tricia sighed. *Ah, yes. The money.* Until she'd learned what Brody's plans were, she'd been secretly afraid a housing development might be going in where the campground and the drive-in were now or, God forbid, one of those sprawling big box stores.

"Right," she said, knowing how pleased Joe would be that his long-range plans for his daughter's financial well-being had paid off so handsomely. For him as much as for herself, Tricia picked up the stack of documents and read every word on every page.

Sasha came through the back door, her little arms full of wood. "Can I come in now?" she asked. Her lower lip was protruding slightly, and her gaze was fiery. She didn't like being sidelined. "It's *cold* out there, you know."

"Yes," Natty said, with a tiny smile. "You may."

Tricia read on. Everything seemed to be in order as far as Brody's offer was concerned; he wasn't asking for any improvements or upgrades and he was prepared to close at any time. Satisfied, Tricia signed beside each of the little stick-on arrows Carla had put in place ahead of time.

Carla all but snatched up the documents, as if she thought Tricia might change her mind and cancel the deal. Only after the woman had tucked the papers into her portfolio and zipped the zipper did she speak. "Well, then, that's done," she said, clearly relieved. Rising, she stuck out a hand to Tricia. "Congratulations."

"Thank you," Tricia murmured. Because her head

was spinning a little—even considering taxes, the last of Joe's debts and Carla's commission, she was a wealthy woman—she didn't get out of her chair.

"I'll just be on my way. I'll call you with a choice of dates for the closing," Carla said. Putting her coat back on proved an awkward enterprise, since she was evidently unwilling to lay the portfolio down and free both hands at once.

"I'll be out of town for a little over a week," Tricia recalled. "Starting tomorrow. But you can reach me on my cell phone."

Carla smiled. "Eventually, yes," she said.

And, moments later, she was gone, back in her big real-estate agent's car, driving away.

Tricia frowned.

"You don't seem very happy," Natty ventured, watching her.

"I'm *happy*," Tricia lied.

One stubborn woman recognizing another, Natty didn't press the point.

CONNER WAITED UNTIL he was sure Tricia and the little girl had left for Denver the next morning, before stopping by to get Valentino.

Natty, busy lording it over a crew of moving men, paused long enough to smile sadly and say, "We are going to miss that dog."

"I'll take good care of him, Natty," Conner answered. Sure, he'd been meaning to get a dog for a while, but he was doing somebody a *favor* here, wasn't he? So why did he feel guilty, like he was kidnapping the critter or something?

"I know," Natty said softly, patting his arm distractedly. "I really thought Tricia would want to keep more of this stuff," she confided. "Turns out she only wanted family photos and some of the china. She's not much for *things*, though."

Word was all over town about Natty's move to Denver, so Conner wasn't surprised to find her sorting her belongings. Still, she *was* shedding a lot of memories, it seemed to him, right along with the figurines and the needlepoint pillows and the like. And she wasn't wasting much time doing it.

"What's the big hurry, Natty?" Conner asked, without planning on saying anything of the sort.

"Once I make a decision," Natty replied, "I like to move on it. There's nothing to be gained, in my opinion, by dillydallying." She paused. "Don't you agree?"

"I don't reckon it's my place to agree or disagree," Conner hedged. The dog, soon to be rechristened Bill, leaned heavily against his leg.

Natty sighed and put her hands on her hips. She looked a little quaint, standing there in a flashy gold lamé running suit and sequined shoes. *Bring on those big-city lights,* her getup seemed to say. *And let's party!*

She also looked annoyed. "I declare, Conner Creed," she said, causing him to rock back slightly on his boot heels, "for an intelligent man, you can be remarkably obtuse!"

He blinked and, knowing all the while that he'd live to regret it, asked, "What are you talking about?"

Natty looked back over one shoulder, probably making sure the moving men were doing what she'd hired them to do, but her blue eyes had a chill in them when they landed on Conner again.

The dog sighed and sat down.

"I'm talking about Tricia," Natty said, in a stage whisper. "And if you weren't such a lunkhead, you'd have known that without asking!"

Conner felt that sinking sensation again. It was as though the floor had suddenly turned to foam rubber. "What *about* Tricia?"

"You know darned well *what about Tricia,*" Natty lectured. "Are you really, *truly* going to stand by and do nothing while she makes the biggest mistake of her life?"

They were standing in the entryway.

The moving men were listening in.

So Conner took Natty lightly by the elbow and escorted her into the small parlor, where there were still plenty of chairs.

Valentino slogged resolutely along, apparently resigned to go with the flow. There was something sad about that, to Conner's mind—as if the dog knew he was being ditched and had decided not to fight it.

"Sit," he told the animal.

"I beg your pardon?" Natty demanded, feathers ruffling right up.

Conner chuckled. "I was talking to Bill, here," he said.

Natty frowned. "Bill?"

"The canine formerly known as Valentino," Conner explained.

Natty sank into a prissy little chair. Now, there were tears in her eyes.

Conner's heart skittered up into his throat, because he hated it when women cried. He never knew what to do, or say.

"It's all so sad," Natty said, after a short silence.

Conner dropped to one knee, ruffled the dog's ears to let him know he'd be okay, but he kept his gaze fastened on Natty McCall, an institution in Lonesome Bend. "What's sad, Natty?" he asked, very quietly. "Leaving this house? If you don't want to go, just say so, and I'll have those guys packing up your stuff out of here in no time—"

Natty interrupted him with a shake of her head. She dabbed at her eyes with a lace-trimmed hanky plucked from the pocket of her sparkly jacket. "It's time for me to go," she said.

Something in her tone gave Conner a chill. "I hope you didn't mean that the way it sounded," he said carefully.

"To *Denver*," she clarified, with a moist giggle. "Conner, I'm an old woman, but I'm not so far gone that I don't know passion when I see it, that I don't know *love*."

"Whoa," Conner said gravely. "Passion? Love? You've lost me again."

Natty shook her head, set her very small jaw. "Men," she scoffed, her tone mild but her eyes fiery. "Are you just going to let Tricia move back to Seattle without even giving the two of you a *chance?*"

Tricia's plans to leave were never too far from his mind, but the facts had a way of pouncing on him when he wasn't paying attention. He got to his feet, after murmuring a few soothing words to the dog.

"I can't make Tricia stay in Lonesome Bend, Natty," he said quietly. "She's a grown woman, with her own plans." He paused, cleared his throat, remembering the ski-guy in the screen-saver picture. "Anyway, there's somebody else in her life. Somebody she wants to get back to."

Natty waved a hand at him. "Nonsense," she said. "Tricia is attracted to *you,* Conner. She told me so, just yesterday. In fact, she went so far as to confide that she's been fooling herself about having a future with Hunter."

Conner didn't know what to say to that. Tricia had responded to his kiss, he knew that, and every time they were in the same room, the air crackled. So they were attracted to each other? That was a far cry from being in love, and if all Conner had wanted from a woman was good sex, well, hell, there had never been any shortage of that.

The problem was that Conner wanted a lot more than a bedmate. He wanted a full partner, a confidante, somebody he could trust with all those dusty old dreams of his. He wanted kids and dogs running every which way. He wanted a *family.*

And he wasn't willing to settle for less, even if it meant being alone for the rest of his life.

"Bill and I had better get going," he finally said, his voice gravelly. "We're burning daylight."

With that, he crossed to Natty's chair, bent and kissed her lightly on the forehead.

"Goodbye, Natty," he said. "If you need anything, anything at all, you just let me know."

She put a small hand on his coat sleeve, held on for a moment then let go.

His last image of Natty McCall was of her sitting there in that slipper chair, dressed up like Elvis, her eyes that much bluer for the sorrow they held.

CHAPTER FOURTEEN

TRICIA HAD BEEN in Seattle for three full days when Diana finally shamed her into contacting Hunter.

"If you won't call or email the man," Diana said, one morning when the two of them were sitting in her sunny kitchen, chatting and drinking coffee, "then go and see him in person. You can't go on like this, Tricia."

Tricia sighed. "Like what?" she stalled. Since her and Sasha's plane had landed on Wednesday afternoon—they'd waited only an hour for a jet-lagged Diana and Paul to arrive via Air France—it seemed as though every minute of her time had been occupied.

While catching up, she and Diana had shopped for groceries, picked up dry cleaning, cooked together and pored over about a million digital photos of the new house in Paris.

After much discussion, the couple had decided to put most of their things in storage and lease out their lovely suburban home in Seattle, rather than sell it. That meant sorting stuff, stuff and more stuff.

"You seem—confused," Diana said, after thinking about Tricia's response for a few moments. "Or *down,* or something. For nearly two years, all you've talked about was Hunter this, and Hunter that, and I'll bet you haven't said three words about the man since you got here. That spells *A-V-O-I-D-A-N-C-E,* my friend.

On top of that, you're about to be debt-free and rolling in money, but you haven't looked at a single storefront for that gallery you've wanted to open for as long as I've known you, or even checked out a condo, for that matter."

"We *have* been a little busy," Tricia pointed out.

"Tell me I'm right," Diana said, undaunted. "You've seen the error of your ways. You're about to dump the biggest loser. That's why you've been so preoccupied, isn't it? That and the cowboy Sasha can't stop talking about?"

Tricia sighed, raised and lowered her shoulders in a slow semblance of a shrug. "It's just that so many things have happened lately," she said, hoping Diana wouldn't press the Conner issue.

Fat chance.

"Sasha says she saw him kiss you," Diana said. "The cowboy, I mean."

"His name is Conner," Tricia said. "And the kiss was just—a kiss. An impulse. We lost our heads."

"Sure you did," Diana said, with a saucy little smile.

Tricia blushed. "Okay, so maybe I enjoyed the kiss, all right?"

Diana laughed. "Nothing wrong with that."

"There *is* something wrong with it," Tricia argued, after looking around to make sure Sasha wasn't within earshot, "if you're technically involved with *someone else*."

"'Involved'? You and Hunter? Give me a break. When was the last time you even saw the man, let alone had sex with him?"

"Shhh!" Tricia scolded, color stinging her cheeks. "What if Sasha had heard that?"

"Sasha," Diana replied, "is in the garage helping her dad decide which set of golf clubs he wants to take to Paris." She leaned forward slightly, her green eyes twinkling as she studied Tricia. "What about Conner? Come on, 'fess up—have you been to bed with him?"

"Of course not," Tricia said.

"Pity," Diana said. "You want to, though, don't you?"

"Diana."

"Don't you?"

Tricia groaned. "Okay," she admitted grudgingly. "Yes. Maybe."

"'Yes, maybe'? Now there's a definitive answer. Either you want to hit the hay with this Conner dude, or you don't."

Tricia looked away.

"You do!" Diana exulted.

Tricia forced herself to meet her friend's gaze. "All right, I do," she said. "Maybe."

"Maybe nothing," Diana said. "You want him. And from the way Sasha described that kiss, he definitely wants you. So what's the holdup?"

"What's the holdup?" Tricia echoed, frustrated and embarrassed. She felt as shy as she ever had as an adolescent. Any minute now, her teeth would sprout braces and her skin would break out. "I told you. I have to clear things up with Hunter first. And even if I—even if I *do* end up—" she lowered her voice to a near whisper "—going to bed with Conner Creed, it might not change anything."

"Oh, it'll change something, all right," Diana teased. Then she stood up, walked over to the desk in the corner, and came back with her purse. She rummaged through it and laid a set of keys on the table in front of

Tricia. "As a general rule, I like to keep certain observations to myself, but this time, I'm making an exception. You're acting just like your mother, Tricia."

A pang of recognition struck Tricia in that moment, so she went into immediate denial. "Oh, right. My mother is at an emotional remove from everything, including herself. She's afraid to care about anything other than a natural disaster of some kind."

Diana simply sat back in her chair, folded her arms and said, "Isn't that why you stuck it out with Hunter all this time? Because you could keep your distance and still enjoy the fantasy that you were in a real relationship?"

Tricia blinked. "No," she replied, but it took a beat too long. "For heaven's sake, Diana, you make me sound like one of those women who marries a guy serving life in prison—"

Diana arched an eyebrow, gave her head a slight shake. "I wouldn't go that far," she said. "But you're scared of really *connecting* with a man—especially a man who, unlike Hunter, won't settle for anything less. My guess is, the cowboy terrifies you."

"That's preposterous," Tricia sputtered. But gears were turning in her mind. *Was* she like her mother? Was she incapable of opening her heart and her life to another person?

Diana smiled. Pushed the car keys closer. "Here. Take my car and drive yourself to Hunter's studio and tell that egomaniac what he can do with his romantic cruise to Mexico, not to mention all those promises. That will be a start, anyway."

Tricia swallowed hard. It didn't seem like a start to

her, but the end of a safe and comfortable and, okay, *boring* time in her life.

In the next instant, another possibility occurred to her. "Is there something you should have told me?" Tricia asked, very quietly. But she did reach for the car keys. "Diana, what do you know about Hunter that I don't?"

"I'm your best friend," Diana said, with equal amounts of frustration and affection. "If I had any kind of goods on the guy, I'd have told you in a heartbeat. It's just a feeling I have, that's all—that he's not good enough for you. He's sort of—shifty."

"Shifty." Tricia sighed. "I'll be back," she said.

A few minutes later, she was driving toward downtown Seattle in her friend's sporty blue BMW, keeping the comparison Diana had drawn between Tricia and her mother at bay by rehearsing what she'd say when she got to Hunter's studio.

I'm sorry I didn't call first. I know it's rude to just show up like this.

Trouble was, she didn't feel like apologizing. After all, she hadn't done anything wrong.

There's this guy in Lonesome Bend... I barely know him, you understand, but I'd like—love—*to explore the possibilities.*

No, that wouldn't do, either. What might or might not happen between her and Conner was flat-out none of Hunter's business, once they'd agreed to see other people.

Let's face it, Hunter. We haven't been a couple in a long time.

"Excellent," Tricia said, out loud and with scorn.

She took a wrong turn at the next light and, since

downtown Seattle was composed of one-way streets, she had to drive even farther out of her way just to backtrack. By the time she pulled into the parking lot in Pioneer Square, she was no closer to deciding what to say to Hunter than she had been when she'd left Diana and Paul's place.

And it was only then that she realized she hadn't even checked her lipstick, let alone done anything with her hair.

She was decently dressed, though, since she and Diana were planning a trip to the mall later that day. She'd replaced her usual Lonesome Bend garb of jeans and tops—T-shirts in spring and summer, sweatshirts in fall and winter—with a pair of black jeans and a simple white top.

Breaking up, she decided, marching herself toward the brick building where Hunter lived and painted in an elegantly rustic loft, shouldn't be all *that* hard to do.

The converted warehouse boasted a doorman, as well as a stunning view of Elliott Bay and the Olympic Mountains, and Tony recognized her right away.

His eyes rounded. "Haven't seen you in a while," he said awkwardly. "How have you been, Ms. McCall?"

"I've been fine, Tony," Tricia said, stepping into the elevator. "I'll see myself in, thanks."

Tony blinked and, as the door slipped closed, Tricia would have sworn she'd seen him lunge for the intercom.

Sure enough, when the elevator reached the top floor, Hunter was standing right there, waiting for her.

He was good-looking, she thought offhandedly, in a game-show-host kind of way. All teeth and hair.

"Tricia!" he said. "I wasn't expecting—"

"I'm sorry," Tricia said, forgetting her firm decision not to apologize. "I should have called."

Hunter sighed, shoved a hand through his hair. He didn't seem to know what to do or say and, once or twice, he glanced back at the half-open door leading into his loft. "Well," he finally stammered out, "I guess there's no harm done."

"Good," Tricia said. Puzzle pieces were falling into place.

What an idiot she'd been, she was thinking. What a naïve, romantic *idiot.* Hunter wasn't alone, and he probably *hadn't* been, from the day she left for Colorado, intending to settle her dad's estate and return right away.

She smiled. If she'd cared about Hunter, she might have said something catty, like, "Aren't you going to ask me in?"

If she'd cared, she'd have been hurt and angry, because she knew in every fiber of her being that there was a woman inside, probably listening at the door. Maybe dressed and maybe not.

Instead, she felt a tremendous sense of relief. And she *laughed.* "It's okay, Hunter," she said. "I just came by to tell you I won't be coming along on that cruise, but thanks anyway."

Hunter's eyes narrowed, and his mouth dropped open for a moment, before he regained control. Enormously successful in just about every area of his life, he wasn't used to rejection.

A face appeared in the opening between the door and the frame. Hunter's guest was pretty, with spiky blonde hair, and way too young for him.

"What cruise?" Lolita asked, pouting.

"Oops," Tricia said, amused.

Hunter reddened. "Monica has been doing some modeling for me," he said.

Along with a few other things, Tricia thought.

"Monica," Hunter snapped, "go back inside."

"I want to know about this cruise," Monica said.

"It's all a big mistake," Tricia told the young woman cheerfully. "I must be in the wrong building."

"Oh," Monica replied, still confused but willing to be mollified. With that, she retreated, and closed the door to Hunter's loft.

"It's just that you were gone so long," Hunter said, miserably. Then he brightened. "But now that you're back—"

Tricia smiled and shook her head. "I'm not back, Hunter," she told him. "Not the way you mean, anyway."

"If you'll just give me a chance—the cruise—"

"No cruise," Tricia said, turning to push the down button that would summon the elevator again. "Goodbye, Hunter. Have an excellent life."

She truly meant those words.

It was over.

She was *free.*

"Wait," Hunter protested. "What about all our plans? What about the gallery we were going to open together? What about—?"

The elevator doors swished open. It hadn't gone anywhere.

Tricia stepped inside. Waggled her fingers at Hunter in farewell and mouthed the word *Over.*

And that was it.

Tony, the doorman, was waiting anxiously when she emerged into the lobby seconds later. He was probably used to women coming and going, used to scenes.

Tricia's smile obviously took him aback.

He opened his mouth, closed it again, then scrambled to hold the lobby door for her. "You're all right?" he asked meekly.

"Oh, I'm better than all right," Tricia answered. *And I am not emotionally distant, like my mother. Much.*

THE DOG RAN away twice before he figured out that he didn't live in town anymore.

Both times, he went straight to Tricia's place, and both times Conner found him sitting on the landing outside her door, waiting in vain to be admitted.

The sight choked Conner up a little, and not just because the critter looked so pitiful. He knew how that dog felt, because he missed Tricia, too. Missed her more than he'd ever thought it was possible to miss a woman, especially when he'd never done anything more than kiss her.

"Tell you what," Conner said gruffly, after hauling the dog bodily down the stairs and setting him in the passenger seat of his truck. "We'll go back to calling you Valentino. No more Bill. How would that be?"

Valentino licked Conner's cheek and settled himself for the ride back out to the ranch, looking straight out through the windshield.

It started to rain right after that, and Conner succumbed to the low mood that had been trying to drag him under ever since Tricia left for Seattle. At home, he did the usual chores, keeping one eye on Valentino while he worked. The dog sat in the open doorway of the barn, his furry back turned to Conner, cutting a forlorn figure against a backdrop of gray drizzle.

Later, Conner built a fire in the stove in the kitchen and grilled up a good-size T-bone steak for supper.

He and Valentino shared the meat and a couple of cans of beer.

When Brody wandered in out of the storm, around eight that night, Conner was damn near glad to see him.

"Guess I've thrown in with a somber outfit," Brody drawled, shrugging out of his wet coat and hanging it up, along with his hat. "I don't know which of you looks more down in the mouth, little brother—you or the dog."

"His name is Valentino," Conner said, resting his booted feet on the chrome ledge around the stove. He'd changed and showered after he was through with the chores, but he couldn't seem to get warm.

Brody chuckled. "Valentino? I thought it was Bill or something like that."

"Bill didn't work for him," Conner admitted. "So it's back to Valentino."

"Oh," Brody said, moving to the refrigerator. He sighed, once he'd seen the contents. "I thought I smelled steak."

"You did," Conner said. "We ate it."

Brody hadn't closed on the property he'd bought from Tricia yet, and Carolyn was still staying up at Kim and Davis's place, so the brothers had been sharing the main house. Giving each other lots of room and speaking only when it couldn't be avoided.

"Kim called today," Brody said, taking a carton of eggs from the fridge and moving on to the electric stove. "They're coming back early—her and Davis, I mean—and there'll be a crowd for Thanksgiving. Boston and his pretty wife and the kids will be here."

Boston was and always had been Brody's name for Steven.

"That's good," Conner said. Brody was in an unusually chatty mood, it seemed to him. Maybe he'd shut up, if Conner kept his responses to a word or two.

A cast-iron skillet clanged onto a burner, and Brody started cracking eggs.

"You hungry?" he asked.

"No," Conner answered.

Right about then, thunder tore open the sky, and hard rain lashed against the sturdy walls of the house, pattered on the windows.

Valentino scooted closer to Conner's chair, and Conner reached out to stroke the dog's head.

"Weather like this chills a man to the core," Brody remarked, with an audible shudder. "There ain't much I wouldn't give for a nice, warm woman right about now."

The statement rankled, though Conner couldn't have said why. Not without giving it some thought, anyhow. He decided it was the *ain't* that got to him.

"What's with the yokel routine?" he grumbled. Brody had a college degree, just as he did.

Brody laughed. "I was waxing colloquial," he said. "Making conversation."

"Well, don't," Conner snapped.

"Don't wax colloquial?"

"Don't make conversation."

Brody gave a heavy sigh. "This isn't about Joleen, I'm guessing," he said.

"Nope," Conner agreed.

"Then what? The land I bought from Tricia McCall?"

"Why would I give a damn about that?"

"Got me," Brody said. The words had a built-in

shrug. "Maybe you figure Tricia goes along with the deal."

If it wouldn't have scared the dog, Conner would have been on his feet, across the room and closing his hands around Brody's throat, all in the space of a heartbeat.

"Tricia's got better sense than to take up with the likes of you," Conner said, still in his chair in front of the stove. *Or me,* he added silently. "She plans on moving back to Seattle pretty soon. That's why I have the dog."

"I do believe that's the most you've said to me in ten years," Brody commented, rattling utensils around in a drawer until he found a spatula to turn the eggs. "You like her, Conner?"

"She's all right," Conner said.

All right? Kissing her had practically turned him inside out. God only knew what would happen if they ever made love. Fireworks, probably.

Meteor showers.

Earthquakes, without a doubt.

Again, Brody laughed. It gave Conner that old feeling that he and Brody could see inside each other's heads.

"I don't have designs on Tricia," Brody said. He'd stacked the eggs onto a plate like a pile of pancakes, and he was headed for the table.

"None of my concern if you do," Conner said.

"Like hell," Brody responded, busy digging in to the eggs. "You think you know all about me, brother, but you don't."

"Is that right?" Conner asked, wondering if it meant

anything that Brody had just said "brother" instead of the usual "*little* brother." Deciding it didn't.

"Fact is," Brody reflected, looking at Conner now, "I'm more like you than you'd care to admit, and you're more like me than anybody else knows."

Conner absorbed that statement, swallowed the immediate urge to refute it. Even in friendlier days, he and Brody had lived to disagree with each other—he supposed it was because they'd needed, as kids, to establish separate identities. In most people's eyes, they were practically interchangeable, each of them only half a person without the other.

"Where have you been all this time, Brody?" Conner asked, taking himself by surprise. It seemed he was always saying something he hadn't *meant* to say, lately. To Brody and to Tricia, anyway.

"Around," Brody said.

"Come on," Conner said, in an angry rasp, turning his chair around so his back was to the stove now, and he was facing Brody, who was still sitting at the table, though he'd stopped eating. Valentino adjusted himself to the new arrangement, sticking close enough to rest his muzzle on Conner's right boot.

"Just around," Brody reiterated. "For now, Conner, that needs to be enough."

Conner didn't answer.

Brody wasn't finished, though. And that was strange, given that this time he'd been the one to pull his punches. "I'll tell you what I told Boston, back when he asked me the same question," Brody said. "I wasn't in jail, or anything like that. There's no big secret— but there is some stuff I'm not ready to talk about. Fair enough?"

"Fair enough," Conner replied.

Brody left the table, carried his plate and his silverware to the sink, set them down. "I'll be out of town for a few days, as of tomorrow," he said, as though it mattered. "But I'm coming back to Lonesome Bend, for sure. Soon as I close on that real-estate deal, I'll be living in that log building at the campground and you'll be rid of me."

"Whatever," Conner said.

"Yeah," Brody said hoarsely. "Well, good night, little brother."

"Night," Conner ground out.

When he and Valentino were alone in the kitchen again, the dog lifted his head off Conner's instep and gave an inquiring little whine.

"We might as well turn in, too," Conner said.

Tired as he was, sleep eluded him for a long time.

TWO DAYS LATER, Conner awakened to a loud pounding at the back door.

Grumbling, he rolled out of bed, pulled on a pair of jeans and padded out into the kitchen.

Dawn hadn't even cracked the horizon yet, but the porch light was on, and he could see Tricia standing out there, hands cupped on either side of her face, peering in through the window beside the door.

Conner's heart did a funny little spin, right up into his throat.

Valentino, at his side as ever, gave a happy little yelp.

"I want my dog back," Tricia said, first thing, when Conner had pulled open the door. With that, she dropped to her knees, right there on the threshold, and hugged Valentino, laughing as he licked her face in welcome.

"Oh, buddy, I've missed you." she crooned, burying her face in the dog's ruff.

Conner rubbed his bare chest with the heel of one palm. "You mind coming inside?" he asked, in a tone that would have led some people to believe things like this—women showing up at his house in what amounted to the middle of the night—happened to him all the time. "So I can shut the door?"

She got to her feet, smiling, and stepped into the house.

Conner pushed the door closed, looking her over.

He saw her eyes widen as she registered that he wasn't wearing a shirt. "Hold on," he said, heading into his old room, the one Brody had taken over, and grabbing the first garment he got his hands on.

Turned out to be a T-shirt with a lot of holes and a lewd slogan on the front.

"I guess I woke you up," Tricia said, sounding chagrined. She'd already hunted up Valentino's leash, and she was bending to attach it to his collar. He supposed it should have galled him, her certainty that he'd just give back the dog and say nothing about it, but it didn't.

"Bound to happen," Conner observed dryly, glancing at the stove clock, "at three forty-five in the morning."

She had the good grace to blush. "I'm sorry," she said. "I took a red-eye from Seattle to Denver and all the way home, I was thinking about Valentino—"

Conner tried to remember the last time he'd been jealous of a dog and came up empty. Besides that, his sleep-drugged mind got snagged on the word *home*. Since when did Tricia McCall consider Lonesome Bend "home"? All she'd wanted was to get the hell out of there.

Just a figure of speech, he decided, rummy but waking up fast.

"He's still your dog," Conner said, folding his arms. Drinking in the sight of her. For somebody who'd been up all night, Tricia looked good—deliciously so. "Took off twice, after you left, and both times, I found him waiting on your doorstep. Coffee?"

Tricia blinked, probably at the conversational hairpin turn—Conner was prone to those, since his brain moved a lot faster than his mouth. "I couldn't impose," she said.

Conner laughed. "As if. This from a woman who couldn't wait till daylight to reclaim her dog?"

She blushed. She looked damn good, with color blossoming in her cheeks and that shine in her eyes. It would be interesting to see what a nice long orgasm did for her.

"I'm sorry," she repeated.

"Sit down," Conner said, moving on to the coffee-maker and starting the brew. Once it was percolating, he turned around to look at her again. She'd taken a chair, and the dog was standing there with his head resting on her knees, his eyes rolled up at her in frank adoration.

Conner could identify.

"I thought you'd decided Valentino was too big a dog to live in the city," he ventured. That was as close as his pride would let him get to asking her what her plans were, but he sure as hell wanted to know.

"We'll adapt," Tricia said, stroking Valentino lovingly.

Conner reminded himself that it was stupid to envy a dog. "So," he responded casually, turning away to get cups from the cupboard, "you're still going back to Seattle?"

"I haven't decided," she answered. "There's no hurry, after all."

Conner looked back at her. "What about ski-guy?" he asked, and then could have kicked himself. Now she'd know he'd seen—and remembered—that snow-globe picture of her and the boyfriend on her computer screen.

She smiled. "Hunter? That's over." She said this lightly, in the same tone she might have used to say she'd once believed that the moon was made of green cheese, but now she knew it was just one big rock. "Actually, it's *been* over for a while now, but it took me some time to notice."

He got real busy with the cups, even though the coffee was a long way from being ready to drink. "I see," he said, when the silence had stretched to the breaking point. Of course, he *didn't* see. He was damned if he could figure out how a woman's mind worked, sometimes. Especially *this* woman.

She looked around. "Where's Brody?" she asked. Then she colored up again. "Sleeping, I suppose."

"I doubt that," Conner replied. "He's out of town right now."

"Oh," Tricia said, squirming a little on the hard seat of that wooden chair. Not quite meeting his eyes.

Hot damn, he thought. Was it possible that she was there for another reason, besides fetching her dog?

Whoa, dumb-ass, he told himself silently. *Don't go jumping to conclusions.*

Conner needed something to do, so he went ahead and pulled the carafe from the coffeemaker, even though it wasn't done doing its thing. The stuff sizzled on the little burner and scented the air with java.

He filled a cup for Tricia and one for himself and finally joined her at the table.

"Sugar?" she asked.

Holy shit, he thought, as a zing went through his whole system. But then the request penetrated his thick skull and seeped into the gray matter.

"Sure," he said, getting up to find the sugar bowl and get her a teaspoon so she could stir the stuff into her coffee. "You want cream, too? I've got some of the powdered stuff, I think."

Tricia shook her head and concentrated on doctoring the contents of her mug. "No, thanks," she said.

He sat down again.

The dog, he noticed, had positioned himself halfway between the two of them, and he kept turning his head from one to the other.

Tricia's spoon rattled in her cup.

Conner sipped his own coffee and mused.

Finally, she looked up at him, and he was amazed to see tears standing in her eyes. "I can't believe Natty won't be there when Valentino and I go back to the house," she said.

So that was it, Conner decided. She didn't want to face her great-grandmother's empty rooms—not in the dark, anyway, and not after a long and probably uncomfortable flight, followed by the drive from the airport.

"You could stay here," Conner said. Might as well put it out there in the open. All this pussyfooting around was getting them nowhere. "Go back to Natty's place after the sun's up and you're feeling a little stronger."

She blinked and, with a subtle motion of one hand, wiped her eyes. "Would you mind?"

Mind? Would he *mind?*

"I could sleep on the sofa, I suppose," she said in a thoughtful tone.

"You can have my bed," Conner answered. There were guest rooms in the house, of course, but none of them were made up, and he couldn't bring himself to put her in Brody's, empty though it was. There were probably cracker crumbs on the sheets, anyhow. "I'll just get an early start on the chores."

Tricia bit down on her lower lip, finally nodded. She used both hands to pick up her coffee mug this time, and they shook visibly.

"Okay," she said, looking at him over the rim. "My— my suitcase is in the Pathfinder—"

"I'll get it," Conner said, on his feet immediately. Over by the door, he paused to pull on a pair of boots and his denim jacket.

"Thanks," she said, after clearing her throat.

He braved the cold, retrieved the suitcase and hurried back inside. By then, she was standing at the kitchen sink, rinsing out her cup.

"This way," he told her, and the words came out sandpaper-gruff.

They followed him, the woman and the dog, through the old-fashioned dining room, into the hallway beyond. Conner flicked on a light when he passed the switch, thumped on the door across from the one leading into his room.

"That's the bathroom," he said.

Then he pushed open his own door, where the bed-side lamp was still burning; he'd turned it on earlier, when she knocked. The bed, a massive four-poster, dated back to the 1800s, when Micah Creed had brought his mail-order bride home to a much smaller version of this house. According to legend, old Micah wasted no time bedding the woman, and she hadn't minded.

Tricia peered around his right shoulder, taking in the natural rock fireplace, the bowed and leaded windows that formed an alcove of sorts on one side of the room.

"Wow," she breathed. "It's like going back in time."

"Except for the 3D TV, yeah," Conner agreed.

Tricia swallowed. "This is—very kind of you."

"Don't mention it," he said, with a partial grin.

"Oh, believe me," she replied, with a nervous laugh, "I won't. Not to anyone. You can just imagine the talk."

"Hadn't thought about it," Conner said, and that was true.

"Of course you haven't," Tricia said, seeming to loosen up just a little. "You're a man."

Oh, yeah, Conner thought. *I'm a man, all right. And I've got the hard-on to prove it.* He carried her suitcase in and set it on the antique bench at the foot of the bed, then crossed to the bureau to take out fresh clothes. "Make yourself at home," he said, heading toward the door.

Valentino settled himself on the rug in front of the fireplace, even though the hearth was bare, yawned and shut his eyes.

"You, too," Conner added, speaking to the dog, and then he and Tricia both laughed.

There was something intimate in the exchange, ordinary as it was. Laughing with Tricia felt good, but when it was over, they were both uncomfortable again.

"Holler if you need anything," Conner finally said.

And then he left the room without looking back, careful to close the door behind him.

CHAPTER FIFTEEN

ONCE SHE WAS sure she wouldn't run into Conner—she'd heard the back door shut smartly in the distance—Tricia took her last clean sleepshirt out of her suitcase, left over from the trip to Seattle, along with her toothbrush and a tube of toothpaste, and ventured into the bathroom.

The shower was huge, and there were plenty of thick, thirsty towels. Tricia leaned inside the stall and turned the spigots, planning to adjust the spray, but pleasantly warm water flew out of a dozen different showerheads, placed at all levels and angles. With a little shriek of surprise, she jumped back, laughing, and started peeling off her now-soggy clothes.

What followed wasn't a mere shower, it was an *experience,* like being massaged by a hundred industrious Lilliputians. Although she most definitely *had not* come to the ranch to seduce—or be seduced by—Conner Creed, the warmth and the soap lather and the dance of the water against her naked skin *was* sensual.

Okay, Tricia admitted to herself minutes later, as she stood on the lush-plush bathmat, drying off, if she was perfectly honest, maybe coming here was a *little bit* about having sex with Conner. She didn't seem to be in any big hurry to put on her nightshirt, after all.

As the steam fog cleared from the big mirror above

the long vanity, with its artfully painted ceramic sinks and ornate copper-tile backsplash, Tricia assessed her wild-haired image. She had a pretty good body, compact and firm where firmness was an advantage. She turned in one direction, studying her profile, and then the other.

Finally, since goose bumps were starting to crop up all over, she put on the nightshirt, brushed her teeth thoroughly and crossed the hallway to Conner's room.

There was a nice blaze crackling in the fireplace grate now, and Valentino, still lounging on the rug, had rolled onto his back in an ecstasy of warmth, all four paws in the air.

Tricia smiled at the sight, but only after she'd scanned the room and made sure that Conner hadn't stuck around after building the fire.

He hadn't.

This was, as it happened, both a major relief and a disappointment.

Too tired to consider the implications—there would be plenty of time for that in the morning, when she was over her exhaustion and this crazy sense of ending one chapter of her life to begin another—Tricia crossed the room and climbed into the bed, stretching out on sheets that smelled woodsy and fresh-air clean. Like Conner.

She bunched up a pillow, snuggled down.

The bedframe was probably old, but the mattress was definitely modern, made of some space-age material that supported her softly, like the palm of a huge and gentle hand. She yawned, closed her eyes and promptly conked out, tumbling into a dreamless sleep, deep and sweet.

Hours later, upon awakening to a stream of sunlight and a cheerful yip from Valentino, Tricia stretched deliciously before turning onto her side and seeing Conner on the other side of the room.

Fully dressed, his honey-gold hair damp and recently combed, he was just turning away from the fire. He'd added wood, and the flames leaped and popped behind him, framing him in a reddish glow.

"Hey," he said. His grin flashed. "All rested?"

"Yes," Tricia said, as the inevitable sense of chagrin settled over her. She jerked the covers up over her head, so he couldn't see her face. "Don't look at me," she added.

Conner laughed. "That's asking a lot, don't you think?"

"I could *just die,*" she said, the words muffled.

"No need to go that far," he replied. The echo of laughter lingered in his voice.

"I'm *in your bed!*" she pointed out, through layers of cloth.

"Yes," Conner answered easily. "I know that." A pause, a circumspect clearing of his throat. "Believe me, I know. And I'll admit this isn't exactly how I pictured things turning out—sure, I imagined you in my bed, lots of times—but I sort of expected to be right in there with you."

No way she was coming out from under the covers now—or maybe ever. "You pictured me in your bed?"

"I'm *human,*" he said. Apparently, Conner considered that an answer.

"Please leave the room," Tricia said. "Before—"

"Before what?" Conner's voice was throaty.

She felt a distinct tug at the covers. And a need to breathe freely.

Tricia lowered the blankets just far enough to peer over the edge and suck some air in through her nose.

Conner's face was an inch from her own.

"I have a theory," he drawled. His gaze rested on her lips, made them tingle with the anticipation of illicit things.

"Wh-what theory?" Tricia ventured, suspicious and wary and hot to trot, all at the same time.

"That you want to make love as much as I do."

Her eyes widened. "What makes you think a thing like that?"

How did you know? Am I that obvious?

"I said it was a theory," Conner murmured, and by then his mouth was almost touching hers.

When he actually kissed her, Tricia couldn't help responding. The demands of her body instantly overrode conscious reasoning; the wanting raged through her like fire, swift and fierce, devouring every doubt, every hesitation, every fear in its path.

Her arms went around him, her fingers splayed across the hard expanse of his shoulders. The walls and floor and ceiling of that room seemed to recede, leaving in their places a void that throbbed rhythmically, like an invisible heart.

By the time that first consuming kiss was over, Conner was on top of Tricia, his hands pressed into the mattress on either side of her, being careful not to crush her under his weight.

"Hold it," he murmured, gasping for breath, and for the life of her, Tricia couldn't have said whether he was addressing her, or himself. "Hold on a second."

She looked up at him, her very cells drinking in the hardness and heat, the blatant, uncompromising *maleness* of him.

A fragment of that milestone conversation with

Diana flashed in her fevered brain, and a part of Tricia acknowledged that, yes, she was afraid to open herself, body, mind and soul, especially to this man. For all that, her need of him felt ancient, a cell memory, a part of her very DNA.

There was, she knew, no turning back. However advisable that might be.

"Conner," she said, softly but clearly, "make love to me."

His eyes were so serious, and so impossibly blue, as they searched hers, took in every nuance of her expression. It was almost as though he could see inside her mind, see past her desire, past her every defense, to the essence of her being, where all her deepest secrets were stored.

"Are you sure about this?" he asked.

She nodded. "Yes," she said, and it was the purest truth she knew in that moment.

Still, Conner hesitated, pushing back from her, standing up. She felt afraid then, afraid he would turn his back and walk away.

Instead, he hauled his shirt off over his head, without bothering to unbutton it first. He opened a drawer in the nightstand and took out a packet, set it within easy reach of the bed, his gaze fixed on her, blue and hot, missing nothing. After a few moments, he was out of his jeans and gently sliding Tricia's nightshirt up and then off over her head.

He lowered himself to her, kissed her again. Wherever her skin made contact with his, it seemed to Tricia, they fused, one to the other.

She felt dazed and, conversely, powerful. She was more than herself, more than an individual woman with a name and a heartbeat and a collection of disparate emotions—she was *womanhood itself,* as ferociously feminine as a she-wolf taking a mate. She wanted him inside her.

Now.

But Conner moved at his own excruciatingly slow pace, every nibble or touch of his tongue designed to heighten her need and, at the same time, delay the gratification she craved with her whole being.

His lips traced the length of her neck, returned to her earlobe, shifted to her collarbone and then the rounded tops of her breasts.

When he finally took one of her nipples into the warmth of his mouth, Tricia cried out in throaty, wordless welcome, and arched her back out of pure instinct and incredible need.

Still, Conner savored her.

She alternately flailed and writhed under his mouth and his hands, gasped his name. Pleas spilled out of her, intertwined with desperate commands.

Conner Creed wasn't taking orders—or dispensing mercies.

He ran the tip of his tongue around her navel, leaving a fiery little circle blazing on her skin, building the sweet, terrible pressure inside her, then easing off.

Tricia clawed at his shoulders, trying to pull him up from her belly, draw him onto her, *into* her.

But still Conner would not be swayed, would not be hurried. Conquer her he would, that was plain, but on his own terms and in his own time.

He moved farther down her frantic body, parted her legs and then raised her by the strength of his hands, took her softly into his mouth.

She gave a strangled, exultant sob, and her legs went

around him, because her arms couldn't reach. She repeated his name, over and over again, like some litany offered in delirium, now begging, now cajoling, now crying out in ecstasy.

The first orgasm was long, *endless,* with peaks and valleys, slow descents followed by rapid trajectory to an even higher pinnacle than the one before it. It wrung every last ounce of passion from Tricia, that continuous climax, causing her mind and soul to buckle and seize right along with her body. She was breathless when Conner finally let her rest, trembling, against the sheets.

Speech was impossible; she'd forgotten the language. She'd been transported, catapulted out of herself and then flung back in at the speed of light, and yet she felt every delicious thing Conner did to her. She was alive, and responding, on every level—physical, spiritual, mental and emotional.

He asked her again if she was sure; she barely made sense of the question. But she nodded.

Felt the shift of his powerful body as he put on the condom.

And then it happened, the hard, deep thrust as he claimed her.

Had her thoughts been coherent, Tricia might have wondered how Conner could possibly have aroused her to such a state of need, so soon after satisfying her so completely. As it was, she could only marvel, flexing wildly beneath Conner, hungry for release, fighting for fulfillment.

The pace, so slow before, was a rapid, powerful lunging now. The whole of life seemed to be concentrated in their coupling bodies. Tricia at once yearned for relief and wanted to burn in the fire of Conner's love-making forever.

When they came, they came simultaneously, with low, hoarse shouts of nearly intolerable pleasure, slamming together hard, as though to become one and stay that way for all eternity.

Afterward, they clung together, hard against soft, warm pressed to warm, both of them breathless.

Tricia drifted, finally settled slowly inside herself, like the feather of some high-flying bird riding the softest of breezes back to earth.

Then Conner left the bed, returning long minutes later to stretch out beside her.

"Tears?" he asked gruffly, sliding the side of one thumb across her cheekbone.

Tricia hadn't realized she was crying until then, and she had no explanation to offer, no way of sorting through the tangle of nameless emotions he'd stirred to life within her.

"Tricia?" Conner pressed, sounding worried. "Did I hurt you?"

She could only shake her head *no*. She slipped her arms around his neck, though, and held him close, unable to tell her own heartbeat from his.

He watched her, a gentle frown in his eyes. And he waited.

How could she tell him, in words, that he'd opened up new places inside her, broken down barriers she had no recollection of erecting in the first place? How could she explain that their lovemaking had altered her, possibly for all time, in ways that were beyond her power to define—ways that made her feel both triumphant and dangerously vulnerable?

"Hold me," was all she could manage to say.

But it was enough.

Conner did hold her, and closely, his chin propped on top of her head, his shoulder smooth and strong under her cheek, his arms firm but gentle around her.

There was no telling how long they might have stayed like that if Valentino hadn't suddenly stuck his cold nose between Tricia's bare shoulder blades and given a plaintive whimper.

She started and cried out, and Conner chuckled.

"And now back to the real world," he said, pulling away from her, sitting up, throwing back the covers to get up.

Tricia listened, keeping her eyes closed, as Conner got dressed, spoke a few gruff but reassuring words to the dog and finally left the room.

As soon as she heard the door close, Tricia bolted out of bed, grabbed her clothes and raced, wobbly-legged, into the bathroom. There, she locked the door and started water running for a shower.

And now back to the real world.

Was *that* ever true. She'd landed smack-dab in the center of reality, with a bone-jarring *thunk,* too, like a skydiver whose parachute had failed to open.

Of course, her body still hummed liked the strings of a recently tuned violin, and that only made everything worse. She'd given herself to Conner Creed in haste, and now, as the old saying went, she would repent at leisure.

What would happen now?

Tricia couldn't say, of course, but she was sure of a few things, anyway. She'd crossed some invisible line, entered some uncharted territory, a place she'd never been before. She didn't speak the language, and she didn't know the rules. She was adrift.

And worse? There was no going back.

TRICIA DIDN'T JUST LEAVE.

She *fled* that venerable old ranch house, muttering some lame excuse about a forgotten appointment in town, remembering to take the dog with her but leaving her suitcase behind.

Conner watched through the window over the kitchen sink, a slight smile crooking his mouth up at one corner, as the Pathfinder sped off down the driveway toward the road. Once the rig was out of sight, he poured himself some coffee and fired up the right-front burner on the stove to cook some scrambled eggs. He made toast and sat down to enjoy his solitary breakfast, feeling strangely peaceful, though he supposed Tricia's quick exit wasn't an especially good sign.

After he'd eaten, Conner headed to the barn to feed the horses and then turn them out into the corral for some exercise. Brody's rodeo stock was way out there, on the range, and against his better judgment, Conner worried. There was plenty of water, since the river flowed clear across the ranch, but the grass was getting skimpy, now that it was November.

And Brody wasn't back from wherever it was he'd gone. Fuming a little, Conner strode to the equipment shed, rolled up the high, wide door, and drove the flatbed truck out, leaving it to idle beside the barn while he climbed into the hay mow and began chucking bales down. When he had a load, he got behind the wheel again and made his way through a series of gates and out onto the range. He attracted a crowd of hungry cattle right away, though the horses kept their distance at first.

Methodically, silently cursing his twin brother the whole time, Conner drove from one part of the ranch to another, cutting the twine around the bales with his pocket knife, flinging the feed onto the ground so the livestock could get at it. After he'd dropped the last pile, he drove back toward the house. All the while, he was conscious of the heavy gray clouds overhead, promising snow. Maybe a lot of it.

What he tried *not* to think about was making love to Tricia McCall. Yes, he acknowledged silently, he'd enjoyed the experience. But it had left him shaken, too, and more than a little confused.

He'd been with his share of women in his time; the mechanics were the same. What *wasn't* the same was the way he'd felt, before, during and after. He supposed it could be compared to dying a good death at the close of a long and happy life, or being knocked off a horse on the road to Damascus by a Light so irrefutably real as to be utterly transformative.

He was thinking all those crazy, un-Connerlike thoughts as he pulled up next to the barn, shifted gears and shut down the truck's big engine. There was no point in putting the rig away in the equipment shed; knowing Brody, he, Conner, would be out there feeding cows, bulls and bucking broncos again, all by his lonesome, come morning.

A light rain, mixed with snow, began to fall as he stepped out onto the running board and leaped to the ground. A sound, or maybe a flicker of movement, drew his attention to the back door of the house, and there was Bill—*Valentino*—sitting on the step, looking as though his last friend had just caught a freight train for points south.

He walked quickly toward the dog, noting as he approached that the animal's hide was damp and streaked with mud. Judging by the way Valentino sat, instead of getting up to greet Conner, he was footsore, too.

"Hey, buddy," Conner said, crouching in front of Valentino and looking straight into those expressive, dog-brown eyes. "What brings you all the way out here?"

Valentino gave a low whine, but he didn't move.

A chill trickled down Conner's spine, like a drop of ice water. He glanced around, but there was no sign of Tricia or her Pathfinder.

So he reached out gently and ruffled Valentino's floppy ears.

Valentino whined again and raised his right foreleg slightly, prompting Conner to examine the dog's paw. It looked swollen, maybe a little bruised, but there was no blood.

Conner frowned. "Okay," he said, partly to himself and partly to the dog. "Let's get you inside. Give you some water and let you rest up a little."

Valentino permitted Conner to hoist him into his arms, carry him into the kitchen. He set him gently on the bed he'd improvised when the critter first came to stay with him, then headed for the phone.

A glance at the wall clock above the stove surprised him with the realization that it was barely 10:00 a.m. Conner could have sworn he'd lived a lifetime since Tricia had left the house on a dead run.

It occurred to him that he didn't know her number, either the landline or the cell. So he dialed Kim and Davis's place and, as he'd hoped, Carolyn answered.

Conner identified himself and asked for Tricia's number.

Maybe it was something in his voice. Maybe it was just woman's intuition. In any case, Carolyn was instantly worried, and there was some intrigue there, too. "Is something wrong?" she asked.

"Probably not," Conner said, after indulging in a long sigh that wouldn't be kept inside him. "I'd just like to make sure, that's all."

Carolyn hunted up the number, then recited it to him.

Conner thanked her and hung up, but before he could punch in the appropriate digits, the phone jangled in his hand. The unexpectedness of it made him flinch.

"Hello?" he rasped.

"It's Tricia," came the answer, at once shy and anxious. "Conner, have you seen Valentino? I took him for a walk, and everything was fine, but when we got home and I unhooked his leash from his collar, he took off like a shot. I've looked everywhere, but—"

"He's here," Conner said, closing his eyes. Bracing himself against the wall by extending one hand, palm out. "Tricia, are you all right?"

She hesitated before answering. "I'm—I'm fine. What's Valentino doing all the way out there?"

Conner chuckled, though inside, he was quaking with relief. Nearly sick with it. He opened his eyes, straightened his spine. "I guess you'll have to ask *him* that. I went out to feed the range stock and, when I got back, Bill—er, Valentino—was waiting for me."

"Is he okay?" Tricia sounded anxious.

"I think his feet might be a little tender," Conner allowed, glancing at the dog. "Must have been quite a hike, from Natty's place to here."

She was quiet for so long that Conner started to think the connection had been broken. "Maybe Valentino would rather be your dog than mine," she said, at long last.

The words bruised Conner's heart in some deep and private places. "I could bring him back," he offered, after a long time.

"Conner—"

He sighed. Shoved a hand through his hair. "Look, if you regret what we did this morning, Tricia, I can deal with that. What I *won't* do, under any circumstances, is pretend that nothing happened."

She was silent for a while, but this time Conner knew she was still on the line, because he could hear her soft breathing. "I'm—I was vulnerable last night, and I didn't mean—I don't want to—"

"It's *all right,* Tricia. If you don't want things to go any further than they already have, I'm okay with that. But, as I said before, I won't accept business as usual, either. We *did* go to bed together. It was better than good. Beyond that, you can put any spin on this that works for you."

Again, she didn't answer right away. "Lonesome Bend is a small town," she said, finally. "If you—well, if you kiss and tell, Conner—"

He huffed out a snortlike chuckle, a sound completely devoid of amusement. "If you think I'd brag about our getting together, Tricia, you don't know me very well."

"Exactly," she said, after a long time. "I *don't* know you very well, Conner. And you just said you weren't going to pretend—"

"With you," Conner clarified, annoyed. Even a little hurt. "I'm not going to pretend *with you.* But neither do

I have any intention of announcing to the whole town that we slept together."

A low whistle of exclamation made Conner whirl in the direction of the kitchen door.

There stood Brody, wearing a grin as wide as the Mississippi River. His timing, as always, was rotten.

Conner swore under his breath, roundly and with considerable creativity.

Tricia, being a woman, instantly took offense. "I beg your pardon?"

"I wasn't talking to you," Conner told her, so calmly that he amazed himself. He glowered at Brody, who ignored him, crossed to Valentino, and crouched to stroke the dog with a sympathetic hand. "Listen, Tricia—I'll bring your dog home in a little while. We'll talk then."

"What if I don't *want* to talk to you?"

"Well, I guess that's your prerogative. I could always keep Bill. Obviously, he likes it here."

"Who's Bill?" Tricia wanted to know.

"Bill," Conner replied patiently, "is what I called Valentino before you decided to take him back."

"Oh," Tricia said.

"Yeah," Conner said. *"Oh."*

On the other side of the room, still on his haunches beside the dog, Brody chuckled and shook his head. "God almighty," he told Valentino, in a voice just loud enough to carry, "no *wonder* my little brother can't score with a woman. He has all the subtlety of a Brahma bull at a church social."

"What if you bring Valentino back and he runs away again?" Tricia asked, her voice soft and sad, echoing faintly with losses he knew nothing about. "He could be hit by a car, out there on the road, or attacked by coyotes—"

Trying to ignore Brody, who was still inspecting the dog for injuries, Conner thrust out a sigh. "Here's the problem, Tricia," he said quietly. "The road goes both ways. He could just as easily take a notion to take off for your place."

"What are we going to do?" Tricia asked.

"Keep an eye on him," Conner answered, wanting to offer her solutions but having none to offer. "That's all we *can* do, right now."

Brody, getting to his feet and ambling over to the refrigerator, where he no doubt hoped to find that his favorite foods had materialized by magic, had evidently gotten the gist of the conversation by listening in on Conner's end of it. And he jumped right in there with his two cents' worth, unasked, like always.

"That poor dog," he said mildly, "will run himself ragged going back and forth between the ranch and town. If he's with you, Conner, he misses Tricia. And vice versa. He's only going to be happy when both of you are under the same roof."

Brody's remark made a certain amount of sense, to Conner's irritation.

"Stay out of this," Conner said, adding, at Tricia's indrawn breath, "Brody."

Brody shrugged. He'd shaved recently, and his hair was still fairly short. Furthermore, he was either wearing Conner's clothes again, or he'd gone to a Western store and outfitted himself with similar ones.

What the *hell* was going on with him, anyhow?

"So," Tricia interjected, "are you bringing Valentino back or not?"

"Might as well," Conner said lightly. If Brody hadn't been right there, he'd have reminded her that she'd left her suitcase behind, though he was pretty sure she must have realized that by now. "I've been feeding my brother's livestock," he added, putting a point on his words and raising his voice a notch, "so I have to shower and change first. See you in about an hour?"

"Yes," Tricia said, rallying audibly from some distraction all her own. Her tone and her words were formal. They might have been business associates, or mere acquaintances, the way she talked, instead of two people who'd been wound up in a sweaty tangle together just a few hours before. "Yes, that would be fine."

Frowning, Conner said goodbye and hung up.

Brody was still rummaging through the fridge. "Don't you ever buy food?" he complained.

"Don't you?" Conner countered.

Brody closed the refrigerator door briskly. His jaw tightened as he studied Conner, but then mischief twinkled in his eyes.

"You slept with Tricia McCall," Brody said. "Little brother, I'm proud of you."

Conner gave a ragged laugh, but he wasn't amused. "Brody?"

"What?"

The dog lifted his head off the blanket-bed and looked at them curiously.

"Stay the hell out of my private business."

Brody leaned back against the counter, in that old, familiar way, folding his arms, tilting his head to one side and planting the toe of his right boot on the other side of his left one. "Thanks for feeding my stock," he said idly. "But it wasn't necessary. I made arrangements with Clint and Juan before I left, and I figured on being back in time to haul out a load of hay this morning. Which I was."

Conner was still annoyed, but the subject they were on was better than kicking around what had gone on between him and Tricia—by a long shot.

"Well, I didn't have any way of knowing that, now did I?" he asked.

Brody sighed, looking put upon and sadly amused, both at once. "Those critters belong to me," he said. "And I'll take care of them. If I need your help, Conner, I'll ask for it."

Conner cleared his throat. Looked away. Momentarily, and with a stab of pain so sudden and so fierce that it nearly stole his breath, he wondered what things would be like by now, between him and Brody, if Joleen had never come between them.

"I want to get along, Conner," Brody said, surprising him. "But you're not exactly making it easy."

"Imagine that," Conner snapped, but the truth was, the grudge was starting to weigh him down. He was getting tired of carrying it.

Brody huffed out another sigh. "I'm heading for town to pick up some grub at the grocery store," he said. "If you want, I could drop the dog off at Tricia's and save you the trip."

Conner felt a whisper of distrust, fleeting and foolish.

He wanted to see Tricia again, and any excuse would do, but he knew she needed space, and time to think.

"Okay," he said, secretly pleased to see that Brody had expected him to refuse the offer out of hand.

Conner crossed to the dog, crouched beside him. "You be good, now," he told the animal. "No more running away."

CHAPTER SIXTEEN

THE OLD VICTORIAN house literally echoed all around Tricia, whenever she made the slightest sound.

Natty was gone. So was Sasha. Even Winston and Valentino had bailed on her.

She finally sat down in front of her computer, sorely in need of distraction, but when she booted up, there was Rusty, filling the screen saver, grinning a dog-grin. And there was her younger self, still shy, but with luminous eyes, full of hopeful expectations.

Her eyes scalded, and she swallowed. Touched the image with the tip of one finger, watching as pixels spread out in a tiny radius, like still water disturbed.

Instead of sorrow, though, she felt a soft surge of happy gratitude for Rusty, and for his devoted friendship. He'd bridged the gap in some important ways, she realized, between her and her feuding parents.

She smiled and clicked her way online. Her inbox was full, and she spent a few minutes weeding out once-in-a-lifetime offers, then scanned the list of incoming messages.

Two from Diana. One from Sasha. *Seven* from Hunter. And, finally, one from her mother.

Her mother?

Tricia couldn't resist opening that one. She and her mom weren't close, so they didn't chat or swap instant messages and silly forwards. When one of them made the effort to get in touch with the other, there was a reason.

She opened the message and was surprised to see her slender, blonde mother smiling back at her from a photograph taken in front of some jungle hut.

Beside Laurel McCall stood a handsome man with a receding hairline and wire-rimmed glasses. He was beaming, too, one arm around Laurel's waist.

Tricia gulped, flicked a glance at the subject line above the picture.

"Meet Harvey, your new stepfather," Laurel had written, the phrase supplemented by half a dozen exclamation points.

"My new—?" Tricia whispered. She was feeling something—all kinds of things, actually—but she couldn't have said what those things were.

A knock sounded from downstairs; someone was at Natty's front door. Conner, bringing Valentino home? No, Tricia decided. He would have come up the outside staircase and, besides, he knew Natty was off in Denver.

Strangely jittery, Tricia closed the message without reading her mother's long missive, pushed back her chair and went to the living room window to look out at the street. Conner's truck was parked at the curb.

The knocking, though still polite, grew more insistent.

Tricia hurried downstairs, worked the stiff locks and pulled open the door.

Her gaze dropped to Valentino, sitting there on his haunches, panting and looking up at her, all innocence and unconditional canine love.

"You," she told the creature fondly, "are a bad dog."

She forced herself to look up and meet Conner's eyes.

He'd said they weren't going to pretend, and she knew he'd meant it.

The man standing before her looked like Conner—*exactly* like him, in fact—but this *wasn't* Conner. It was Brody.

What was going on here? Tricia wondered, glancing past Brody's shoulder at Conner's truck. Was this some kind of immature twin trick? The old switcheroo?

"Hey," Brody said, and it was clear from the laughter lurking in his Conner-blue eyes that he'd picked up on her thoughts. "Brought your dog back."

"Thanks, Brody," Tricia said, stepping back. On the one hand, she was glad she didn't have to face Conner quite yet, because she wasn't ready, after the way she'd carried on in his bed and then run out of his house in a stupid panic. On the other, she felt his absence like a physical ache. "Come in. I'll put on a pot of coffee."

Brody's grin was crooked, identical to Conner's, and yet—*different.* "I guess you can tell my brother and me apart," he said, following Valentino over the threshold. Taking off his hat and holding it respectfully in one hand, cowboy style. "Most people can't, when we're trying to look alike."

Tricia, headed for the inside stairs, looked back over one shoulder. "Did you set out to fool me, Brody Creed?" she asked bluntly, but with a touch of amusement.

"If I did," he allowed good-naturedly, "it didn't work, did it?"

She shook her head.

"Ready for the closing tomorrow?" he asked, when they'd reached the upper floor and her apartment. The place was too quiet without Sasha. Without Natty. But Valentino was back. That was something.

It took Tricia a moment to remember that Brody was buying her property, hence the mention of a closing.

Thanks to him, she was suddenly presented with a plethora of choices. Go or stay. Take a chance on a flesh-and-blood man or run for the hills.

Decisions, decisions.

"All ready," she answered, at last. But she was frowning slightly as she moved toward the coffeemaker. At a nod of invitation from her, Brody pulled back a chair and sat down at the table, resting his hat on the floor.

Valentino, meanwhile, plodded over to his bed, sniffed his blue chicken a few times and laid himself down with a loud, contented sigh.

"Crazy dog," Tricia said, shaking her head.

Brody shifted in his chair, taking off his denim jacket, setting it aside, with the hat. And grinning. "If I didn't know better," he said, "I'd be convinced that that critter is trying to play matchmaker."

Tricia turned her back to Brody, because her cheeks were suddenly warm and probably pink. Her heartbeat quickened a little, and she wondered exactly how much he knew about her relationship with Conner.

But Tricia shook her head an instant later, in answer to her own unspoken question. Conner wouldn't kiss and tell.

Brody chuckled to himself and didn't press her for a verbal reply.

"You'd be good for Conner," he said, after a long and thoughtful silence, just as Tricia was turning away from the coffeemaker. He looked, and sounded, totally serious, and there was something gentle in his eyes. "He's been alone too much, for way too long," Brody finished.

Tricia averted her eyes, ran her suddenly moist palms

down her blue-jeaned thighs. She was blushing again, and this time, there was no hiding it. Still, she couldn't bring herself to speak.

"I walked in on that conversation you and Conner had this morning, over the telephone," Brody explained kindly. "And I overheard a pertinent detail."

He stood up, leaned to draw back a chair for Tricia. She sat, still not looking at him, or saying anything.

He sat, too.

The coffeemaker chortled and hissed, and Valentino started to snore.

"Like I said," Brody told her finally, with a smile in his voice, "I think you'd be about the best thing that ever happened to my brother."

She met his eyes. Bit down on her lower lip, searching her brain for a sensible answer, discarding every prospect she managed to come up with.

Finally, she settled on, "I'd rather not talk about Conner."

"Okay," Brody said, with an agreeable nod. "Then let's talk about River's Bend, and the old drive-in." He paused, chuckled. "I have some great memories of that place. By my calculations, half the kids in Lonesome Bend must have been conceived there, back in the day."

Tricia was beginning to relax a little—she was comfortable around Brody in a way she wasn't with Conner—probably because she and Brody had never been intimate. She smiled, let out her breath.

"Are any of them yours?" she asked, with a twinkle.

He laughed. "Not that I've heard," he replied. But then a new expression flickered in his eyes, and Tricia read it as uncertainty. She'd certainly touched a nerve, and now she wished she'd held her tongue.

She got up and poured them both a cup of the still-brewing coffee. Took a careful, steadying sip before turning the conversation back to her late father's properties.

"I guess you'll be getting rid of the screen and the speakers and stuff, out at the Bluebird," she said.

There was an easing in Brody. He'd made some kind of internal shift, away from whatever had been bothering him. His grin was companionable, his manner brotherly. "Yes," he answered. "Does that bother you?"

Tricia pondered the question—not for the first time, of course—and then shook her head. "No," she said. "Things change. What about the campground and the 'lodge,' as my dad used to call it?"

Brody shifted in his chair, looked down into his coffee cup as though he saw some benevolent scene playing out on the liquid surface. A moment later, though, he met her gaze. "Come spring," he said, "I plan on clearing that land and building a house and a barn. Putting up some pasture fences and the like."

She recalled that Carla, her real-estate agent, had mentioned Brody's intention to make the newly acquired land part of the Creed ranch, but hearing it directly from him made it real, took the idea outside the nebulous realm of local gossip and speculation.

"Will it seem strange," she began, "living somewhere besides the main ranch house, I mean?" The Creeds were a legend in Lonesome Bend and for miles around, probably. Natty's house, historical monument that it was, was new by comparison to the one Brody and Conner had grown up in.

Both the house and the ranch had been passed down from father to son for generations.

Too late, Tricia saw that her question had pained Brody, at least a little.

He cleared his throat, but his voice was still gruff when he said, "As you're probably aware, Conner and I don't get along very well. We inherited the ranch in equal shares, and that includes the house, but since he stayed put all this time, while I was off roaming the countryside, I figure it's only fair to let him have the place."

Tricia nodded, understanding. "It's too bad," she said, meaning it. "That you don't get along, I mean."

"I agree," Brody said, with quiet regret. "But what's done is done. Once Conner makes up his mind to write somebody off, the person might as well be dead. When he's finished, that's it."

The statement saddened Tricia, and frightened her a little, too. If Diana had been there, she probably would have said that was the reason for Tricia's history of arm's-length relationships—the fear of caring too much about someone, and then being tossed aside, forgotten.

"Because of Joleen," she said, without meaning to say any such thing.

"Because of Joleen," Brody confirmed grimly. "Or, to be more accurate, because of what Conner thinks happened between Joleen and me once upon a time."

A combination of remembered pleasure and potential pain washed over Tricia; it was completely ridiculous, but she hated the idea of Conner making love to any other woman—past, present or future.

"It didn't happen?" she asked, her voice small. She was treading private ground, she knew, and yet she hadn't been able to keep the question inside.

Brody shook his head. "Nope," he said. "But there'll be no convincing Conner of that."

She recalled the day of the trail ride, when Joleen and Brody had come racing across the range together, bent low over their horses' necks, laughing. They'd looked like a couple in love, Brody and Joleen had—particularly to Carolyn.

How *was* Carolyn, anyway? She needed to find out.

"Have you tried?" she asked. "Convincing Conner, I mean?"

Brody gave a raspy, raw chuckle, the kind of sound it hurts to make—and to hear. "He knows the truth, somewhere in that hard Creed head of his. The thing is, Conner resents me for a whole other reason, one he might not even be aware of."

Tricia waited, desperate to know what that reason was, but unwilling to pry any more than she already had. She was way out of bounds as it was.

"Being an identical twin can be a great thing," Brody mused, looking off into some other place, beyond Tricia and beyond her kitchen. Maybe even beyond Lonesome Bend itself. "Or it can be a bad one. Sometimes, it's like you're one person, the two of you, but split apart. Believe it or not, you forget sometimes that you've got an exact double, and then you look up and see *yourself* standing on the other side of the room. It can be unnerving."

Tricia nodded again. The revelation was highly personal, but Brody had been the one to put it out there. She hadn't pried. "Is it true," she asked carefully, "that if one of you gets hurt—thrown from a bull at a rodeo, say—the other one feels pain?"

Brody nodded. "It happens. With Conner and me, the connection tended to manifest itself in other ways, though. As kids, the teachers used to separate us on test days, even put us in different rooms, because they thought we must have worked out a way of signaling each other—the answers we gave were always the same, no matter what they did to keep us apart." He paused, chuckled at the memory. "Even the wrong ones."

Tricia smiled. "I didn't go to school in Lonesome Bend," she said, "but I remember the fuss everybody raised when you two switched places."

"Those were the days," Brody said. He'd finished his coffee, and now he pushed his chair back, ready to leave. Retrieved his jacket and his hat and put them on. "Guess I'd better get back to the ranch. Shoulder my share of the load, and all that."

"I'll see you tomorrow, at the closing," Tricia said, rising. "Thanks for bringing Valentino home."

She opened the kitchen door, and he stepped out onto the landing. The wind was chilly, laced with tiny flakes of snow, and it ruffled his hair, caused him to raise the collar of his jacket and shiver slightly.

"Thanks for the company," was Brody's belated reply.

He didn't move to descend the outside stairs, and Tricia didn't close the door.

"You *were* trying to fool me, showing up in Conner's truck," she finally said. "Why?"

Brody looked away into that private distance of his again, then looked back. Gave the faintest semblance of that infamous Creed grin. "I wasn't expecting to pass myself off as my brother, if that's what you're thinking," he replied. "I just wanted to know for sure what I already suspected, since you and I ran into each other at the big chili feed that weekend—that you're one of the few people in this world who sees Conner as one person, and me as another."

Of course she remembered the encounter. She'd said, without any hesitation at all, "Hello, Brody."

She reached out now, touched his arm. "See you," she said, just as the landline rang behind her.

Brody grinned, raised one hand in a wave, and took his leave.

Tricia closed the door, turned, and leaped for the phone. Maybe it was Conner calling.

She hoped so.

She hoped *not*.

"Doris and I are going on a cruise," Natty announced, without preamble. "And I need someone to look after Winston while we're gone."

Tricia smiled, forgetting, for the moment, all the complications in her life. A new stepfather was just the beginning, though, of course, she had no intention of laying that on Natty.

"I'd be happy to do that," she told her great-grandmother. "I've missed Winston almost as much as I've missed you."

"I miss you, too, dear," Natty said. "In truth, I wasn't sure you'd still be in Lonesome Bend. I know Seattle beckons."

"Seattle," Tricia said, "is right where I left it. It will keep. Where are you and Aunt Doris going on this cruise of yours?"

"Everywhere," Natty responded happily. She sounded like a teenager instead of a woman in her nineties; living with her sister was clearly good for her. "We sail to Amsterdam next week, out of New York, and then from one Baltic port to another, all the way to St. Petersburg."

"That sounds wonderful," Tricia said, pleased.

"You could come with us," Natty mused. "But, then, I don't know who would take care of Winston if you did. Doris leaves her dogs at a local kennel, but I think my poor cat has had enough to get used to lately, without being sent to some strange place."

Tricia smiled. "Not a problem. How long will you be away?"

"Three weeks," Natty said, after a little pause. "Is that too long?"

"No," Tricia said, thinking of all the times Natty might have gone traveling if she hadn't chosen to stay in Lonesome Bend and help look after her great-grand-daughter every summer instead. "Of course it isn't too long. Take all the time you want." She looked over at Valentino, who had lifted his head to take it all in. Did he know, somehow, that his feline sidekick was coming back for a visit? "Shall I come to Denver to fetch Winston?"

"No, dear," Natty replied, revving up again, in that old familiar way. Full of excitement and anticipation. "Doris's friend's oldest son, Buddy, drives a delivery truck to Lonesome Bend and the surrounding area five days a week. He'll bring Winston directly to your doorstep."

"Okay," Tricia answered. "Good."

"There is one other thing," Natty said.

Tricia felt her shoulders tense up slightly. It was something in her great-grandmother's tone—a certain hesitancy. "What?"

"Carolyn Simmons is moving in downstairs," Natty said. "She's my new renter. Housing is at such a premium in Lonesome Bend, and with Kim and Davis Creed coming home early, she doesn't have anywhere

else to go. I didn't think you'd mind, since the two of
you seem to like each other."

"I don't mind," Tricia confirmed. What she found
hard to accept, though, was the sudden and certain realization that Natty really wasn't planning to come back
home. Ever.

"I kept thinking of how *abandoned* that house would
be, especially if you left. It's never been empty since it
was built, you know. Not for any length of time, anyway. Even when Mama and Papa went to Europe on
their honeymoon trip, my grandmother and great-
grandmother were there to keep the home fires burning." Natty stopped to draw a breath, then rushed on.
"What to do, what to do. That's what I wondered. You
can just imagine. And then, all of the sudden, inspira-
tion! I could offer that nice Carolyn Simmons a sort of
home base. Everybody needs that. In any event, I knew
she was housesitting for Davis and Kim, so I called her
there, and she said she'd just love to stay in a beautiful
house like mine and look after the plumbing and such,
but she *insisted* on paying rent."

Tricia smiled. If she did decide to move back to
Seattle—or elsewhere—at any time, she wouldn't have
to worry about Natty's house. Even when she was minding someone else's place, Carolyn would keep an eye
on the lovely old Victorian.

"I'm glad you found someone," Tricia said.

"Not that you need to be in any kind of hurry to
leave, dear," Natty was quick to say. "After all, one day
the place will be all yours."

"Not too soon, I hope," Tricia replied. She hadn't told
her great-grandmother about the breakup with Hunter—

she hadn't had the chance. And she certainly wasn't going to mention the latest development with Conner.

If it *was* a development.

Sex meant more to a woman than it did to a man, after all. She had to be careful not to read anything into that one incident.

I think you'd be good for my brother, she'd heard Brody say.

"How was your trip to Seattle?" Natty asked. She'd mentioned a few times that her husband had dubbed her Chatty Natty, and it was easy to see why.

"It was fine," Tricia answered, smiling again. "Diana and Paul are busy getting ready to leave for Paris, and of course I enjoyed getting to spend more time with Sasha. I did some shopping, too. Bought some actual *clothes*."

"Did you see Trooper?"

"Hunter," Tricia corrected, with amused patience.

"Hunter, then," Natty conceded, with good-natured *im*patience. "Did you see him?"

"Yes," Tricia said. "I saw him."

"And?"

Tricia laughed. "And we decided to go our separate ways," she answered.

"My dear," Natty told her, "you and Hunter went your separate ways a *long* time ago."

Tricia closed her eyes for a moment. Thought of her mother. And it spilled out of her then, without her ever intending for it to happen. "Do you think I'm like Mom?" she blurted.

Natty was quiet, an unusual situation in and of itself. "In what way, dear?" she asked, at long last. "Physically, you've always been more like your father—"

"You're stalling," Tricia accused. "Diana said I was

only interested in Hunter because he was unavailable, and therefore *safe,* and that allowed me to keep my distance and still claim to be in a relationship. Is that how it was with Mom and Dad?"

Again, Natty hesitated. Then she spoke decisively, but with her usual gentleness. "Your father *was* available. That was the problem, for your mother. I don't think she was comfortable being close to another human being."

Including me, Tricia thought, rueful.

"You mustn't blame Laurel," Natty said quickly. "She was doing the very best she could. She was raised in foster homes, remember. Joe always said she tried, and I believed it, too."

Tricia, standing all this time, made her way to a chair and dropped into it. Shut her eyes tightly against the memory of all those lonely days and nights, when her mother had been working, working, *working,* while her daughter made do with nannies and babysitters and housekeepers.

"Her best wasn't all that terrific, Natty."

"I know that, sweetheart," Natty replied softly. "And it's unfortunate. Nevertheless, there is only one way to deal with something like this, and that's to make up your mind to do better, in your turn, than poor Laurel did."

By that time, Tricia could only nod. She wasn't crying, but she was definitely choked up. She'd resented her mother for so long, yet now she felt sorry for her.

And happy about Harvey.

Once the conversation with Natty was over, Tricia returned to her computer. Made her way back into Laurel's effusive email.

Harvey was a doctor, Laurel had written. He was funny and strong and she loved him with all her heart. They'd gotten married on a recent and apparently brief sabbatical in Barcelona and sincerely hoped Tricia wouldn't mind that she'd missed the wedding.

It had all happened so quickly.

Tricia smiled as she studied the photo for a second time. Then she hit reply and began her response, starting with, "Congratulations!"

After that, well aware that she was procrastinating, Tricia read Diana's emails, both of which were comfortingly mundane, and then Sasha's. The child reported that she was already learning French, so she could start making new friends right after the family arrived in Paris.

Finally, Tricia turned to Hunter's emails. She considered deleting them, unopened, but decided that that would be cowardly. They weren't enemies, after all. Just two people who didn't belong together.

The first message contained a long and involved explanation of how lonely he'd been, after she'd left Seattle. Tricia nodded as she read.

Six more emails followed, all of them much shorter, thankfully, and progressively less woeful. In the final one, clearly an afterthought, he said he wished her well and hoped they could get together for a friendly dinner if and when she returned to Seattle.

Tricia sent off a lighthearted reply and went offline.

Glancing up at the window, she saw that the snow was coming down harder and faster, the flakes feathery and big. Later, she'd walk Valentino again, she decided, and this time, she'd be careful not to let him off his leash before they were safely inside the apartment again.

One thing was for sure, she thought, with a sigh, looking around her small, well-organized kitchen.

She needed something to *do*. The leisurely life was not for her.

It gave her too much time to think.

HIS TRUCK WAS GONE.

Conner stood in the driveway, Tricia's forgotten suitcase at his feet, shaking his head in consternation.

Damn Brody, anyhow. It was just like him to take off in somebody else's rig, without so much as a howdy-do, and leave his own rusted bucket of bolts behind in its place.

Conner picked up the suitcase and gave Brody's old pickup a rueful once-over. The tires looked low, the back bumper was held in place by grimy duct tape, and the rear window was so cracked that the glass was opaque.

He swore under his breath. Brody wasn't a poor man, no more than he was. He could afford to drive a decent vehicle—he was buying the McCall properties for a huge chunk of cash, after all—but, no. A modern-day saddle bum, Brody liked to look the part.

Except when he was heading for Tricia's place, bringing back her dog. He'd wanted *Conner's* truck for that. Conner's clothes and haircut, too.

The realization stung its way through him like a jolt of snake venom. Made him swear again, but with a lot more vehemence this time.

Brody knew he was interested in Tricia. Was it happening again? Was that even possible?

"That's crazy!" Conner said out loud, but he tossed Tricia's suitcase into the back of that beat-up old truck just the same and, seeing that Brody had left the keys in the ignition, he plunked down behind the wheel. After a few grinding wheezes, the engine started, and he pointed that rig toward town.

The drive was short, but it gave him enough time to cool down.

Brody wasn't above betraying him, as history proved, but Tricia was another kind of person entirely. She wasn't like Brody and she wasn't like Joleen, either—she had her share of hang-ups, like everybody else on the planet, but she didn't play games with people's heads.

Or their hearts.

He knew that much about her, if little else.

When he pulled up in front of Natty's place, there was no sign of Brody or of Conner's truck. But Tricia and the dog were in the front yard, Valentino was on his leash and Carolyn was there, too, smiling, with both hands shoved into the pockets of her coat. Flurries of snow swirled around both women, like capes in motion.

Conner sat for a moment, before shutting off the engine and getting out of Brody's sorry-looking rig.

Carolyn and Tricia had been engaged in conversation before, but now they turned to look at him as he crossed the sidewalk and stepped onto the lawn. The difference in their expressions was something to see—Tricia looked shy but pleased, Carolyn stunned. She even took a step backward.

Conner recalled how she'd split herself off from the rest of the people on the trail ride Sunday afternoon, out at the ranch, and realized that she thought he was Brody—probably because of the truck.

He started to speak, wanting to put the woman at

ease by identifying himself, but before he got a word out, Valentino broke free of Tricia's grip on his leash and bolted toward him, barking gleefully, the strand of nylon dragging through the dying grass behind him.

Three feet shy of slamming right into him, the dog leaped through the air like a circus performer and Conner barely had time to brace himself before twenty-plus pounds of squirmy canine landed in his arms.

He laughed, scrambling to hold on to the dog so it wouldn't fall. The wonder was that *both* of them didn't hit the ground.

Tricia hurried over, her eyes shining, her cheeks the same shade of pink they'd been after she'd had the umpteenth orgasm that morning, in his bed. "Valentino!" she scolded lovingly. "Bad dog!"

Conner set Valentino down and shoved a hand through his hair. In his hurry to reach Tricia, he'd forgotten his hat and, come to think of it, his coat, too.

She was exuding a glow that warmed him, though. Through and through.

"I'm sorry," she said, sputtering a little. "I guess Valentino was glad to see you."

"Guess so," Conner agreed.

By that time, Carolyn had reached them. Her hands were still balled up in her jacket pockets, and her eyes were narrowed as she peered at him through the thickening snow.

"Conner?" she said.

He gave her a half salute and a slight grin. "That's me," he affirmed.

Carolyn studied him, studied the old truck at the curb. "I thought—"

"Common mistake," Conner said. He was having trouble looking at anybody or anything besides Tricia.

Damn, she was hot. He wanted her all over again.

He was about to go back to the truck and hoist the suitcase out of the back, but it came to him that such a thing as that could be misunderstood. So he wedged his hands into the pockets of his jeans, like some kid with a confidence problem, and waited to see what would happen next.

"I'd better be going," Carolyn said, breaking the silence. "I'm expecting Kim and Davis at any time, and I want to have a special meal waiting for them when they get home."

Tricia nodded, but she was looking back at Conner. It was as though their gazes had snagged on each other, like fleece on barbed wire, and neither one of them could pull free.

Tricia managed it first. Handing Valentino's leash to Conner, she hurried to catch up with Carolyn, who was already making her way toward her car, head down against the cold wind.

"I'll be in and out tomorrow," Conner heard Tricia say to Carolyn. "Because of the closing and everything. But you have a key, right? When your furniture gets here, you'll be able to let the movers in?"

Carolyn nodded and gave some response Conner didn't hear, over the noise of the worsening weather. Then her eyes slipped past Tricia, past Conner, and touched briefly on Brody's old truck.

Conner couldn't remember the last time he'd seen a sadder look on anybody's face. Someone had done one hell of a number on Carolyn Simmons, and that some-one was most likely Brody.

CHAPTER SEVENTEEN

NATTY'S FRONT DOOR stood ajar, since Carolyn and Tricia had been inside, moments before Conner's arrival, discussing where to put various items of furniture once Carolyn's things had been delivered the next day.

Tricia was definitely looking forward to having a housemate again.

"Let's go in," she told Conner, as Carolyn backed out of the driveway and drove away, giving a jaunty toot of her horn in parting. The woman had obviously been shaken by Conner's arrival—she'd mistaken him for Brody at first, and had all but gone limp with relief when he identified himself. "It's cold out here."

Snowflakes rested on Conner's caramel-colored hair and on his eyelashes. He'd gotten an early start on his five o'clock shadow, too.

Tricia felt the same bone-deep, visceral attraction she had on previous encounters with this enigmatic man. Maybe, she reflected, inviting him into the house hadn't been the best idea; she was still assimilating aspects of that morning's wild lovemaking, emotionally *and* physically, and she needed more time, but she was dangerously amenable to a repeat performance, too.

Conner Creed had a way of making her nerves dance, with no discernible effort.

He handed her Valentino's leash and, for one awful

moment, Tricia thought he was about to tell her he couldn't stay, that he'd just turn right around and leave again.

While that probably would have been the ideal scenario, given her ambivalence about getting romantically involved so soon after cutting Hunter loose, the thought of Conner's going blew through her like a cold and desolate wind.

Did she love Conner, or did she love the *idea* of loving him? Was she ready to be fully present in a relationship, as she *hadn't* been with Hunter, or any of the other men she'd dated over the years?

There were just too many questions. And way too few answers.

But then, in the midst of her private dilemma, Conner gave that tilted grin that warmed her all the way to her toes, and the very landscape of her soul seemed to shift, powerfully and with a series of aftershocks. "You forgot your suitcase when you left this morning," he said. "You and Valentino go on inside, and I'll get the bag out of the truck."

Tricia hesitated, then nodded, and went up the porch steps. Valentino stopped at the top and sat down, looking back at Conner. The animal made a low, mournful sound in his throat.

She thought of Brody's offhanded theory—that Valentino might be doing a little canine matchmaking by running back and forth between her house and Conner's—and sighed. She'd dismissed the idea as silly before, but now she wasn't so sure. Of anything.

She gave Valentino's leash a gentle tug. "Hey, you," she said. "Be a good dog and come inside with me."

But Valentino didn't budge until he saw Conner

turning back, coming up the walk, grasping the handle of Tricia's heavy suitcase and carrying the thing as though its weight could be measured in ounces instead of megatons.

The dog gave a happy little yelp as Conner reached the porch, shifted the suitcase to his left hand and pressed the palm of his right to the small of Tricia's back, guiding her gently but firmly through the doorway.

Now, of course, Valentino cooperated. He was all bright eyes and lolling tongue and wagging tail. Everything was right in his world—because Conner was around.

Tricia sighed. She knew where the dog was coming from on that one.

Standing in the entryway, Conner took in the large, empty parlor where Natty's belongings had huddled together in lace-trimmed little groups for decades.

Tricia stood beside him, feeling a lump gather in her throat. The wallpaper was faded, and speckled with bright spots where paintings and photographs had hung. If Tricia recalled correctly, her great-grandmother had once confessed that she hadn't redecorated since 1959, but it hardly mattered. Carolyn, thrilled that her mail would be coming to an actual address instead of a box at the post office, planned to paint several rooms and sew new curtains for the kitchen windows.

"You sew?" Tricia had asked, impressed.

And Carolyn had laughed and retorted, "Yes. It's not brain surgery, Tricia."

For me, it might as well be, Tricia thought now.

Conner nudged her with an elbow. "Missing Natty?"

"The way I'd miss a severed limb is all," Tricia answered, with a roll of her eyes for emphasis. Since the front door was safely shut now, she leaned down and unfastened Valentino's leash. "Guess what she's up to now."

"I couldn't begin to," Conner said, as the two of them started up the inside staircase. It was narrow, so he paused to let Tricia step in front of him, and Valentino gamely brought up the rear.

"Natty and Doris," Tricia said, stepping into her kitchen and turning to wait for Conner and Valentino to catch up, "are going on a three-week cruise. They leave New York next week, sailing to Amsterdam and then beyond, through the Baltic Sea. They're even going to *St. Petersburg.*"

Conner's voice was gruff and arguably tender when he replied, "Is that something you'd like to do, Tricia? See the world?"

She considered the question. "My mother has the travel bug," she said, "but I think it skipped me entirely. I'm more like my dad, I guess—something of a homebody, really." She bit her lip. "Color me boring," she finished, blushing a little. She hoped it was true, what Natty had always told her about blushing—that it was good for the complexion—because she'd sure been doing a lot of it lately.

"I guess it's a matter of perspective," Conner said, looking around for a place to put the suitcase down and finally just setting it on the floor beside him. "There's a lot to be said for home, if it's a good one."

Tricia didn't know how to answer that. "I could make coffee," she said.

You're a conversational whiz, McCall, mocked a voice in her head.

"I really just stopped by to drop off the suitcase and make sure the dog had stayed put," Conner said.

Tricia's gaze dropped to the bag. "Thanks for not sending it with Brody," she said, and promptly wished she hadn't. Conner didn't react overtly to the mention of his brother's name, but she would have taken it back anyway, if that had been possible.

Conner gave that crooked grin, but the usually vibrant blue of his eyes had darkened to a stormy gray. It wasn't that he looked angry—just unhappy. He started to say something, then stopped himself.

"And for not bringing it in when Carolyn was here," Tricia added quickly, because the moment seemed oddly tenuous. "I wouldn't want people to get the wrong idea."

Conner's grin didn't waver. "Like that we slept together?" he countered.

A small, nervous laugh escaped Tricia. "We *slept?*"

That made him chuckle. "Not that I recall," he said.

They stood looking at each other then, neither one moving or speaking.

Valentino finally wedged himself between them and tilted his head back to gaze up at them in frank adoration.

Conner grinned. "He likes us," he said.

"Ya think?" Tricia teased. Her voice came out sounding small and breathless, though. Even with the dog between them, she felt things stirring around inside her, in response to Conner's nearness.

She took a quick step backward.

His grin softened to an understanding smile. "No pressure, Tricia," he said quietly.

Tricia swallowed. "Right," she said. "No pressure."

He started for the outside door. Valentino trailed after

him, making that whimpery sound again. The message couldn't have been clearer if that dog had suddenly developed the capacity for speech: *Don't go. Please, don't go.*

Conner turned, leaned slightly to pat the top of Valentino's head and muss up his floppy ears a little. "Hey, now," he said, in a low rumble of a voice, "no fair playing the heartstrings, buddy."

It touched Tricia, the way Conner acted with Valentino. The way he seemed to care so much about the animal's feelings.

Tricia held her tongue, afraid she'd say something foolish if she allowed herself to speak just then. Conner lifted his head and looked straight at her. And that was when the something-foolish tumbled out of her mouth, despite her best efforts.

"Stay," she said. Then, flustered, she clarified, "F-for lunch, I mean."

"All right," he replied, after a pause. "But if we're having grilled cheese sandwiches, I'd better make them."

Tricia laughed, relieved. Ridiculously happy. "No worries there," she said. "I'm fresh out of cheese. And butter. And bread. Basically, I'm out of *food*."

"Well, then," Conner answered, with a smile in his eyes, "I reckon we'll have to go out. Maybe hit the drive-through, since the dog's bound to raise a fuss if we leave him behind so we can sit in some restaurant."

"Unthinkable," Tricia said, practically diving for her purse and coat. She hadn't been this excited about fast food since—well—*ever*.

"Assuming that old rattletrap Brody calls a truck

bering her father, how proud he'd been of her, of that drawing, of River's Bend and the Bluebird Drive-in. The original people-person, Joe McCall had enjoyed dealing with campers and moviegoers from late spring until early fall, and even though he'd never made much money, Tricia knew he'd considered himself a success, particularly as a father.

So had she.

"I asked my dad, once upon a time, if he'd ever wished I'd been a boy," she mused quietly, aware that Conner was watching her and listening in that focused way he had, as if everything a person said was important. "And he said he wouldn't trade me for a thousand boys."

"You miss him," Conner observed, standing behind her now, resting his hands on her shoulders.

She nodded. She *did* miss Joe McCall, but she'd done her grieving, reached a place of simple gratitude that he'd been her father. She could celebrate the part he'd played in her life, celebrate his humor and his steadiness and the easy constancy of his love.

Partly because she'd always been so sure of Joe's affection, she was strong enough to let go. Strong enough to move on. Just as he would have wanted her to do.

"I suppose I ought to take all these pictures down," she said, reaching up to lift the map off its hook. She'd be leaving behind all the furniture and office equipment, such as it was, but she wanted to keep the framed photos. So, primarily because she thought she might cry, and she was *sick* of crying, she set the map on the floor, leaning it carefully against the wall, and reached for the shot of Joe on the dock, with the kayak.

Conner let her take down and stack half a dozen

dusty frames before he stopped her, turned her gently around, and pulled her close.

"Shh," he said, even though she wasn't making a sound.

She rested her forehead against the hard flesh of his shoulder—his shirt was still damp from the snow—and slipped her arms loosely around his lean waist. Let out a long, shuddery breath.

"I'm okay," she said, but she didn't pull back out of Conner's embrace. "Really."

Conner curved a finger under her chin and lifted, looking directly into her eyes. "If you want to do this now," he said, indicating the photographs with a slight nod of his head, "I'll help you. If you don't feel up to it, that's okay, too. Brody will understand."

I love you, Conner Creed.

The words rose so suddenly and so vividly in Tricia's mind that, for a split second, she was afraid she'd said them aloud.

She trembled, tried to look away.

But Conner cupped her face in his hands now—she loved the calloused roughness of his palms, in contrast to the near-reverent gentleness of his touch—and held her gaze.

"Tricia?"

"I—I'd rather make a clean break," she said, and was immediately caught up in a backwash of regret. "With River's Bend, I mean," she added anxiously.

Conner chuckled, and his hands remained where they were. "That's a relief," he said. And then he kissed her.

The kiss was deep, and it sent a tingling rush of sweet, vibrant energy through Tricia, from her head to her feet, but it wasn't the same as the passionate, near-frantic kisses they'd exchanged in Conner's bed that morning.

No, this kiss wasn't a prelude to lovemaking. It was an assurance, a promise, as if Conner were telling her, without words, *I'm strong. And I'll be here, when you want somebody to lean on.*

He was the one to end the kiss, as it turned out. He went on holding her, though, and there wasn't any need for words.

After a minute or two, they separated. Conner disappeared into the storage room and returned right away with a couple of large, empty boxes.

They were both quiet as they took down all the pictures, one by one, wrapping them in old newspaper, also from the storeroom, and setting them carefully inside the boxes.

Valentino, meanwhile, lay curled up in front of the stove, blissfully content to be warm, full of cheeseburger and in the presence of his two all-time favorite humans.

Take it slow and easy, you big dumb cowboy, Conner told himself, an hour later, after he'd delivered Tricia and Valentino back home and lugged in both boxes of pictures, along with the framed map.

He wanted nothing more than to spend the night right there in Tricia's apartment—in her *bed,* actually—making love to her. He knew she'd let him stay—it was in her eyes—but he also knew she'd be going against her own better judgment if she did.

"I need time," she'd told him, while they were rattling back from River's Bend in Brody's clunker, the dog looming like a hairy mountain between them. "You know—to figure things out."

"Okay," he'd responded, his hands tightening on the steering wheel. *What* kind *of things?* he'd wanted to ask. Hell, he'd wanted to *demand* an answer. But he'd restrained himself, because this was important.

Tricia was important.

This was no time to go off half-cocked and ruin everything.

So he stood there, coatless, in Tricia's kitchen, with one hand resting on the doorknob, looking his fill of the woman, memorizing the dark, silken fall of her hair, the flushed smoothness of her skin, the glow in her eyes, as hungrily as if the memory would have to last him for a long, long time.

I love you, Tricia McCall, he thought.

She glanced over at Valentino, who was stretched out on his dog bed, with his blue chicken tucked under his muzzle, ready for a nap. So much for Brody's matchmaking theory.

When Tricia's gaze returned to Conner's face, he felt as though the floor had gone soft under the soles of his boots.

"You could stay," she said, very softly.

He wanted to do just that, big-time. But there was a delicate process going on here and, whatever it was, he wasn't about to complicate the situation.

Besides, he was a rancher.

"I've got horses and cattle to feed," he said.

Tricia nodded. They were standing a few feet apart, and he was tempted to backtrack far enough to kiss her, but he didn't give in to the urge, because he knew that if he did that, if he touched his mouth to hers, there would be no leaving after that.

And the livestock *did* need to eat. Six generations of Creeds would roll over in their graves if he let the animals go hungry, even for one night, and he sure as hell couldn't depend on *Brody* to make sure the work got done.

"Go out to dinner with me tomorrow night?" he asked, opening the door a crack to remind himself that he had to leave, whether he wanted to or not. "Without the dog?"

She smiled one of those light-up smiles. "I'd like that," she said.

Pleased beyond all reason, Conner nodded, promised to call her the next day, and forced himself out of the warmth of her home and her presence and into the bitterly cold twilight of a wintry day.

The snowstorm was beginning to look more like a blizzard as Conner nosed that old truck toward home. Though it had worked just fine earlier, when Tricia and Valentino were riding with him, the rig choked and lurched and backfired its way along the nearly invisible highway.

It died at the bottom of the driveway, just inside the main gate, and Conner, wishing he'd remembered his coat, put his head down and slogged uphill toward the light glowing from the ranch house windows.

Brody was in the kitchen, frying up chicken, when Conner came inside, soaked to the skin and shivering.

"Thanks for taking off with my truck," he said, through chattering teeth. He reached for his warmest coat, the leather one lined with sheepskin, and jammed an arm into one of the sleeves. "Yours just gave up the ghost, by the way. Down by the road."

Brody lifted the lid off a pot and peered in at whatever was cooking. "Spuds are almost ready," he said, as though Conner hadn't said anything about the dead truck. "Take off your coat and stay awhile, little brother. I've already done the barn chores. Clint and Juan and I fed the range stock, too."

Conner knew how to be irritated with his brother, but he'd forgotten how to deal with the rough-edged kindness Brody sometimes showed—always at the most unexpected times, of course. The minute a person got to expecting anything from Brody Creed, he'd shoot off in the opposite direction, just to be contrary.

Slowly, stuck for an answer, Conner took off the coat. Hung it on its peg again.

"Davis and Kim got back a little while ago," Brody went on. "You ought to see our old uncle with those two pint-sized dogs they bought. He's crazy about them, right down to the pink bows in their topknots. Even lets them ride in his coat pockets."

Brody was working at the electric stove, but the woodstove was going, too, and Conner went over to it, to warm himself up a little.

"That must have been a sight to see," he said.

"It was." Brody laughed, shook his head, went on turning pieces of chicken over in the skillet. The food smelled half again better than good. "Kim's complaining that they're supposed to be her dogs, not Davis's."

There was a brief silence.

"Since when do you cook?" Conner asked.

This was as close to a civil conversation as he could remember having with Brody since before Joleen. It felt fragile, like something that could break apart at any time.

"I like to eat," Brody replied. "Therefore, I cook."

Conner felt his back molars clamp together. He unclamped them so he could talk. "Why'd you take my truck?" he asked for the second time.

Brody looked at him over one shoulder. The chicken sizzled and the pot lids rattled and the whole setup was homey as all get-out.

"I wanted to see if Tricia could tell us apart," Brody replied, his tone easy, like his manner.

Brody's blunt honesty could be as much of a surprise as his kindness, and Conner was taken aback.

"She can," Brody added, with a wicked grin. "Fancy truck or no fancy truck, she knew I wasn't you."

Conner swallowed hard, warning himself to be watchful, not to let himself be suckered in. His brother was, after all, a master at hooking fools and reeling them in for the kill. Still, it made something leap inside Conner, hearing those words. Knowing that, to Tricia at least, he wasn't interchangeable with his twin.

"What if she *hadn't* known?" he finally asked. His teeth had stopped chattering, but he sounded hoarse, like he was coming down with something. "What if Tricia had thought you were me? What would you have done?"

Brody pushed the skillet off the burner and turned to face Conner squarely. "Nothing," he said, quietly but with a tinge of anger. His jaw worked, then he ground out, "*Dammit*, Conner, you're my brother."

"You were my brother when I thought Joleen and I were going to get married and raise a family together," Conner heard himself say, his tone mild and matter-of-fact. "How was that different?"

"I was a kid," Brody growled. "So were you, and so was Joleen. But she knew, even if you *didn't*, little brother, that both of you were too young to think about marriage, let alone making babies."

Conner wasn't cold anymore. He walked over to the table, hauled back a chair, the legs scraping loudly against the floor, and sat down. His shirt and jeans felt clammy against his skin, and he would have sworn that even his socks were wet.

"I trusted you," he said, without looking at Brody.

"And you were *right* to trust me, brother, because I didn't sell you out. Not with Joleen or anybody else."

The truth of that hit Conner like a wall of water. *Cold* water.

"All this time, you let me think you and Joleen—"

Lightning fast, Brody took hold of the front of Conner's shirt and yanked him to his feet. They were practically nose to nose, Brody already furious, Conner getting there fast. In a moment, they'd be tying into each other, right there in the kitchen, butting heads like a couple of rutting bulls.

"You believed I'd do something that low-down and chicken-shit," Brody seethed. "So don't go talking to me about selling out!"

Conner knocked Brody's hand away, but the fight had gone out of him and it must have been plain to see. He felt that old-time sensation of having switched bodies with his brother, of seeing himself through Brody's eyes. "You could have denied it!" he rasped.

"I was too *insulted* to deny anything!" Brody yelled. "I shouldn't have *had* to deny it, because you, Conner, *you of all people,* ought to have known what the deal was!"

"You didn't go to bed with Joleen," Conner said, in a slow, let-me-get-this-straight voice.

"I sure as hell didn't," Brody snapped, breathing hard but no longer yelling. He paused, shoved a hand through his hair in exactly the same way Conner had done, and then he grinned. "Not back then, anyhow," he clarified.

Conner laughed.

Brody laughed.

"Let's have ourselves some fried chicken," he told Conner. Then he frowned. "Maybe you ought to change clothes, first, though. It would be a hell of a note if you came down with pneumonia just when we're getting so we can stand to be in the same room."

Conner nodded his agreement and left the kitchen for his room upstairs. The bedcovers were still tangled from his and Tricia's lovemaking, and he caught the faintest scent of her skin as he headed for the bureau.

Armed with a pair of jeans and a warm sweatshirt, he went on to the bathroom, set the clothes on the counter, stripped off what he was wearing, and stepped into multiple sprays of hot water, coming at him from every direction.

Because he was hungry, because there was so much to tell Brody and so much to ask him about, Conner made quick work of his shower, dried off, dressed again and swiped a comb through his hair a couple of times.

By the time he got downstairs, he was beginning to think he might have imagined the confrontation with Brody, but there was his brother, with the table set properly and the food steaming fragrantly in the middle.

"All you need," Conner told Brody, in order to lighten the moment a little, "is a ruffled apron."

Brody chuckled, hauled back a chair. "Don't push

your luck, little brother," he said. "I might have decided
to let you live, but the jury is still out on whether or not
I kick your ass from here to next week."

Conner sat down at his own place, picked up his
fork and stabbed three pieces of chicken onto his plate.
"You're welcome to try that at any time," he said affably. He looked the whole meal over again, and shook his
head. "You even made gravy and mashed the spuds," he
marveled. "What else can you do, brother? Darn socks?
Make curtains out of flour sacks?"

"Keep pushing it," Brody drawled, but there was
laughter in his eyes.

For a while, they ate in silence. This was the first real
meal Conner could remember having at that table since
Kim and Davis moved to their own place up the road.

"You've been in prison all this time," Conner speculated. "And they put you on kitchen duty. That's the
big mystery."

"There *is* no big mystery," Brody said, and now his
eyes were solemn and his tone was serious. "I was on
the rodeo circuit, I told you that."

"I follow the rodeo circuit," Conner pointed out, considering a fourth piece of chicken and deciding against
it because he was full to the gills. "I saw your name
once or twice, Brody, but not often enough to account
for *ten years* of being gone."

Brody sighed. "You are not going to leave this alone,
are you?"

"No," Conner said. "I'm not."

That was when Brody told him about the woman,
and the boy, and the accident that had taken their lives.

CHAPTER EIGHTEEN

THE NEXT DAY, in the small conference room at Lonesome Bend's one and only bank, Tricia held the cashier's check in both hands and stared at it in awe. All the papers had been signed and witnessed, and now River's Bend and the RV park and the Bluebird Drive-in belonged to Brody Creed.

Suddenly, she was free. Suddenly, she had *so many choices*.

Of course, she had to settle the few debts Joe had left behind, and pay off the small balance on her one credit card, and there would be taxes to pay. Even so, she was *rolling* in it.

Possibilities flashed through her mind—none of them were new, but they were all more substantial, now that she didn't have to live from hand to mouth.

She thought about Paris, about not only visiting the City of Light, but living there for a while.

She thought about Seattle, that bustling, busy place where something was *happening,* everywhere and all the time.

She thought about a gallery, with her name over the door in elegant gold script, a small but tasteful storefront full of vibrant art of all sorts and mediums.

But mostly she thought about Conner.

There were two worlds in Tricia's personal universe

now, it seemed—one with Conner in it, and one with-out. Should she choose the world her brain wanted—freedom, counterbalanced by the inevitable times of loneliness—or summon all her courage and follow her heart? Allow herself to take the terrible risk of loving and being loved in return?

Tricia shook off the nagging questions. She had things to do, starting with depositing the funds that would change everything, no matter *what* she decided to do in the end.

Brody, dressed to the nines in a perfectly tailored gray suit and a spiffy tie, looked wan and a little hollow-eyed as he watched her tuck the check back in its envelope and slip that into her purse.

"Buyer's remorse?" she asked, with a little smile.

"No," Brody replied, shoving his hands into his pockets. "Nothing like that."

She should get going. Head back to Natty's and help Carolyn supervise the placement of her furniture and unpack. Figure out what to wear for her dinner date with Conner that night.

Oh, and what to do with the rest of her life. Add *that* to the list.

But she liked Brody Creed, and she was grateful to him, so she tarried.

"Thanks," she said, putting out her hand to Brody.

He smiled and shook it, very businesslike.

She squinted at him. "Are you all right?" she asked, very quietly, so the bankers and Carla, still chatting in the conference room, wouldn't overhear.

Brody gave a raspy chuckle. "Conner and I were up pretty late last night, talking things through," he explained. "It'll be a long road back, but at least we're on the way."

"That's good," she said, remembering their conversation at her kitchen table, after Brody brought Valentino home from the ranch. She knew it troubled Conner, maybe even grieved him, to be estranged from his only brother, though he hadn't talked about it much, at least to her.

"It's good," Brody agreed. "But we went over some rough ground, my brother and me." He paused, and the smile drained out of his eyes, replaced by a dark expression she couldn't put a name to. "It's some consolation to know that Conner feels like he's been dragged backwards through a knothole, just as I do."

Tricia stood on tiptoe, kissed his cheek. "Give it some time," she said. "Things are bound to get better if you don't give up."

"If you say so," Brody joked, but the change in his eyes indicated that something else was going on beneath the surface here.

"Are you moving in over at River's Bend today?" she asked, hoping to lighten the mood.

"Yeah," Brody replied. He smiled again, but there was an edge to it. He nodded, as if to say goodbye, and half turned away from her, only to turn back. "Tricia?"

She waited. Glanced past him to the door of the conference room; she could see Carla's shadow through the frosted glass. Any moment now, the others would join them.

Brody gave a deep, ragged sigh. Ran a hand through his hair. "I might be way out of line here," he said hoarsely, "but there's something I need to say. About you and Conner, I mean, and whatever is or isn't going on between you."

Inwardly, Tricia stiffened. Outwardly, she probably appeared calm. "What's that?"

"Don't hurt him," Brody said. With a nod, he indicated the purse she held, an oblique reference to the cashier's check inside, most likely. "You have a lot of options now. If your plans don't include Conner, then I'd appreciate it if you'd back off and leave him alone."

Heat suffused Tricia's face. Carla, still chatting with the bank officials who'd overseen the closing, started to open the door.

"You were right before, Brody," Tricia said evenly, careful to keep her voice down. "You *are* out of line. By a country mile."

With that, she turned on her heel and stormed along the corridor, practically erupting into the main lobby, where the tellers stood at their windows, between customers and therefore watching her with interest.

Tricia stopped, took a deep breath, released it slowly. *Be calm,* she told herself.

Then she marched over to the nearest teller, opened her purse and took out the envelope with the seven-figure check inside.

"I'd like to make a deposit, please," she said.

Brody caught up to her outside, several minutes later, as she was about to get into her Pathfinder.

"Tricia, wait," he said, and he looked pained.

She glared at him. This was one of the biggest days of her life so far, and he'd nearly spoiled it by implying that she might be jerking Conner around, encouraging him when she had no intention of following through. "What?" she snapped, begrudging him even that one word.

"I might not be the most tactful person in the world," Brody said.

"Maybe not," Tricia agreed, settling herself in the driver's seat and fastening her seat belt with a noisy click. She couldn't have shut the door if she'd wanted to, because Brody was in the way.

"I'm sorry," he said.

"Oh," Tricia mocked, with a sweeping gesture of one hand, "*well, then.* That changes everything!"

"Give me a chance, here," Brody responded. "I'm trying to look out for my bullheaded brother, that's all. Lonesome Bend is a small town, Tricia, and there's a lot of talk going around. Is it true that you're heading back to Seattle as soon as that check of mine clears the bank? That there's some guy waiting for you there?"

All the steam went out of her.

"There's no guy," she said softly. "Not anymore."

"What about leaving town? Is that what you mean to do?"

Tricia was quiet for a long time. Then she turned the key in the ignition, switched on the heater. With the door open to the cold, much of which seemed to be coming from Brody rather than the environment, the benefits were limited. "I don't know," she finally said. "There are a lot of things to consider."

"Here's another one for you," Brody said evenly, gripping the framework of the door and leaning in a little way. "Conner cares about you. It might be a while before he gets around to admitting that, to himself *or* to you, but, believe me, he *does* care. He's a good man, through and through, and he's smart as all get-out, but game playing is something he just doesn't understand— when he falls for somebody, he falls hard. He's rock-solid, the original straight shooter, the kind of guy most women think isn't even out there anymore."

"Are you finished, Brody?" Tricia's flippant tone was a bluff. Hurting Conner in any way, shape or form had never crossed her mind, but it *was* true that she might leave Lonesome Bend. After all, without River's Bend to oversee, she was pretty much at loose ends. Money or no money, she needed something to occupy her days or she'd go crazy.

"Just one more thing," Brody finally answered, stony-faced. "If you break Conner's heart, he'll be alone for the rest of his life, because he's not the sort to settle."

With that, Brody stepped back.

Trembling a little, Tricia shut the door.

And then she just sat there for several minutes, waiting until she felt calm enough to drive home.

CONNER SPENT THE morning on the range, with Clint and Juan and some of the extra hands Brody had hired on, setting up feed stations for the cattle and horses. Just before noon, he rode back to the ranch house, his coat collar raised against the icy wind, his hat pulled down low over his face. The sky churned with low-bellied clouds, gunmetal gray and, in his opinion, fixing to give birth to the perfect storm.

Kim and Davis drove up in their going-to-town car just as Conner was dismounting in front of the barn. He waited, speaking quietly to the horse, and grinned wide when his uncle eased his big frame from behind the wheel and got out, settling his hat on his head as he approached.

Two tiny dog faces looked out of the deep, wool-lined pockets of Davis's coat, bright-eyed and clearly enjoying the ride. And damn if they didn't have little pink bows on the tops of their heads, just as Brody had said.

The sight was so incongruous that Conner had to laugh. Kim, glowing with happiness as usual, looked Conner's way and shook her head with amusement.

Davis, so comfortable with his own masculinity that it probably wouldn't have occurred to him to be embarrassed to be seen with a pair of pink-bowed pocket dogs, grinned. He and Conner shook hands, their customary way of greeting each other after a separation of any length. "I hear Brody went ahead and bought Joe McCall's property," Davis said.

Conner nodded. The chill bit at the edges of his ears, even with his hat on, and he cast a wary look up at the fitful sky. "He's in town finalizing the deal right now," he said. Tricia would be at the closing, too, of course. He was glad for her, glad for Joe, who had held on through thick and thin, having set his heart on leaving something behind for his "little girl."

"Is the coffee on?" Kim wanted to know, reaching into Davis's pockets, one by one, and collecting the dogs. Holding them up to her face to nuzzle them between their perked-up ears. "If not, we'll make some, won't we?" she asked the pups.

Davis rolled his eyes, but his love for his wife was almost palpable.

He watched her fondly as she headed for the house, being as much at home there as she was at the other place, then walked alongside Conner as he led his horse into the barn and removed the animal's saddle and bridle inside the stall.

Davis brought a couple of flakes of hay and tossed them into the feeder, while Conner gave the gelding a quick brushing-down. It was an ingrained habit, something he always did after a ride and rarely thought about.

That day, though, he was jumpy as a five-year-old on Christmas Eve—he'd be taking Tricia out for dinner that night—so he made short work of the grooming.

The other horses nickered companionably as he and Davis left the barn. A few enormous flakes of snow were drifting down.

Conner squared his shoulders, adjusted his hat again.

Inside the kitchen, Kim had all the lights on, and she'd started a fire in the cookstove while the coffee was brewing. The little dogs peeked out of a bottom drawer in the china cabinet, keeping a close eye on the proceedings.

"Are you sure those critters are dogs," Conner teased, grinning at Kim, "and not some kind of fancy rodents?"

Kim made a face at him, then laughed. "They're Yorkshire terriers," she said.

For as long as Conner could remember, she'd been like that, lighthearted and easy to get along with, full of mischief and uncomplicated joy, taking things as they came and making the best of the bad as well as the good.

It must have been a disappointment to Kim, Conner thought now, that she and Davis had never had a family of their own, but if it was, she'd never let on. She'd loved him and Brody and Steven full-out, like any mother.

Davis chuckled and hung up his hat, then his coat. "Wait till you hear their names," he told Conner.

The pups spilled out of the bureau drawer and trotted over to sniff at Davis's boots. They were pretty damn cute, all right, but Conner was worried that he might step on them. To make sure that didn't happen, he crouched and scooped them up, one in each hand, and both of them commenced to licking his face as though he'd used gravy for aftershave that morning.

"One's called Smidgeon," Davis went on, "and one's called Little Bit." His tone was teasing, for Kim's benefit, but there was a certain pride in his gaze, too. The look on his uncle's face reminded Conner of Steven, when he'd brought Melissa and Matt and the babies to the ranch to show them off.

"Smidgeon and Little Bit," Conner mused, with a wink for Kim. "Isn't that redundant?"

"Your uncle," Kim said dryly, eyes still twinkling, "wanted to name them Puffy and Fluffy. I had no choice but to intervene."

Conner put the dogs down carefully and looked over at Davis. *"Puffy and Fluffy?"*

Davis colored up a little, under his jawline. "I haven't had a lot of practice at naming dogs," he said. "The last one already had a name when we got him."

Conner laughed.

The dogs explored the kitchen, inch by inch, then leaped back into the bureau drawer, snuggled up in a furry little pile and went to sleep.

Kim poured coffee and the three of them sat at the table, sipping the brew, letting the heat thaw the marrow of their bones.

They talked, mainly just about catch-up stuff. Sure enough, Kim confirmed, Steven and Melissa were coming home for Thanksgiving, and of course they were bringing the kids.

Brody showed up, driving Conner's truck because his own was still down by the gate, the engine deader than a doornail, just as Davis and Kim were about to take Smidgeon and Little Bit out of the drawer and head for town. Kim thought they ought to stop by the supermarket and stock up on nonperishables, in case the storm turned out to be a humdinger.

"Was it something I said?" Brody joked, looking on wryly as Davis tucked the yawning pups into his coat pockets.

Kim laughed and kissed his cheek before stepping back to give him the once-over. "That's quite the suit," she remarked. "If Conner hadn't told us you were at the bank, sealing a real-estate deal, I'd think you were about to get hitched."

Brody chuckled, but the look in his eyes was out-and-out somber. "I can't wait to get out of it," he said, and disappeared into his bedroom.

When he came out, wearing jeans and a T-shirt, Kim and Davis and the pups were gone, and Conner was standing at the sink, a fresh cup of coffee in one hand, watching the snow come down.

The flakes were thick as goose feathers, and there wasn't much space between them now. In fact, he could barely see the barn.

Brody drained the carafe of the coffeemaker into a mug and sighed. "Damn," he said. "I could do without a blizzard right now."

Conner turned his head. Studied his brother's grim profile. "Join the club," he said, with a halfhearted effort at a chuckle. "We've got months of feed-hauling ahead of us, if we want to keep the range stock alive."

Brody met his gaze. "You're gonna kill me," he said, out of the blue.

Conner frowned. "Maybe," he allowed solemnly, "but I guess I'd like to know why before I go ahead and do it."

Brody tried for a smile, but it didn't work. "I meant well," he said.

Conner felt a small muscle bunch up in his cheek, then wriggle itself loose again. He knew this speech had something to do with Tricia, since Brody had just been with her at the bank.

"What?" he rasped out.

Brody gave a heavy sigh and made his way to the table, hobbling a little, as if he'd been thrown from one too many bad-ass bulls during his rodeo career. Which he probably had.

"Sit down, Conner," he said, still gruff.

Conner nearly tipped his chair over, pulling it back from the table. But he sat.

Brody was across from him, but still within throttling distance if it came to that. "As I said," he reiterated, "I had the best of intentions."

Conner didn't say anything. He just waited, flexing his fingers into fists, relaxing them again.

Brody plunked his elbows on the table and splayed his hands over his face long enough to bust out with a loud sigh, as though he were the beleaguered one.

"I might have interfered in your—relationship," he finally confessed.

Annoyance sang through Conner, electrified him. "What the hell is *that* supposed to mean?" he demanded, his voice dangerously quiet.

"I told Tricia not to hurt you."

Conner slammed his palms down hard on the table. It was a good thing those little dogs were gone, because he was about to go off like a geyser. They'd have been scared right out of their rhinestone collars and their itsy-bitsy hair ribbons.

"You did *what?*"

Brody looked chagrined, but if a fight broke out, he'd hold his own, Conner knew, as always. "You know how people talk—"

"Brody, I swear to God—"

"Joleen's mother heard it at Bingo Friday night," Brody said. "All about how Tricia has been seeing this yahoo in Seattle for years, just waiting to unload Joe's property so she could get the hell out of here—"

"Joleen's mother heard it at Bingo Friday night," Conner repeated, in a tone that didn't begin to express his disbelief.

"Okay," Brody allowed, "so maybe I overreacted a little."

"Maybe you should have kept your nose out of my business," Conner speculated, after unclamping the hinges of his jawbones.

"I'm sorry," Brody said. "I wish I'd stayed out of it, but I was afraid—after the way you took the breakup with Joleen, I was afraid you'd never take a chance on a woman again, if things went wrong with Tricia—"

Conner swore. And that siphoned off some of the fury.

"I was a *kid* then, Brody. Yeah, I thought losing Joleen was the end of the world, especially losing her to you. But I also thought professional wrestling and Jeanine Clark's boobs were for real."

A grin tugged at the corner of Brody's mouth, and he didn't look quite so grim as before. "Jeanine Clark's boobs weren't real?" he asked, widening his eyes a little.

Conner gave a snort of laughter, but his amusement didn't last any longer than the rush of anger had. He felt—numb.

Neither one of them spoke for a while. They just breathed, and drank their coffee, and occasionally glanced over at the snow tumbling past the windows, thicker and thicker. Wood crackled in the antique cookstove, and the lights flickered and Conner wondered if he'd be able to get to Tricia's place on anything but cross-country skis or a snowmobile.

The county workers wouldn't start plowing the roads until they were sure the snow was going to stick, and even when they did, they'd be working on the far side of Lonesome Bend, keeping the main highway clear.

He pushed back his chair and stood. "If I don't get back in time," he told Brody, "feed the horses and make sure the water doesn't freeze up out in the barn."

Brody opened his mouth, shut it again.

Conner crossed to the row of pegs by the door and put on his hat and coat. "Keys," he said, since Brody had been the last one to drive his rig.

"In the ignition," Brody answered, rising from his chair.

"Figures," Conner muttered, on his way out.

He was halfway to his truck when Brody called to him from the doorway. He turned just in time to catch his flying cell phone in one hand.

There couldn't have been more than twenty feet between them, and yet Brody was just a shape, framed in a big square of light.

"Be careful," he said, in a low shout. "And call if you need help."

Conner nodded, dropped the cell into his coat pocket, smiling briefly because it made him think of Davis and the dogs.

Once he was inside the truck, though, with the engine

going and the windshield covering over with snow between every swipe of the wipers, he was getting worried—and not just about Tricia.

Were Davis and Kim on the road? He didn't figure they'd had time to wheel a cart through the supermarket, load up the groceries and get home again, but he supposed it was possible, if they'd decided to hurry. Practically every winter, somebody ran off the road when the snow was heavy or the roads were iced over or both, and there wasn't always a happy ending.

Conner fumbled for his phone. Calling either Davis or Kim was always a crapshoot—Davis thought cell phones were more hindrance than help, as he put it, and Kim's was usually in her other purse. That is, the one she wasn't carrying.

Covering about a foot a minute, because of limited visibility, Conner keyed in his uncle's number. He got voice mail.

He tried getting in touch with Kim. Ditto.

He called their house, hoping they'd changed their minds about going to town and driven home. Voice mail again.

He swore under his breath and told himself the last thing the world needed was another fool out driving around in this weather, but he kept going, stopping now and then to reorient himself to the disappearing road. It was a good thing he'd lived in that country all his life, driven across it thousands of times.

Nearly an hour passed before Conner got to town, a trip that rarely took more than fifteen minutes, even in a hard and slippery rain. When he spotted the bright lights of the local supermarket off to one side, he cranked the wheel in that direction.

He cruised up and down the rows of cars and pickup trucks until he came to Kim and Davis's rig. Davis had the window rolled down, and fumes billowed from the tail pipe, but the tires wouldn't grab and he wasn't going forward or backward.

Conner pulled up alongside, pointed in the opposite direction, and buzzed down his own window. A whiff of burnt rubber met him, along with a face full of snow.

"I knew we should have brought the truck!" Davis grumbled.

Conner laughed, shoved open his door and held his hat on as he approached. Bent to look across at Kim, who looked as worried as he'd ever seen her, the two tiny dogs huddled together on her lap, shivering.

Kim brightened at the sight of him. "We're saved," she told the dogs. "Conner's here."

Davis was indignant, probably at the suggestion that any woman or critter in his care would need saving by Conner or anybody else. "Hell, Kim," he growled, "we're in the middle of town, not out on the range somewhere."

"Can you take us home?" Kim asked Conner, ignoring her husband. "Davis can stay here *in the middle of town* if he wants to, but Smidgeon and Little Bit and I want to take our kibble and our canned goods and hightail it for the ranch."

Conner answered by going around to the other side of the car and helping Kim out. She'd tucked the dogs inside her coat, and they looked out over the folds of her lapels, transfixed by the snow.

By the time Conner had settled his aunt and her pups in the backseat of his extended-cab truck, Davis had given up on getting the car moving and opened up the trunk to transfer the groceries.

Neither he nor Conner said much while they hustled the bags into the back of Conner's rig—they'd have had to yell to hear each other over the howl of the wind, and there was no point in that—but Davis had plenty to say once they were inside again.

"I told Kim before we even left our place that we ought to take the truck, because I didn't like the looks of that sky, and there were already a few flurries coming down, but *no*. She said her car hadn't been started up in a while, what with our being away from home and all, and we ought to take that to town, blow the cobwebs out of the motor—"

"Oh, Davis," Kim said sweetly, from the backseat, "do shut up."

The air seemed to throb inside that truck, as if there were going to be an explosion, and Conner braced himself for it.

Instead of blowing up, though, Davis just laughed. "Sometimes," he joked, "I wonder if this relationship is going to last."

"You're stuck with me, cowboy," Kim told him, leaning forward to pat her husband's shoulder.

Conner let out his breath. It was no big revelation—married people argued, even when they loved each other—but it struck him as a good thing to remember.

He took Davis and Kim as far as the main ranch house—the road to their place was all uphill and it was narrow. Too treacherous to travel over in the dark.

Brody came out to help unload the grub from the back of the truck, and Davis hustled Kim and the pups toward the house. When Conner started back to his truck—the snow was up to his knees now—Brody objected.

"Tricia's *all right*." He probably shouted the words, but the wind carried them away.

"I need to know that for myself," Conner yelled in response.

"You could call her, you dumb-ass!" Brody hollered, looking as though he might try to physically restrain Conner from getting into that truck and heading back down the road toward Lonesome Bend. "Did you ever think of that?"

Conner *had* tried to call Tricia, both on her landline and her cell. No luck with either one. And he wasn't going to take the time to explain, because the storm was getting worse, not better.

He shut the door and backed up, the tires grabbing as the ones on Davis's car had earlier, in the icy parking lot.

And Brody jumped right onto the running board and pressed his face to the window.

Conner lowered the window.

"Are you crazy?!" Brody demanded, the instant he could. "You're damn lucky you made it to town and back the *first* time—"

Conner planted one hand in the center of his brother's chest and pushed.

Brody went sprawling backward into a snowbank, came up ready to yank Conner out of that truck and pound on him, but the tires finally got down to solid ground and grabbed, and Conner was on the move.

It took twice as long to get to town this time, and the lights were out in the supermarket as he passed. Except for Davis and Kim's car, the lot was empty.

He made his way over buried roads to Natty's place, working mostly from memory because he could hardly see.

The old Victorian house was dark, like all the others he'd passed, and Conner thought about the wood he'd delivered, hoping Tricia had at least built a fire to keep herself and Valentino warm.

The wind fought him all the way to the outside stairway. The steps had already vanished beneath an even layer of snow, a perfect, gleaming slant of white.

"Conner!"

He turned, looked behind him, on the off chance that he'd heard correctly, over the screech of the wind. Sure enough, Tricia was standing on Natty's porch, a flashlight in her hand.

"This way!" she shouted, beckoning.

Conner headed to the porch steps, which had been covered, like the ones leading up to the apartment, and slogged his way up them. In the entryway, Valentino was waiting to greet him, wagging his whole rear end instead of just his tail.

"What are you doing here?" Tricia asked, setting aside the flashlight to peel Conner's coat off him.

He was wildly glad to see her, find her safe. "We had a date," he quipped, shaking off his hat before hanging it on the doorknob behind him. "Remember?"

She pushed at his chest with both hands, but she was smiling and her eyes glistened in the near darkness. Inside Natty's former parlor, a fire blazed on the hearth and there were a few candles burning here and there, on top of boxes and what looked like teetery TV trays.

He remembered that Carolyn was moving in, looked

around for her as he headed for the fireplace. "Where's your roommate?" he asked.

"Staying at the Skylark Motel," Tricia answered, glowing like a goddess in the light of the fire and the candles. "She called about two seconds before the phones went dead—her car couldn't make it through the snow, and she decided not to risk freezing to death by trying to walk here."

"Good decision," Conner said. He was starting to get the feeling back in his fingers.

Tricia came to stand beside him. Rested her head against the outside of his upper arm. "I can't believe you were idiotic enough to drive all the way here in this god-awful weather," she said.

"Actually," Conner replied, slipping an arm around her waist, "I was idiotic enough to do it twice. Davis and Kim got stranded at the supermarket, and I took them back to the ranch."

She pulled away just far enough to look up at him. The firelight danced in her eyes and sparkled in her hair. "And then you came back here? Why?"

He bent his head, tasted her mouth. "Because you're here," he said, breathing the words as she melted against him. "Nothing could have kept me away."

CHAPTER NINETEEN

Because you're here. Nothing could have kept me away.

Those words, like Conner's kiss, reverberated through her. She rested her cheek against his chest when it was over, sighed softly. His arms were around her, easy and safe.

It came back to her then, some of what Brody had said to her that day, at the bank. *Conner cares for you—when he falls for somebody, he falls hard—he's rock-solid, the original straight shooter, the kind of guy most women think isn't even out there anymore.*

Conner propped his chin on top of her head. "I hear you had a little run-in with my brother this morning," he said, as if he'd been reading her mind.

She tilted her head back, looked up Conner. "I'm over it," she said honestly. "Brody loves you. I realized pretty quickly that he was only trying to look out for you."

Conner chuckled. The sound echoed through Tricia, just as the kiss had, just now. "Yeah," he agreed. "I figured that out, after I got past the desire to do him bodily harm."

Tricia laughed, still gazing into that strong, handsome face. Conner was integrity and commitment personified; if the man signed on for something, he was in for the duration.

Tricia's doubts about a future with Conner Creed had

been slipping away all day, the victims of quiet logic, but as she stood there, drinking in the sight and the feel of him, Tricia said goodbye to the last of her hesitancy.

As frightening as it was, she loved Conner. Furthermore, she would *always* love him. He was literally part of her, and while she would certainly survive without him, possibly even thrive, she'd still be shortchanging herself, settling for less than she might have had. Less than she might have *given*.

"What do we do now?" she asked him.

But Conner wasn't taking the long view, as she was. Not yet, anyway.

"Lay a blanket or two on the floor in front of this fireplace and make love like a caveman and his woman in mating season?"

Again, she laughed, a throaty sound, tinged with mischief. "I thought we had a *dinner* date," she said. "Not one for hot, wet, unbridled sex."

He chuckled, held her closer, nibbled at her lips again. The fire burning on that hearth had nothing on the one Conner had ignited inside her. "With any luck," he murmured, "our dinner date would have evolved into 'hot, wet, unbridled sex' anyhow."

"But we haven't *had* dinner," Tricia stalled, just to prolong the anticipation a little.

Conner was already unbuttoning the practical flannel shirt she'd put on after she returned from the closing, in order to help Carolyn with all the moving-in chores. With the storm getting worse by the moment, she'd written off the date with Conner as a lost cause.

And now here he was. Seducing her. Making her want him—*need* him. Her heart raced, and her breath grew so short that she was afraid she'd hyperventilate.

He moved the shirt back off her shoulders, weighed her lace-covered breasts gently in his rough, rancher's hands before deftly popping the front catch of her bra, setting her free. Her nipples hardened instantly, not from the chill, but in response to Conner's hungry appreciation of her partially unveiled body.

The bra went, too, after that, sailing off into the surrounding darkness.

Tricia turned her head, overwhelmed by this new and deeper vulnerability. She and Conner had made love before, of course, but this was different. As fantastic as the first round of sex had been, she'd been responding physically but struggling the whole time not to respond *emotionally.* She'd held back some vital part of herself, even at the frenetic height of satisfaction. Now, she was offering him everything—not just her body, but *everything.*

She was gloriously terrified, like an astronaut about to step out of some craft into deep space, except that, in this instance, she had no special NASA-designed suit to sustain her, no line to tether her to the last vestige of a world she knew and understood.

"Conner," she whispered, closing her eyes, letting her head fall back as he toyed with her nipples, chafed them with the sides of his thumbs, preparing them, preparing *her* for incomprehensible pleasure. "Oh, Conner."

He kissed her again, lightly this time around, the tip of his tongue exploring the corners of her mouth, promising a deeper, wilder conquering, moments from now. Or minutes, or maybe even hours.

"Wh-what about—protection?" she asked.

Conner was unsnapping her jeans, unzipping them, pushing them down, right along with her panties. He dropped to one knee, worked off her shoes and socks, freed her from the last of her clothing.

She stood bare before him. *Cavewoman by firelight,* she thought fancifully, breathlessly, fully aware of Conner in every part of her.

Aware, too, of the question suspended between them.

"Conner," she repeated, with the last of her resistance, the last of her strength.

"I brought something," he said, and then he took her into his mouth and suckled, and she was utterly, completely, deliciously lost.

Long before Conner allowed Tricia to reach that first, desperately needed orgasm, her knees threatened to give out, and he lowered her to the rug, consumed her with his mouth, his hands, his eyes.

At some point, he must have shed his own clothes, though Tricia had been too delirious to notice until he was kneeling astride her, magnificently naked, his erection huge.

She watched, dazed, as he put on a condom and lowered himself to her.

"I love you, Tricia," he said, and even though both of them were trembling with need by then, his voice was even, his words clear.

Aroused to a state of primitive need, Tricia answered him with all the honesty in her. "I love *you,* Conner Creed."

He delved inside Tricia, wringing a shout of hoarse, welcoming joy from her. "Will—you—marry—me?" he gasped, punctuating the sentence with hard, deep strokes.

Tricia, already teetering on the verge, came then, laughing and sobbing and shouting, "Yes!" all at once.

After the lovemaking—*long* after the lovemaking—Tricia and Conner dined on peanut butter and jelly sandwiches, partially dressed and sitting cross-legged in front of the fire, facing each other.

Valentino, hoping for a bite of one of their sandwiches at first, finally settled for a ration of kibble and went back to sleep.

"Some dinner date," Conner said, his eyes twinkling.

Tricia smiled, raised her shoulders in a slight shrug. She was wearing Conner's shirt, with only a few strategic buttons fastened. "I'm not complaining," she said.

He laughed, raised his iced-tea tumbler, a third filled with wine he'd rummaged for upstairs, in the dark, and clinked it against Tricia's jelly glass. "Me, either," he replied.

Tricia took a sip of wine, set her glass aside, and gazed sidelong into the fire. "About that marriage proposal—"

Conner stilled. "Second thoughts?" he asked, and while his tone was light, she knew the answer mattered to him.

She met his eyes. "When I said yes, I *meant* yes," she said.

He let out his breath. He looked like Example A of the perfect man, sitting there, clad only in his jeans, with the flickering fire giving him a light side and a dark side, like the moon. "Is this going somewhere?" he asked, with no sarcasm at all. He really wanted to know.

Tricia blushed, searching for words. They were about as easy to capture or even herd in one direction as a flock of frightened chickens.

"We were—making love at the time," she began, feeling her way.

"Yeah," Conner agreed. "I'd say that's the understatement of the century, but, yes, we were making love when I asked you to marry me."

She was too flustered to be diplomatic. "Did you mean it?" she blurted out. "Or was it just—?"

"I never say anything I don't mean, Tricia," Conner said, his expression tender and serious now. "I love you. I want to marry you and make babies together and all the rest of it."

Her heart soared. "Really?"

His mouth crooked up at one corner. "Yeah, really."

"When?"

Conner chuckled, reached over to give her braid a light tug and then slip it behind her shoulder. "When do we get married, or when do we start making babies?"

She blushed. "Take your pick," she said, gasping a little when he slid his hand from her hair to the inside of the shirt, cupped it around her breast. The nipple pulsed against his palm.

He eased her down onto her back. "You're the bride, so you can set the wedding date. Next week, next year— I don't care, as long as I can do this whenever I want to—"

To demonstrate his point, he laid the shirt open, baring her to the firelight and his gaze and drawing on her with a combination of tenderness and lust that instantly awakened all the previously satisfied forces within her.

At his own leisurely pace, he attended to her other breast. "And this," he said, kissing his way downward now. "And, of course, *this*—"

A soft, sweet climax seized Tricia instantly, made her body ripple like a ribbon trailing in the wind. Instead of crying out, she crooned, surrendering to the slow, luxurious pleasure.

She sighed, when it ended, trembled with contentment.

Conner kissed his way back up to her mouth. "Now, the babies," he began, as if there had been no break in the conversation, no fiercely delicious orgasm to fuse together all the broken places inside Tricia, "might not be as easy to time."

He was stretched out on top of her now, wanting her.

And she wanted him. Again. Already.

"Why's that?" she murmured, her hips already beginning to rise and fall of their own accord, seeking him.

He chuckled, the sound a sexy rasp, low in his throat. "Because," he said, "there was only one condom."

"Uh-oh," she purred.

"Yep," he muttered, kissing the length of her neck.

"You're sure you only had one?" The question came out on a series of ragged breaths.

"Positive," he lamented, back at her breast.

She cried out and arched her back. Grasped his face in both her hands and demanded, "Did you mean it when you said you love me, Conner Creed? When you said you want us to have babies together?"

He nodded.

"Then have me," she whispered.

And he did.

"GOD BLESS THE POWER COMPANY," Tricia said, hours later, when the electricity set things to clunking and then whirring all around her and Conner. The lights came on in her kitchen, and the furnace roared to life two floors below, in the basement. Exquisite curlicues frosted the glass in her bedroom window.

Warmed by each other, four quilts, two blankets and

one dog, Tricia and Conner slowly began to untangle their limbs.

"I think we ought to stay here until the house warms up a little," Tricia said.

Valentino, curled up at their feet, gave a doggish sigh.

"Or a lot," Conner agreed. "Is that my leg, or yours?"

Tricia laughed. "If it's hairy, it's yours," she teased.

He put his arms around her, held her close against his chest.

"Now, I *know* that isn't my hand," he said, with a grin in his voice. And the slightest groan of renewed lust.

Valentino yawned broadly, jumped down off the bed, and padded out into the kitchen. Moments later, he was lapping up water from his bowl. Next, he crunched away on his kibble.

Conner gave a strangled chuckle and groaned again.

"I've decided on a wedding date," Tricia told him.

"I—can't wait—to hear about it—" Conner choked out, rolling onto his side and then poising himself above her.

"I think we should get married right away," Tricia said, getting a little breathless now herself, as Conner began to caress her with slow promise. "As soon as we can round up Natty and your family."

"Umm," Conner muttered. "You don't want a regular wedding?"

"Weddings—take too long to—*oooooh, Conner*—plan. There's the dress—the cake—the invitations—the—oh, God, *do that again*—"

He grinned. And did it again.

Valentino came back into the bedroom, collar tags jingling, and made a low, whining sound, almost apologetic.

"He needs to go out," Conner rasped. "Now. Of all times." He groaned loudly.

Tricia sighed, resigned to the inconveniences of pet ownership. "Yes," she said. "Now, of all times."

Conner rose, grumbling, and scrambled into his jeans. Reclaimed his shirt from the floor, where it had fallen the night before, soon after they came upstairs, and put it on. Looked around for his boots, which were still downstairs.

Tricia started to get up.

"Stay there," Conner told her. "The dog and I will head downstairs and try to tunnel our way out the back door."

The room was brutally cold, without Conner to keep her warm. It would be a while for the furnace to overtake the chill. So Tricia huddled inside the bedcovers, with only her head sticking out. Before she could protest that Valentino was her dog and therefore her responsibility, both of them were gone.

Tricia spent a couple of minutes trying to work up her courage to climb out of bed; the least she could do was woman-up and get out there in the kitchen to put the coffee on. Conner, after all, was braving postblizzard conditions; he'd need the hot brew when he came back inside.

The soles of her bare feet nearly stuck to the floor, and goose bumps leaped out on every square inch of her skin.

Teeth clattering together, hugging herself, Tricia hiphopped to her dresser, snatched a pair of black sweatpants and a blue woolen hoodie from a drawer, and plunged back into bed. She hid there, waiting for the chills to subside, and began squirming into the clothes, still under the covers, when she heard Valentino coming up the inside stairs, with Conner.

She got tangled in the sweatpants and then the sheets, and as she struggled on, she heard a familiar masculine laugh from the doorway.

"No fair starting without me," Conner said.

Tricia fought her way into her clothes. Her voice muffled by layers of covers, she replied, "This is *not* funny."

Again, he laughed. "Of course it is," he said. "It's a hoot. If I didn't know better, I'd say there was a wrestling match going on under those quilts."

"Just for that," Tricia said, dressed at last, "you can make your *own* coffee."

"Is this what it's going to be like when we're married?" Conner teased.

By the time she tossed the blankets back, she was smiling. "Probably," she said, glancing at the window, which was still opaque with frost. "What's going on outside? Is it still snowing?"

Valentino squeezed past Conner in the bedroom doorway and shook himself, hard, sending icy moisture flying in every direction.

"No," Conner said, after a pause to enjoy Tricia's consternation over the impromptu christening, "but there must be two feet of the stuff on the ground. The sun's out and the sky is clear and blue enough to break your heart."

Tricia stroked Valentino's damp head, looking around for her slippers. Then she remembered—she'd donated them to the rummage sale.

She got out a pair of socks and sat down on the edge of the bed to pull them on.

"I suppose you have to go and feed cattle or something," she said, because this intimacy—taking the dog out, making coffee—was in some ways more profound than making love. It was a reflex, that attempt to establish a distance between them, however slight.

Conner nodded. "Yep," he said. "I'm a rancher, Tricia. That's what we do."

"What if the roads haven't been plowed?" she asked reasonably, slipping past him to enter the kitchen.

"That truck will go anywhere," he said. "I'll put chains on the back tires and then roll."

She reached for the coffee carafe, filled it with water at the sink. Through the kitchen window, which hadn't frosted over, she could see the pristine shimmer of a snow-whitened world. It looked almost magical, but Tricia's feelings were bittersweet. On the one hand, she was glad the storm was over, at least for now, so people could start digging themselves out and get on with their daily life. But on the other, she didn't want Conner to leave.

"You could ride along, as far as the ranch house, anyway," Conner ventured, his voice quiet and a little gruff. "Keep Kim and those little dogs of hers company while Davis and Brody and I go out and check the herd."

Tricia hesitated long enough to push the button on the coffeemaker. Sighed. "I'd better not," she said. "Winston—Natty's cat—is supposed to arrive any day now. I have to be here to take delivery if, by some miracle, the truck gets through."

Conner approached her, pinned her gently against the counter in front of the coffee machine. "You could call the delivery company to make sure," he said. "Unless, of course, you're set on putting some space between us."

Tricia blinked up at him. She was getting aroused

again, starting to ache in needy places. "Why would you say that?"

"Because you've seen my soul and I've seen yours," Conner replied, kissing her forehead. "If you're like me, you're happy, but you're scared, too." He drew back just far enough to hook a finger under her chin and lift, so that she had to look at him. "We love each other, Tricia," he reminded her. "We'll have to find our way forward from there, like everybody else, but we'll make it. One step at a time, we'll make it."

Tricia relaxed, with a soft sigh, and put her arms around Conner, let herself lean into him. Her cheek rested against his heart; she could feel the strong, steady beat of it. "You're right," she said, thinking of her parents, and their ill-fated union. "Nobody gets a guarantee, do they?"

He stroked her hair, coming loose from its usually tidy braid. "Nobody gets a guarantee," he agreed. "But we can stack the odds in our favor, Tricia."

"How?" she asked, thinking that if she loved this man any more than she already did, she'd burst from it.

"Davis told me one time that he and Kim have stayed married all these years mainly because neither of them was willing to give up on the other. They scrap once in a while—they're both strong-minded people—and they've had their share of disappointments and setbacks, too, but they don't quit."

Tricia nodded, loving the feel of Conner Creed, the scent of him, the warm strength of his arms around her, the pressure of his chest and hips. "Natty adored my great-grandfather, Henry, but according to her, the secret of a good marriage is not expecting to be happy all the time, because no one is. Whenever she and Henry went through tough times, Natty said, they made sure they were on the same side, stood shoulder to shoulder and took on whatever came their way."

"Natty's a pioneer," Conner said, with amused admiration.

Out on the street, a mighty roar sounded, and Valentino tilted his head back and howled once, like his distant ancestor, the gray wolf.

"Snowplow," Conner told him. "Take a breath."

Valentino went over to his bed, sighed, and lay down on top of his blue chicken, resigned.

After coffee and a couple of slices of toast, Conner took a quick—and lukewarm—shower, got dressed again and, after giving her a kiss and a promise that he'd be back no matter what, headed for the ranch.

Tricia waited until the water was hot before taking her own shower.

She dressed warmly, in jeans and a bulky blue sweater, found Doris's Denver number in her address book and dialed. Tricia figured the great-aunt-and-grandmother combo might already have left for New York, where they would board the cruise ship, but it was worth a try.

Doris answered on the other end, greeted Tricia in her fond but businesslike way, and called out, "Natty Jean! It's for you."

Tricia smiled to herself as she waited

"Did Winston get there yet?" Doris asked, while both of them waited for Natty to make her way to the phone. "Buddy stopped by and picked him up this morning. He said the highways were clear all the way to Lonesome Bend, thanks to a whole night of plowing."

"No sign of Winston yet," Tricia answered, smiling, "but I'll be sure to call and let you know when he arrives."

"That's good," Doris said. "Natty Jean frets about him, you know."

"I know," Tricia said gently. "But Winston will be fine here, with Valentino and Carolyn and me."

Doris didn't get a chance to respond; Natty must have wrested the handset from her, because the next voice Tricia heard was her great-grandmother's.

"Is Winston there, dear?"

The smile was back. "No," Tricia said, "but I'm expecting him anytime now. Shall I tell him you called?"

Natty laughed. "Yes," she said. "Right after you call *me* to say he's safe and sound."

Tricia repeated her promise.

"So the old house is still standing, then?" Natty inquired. "Phew! I haven't seen that much snow fall in one night since the blizzard of 1968. You wouldn't remember that, of course."

"The house is as sturdy as ever," Tricia said. "Will the weather be a problem for you and Doris, cruisewise, I mean?"

"Heavens, no," Natty informed her, and her tone made Tricia think of Conner's words, earlier that morning. *Natty's a pioneer.* "The airport is already open again and, anyway, we don't leave until day after tomorrow."

"Send me a postcard?"

"Of course, dear," Natty said. "At least one from every port."

Tricia's heart warmed. "There's something I need to tell you, before you go jetting off to board the QE2, or whatever your ship is called."

An indrawn breath. "I presume it's something good?" Natty murmured.

"Very good," Tricia said, feeling so happy in that moment that her throat thickened and her eyes burned. "You were right, Natty. About Conner being the right man for me, I mean."

Natty's voice was fluttery—and loud. "Doris!" she called, making Tricia wince and hold the handset away from her ear for a moment. "Doris! It's happening—just like I told you it would—" A pause, with Doris muttering unintelligibly in the background. "Well, *of course* I mean that Conner and Tricia have fallen in love! What else would it be?"

Tricia chuckled. "We're getting married," she said.

More delight on Natty's end, followed by, "Oh, dear, that's *wonderful.* When, though? Not before Doris and I get back from our trip, I hope."

"Not before then," Tricia promised. "I couldn't get married without you there, Natty."

"I should hope not," Natty said stoutly. Then, brightening, she went on to ask, "Are you planning on living in sin in the meantime, dear?"

"Maybe not *living* in sin, but it's safe to say there might be some dabbling."

This time, it was Natty who laughed. "Henry and I lived in sin for a whole week," she confided. "Hush, Doris, it's true and you know it. Don't be such a stick-in-the-mud."

"You and great-grandpa *lived in sin?*" Tricia couldn't help being intrigued, though a part of her pleaded silently, *Don't tell me!*

"Well," Natty said, after clearing her throat and lowering her voice to a confidential tone, even though Doris had obviously gotten the gist of the conversation and, thus, the proverbial horse was out of the barn, "we didn't move in together, like young people do today, but we *did* run off to get married. We were so busy honeymooning that we forgot all about the wedding, though, and Papa showed up and made a terrible scene before he dragged me back home. Mama was furious, and when Henry came looking for me—he was very brave, my Henry—she met him at the front gate and told him she'd shoot him with an elephant gun if he didn't make an honest woman out of me. I'll never forget what he said to her. *'Eleanor,'* he told Mama, just as bold as you please, *'I can't make Natty an honest woman, because she already is one. But I'd be proud to make her my wife.'* Isn't that what he said, Doris? Don't deny it, you were hiding behind the lilac bush the whole time, and you heard everything."

Tricia smiled, imagining the scene. She'd probably never pass through the gate out front again without thinking of her spirited great-grandparents and the romantic scandal they must have created, back in the day.

Some things, she thought happily, never change.

Downstairs, the doorbell rang.

Tricia carried the phone into her bedroom, which was at the front of the house, and wiped a circle in the thawing frost covering the window. A large brown truck was parked at the curb, undaunted by the high snowbanks.

"I'm pretty sure Winston is here," Tricia announced.

"Well, then, you go and welcome him, dear. Doris says they have computers on the ship, so I'll be in touch after we set sail."

"Natty?" Tricia said, moving through the house, toward the inside staircase.

"Yes, dear?"

"I love you."

Natty gave a pleased little chuckle. "Well, I love you, too, dear. Take good care of Winston."

"I will," Tricia promised, disconnecting and laying the handset on the wide windowsill in the entryway so she could open the door.

"Meow," Winston complained peevishly, from inside his plastic carrier.

The driver, presumably the aforementioned Buddy, wore earmuffs as well as a stocking cap, a heavy scarf and a quilted uniform to match his truck.

"Tricia McCall?" he asked.

"That's me," Tricia said.

"Reooooow," Winston insisted.

Buddy handed Tricia the electronic equivalent of a clipboard, so she could sign for the cat.

"He's been doing that since we left Denver this morning," Buddy said. "Miss Natty gave me all his gear, but that's still in the truck. Maybe you ought to take him inside, though, while I fetch it. I wouldn't want the noisy little feller to catch a cold or anything."

"Good idea," Tricia said. She stepped into the house, set the carrier down on the floor and opened the little gate.

Winston shot through the opening like a furry bullet and made a dash for the stairway.

Valentino gave a brief, happy bark of welcome, already partway down the stairs.

Just as Buddy was handing over the pet-store bags filled with cat toys, a fluffy little bed, a new litter box, a five-pound bag of cat food and three cans of sardines, Carolyn drove up.

She passed the retreating Buddy on the as-yet-unshoveled walk, high-stepping it toward the porch.

"I see you survived the storm," Carolyn called, her voice sunny.

Tricia thought of the chain of tumultuous orgasms she'd enjoyed, first on the floor in front of the downstairs fireplace and then *up*stairs, in her bed. *Survived* was hardly the word, but for now, she'd keep that to herself.

"Come in," Tricia said, smiling at her friend. "Before you freeze."

Winston zoomed past, evidently running off some of his excess energy.

Carolyn laughed and raised one eyebrow in good-natured question.

"That's Winston," Tricia explained. "When he calms down, I'll introduce the two of you. In the meantime, the coffee's on upstairs, and you look like you could use a cup."

Carolyn nodded, and the two of them climbed the stairs.

In Tricia's kitchen, they settled themselves at the table, their steaming cups in front of them. Tricia was bursting with her news, but she wanted to tell Diana first, now that Natty knew.

Carolyn took on a serious expression. "I think you should know about Brody Creed and me," she said.

Surprised, Tricia studied her. "That's not necessary," she said carefully.

"It is for me," Carolyn said. "I know you and Conner have something going, and he's Brody's brother, of course, and—well—it will just be too awkward, keeping secrets."

"Okay," Tricia said, drawing out the word, wondering if, as curious as she was, she really wanted to hear this story.

Carolyn took in a long breath and let it out very slowly, in a here-goes kind of way. Her high cheekbones were pink, partly because she'd been out in the cold, certainly, but mostly because she was embarrassed.

"A couple of years ago," she began, "I was housesitting for Davis and Kim, while they were on the road. One night, Brody showed up—I thought he was Conner, of course, but I realized my mistake as soon as I got a good look at him, standing there under the porch light. I told him the Creeds weren't home, and he said that was just his luck, or something like that. He looked so tired and discouraged and—well, sort of *scruffy*—that's mainly how I knew he wasn't Conner—he said he'd spend the night in the barn and head out in the morning." Carolyn stopped, sipped her coffee, swallowed in a way that looked painful. "He didn't leave in the morning," she said finally. "And after that first night, he didn't sleep in the barn, either."

Tricia waited, knowing there was more.

"I thought—" Carolyn paused again and gave a bitter little laugh, shaking her head, "I thought I meant something to him. We talked about so many things— he told me about growing up as an identical twin, and all about his falling-out with Conner—but there was one thing he left out."

Again Tricia waited. The moment was too delicate not to.

"He was about to marry another woman—and she was carrying his baby."

Tricia ached for Carolyn, and for Brody and the unknown woman and the baby. It was a lose-lose situation, all the way around.

"That's pretty much it," Carolyn said, her eyes filling.

Tricia reached across the table and squeezed her hand. "Let's have one more cup of coffee," she said, "before we go downstairs and start taking your things out of boxes and putting them away."

"I—" Carolyn cleared her throat, blushed harder. "I wouldn't want anyone else to know—"

"Don't worry," Tricia replied. "As my dad used to say, mum's the word."

Carolyn laughed, wiping away tears at the same time. "Mine used to say that, too," she said.

Tricia smiled.

Winston jumped unceremoniously into Carolyn's lap and settled himself there, purring loudly. Valentino, standing nearby, looked a little envious.

Carolyn stroked the cat's back, smiling down at him.

"I guess I've made another friend," she said.

EPILOGUE

New Year's Eve
The Brown Palace, Denver

CONNER SWEPT HIS wife of two full hours up into his arms and kissed her soundly, outside the door of Room 719.

They'd been married at her great-aunt Doris's place, with Natty giving the bride away and Brody serving as best man, while Davis and Kim and a very quiet Carolyn looked on. Tricia's mother and stepfather had been there, too, via webcam, as had Diana and Paul and a very excited Sasha, the three of them tuning in from their apartment in Paris.

Yep, it was a high-tech world, all right. Fit to boggle a cowboy's mind.

And speaking of scrambling a man's brain...

"I love you so much," Tricia said, after Conner had managed to jimmy open their hotel room door and carry her over the unusually high threshold.

Champagne awaited, nestled in a silver ice bucket, and the bed had been strewn with delicate white rose petals, a touch Kim had suggested. Now, seeing the effect, Conner was glad he'd called the florist and had those flowers sprinkled around.

He kissed Tricia, letting his mouth linger on hers.

The first of many lingering kisses, he thought, with a rush of grateful anticipation. "And I love you," he answered.

Then he set his lovely bride on her feet.

She wobbled a little, not used to high-heeled shoes. At home on the ranch—she'd moved in with him at Thanksgiving, bringing Valentino with her—Tricia wore boots and jeans most of the time. Although she and Carolyn were cooking up a plan to open some kind of shop on the first floor of Natty's house, the newest Mrs. Creed seemed to love living in the country.

Seeing her in the fancy pale blue dress she'd bought for the wedding was quite a change from every day. To Conner, she always looked amazing, no matter what she was—or wasn't—wearing.

Flakes of snow glistened in Tricia's hair and on the shoulders of her coat as she stood there looking at him, her heart in her eyes. He doubted a lot of things in his life, but there was no doubting her love for him.

"It's almost the new year," she said. At times, the old shyness overtook her, even with him, but it never lasted long.

He touched her cheek gently, wanting to put her at ease and, at the same time, wanting to get her naked on that flowery bed and drive her out of her mind with a whole constellation of explosive orgasms.

"New year, new life," he said, helping her out of the coat, watching as she kicked off the shoes. Wriggled her toes and sighed with undisguised relief.

A few moments after that, she moved close, slipped her arms around Conner's neck, and nibbled at his mouth, her eyes dancing with sultry mischief now.

"Make love to me, Mr. Creed," she murmured.

He gave a throaty laugh, a little raspy, a little raw. It was terrifying to be so happy, to fly so close to the sun. "It would be my pleasure, Mrs. Creed," he replied.

Tenderly, Conner turned Tricia around, unzipped her wedding dress, and eased it off her perfect shoulders, down over her arms and her hips, letting it fall into a patch of glistening blue on the floor.

She faced him, a vision in her white lacy bra and panties, no longer shy.

She was flushed, from the curve of her breasts to her hairline, but her eyes blazed with passion and confidence and the power to turn him inside out and then put him right again.

"Your turn," she said.

Conner grinned. He took off his coat, tossed it aside.

Tricia moved in to loosen his tie, open the first few buttons of his shirt. She made a soft cooing sound as she touched her lips to the skin at the base of his throat, and he could feel his heart beating there.

And somewhere else, too.

"It's our first time as husband and wife," she murmured, baring more and more of his chest, putting her hands under his shirt, fingers splayed and searching. "Let's make it wild."

Conner gave an exultant laugh. "Good idea," he said, just before he kissed her. All the while, he was peeling off the last stitches of fabric keeping him from her. He lifted her off the floor, and her legs, with their sexy pull-up stockings, the only things she was still wearing, went around him.

They kept kissing.

Tricia moaned.

Conner used his tongue, foreshadowing what would happen in the very near future.

He laid her sideways on the bed, and the rose petals settled around her, softly fragrant.

Conner straightened, one knee on the mattress, took his time rolling down one of Tricia's stockings, then the other. She gasped and moved her head slowly from side to side as he stroked the insides of her thighs, the soft mound of her belly, her firm breasts.

Her nipples hardened against his palms, and she cried out for him, grabbed for him, trying to pull him down on top of her.

"You wanted it wild," he reminded her.

She nodded, her eyes closed, making that low, come-hither sound she always made when she needed him inside her. "And *fast*—" she told him breathlessly.

But Conner draped her legs over his shoulders, one at a time.

Tricia bit down on her lower lip, but she couldn't contain the soft, choking cry his touch elicited.

He bent his head to the crux of her, nuzzled his way through warm silk, and took her greedily into his mouth.

She climaxed almost instantly, in a wild, writhing fury of surrender, but when it was over, when she settled, sighing with satisfaction, into the cushion of rose petals, clearly, she expected Conner to take her then.

Instead, he started her on a second climb, this one long and slow, to heaven.

* * * * *

UNFORGIVEN

B.J. Daniels

I had only sold four books when
my former newspaper managing editor convinced me
to quit a job I loved to follow my dream. That day,
I promised to dedicate my first single-title book to him.
So this book is for you, Bill Wilke. Neither of us
could know back then what a huge favor you did for me.

CHAPTER ONE

THE WIND HOWLED down the Crazy Mountains, rocking the pickup as Sheriff Frank Curry pulled to the side of the narrow dirt road. He hadn't been to this desolate spot in years. Like a lot of other residents of Beartooth, he avoided coming this way.

The afternoon sun slanted down through the dense pines, casting a long shadow over the barrow pit and the small cross nearly hidden among the weeds. The cross, though weathered from eleven years of harsh Montana weather, stood unyielding against the merciless wind that whipped the summer-dried weeds around it.

After a moment, Frank climbed out of the truck, fighting the gusts as he waded into the ditch. Someone had erected the wooden cross, though no one knew who. Back then the cross had been white. Years of blistering hot summers and fierce, long snow-laden winters had peeled away the paint, leaving the wood withered and gray.

The brisk fall wind kicked up a dust devil in the road. Frank shut his eyes as it whirled past him, pelting him with dirt. The image he'd spent years trying to banish flashed before him. He saw it again, the young woman's broken body lying in the barrow pit where it had been discarded like so much garbage.

The lonesome moan of the wind in the tops of the

thick wall of pines was the only sound on this remote
rural road. That night, standing here as the coroner
loaded the body, he'd sworn he would find Ginny West's
killer if it was the last thing he ever did.

Now, he looked again at the cross that marked this
lonely place where Ginny had died. The wind had plas-
tered a dirty plastic grocery bag against its base.

Feeling the crippling weight of that vow and his failure, Frank crouched down and jerked the bag free. As he
rose to leave, he heard the sound of a motor and looked
up to see a small plane fly over.

RYLAN WEST LAY dazed in the dirt. He'd lost his hat, gotten the air knocked clean out of him and was about to
be trampled by a horse if he didn't move—and quickly.

To add insult to injury, as he lay on the ground staring up at all that blue sky, he saw Destry Grant's red-
and-white Cessna 182 fly over. He didn't have to see the
woman behind the controls to know it was *her* plane.
Hell, he could call up Destry Grant's face from memory
with no trouble at all and did so with frustrating regu-
larity even though he hadn't laid eyes on her in more
than ten years.

In the past few weeks that he'd been home, he'd made
a point of staying out of Destry's way. He told himself
he wasn't ready to see her. But a part of him knew that
was pure bull. He felt guilty and he should have. The
last time they'd seen each other, he'd made her a promise he hadn't kept.

Not that anyone could blame him under the circumstances. Eleven years ago he'd left Beartooth, Montana,
joined the rodeo and hadn't looked back. That is, until
a few weeks ago when he'd grown tired of being on the

road, riding one rodeo after another until they'd become a blur of all-night drives across country.

He had awakened one morning and realized there was only one place he wanted to be. Home. He'd loaded up his horse and saddle, hooked on to his horse trailer and headed for Montana. He'd yearned for familiar country, for the scent of pine coming off the fresh snow on top of the Crazy Mountains, for his family. And maybe for Destry, as foolish as that was.

He swore now as he listened to the plane circle the W Bar G, hating that Destry was so close and yet as beyond his reach as if she were on the moon. That hadn't been the case when they were kids, he thought with a groan. Back then he couldn't have been happier about the two of them growing up on neighboring ranches. They'd been best friends until they were seventeen and then they'd been a whole lot more.

"What the hell is wrong with you?"

Rylan blinked as he looked over on the corral fence to see his younger brother Jarrett glaring down at him. To his relief, he noticed that Jarrett had hold of the unbroken stallion's halter rope. The horse was snorting and stomping, kicking up dust, angry as an old wet hen. His brother looked just as mad.

"Nothin's wrong with me," Rylan said with a groan as he got to his feet. At least physically, that was.

"If Dad finds out that you tried to ride that horse..." Jarrett shook his head and glanced toward the sky and Destry's plane. His brother let out a curse as if everything was now suddenly crystal clear.

Rylan grabbed the reins from his brother, hoping Jarrett had the good sense not to say anything about him trying to ride one of the wild horses their father had brought home from the Wyoming auction—or about Destry. If he and Jarrett had that particular discussion, more than likely one or both of them would end up with a black eye.

He knew how his family felt about the Grants. Hell, he felt the same way. Even after all these years, just thinking about what had happened still hurt too badly. Just as thinking about Destry did. But as hard as he tried to put her out of his mind, he couldn't do it.

"I just heard the news. It's all over town," his brother said as her plane disappeared from view.

DESTRY GRANT BANKED the small plane along the east edge of the towering snow-capped Crazy Mountains and then leveled it out to fly low over the ranch.

It never failed to amaze her that everything from the mountains to the Yellowstone River was W Bar G Ranch. Say what you want about Waylon "WT" Grant— and God knew people did, she thought—but her father had built this ranch from nothing into what it was today.

She'd spent the past few days in Denver at a cattleman's association conference and was now anxious to get home. She was never truly comfortable until she felt Montana soil beneath her boots.

The ranch spread below her, a quilt of fall colors. Thousands of Black Angus cattle dotted the pastures now dried to the color of buckskin. Hay fields lay strewn with large golden bales stretching as far as the eye could see. At the edge of it all, the emerald green of the Yellowstone River wound its way through cottonwoods with leaves burnished copper in the late October air.

Destry took in the country as if breathing in pure

oxygen—until she spotted the barns and corrals of the West Ranch in the distance. But not even the thought of Rylan West could spoil this beautiful day.

The big sky was wind-scoured pale blue with wisps of clouds coming off the jagged peaks of the Crazies, as the locals called the mountain range. Behind the rugged peaks, a dark bank of clouds boiled up with the promise of a storm before the day was over.

Just past a creek tangled with dogwood, chokecherry and willows, the huge, rambling Grant ranch house came into view. Her father had built it on the top of a hill so he'd have a three-hundred-and-sixty-degree view of his land. Like the ranch, the house was large, sprawling and had cost a small fortune. WT scoffed at the ridicule the place had generated among the locals.

"What did WT think was going to happen?" one rancher had joked before he'd noticed Destry coming into the Branding Iron Café for a cup of coffee last spring. "You build on top of a knob without a windbreak, and every storm that comes in is going to nail you good."

She hadn't been surprised that word had spread about what happened up at WT's big house in January. During one of the worst storms last winter, several of the doors in the new house had blown open, piling snowdrifts in the house.

Even early settlers had known better than to build on a hilltop. They always set their houses down in a hollow and planted trees to form a windbreak to protect the house from Montana's unforgiving weather.

That was another reason she'd opted to stay in the hundred-year-old homestead house down the road from WT's "folly," as it'd become known.

She was about to buzz the house to let her father know she was back, when she spotted something odd. An open gate wouldn't have normally caught her attention. But this one wasn't used anymore. Which made it strange that the barbed-wire-and-post gate lay on the ground, and there were fresh tire tracks that led to the grove of dense trees directly behind the homestead house where she lived alone.

She frowned as she headed for the ranch airstrip, wondering why anyone would have reason to drive back there. As she prepared to land, she spotted a bright red sports car heading toward the ranch in the direction of WT's folly. In this part of the state, most everyone drove a truck. Or at least a four-wheel-drive SUV. The person driving the sports car had to be lost.

AFTER LEAVING THE plane at the hangar, Destry drove straight up to the main house in the ranch pickup. She pulled in as the dust was settling around the red sports car she'd seen from the air. As the driver shut off his engine, she saw her father roll his wheelchair down the ramp toward them.

WT had been a handsome, physically imposing man before his accident. Not even the wheelchair could diminish his formidable strength of will, even though he was now grayer and thinner. The accident hadn't improved his disposition, either, not that it had been all that great before the plane crash.

WT was a complicated man. That was the nice way people in the county explained her father. The rest didn't mince words. Nettie Benton at the Beartooth General Store called him the meanest man in Sweetgrass County.

Right now, though, WT looked more anxious than Destry had ever seen him. As he wheeled toward the car, Destry shifted her gaze to the man who had climbed out. For a moment she didn't recognize her own brother.

"Carson?" For eleven years, she'd wondered if she would ever see her big brother again. She ran to him, throwing herself into his arms. He chuckled as he hugged her tightly, then held her at arm's length to look at her.

"Wow, little sis, have you grown up," he said, making her laugh. She'd been seventeen when he'd left, newly graduated from high school and on her way to college that coming fall. She hated to think how young she'd been in so many ways. Or how much that tragic year was to change their lives. Seeing Carson on the ranch again brought it all back with sharp, breath-stealing pain for everything they'd lost.

Carson had filled out from the twenty-year-old college boy he'd been. His hair was still a lighter chestnut from her own. They both had gotten their hair color from their mother, she'd heard, although she'd never seen as much as a snapshot of Lila Gray Grant. Unable to bear looking at photographs of Lila, her father had destroyed them all after his wife's death.

Her brother's eyes were their father's clear blue, while her own were more faded like worn denim. It had always annoyed her that her brother had been spared the sprinkling of freckles that were scattered across her cheeks and nose. He used to tease her about them. She wondered if he remembered.

Around his blue eyes was a network of small wrinkles that hadn't been there eleven years ago and a sadness in his gaze she didn't recall. Like their father, he was strikingly handsome and always had been. But now he was tanned, muscled and looked like a man who'd been on a long vacation.

"What are you doing here? I mean—" She heard the crunch of her father's wheelchair tires on the concrete beside her and saw Carson brace himself to face their father. Some things hadn't changed.

"Carson," WT said and extended his hand.

Her brother gave a slight nod, his face expressionless as he reached down to shake his father's hand. WT pulled him closer and awkwardly put an arm around the son he hadn't seen in years.

For the first time in her life, Destry saw tears in their father's eyes. He hadn't cried at her mother's funeral, at least that's what she'd heard through the county grapevine.

"It's good to have you home, Carson," their father said, his voice hoarse with emotion.

Carson said nothing as his gaze shifted to Destry. In that instant, she saw that his coming back to Montana hadn't been voluntary.

Her heart dropped at what she saw in her brother's face. Fear.

CHAPTER TWO

CARSON COULDN'T TAKE his eyes off his sister. When he'd left she'd been a tomboy, wild as the country WT couldn't keep her out of. Eleven years later, she'd turned into a beautiful woman. Her long hair, plaited to hang over one shoulder, was now the color of rust-red fall leaves, her eyes a paler blue than his own. A sprinkling of freckles graced her cheeks and nose. Even after all these years she never tried to conceal them with makeup.

He smiled. "You have no idea how much I've missed you." Or how badly he felt about the pain he'd caused her. "Little sis," he said, pulling her into his arms again.

She hugged him tightly, making him wonder what their father had told her about his return. Given her surprised reaction, he'd guess the old man hadn't told her anything.

"Why are we standing out here? Let's go inside," WT demanded impatiently. "Don't worry about your luggage. I'll have one of the ranch hands unload it for you. You haven't even seen the house yet."

Carson released Destry and glanced behind him at the looming structure. How could he miss it? He'd seen the massive house perched like a huge boulder on the hill from way down the road. He didn't need to ask why his father had built such a house. Apparently WT still hadn't shed that chip on his shoulder after growing up poor in the old homestead house down the mountain. Back then, the house and a few acres of chicken-scratch earth were all he'd had.

But WT had changed that after inheriting the place when he was only a teen. He'd worked hard and had done well by the time he'd married. Carson had never known poverty, nothing even close to it.

But WT couldn't seem to shake off the dust of his earlier life. He just kept buying, building, yearning for more. The manor on the mountain, planes, a private airstrip, and he'd even mentioned that he'd built a swimming pool behind the house. A swimming pool in this part of Montana so close to the mountains? How impractical was that?

As his son, Carson had certainly benefited from his father's hard work. But it came at a price, one he'd grown damned tired of paying.

"Wait a minute, WT," he said as his father began to wheel himself back toward the house. He hadn't called him Dad since the fourth grade. "There's someone I want you to meet."

DESTRY WATCHED THE passenger side of the sports car open and one long slim leg slide out.

She hadn't noticed anyone else in the car, not with the sun glinting off the windshield, and neither she nor her father had apparently considered that Carson might bring someone home with him. That now seemed shortsighted. Carson was thirty-one. It was conceivable he'd have a girlfriend or possibly even a wife.

Destry glanced at her father and saw his surprised

expression. She cringed. WT hated surprises—and Carson had to know that.

"I want you to meet Cherry," her brother said, going to the car to help the woman out.

Destry felt her mouth drop open. Cherry was tall, almost as tall as Carson who stood six-two. She was a bleached blonde with a dark tan, slim with large breasts.

Cherry gave WT a hundred-watt smile with her perfectly capped ultrawhite teeth, which were almost a distraction from the skimpy dress she wore.

Carson was looking at their father expectantly, as if awaiting his reaction. There was a hard glint in her brother's eyes. He had to know what WT's reaction was going to be. It was almost as if he was daring their father to say something about the woman he'd brought home.

Beside her, their father let out an oath under his breath. Destry didn't need to see WT's expression to know this wasn't the way he'd envisioned his son's homecoming.

Cherry stepped over to WT's wheelchair and put out her hand.

He gave her a limp handshake and looked to Carson. "I think it would be best if your…friend stayed in a motel in Big Timber." Big Timber was the closest town of any size and twenty miles away. "Of course I'll pick up the tab." Only then did he turn his gaze to Cherry again. "I thought Carson would have told you. We have business to discuss. You'd be bored to tears way out here on the ranch."

"WT," Carson said in the awkward silence that followed, "Cherry is my *fiancée*."

"Destry, show Cherry the swimming pool," her father ordered. "Carson and I need to talk. In *private*."

WT ROLLED HIMSELF into his den and straight to the bar. His son had brought home a Vegas showgirl and thought he was going to marry her? Over his dead body. As he shakily poured himself a drink, he realized that might be a possibility if he didn't calm down.

"I'll take one of those," Carson said as he came into the room behind him. "I have the feeling I'm going to need it."

Unable to look at his son right now, he downed his drink, then poured them both one. His hands were shaking, his heart jackhammering in his chest.

"Close the door," he ordered and listened until he heard the door shut. "You aren't going to marry that woman," he stated between gritted teeth as he turned his wheelchair around to face his son.

Carson took the drink WT held out to him and leaned against the long built-in bar. His son had grown into a fine-looking man. WT felt a surge of pride. Until he noticed the way his son was dressed. Loafers, a polo shirt and chinos, for God's sake. Who the hell did he think he was? He was the son of a *rancher*.

WT hated to think what that sports car parked out front had cost or about how much money he'd spent keeping Carson away from Beartooth.

"You aren't going to marry that woman," he repeated.

Carson met his gaze and held it with a challenge that surprised WT. With an inward shudder, he realized this wasn't the son he'd sent away more than a decade ago. That scared twenty-year-old boy had just been grateful to get out of town alive.

"I'm in love with Cherry," Carson said, as if daring him to argue the point.

WT shook his head. "Doesn't matter. It's not happening. And I don't want to talk about that right now," he said with a wave of his hand. "We need to talk about the W Bar G. You're my son. This is where you belong. When I'm gone, I want to know you're here, keeping the ranch and the Grant name alive."

"I think I have more pressing matters to concern myself with right now, don't you?"

WT fought to control his temper. "You let me worry about the sheriff and that other matter."

"That other matter?" Carson demanded. "Is that what you call Ginny West's murder?"

WT refused to get into the past with his son. He'd looked forward to this day from the moment Carson was born. No one was going to take that away from him.

"As I was saying," WT continued, "I'm not going to turn the W Bar G over to you until I know you can handle running it. You're going to have to learn the ranching business."

Carson took a long gulp of his drink and pushed himself off the edge of the bar to walk around the room. WT tried to still the anger roiling inside him. He knew Carson was upset about being summoned home. Just as he'd been upset about being sent away eleven years ago.

He watched his son take in the den he'd had built so it looked out over the ranch with a view that ran from the mountains to the river. WT joined him at the bank of windows.

The valley was aglow with golden afternoon light. WT loved the way his land swept down from the base of the mountains in a pale swatch of rich pasture, hay and alfalfa fields to the river. Much of the land had dried to the color of corn silk. It was broken only by rocky outcroppings, hilly slopes of pine and the rust hues of the foliage along the creeks that snaked through the property.

It was an awe-inspiring sight that he feared was wasted on his son.

Carson finally spoke. "Even if everything turns out the way you think it will, I don't understand why I have to learn the business. Destry's doing a great job running the ranch, isn't she?"

"She has only been filling in until you returned."

"Does she know that?" his son asked, his tone rimmed with sarcasm.

WT took a swallow of his drink, giving himself time to rope in his anger. "I want *you* to run the ranch."

"What about my sister? She isn't some horse you can put out to pasture."

WT let out a curse. "She needs to find a man and get married before it's too late for her."

He thought of the times she'd come home from a branding or calving filthy dirty as if she thought she was one of the ranch hands.

"It's unseemly for a woman to be working with ranch hands," he said, repeating what he'd told Destry more times than he cared to recall. Like her mother had been, she wasn't one to take advice. Especially from him. "She needs to start acting respectable."

"Maybe you haven't heard, but women can vote now."

"Biggest mistake this country ever made," he said, only half joking. He thought of Lila and the trouble he'd had with her. Women were too headstrong and independent. He still believed a woman's place was in the home and said as much to his son.

Carson didn't seem to be listening. He stood staring down into his drink. WT wondered what he hoped to find there. Carson had always been moody as a boy. His mother's doing when he was young, WT thought with a curse. Why couldn't Carson have been more like Destry?

That thought made his stomach churn. People said Destry was too much like him. They had no idea.

When Carson looked up at him again, his expression was both angry and guilty. "You take this ranch away from my sister and you'll kill her. Hasn't she lost enough because of me?"

"You talking about that no-count rodeo cowboy Rylan West?"

"She loved him and would have married him if—"

"She's not marrying him any more than you're marrying that whor—"

"Careful, that's my fiancée."

WT looked at him hard, then laughed. "You're not fooling me with this halfhearted protest about not wanting to take the ranch away from your sister any more than you are with this ridiculous engagement. You have no intention of marrying that woman."

"Don't I?"

"Well, let me put it to you this way. You marry that woman and I'll leave this whole place and every dime I have to some goddamned charity."

Carson cocked his head at him and smiled. "Now who's bluffing?"

WT smiled back. "The difference is I can *afford* to call your bluff. I suspect *you* don't have that luxury." He narrowed his gaze, feeling his ire rise even higher. "You have no choice if you want my help with the sheriff. You'll stay here and take over the ranch. Or you can go it alone without another dime from me. There is no third option and, from what I've heard, you might be in need of a damned good lawyer soon. I hope I've made myself clear," he said as his cook and housekeeper, Margaret, rang the dinner bell.

"Perfectly," Carson said and drained his glass.

NETTIE BENTON AT the Beartooth General Store was the first person to see Carson Grant driving by in that fancy red sports car.

It wasn't blind luck that she'd been standing at the front window of the store when Carson drove past. The once natural redhead, now dyed Sunset Sienna to cover the gray, spent most of her days watching the world pass by her window at a snail's pace. It was why, as the storeowner, she often knew more of what was going on than anyone else in these parts.

"Bob," she called to her husband. No answer. "Must have already gone home," she muttered to herself. The two of them lived behind the store on the side of the mountain. Bob didn't spend much time in the store his parents had turned over to them when they'd gotten married thirty years ago. He didn't have to.

"Nettie loves minding the store—and everyone's business," he was fond of saying.

Nettie hurriedly grabbed the phone and began calling everyone she knew to tell them about Carson Grant.

"Nettie?" Bob called from the office in the back. "What's all the commotion out there?"

Not only was Bob getting hard of hearing—at least hard of hearing her—he wouldn't appreciate her news. Though he might have enjoyed seeing the bleached blonde with Carson.

"It's Carson Grant," she said as she stepped to the office doorway.

Bob didn't look up from the bills he'd been sorting through. "What about him?" he asked distractedly.

"He's back in Beartooth."

Her husband's head jerked up in surprise. *"What?"*

"I saw him drive past not thirty minutes ago." She'd recognized Carson right off, even though it had been years since she'd laid eyes on him.

"Why would he come back *now?*" Bob asked, clearly upset. But then most of the county would be upset, as well.

"I would imagine it has something to do with the rumor circulating about new evidence in Ginny West's murder."

"What new evidence?"

"I heard it was some kind of fancy hair clip one of the kids found over at the old theater. Now they're speculating that she might have actually been killed there and not out on the road." She frowned. "Are you all right?"

Bob was holding his stomach as if something he ate hadn't agreed with him. "You give me indigestion," he said angrily as he shoved the bills away and pushed himself to his feet. "I wouldn't be surprised if you weren't making all of this up."

"It was Carson Grant, sure as I'm standing here."

"What I want to know is why he wasn't arrested years ago?" Bob demanded. "Everyone knows he killed that poor girl. If your sheriff can't figure that out, then there's something wrong with him."

Her sheriff? "Well, I, for one, am not convinced Carson did it," she said as he pushed past her and headed for the back door and home.

"The fact that you're the only one who believes that should tell you something, Nettie." He didn't give her a chance to respond as he slammed out the back door.

Surprised, since that was the most passion she'd seen in her husband in years, maybe ever, she wandered back to the front store window to entertain herself until she was forced to wait on a customer, should one come by.

The narrow two-lane paved road was empty—just as it was most days. The town of Beartooth was like a lot of small Montana towns. It had died down to a smattering of families and businesses. Not that it hadn't been something in its heyday. With the discovery of gold in the Crazy Mountains back in the late 1800s, Beartooth had been a boomtown. Early residents had built substantial stone and log buildings in the shadow of the mountains where Big Timber Creek wound through the pines.

By the early 1900s, though, the gold was playing out and a drought had people leaving in droves. They left behind a dozen empty boarded-up buildings that still stood today. There was an old gas station with two pumps under a leaning tin roof at one end of town and a classic auto garage from a time when it didn't take a computer to work on a car engine at the other.

In between stood the Range Rider bar, the post office, hotel and theater. There'd been talk of tearing down the old buildings to keep kids out of them. Nettie was glad they hadn't. She thought fondly of the hidden room under the stage at the Royale theater where she'd lost her virginity. Unfortunately, that made her think of the sheriff, something she did her best not to do. *Her* sheriff, indeed.

Directly across the street from Nettie's store was the Branding Iron Café where ranchers gathered each morning. Right now a handful of pickups were parked out front—and another half dozen down the street in front of the bar.

Nettie knew the topic of conversation among the ranchers must have Carson Grant's ears burning. She wondered if the West family had heard yet and how long it would be before one of them either ran Carson out of town again—or strung him up for Ginny West's murder.

But it was her husband's reaction that had her scratching her head.

"WHERE'S YOUR SISTER?" WT asked Carson as he looked up from his meal and apparently realized for the first time that Destry wasn't at the table.

"She got a call that some cattle had gotten out and were on the road," Carson said.

His father grunted in answer, the sound echoing in the huge dining hall. Carson idly wondered how often this dining room was ever used. Not much, he'd bet, since everything looked brand-new, and it wasn't as if WT had friends or family over. He'd never been good at making or keeping friends.

"Why didn't she call one of the ranch hands to take care of it? Or our ranch foreman? This is what I pay Russell to do," WT said irritably after a few bites.

Carson tamped down his own irritation. "I would imagine she didn't want to bother them in the middle of their dinners, especially when she's probably more than capable of taking care of it herself." Knowing his sister, that would be exactly her reasoning.

"You see what I mean about your sister?" WT asked with a curse. "She doesn't know her place."

"*This* is her place," Carson said defiantly in the hopes that an argument would end this meal faster. It couldn't end soon enough for him.

WT continued to eat, refusing to rise to the bait. He hadn't even acknowledged Cherry's presence since she'd sat down. Did he really think that by ignoring her she would leave? Under other circumstances, Carson might have found all of this amusing.

He'd done his best to convince his father to give him enough money so he could leave the country. Coming back here only reminded him of everything he'd spent eleven years trying to forget.

But WT had been adamant. There would be no money, not even any inheritance, if he didn't return.

"What about the sheriff?" he'd asked.

"He has a few questions, that's all."

A few questions about Ginny's murder after all these years?

Clearly WT didn't realize how dangerous it was for him being back here, he thought, recalling the look on Nettie Benton's face when he'd driven by her store earlier today. There had been no reason to try to sneak back here. In a community this small, there were few secrets.

This was Montana where there was still a large portion of the rural population that believed in taking the law into their own hands—just as they had in the old days. That could mean a rope and a stout tree.

He mentioned that now to his father.

"I told you not to worry about any of that," WT said without looking up.

"Don't worry about it? Do I have to remind you that the last time I saw Rylan West he swore he'd kill me if he ever saw me again?"

His father finally looked up from his plate, his expression one of mild amusement. "I guess you'd better not let him see you then."

DESTRY FOUND THREE W Bar G cows standing in the middle of the county road, just as a neighboring rancher had described over the phone. She slowed the truck, all three cows glancing at her but not moving. They mooed loudly, though, associating the sound of a truck with the delivery of hay.

"You girls are out of luck," Destry said as she began to herd them with the pickup back up the road toward W Bar G property. She regretted missing her brother's first dinner at home, but hoped he would understand. He and his fiancée needed time alone with WT so they could work out whatever was going on. Her being there would have only made things more strained, she told herself.

As it was, her conversation with Cherry by the pool earlier had left her even more concerned about her brother. Apparently the two had met at the Las Vegas casino where they both worked, Cherry as a dancer and Carson in the office.

Destry couldn't imagine her brother living in Vegas, let alone working in a casino; neither could she see him settling down on the ranch. But then again, she didn't know him anymore.

She wondered how much Carson had told his fiancée about what had happened eleven years ago. Did Cherry know about Ginny's murder? Or that Carson was still the number one suspect?

She lowered her pickup window to feel the air, driving slowly as she moved the cattle at a lazy pace down the road. They were in no hurry, and neither was she.

This far north, it wouldn't get dark for hours yet. Even with the possibility of an approaching storm, it was one of those rare warm fall afternoons in Montana. The rolling hills had faded to mustard in contrast to the deep green of the pines climbing the mountains. As always, the Crazy Mountains loomed over the scene, a bank of dark clouds shrouding the peaks.

She loved living out here away from everything. In this part of Montana, you could leave the keys in your pickup overnight, and your truck would still be there in the morning. The rural area's low crime rate was one reason Ginny West's murder had come as such a shock. It rattled everyone's belief that Beartooth was safe because you knew your neighbors. Now, like a rock thrown into Saddlestring Lake, Carson's return would create wide ripples.

Ginny West's murder—and her breakup with Carson right before it—would be rehashed in booths and at tables in the Branding Iron Café and on the bar stools at the Range Rider bar.

There were still plenty of people around who believed Carson had killed her. Rylan West among them, she reminded herself with a sinking heart.

What would he do when he heard that Carson was back?

The cows mooed loudly as she brought the pickup to a stop and got out to open the barbed-wire gate. She'd seen a broken fence post where she figured the cows had gotten out. She'd let Russell know. Overhead, a hawk soared on an updraft.

As she waded through the tall golden grass, grasshoppers buzzed and bobbed around her. She lifted the metal handle to loosen the loop attached to the gate and, slipping the post out, walked the gate back to allow the cows into their pasture.

At the sound of a vehicle on the wind, she looked up the road. Dust churned up in the distance.

"Come on girls," she said to the cows, swatting one on the backside with her hat to finally get them moving. She could hear the growing sound of the vehicle's engine and was thankful she'd managed to get the cows off the road in time. Once she had them inside the fence, she dragged the barbed-wire gate back over to the post.

Destry had just cranked down the lever that kept the gate taut and closed when she heard the truck slow. She turned, squinting in the cloud of dust, as the pickup stopped only feet from her.

When she saw who was behind the wheel, her heart took off at a gallop.

CHAPTER THREE

RYLAN SWORE AS he saw Destry standing at the edge of the road. Had he really thought he could come storming out to the ranch and not run into her? One look at her and he'd known he wasn't ready for this.

Destry looked the same and yet completely grown up. Her hair was longer, that same rich russet color that reminded him of fall in Montana. It was plaited down her slim back except for a few strands that the wind lifted around her face under the shade of her straw hat. She wore a yellow-checked Western shirt and jeans, both accenting her more mature, rounded figure.

Her eyes were still that faded blue that often matched Montana's big sky. As he looked into them, he felt that old spark. It burned into him, hotter than a Montana summer day.

One look at her and he realized all the running he'd done the past eleven years had been for nothing. He couldn't escape the way he felt about this woman any more than he could forgive her brother for what he knew he'd done.

His sister's murder was like a line drawn in the dirt. Neither of them could step over it. Destry was convinced her brother was innocent of Ginny's murder. Rylan would never believe that. Nothing had changed.

"Destry," he said through his open window. The

word felt alien on his lips, and he realized how long it had been since he'd uttered it aloud. It brought with it an ache that made him grit his teeth.

DESTRY HAD WATCHED frozen to the spot as the pickup came to a dust-boiling stop next to her. The early evening light ricocheted off the windshield, blinding her for a moment before the driver's side window came down.

The shock of coming face-to-face with Rylan after all these years sent a tremor through her. She stared into those familiar brown eyes, seeing the Rylan West she'd fallen in love with as a girl. For a moment, lost in his gaze, she had the overpowering feeling that if he would just get out of that pickup and take her in his arms they could find their way back to each other.

"Destry?" The sound of her name on his lips made her heart pound with the familiarity of it.

She found her voice. "I wondered when I'd see you. I should have known what it would take. I guess I shouldn't be surprised."

He shoved back his Stetson. "I reckon not. I need to see your brother."

She shook her head. Before he'd left town, she'd tried to convince Rylan that her brother couldn't have killed Ginny. "If you just knew him the way I do…"

But his mind had been made up. Just as it was today. She could see it in the clenched muscles of his strong jaw, in the set of his broad shoulders. He'd looked the same way the day of his sister's funeral when he'd gone after Carson, the two of them getting into a fistfight at the cemetery until Rylan's father had broken it up.

"I was hoping…" She couldn't even bear to say the words, her hopes like daggers through her heart. She'd dreamed about the day she would see Rylan again. Her dream crumbled like the dried leaves on the cotton-woods nearby, turning to dust in the wind.

The man she'd known was gone. It was high time she let go of the past. Let go of Rylan West.

RYLAN NEARLY BUCKLED under the pain he saw in her eyes. "Don't make this any harder than it already is."

She sighed, cloaking the hurt with a smile, a smile with an edge to it. Anger fired her blue eyes. It burned hot as a flame. She knew what he planned to do.

For weeks after Ginny's murder, he'd tried to find proof that would put Carson Grant behind bars. What he kept running into was the same thing that had kept Carson free all these years—a lack of evidence.

"I have to get my sister justice since the law isn't going to. As Ginny's oldest brother, I owe her that."

"And you think this is the way?" she said, sounding sad and disappointed in him.

"Stay out of this, please."

"Carson's my *brother*."

"And Ginny was my sister. At least you still have your brother."

"Not if you have your way."

He had no intention of killing Carson—just getting the truth out of him, one way or the other. He snatched off his hat and raked his fingers through his hair in frustration. Now that he and Carson were both back, Rylan intended to see his sister's murderer behind bars. He said as much to Destry.

"He didn't do it, Rylan," she said. "He never left the ranch that night."

"According to his alibi. *You*. But we both know that

was a lie." He fought back the image of her naked in his arms the night they'd made love for the first time at the old abandoned ski lodge high on the mountain. Little did they know what was happening in the valley below them.

Her hands went to her hips, her gaze blazing. "Carson didn't know I'd left the ranch to meet you. It was an honest mistake since you and I were both sneaking around back then."

"I notice that even you didn't bring up Carson's other alibi."

"What would be the point? My brother could have a half dozen alibis and you still wouldn't believe him."

Rylan swore because she was right. "You have to admit his best friend isn't the most reliable alibi, not to mention that Jack French would say the moon was made of cheese if your brother asked him to. Destry, when are you going to stop covering for your brother and see him for what he really is?"

She took a step toward the pickup, her fists balled at her sides. "When are you going to realize that you might be wrong?"

Rylan looked away, his jaw tensing in frustration. "This isn't getting us anywhere." He'd never believe Carson wasn't Ginny's killer, and Destry would defend her brother until hell froze over. "We both know why your brother is back in town. The county attorney threatened to bring Carson back in handcuffs if he didn't return for questioning about the new evidence."

"New evidence? Is that true?"

He saw her surprise. "Your father didn't tell you? I thought you would have heard." But then again, Destry hardly ever left the ranch, from what he'd heard.

"I just assumed WT forced Carson to come back," she said.

Rylan shook his head. "A gold hair clip with my sister's name on it was found under the stage at the Royale. We're pretty sure Ginny was wearing it the last time we saw her."

"So she was at the old theater that night?"

"The sheriff thinks she might have met someone there, probably her killer, then was taken by car to where her body was left." He looked away, fighting the roiling emotions boiling inside him.

"Maybe now the real killer will be found," Destry said.

He hated the hopefulness he heard in her voice. She would be devastated when the truth came out.

"Destry," he said, as kindly as he could, "the county attorney wouldn't have forced your brother to come back here unless the evidence pointed to him."

Her blue eyes narrowed to slits. "If you're so sure this so-called new evidence will prove my brother guilty, then why are you out here ready to take the law into your own hands?"

"Because the *law* in this county is Sheriff Frank Curry. Everyone knows that he does whatever your father tells him to."

Destry shook her head angrily. "Or because you know a hair clip isn't going to prove that my brother had anything to do with her death."

"Not unless someone can place your brother in the old theater that night."

"Don't you think if my brother had been there, someone would have mentioned it by now?" she demanded.

She had always been strong and determined. It was

one of the reasons he'd loved her more than life. If his sister hadn't been murdered that night, he didn't doubt they'd be married now, probably have a couple of kids.

Did Destry ever think about what might have been? She'd made a life for herself on the W Bar G. He'd heard how she had taken over after her father's plane crash. She was born to ranch, that's what people said. They also said how lucky WT was to have such a daughter. Everyone liked Destry and with good reason.

Carson, though, was another story.

"I warned your brother that if I ever saw him again... Destry, I can't live with myself unless I do something. Can't you understand that?" He hated the pleading he heard in his voice. It upset him that it mattered what she thought of him, even after all these years.

Her gaze softened. "I *can* understand. But not this way. Find out who your sister was meeting in town that night."

He flinched at the mental picture of the coroner and EMTs bringing his sister's body out of the shallow ditch beside the road a few miles outside of town. The killer had thrown her into the ditch, leaving her for dead, leaving her to die alone beside the road.

"She ran into *your* brother," he snapped.

She made an impatient sound. "How can you be so sure that Ginny wasn't seeing someone else that she kept not only from Carson, but also from your parents and even from you?" she demanded.

He swore under his breath as he slapped his hat back on to his head. "Some *mystery* man? That's just some story your brother cooked up to shift suspicion onto someone else. This isn't getting us anywhere. It's the same old argument. It's why I left eleven years ago. Your brother killed her."

"Are you willing to stake everything on it? If so, then there is nothing more I can say, is there?" She turned toward her truck.

"What if you're the one who's wrong, Destry?" he called after her. "Ginny said your brother had been following her. How can you be so sure your brother didn't leave the ranch that night? It wouldn't be the first time he lied. Or the first time he hurt Ginny, would it?"

CARSON KNEW BETTER than to try to reason with his father, but he had to give it a shot. As he looked down the table, he wondered if WT believed he'd killed Ginny West. Or if it mattered to him. Apparently being Waylon Thomas Grant's male heir trumped everything— even murder.

"Tomorrow morning, I'll show you the new grazing land I've picked up since you've been gone," WT was saying.

"Aren't you worried about this new evidence that's turned up?"

WT scoffed. "The state attorney general has been putting pressure on local law enforcement to clear up their cold cases. The sheriff is just going through the motions. I doubt there's any new evidence. I wouldn't worry about it."

"I'd feel a whole lot better if I knew what it was."

"Doesn't matter. We'll get you the best lawyer money can buy." He looked up from his meal. "But it won't come to that. You never left the ranch that night. Stick to that story. Jack will back you up, right?"

Carson said nothing for a moment, shocked by his father's cavalier response. "You can't really think I could get a fair trial in this county." When WT didn't respond, he tried again, "With enough money, I could leave the country. There are still foreign countries that the U.S. can't extradite from."

WT looked up at him and frowned. "I built this ranch for my son to take over. So I'm certainly not paying to send him out of the country."

"I can't very well take over the ranch if I'm on death row," Carson snapped.

"You're not going to prison. If the sheriff had anything on you, I'd know."

Carson shook his head in disbelief. "Frank Curry might owe you his life, but not even his gratitude is going to save me if this new evidence makes me look guilty."

WT let out an exasperated sigh. "Stop worrying. No one is fool enough to cross me. Not even the damned state's attorney general."

"If you're so powerful, why did you insist on me leaving eleven years ago? Why didn't you let me stay and fight the allegations? If that's all you thought they were?"

WT shook his head and angrily shoved away his plate.

For a few minutes, the only sound in the huge dining room was the click of Cherry's silverware as she kept eating.

Carson wished he could walk away right now and not look back. But that was no longer an option. He would need a lot of money to leave the country. If WT wouldn't pony it up, then he needed the ranch and the money he could get for it. He thought of his sister. He had to convince WT to give him the money so he could disappear.

"Dad?" The word came at a cost after refusing to call WT that for so many years. *"Dad?"*

His father turned on the only other person in the

room. "Cherry. That your real name? It sounds like a stage name."

Carson swore under his breath as he watched WT take off the gloves. WT would fight as dirty as he had to get what he wanted.

His father threw him a challenging look. But he was no longer that scared kid who'd been sneaked out of Beartooth in the cover of darkness. Ginny's murder and a target on his back had changed him. Nor did he need to come to Cherry's defense. She could take care of herself.

Cherry slowly licked her painted lips and turned her full attention to WT. She'd chosen a hot-pink low-cut top that barely covered her nipples and white capris that cupped her toned bottom. Her dyed blond hair was piled haphazardly on top of her head with stray tendrils curling down around her face. The fake eyelashes gave her a sleepy, half-soused look, but then again, it could have been the wine she'd consumed with abandon since they'd sat down to supper.

"I'm a *dancer*," she said proudly, daring him to dispute it.

"A *dancer?*" WT repeated and added, "And I'm a high flier on the trapeze."

Cherry smiled. "Carson told me that his great grandfather used to be in the circus but I didn't know you—"

"He's making fun, Cherry," Carson said dryly.

She narrowed her eyes at WT. "Making fun of *me?*"

"No," WT said. "My *son.* And by the way, my grandfather rode in a Wild West Show. Not a *circus*."

Carson laughed and shot a wink to his fiancée.

At the head of the table, WT bellowed for Margaret to serve dessert.

CHAPTER FOUR

RYLAN TOOK OFF in a dust devil of anger as Destry climbed into her pickup, her legs weak, her heart aching. Seeing Rylan again had sent her already spinning-out-of-control world even further into orbit. She couldn't look as he drove on down the road toward the W Bar G. There was no stopping him, no way to call the ranch to warn her father and brother since she hadn't grabbed her cell phone—not that she could get service often this close to the mountains. Nor could she beat him to the ranch.

She feared not only for Carson. Her father wouldn't hesitate to shoot a trespasser. Especially a West toting a gun.

Running into Rylan like that had been a shock, one that still reverberated through her. She couldn't tell if the trembling in her hands as she started her truck had more to do with anger—or fear. Or those old feelings that still lingered when it came to that tall, lanky cowboy.

There'd been other men in the years since Rylan had left, even one she'd been fairly serious about, but she'd always measured them against her first love and they'd always come up short.

But did she even know this Rylan? This man so full of rage and set on vengeance at any cost?

Unable to resist it any longer, she glanced in her rearview mirror.

To her surprise, she saw Rylan hit his brake lights up the road. She watched him in the mirror, waiting and praying he'd changed his mind about confronting her brother.

It wasn't as if she didn't understand what was driving him. But he was wrong about Carson. Her brother had loved Ginny.

For long minutes, they sat like that, both pulled off the road fifty yards apart. Both apparently debating what to do next.

"Please, Rylan," she said under her breath, half plea, half prayer.

She let out the breath she'd unconsciously been holding as she watched him turn his pickup around and head back in her direction. She thought he might stop again, but he didn't.

He didn't even look at her as he roared past in a cloud of dust headed away from the W Bar G. He'd said everything he had to say, she thought as she watched him go, her heart in her throat.

What had changed his mind? Hopefully he'd realized after he'd calmed down that the stupidest thing he could do was go to the ranch gunning for Carson.

Whatever had changed his mind, she was thankful. Not that it took care of the problem. She knew Rylan was right. He wouldn't be the only one riled up about Carson's return. If Carson stayed here, he wouldn't be safe.

She sat for a moment, then leaned over the steering wheel letting all the emotions she'd bottled up the past eleven years spill out. She cried for all that had been lost to her, to both their families. Finally, drained, weak with relief and regret, she sat up and wiped her eyes. She'd been strong for so long.

For years she'd told herself she could live without Rylan. She'd moved on with her life. She was happy. At least content. But seeing him, coming face-to-face with him, hearing his voice, looking into his eyes…

He'd always been handsome, but now his body had filled out. He was broader in the shoulders, his arms sinewy with muscle, his face tanned from working outside. There were tiny lines around his eyes that hadn't been there before, but if anything, they only made him more handsome.

His hair was still thick and the color of sunshine, his eyes that honey-warm brown that she'd gotten lost in from the first time she'd looked in them. Her heart had always swelled at the sight of him. She'd never stopped loving him—just as she'd promised. Today proved what her heart already knew. She never would.

Pulling herself together, she turned the pickup around and headed back toward the ranch. Thoughts of Rylan aside, she just prayed that this new evidence would prove that Carson was innocent.

As RYLAN HEADED home, he thought about the first time he'd laid eyes on Destry Grant. She'd come riding up with the W Bar G's ranch foreman at a neighbor's branding on a horse way too big for her. She would have been five at the time to his six. He recalled how serious she'd looked.

What stuck in his mind was that she'd stayed at the branding all day, cutting calves into the chute as if she was ten times her age, and later, when one of the cowboys' hats had blown off and spooked her horse, she'd gotten bucked off and hit the ground hard. Her face had scrunched up, but she hadn't shed a tear. She'd climbed the fence to get back on her horse and ridden off.

He'd never seen anyone so determined.

What chapped his behind now, though, was that she hadn't changed one iota when it came to that stubborn determination and pride. He hated that, when it came to her brother, she just refused to see the truth.

He'd left eleven years ago because he couldn't bear being around her with his sister's death standing between them. He'd always rodeoed, but after college, he'd joined the pro circuit. It had been exactly what he'd needed—traveling from town to town across the country, never staying in one place too long. If he needed company, there were bronco and bull riders to hang out with, and if he felt in need of female attention, there were always buckle bunnies and rodeo groupies who were up for a good time.

The rodeo had helped him heal. He'd felt badly about bailing on his family, but his mother and father had two sons at home and he'd kept in touch. The only people he hadn't wanted to hear anything about were the Grants. Especially Destry.

His family had welcomed him back with open arms and the ranch was large enough that there was plenty of room as well as work. Not that he'd have moved back into his childhood room at the ranch, even if his mother hadn't turned it into her quilting room.

He'd moved into an old cabin on a stretch of land adjacent to the W Bar G until he could decide what he wanted to do next. The cabin had a roof he could see daylight through and that required a bucket or two when it rained, and often at night he heard mice gnawing on something under the floorboards.

Still, it was better than most of the places he'd slept in while on the rodeo circuit, and he was home.

If only he didn't feel in such limbo. He'd saved nearly every dime he'd made rodeoing so he had options. But he feared moving ahead meant dealing with the past, something he'd put off all these years.

He swore under his breath, as frustrated with the situation between him and Destry as he'd been eleven years ago. He'd known seeing her again would be difficult. *Difficult?* He laughed to himself at how that word didn't come close to adequately describing their encounter.

It hurt like hell. Like being bucked off a horse and hitting the ground with such force that it stole his breath for what seemed like forever. After that initial impact with the ground came the pain in his chest, an ache that radiated through his entire body, and for long moments, he was unable to move or breathe. A small death. Just like seeing Destry after all this time, a moment he would never forget.

And just like getting bucked off a wild horse and being anxious to ride another time, he couldn't wait to see her again.

As he pulled up to his cabin, he saw his father's pickup parked out front. Taylor West climbed out of the truck as Rylan cut his engine. One look at his father's face and he knew he'd heard that Carson Grant was back.

"Where have you been, son?" he asked as Rylan got out. Taylor West was a large man, his blond hair graying around the temples. Years ago he'd been asked to do some modeling. A cowboy through and through, he'd turned down the offer, married his high school sweet-heart, Ellie, and settled down to bring a daughter and three sons into the world. Rylan couldn't have asked for better parents or a more stable family—until his sister, Ginny, was murdered.

His parents were both strong and, with the help of his brothers, had somehow managed to survive the trag-edy. Probably better than Rylan the past eleven years.

"Son?" Taylor asked again.

"Just went for a ride," Rylan said, a half-truth at best.

His father studied him for a long moment. "I know you heard the news."

He nodded and shifted on his boots as he felt that old aching anger settle in his belly. "If there's new evidence, then why isn't Carson Grant already behind bars?"

His father shook his head. "These things take time. The sheriff—"

"The *sheriff*? Frank Curry isn't going to—"

"Frank told me he's just waiting for the new evidence to be run through the crime lab."

His father was often too trusting. "And how long is that going to take?" Rylan demanded.

"We have to give Frank a chance. The sheriff men-tioned that they have more resources than they did eleven years ago and that a lot of cold cases are being solved now because of it. All the evidence is being re-viewed. They need enough to convict."

Rylan grasped on to hope. "It has to be enough that they can nail the son of a bitch." He hated to think, though, what Carson's arrest would do to Destry. Her brother could be facing the death penalty.

"Frank Curry is hoping he can keep a lid on this community until then," Taylor said. "Son, I need your word that you won't do anything to make this any worse."

Rylan thought about earlier, sitting on the narrow track of dirt road, the wind whistling in his side window, his heart pounding after coming face-to-face with Destry again. He didn't have to tell his father that he'd been running for years from the past. Or that he didn't think he could live with himself if he let his sister's murderer remain free.

Taylor West knew his son. He'd been the one to pull Rylan off Carson the day of Ginny's funeral when the Grants had had the audacity to show up.

"You've got to let the law handle this," his father said now.

"And if the law doesn't?" Rylan asked.

"Then we'll cross that bridge when we get to it."

Rylan studied his father for a long moment. "I'll wait to see what the sheriff comes up with."

His father laid a big hand on his shoulder. "Thank you, son. I can't lose another one of you."

SHERIFF FRANK CURRY dragged the evidence box marked Ginny Sue West over to his desk and lifted the top. Until recently, it had been years since he'd reviewed the material. He'd had to force himself to put it away. The case had kept him awake at night.

He'd read through the report dozens of times. Everything had been pretty straightforward. Local girl Ginny West had been struck in the head with a blunt object before her body had been dumped beside the road a couple of miles from town.

She'd still been alive at the time. In the shallow ditch where she was found, there was evidence of where she'd tried to crawl out. But her injuries had been significant. She'd died of the blows she'd sustained before her body had been found.

There were no defensive wounds, which led him to believe she'd known her killer, and that's why she'd gotten into a vehicle with him. That didn't narrow down the suspects since Ginny West would have felt safe getting into a vehicle with most anyone in the county.

The ranch pickup Ginny had driven into town had been found behind the Range Rider bar. Originally, Frank had thought she might have met with foul play because of something that had happened in the bar earlier that night.

However, no one remembered seeing her. Which had led him to believe she'd never gone inside the bar. Whoever she'd run into in the parking lot behind the bar had made sure of that. Which could explain why her purse was found in the pickup.

The main suspect had been Ginny's boyfriend who'd she'd broken up with about a week prior to her murder. Several locals had seen Carson Grant arguing with Ginny in public. It hadn't helped either that Carson was WT Grant's son or that Carson had been in some minor scrapes growing up. People in this community never forgot.

Carson, who'd sworn he'd been on the ranch all night, also had an alibi. And there was no evidence to prove he'd had a hand in Ginny's murder. The town was convinced, though, and Frank thought it had been smart of WT to send Carson away.

Now, with the new evidence and Carson back in Beartooth, if there was any chance of closing this cold case, then Frank was taking it. But the last thing he needed was another murder on his hands, though.

He had asked the lab to put a rush on the tests. It was a long shot, but if he could get some DNA evidence, they could all move on with their lives. And if there was nothing on the barrette… At the very least it had gotten Carson back to town. Now he just had to hope talk of new evidence would force the killer to make a mistake and out himself.

His instincts told him that even with his suspicions about Carson Grant, this case wasn't as cut-and-dried as everyone thought.

CHAPTER FIVE

CARSON LEFT THE house after dinner on the pretense of going for a walk. Cherry had turned in early. He couldn't help smiling when he thought about her and WT at dinner. He wished he was more like her. She could handle WT with one hand tied behind her.

Margaret, the housekeeper and cook, had put a box of his old clothes in the bedroom he and Cherry shared. He'd found a pair of his Western boots and put them on, along with some worn jeans and a flannel shirt. When he looked in the mirror, it gave him a shock. He'd expected to see the twenty-year-old he'd been, but his face gave away an unmistakable regret.

He'd left the house, unable to bear another moment with his father. He hadn't gone far down the road when he saw Destry go roaring past in one of the ranch pickups.

The fact that she was just now coming back didn't bode well. Something told him the cows she'd gone to rescue from the road weren't the only problem she'd run into. Did it have something to do with him?

He'd known his being back here would be trouble for her. He loved his sister and hated what he'd put her through already. Now it was about to get worse. Destry would be collateral damage, but he had little choice.

All of this had been set in motion long before she was even born.

It wasn't far to the homestead house as the crow flies, but over a mile by road. After he started down the mountain, he spotted the barn and corrals on the mountain just out of sight from the house. Nearby was the airstrip and hangar where the plane was kept.

Not far into the walk, he regretted not driving. The wind felt cold. Either that or his blood had thinned. It wouldn't be long before snow would blanket the ground, and stay there through April, even May.

Down the road in the fading light of day, he caught sight of the old house where he and Destry had grown up.

"So you were born…poor?" Cherry had asked.

"My father had been dirt poor, as WT called it. He was doing okay by the time I came along and even better when Destry was born. We weren't rich, by any means. We lived in the old homestead. He hadn't built the new place yet or had his plane accident." Funny, but Carson recalled those years more fondly than he'd expected he would.

"WT made some good investments, bought up any land that came available—and usually cheaply since this was before Montana property went sky high. As they say, the rest is history," he'd told her.

Cherry had been impressed. "Well, that's good for you," she'd said.

Was it? If WT still lived in the old homestead house and the ranch was small as it had been when he started, would he be so dead set on his son taking the place over? Carson doubted it.

And wouldn't things have been different when Ginny

West was murdered? WT couldn't have afforded to send his son away for eleven years. Carson would have had to stay—no matter the consequences.

Cherry had been surprised that his sister preferred living in the two-story log house instead of the mansion their father had built. Carson understood only too well. But he would have made the old man build him his own house, something new and modern and even farther away. Clearly, he wasn't his sister.

The twilight cast a soft silver sheen over the land, making the dark pines shimmer as he crossed the cattleguard and approached the house. This far north, the sun didn't set in the summer months until almost eleven. Now, though, it was getting dark by eight-thirty. Soon it would be dark by five.

The wind had picked up even more, he noticed distractedly. Something was definitely blowing in. The wind was so strong in this part of Montana that it had blown over semis on the interstate and knocked train cars off their tracks.

It was worse in the winter when wind howled across the eaves and whipped snow into huge sculpted drifts. He remembered waking to find he couldn't get out to help feed the animals because the snow had blown in against the door. Often he'd had to plow the road out so he and Destry could get to the county road to catch the school bus.

It had become a state joke that while other states closed their schools when they got a skiff of snow or the thermometer dropped below zero, Montana schools remained open in blinding blizzards and fifty-below-zero temperatures. Carson remembered too many days when the ice was so thick on the inside of the school bus windows that he couldn't see outside. He hadn't missed the cold, especially enjoying winters in Las Vegas.

He reminded himself that, with luck, he and Cherry would be back there before their vacations were up.

Carson found his sister unloading firewood from the back of a flatbed truck and stacking it along the rear of the house. As a kid, she'd always turned to hard work or horseback when she was upset. He watched her for a moment. She was working off something, that was for sure.

"I thought we had hired hands for that?" he asked, only half joking.

She grinned and tossed a sawn chunk of log in his direction. He had to step out of the way to keep it from hitting him.

"Think you got enough wood there?" he asked as he fell in to help stack the truckload of logs along the back of the house. Firewood had been stacked in that spot for as long as he could remember.

"Takes quite a few cords to get through the winter with this latest weather pattern," Destry said.

"I can't imagine what it must take up at the Big House." He'd heard her call it that and thought how appropriate it was to compare WT's mansion with prison.

"Dad doesn't heat with wood," she said. "Went with a gas furnace. The wood fireplaces are just for show."

He stopped, already winded from the exertion of trying to keep up with his sister. "Why do you stay here?"

"You know I've always loved this old house."

"I'm not talking about this house. I'm talking about this ranch, Montana. I gave you some good advice before I left." He'd told her to go away to college and not come back. To run as far away from WT as she could get. She should have listened. "You obviously didn't take it."

"But I appreciated the advice." Destry stopped throwing down wood long enough to smile at him. "I was able to get my degree in business and ranch management and still stay around here, so it all worked out for the best."

"Destry, what's here for you but work?"

"I love this work." She looked out at the darkening land beyond the grove of trees for a moment, her expression softening. "I couldn't breathe without open spaces."

He wondered what had happened either before she'd left to see about the cows—or while she was gone. Maybe it was just his return that had her upset. "Destry, you know I can't stay here."

She jumped down to stack logs, making short order out of the pile she'd thrown from the truck bed. "What does Dad say about that?"

"What do you think he says?" He felt his blood pressure rise. "I don't know how you can put up with him. I can't."

"What will you do?"

He shook his head. He didn't have a clue. The old man definitely had him between a rock and a hard place. Destry was in an even worse corner, but he didn't have the heart to tell her.

She stacked more of the wood for a moment. "I'll pick you up early in the morning," she said, stopping to study him. "Be ready."

"Where are we going?"

"You'll see."

He smiled at his sister. "I've missed you."

"Yeah, I've missed you, too."

Rylan had just thrown a couple of elk steaks into a cast-iron skillet sizzling with melted butter. A large baked potato wrapped in foil sat on the counter since the steaks wouldn't take long.

The secret with wild meat was not to overcook it. He'd learned that at hunting camp when he was a boy. At least today he wasn't cooking over an open campfire. The wonderful scent of the steaks filled the cabin, and for the first time in weeks, he felt as if he was finally home.

The knock at the door made him curse under his breath. He really wasn't in the mood for company.

When he went to the door, he was shocked to find Destry standing outside on the wooden step. He tried to hide his surprise as well as his pleasure in seeing her again. Leaning his hip against the door frame, he studied her for a moment as he waited for her to speak— that was until he remembered his steaks and swore as he hurried back to the stove.

When he looked up from flipping the beautifully browned steaks, she had come in and closed the door behind her. The cabin immediately felt smaller. Too small and too warm.

"I assume you're not here for supper," he said, wondering what she *was* here for. Being this close to her jolted his heart, reminding him of things he'd spent years trying to forget. "I'm a pretty good cook if you're interested."

"No, thanks." She appeared as uncomfortable as he felt in the tight quarters, which surprised him. He'd only seen her lose control of her emotions once. The reminder of their night together did nothing to ease his tension. He pulled the steaks off the stove, his mouth no longer watering for them, though, and gave her all his attention.

Destry was the only woman he knew who could make a pair of jeans and a flannel work shirt sexy. Her chestnut plaited hair hung over one shoulder, the end falling over her breast. He remembered the weight of her breasts in his hands, the feel of her nipple in his mouth. His fingers itched to unbraid her hair and let it float around her bare shoulders.

"I'll make this quick since I don't want your steaks to get cold," she said. "Thank you for changing your mind about going to the W Bar G earlier."

He shook his head. "Don't. You don't know how close I came."

"You stopped before it was too late," she said quietly.

"Yeah, but that was today. I can't make any promises about tomorrow."

Her blue eyes shone like banked flames. Even in the dull light of the cabin, he could see the sprinkling of freckles that arced across her cheeks and nose. She looked as young as she had in high school. The girl next door, he used to joke. And that was still what she was.

Only now she was all woman, a strong, independent, resilient woman who made his pulse quicken and heart ache at the sight of her. Pain and pleasure, both killers when your heart was as invested as much as his was.

He wanted to reach for her, to pull her into his arms, to kiss that full mouth....

"Enjoy your steaks," she said, turning toward the door.

He couldn't think of anything to say, certainly not something that would make her stay. He listened to her get into her pickup, the engine cranking over, the tires crunching on the gravel as she drove away.

He dumped his steaks onto a plate, but he'd lost his appetite. Destry was determined to make him a saint when he was far from it. Now he wished he'd kicked Carson's butt.

But he figured Destry would have still ended up on his doorstep tonight—only she wouldn't have been thanking him. She would probably have come with a loaded shotgun and blood in her eye.

THE STORM BLEW in with a vengeance just after midnight. Destry woke to rain and the banging of one of the shutters downstairs. She rose and padded down the steps wearing nothing but the long worn T-shirt she'd gone to bed in.

As she stepped off the bottom stair, she slowed, surprised to feel the chilled wind on her face. Had she left one of the windows open?

The air had a bite to it, another indication that winter wasn't far off. This time of year the days could be hot as summer, but by night the temperature would drop like a stone. Soon the water in the shallow eddies of the creek would have a skim of ice on them in the morning and the peaks in the Crazies would gleam with fresh snow.

She thought about her brother's earlier visit. What had he walked all the way down here for? She'd been too worked up over seeing Rylan at the time to question him. Later she'd had the feeling he wanted to tell her something. Whatever it was, he'd apparently changed his mind.

After they'd finished stacking the wood, she'd invited him in, but he'd declined. Just as he had when she'd offered to give him a ride back up to their father's house.

"I need the exercise," he'd said and had taken off before it became completely dark.

Her thoughts turned to her visit with Rylan earlier that night. Just the memory of him cooking steaks in that small cabin, warmed her still. It had seemed so normal, so welcoming, like the Rylan she once knew. He might come after Carson again when she wouldn't be there to talk him out of it. But at least it wouldn't be tonight.

Destry hugged herself from the chill as she started across the open living room. The worn wood floor beneath her bare feet felt freezing cold. The shutter banged a monotonous beat against the side of the house. The wind curled the edge of the living room rug and flapped the pages of a livestock grower's magazine left on an end table.

It wasn't until she reached the back of the house that she realized it wasn't a window that had been left open—it was the back door.

A chill rattled through her that had nothing to do with the wind or the cold. Through the open doorway, the pines appeared black against the dark night. They whipped in the wind and rain below a cloud-shrouded sky.

Destry reached to close the door but stopped as she caught movement out beyond the creek. Something at the edge of the trees. Without taking her eyes off the spot, she reached for the shotgun she kept by the back door to chase away bears. She didn't have to break it down to know it was loaded. There were two shells, one in each barrel.

She stared through the darkness at the spot in the pines and cottonwoods where she would have sworn she saw something move just moments before.

As she stood in the doorway, large droplets of rain

pinged off the overhang, splattering her with cool mist. The wind blew her hair back from her face and molded the worn T-shirt to her body.

What had she seen? Or had she just imagined the movement?

Another chill raced across her bare flesh. She hated the way her heart pounded. Worse, that whatever had been out there had the ability to spook her.

The door must not have been latched and had blown open. But as she started to close the door, she recalled the downed fence and the tracks leading into the trees behind her house that she'd seen from the air. With everything that had happened, she'd forgotten about them.

Few people who lived out in the country locked their doors, especially around Beartooth. Destry never had. But tonight she closed the door, locked it and, leaving the shotgun by the back door, took her pistol up to her bedroom.

CHAPTER SIX

NETTIE BENTON DIDN'T notice the broken window when she opened the Beartooth General Store early the next morning. She hadn't gotten much sleep, thanks to Bob and the bad dreams he'd had during the night. She'd awakened to find him screaming in terror—as if his snoring wasn't bad enough.

He'd finally moved in to the guest room, or she wouldn't have slept a wink. When she'd gone to open the store's front door, she'd looked across the street and seen the new owner of the café chatting with a handful of customers. Just the sight of Kate LaFond threatened to ruin an already bad day.

The woman had purchased the Branding Iron after the former owner had dropped dead this spring. Just days after the funeral, Kate LaFond had appeared out of nowhere. No one knew anything about her or why she'd decided to buy a café in Beartooth.

The community had been so grateful that she had kept the café open, they hadn't cared who she was or where she'd come from. Or what the devil she was doing here.

Everyone but Nettie. "I still say it's odd," she said to herself now as she stood at the window watching Kate smiling and laughing with a bunch of ranchers as she refilled their coffee cups.

An attractive thirtysomething brunette, Kate had apparently taken to the town like a duck to water. It annoyed Nettie that, after only a few months, most people seemed fine with her. They didn't care, they said, that they didn't know a single relative fact about the woman's past.

"It's just nice to have the café open," local contractor Grayson Brooks had told her. Nettie had noticed how often Grayson stopped by the café mornings now. Grayson owned Brooks Construction and was semiretired at forty-five because of his invalid wife, Anna. He had a crew that did most of the physical work, allowing him, apparently, to spend long hours at the Branding Iron every morning.

"Kate's nice and friendly and she makes a pretty good cup of coffee," Grayson had said when Nettie had asked him what he thought of the woman. "I think she makes a fine addition to the town."

"Doesn't hurt that she's young and pretty, I suppose," Nettie had said.

Grayson had merely smiled as if she wasn't going to get an argument out of him on that subject, although everyone knew, as good-looking as he was, he was devoted to his wife.

"Did you ever consider it's none of our business?" her husband, Bob, had asked when Nettie had complained about Kate LaFond to him. He'd been sitting in his office adding up the day's receipts.

"What if she has some dark past? A woman like that, she could have been married, killed several husbands by the age of thirty-five, even drowned a few of her children."

Bob had looked up at her, squinting. After forty years of marriage, he no longer seemed shocked by anything she said.

"Why on earth would you even think such a thing?" he'd asked wearily.

"There's something about her. Why won't she tell anyone about her past if she has nothing to hide? I'm warning you, Bob Benton, there is something off about that woman. Why else would she buy a café in a near ghost town, far away from everything? She's running from something. Mark my words."

"Sometimes, Nettie" was all Bob had said with one of his big sighs, before leaving to walk up the steep path to their house.

Now, Kate LaFond looked up. Their gazes met across the narrow stretch of blacktop that made up the main drag of Beartooth. The look Kate gave her made a shudder run the length of Nettie's spine.

"That woman's dangerous," she said to herself. It didn't matter that there was no one around to hear. No one listened to her anyway.

Nettie moved from the window and went about opening the store as she did every morning. Lost in thought, she barely heard something crunch under her boots. She blinked, stumbling to a stop to look down. That's when she saw the glass from the broken window.

DESTRY DROVE UP to the big house, anxious to spend some time with her brother. She hadn't slept well last night after discovering the open door, so she'd had a lot of time to think.

She was worried about her brother. Even more worried about what he might have come down to the house to tell her last night.

This afternoon she would be rounding up the last of the cattle from the mountains. After a season on the summer range, they would be bringing down the last of the fattened-up calves, and all but the breeding stock would be loaded into semis and taken to market.

Destry always went on the last roundup in the high country before winter set in. The air earlier this morning had been crisp and cold, the ground frosty after last night's rain. But while clouds still shrouded the peaks of the Crazies, the sun was out down here in the valley, the day warming fast.

As she pulled up to the house and honked, she was surprised when her brother came right out. He'd never been an early riser even as a boy. He must really be desperate to get away from their father. Or was it his fiancée?

"Okay, where are we going?" Carson asked as he climbed into the pickup.

Destry nodded her head toward the bed of the truck and the fishing tackle she'd loaded this morning.

"Fishing?" He shook his head as she threw the pickup into gear. "Did you forget I don't have a fishing license?"

"With all your problems, you're worried about getting caught without a fishing license?"

He laughed. "Good point." He leaned back in the seat as she tore down the road, and for a moment, she could pretend they were kids again heading for the reservoir to go fishing after doing their chores.

Destry barreled forward, having driven more dirt roads in her life than paved ones. The pickup rumbled across one cattle guard after another, then across the pasture, dropping down to the creek.

Because it was late in the year, the creek was low. She slowed as the pickup forded the stream, tires plunged over the rocks and through a half foot of crystal clear water before roaring up the other side.

Tall weeds between the two-track road brushed the bottom of the pickup, and rocks kicked up, pinging off the undercarriage. Out of the corner of her eye, she saw Carson grab the handle over the door as she took the first turn.

"Sorry to see your driving hasn't improved," he said.

She laughed. "You've been gone too long."

"Not long enough."

"Come on, haven't you missed this?" She found that hard to believe. Didn't he notice how beautiful it was here? The air was so clear and clean. The land so pleasing to the eye. And there was plenty of elbow room for when you just wanted to stretch out some.

The road cut through the fertile valley, stubble fields a pale yellow, the freshly plowed acres in fallow dark with the turned soil.

"Apparently you haven't been listening to me any more than WT has," her brother said. "This is just land to me. I feel no need to take root in it."

They fell silent, the only sound the roar of the engine and the spray of dirt clods and rocks kicked up by the tires. The land dropped toward the river, falling away in rolling hills that had turned golden under the bright sun of autumn.

Ahead she saw the brilliant blue of pooled water and smiled, feeling like a kid again. Over the next rise, she swung the pickup onto a rutted track that ended at the water's edge. Summer had burned all the color out of the grass around the small lake. Only a few trees stood on the other side, their leaves rust red, many of the branches already bared off.

Destry parked the truck next to an old rowboat that lay upside down beside the water like a turtle in the sun. Getting out, together they flipped the boat over and carried it to the water before going back for the poles, tackle box and the cooler she'd packed.

"When was the last time you went fishing?" she asked as they loaded everything into the boat.

"Probably with you. As I recall I caught more fish than you, bigger ones, too."

She laughed. "Apparently your memory hasn't improved any more than my driving."

Their gazes held for a long moment. Carson was the first to look away. "Hop in. If you're determined to do this…" He pushed the rowboat off the shore and climbed in.

Destry breathed in the day, relaxing for the first time since her brother's return. She dipped her fingers into the deep green water. It felt cold even with the October sun beating down on its surface.

"I assume you brought worms," Carson said, reaching into the cooler. He opened the Styrofoam container and tossed her a wriggling night crawler, chuckling when she caught it without even making a face.

"You never were like other girls," he said.

"I'm going to take that as a compliment." The water rippled in the slight breeze as the boat drifted for a few moments before Carson took the oars. He rowed the boat out to the center of the reservoir, then let the tips of the oars skim the glistening surface as they drifted again.

Destry watched her red-and-white bobber float along on top of the water in the breeze. From the horizon came the loud honking of a large flock of geese. The eerie sound seemed to echo across the lake as the geese carved a dark V through the clear, cloudless blue.

Nothing signaled the change of season like the migration of the ducks and geese. She thought of all the seasons she'd seen come and go, so many of them without her brother, the lonesome call of the geese making her sad.

"I don't want you to leave again," she said without looking at him.

Water lapped softly at the side of the boat. The breeze lifted the loose tendrils of hair around her face. A half dozen ducks splashed in the shallows near the shore, taking flight suddenly in a spasm of wings. Beads of water hung in the air for an instant as iridescent as gleaming pearls.

"I'll bet there aren't any fish in this reservoir anymore," Carson said. He was lying back on the seat, eyes closed, his pole tucked under one arm, the other arm over his face. He wore a T-shirt and an old pair of worn jeans, the legs rolled up, and a pair of equally old sneakers. The Western straw hat he'd been wearing rested on the floor of the boat.

"Doesn't really matter if there are fish, does it?"

Carson moved the arm from his face enough to open one eye and look at her. "Only if you hope to catch something."

"I'm happy just being here," she said.

"*You* would be. Some people actually like to catch fish when they go fishing." He went back to half dozing on the seat.

"Are you really going to marry Cherry?" Destry asked after a few minutes had passed.

"Why else would I have asked her?"

"Because at the time it seemed like a good idea?"

Her brother snickered. "It did seem like a better idea in Vegas than in Beartooth, Montana. She doesn't exactly fit in here, does she?"

"Is she bored to tears?"

"Yep, and worried about grizzly bears coming down and eating her in the middle of the night. She can't believe the closest big-box store is over an hour away." Carson laughed. "I hate to think what will happen if she breaks a nail."

The sound of her brother's laughter filled Destry with such love for him. She leaned back, letting the warm morning and the gentle slap of the water on the side of the boat lull her. Overhead, a red hawk circled on a warm thermal.

"You haven't asked me if I killed Ginny," Carson said, and she felt the boat rock as he leaned up on one elbow to look at her.

She thought she could see the hawk circling overhead reflected in his gaze. "You didn't. You couldn't."

He scoffed and lay back again, the arm back over his face. "If there's one thing I've learned, it's that we're all capable of despicable acts when we're backed into a corner. But thanks for believing in me, sis. It means a lot."

NETTIE FELT SICK to her stomach as she stared at the shattered window, the shards of glass glittering on the floor. Who had done such a thing?

She took a step back, her heart pounding as she realized whoever had broken the window could still be somewhere in the store.

Rushing to the phone, she dialed the sheriff with trembling fingers. "I've been burglarized!" she screamed into the phone the moment the dispatcher put her through.

"Who is this?" Sheriff Frank Curry asked in a voice so calm it set Nettie's already frayed nerves on edge.

She'd known Frank Curry since she was a girl. "Who

the devil do you think it is?" she snapped. "My store was burglarized." She dropped her voice. "He might still be here."

"Lynette," the sheriff said. He was the only person who called her by her given name. The way he said it spoke volumes about their past. In just one word, he could make her feel like that lovestruck, teenage girl again. "Perhaps you should wait for me at your house. Where's your *husband?*"

She knew only too well what Frank thought of her husband. "Just get up here and don't you dare send that worthless Deputy Billy Westfall instead." She slammed down the phone, shaking even harder than she'd been before. She was fairly certain whoever had broken in wasn't still here. At least not on the lower floor.

The upper level was used for storage. Moving to the second-floor door, she eased it open and peered up the dark steps. She listened, didn't hear a sound and closed the door and bolted it.

If the burglar was up there, he wouldn't be going anywhere. She checked her watch and, leaving the closed sign on the front door, settled in to wait. As she glanced across the street to the café again, she realized she'd never had a break-in before Kate LaFond came to town.

"WHERE'S CARSON?"

Margaret turned from the stove, eyes narrowed. "Good morning to you, too, Waylon."

WT cursed under his breath. He hated it when she called him Waylon. She only did it because she knew it annoyed him. Or to remind him where he'd come from. As if he needed reminding.

"Don't act as if you didn't hear me," he snapped.

"Why? *You* do."

He didn't know how many times he'd come close to firing her. But they both knew he'd pay hell getting anyone else to cook and clean for him—let alone put up with him.

The real reason he hadn't sent her packing was that she knew him in a way that no one else did, not that he would ever admit it to her. Like him, she also knew the pain of poverty. Of wearing the same boots until even the cardboard you'd pasted inside couldn't keep the rocks from making your feet bleed. She knew about hand-me-down clothes and eating wild meat because there wasn't anything else.

Christmases had been the worst. That empty feeling that settled in the pit of the stomach as the day approached and you knew there would be no presents under the tree. It was hell when even Santa Claus didn't think you deserved better.

A couple of do-gooders in the area had left presents for him one year. WT had been too young to know what it had cost his parents to accept them. He'd greedily opened each one. A football. A pair of skates. A BB gun.

He remembered the feeling of having something that no one had ever worn or used before him. He'd run his fingers along the shiny BB gun, seeing his reflection in the blade of the skates and holding the warm leather of the football thinking it the happiest day of his life.

The next Christmas, though, he'd seen the look on his father's face and realized his mother's tears weren't those of joy. There was no Santa Claus, only people who felt sorry for him and his family. He'd made sure the do-gooders skipped his house from then on and swore he'd never need or take charity again.

No one knew about any of that—except for Margaret. Yes, that shared past was one reason he didn't fire Margaret—and that she put up with him. Also, they knew each other's secrets. That alone was a bond that neither of them seemed able to break. Margaret knew him right down to his black, unforgiving soul.

"I was looking for Carson," WT said, tempering his words now as he wheeled deeper into the kitchen. "Have you seen him?"

"He left with his sister. I believe they've gone fishing."

"Fishing?"

"Yes, fishing. They haven't seen each other in more than a decade. I would imagine they want to spend some time together." She didn't add, "Away from you," but he heard it in her tone.

He grunted and spun his wheelchair around to leave.

"Even if you can get him cleared of a murder charge, you can't keep him here against his will," she said to his retreating back.

"We'll see," he said, gritting his teeth.

CARSON SURREPTITIOUSLY STUDIED his sister as he pretended to sleep in the gently rocking boat. Everything about this grown-up Destry impressed him. There didn't seem to be anything she couldn't handle on the ranch. This afternoon he'd heard that she was planning to ride up into the high country to finish rounding up the cattle. He'd never been able to ride as well as her. Nor did he have her knack for dealing with the day-to-day running of a ranch. The ranch hands had always respected her because she'd never been afraid to get her hands dirty, working right alongside them if needed.

He felt a wave of envy, wishing he were more like her. There was a rare beauty about her, a tranquility and contentment that he'd have given anything for. Was she really that at peace with her life? Or was she just better at hiding her feelings than he was?

Stirring from his dark thoughts, he sat up. "So who are you dating?"

"Dating?" She let out a laugh. "I don't have time to date. Oh, don't give me that look. I've dated. Don't you be like Dad and try to marry me off to someone with good pasture or grazing land."

Carson remembered how WT had been about him and Ginny West.

"Why can't you be interested in one of the Hamilton girls? Now that's some nice ranch land those girls are going to inherit, a whole section of irrigated pasture along Little Timber Creek."

Carson laughed now at the memory and shared it with Destry.

She chuckled. "He's been pushing me to go out with Hitch McCray in hopes of someday getting that strip of land between ours and the forest service land to the north."

"He'd even marry you off to Hitch?" Carson let out a curse. "I wouldn't let Hitch have a mean stray dog. Anyway, he's too old for you."

She smiled at that. "He's only forty."

"Seriously, you've put in your time taking care of WT. Isn't it time for you to have some fun?"

Destry shook her head, smiling. "I haven't been holed up here. There's just nowhere I want to be but here or nothing else I want to do with my life. I could never leave Montana, no matter what." She studied him. "What about you? What do you want to do with your life?"

He shrugged. He truly didn't know. He'd thought he was happy in Las Vegas working at the casino, had seen himself married to Cherry and living the rest of his life in the desert.

But some bad luck, WT and this new evidence had changed that.

Destry was studying him openly. "Isn't there someone you'd like to spend your life with?"

"How can you ask that?" Carson said with a laugh. "I'm engaged to be married."

"Do you love her?"

He sobered. "Not like I loved Ginny."

"I'm sorry."

"Don't be. I'm like you. I'm fine." He almost told her everything then, but he couldn't bring himself to spoil this beautiful morning with her. Soon enough he would be responsible for breaking her heart. Again.

"What if you could clear your name?" Destry asked.

"After all these years?" he asked with a shake of his head. But her words conjured a future he'd thought lost to him. As he looked out across the land, he told himself not to, but for the first time in years, he felt a sense of hope he hadn't since Ginny was killed.

CHAPTER SEVEN

BETHANY REYNOLDS FINGERED the locket at her neck and tried not to think about her husband as she reached for her hastily discarded clothing.

Her husband, Clete, would have never thought to give her a silver heart-shaped locket. Clete didn't have a romantic bone in his body. What had the man gotten her for their first Valentine's Day together? A set of snow tires.

The only reason he'd married her was to get her elk hunting tag. Only a few tags were given out each year in the area he loved to hunt. She'd lucked out and gotten one.

It had taken a moose even to get Clete to notice her. She'd been mooning over him for years. But it wasn't until she'd come into the Range Rider where he'd worked as a bartender and started showing her moose photos that he finally came around.

She'd drawn a moose tag—and bagged one. That was big news since moose tags were more rare than elk. Of course Clete had been jealous as all get out.

"*You* got a tag?" Clete had said.

She'd grinned, enjoying his jealousy—until he'd asked, "Who shot it for you?"

Bethany hadn't even bothered to answer him as she'd turned to show off her moose. It was three times bigger than she was and would feed herself and her family all year.

"What's moose meat taste like?" one of her "city" friends had asked.

"A little sweet, a darker meat than elk or deer. I'll get you a package of steaks to try," Bethany had promised. Behind her, she'd heard Clete banging around behind the bar, louder than usual.

It wasn't until the bar had cleared out some that he'd called her over. "So you shot it yourself," he'd said and offered her a drink.

She'd never been one to hold a grudge or turn down a free drink. Not to mention the fact that she'd had a crush on Clete since junior high. He'd been Beartooth's claim to fame, a football player who'd played for the Grizzlies at the University of Montana. That is until he got hurt.

Bethany had always known she was going to marry him. She even did that silly thing all lovesick girls do, she wrote Mrs. Clete Reynolds and Bethany Reynolds so many times that she believed it.

When he'd gotten injured his sophomore year at U of M, he'd dropped out, come home and gotten a job bartending at the Range Rider.

"Just until the leg heals," he would say. Everyone knew better. When the bar came up for sale, the owner sold it to Clete and carried the loan.

"So tell me about this moose," Clete had said that day at the bar as he'd glanced up from one of the photos to look at her. There'd been only one other time that he'd looked at her like that, years ago at the Fall Harvest Festival when she was sixteen. She'd told him that day she was going to marry him and that he'd better wait for her to grow up.

But it had taken the moose to bring them together years later.

"You gutted it yourself?" he'd said.

It was so big that she'd had to crawl inside it.

The moose had gotten them dating. But it had taken the *elk* permit to get Clete to pop the question. It was almost an accepted thing, women giving up their tags so their men could hunt more, even though it was illegal. If you got caught.

Most things came down to simply that, she'd learned. Like affairs, she thought as she slipped into her Western shirt.

"That was amazing," said the man on the bed.

She felt warm fingertips brush along the top of her bare butt and smiled to herself. Some men were breast men, others leg men. This one was all about her large, round butt and she loved it.

Clete had never appreciated her backside. Hell, he wasn't all that wild about her other parts, either. Lovemaking with Clete had become so mechanical that Bethany could just lie there and think about anything else she wanted until it was over. At just barely thirty-two, she was in her prime and was glad at least there was one man around who appreciated that fact. This man had never thought she was too young for him.

"I'm glad you were able to get away today," he said.

She finished snapping her Western shirt and stood. This was when she usually told him that she couldn't do this anymore. If they got caught, they both had too much to lose, not to mention it was wrong.

Bethany always left him, swearing she wouldn't go back. But after a day or two, she'd weaken. He made her feel as if she was the most beautiful woman in the world. He also was smart enough to know a woman didn't want snow tires on Valentine's Day, she thought as she again touched the tiny heart-shaped silver locket he'd given her. It felt cold against her bare skin.

"I have to work a double shift at the café tomorrow," she said and groaned at the thought. She'd worked at the café through high school and thought those days were behind her once she married Clete. She'd been wrong about that, too.

"I'm sorry, Sweetie, but I'm going to be busy for a few days myself."

She turned to look at him, a little surprised by his words. He always had more free time than she did. Lately, she'd felt as if he was losing interest in her and that scared her.

"Oh, and don't forget to take that off before you go home, will you," he told her, motioning to the locket resting against her skin.

The locket, like their affair, was their secret. "I won't forget."

DESTRY COULDN'T WAIT to ride horseback up in the high country above the ranch. She did her best thinking on the back of a horse. Or no thinking at all, which would have been fine with her this afternoon.

When she stopped by the house on her way to the barn, Cherry was lying by the pool.

"Is it always this quiet here?" Cherry asked.

"Always," Destry said, looking toward the spectacular Crazy Mountains.

"Where do you shop?" Cherry asked.

"Nettie at the Beartooth General Store sells the essentials, food, supplies, even some clothing and muck boots."

"Muck boots. You have a lot of use for those?" Cherry smiled up at her.

"Actually we do, especially in the spring and during a winter thaw when you're out feeding the animals."

"I can't imagine," Cherry said with a shake of her head. "Carson said there are grizzlies and they sometimes come down in the yard?"

Destry could tell that the thought had been worrying her. "Occasionally." She didn't add that this time of year bears were fattening up for the winter and stuffing themselves before going into hibernation.

Cherry sighed. "I have to tell you, this place gives me the creeps. It's too…isolated."

Destry thought about what her brother's fiancée had said as she prepared for her trip up into the mountains. She'd noticed that Carson had spent little time with Cherry and suspected he was seeing her differently against the Montana backdrop. Cherry was like a fish out of water—and clearly unhappy being here.

Inside the big house, Destry followed a familiar, alluring scent as she walked down to the kitchen to find Margaret making fried pies. A dozen of the small crescent shaped pies were cooling on a rack next to the stove. Against the golden brown of the crusts, the white frosting drizzled over them now dripped onto a sheet of aluminum foil.

"You're just in time," Margaret said, smiling, as she lifted two more pies from the hot grease and put them beside the others.

"They smell wonderful." Destry picked up a still warm pie and took a bite. The crust was flaky and buttery and delicious. She licked her lips, closing her eyes as her taste buds took in the warm cinnamon apple filling and sweet icing.

"Do they meet your satisfaction?" Margaret asked with a smile as Destry groaned in approval.

"I swear they're the best you've ever made," she said between bites.

Margaret laughed. "You always say that."

Even with fried pies cooling nearby, Carson sat at the counter in the kitchen with nothing but a cup of coffee in front of him, looking miserable.

"Why aren't you out by the pool?" she asked.

"I'm showing Carson around the ranch," their father said as he wheeled into the kitchen. "He's been gone so long he doesn't know anything about the operation. I planned to take him out first thing this morning, but apparently he went fishing."

Carson grunted as he stared down into his cup. "And didn't catch a darned thing."

WT ignored him, shifting his gaze to Destry instead. "Where are you going dressed like that?"

"Riding up to collect the rest of the cattle from summer pasture," Destry said as she poured herself a half cup of coffee.

"I thought we had ranch hands for that," her father said.

She merely smiled. It was an old battle between them. He made little secret of the fact that he didn't like her actually working the ranch. But she'd always loved calving on those freezing cold nights in January when she could see her breath inside the barn. There was nothing like witnessing the birth of a new calf, branding to the sound of bawling calves, the feel of baking sun on your back or riding through cool, dark pines gathering cattle in the fall.

He had the idea that marriage would change her. It often amazed her that her own father didn't know her at all.

"On your way out you might tell your brother's fiancée that at this altitude she's going to get burned to a crisp out there," WT said to her.

"Don't bother," Carson said. "Cherry likes to find out things on her own. Anyway, she can take care of herself."

As her father and brother left, Destry grabbed a couple of Margaret's famous fried pies, wrapped up a couple for Russell Murdock, their ranch foreman, and finished her coffee. She was on her way out when the phone rang.

She picked it up to save Margaret the effort. "W Bar G, Destry speaking."

The voice on the other end of the line was low and hoarse. It could have been a man or a woman's. "You tell that brother of yours we don't want the likes of him around here."

"Who is this?" she demanded, but the caller had already hung up. As she returned the receiver, she saw Margaret looking at her and knew it wasn't the first time someone had called threatening Carson.

"People who call making threats hardly ever do anything more," Margaret said, turning back to her fried pies. "I'd be more afraid for anyone who tries to come on this ranch. Your father's been carrying his .357 Magnum since your brother came home."

So he'd been expecting trouble. That made her all the more worried for her brother. She scooped up the pies, said goodbye to Margaret and headed for the barn. Since his accident, her father had put in a paved path down to the barn, even though he no longer rode.

As she saddled up, she promised herself that for a few hours, she was going to put all of her worries aside. She loved the ride up into the high mountain meadows and the feel of the horse beneath her. So many ranches now used everything from four-wheelers to helicopters to round up their cattle, leaving the horses to be nothing more than pasture ornaments.

She much preferred a horse than a noisy four-wheeler. Her horse, Hay Burner, a name her father tagged the mare, was one she'd rescued along with another half dozen wild horses from Wyoming.

Destry had fallen helplessly in love with the mare at first sight. She was a deep chocolate color with a wild mane and a gentle manner. She'd taken well to cattle and cutting calves out of the herd.

As Destry rode out to join the ranch foreman and the ranch hands for the ride up into the Crazies, she breathed in the scent of towering pines and the smell of saddle leather.

Meadowlarks sang from the thick groves of aspens as white cumulous clouds bobbed along in a sea of clear blue. The air felt cool and crisp with the sharp scent of the pines and the promise of fall in the changing colors of the leaves. Overhead, a bald eagle circled looking for prey. Nearby a squirrel chattered at them from a pine bough.

"Everything all right at the house?" the ranch foreman asked as Destry rode beside him.

Russell Murdock had let the others ride on ahead of them. He'd been a ranch hand when she was young and had worked his way up to foreman. He'd been with the W Bar G longer than anyone except Margaret. Destry considered them both family.

In his late fifties, Russell was a kind, good-natured man with infinite patience with both the ranch hands and WT. He'd been the one who'd dried her tears when he'd found her crying in the barn when she was a girl. He'd picked her up from the dirt when she'd tried to ride one of the ranch animals she shouldn't have. He'd also been there for her when Carson had left and Rylan had broken her heart.

"It's an adjustment for Carson," she said.

Russell smiled over at her. "He's staying?"

She met the older man's gaze. They'd been too close over the years for her to lie to him. "WT thinks he is. I guess it will depend on this new evidence in Ginny West's murder investigation."

Russell nodded knowingly. "You know there's talk around town…"

"I've heard. I'm hoping as long as Carson stays on the ranch there won't be any trouble."

Russell looked worried but said no more as the trail rose up through a mountain pass and the sound of lowing cattle filled the air. Once they reached the ridge, the foreman rode on ahead to catch up with the others.

Destry lagged behind to stop and look at the view of the ranch. She heard someone ride up beside her.

"Quite the spread, wouldn't you say?" Lucky leaned over his saddle horn and looked to the valley below. "I heard your brother is back. Does that mean he's going to be running the place now?"

Pete "Lucky" Larson had been with the W Bar G

since he and Carson graduated from high school together.

"You'd have to ask him," Destry said, hoping that would be the end of it.

"Kind of hard to ask him since I haven't seen him. Wouldn't you think he'd at least ask me in for a drink? After all, we go way back."

She glanced over at the cowboy. Pockmarked with a narrow ferretlike face, Lucky made her a little uneasy lately. It was the way he looked at her, as if he thought she needed being brought down a peg or two.

"I figure if Carson is running the place, he'll want to give me a nice raise, don't you think? I know I'll never get to live like your old man, but I'd like to live better than I do."

Ranch hands on the W Bar G were well paid. Lucky was probably overpaid, if the truth were known. "Carson's been pretty busy," Destry said. "But if you think you're due for a raise, you should take it up with Russell. He's the ranch foreman."

"Is that right?" His gaze brushed over her like a spider web, making her want to brush it off. "Carson's busy, huh? Not too busy to be asking around about a poker game, though. You should tag along to the next game. Maybe you'll get lucky," he said with a wink. "From what I've seen, you don't get out much."

"But *you're* going to have more time to get out," Russell said, startling them both since they hadn't heard him approach. "You can collect your pay, Lucky. I've put up with your lip as long as I'm going to."

"I was just visiting with the boss lady," Lucky said and looked to Destry. "Isn't that right?"

Destry looked at him and felt a shudder. Was it possible Lucky had been in the woods behind her house watching her? "Like Russell said, collect your pay. I think you'd be happier on some other ranch."

"You're making a big mistake, Boss Lady," Lucky said as he reined his horse around and shot her a furious look.

NETTIE WATCHED AS Sheriff Frank Curry pushed back his Stetson and kneaded his forehead for a moment before glancing up. Hands on her hips, she scowled down at him from the back doorway of the store. He'd taken his sweet time getting out here, and for a good ten minutes, he'd been stumbling around in the pine trees behind the store. What was the fool doing? Certainly not figuring out who'd broken into her store.

Frank had weathered well for his age, sixty-one, only three years older than herself. He even still had his hair, a thatch of thick blond flecked with gray. He no longer wore it in a long ponytail like he had when he'd roared up to her house on his motorcycle and asked her out all those years ago.

While his hair was shorter, he now wore one of those thick drooping mustaches like in all the old Westerns. His shoulders were still broad, and he looked great in the jeans he wore with his uniform shirt and cowboy boots.

"You're not going to catch whoever broke into my store by wandering around out there in the woods."

He grinned. "Wanna bet?"

She reached for the broom she kept by the door, wanting to wipe that grin off his face.

He held up both hands in surrender and took a step back.

"Settle down. Anyone who knows you would have more sense than to break into *your* store, Lynette."

"Bet it was those Thompson brothers' kids. Young whelps. Those kids don't have the sense of a rock. I chased a few out of my store the other day. Wild as stray cats."

Frank shook his head. "Weren't kids. Come out here and I'll show you. And put down that damned broom. I don't want to have to arrest you for assaulting an officer of the law."

She came down the back steps and followed him a few feet into the pines.

"Look here. That's what broke into your store," he said.

Nettie stared down at the tracks in the soft earth. "A bear?"

"A fair-sized grizzly."

Nettie shook her head. "That is the craziest thing I've ever heard, Frank Curry. He just broke the window and left?"

"Must have gotten scared away." He shrugged, dusted off his hands and started to leave.

"That's it?" she demanded of his retreating back. "That's all you're going to do?"

He turned. "You want me to go after the grizzly and put him in jail for breaking your window? You're lucky that's all he did. If he'd gotten in, you'd have had one heck of a mess to clean up. I'd suggest you get that window boarded up until you can get it fixed. I'm sure your husband can do *that*."

She ignored the dig about Bob. "You're assuming the bear will be back."

"Aren't you? I'll call FWP to set out a trap."

She doubted the Fish, Wildlife and Parks department would get someone out with a trap today, she thought, glancing into the dark pines. A cool breeze stirred the lush boughs, making a sound like that of a grizzly moving through them. Her skin prickled. A hunter had been mauled by a grizzly just last year back up a canyon near here.

"In the meantime, I'd keep an eye out if I were you. The pines are pretty thick here by your back door. I'd hate for a grizzly to tangle with you. Grizzlies are still protected by law, so don't hurt him." He laughed at his own joke.

She mugged a face at him and stepped back into the store. From the front window, she watched the sheriff cross the street to Kate LaFond's café. She hoped his ears were burning as she cussed him to Hades and back.

CHAPTER EIGHT

NETTIE THOUGHT ABOUT having her husband tack up a piece of plywood over the broken window. But it would be less trouble just to call the contractor who lived down the road. Bob would make a big deal out of it, while Grayson Brooks would be quick and efficient and not complain.

Grayson answered on the first ring.

She quickly apologized for calling and asked how his wife, Anna, was.

"She's fine, Nettie. What can I do for you?" He was soft-spoken, always polite and agreeable.

"A darned grizzly broke the back window at the store," Nettie said. "I can't get it fixed until next week at the soonest according to the glass shop in Big Timber. I was hoping—"

"You want me to board it up for you?"

"Would you mind? I know you're busy with your work and Anna."

"No problem. I have a lovely woman who stays with Anna when I'm at work. The bear didn't get into the store and do any damage?"

"Luckily not. But I wouldn't be surprised if he comes back."

"I'll drive up to Beartooth now," Grayson said. "Don't you worry about a thing."

AFTER A DAY on horseback in the mountains, Destry was anxious to get back to the ranch. She'd gone home first, showered and changed, and then driven up to the big house. She felt badly about missing dinner her brother's first night at home. She could well imagine what that meal had been like with just their father and Carson and Cherry.

As Destry stepped into the living room, she saw Cherry thumbing through a magazine beside the fire.

"Where's Carson?"

"He left just a few minutes ago. I'm surprised you didn't see him."

"Where did he go?" Destry asked, wondering why he hadn't taken his fiancée with him. She'd seen their father's pickup out front, so the two of them hadn't left together and Carson's fancy sports car had been parked in the four-car garage and hadn't moved since he'd arrived.

"He said he had some business to take care of in town."

Destry felt her panic rise. "Beartooth?"

Cherry nodded. "He told me not to wait up for him, so I would imagine he found himself a poker game. Why are you—"

But Destry was already out the door. She ran to her pickup and took off toward town.

As she tore down the road, she saw dust ahead, and if Cherry was right, that must be Carson in one of the ranch trucks. He was headed toward Beartooth all right.

Had he lost his mind? Given the way some people in the community felt about him, he needed to stay close to the ranch.

Unfortunately, he not only wasn't on the ranch, he

seemed to be heading right into the badger's lair. She watched the ranch pickup drive past the post office, café and general store to turn into the parking lot behind the Range Rider bar.

Destry followed but had to park down the road a ways because the back lot was now full. Carson had picked the busiest night of the week to come here. What was he doing? Was he looking for trouble?

She'd hoped to find him still outside the bar, but he'd already gone in by the time she pushed open the back door. The smell of stale beer filled her nostrils as she walked into the packed room.

The band broke into a slow country-western song. She didn't see Carson anywhere around. She started to turn back when she spotted him.

He was standing at the end of the bar, back in the corner. If anyone had seen him come in, they hadn't reacted yet.

"What are you doing here?" she demanded under her breath as she stepped to his side.

"What would you like to drink?" he asked. She smelled alcohol on his breath. Clearly he'd had more than a few already. "I was just about to get a beer."

"Have you lost your mind?" she whispered, keeping her back to the crowd as she grabbed hold of her brother's arm. "Let's get out of here."

"Come on, little sis. Have a drink with me. I was going crazy at the ranch and I figured I might as well get it over with," Carson said.

"Dying? Is that what you're planning to get over with? Because if you stay in this bar—"

"I can't hide at the ranch like I'm some kind of fugitive." The pain in his voice made her let go of his arm.

From behind her she heard the name Grant and the scrape of a bar stool. Someone had recognized Carson and was no doubt making his way toward them.

"It would be better, little sis, if you left now," Carson said, looking past her.

"I'm not leaving without you."

He gave her a pleading look. "I know what I'm doing."

She shook her head and braced herself as she felt a hand drop on her shoulder. Turning, she came face-to-face with Hitch McCray. Hitch ranched on his mother's place to the north and had never made a secret of his interest in Destry or any other woman, for that matter.

At forty, he was still a bachelor. Word on the Beartooth grapevine was that no woman would ever be good enough for his mother. And since Ruth McCray ran the ranch—and her son—with an iron fist, there wasn't much chance of McCray getting married until his mother was dead, if he hoped to get the ranch.

"Mind if I dance with your sister?" Hitch asked Carson.

"I'd appreciate it if you did. Destry doesn't have enough fun," her brother said as several cowboys at the bar turned to glare at him.

Destry was shaking her head, but Hitch had hold of her arm and she felt her brother give her a push toward the dance floor. "Hitch, no, I can't—" The rest of her words died on her lips as she spotted Rylan leaning against a pool table in the far back. His gaze practically burned her skin.

All the fight went out of her. Hitch pulled her onto the dance floor. She didn't want to dance, but neither did she want to make a scene and call even more attention to herself or her brother.

Her heart was pounding from the heat of Rylan's gaze on her. That and fear for her brother. The effect was making her both heavy on her feet and light in the head. She stumbled, stepping on Hitch's boot toe.

"I'm sorry," she said as she tried to pull away from him. "I don't want to dance. I need to get my brother and…" Past him, she saw Kimberly Lane try to drag Rylan out on the dance floor, and the rest of the words died on her lips. Kimberly was saying something to Rylan, leaning into him, smiling, her glossy lips next to his ear.

"I've had my eye on you, you know," Hitch said.

The words didn't register at first. Destry was distracted, worried about her brother and sick at heart to see Rylan with another woman. She looked back to the spot where Carson had been standing, fearing a fight was about to break out. To her relief, she saw her brother check his watch, then pick up his beer and head for the door. She watched, but no one followed him out.

She realized Hitch had said something she'd missed as the song ended and the band broke into another slow one. She watched Rylan glance in her direction as Kimberly stepped into his arms and began moving to the music.

Destry looked away, willing herself not to care. She just wanted to get out of the bar. She started to step away, but Hitch drew her back.

"Did you hear what I said? I've been watching you," Hitch repeated, lowering his voice as if he wanted to make sure he wasn't heard.

She drew back to look into his face. *"What?"*

He grinned. "I've been watching you for years."

Destry thought of the downed gate, the tracks into

the property, the feeling that someone had been in the trees behind her house.

"You've turned into quite the woman," he said, eyeing her up and down.

"You've been watching my *house?*" She tried to pull away, but he had a tight grip on her.

"I've been watching more than your house," Hitch said with a laugh. "You and I need to get together sometime and—"

Suddenly Hitch stopped talking—and dancing. Destiny blinked, startled to see Rylan standing next to them. Hitch seemed to hesitate before he let go of her and stepped back. It took her a moment to realize what was happening.

Rylan had cut in?

Her heart beat so hard that her chest ached. She tried to swallow the lump in her throat as he took her hand and drew her to him. It had been so long since she'd been this close to him, let alone in his arms. She caught the familiar scent of him. It kick-started her pulse. Just his touch sent goose bumps skittering over her skin.

She looked into his eyes. All that warm brown blazed with something so strong she felt it quake through her. He drew her closer, his lips going to her ear.

"What the hell are you and your brother doing here?" he whispered. "I'm trying really hard to ignore the fact that he is still walking around free, but he's pushing it, coming here tonight."

She drew back to look at him again and saw that his gaze was hard and still hot with a mixture of emotions that seemed about to boil over. "I know, that's why I came in to get him."

Rylan shook his head as he gazed down at her. "You

can't save your brother from himself. He'll only take you down with him, Destry."

"Thanks for the advice." She tried to pull away, but he held on to her.

"Ginny didn't take my advice about your brother and look where it got *her*." With that, Rylan released her, turned and walked off the dance floor, leaving her standing alone in the middle of a song.

Anger welled in her, but nothing compared to the hurt as she watched Rylan go back to Kimberly.

Destry turned and, pushing her way through the crowd, hurried out the back door of the bar. She stopped short under one of the pine trees in the parking lot when she saw her brother standing with a man talking. Even from where she stood, she could tell that the man was threatening him.

"Carson," she called, making them both turn as she started toward them.

The man stepped back from her brother. She couldn't hear what he said as he climbed into a large dark SUV, but it was clear her brother knew him.

"Who was that?" she asked as Carson sauntered toward her. He came into the dim light from the back of the bar, and she saw that his lip was bleeding. "You're hurt." She started to reach for him, but he pushed her hand away.

"I'm fine."

"You're not fine. Why was that man threatening you?" she demanded as he moved past her toward the ranch pickup he'd driven into town.

"Stay out of it," Carson said as he retrieved his open bottle of beer from where he'd left it on a pine stump. He took a long drink.

"That's why you came here tonight. You were meeting him." Her voice sounded strained even to her. "What kind of trouble are you in?"

"You're a bigger fool than I am, you know that?" he said, ignoring her question as he leaned back against the pickup, fished a package of cigarettes from his pocket and lit one. "I saw the way you were looking at Rylan West. How many times are you going to let him break your heart?" He took a drag, releasing the smoke in a ghostlike cloud that rose up into the cold night air.

She said nothing. He sounded drunk and angry, a side of her brother she'd never seen before.

"I thought you had more sense," he said, sounding disgusted with her.

She couldn't bear to see him like this. Her heart ached because, under the anger and the alcohol, she could see his pain. "Let me help you."

His laugh held no humor. "There is no help for me. Hasn't been for years."

"I heard you'd been looking for a poker game."

He swore. "So Cherry blabbed. Great. Bringing her here sure was a mistake."

"Carson, what are you doing?"

He smiled at that. "You mean, do I have a plan? Sis, I haven't had a plan since I was nineteen. What about you? What's your plan now that Rylan seems to have moved on?"

She flinched at his words. "I'm not letting it destroy my life," she snapped back.

"Aren't you?" He cocked a brow at her. "Your life is the ranch, and the old man is going to kick you off and give it to me while you're mooning over Rylan West, who is chasing that Lane girl. Is that what you want?"

She'd suspected that was exactly what their father had planned, but hearing it still hurt. "What I want doesn't matter. Haven't you figured that out yet?"

"Now look who's feeling sorry for herself," he said as he dropped the cigarette and crushed it under his boot.

She felt her chin go up. "I know Dad wants you to take over the ranch. He's always wanted that. Have you tried being honest with him? Told him what *you* want. Or do you even know?"

Carson lowered his head, his gaze on the ground. "What I want is to be rid of the whole damned place."

"What do you mean?" Her heart dropped. "You wouldn't sell the ranch."

"That's what the old man thinks," he said. "I could give a damn about the place. I know how you feel about the ranch and I'm sorry."

She doubted that. He didn't know how she felt about the ranch any more than he understood how she felt about Rylan. She couldn't let go. Not of the ranch. Not of Rylan. The land held her soul. Rylan her heart. Even if her father hadn't needed her after his accident, she couldn't have stayed away. This country was in her blood. It filled her with every breath she took.

"That man who was threatening you," she said, realizing that whatever the trouble was, it had followed him from Nevada. "You owe him money, don't you?"

"Yes, okay? I owe him a whole lot of money for some gambling debts. That's right, little sis. I need money."

"Have you asked Dad?"

He scoffed at that. "Even if he'd give me some, it wouldn't be enough. I need the *ranch*."

"You can't, Carson. It's his legacy. If he even suspected, it would kill him."

"What do you care about *his* legacy? It isn't like he's ever given a damn about you."

There it was, finally out in the open. *"Why?"* Her voice broke. She'd asked herself this for as long as she could remember. Why was their father the way he was with her?

"Whatever the reason, he wasn't going to leave you the ranch even if I hadn't come home." He opened the truck door to leave.

"Tell me the truth. There has to be a reason he feels the way he does other than you being the male heir."

"Don't you know, Destry?" he asked, his back to her. "Haven't you always known?"

"No." The word came out on a breath. Her heart thundered in her chest, the suspected truth crushing it with the weight of a draft horse.

"Why don't you ask him then?" He slid behind the wheel and looked at her. "Some things are just the way they are. I'm sorry. We can't change them. Give up. I have." He started the truck engine.

The back door of the bar opened, filling the night with the blare of music and the dull roar of voices. She turned, startled. Rylan stood silhouetted in the doorway. His gaze seemed to soften when he spotted her in the shaft of light coming from the open door, fingering its way through the pines.

He stood for a moment, the country music spilling from the bar kicking up a beat as the band broke into a cowboy jitterbug.

She swallowed, knowing that what her brother had said about Rylan breaking her heart again was nothing more than the truth, but it hurt more than he could know.

Had Rylan come out looking for her brother? Or for her?

He seemed to hesitate before he stepped back into the bar, the door closing behind him, muting the music again. In the cold shadow of the pines, her heart seemed to throw itself against her rib cage as if to prove that it could be broken over and over again.

Destry turned but wasn't surprised to find her brother and the ranch truck he'd driven to town in gone. Carson always had a way of disappearing when things got tough.

RYLAN WALKED BACK into the bar and picked up his pool stick, his emotions a tight knot in his belly. Why had he gone after Destry? There was nothing more he could say. Worse, no way to protect her.

"What's going on?" Kimberly asked, hands on her hips, alcohol firing her anger, as she stepped in front of him to block his shot.

"I'm going to play some pool and then I'm heading home."

She cocked a brow at him. Kimberly had been two years behind him and Destry in school. Pretty, but not his type. Not that his type mattered when he was looking for nothing more than a diversion. Tonight, though, nothing was going to distract him from thoughts of Destry.

"You went outside to check on her, didn't you? So, was she gone?" Kimberly demanded.

"I'm not talking to you about this, okay?" By the look on her face, clearly it wasn't. He dropped the pool stick on the table and, with the tip of his hat, said good-night and left the bar through the front door. He wasn't up to a fight with Kimberly. Nor was he looking to run into Destry again tonight.

Once in his pickup he'd left parked down the road from the bar in the pines, he headed out of town. Warring emotions roiled inside him. Seeing Destry had knocked the wind out of him. The Range Rider was the last place he'd expected to see her.

Now as he drove toward the ranch, he mentally kicked himself for going to the bar tonight. He hadn't wanted to be alone with his thoughts. Since his talk with Destry on the road yesterday, he kept going over their conversation in his head.

"How can you be so sure that Ginny wasn't involved with someone else who she kept not only from Carson, but also from your parents and even from you?"

Destry's words had stirred up things he didn't want to be digging around in. But he couldn't keep going the way he was, doing nothing, pretending he could let it go, he told himself now. Just as he kept pretending he could let Destry go.

He thought of his beautiful, sweet sister. Ginny had been the light of his family's life. The only girl in a family of three boys. He and Ginny had been only a year and a half apart in age, which had made them close. She wouldn't have kept secrets from him, he told himself as he drove toward the West Ranch.

Hadn't he been the one she'd confided in when she and Carson had gotten into a fight and he'd sprained her wrist?

"It isn't what you think," she'd cried when she'd come into his room holding her wrist. But he'd seen the hurt in her eyes. Just as he had seen Destry's pain tonight behind the bar.

He shoved that image away, letting his anger at Carson Grant replace it.

"What did that bastard do to you?" he'd demanded of his sister. He'd been ready to go after Carson Grant even then. It had been coming for a while, the trouble between Carson and Ginny, and, as her oldest brother, Rylan had tried to get her to break up with him.

"It was my fault," Ginny had said, blocking the door to keep him from heading for the W Bar G. He'd often wondered in the years since her death if things would have been different if he had gone that night and had it out with Carson then.

"Carson was holding me, I pulled away and tripped and fell," she'd claimed.

"You were fighting, don't even try to deny it."

It had taken a while, but he'd gotten the story out of her. She and Carson had quarreled, though she wouldn't say about what, but it had been her own clumsiness. "Carson was so sweet and so sorry that I'd hurt myself. Rylan, he wouldn't hurt me. I'm the one who's hurting him," Ginny had tried to convince him. Or had she been trying to convince herself?

Rylan had kept her secret and his parents never found out. A mistake, he'd thought a thousand times since and again now, as he pulled up to the house.

The lights were off. His brothers were at a community dance in Big Timber with their girlfriends they'd had since high school. All of the West kids had gone to the Beartooth one-room schoolhouse until ninth grade when they'd had to go the twenty miles across the Yellowstone River to school in Big Timber, or Big Twig, as they'd all called it.

His parents had said earlier that they were going to

Bozeman for dinner and a movie. Which meant he had the house to himself.

As he killed the engine and started to get out of the pickup, he hesitated. All of Ginny's belongings had been packed up and stored in a corner of the basement. He'd seen the boxes marked with her name when he'd returned and had been looking for some of his own belongings his mother had stowed away for him.

He knew his mother hadn't gone through Ginny's things. In fact, it had been his father who'd boxed up everything in the weeks after the funeral. He doubted his father had looked through them, either. It would have been too painful. Taylor West would instead have done the job with quiet efficiency, the same way he ranched.

Opening the pickup door, Rylan walked toward the dark house. It was a pale yellow two-story structure with white trim and a wide railed porch across the front. The large yard light cast long shadows as he climbed the porch steps and entered the unlocked front door.

Out of habit, he didn't turn on a light, didn't have to. He knew this house by heart. As a teen, he'd sneaked through it in the dark more times than he could count. His mother wasn't one to move the furniture around, so the place had changed little in eleven years.

At the basement stairs, he opened the door and turned on the light. It was an old-fashioned basement with small windows, lots of concrete and steep wooden steps. The old, damp smell was almost pleasant in its familiarity.

He closed the door behind him as he descended the stairs. There were a half dozen large boxes piled in the far corner. Ginny's white bed frame and mattress stood against a far wall where it would never be used again.

Her empty matching white chest of drawers and vanity were next to it.

The sheriff had taken her computer. Rylan didn't know if it had been returned or not. Her fifteen-year-old computer would be almost an antique by now. The only other item of clothing that had been missing was the letterman jacket Ginny had been wearing that night. She'd seldom gone anywhere without it after lettering in cheerleading, basketball and track.

Rylan made his way to the boxes. Each had only one word printed on it. *Ginny.* The first box he opened held nothing but a frilly pink, white and mint green comforter and matching pillow shams in a modern art design.

The second box was filled with her clothing just as the third and fourth were. No sign of the jacket, though. There was still the faint smell of the perfume she used to wear. Or maybe he'd only imagined it. Either way, it hurt so much he almost didn't open the fifth box.

But when he did, he saw her jewelry box sitting on top of her favorite books.

Carefully, he lifted out the smooth, varnished wood box. He remembered the Christmas when their parents had given it to her. She'd been so excited about having a big-girl jewelry box. When she'd opened the lid, they'd all laughed at her surprised expression. She hadn't known it would play music.

As he lifted the lid, her favorite song, "Amazing Grace," began to play. He felt a lump form in his throat and had to close the lid quickly. Carefully turning the box over, he flipped the switch that shut off the music.

Opening it again, he went through the contents, wondering why he was wasting his time. There wasn't much in it, just some cheap costume jewelry. Ginny had been buried in the Black Hills gold earrings and necklace that she'd loved and the Montana sapphire ring she'd gotten from all of them on her sixteenth birthday.

As he started to close the box again, he saw that a corner of the velvet interior had come loose. His heart began to pound, his fingers trembling as he pulled at it, hoping he was wrong. That Destry was wrong.

The corner of the velvet came up easily, making his stomach drop at the sight of a tarnished silver heart-shaped locket and chain coiled on a piece of paper. As he gingerly pulled out the locket, he saw the words hand-printed on the notepaper under it and felt his heart drop.

CHAPTER NINE

A CANOPY OF black velvet, bejeweled by more stars than most people had ever seen, filled Montana's big sky as Destry drove toward the W Bar G.

She felt wrung out. Her worry for her brother and seeing Rylan with Kimberly had taken everything out of her. She'd heard rumors since Rylan had returned home. Word on the grapevine had been that he was ranching with his father and brothers during the day and spending at least part of his nights at the Range Rider Bar.

She'd also heard that he'd been seen with several women in the area. Nettie Benton at the store had made a point of telling her. Apparently it wasn't enough that Rylan had tried for years to get his fool self killed riding anything that held still long enough in the rodeo—he'd come home still looking for adventure?

Fortunately, since he'd been home, the worst he'd done to himself was drink too much, get into fights and hook up with Kimberly, apparently.

What bothered Destry was that his behavior was so different from the cowboy she'd known all her life. He'd changed after his sister's death. They all had. But now it wasn't just her brother she wasn't sure she knew anymore.

A cool breeze blew down from the mountains, the air scented with wood smoke from one of the ranch houses she passed. It was a good night for a fire to ward off the cold. Destry yearned for a warmth that the heater in the truck couldn't provide.

She shoved away thoughts of Rylan, only to find herself worrying about her brother again. Carson was in trouble. That man who'd been threatening him when she'd come out of the bar had looked like a thug. Worse, her brother's attitude scared her.

"Give up," he'd said. "*I* have."

The defeat she'd heard in his voice had rocked her to her core. Just that morning he'd seemed hopeful when she'd mentioned him clearing his name.

Now she feared he was in more trouble than even she could have imagined, if the only way he could pay his gambling debts was to sell the W Bar G.

She thought about what Rylan had said about her not being able to save her brother from himself. That he would take her down with him.

Destry feared he might be right, since, as determined as she was, she hadn't been able to stop Rylan and the rest of this community from finding Carson guilty of Ginny's murder without even a fair trial.

Like a shot straight to her heart, she again was reminded of the image of Rylan with Kimberly tonight on the dance floor. She'd heard about the women on the pro circuit who followed the riders, as rabid as any rock groupies. But actually seeing Rylan with another woman...

She forced the image away again as she reached the fork in the road. To the right, the road led to her father's house up on the mountain. To the left, it wound down to the homestead house where she lived.

It was late. There would be no point in trying to

talk to Carson tonight with him half loaded. But she had to be sure he'd gotten back to the ranch safely. She wouldn't be able to sleep until she was.

Swinging the pickup to the right, she headed up the mountain road. A wedge of moon hung high over the ranch, the bright stars glittering around it. In the shadow of the Crazy Mountains, the pines stood like dark sentinels against the skyline.

Normally she loved nights like this, all the different fall smells, the landscape captured in cold silence. But tonight she felt unsettled and scared. The things her brother had said…

The pickup Carson had driven into town was parked beside the house. She would have turned around and left then, but she saw lights on in WT's den. Was Carson having it out with their father? The thought scared her. Her brother had sounded so desperate tonight. She feared what would happen if the two of them locked horns.

The big house was quiet as she slipped in the front door. Only a few lamps shone in all that spaciousness as she headed across the stone entry. The smell of charbroiled beef steaks lingered. She moved through the large living room with its stone fireplace and Native American rugs and artifacts.

She was partway down the hall when she heard the voices. Her father's was raised in anger. She debated whether to turn and leave or go in and try to keep the two of them from killing each other.

Then she heard her brother say from the partially open door to her father's den, "Destry has a right to know the truth."

"What truth is that?" Destry asked as she stepped into the den.

THE LAST THING Clete Reynolds wanted was trouble in his bar, but when the band took a break, he could feel a change moving through the place. He didn't need to hear the talk at the end of the bar to know it was about Carson Grant.

Trouble was brewing. It was one reason he kept a sawed-off shotgun and a baseball bat behind the bar at the Range Rider—as well as a can of high-dollar pepper spray. The spray was for the women.

He'd started carrying the spray after an episode with a couple who'd been sitting at the bar drinking and bickering. Pretty soon the wife said something to the husband and he smacked her, which, as the old joke went, was considered foreplay in some parts of Montana.

Before Clete could put an end to it, one well-meaning male patron from down the bar stepped in, no doubt thinking he was going to be a gallant protector. The moment he butted in, the wife began pummeling the poor fool with her high-heeled shoe. So much for date night.

Ever since then, Clete kept pepper spray under the bar for the angry girlfriends and wives.

He'd come to have a sixth sense when it came to trouble. Sometimes it was a single raised voice. Other times it was the sudden quiet that came before a storm. Or, like this evening, it was more like an electric current moving through the place, making the hair on his neck lift and his skin prickle.

Several rowdy patrons had been working themselves up after seeing Carson Grant. Now tensions were running high. All this bar needed was a spark, and it would blow like a roman candle on the Fourth of July.

As if he'd conjured up that spark, Clete turned at the

sound of the front door opening and saw the Thompson brothers come in. They were always spoiling for a fight.

He glanced at the clock on the wall. Even set at bar time—twenty minutes fast—it was going to be a long night the way things were going. Before now there'd only been grousing about Carson Grant's return.

No one in the county was a fan of WT Grant, but they put up with him for Destry's sake. Most everyone liked her, just as they had liked her mother, Lila. Prior to Ginny West's murder, they'd at least tolerated WT's son, Carson.

But Ginny's murder had changed that. Several of the more raucous residents had been talking about paying the W Bar G a visit.

Now that the Thompson brothers had walked into the already charged air, Clete feared a vigilante posse would soon be heading for the ranch.

Clete had enough problems of his own, he thought. He didn't have any idea where his wife, Bethany, was at this moment, but he had a sneaking suspicion that she was with another man.

Right now, though, he had to keep the Thompson brothers from tearing up his bar.

As Clete reached for his sawed-off shotgun, the front door swung open and a breath of cold fall air rushed in along with Sheriff Frank Curry.

"WHAT TRUTH?" Destry asked again as both her brother and father turned to look at her.

"This it between you and WT," Carson said, heading for the door. He slowed enough to squeeze her shoulder as he passed. His lip looked swollen from his earlier altercation.

"There's something you need to tell me?" she said to her father, remembering what Carson had said earlier.

WT looked paler than he had a few moments before. He wheeled away, turning his back to her, as he went to the bar. "You want a drink?"

"Am I going to need one?"

His movements slowed for a moment, his shoulders slumping a little. "You shouldn't eavesdrop."

"I wasn't. I was worried about you and Carson in the same room together. I didn't expect you to be talking about me."

He turned from the bar with a drink in his hand. Hadn't he been drinking more lately? Or had she just not noticed before?

"What truth is it I need to know?" she asked, holding her ground.

"It's late. I really don't want to get into this now."

She put her hands on her hips, digging in her heels. "I think you'd better tell me. I suspect this is something that you've needed to tell me for some time. Be honest with me. You got Carson back to run the ranch."

He gave her an impatient look. "He's my son."

His son. She stood, breathing hard. *Give up, I have,* her brother had said. But that wasn't her. She would fight for the ranch if that's what it took. WT had always made it clear that he expected his *son* to come back to the ranch. But she'd never dreamed WT meant to give it to him, lock, stock and barrel.

She shook her head. "You're leaving him in charge of the ranch."

Her father said nothing, making it clear that Carson had been right.

"What about me? You just hope to marry me off to anyone who'll have me?" she asked.

"Hitch McCray has had his eye on you for years and he stands to inherit the McCray place," he said. "That's some fine land and part of it is adjacent to that piece I just purchased."

"I see. So if I want a ranch, you expect me to marry it."

"That's what women do."

Destry balled her fists at her side, overcome with years of anger at her father. He'd fought her at every turn when it came to the running of the ranch, but she'd helped make it one of the most productive ones around in spite of him.

"You think Carson will do a better job of running the ranch?" she asked.

WT looked away. "I'm not saying that. I'll admit he's made some mistakes in the past."

"Mistakes?" She stared at him in shock. "You don't mean Ginny's murder." She felt her eyes widen in alarm. "You think he killed her."

"What I think doesn't matter."

"And yet you plan to give the ranch to him believing he's a *murderer?*"

"He's my *son.*"

"And I'm your *daughter,* not to mention I am actually capable of running the ranch and I don't have a murder charge hanging over my head." She stopped herself from saying Carson only wanted the ranch to sell it so he could pay his gambling debts.

Hot angry tears burned her eyes. She willed herself not to cry, damned if she would let him see how much he'd hurt her.

"I don't expect you to understand." With a curse, he said, "You've always been just like your mother."

Destry had heard that her whole life. She apparently looked like her mother and acted like her. But until that moment, she'd always thought her father meant it as a compliment.

"This isn't just about the ranch, is it?" she demanded.

WT shifted his gaze away.

Given his attitude toward her, she'd suspected it for sometime. "It has something to do with me. Why you treat me the way you do. It isn't just because I look so much like my mother, is it?" She'd always thought he couldn't bear to be around her because she reminded him so much of the wife he'd loved and lost in a horse-back riding accident. Now, though, she suspected that had never been the case. "Since you're being honest with me…"

He trembled with rage as he met her gaze. "If you're so damned determined to know the truth, then fine. You aren't my daughter. You're some bastard's your mother slept with. She didn't even bother to try to pass you off as mine."

His words were delivered like a blow. They knocked the air out of her. She rocked like a young sapling under a gale wind. For years she'd known something was wrong, even suspected it had something to do with her mother. But not this.

"I don't believe you." Even as she said the words, she did believe him. It all made sense, why he never wanted to hear her mother's name, why he'd destroyed all the photographs of his wife, why he treated Destry the way he had since as far back as she could remember. Why he was giving the ranch to Carson.

"You wanted to know. Now you do." He took a gulp of his drink and coughed as it went down the wrong way.

"Did she tell you I'm not your daughter?" she asked.

He laughed at that. "She didn't have to."

"Did my brother know, too?" Was this what her brother had wanted to tell her the night he came down to the homestead house and helped her stack wood? If so, how could he keep something like this from her?

WT narrowed his gaze. "Your brother was young but I suspect he knew more than he's ever told me." He sounded bitter and angry about that. If Carson had seen something and hadn't told, WT would never forgive him for not coming to him. It wouldn't matter that Carson had been just a boy.

She stared at WT. She'd made excuses for him, telling herself not to take the way he treated her personally. He was a bitter man who treated most everyone poorly. But the pain of WT's rejection had never been as sharp as it was now that she knew his feelings toward her *had* been personal.

She'd never had her father's love, but she'd never missed it, either. As far back as she could remember, she'd had people who loved and took care of her. W Bar G's ranch foreman, Russell, had taught her to ride a horse. Ranch hands had taught her to rope and brand and cut cattle. Her brother had taught her to swim. Margaret had taught her to cook enough that she would never starve.

She'd had Rylan for her best friend. She'd never felt unloved. If anything, she'd felt badly for her father because it had been clear to her early on that he was in a lot of pain. She'd felt for him and blamed herself for looking so much like her mother.

"You're the spitting image of Lila," Margaret had told her when she'd asked why her father could barely look at her sometimes. "It's just hard for him because of that. Don't pay the old fool any mind."

And it wasn't as if WT was nice to other people. He was abrasive to everyone and didn't apologize for it. Except maybe to Margaret. Margaret was also the only person Destry had ever seen stand up to him.

"Who is my father?"

"Don't you think if I knew who he was that he'd be dead?"

She didn't believe him. He knew. Or at least he suspected. But for some reason he hadn't confronted the man. Her heart was pounding as if she'd tried to outrun a storm on a fast horse. If she wasn't WT's daughter, then who was she?

The thought shook the once solid ground on which she'd built her life. She had no right to the ranch. No wonder WT had never considered leaving it to her. With a horrible sinking feeling, she realized she was about to lose everything she loved.

She'd already lost so much. Her mother. Rylan. And now not just her father, but also her whole identity. But to lose the ranch, too?

"You can't just turn the W Bar G over to Carson."

"It's late and I'm tired," WT said and coughed again.

"I love my brother, but there is something you have to know."

WT's drink glass slipped from his hand and hit the floor, shattering with what sounded like a gunshot. Ice cubes clattered across the floor.

With alarm, Destry saw his face. All the color had washed from it. His hand had gone to his chest, and he seemed to be desperately trying to catch his breath.

RYLAN CAREFULLY PICKED up the piece of notepaper from where it had been hidden under the velvet of Ginny's jewelry box. The words were handwritten in ink, the letters slightly slanted. Neat, but appearing to have been scrawled in a hurry—or in anger. He didn't recognize the handwriting.

The small piece of paper was faded to sepia. It was also wrinkled, as if at some point his sister had wadded it up to throw it away. Why hadn't she? Why would she keep something like this, let alone hide it? A frisson of fear rushed along his nerve endings as he read the words printed on the notepaper once again.

For the lips of an adulteress drip honey, and her speech is smoother than oil; but in the end she is bitter as gall, sharp as a double-edged sword. Her feet go down to death; her steps lead straight to the grave

What the hell? *Her feet go down to death?* He shuddered.

Why would Ginny have kept this? Especially why would she keep it hidden in the same place as a tarnished heart-shaped locket?

Both of these had to mean something to his sister. Something she hadn't wanted anyone to know about.

Rylan slumped back onto one of the boxes as he considered what he'd found and, more to the point, what it meant.

It meant Ginny had secrets. Just as Destry had said. Secrets that could have gotten her killed?

He shook his head at the thought as he picked up the locket and pried it open in the hopes that a clue would be inside. The locket was empty. Even under the overhead bulb of the basement he could see that the piece of jewelry was cheap. He tried to remember if he'd ever seen his sister wearing it. He couldn't recall seeing it around her neck. If it meant something special to her, then why hadn't she worn it?

Rylan groaned at the implication. He thought of Carson Grant's suspicion that Ginny had been seeing someone. Possibly a married man. What if it was true and the locket was from the mystery man? The note certainly would support that theory if someone had found out about them.

Was it possible Carson had given Ginny this note? He couldn't see Carson Grant quoting the Bible, not that hotheaded young man he'd been at twenty. But he could see Carson losing his temper if Ginny really was seeing a married man. Didn't this give Carson even more motive?

He stared at the note and the locket, wondering what to do with them. How about putting them back where he'd found them and keeping his mouth shut? The last thing his parents needed was this. How could he open this can of worms now? But Destry's words to him echoed in his head.

"Are you so set on vengeance, that the truth be damned?"

As he sat staring at what he'd found, he realized he had no choice. His father had told him that the sheriff

was reinvestigating the case. He couldn't keep this to
himself, no matter where it led.

He thought of Destry. Her brother might have been
right about there being another man in Ginny's life. But
that only gave Carson Grant even more motive to kill
Ginny in a jealous rage.

IT WAS LATE. Late enough that Bethany thought it would
be all right to call him. Still, she was shaking when she
dialed his number and was relieved when he answered
and not his wife.

"I got another one of those notes," she said before he
could chew her out for calling the house.

"What are you talking about?" he asked, keeping his
voice down. She heard a door close on his end of the
line. She could tell he was distracted. He hated when
she called him at home. But this last note had scared her.

"I told you about the note someone left under my
windshield wiper. I saw it when I came out of the Branding Iron after my shift." She felt a stab of anger at the
realization that he hadn't remembered the other note
she'd told him about. He also hadn't tried to contact her
since they'd gotten together earlier. "You remember the
Branding Iron, don't you?"

The café was where they used to visit when she
was working and the café was empty. He'd stop by and
they'd just talk. After a while, she'd realized that he was
flirting with her. Before then, she'd thought of him as
being too old and too married. But he'd become even
more forward when the cook, Lou, was out having a
smoke behind the café.

She'd been flattered by the attention. He was sweet
and shy at first. He made her feel as if she was the only

woman in the world. The flirting had led to a secret rendezvous away from the café and finally to his cousin's apartment in Big Timber.

"Of course, I remember the Branding Iron." The way he said it made her heart kick up a beat or two. It had been romantic, the way he'd seduced her over time. She could still remember the night he'd put the locket on her and shivered at the memory.

"So tell me about these notes?" he asked as if this was the first time he'd heard about them.

"The first one was just weird. But this one kind of scares me."

"Bethany."

"Just listen to the note, okay?" She cleared her throat and read:

He who sleeps with another's man wife; no one who touches her will go unpunished. Those who confess their sins and turn from them will receive mercy.

It had been under her windshield wiper, just like the last one, when she'd come off her late shift at the Branding Iron tonight. She'd put off calling him, afraid she would only make him mad.

"So, what do you think?" she asked into the dead silence coming from the other end of the phone.

"I think we definitely shouldn't see each other for a while."

"What?"

"I don't think these notes have anything to do with us, but if they do…"

She hadn't imagined it when she'd thought he was

pulling away from her earlier. "There's someone else, isn't there?" she cried.

"Don't start this again. We're both married. Of course there is someone else! We should never have gotten involved to begin with and you know it. We're better people than this."

"There *is* someone else. I can tell."

"I have to go. Please, let's do the right thing. Don't contact me again." He hung up.

She stared at the phone, fighting tears. He was breaking up with her.

As many times as she'd said she wasn't going to see him again, she felt as if someone had pulled the rug out from under her. She'd always thought she would be the one to end it. She never dreamed he would.

She touched the locket at her throat. There *was* someone else. And not his wife. But who?

CHAPTER TEN

DESTRY PACED.

"Wearing a hole in the floor isn't going to help," her brother said from where he was slumped in an alcove chair.

"I can't sit. This is all my fault. If I hadn't confronted him—"

"It's not your fault." Carson sounded weary. They'd had this conversation a half dozen times already as they waited for the doctor outside WT's bedroom door. "I'm sure he's fine. I wouldn't be surprised if he pulled this so you'd be afraid to argue with him for fear you'd kill him."

"How can you say that? He looked as if he was having a heart attack."

Carson shrugged. "I know him. He isn't past pulling something like this because he feels guilty about what he's doing to you. So he told you everything?"

"I don't want to talk about it right now. I can't, okay?"

"Fine with me." He closed his eyes. His lack of concern bothered her. Did he really care nothing for his own father? Or was this his way of coping?

A door opened down the hall. Carson sat up as the doctor came out, closing WT's bedroom door behind him.

"How is he?" Destry asked.

"Your father is resting comfortably," Dr. Flaggler said.

Her father. The words made her ache. "Did he have a heart attack?"

"No. Just shortness of breath. Probably along the lines of a panic attack. I understand you and he were having a discussion?"

"WT doesn't have discussions. He has arguments," Carson said.

The doctor shot him an impatient look. "Whatever you want to call it, your father needs to take it easy."

Her brother shoved to his feet. "In other words, he told you to tell us not to argue with him, right?"

The doctor frowned. "Has your father talked to you about his health?"

"No," Destry said. "Is there something we should know?"

He cleared his throat and glanced back at the closed bedroom door. "Your father is a very stubborn man. The last time I saw him he promised me that he would talk to you about his condition."

Her eyes widened in alarm. "The last time you saw him? I didn't even know he'd been to see you. Is his condition serious?"

"Your father's airplane accident and years in a wheelchair have taken a toll on his body," the doctor said. "I encourage you to have an honest talk with him about his health."

"Without upsetting him, right?" Carson said snidely, but quickly sobered. "Wait a minute. Are you telling us he's dying?"

Destry felt her chest hitch. No matter their blood, WT was the only father she'd ever known.

"Just try to keep him as comfortable as you can and

as…calm." The doctor put his hand on her shoulder and squeezed it before walking away.

RYLAN KNEW IT was too early in the morning. He'd tried to talk himself out of what he was about to do. But he was already in his truck on his way to the W Bar G as the sun was coming up.

Last night, he'd had hell getting to sleep after what he'd discovered in Ginny's jewelry box. He hated to think what the note or the hidden locket meant. A part of him still wished he'd just put both back in the jewelry box where he'd found them.

He knew he was probably going to wake up Destry, but he couldn't put this off any longer. The thought of her sleepy-eyed, hair a jumble falling around her shoulders, set off a sharp, painful ache inside him.

Rylan shoved the image away as he passed the road up to WT's Folly and continued down the mountain to the ranch road and the homestead house. It was a two-story log structure surrounded on three sides by aspens, pines and cottonwoods.

The front yard was shaded, the sun gilding the tops of the trees. A figure slinked across the front of the house, stopping to peer into one of the windows.

Rylan blinked, confused for a moment by what he was seeing. The pickup rumbled over the cattle guard and down the ranch road. The man must have heard him coming because he took off running toward the trees that flanked the side of the house.

Speeding up, Rylan raced into the yard and jumped out to rush into the trees after the man. He had only an impression of the intruder: big, definitely male.

It was still dark in the thick stand of trees. About half

the leaves clung to the limbs of the aspens. They rustled over his head, sunlight flickering through them as he ran. The man had too much of a head start.

As Rylan burst from the trees at the edge of the creek, he stopped short. There was no movement in the trees on the other side. A gust of wind whirled leaves around him, sending them skimming across the water's surface. Over the sound of the wind and the rushing water, Rylan heard a vehicle engine start up in the distance.

The man was gone. But he'd left a fresh boot print in the soft dirt. It wasn't the only print, Rylan noticed with a curse. He'd been here before.

DESTRY WOKE WITH A START. She lay in bed listening to the familiar creaks and groans of the old house. So what had awakened her?

Through the sheer curtains of the second story window, she could see the sun was still low on the eastern horizon. She glanced at the clock, surprised it was so early. She hadn't gotten home from the big house until late after her father's spell, which meant she hadn't been to sleep long.

The events of last night came back in a rush of shock and grief. WT was ill, so ill he might be dying. She'd upset him enough that she could have killed him. She closed her eyes, not wanting to deal with any of it yet this morning.

The sudden banging on her front door startled her up into a sitting position. Going to the window, she looked down to see a pickup parked in the yard. That must have been the sound that had awakened her.

The banging became insistent. She grabbed her robe

and tied it as she headed down the stairs. Throwing open the door, she was shocked to see Rylan standing there.

"Were you asleep?" he asked, sounding either winded or upset. She couldn't tell which as he stepped past her into the house.

"What's wrong?"

"That's what I was going to ask you. As I drove up I saw a man peering in one of your lower windows."

"A man?" She felt half asleep, exhausted after last night and off balance with Rylan standing in her living room staring at her. "Are you sure it wasn't my brother?"

"Would your brother have taken off through the trees when he heard me drive up?"

"Maybe, if he saw you racing up this time of the morning," she said. There was no way her brother was up at this hour unless there was trouble at the big house, but then he or Margaret would have called. And Carson wouldn't have taken off into the trees even if he had seen Rylan.

Destry knew that the man she'd seen the other night had come back. It sent a chill through her. Lack of sleep and the recent emotional roller-coaster ride she'd been on, added to Rylan's surprise visit, had her feeling vulnerable. It wasn't a feeling she was comfortable with.

Wrapping her robe more tightly around her, she went into the kitchen and busied herself by putting on a pot of coffee. Someone had been out there again. Had he been peeking in the windows the last time, too?

"This isn't the first time he'd been on your property," Rylan said, following her. "I found older boot tracks by the creek. They matched the ones of the man I saw looking in your window. You don't seem surprised."

She was more surprised that Rylan was here.

With a shudder, though, she tried not to imagine what could have happened if he hadn't shown up when he did. She set the can of coffee back on the shelf above the coffeemaker and closed the cupboard before she turned to face him.

"I thought I saw someone watching the house before I went to Denver. He's been back once since then."

"Did you call the sheriff?" He didn't wait for an answer. "Of course not. You think whoever it is, you'll just handle it yourself."

"The sheriff can't do anything," she said. "If I called him when I saw someone out there, by the time he got here, it would be too late."

Rylan swore and dragged off his Stetson to rake his hand through his thick blond hair. Watching him, she was reminded of those same fingers caught up in her hair in a moment of passion. She quickly pulled her hair up, knotting it at her neck.

THE WOMAN WAS IMPOSSIBLE. Rylan swore under his breath as he watched her tie up her mane of hair. Just as he'd pictured, she had that sleepy-eyed look that made him want to drag her to him and kiss her senseless.

"You've got yourself a Peeping Tom or something worse and you don't seem all that concerned."

Her look said she had bigger things to worry about right now. He noticed the shadows under her eyes. Apparently she hadn't been sleeping any better than he had.

"I'm having Grayson Brooks put new locks on the doors later this week when he comes to build some stalls up at the barn. He's busy up at the store taking care of a window where a bear tried to break in."

"This Peeping Tom's been in your house?"

She hoped not. "No, but since I don't even know where to find a key for the front door, I thought it might be a good idea to get new locks."

"You have any idea who was out there?" he asked.

"No," she said with a shake of her head.

"Could this have something to do with your brother?"

Her hands went to her hips. She had an athletic body, full in all the right places, and great hips. "Isn't it possible that not everything comes back to Carson?" she snapped. "It just so happens that I thought someone was watching my house *before* my brother came back."

He didn't want to argue with her about her brother. "Still, you'd be smart to stay up at your father's house until Grayson changes the locks."

"I have my shotgun. Loaded. A pistol by my bed. And I'm planning to sleep with one eye open. But thanks for your concern."

He ground his teeth at the woman's mule-headed stubbornness.

"Is there some reason you're here at this hour of the morning?" she asked impatiently.

He slapped his hat back on his head, having second thoughts about coming out here. But he wasn't going to let her rile him so he would leave. What he'd come out here for was too important.

"I got to thinking about what you said the other day." It was damned hard to admit that he might be wrong. Especially about her brother. "What you said about Ginny having a secret…"

Destry nodded and moved out of the kitchen to take

a chair at the table. He finally had her undivided attention apparently.

He cleared his throat. "I need you to look at something." Reaching into his pocket, he stepped to her and laid the yellowed piece of once-crumpled notepaper on the table, dropping the silver heart-shaped locket and chain next to it. He watched her closely as she looked from the note and locket to his face.

"Have you seen that before?" he asked as she lifted the locket by its thin silver chain.

THE SILVER WAS TARNISHED. The only thing unusual about the locket was that the heart wasn't perfectly shaped. "Is it Ginny's?" Destry asked.

"I found it in her jewelry box—hidden under the lining."

She felt herself start. Hope burned through her. So it was possible that Ginny had a secret lover just as her brother had said.

Rylan clearly still didn't want to believe his sister had any secrets, she thought, seeing the hard set of his jaw. And yet he was here, showing her what he'd discovered. Clearly the discovery had upset him.

He pointed to the piece of notepaper he'd put on the table. "I found that with it. Do you recognize the handwriting?"

She glanced at the note, then up at him. "Carson didn't write it, if that's what you're asking. He's left-handed like you. This is definitely not his handwriting."

Rylan said nothing as she picked up the note. She had only glanced at the writing before. Now she read the words.

*For the lips of an adulteress drip honey, and her
speech is smoother than oil; but in the end she is
bitter as gall, sharp as a double-edged sword.
Her feet go down to death; her steps lead straight
to the grave*

Startled, she looked up at Rylan. "This sounds…
threatening."

"Why would she hide something like this?" he asked,
as if hoping she would come up with a reason other than
the one staring him in the face. He'd come to the wrong
house if he hoped for that.

"You *know* why. Carson was right about Ginny seeing someone else. Apparently, if the note is any indication, a married man."

Rylan shook his head as he pulled out a chair and
sat down. "I called some of Ginny's old friends. None
of them knew about her dating anyone but Carson."

"She wouldn't have 'dated' this man if he was married."

"Ginny was too smart to get involved with a married man," he said adamantly. "There has to be another
answer."

Destry didn't argue the point. She knew that intelligence had little to do with love.

"Maybe he wasn't married, but he wasn't free. Whoever wrote this knew about the two of them," she said,
holding up the paper. "But if he wasn't married, then
why else call her an adulteress?"

"If the note was even to Ginny."

Destry gave him an impatient look. "Why else would
she have kept it?" A thought struck her. "What if she

showed it to her lover? He'd know that someone had discovered their secret. He might panic."

Rylan didn't say anything for a long moment. He leaned forward, placed his elbows on the table and dropped his head in his hands. Destry fought the urge to place a hand on his broad shoulders. She loved this man. She wanted to comfort him. But there was eleven years between them and a whole lot more.

"There's something I haven't told you," he said, his words muffled.

She held her breath as he raised his head, his eyes shiny and filled with a bright pain that broke her heart.

"Ginny was pregnant."

Her breath came out in a rush. "Was it Carson's?"

Rylan nodded.

Destry felt her heart break for her brother. Had he known Ginny was pregnant? That she was carrying his baby?

As the coffee finished brewing, she rose from her chair, needing a cup for the warmth and a few moments to lasso in her anger. "If he'd known about the baby, he would have wanted it. He says Ginny was the only woman he will ever love."

Rylan said nothing, clearly not believing a word of it.

She took down two mugs, filling one. As she held it up, Rylan shook his head. She put the second mug away. Wrapping her fingers around her cup, she hoped the radiating heat chased away the chill she felt after reading that note. What had Ginny gotten herself into?

Rylan got up from his chair, and for a moment, she thought he was leaving. Instead, he walked over to the windows facing the creek.

"You have no idea who this other man might have been?" she asked as she took her seat at the table again.

He shook his head but didn't turn around. She studied his broad back, the long muscled legs clad in faded denim, and felt an overwhelming rush of desire. She took a sip of the hot coffee, wanting to scald away her need for this man.

"If this man was married, then he has a motive to want to keep your sister quiet about the affair," she said, even though Rylan wouldn't have come out here so early in the morning if he hadn't already figured that out himself. "Especially if she thought it was his baby."

As she looked at the note and locket, her heart swelled at the realization that there really was another suspect other than her brother. If the real killer was found… "You have to take this to the sheriff."

"I've been wondering what made your brother think Ginny was seeing a married man."

She shook her head as he turned to look at her.

"Ginny told me that she'd thought someone had been following her, spying on her."

"If Carson had been following her, then he would know who she was seeing. He would have had no reason not to tell the sheriff eleven years ago."

Rylan sighed. "I'll take this to the sheriff, but this doesn't clear your brother. If anything, the pregnancy makes him look more guilty. Given what the locket and note suggests, if he'd found out about the baby and thought it wasn't his, I can only imagine what he might have done."

"Even with this evidence right in front of your face, you're still determined my brother is guilty?" She shoved back her chair and got to her feet. She studied him for a moment and then, with a shake of her head, said, "I used to think I knew you."

"Ginny's death changed us all," Rylan said with a curse.

"Yes, it changed us. But not the way it changed you and my brother." She started to step away, but he grabbed her arm, pulling her around to face him.

"I'm still the same man you fell in love with."

She looked into his eyes. "I don't think so."

"Like hell." He dragged her to him with one arm around her waist. His mouth dropped to hers in a demanding kiss that stole her breath. She could feel the thunder of his heart against hers. Wrapped in his strong arms, she lost herself in the kiss. She felt the passion, the chemistry that had always made her pulse pound. The kiss fired that old aching need for this man she couldn't have.

It swept her up, made her forget for a moment the gulf that lay between them. He drew her closer, pressing his body to hers, deepening the kiss, and with desire burning through her, all she wanted was for him to sweep her up in his arms and carry her upstairs to her bed.

The realization made her draw back. She was shaking with both passion and fear at what would happen if she gave in to her need for this cowboy. "You should leave now."

He shook his head, clearly as overwhelmed as she was by the desire the kiss had ignited. "Destry—"

"You are never going to believe my brother didn't hurt Ginny, no matter how much evidence you find otherwise." She picked up the note and the necklace. The locket felt light. She wondered—

"I already looked inside."

Destry handed the locket to him and crossed her arms, waiting for him to leave, needing him to leave before they did something they would both regret. "I'll ask my brother if he gave her the locket or knows anything about the note."

He took out a West Ranch business card and pen, scribbling something on the back. "There's my cell number. Call me." He seemed to hesitate, as if there was something more he wanted, needed, to say.

Destry held her breath. When he finally walked to the door, he stopped and turned. "Please don't stay here alone tonight." His voice was soft, caring. She remembered the way he was with the horses on the ranch. A gentle man with a soft, slow hand. "I don't think you're safe."

"Thanks for your concern, " she said, unable to look at him. She feared she might call him back. "But I can take care of myself."

"That's what my sister thought."

CHAPTER ELEVEN

DESTRY DROVE INTO church as she always did on Sunday mornings. The small, white wood-framed community church sat at the far edge of Beartooth. It had a steeple with a bell that Pastor Tom rang each Sunday morning and looked like something out of an old Western movie.

As she entered the building, she didn't take her usual wooden pew up front, but sat at the back. There was no use pretending that nothing had changed from other Sundays. She felt the stares, saw the curious looks and whispers. She didn't want to sit through the entire service, feeling as if everyone was staring at the back of her head.

Kate LaFond, the new owner of the Branding Iron Café, sat at the organ playing a hymn Destry recognized. Kate had taken over since Grayson Brooks's wife Anna's health had gotten too bad for her to play or even attend church.

Destry looked around until she spotted Grayson, the local contractor, also sitting alone at the back of the church. He was a large, nice-looking man with an easygoing manner. He smiled at her and looked as if he might come over to sit by her. She picked up a hymnal on the pew beside her.

She didn't want to have to visit with anyone this morning. Rylan's unexpected visit had left her off-kilter, like a washing machine out of balance. It wasn't every day that she was awakened by Rylan West. Unfortunately, she thought, with no small amount of disappointment.

Her hope was to simply enjoy the service. She wasn't going to worry right now about her brother or think about Rylan or WT. Maybe she didn't know Carson. Maybe she never had.

She barely knew *herself* this morning. She thumbed through the hymnal for a moment, unable to hold off the reminder that WT apparently wasn't her biological father. Looking around the congregation gathered, she wondered if one of the older men might be her father. The thought sent a shiver through her. She feared she'd never look at an older man in the community without wondering.

She pushed the thought away as she took in the parishioners gathered today. There was Nettie and Bob Benton from the Beartooth General Store. Both were in their late fifties. Natives of the area, they lived in a house on the mountain behind the store. Nettie was chattering away. Bob didn't seem to be listening.

Destry spotted Rylan's father, Taylor, but not his mother, Ellie. The two younger West boys were also not in attendance, either, it seemed. That was unusual. Nor was Sheriff Frank Curry here, also unusual.

Pastor Tom Armstrong spotted her, nodded and smiled, but she was glad he didn't come over. In his early fifties, Tom had come to the cloth late in life after growing up in California. He claimed he enjoyed preaching because it kept him on the straight and narrow.

He still had that blond, blue-eyed West Coast look

and was quite handsome, which didn't hurt when it came to getting more of the twenty- and thirtysomething young women to attend Sunday service.

Destry noticed his wife, Linda, in the front row pew. Linda was a tall, statuesque woman, quite a bit older than her husband. They'd come to town about fifteen years ago and moved into the parsonage on the hill behind the small community church.

She was glad to see that neither Kimberly nor the rest of the Lane family were in church today. She tried not to think of Kimberly in Rylan's arms at the bar as Tom took his place behind the lectern and the church quieted. He opened his Bible, welcomed everyone and announced the hymns. They all stood and sang, one of Destry's favorite parts of Sunday service. She loved the hymns and the feeling they gave her as she heard the congregation's voices raised in song.

It seemed like more than a coincidence when Tom announced that the sermon was about forgiveness. She wondered if next week's service would be on being her brother's keeper and if she would heed its message.

Destry started for the door at the conclusion of the service. She was almost there when Pastor Tom caught her arm.

"Destry, so good to see you."

She looked past the pastor to see that Linda had cornered Grayson Brooks. Destry knew that Linda had become good friends with Grayson's wife, Anna, when they'd moved here. Linda looked upset, and Destry wondered if Anna's health had worsened. Linda and Grayson certainly seemed to be having a very intense conversation. Linda had a grip on Grayson's arm that looked almost painful. Nearly as painful as the look on his face.

"How are you?" Pastor Tom asked now as he drew Destry aside.

"Fine." The word came out automatically.

He smiled as if he knew better. "I'm always available to talk if you feel the need."

"Thank you." He'd made the same offer after Ginny's murder and Carson's exodus from Montana. But Destry hadn't wanted to talk about it. Maybe especially to a pastor. She hadn't wanted to admit that she'd been making love with Rylan the night his sister was killed and that had made it all the worse.

"How is your brother?"

She didn't know how to answer that. "Carson's trying to adjust to being home." Past him she saw that Linda had released her hold on Grayson Brooks and was now watching her.

"Then he's staying?" Pastor Tom sounded pleased.

"I'm not sure." If WT had his way, yes.

"Well, the offer stands if you need anything or your brother needs someone to talk to. Sometimes it helps to talk to someone who doesn't have a dog in the fight, so to speak."

"Actually, I wondered if you are familiar with this." She'd looked up the Bible quote after Rylan had left this morning and written it down. She handed him the piece of paper to read.

He looked at it, then handed it back. "I'm familiar with a lot of quotes from the Bible. Is there a particular reason you wanted me to look at that one?"

"I believe someone left it as a threat."

He paled. "That is very upsetting. Was this recent?" He was definitely upset, she noticed.

But before Destry could ask him anything further,

Linda joined them. She slipped an arm possessively through her husband's and asked, "Did you enjoy the sermon?" Linda always wore flats, no doubt so she didn't tower over her husband.

"I did, thank you," she said.

Linda gave her a smile, then turned to her husband. "Tom, Mrs. Murphy needs a word with you. If you'll excuse us, Destry?"

"Destry," Tom said quickly, "I was hoping you'd stop by sometime soon, since you're chairwoman of the clothing drive, so we can get the bins emptied out."

She said she would and watched Linda drag her husband over to the elderly Mrs. Murphy. Tom looked back at her once, worry etched on his handsome face.

"She can't stand to see her husband talking to a pretty young woman," Nettie Benton said beside Destry, startling her. "It's that green-eyed jealousy. I feel sorry for Pastor Tom, don't you? I really doubt he gives her any reason to worry, but you never know about men, do you?"

Destry didn't have a chance to respond as Bob dragged his wife out, saying they had to get the store open. Nettie prided herself on the Beartooth General Store being open seven days a week, even though the hours often varied.

"Me and God have an understanding," Nettie was fond of saying. "I pay my respects to him and then I make sure people have what they need, even on Sunday."

As Destry followed them out of the church, she saw Grayson drive away and wondered what Linda had been so intently talking to him about. Only three vehicles were still in the lot by the time she made her way to her truck.

But as she grew near, she caught a glimpse of a straw Western hat through the window of her truck cab. Someone was leaning against the other side of her pickup waiting for her.

Her first thought was Rylan, not that he'd been in church this morning. But he would have known where to find her. She seldom missed church services.

As she came around the front of the truck, she was disappointed and immediately uneasy to see that it was Hitch McCray.

She slowed, remembering what he'd said at the bar.

"You're a hard woman to get alone," Hitch said congenially enough as he took a step toward her. "Why don't we go somewhere so we can finish our talk."

Destry shook her head. "I don't think so."

He grabbed her arm to stop her from moving away. "You know your father wants to see the two of us get together. So what is the problem?" he demanded, raising his voice.

Her father? She almost laughed at that. She jerked free of his hold. "Have you been coming out to my place sneaking around watching me?"

He let out a snort. "Why would I do that?"

"That's what I was wondering. You told me at the Range Rider that you'd been watching me."

His eyes widened. "And you thought that meant I'd been out to your house, sneaking around and looking in your windows?"

"Have you?"

A nasty grin curled at his thick lips. "What if I have? Sounds to me like you're hoping I have been."

"Is there a problem here?"

They both turned to see Rylan's father, Taylor West.

He was a big man, much like WT, with a quiet, patient way about him that Destry had always admired. He'd apparently been heading for his pickup when he'd heard Hitch's raised voice.

"No problem," Hitch said, taking a step back. Under his breath, he added, "We aren't finished."

Destry smiled her thanks to Taylor West and walked back around to the driver's side of her pickup, but he called to her before she could climb behind the wheel. Reluctantly, she turned, fearing a confrontation she wasn't up to.

Hitch had unnerved her. The more she'd thought about it, the more she feared it had been Hitch prowling around her place. She shuddered at the thought. Well, she'd be ready for him next time. She had her old shotgun loaded with buckshot. It would be the last time he came sneaking around.

An engine roared and Hitch took off, tires throwing gravel and kicking up dust. Destry turned to face Taylor West as he looked after Hitch's retreating pickup for a moment, then shifted his attention to her. He had taken off his hat and now turned the brim nervously in his fingers.

The church parking lot felt eerily quiet. The rest of the parishioners had left. Out of the corner of her eye, she saw Pastor Tom following his wife up the mountainside to the parsonage behind the church. He looked as if he had the weight of the world on his shoulders.

A magpie let out a squawk from a nearby pine tree, then flew away in a flurry of black-and-white wings. Destry looked at Taylor West, waiting.

"Mr. West," she said, bracing herself. Rylan had taken after his father. Taylor West was tall, lean and broad-shouldered strong. Like Rylan, he was also handsome from his blond hair to his brown eyes, with a strong jawline and high cheekbones.

She'd heard Taylor West had been offered a modeling job years ago but turned it down. She imagined that the whole idea had embarrassed him. If WT had been asked, he'd have jumped at it.

"Please. You're old enough to call me Taylor." There was a warmth to his gaze that she'd seen too many times in his eldest son's brown eyes, a kindness and sincerity. He cleared this throat. "I have a favor to ask. I hope you don't mind."

A favor?

"I heard your brother was back. I'm worried something terrible is going to happen after what transpired at the funeral."

"I'm worried, too."

"I was hoping you might talk to Rylan," he said, taking her by surprise. She'd thought he was going to ask her to talk to Carson, talk him into leaving again. "He might listen to you. I know he cares about you."

She smiled at that, wishing it were true.

AT HIS FATHER'S INSISTENCE, Rylan was expected at his parents' house for Sunday lunch. He loved his mother's cooking and would gladly have accepted under most circumstances. It was what he heard in his father's voice that had him feeling anxious this particular Sunday.

"We've been talking about Ginny," Taylor said after the dishes had been washed. His father cleared his voice. "Given what you found hidden in Ginny's jewelry box…"

Rylan looked at his two younger brothers. Jarrett was

twenty, his younger brother a recent high school graduate. Their births were staggered more years than either his father or mother had hoped. Ellie'd had trouble getting pregnant after each of her children.

"Are you sure you want to do this in front of the boys?" Rylan asked.

"They're part of this," Taylor said and looked to his wife, who nodded her agreement. "We've been trying to remember those days before Ginny's death in case there is something that will help find her killer," his father continued.

"I think we need to accept that your sister was seeing someone besides Carson Grant," his mother said. Ellie was a small, gentle woman with honey-brown eyes and an easy smile.

Rylan hated that she had to go through this. "That's all I've been thinking about." That and Destry Grant. He wanted to argue that, even if they were right and Ginny had been seeing someone else, it didn't mean Carson hadn't been the murderer, but he figured they all knew how he felt since he'd voiced it enough times.

"I knew your sister didn't want to go back to college," his mother said. "She'd dreamed for years about her wedding. All she wanted was to get married and have babies. But Carson was too young. He wasn't ready and Ginny had realized that."

"So it makes sense that she might have been attracted to an older man," Taylor said.

"We've been trying to remember if we'd seen her with anyone," his mother said.

"I have to admit, I wasn't around all that much," Rylan said. He'd had too much going on himself with Destry.

"I saw her talking to people at church," his brother Cody said.

They all turned to look at him.

"Like who?" his father asked.

Cody shrugged. "The pastor."

"Yes, son," Taylor said as if to move on, but Rylan had noticed that his mother had paled.

"Did you remember something?" Rylan asked her.

She shook her head, but he could tell something had upset her.

"Hitch McCray," Jarrett said. "He was always going up to her and trying to get her to go out with him."

"He wasn't married, though," Rylan pointed out.

"But he was unavailable because of his mother," Taylor said.

"I saw her talking to Grayson Brooks," Cody said.

"The contractor?"

"This is crazy," Rylan said. "Ginny talked to a lot of people."

"Not Bob Benton. Ginny thought he was creepy," Jarrett said.

"She told you that?" his mother asked.

"No, but I saw her reaction to him. He was like Hitch, always watching her when no one was looking, and once I saw him go up to her in church. She took off like a shot when Bob's wife, Nettie, walked up."

Rylan looked at his brothers, realizing they were just kids when Ginny died. Jarrett had been thirteen, Cody only seven. But sometimes kids noticed more than adults. "Bob, I guess, isn't bad-looking, but he's dull as dirt."

"Maybe dull was exactly what your sister was looking for after Carson," Taylor said.

"Clete Reynolds liked her," Jarrett said. "He used to flirt with her during the sermons."

Ellie got to her feet. "None of this proves anything and I hate talking about our neighbors this way."

After a moment, Rylan followed her into the kitchen. She was standing at the sink, gripping the edge of the counter, her head down.

"Are you all right?" he asked.

"It's just so hard even talking about this." She turned to look at him.

"You remembered something earlier. Mom, you have to tell me."

She swallowed, still looking pale and upset. "I'm sure it's nothing."

"It was something to do with Pastor Tom, wasn't it?"

Her eyes filled with tears. He could see how hard this was for her. "It was a week or so before your sister died. I saw him trying to talk to Ginny. She appeared to be arguing with him and finally pulled away from him. I wasn't the only one who noticed. Pastor Tom's wife, Linda, was watching them. I saw her expression. She'd looked upset and…"

"Jealous?"

His mother nodded. "Pastor Tom has always been so kind and caring, he wouldn't—"

"He's a man, and maybe his wife has reason to be jealous," Rylan said, turning to head for the door.

"Wait, what are you going to do?"

"Talk to him."

"I don't think you want to talk to him about this with his wife around. She goes to a women's support group in Big Timber on Mondays. Linda is usually gone most of the day."

"I know you and Anna Brooks started that group years ago, but I didn't think you still went."

"I don't usually. Anna isn't well enough to attend anymore, but Linda, as the pastor's wife, gives these young women spiritual comfort. She struggled with infertility for years and finally gave up hoping she and Tom would have children. Me, I stop in on occasion, bring cookies, try to do what I can. I was blessed with four children, but I haven't forgotten the ones I miscarried. A mother doesn't."

CHAPTER TWELVE

AFTER CHURCH, DESTRY drove up to the big house to find Margaret and Cherry in the kitchen. "How's WT?" she asked after saying hello to Cherry.

"His usual contrary self," Margaret replied. If she'd noticed that Destry hadn't called him Dad, she didn't acknowledge it. "He's in his den, going over some paperwork."

"Shouldn't he be taking it easy today?" she asked, unable not to be concerned about him. "Maybe I should stick my head in—"

Margaret gave her a warning head shake. "He told me he didn't want to be disturbed."

Destry helped herself to one of Margaret's buttermilk biscuits, slathering fresh creamery butter on it, then a thick layer of peach jam before adding the bacon and the top half of the biscuit. As she took a bite, she reveled in the salty and sweet mixture, the buttery flaky biscuit melting in her mouth.

Last night she couldn't have swallowed a bite, but today, like WT, she was determined to get on with her life. She might not share WT's blood, but when it came to stubbornness, they were two of kind.

She'd had a lot of time to think this morning on the ride to and from church. She'd never taken anything lying down, and she wasn't going to this time.

"You always have to grab the bull by its horns, don't you?" WT would say when she'd dig her heels in over changes she wanted to make on the ranch.

Cherry looked up from the magazine she was reading. "Is your ranch using the radio frequency identification tag system yet?"

Destry blinked, then noticed the magazine Cherry had been reading. She almost laughed. "No. You've taken an interest in cattle?"

"Well, according to this article, all a cattle thief needs is a horse, a dog and a trailer and he can walk away with ten thousand dollars worth of beef in a night. A brand can be changed, but if a vet injects an RFID into the animal, it can be scanned and the cow tracked. It sounds like a very sensible system. I'm surprised you haven't implemented it."

"I've talked to WT at length about it, but he's stubborn," Destry said. "He thinks it's a waste of money. He has it in his head that no one is going to rustle his cattle."

Cherry sighed. "That explains why he didn't want to discuss it with me, then." She smiled. "Not that he wants to discuss anything with me." She got up. "Thank you for breakfast," she said to Margaret. "I think I'll go work out."

After they were sure Cherry couldn't hear them, Destry and Margaret shared a laugh.

"Can you imagine how WT reacted to Cherry asking him about RFID tagging?" Margaret said with a shake of her head.

Destry could well imagine. No one could convince WT of anything. Except maybe Margaret. Just the thought made her voice something she'd often wondered. "So what does WT have on you?" Destry asked, studying her. She was a few years younger than WT, a pretty woman, talented, smart, strong and reliable. She could do so much better than working here.

"I beg your pardon?" Margaret asked with a laugh.

"There has to be a reason you put up with him. I'm thinking it must be blackmail, but then why wouldn't you have poisoned him by now?"

Margaret shook her head, smiling. "WT and I go way back."

"No, that's not it," Destry said and, with a start, wondered why she hadn't seen it before. The spark in Margaret's eyes when WT was around wasn't irritation or even anger. "You're in love with him."

It seemed so improbable, and yet that was it, Destry realized.

Margaret didn't bother to deny it. "Your biscuit is getting cold," she said and turned back to the chocolate cake she was preparing for dinner. Chocolate cake was WT's favorite.

Destry finished her biscuit without another word on the subject. "Where's Carson?" she asked as she took her plate over to the sink. She needed to ask Carson about the silver locket, then she planned to call Rylan. She wanted to tell him about Pastor Tom's odd reaction at church when she'd told him about the Bible verse.

"He's gone for a hike."

Destry didn't bother to hide her surprise. "We're talking about Carson, right?"

The housekeeper laughed.

"Any idea where he went on this hike?"

"I saw him head up the creek trail about ten minutes ago."

Destry glanced out the window, but she couldn't see him. "I think I'll see if I can catch him."

THE TRAIL BORDERED the creek, going from the grassy foothills into the thick pines before breaking out to reveal a waterfall that tumbled over a sheer rock face. It was a short easy hike—until you reached the falls.

She hadn't gone far when she saw her brother making the last of the climb to the top of the waterfall. A moment later, he appeared at the railing. Years ago, someone had built a wooden fence at the top edge of the falls. It had rotted over time and needed replacing, but since WT owned this piece of land, he'd seen no reason to make the repairs.

"You and everyone else have no business going up there anyway," he'd said when Destry had suggested it. "You could fall, railing or no railing, and kill yourself." Sometimes WT's logic amazed her.

Now, seeing her brother standing so close to the edge frightened her. It wasn't like him to go for a hike. Especially up here.

She hurried up the rest of the trail, climbing to the top of the falls without any trouble. She was used to the high altitude.

If Carson saw her coming, he gave no indication. Even when she walked up behind him, he didn't acknowledge her presence.

"Carson," she said a few feet behind him, afraid she might scare him.

"Hey, sis," he said without turning.

She moved to his side and looked out over the valley. It took her breath away. The land dropped to the Yellowstone River in a series of streams edged with yellows, golds and reds. The only green was the clear, snow-fed waters of the creeks and finally the river on its way to the Gulf of Mexico.

But when she looked over at her brother, she realized he wasn't seeing any of it. He had a faraway look in his eyes. His swollen lip a reminder of the trouble he'd brought home with him. She'd come up here to ask him about the locket, but there was something she needed to know first.

CARSON HAD GROANED inwardly when he'd seen his sister coming up the trail. He knew it was no coincidence that she'd hiked up here today, which meant she'd been looking for him.

"Something on your mind?" he asked, just wanting to get whatever it was over with.

"How long have you known I'm not WT's daughter?"

He couldn't miss the accusation in her voice and sighed. "Didn't know exactly. Suspected. Come on, the way he's always treated you. How could *you* not suspect?"

"He's a bastard to everyone." She let out a humorless laugh. "Why should I be special?" Her voice broke as if she remembered what the doctor had said.

"I'm sorry, sis."

"You could have told me."

"Maybe I hoped, especially after his accident and you coming home to help him out here...." He swore under his breath. "I'd hoped he would change."

"How can WT be so sure I'm not his daughter?" she asked, her voice breaking as she stared out at the land as if unable to look at him.

"You'd have to ask him that."

"I did. He says he just knows. If he's not my father, then who is?"

"I honestly don't know."

"There must have been rumors over the years," she

asked, stealing a glance at him. "How could our mother and her lover, if there was one, have kept it a secret in a community as small as this one? I would have heard rumors growing up, wouldn't I?"

"Destry, I don't know. You're asking the wrong person."

They fell silent, the only sound the rush of the water over the rocks and the dull roar that rose with the mist from the bottom of the falls far below them.

"What was she like?" Destry asked after a while. "I don't even have a photograph of our mother."

He hated the pain he heard in her voice. "I wasn't that old when she died, but I remember her as being kind of quiet. I think I remember her smile, maybe even her laugh."

"Do you think she ever loved him?"

"I suppose so, at first."

"He must have loved her to be so bitter. And yet love shouldn't turn a person into what he's become."

"Do we really have to do this?"

"I'm trying to make sense of my *life*," she snapped. "I thought I was his daughter. Now I find out he's cutting me out of his life. And we both know what you'll do once you get your hands on the ranch."

Carson rubbed his forehead and sighed again. "I don't have a choice, sis. I need the money."

"Have you asked Dad—WT—for it?"

"Even if he'd give me more money right now, it wouldn't be enough to cover even the interest on what I owe."

She shook her head. "You lost so much that your only way out is to sell the whole ranch?"

He looked away, feeling like the dumb son of a bitch

he was. Did she have any idea what it was like living in WT's shadow? He'd wanted to show the old man that he could be just as successful. Once he got a large enough stake, he'd planned to start a business of his own or buy a company. At least that's what he'd told himself.

"I got in too deep," he said, unable to look at her. "I thought I could get myself out." He shook his head. "I'm in serious trouble, Destry."

Her expression darkened, as if she thought he might be in even more serious trouble than just with gambling debts. "There's something I need to ask you."

He braced himself.

"Did you give Ginny a silver heart-shaped locket and chain?"

He felt the question pierce his chest like a poison arrow. "Why would you ask me that?"

"Just answer the question." She was staring at him, looking for any hint of a lie.

But this was something he could never lie about. "No." He thought of the diamond engagement ring he'd bought. The stone had been small, all he could afford at the time. He'd carried it around with him for weeks. "I didn't give her a silver locket."

DESTRY STUDIED HER BROTHER. It was the pain in his expression when he'd answered that made her believe him. "I need to get back." She was anxious to call Rylan, anxious to hear his voice. She stepped away, but her brother's words made her stop and turn to look back at him.

"That man gave her the locket, didn't he?" Carson said. "The married man I suspected she was seeing."

"We don't know. Rylan found it hidden under the

lining of Ginny's jewelry box. He found a note, too. It was a Bible verse about adultery. It sounded threatening. Do you have any idea who might have written the note to her?"

"Probably just some do-gooder around here, someone you brushed elbows with this morning in church."

"Whoever wrote the note must have known about the affair and who Ginny was seeing. Rylan is taking what he found to the sheriff." She waited for his reaction.

"I don't blame you for not trusting me, but please don't stop believing that I'm innocent of her murder," he said as he turned his back to her to look out again into the distance. She noticed that he'd moved closer to the rotten railing. "You're the only one I have left."

Destry felt her breath catch. "Don't get so close to the edge." She took a step toward him, suddenly afraid of what he might do.

Mist rose into the chilly air from the cascading water, allowing only glimpses of the frothy white pool at the bottom of the cliff. He stood on the precipice as if considering the distance to the ground far below him. If he leaned out any farther... She shuddered, desperately wanting to pull him back but afraid to touch him for fear it would have the opposite effect.

"Carson, step back. You're making me nervous."

He didn't seem to hear her.

"Carson!"

He grabbed the railing, one of the small log limbs coming off in his hand. She reached for him but before she could grasp his arm, he stumbled back.

"Someone should fix that railing," he said as he tossed the limb aside.

Destry couldn't reply, her heart was pounding so hard, her breath still trapped by the lump in her throat.

"I'm sorry, sis. I didn't mean to scare you."

She was shaking her head as she finally found her voice. "I can get you enough money to hold off your creditors for a while."

"I'm not taking your money." But she saw relief, gratitude and, ultimately, guilt wash over his expression. "I can't ask you—"

"You aren't asking. WT pays me what he does the ranch hands. He says if I'm going to act like one, I should get paid like one. Since I have few expenses…"

"It would just be a loan. Once I have the money from—" He broke off. "I'll pay you back with interest. If you want, I could sign something."

"I might not be more than a half sister, but I'm your *sister*."

"Sorry. I feel like enough of a jackass as it is. Your offer is so generous, given what I'm putting you through, that I don't know what I'm saying, okay?"

She smiled, although it hurt. She didn't want to fight with her brother. He was her only blood relative. She loved him. But she was angry with him and concerned about the man he'd become.

"You haven't been asking around about a poker game again, have you?"

He looked chagrined. "A weak moment. Not to worry. The old man hasn't given me a cent. I couldn't gamble even if I wanted to."

His words didn't relieve her mind. "How do I know you'll give my money to the man you owe and not gamble it away?" she asked.

He looked hurt. "You have my word."

His word? She didn't think his word and a dime

could get her a cup of coffee. She feared that if he could, Carson would lose not only the money, but also the ranch in a poker game. As it was, she didn't doubt that once he sold the place, he would gamble it away. She looked out over the ranch and fought the burn of tears. The worst part was that there would be nothing she could do to stop him.

"I need your help with something," she said. Her brother looked wary. "I need a DNA sample from WT. Will you get it for me?"

"Are you sure you want to do this?"

"I have to know for sure."

Her brother nodded, studying her for a long moment before he sighed and said, "Just tell me what you need. I'll do it."

CARSON EASED OPEN his father's bedroom door and quietly slipped inside. The room was dim, the drapes drawn. The smell of age—or more likely impending death—seemed to cloak the room, making him nauseated.

He moved quickly to the bathroom, listening for any sound of his father's wheelchair outside the room. When he'd come into the house, he'd heard WT in his den on the phone and decided now might be the perfect time.

His plan had been to see what brand of toothbrush his father used, then bring a replacement. That plan changed the moment he'd stepped into the bathroom. He had no intention of coming back in here.

WT's toothbrush was in its holder next to the sink. Using a tissue from the box between the two sinks, he carefully wrapped the used toothbrush, then hesitated. What would WT think when his toothbrush was missing?

Carson wasn't sure he cared, but still he looked under

the cabinet and was relieved to see that Margaret had stocked several packages of new toothbrushes.

It only took a moment to replace one in the holder beside the sink. He figured, even if his father noticed, he'd think Margaret had done it.

As he started to leave, he spotted his father's hairbrush. There was always a chance the lab tech wouldn't be able to get DNA from the toothbrush. He pulled some hair from the brush, put it in a tissue as well, and slipped both tissues into his pocket.

No way was he going to get caught in his father's bedroom. But as he was about to leave, he saw his image in a full-length mirror on the far wall and froze.

It often surprised him when he saw himself. It was as if he expected to be that young man who'd left here eleven years ago. Or maybe he just wished it so. Wished those years away, wished Ginny back from the dead, wished—

"What the hell are you doing?" he asked his image as he stepped closer until he could look directly into his own eyes. Even that surprised him, that cold look he got back. "Helping my sister," he answered back.

Yeah, you're real helpful. You're helping yourself to the ranch, the ranch your sister loves. "You really are an SOB, Carson Grant."

The image in the mirror didn't bother to argue.

He had reason to feel guilty. He knew Destry was wasting her time with the paternity test. It would only make everything official. There was little to no chance Destry was WT's daughter. Carson knew that because he remembered a lot more about their mother than he'd told Destry—or the old man.

CHAPTER THIRTEEN

EARLY MONDAY MORNING, Sheriff Frank Curry stood in front of his old farmhouse and stared out at the land in surprise. Sometimes fall came on so fast he didn't notice that the grasses had dried and yellowed or the lush green leaves of the cottonwoods had turned to rusts and golds that scattered on a breath of breeze, leaving the limbs bare.

This year was like that. Or maybe he was just getting old. His short marriage short years after Lynette dumped him seemed like a lifetime ago. Just the thought made him feel old when only recently he'd felt like a teenager again.

He smiled, thinking of Lynette. She had been a beauty in her younger days, with her long red hair like a flame. She'd changed over the years, but he still felt that spark that would never go out. When he looked at her even now, he saw that beautiful, young, lively woman she'd been. He wondered if a lot of men thought of their first loves in that way, forever frozen in that moment past.

Frank sighed, took off his hat and raked a hand through his still-thick blond but graying hair before settling his Stetson back on his head.

He looked toward the Crazies—and the W Bar G—

bracing himself for the day ahead. Whenever he had to butt heads with WT it made for a tough day.

That spring afternoon at the creek so many years ago tugged at him like a noose around his neck. That moment in time had set his life on a course he'd been fighting for years and branded him with its memory, like a scar that had never healed.

He could almost smell spring on the air when he recalled it. The water had been running high and cold that year. He and a group of boys had gone to their favorite spot where the creek ran between the granite boulders and the pines to form deep dark holes.

He'd never been that fond of water. But he'd been smart enough to know that he would never hear the end of it if he didn't go in. All of the other boys, even younger ones than him, had already jumped in.

He'd watched them disappear into the rushing dark water only to bob up moments later downstream in a burst of air before swimming quickly to the shore. Their bodies had been covered with goose bumps, their teeth chattering from the cold, as they'd pulled their clothes back on, all of them looking cocky and self-assured, laughing as if invigorated by the snow-fed stream.

Frank had seen that his turn was coming up fast. His fingers had trembled as he'd slipped out of his boots, unsnapped his Western shirt and discarded it, then shimmied out of his jeans. He'd put his clothing on a large rock, just as everyone else had. He'd stood in his white shorts, trying to talk himself into jumping in.

"Come on, Curry, we haven't got all day," one of the boys had yelled.

He'd stepped to the edge of the water as the boy in front of him had jumped in and waited for a few moments until the boy's head had bobbed to the surface. Then he'd stepped out onto the boulder next to one of the deepest holes and froze as he'd stared in the cold, dark water.

"Frankie's not going to do it." WT Grant's voice had filled the air. "He's chicken." WT had started clucking and the others had begun to laugh and join in. A couple of them had threatened to throw his clothes in with him.

Frank had held his breath, closed his eyes and jumped.

The icy water had stolen his breath, shocking his eyes open. All he'd seen was darkness. It had taken a few moments before he'd realized that he'd sunk like a rock to the deep bottom and hadn't bobbed up for some reason.

The water around him had been almost black with darkness. Instinctively, he'd begun to swim hard for the surface. But it had been as if he'd dropped into a bottomless well. He could feel the water rushing him downstream, see light above him, *far* above him. But as hard as he'd swum for it, the surface had eluded him.

Panic had seized him. He couldn't hold his breath any longer. He'd felt as if he was going to burst. Suddenly water had rushed into his mouth and nose and everything had begun to fade to black.

Even now, he could remember that feeling, knowing he was drowning. That's when he'd felt the arm close around his neck and drag him up and into blessed air.

He'd gulped, then choked and coughed, the icy creek water heaving out of him and, all the time, hearing the scared silence around him. That day Waylon "WT" Grant had jumped in fully clothed to save his life.

That's why everyone in the county thought he

couldn't be trusted when it came to WT. Frank laughed under his breath at that. What he and WT had between them was much more complicated than that.

Frank was startled out of his thoughts as one of his crows called to him from the branch of an old cottonwood next to the barn. He recognized the bird by its call. It was the one he'd named Billy the Kid after his deputy, Billy "The Kid" Westfall, a cocky, loud young man with an itchy trigger finger.

Frank had inherited Billy when he took the sheriff's job. The grandson of one of the town's elite, Billy had a job as long as his grandfather was alive, and there was little Frank could do about it if he hoped to remain sheriff.

The bird Billy the Kid cawed at him and flapped his wings, upset over something. Probably the weather, Frank thought as he looked past the mountains and saw dark clouds obscuring the peaks of the Crazies.

But it was the other storm brewing that worried him as he slid behind the wheel of his patrol pickup and headed for the W Bar G.

WT WAS ALREADY in a foul mood long before he looked up and saw the sheriff's patrol pickup drive up. The reason he hadn't told Destry or anyone else about his declining health was he didn't want them walking around feeling sorry for him.

Margaret and Carson hadn't mentioned the doctor's visit last night or asked how he was feeling. Margaret was smart enough not to. Carson didn't give a damn.

The sheriff's visit wasn't a surprise. WT had been expecting it ever since he'd heard that some new evidence had turned up in Ginny's murder case, and Frank had called to say Carson needed to come home. It would be better for everyone involved if they didn't have to go after him.

WT had agreed. He'd just figured he would handle it, one way or another. He wanted Carson home for his own selfish reasons.

"What the hell do you want?" he asked, answering the door.

"Mind if I come in for a moment?" Frank asked.

"If this is about Carson…" When the sheriff said nothing, WT swore and wheeled into the living room, the lawman behind him.

"I need to speak to Carson," Frank said behind him.

It was too early for a drink, but WT made himself one anyway. The doctor had told him to quit drinking. He laughed to himself at that. He figured alcohol was the only thing keeping him alive. He didn't even bother to offer Frank one. The man was a known teetotaler.

"If you think you're going to railroad my boy—"

"Carson isn't a boy anymore. Nor am I railroading anyone. I came out here to talk to your son. I would think you'd want this resolved. Last night I had to put some fires out at the Range Rider. A lot of people think your son got away with murder. Some of them are talking vigilante justice just like in the old days. The best thing I can do for your son is find out who killed Ginny West. Unless, of course, you know something I don't?"

"Have you forgotten that you owe me?"

The sheriff's gaze narrowed. "I'm never going to forget that you saved my life. But that has nothing to do with this."

"Well, Carson isn't here right now. But let me give you some good advice. If you want to remain sheriff, then I suggest you get rid of any evidence that might incriminate my son or—"

"I'm going to pretend I didn't hear that. Have Carson give me a call."

WT let out a string of curses.

"Oh, and make sure he doesn't run again. It will only make him look more guilty, and this time I'll see that he gets brought back in handcuffs."

As the sheriff left, WT sat staring down into the cut-crystal glass in his hand for a moment before throwing it at the closing door. The glass shattered, the rich amber whiskey droplets suspended in the air for an instant before splattering against the door and running down the wall.

NETTIE WAS ABOUT to turn on the store lights to begin another day at work when she spotted the sheriff sitting in his pickup just down the road. She watched him for a few moments, wondering what he was doing, until her curiosity won out.

Opening the front door, she walked down the street. The fall breeze sent the golden dried leaves of a large old cottonwood next to the creek fluttering across the truck's hood. Frank appeared to be simply sitting there, staring into space.

She heard the soft seductive rustle of leaves, felt the warm sun on her back as the breeze stirred her bottle-red hair. It could have been a fall day years ago when Frank had stopped by the house on his motorcycle to pick her up to do one fool thing or another.

"You don't have anything better to do than day-dream?" she asked, as she stuck her head into the open passenger-side window.

Frank laughed. "I'm watching those young crows over there."

She looked past him to see two birds hopping around on the ground in the fallen leaves. "Fascinating. Why can't you just admit you're daydreaming?"

He laughed. "It *is* fascinating. Come join me." He reached across to open the passenger-side door. "I'll show you."

Nettie lifted a brow. But this was Frank Curry, a man who, even at sixty-one, didn't need a line to get a woman into his pickup. She glanced back at the store and then slid in, moving closer at his encouragement so she could have a better view of the birds.

"Did you know crows are smarter than cats and most children?" he asked. From the children she'd experienced in her store, she couldn't argue that. "Crows are more like us than any other species, even primates. I've been studying them for years." He grinned. "Gives me something to do on a stakeout—besides daydream."

"So you're on a stakeout now?" she asked.

"Actually, I was hanging around in case you had any more trouble from bears."

She couldn't help being touched by his concern. "The grizzly hasn't come back, thankfully."

"I saw that the FWP trap is still empty. Haven't heard of any bear sightings in the area. Maybe the bear wandered back up into the mountains already."

She watched the birds hopping around in the leaves. "So what's so fascinating about these two crows?"

He seemed pleased by her question. "Well, they're young, so they're playing like kids do. See the way they chase each other around, pulling at each other's tails?

Watch that one. He'll pick up that leaf, then the other one will chase him. Whoever has the leaf is it."

He was right about the birds, she thought, watching them, and he smelled nice as if he'd just come from a shower.

"Crows have been known to make their own tools, like taking a plant stem and using it to probe in holes for insects," he said. "In one study I read about, crows in captivity will bend a piece of wire to make a hook, then use it to pull a bucket of food closer to them. Making tools is a sign of just how intelligent they are."

She'd known men with *less* intelligence. Sometimes she wondered if Bob would sit in his chair and just starve to death if she didn't cook for him.

"So you like crows." This side of Frank surprised her, but then he had always been a man of many interests in the old days.

"I like watching crows because they're so human. If you feed them, they'll bring you small presents, pieces of shiny glass or trinkets they've found. But if you're mean to them, they'll poop on your car."

She laughed, wondering how serious he was about these birds, how serious he'd been about her. He'd once told her that she had broken his heart when she married Bob.

"The thing about crows, they're territorial when it comes to their families and loved ones," Frank said and glanced in his rearview mirror. "Crows pair for life, but the males fool around some. If they get caught, though, there is hell to pay. Just like humans, crows have been known to kill one of their own if they suspect he's been trespassing in another's territory."

Nettie pulled her attention from the two young crows to look at Frank. "Are you trying to tell me something?"

He chuckled and pointed to the pickup's rearview mirror. "I just saw your husband go into the store. I think he's looking for you."

She didn't want to leave the warmth of the pickup or the spell Frank had cast. But she slid across the seat to the passenger side and reached for the door handle anyway. "Thank you for the lesson on crows."

"Any time."

As she shoved open her door, the two young crows took off in a flurry of black wings, and she heard Frank sigh and start his pickup engine.

RYLAN HAD MENTALLY kicked himself after his visit to Destry's house Sunday morning. She'd taken his concern for her as him butting into her life, her business. She had a point, though. He had no right to tell her what to do—even if it was for her own good.

He'd gone home and worked hard the rest of the day, thinking he could work off his frustration—and his growing worry about her. It hadn't worked. It was so like her to shrug off his concern, as well as the fact that someone had been watching her house, watching her. She was stubbornly convinced she could take care of herself. She'd been like this since they were kids.

"I wouldn't climb that tree if I were you," he'd said one day. And sure as the devil she'd climbed clear to the top and almost gotten herself killed.

That was Destry Grant. Impossibly mule-headed and just as impossible to forget.

Someone had been hanging around Destry's house spying on her. He recalled that one of Ginny's friends had told him that his sister had had the same problem—months before she was murdered.

That thought shook him to his core. Just a coincidence?

It scared him to think what could have happened if he hadn't gone out to see Destry just after daylight yesterday morning. What if he hadn't scared the man away? And what if he didn't happen by the next time?

As he parked in front of the sheriff's department, he shoved away thoughts of Destry. All thinking about her did was rile him up.

He glanced over at the small plastic bag he'd put the note and the locket in, hoping either could really help find his sister's killer. But what were the chances of that happening? Even if he trusted Sheriff Frank Curry, even if the trail hadn't gone cold, even if Carson Grant wasn't the killer, he feared it was too late for him and Destry.

He fished out his cell phone as it rang. Destry. He braced himself for the sound of her voice and what it did to him. "I was hoping I'd hear from you."

"I talked to my brother. Carson swears he didn't give Ginny the locket." He wondered what was the point of having her ask Carson. Did he really trust her brother not to lie?

"I believe him, Rylan. He was upset. He thinks the other man gave it to her, that's why it was hidden, just as I do."

"Well, thanks for asking him. I'm on my way into the sheriff's office right now. I'll let you know how it goes. Everything all right with you?" Was he trying to make conversation just to keep her on the line because he was worried about her? Or because he liked the sound of her voice?

"Everything is fine."

Why didn't he believe that? He'd seen the dark shadows under her eyes. Something was keeping her awake at night, and he doubted it was the Peeping Tom.

"There is something else," she said. "I showed the quote to Pastor Tom after church. I didn't tell him anything about it except that it had been left as a possible threat. He got upset. I could tell he wanted to talk to me, but Linda came up and dragged him off to talk to someone else."

"You think he might know about the notes?"

"Ginny was in church almost every Sunday. I was wondering if she might have confided in the pastor about the notes, maybe even about her pregnancy and the man she was involved with."

"I think we should talk to Tom."

"I was thinking the same thing."

"You don't mind going with me?"

"Of course not."

"Okay. I'll give you a call after I talk to the sheriff." He snapped the phone shut, telling himself he was a damned fool in more ways than he wanted to admit. Spending time with her was pure hell, and yet every time he saw her or talked to her, he couldn't wait until the next time.

Sometimes he thought he could feel the gulf between them narrowing. But he knew the moment something else came up about his sister and her brother, that gap would only widen further.

As he pushed open the door to the sheriff's department, he was glad he'd shown his father the note and silver locket.

Taylor West had immediately told him he must take them to the sheriff.

Now Rylan just hoped his father was right and that Frank Curry could be trusted.

"Can I help you?" the sheriff's department dispatcher asked from behind the thick sheet of glass.

When had Montana become so dangerous that people were forced to work behind bulletproof glass? "I need to see the sheriff."

"He's out but—" She looked past him and smiled. "Here he is now."

Rylan turned to come face-to-face with Sheriff Frank Curry. Now that he was here, he worried that he was wasting his time, since Frank Curry was as thick as thieves with WT Grant.

"You wanted to see me?" the sheriff asked.

"It's about my sister's murder."

With a nod, the lawman said, "Why don't we step into my office."

Rylan followed him, telling himself all that mattered was catching Ginny's killer and putting him behind bars.

"Sit down," the sheriff said as he settled into his chair behind his desk. The chair groaned under his weight.

Rylan took one of the straight-back wooden chairs across from him. The small room had a musty smell, the building old and dark. Maybe the dispatcher was behind a wall of bulletproof glass, but he didn't get the feeling that anything else about investigating had changed from the days of the old West.

Frank Curry looked like an old-timey sheriff. He wore jeans, boots, a uniform shirt and gold star, his gray Stetson resting on a hook by the door. He could easily have been on the hunt for Butch Cassidy and the Sundance Kid instead of Ginny West's killer. He even had a thick drooping blond mustache flecked with gray and a weathered Montana look about him.

"I'm sorry about your sister," the sheriff said. Maybe it was the kindness in his eyes or something in his voice, but Rylan relaxed a little.

"That night, the night my sister was killed…" Rylan began.

"You were with Destry Grant up at the old abandoned ski lodge."

He stared at the sheriff. "How did you—"

"Destry told me a few days after."

Destry had come forward? Why hadn't she told him? Because he'd cut off all contact with her, and not long after that, he'd left to rodeo.

"So you know that Carson Grant's only alibi is Jack French?"

The sheriff nodded.

"And you know Jack would say whatever Carson told him."

Frank Curry merely smiled.

"But that's not why I'm here," Rylan said and reached into his pocket. He'd put the note and the locket in a small plastic bag. "I found this hidden in my sister's jewelry box."

The sheriff took the bag.

"Carson said there was another man in my sister's life. He swears he didn't give Ginny the locket. Destry believes him. Maybe—" He stumbled over the words, hating that Carson might have been right as much as even the thought that his sister might have been seeing a married man. "—Ginny was seeing another man, possibly a married man."

The sheriff opened the bag, inspected the locket, then read the note. "May I keep this?"

Rylan nodded. "It doesn't prove there was anyone else…" He saw something in the sheriff's expression. "Wait a minute, did you find evidence of another man?"

Frank seemed to measure his words. "It's an ongoing investigation."

Even if that was the new evidence, another man's DNA at the murder scene didn't prove that the man had killed Ginny, though. Just as it didn't clear Carson of the murder. Rylan pointed this out to the sheriff.

"True. You have any idea who might have given your sister this locket?"

He shook his head. "No." But the hidden locket, the note all pointed to a secret lover. A man they all knew? The thought terrified him since Beartooth was such a small, close-knit community.

Rylan got to his feet, remembering what the sheriff had said about Destry. She'd come forward eleven years ago to refute her brother's claim that she was his second alibi. She'd told the sheriff everything.

He'd just assumed she'd kept quiet, covering for her brother. It had felt like a betrayal, but as it turned out, he was the one who'd betrayed her by not trusting her, by taking off the way he had.

The sheriff rose and extended his hand. "I'm glad you're home."

Was he as glad Carson Grant was home? he wondered as he left the sheriff's department.

Rylan felt more confident in the sheriff. Not that he was going to stop digging for answers on his own.

Had he known Destry told the sheriff the truth that night, would it have made a difference eleven years ago? Would he have left?

He didn't know. He felt as if he'd abandoned her after promising to always love her. And yet, it wouldn't have changed anything. Her brother would still be a suspect in his sister's murder. Destry would still side with her brother.

It would be just like it was now. A stalemate. As long as her brother was under suspicion, there was no chance for them.

DESTRY ACHED TO saddle up and ride up into the Crazies—where she always went when she was upset. But she couldn't leave. Rylan hadn't called yet. She felt at loose ends.

In the kitchen she made herself a sandwich but only had a few bites before she put the rest in the refrigerator. She was too anxious to eat. She poured herself a glass of milk. Somehow milk had always soothed her. The milk was cold and sweet. WT loved to drink milk late at night.

"Father like daughter," Margaret used to say when she caught the two of them in the kitchen in the middle of the night.

WT would always grunt and tell Margaret to mind her own business. Destry had never thought anything of it. Until now.

She ached from the sense of loss. She looked around the house. Her mother had lived here, decorated this place, and yet there was so little of her still here. She knew nothing about the woman who had given her birth.

Worse, she knew nothing about herself. *Who was she if not WT's daughter?*

The thought came as a jolt each time, shaking the foundation under her as well as making her question her entire life.

Who was her father?

If only she had known her mother, maybe she wouldn't feel so adrift now. As she stepped to the sink to rinse out her empty milk glass, it slipped from her hand and fell, breaking on impact. Shards of glass ricocheted across the floor.

She'd never been this clumsy, she thought with a curse as she grabbed the roll of paper towels and began to clean up the glass. On her hands and knees, she was reaching for a piece of the broken glass that had fallen in a small indentation in the floor, when she saw something she'd never noticed before.

The indentation was crescent-shaped, as if someone had purposely carved it in the wood. She moved closer to inspect it and saw the slightly wider space between the boards. Was it possible?

Slipping her fingers into the indentation, she pulled. A section of floor lifted a fraction. The years had filled in the edges. No wonder she hadn't noticed it in all this time. The trap door had apparently not been opened in a long time.

Destry shoved the table out of the way and pried at the edges with a butter knife from the drawer. She tried to raise it again. A section of the floor about three foot square lifted just enough that she knew she'd found a door that opened to whatever was under the house.

She tried again and thought she'd have to ask her brother for assistance when it finally gave.

The door creaked slowly open on rusted hinges. An earthy, musty smell rose into the kitchen like a ghost. Leaning the door back so it stayed open, Destry took a flashlight from the drawer and shone it down into the darkness.

Cobwebs had nearly closed off the opening. She reached for a broom and brushed the cavernous gap free before shining the light into the hole again. This time she saw something. Several large old trunks.

The top stair creaked under her weight, and for a moment, Destry thought better about going down into the space below the house. It could be a long time before anyone thought to check on her.

She tested the next stair with her weight, then the next. The trunks called to her like mythical sirens. As she eased down the stairs, she shone her flashlight around the space. The walls were earthen, smelling of damp soil. She heard the scamper of mice. A cobweb brushed across her face and hair, making her jump.

Wiping it away, she took a calming breath. She'd never liked cramped places, especially damp, musty ones. But she was too close to quit now. Just a few more steps.

As she put her weight on the last step, she felt it give and grabbed for the railing, grasping only air. The step snapped, pitching her forward and into the darkness.

CHAPTER FOURTEEN

DESTRY LAY IN the cold, damp dirt for a moment. She'd dropped the flashlight. It now lay a few feet away, the beam cocked at an angle shooting slightly upward, away from her.

She didn't move for a moment, allowing herself time to catch the breath that had been knocked out of her. Something small with a lot of legs ran across her hand. She sat up, brushing furiously at her fingers, then her sleeve and the front of her shirt.

Shoving to her feet, she brushed at her jeans, fighting panic. Alone down here, what would have happened if she'd hurt herself badly?

Well, she wasn't hurt. She was fine, although strangely she still felt more alone than she had, more afraid of not just the creepy crawly things in this cellar, but larger, more all-encompassing fears as if the worst was yet to come.

Limping a little, she stepped to the flashlight and picked it up. The cold dampness seeped into her bones. Flicking the light over the larger of the trunks, she moved to it and pried at the lid with one hand as she kept the flashlight steady, half afraid of what she would find, half afraid all this had been for nothing.

The lid rose with a groan, an aged stale scent from another time rising with it. Destry shone the light over the contents. Clothes. The dresses appeared to have been her mother's, or possibly her grandmother's, from some of the styles. She dug through them, held one dress up to her and sniffed the fabric. But there was no hint of the women who had come before her.

She closed the lid and pried open the other trunk and was disappointed that it was much the same. Digging through the clothing, she found a few items that could have been her mother's. None, though, held any clues as to the woman Lila Gray Grant had been.

Discouraged, she started to close the trunk lid when her gaze lit on the corner of what appeared to be a shoebox under all the clothes. She dug it out to find someone had trimmed the box with a piece of lace. With trembling fingers, she lifted the box out, slipped off the lid and shone the light inside.

She knew at once the photograph was of her mother. Lila Gray Grant was wearing a leather Western jacket, the same one Destry had found in the back of the closet when she'd had the bedrooms remodeled upstairs.

Her mother stared up at her, smiling happily from an old snapshot. The photo was crinkled, the color faded, but to Destry it was the most wonderful thing she'd ever seen. She stared down into her mother's face—a face so like her own.

As she touched her mother's face with her fingertips, she felt her eyes fill. While she couldn't miss the resemblance to her mother, Lila had been a striking beauty. In the photo, her mother was smiling, her eyes bright, her face aglow.

The shot looked as if it had been taken at one of the yearly fall harvest festivals held at the fairgrounds.

Destry glanced then at the two men in the photograph. She'd expected one of them to be WT.

But it was Russell, their ranch foreman, who stood next to her mother. The other man, Sheriff Frank Curry, stood to the other side. All three appeared to be in their early twenties.

While her mother was smiling at the camera, both Russell and the sheriff were looking at her mother with nothing short of adoration in their eyes.

BOB BENTON HAD been having the nightmares for several days now—ever since he'd heard Carson Grant had returned. He'd wake in the wee hours before dawn sweating and shivering, more afraid than he'd ever been in his life.

"Night terrors, that's what they're called," Doc Carrey had told him just this morning as the two had had coffee at the Branding Iron. Doc was retired from pediatrics and had bought a ranch outside of Beartooth, so he now handed out free medical advice from the counter at the café most mornings.

"Do you remember anything about your dreams?" Doc had asked.

He'd lied. "Crazy stuff. Just bits and pieces that make no sense. Like strange noises. And smells."

"Smells?" Doc had turned from his coffee to study him. "What kind of smells?"

Bob had had to shake his head. Blood. "I can't even describe them." He'd shifted his gaze, glancing across the street to the store where Nettie would be opening the front door any minute. He didn't want her knowing about the nightmares. She'd want to know what was causing them and would pester him relentlessly until he came up with some answer. His fear was that she already knew, had known for years.

"Nasty smells," he'd said finally. An image came to him from one of the nightmares. Dark wings against a midnight blue sky. "Vultures, I think."

"Vultures? Could be crows. They're considered a sign of death. You should ask the sheriff. He knows all about crows." Doc had taken a bite of his flapjack and chewed for a moment. "But I doubt your dreams have anything to do with vultures *or* crows. You get to a certain age and you start thinking about death. Completely natural. I wouldn't take the dreams too seriously. You're only in your late fifties, right? You should have another thirty years ahead of you at least, if you take care of yourself."

Bob had made a noncommittal sound, wondering how he would be spending those thirty years.

"Like I said, I wouldn't worry about it," Doc had said, going back to his breakfast. "I'm sure it's just a passing phase."

Before he'd retired, Doc had probably told every mother that it was just a passing phase over the years. "Well, thanks for your help," Bob had said and headed across the street to the store. It made Nettie mad when he wasn't there to help right after opening time, even though they seldom had a customer until later in the morning. Nor did he do much to help.

Partway across the street, he spotted the sheriff's pickup parked at the curb down the street from the store. There were two people in the cab, the sheriff and a woman sitting next to him. He blinked as he recognized Nettie's fiery red head. When she'd started turning gray, she'd begun dying it to match her original color. That was Nettie.

He turned away, telling himself that whatever the reason she and the sheriff had their heads together it didn't concern him. But as he hurried into the store, he had trouble catching his breath—just like in the nightmares—and for a moment, he was crippled with fear.

Clutching the doorjamb, he fought the wave of dizziness that overtook him. His heart still pounding, he made his way behind the counter and sat down on the stool Nettie kept there, afraid he was going to black out.

First night terrors? Now panic attacks?

The image of Nettie sitting so close to the sheriff flashed before him. What was she telling her former lover? What her husband cried out during the night? Was she repeating what she heard to Frank at this very moment?

His stomach cramped, and the next moment he found himself throwing up in the wastebasket behind the counter.

"BOB?" NETTIE CLOSED the store's front door behind her and stood for a moment as her eyes adjusted to the dim interior lighting. It had been so bright and sunny outside. She thought of the young crows, their feathers iridescent in the sunlight, their dark eyes shiny with what Frank Curry believed to be intelligence. "Bob!"

She heard the toilet flush at the back of the store, and a moment later her husband came out drying his hands on a paper towel. Nettie couldn't help the instant irritation she felt. He'd washed his face as well as his hands, apparently, because that lock of gray hair that always fell over his forehead was still dripping.

When he'd started going gray, she'd tried to get him to color his hair. He'd refused, saying something about acting his age.

She'd known it was a dig about her dying hers red. "Don't kid yourself, you've always been old," she'd said. "It would take more than hair dye to make you young, let alone fun."

Now as she looked at him, she noticed something odd. He'd aged. It took her by surprise, because, apparently, she hadn't really looked at him in a long while. This morning he appeared pale and smaller, as if he'd shrunk. She knew she was unfairly comparing him to Frank and maybe always would.

"What's wrong with you?" she asked, although she could have filled volumes without any help from him.

"Nothing." He looked annoyed, frowning at her, before tossing the paper towel into the small wastebasket that should have been behind the counter by the door.

"What are you doing with that?" she demanded. He'd put a new plastic bag in it. Wasteful, she thought, since he'd taken out the trash last night before closing and had put in a new bag. She'd checked since he often forgot.

"Putting it back where it goes," he said as he walked over to place it under the counter. "I'm not feeling well. I'm going home."

She stared at him, thinking for the first time in a long time that she didn't want to work today, either. She'd like to go on a picnic up in the Crazies. Go bird-watching with Frank. Eat that picnic lunch beside the creek and then go skinny-dipping in Saddlestring Lake as she and Frank had done when they were young and in love.

"You can manage without me," Bob said.

Yes, she thought. She could. She just wished she'd

realized that thirty years ago when she'd chosen security over passion.

"I'll come back later if I'm feeling better."

"Don't bother." She hadn't meant for her words to
come out so sharply. "Stay home and get to feeling better. I'll be fine."

He studied her for a long moment, then nodded and
headed for the door.

"Bob?"

He stopped but didn't turn. "Yes, Nettie?"

She started to question him about the nightmares
he'd been having and the odd things he'd been saying.
She settled for, "Call me if you need anything."

He didn't answer as he opened the door and left.

AT THE SHERIFF'S department, Frank Curry pulled open his
desk drawer and took out the worn Bible. It had been his
father's. The leather felt warm to the touch as he opened
it. His father used to keep it beside his chair where he
would open it to a random page and begin reading.

Often he would read aloud, his deep voice rich and
full in the tiny house where Frank had grown up. Wall-
ingford Curry hadn't been one of those fanatical Bible
thumpers. Quite the contrary. He was simply a man of
God who believed in grace and goodness as well as
evil and hell.

It only took Frank a few minutes to find Proverbs
23-27. His father's Bible was the King James version,
so the quote was a little different.

For a harlot is a deep pit, and a seductress is a
narrow well. She also lives in wait as for a victim,
and increases the unfaithful among men

Frank dragged the box marked Ginny Sue West over to his desk and lifted the top. He took a breath and let it out slowly as he picked up the top sealed plastic bag.

The victim's clothing had been sent to the crime lab in Missoula eleven years ago. He'd sent the new evidence marked as Urgent. His hope was that the new evidence would provide the proof he needed to not only make an arrest but also get a conviction.

The autopsy was attached to his report. He didn't bother with any of that right now but dug out the small sealed plastic bags with the purse's contents. The purse had been found in Ginny's pickup.

Pulling out the one with the partial scrap of notepaper, he flattened the plastic and the torn piece of paper inside. The scrap of paper had been found in Ginny's purse-sized Bible, the New Living Translation.

Ginny had been a regular churchgoer, so he hadn't thought much about the piece of torn paper—or the words printed on it. At the time he'd thought she'd simply used it to mark her place.

Now, though, he turned to his computer and typed "bible verse," and the three words that were readable on the scrap of paper, "like a robber."

Proverbs 23-28 came up at the top of the page.

A promiscuous woman is as dangerous as falling into a narrow well.
She hides and waits like a robber,
Eager to make more men unfaithful.

The scrap of paper had now taken on a whole new importance in light of what Rylan West had found hid-

den in his sister's jewelry box. Apparently Ginny had
received at least two such notes.

Frank pulled out the note Rylan had found and compared it to the partial one found in Ginny's purse. The
handwriting was identical. The notes were from the
same person.

His phone rang. He saw that it was the crime lab and
braced himself as he took the call.

"DESTRY?" CARSON KNOCKED again. No answer. He'd
tried the door, not surprised to find it unlocked. "Destry?"
he called as he opened the door and stepped in. No one
out here locked their doors even at night.

He heard her voice, though faint. "Where are you?"

"Down here."

He stepped into the kitchen, surprised to see a gap-
ing hole in the wood floor. As he moved closer, he
glanced down and saw the old wooden stairs. His sister was standing on the dirt floor of what couldn't be
called a basement.

"What the devil are you doing down there?" he asked
as she started up the steps. He could see that the bottom
stair was broken, and his sister's clothes were covered
in dirt. "Did you fall down there?"

"Just from the bottom step," she said as she climbed
up. She had a shoe box tucked under one arm.

"What's that?" he asked, hoping it was full of cash.
Surely this wasn't where his sister kept her money.

"Some old photographs of our mother."

He had a sick feeling. "Oh, really?" She was eyeing
him as if she knew he hadn't told her the truth regarding their mother and the man she'd been involved with.

"I brought what you asked me to get," he said, hoping to change the subject as she dropped the hatch door, put the shoebox on the table and shoved the table back into place.

He took out the tissue-wrapped samples and handed them to her. She hugged him as if surprised he'd done it—let alone done it so quickly. "Thank you."

"You sure you want to do this, though?"

"I told you. I have to know. I have a friend who works in a lab in Livingston. I've already contacted her and she's agreed to run the tests for me. I'll take them to her right away."

"How long before you know something?"

"She said a paternity test like mine shouldn't take more than twenty-four hours."

He nodded thoughtfully. "That quick?"

"It's just a preliminary one, but it will tell me what I need to know."

"Then what?"

She shook her head. "No matter how they turn out, WT wouldn't believe the test results. So basically, it changes nothing."

Carson chuckled, and touched his healing lip. "You do know him, don't you?"

"I'm not doing this for WT. I'm doing it for myself." She sighed, realizing what the results might say about her mother. "I just wish I'd known our mother."

"She would have been so proud of you." He looked away. Earlier he'd gotten a call from the collector the casino had sent after him. The threats were getting more specific. He felt desperate and feared what the man might do.

"I hate to think how disappointed our mother would be in me," he said.

"Don't say that. I can't help feeling that if she'd lived, none of this would have happened."

Carson laughed and gave her a hug. "You really are such an irritating optimist. Don't you get tired of always seeing the glass half full?"

"I'm not always optimistic," she said, thinking about the ranch she loved. She wasn't fool enough to believe even a paternity test could change WT's mind about the ranch. Carson's gambling debts aside, she could see that he was angry and just wanted to be rid of the ranch.

"I'll get you a certified check after I take the samples to my friend at the lab."

He looked down at his worn boots, wishing there was another way, and yet more grateful than she would ever know. "Thank you."

"Was there a reason you stopped by?" she asked.

"Just wanted to see you." He'd come for the money, hoping she hadn't changed her mind. At least now he'd know when he could make a payment on his debt.

He took a step toward the door, glad she hadn't mentioned the photographs in the box. "You should get those samples to the lab."

She nodded as if she knew he was more interested in her getting him a check.

He didn't know what else to say. She would give him her own money even knowing he was planning to sell the ranch out from under her. "You're something, you know that?"

DESTRY WAS SOMETHING, all right. Naive. Foolishly trusting. Possibly just pain stupid. But Carson was her brother and he needed her help.

She realized she hadn't mentioned the photo of her

mother, Russell and the sheriff. A part of her suspected it wouldn't come as a surprise to her brother anyway.

The phone rang and she hurriedly picked it up. She was anxious to get the DNA samples to her friend at the lab in Livingston, but brightened when she heard Rylan's voice on the phone. They agreed to meet in Beartooth. Pastor Tom was anxious to talk to them about the note, Rylan reported.

Destry quickly showered and changed and drove into town. Rylan was waiting for her just down the street from the church.

They found Pastor Tom in his study there. He motioned them in, offering them chairs, clearly nervous.

"So what is this about some note that was left for someone?" he asked as he took his chair behind his desk. He didn't seem to know what to do with his hands, first moving things around his desk, then finally folding them in his lap.

"Destry showed you the Bible quote?" Rylan asked.

Tom nodded. "She didn't say where it came from, though."

"It was found in some of my sister's things."

The pastor's eyes widened. "Your sister, Ginny."

"You know about the notes, don't you?" Destry said. "Ginny showed them to you?"

Tom quickly shook his head. "No. This is the first I've heard that Ginny received one of them."

"Have other people gotten them?" she asked in surprise.

"Several of the parishioners have complained about receiving them. They assumed I was behind them." He glanced from her to Rylan and back again. "I would never do something like that."

"So you have no idea who wrote the notes?" Rylan said, sounding disappointed.

"No. I believe in counseling my congregation, not badgering them." He sounded angry and upset.

"You counseled Ginny when she came to you?" Destry asked.

The pastor's expression gave him away.

"We know she was pregnant," Destry said quickly. "What we need to know is if she told you the name of the man she believed fathered her baby."

"What she told me was in confidence."

"I realize that," Rylan said, jumping in. "But if there is even a chance that man killed her—"

"We have found evidence that indicates she was having an affair with a married man, possibly someone older. If you can just confirm that much," Destry said, watching him closely.

Pastor Tom sighed. "She didn't tell me who the man was. All I can tell you is that she was concerned about the people this would hurt when it came out and how her family and friends were going to take the news. I'm sure the man was, as well. But she was especially concerned how Carson was going to take it."

CHAPTER FIFTEEN

RYLAN WALKED DESTRY out to her truck. The pastor's last words seemed to ring like a death knell. Ginny was worried about how Carson was going to take the news.

"Just say it," Destry snapped as she opened the driver's side door.

"I don't want to argue with you." He wanted to kiss her. He'd seen her face when she'd heard what the pastor said. He'd instantly wanted to comfort her. She wasn't her brother's keeper.

"Isn't it possible Ginny didn't want to hurt Carson? Isn't it possible she cared about him?"

Rylan nodded, stepping to her to touch her cheek as he pushed an errant lock of hair back from her face. His fingers tingled. He quickly drew them back as her expression darkened.

"What do you want me to say?" he asked.

"Say what you're really thinking."

He shrugged and looked away for a moment. "Carson hurt Ginny once during an argument not long before she was killed. Ginny swore it was an accident, that she pulled away and tripped. But even so, why wouldn't she be afraid of him? She broke up with him and yet he continued to stalk her."

"Because he was worried about her," Destry said. "I know that isn't an excuse. But he suspected the man she was seeing was married. Did you happen to notice that the pastor seemed more than a little nervous when we brought up the notes and almost guilty when we asked about Ginny?" Destry demanded.

He had, but like his mother, he didn't want to believe it was Pastor Tom. "If he looked guilty, it was because he didn't help her and she got killed."

"Or he looked guilty because he was. If he was the man Ginny was seeing, the man who fathered her baby, then who would have more to lose by a scandal than Pastor Tom Armstrong?"

Rylan stared at her, her words hitting him hard because they had a ring of truth to them.

"We both knew Ginny. She wasn't the type to have an affair with a married man unless that man was someone trustworthy, someone she felt close to, someone with possible marital problems. If you'd been to church lately, you'd know that Tom's wife is a very jealous woman. I don't know if she has always been that way, but she certainly is now. I'm wondering if she has reason to be."

His own thoughts. But he couldn't help playing the devil's advocate. "Tom would have come forward when Ginny was murdered," Rylan said with more conviction than he felt. "He couldn't have lived with such a lie all these years. According to my mother, Linda and Tom tried for years to have a child. If he thought Ginny was carrying his baby—"

"But she wasn't carrying his baby," Destry interrupted. "It was Carson's."

"No," Rylan said, shaking his head. "Tom would have come forward."

"Why? Once Ginny was dead, there would be nothing gained by his admitting the truth and everything to lose. His worries were over. Convenient, wouldn't you say? And who would suspect the local pastor?"

"Destry, if you have a minute," Pastor Tom called from the church side door. They both turned, no doubt looking guilty. "I was hoping you could take the items we've collected for the clothes drive to the community center. The women on the committee are down there now sorting through things."

"I can help," Rylan said. "You don't think he overheard us, do you?" he whispered as they walked back to the church.

"I hope not." She shot Rylan a look, though, as they followed the pastor back into the church. Tom didn't look well. He was pale, perspiration beading on his forehead, and his hands were shaking as he opened one of the wooden bins at the back of the church where area residents could put clothing for the yearly drive.

"Are you all right?" Destry asked him.

"I'm sorry, but talking about Ginny just makes me realize that I should have done more to help her. I blame myself."

"You shouldn't," Rylan said quickly. "You tried to help her."

He shook his head. "I didn't do enough. If I had, she might still be alive today. Here, I have some bags we can put the clothing in."

"We all feel that way," Rylan said as he opened a second bin and began to pull clothing from it.

Destry held open a bag as Tom began to pull clothing out of the first bin. Both bins were stuffed full to overflowing, surprising her since on Sunday neither had been this full.

Suddenly Rylan let out a gasp. She and Tom turned as Rylan pulled out what appeared to be a blue-and-white letterman jacket. All the color washed from his face as he held it up, and she saw not only the dark stain down one side, but also the name monogrammed on the front: Ginny.

AFTER SHE RETURNED HOME, Destry was too worked up to hang around the house. Finding Ginny's letterman jacket in the church clothing drive bin had left them all shaken. Rylan had called the sheriff at once.

When Frank Curry arrived, he'd asked them to keep what they'd found to themselves. "I'll talk to your parents," the sheriff had told Rylan.

By now the jacket was on its way to the crime lab in Missoula. Destry couldn't get the large dark stain out of her mind.

It was late afternoon by the time she dropped the paternity samples with her friend in Livingston. Fearing that the jacket would incriminate her brother even more, she felt all the more desperate to find out who Ginny West had been seeing.

She stopped in a couple of jewelry shops in Livingston but saw no silver lockets that resembled Ginny's. Who knew how old the locket was before Ginny had gotten it. Whoever might have given it to her could have had the piece of jewelry for years. Or could have bought it anywhere.

Still, she checked the few shops that sold jewelry in Big Timber as well, but with no luck. Then she stopped by the bank and picked up the cashier's check for her brother and headed home.

By the time she neared the Crazy Mountains, the

sky was liquid silver in the twilight. She felt exhausted, wrung completely out by all the events of the past few days. With a chill, she realized that she'd taken the wrong turn back on the highway.

Startled, she saw that she was on the road where Ginny's body had been found. She slowed as she topped the hill a few miles from Beartooth. Even in the dim light of the fading day, she saw the wooden cross in the weeds beside the road.

She brought the pickup to a stop at the edge of the road. As she got out, she shivered less from the cold than this desolate spot. A chill wind blew down from the mountains, though, a reminder that winter would soon be breathing down her neck.

The thought filled her with dread. She had no idea where she would be come winter. Or where Carson would be. The ramifications of everything that was happening had begun to set in. She felt numb, chilled to the bone.

Being here where Ginny had died, only made her feel more depressed. The Crazies cast a long shadow, making the pines lining both sides of the narrow road appear as dark as the inside of a boot.

The small, once-white homemade cross had been erected at the edge of the trees near the spot where Ginny West had died. Destry felt even colder standing near the shadowed dense pines. What was she doing here? It wasn't as if she thought she could find any evidence after eleven years.

She breathed in the sharp scent of pine as she stood at the edge of the road, staring at the dried yellow grasses in the shallow barrow pit and trying to imagine how anyone could have dumped Ginny out here.

Ginny had still been alive when her body had been left here. She'd tried to crawl out of the ditch. Destry shuddered at the thought.

Carson couldn't do such a thing, she told herself and hugged herself against the cold and the growing darkness.

A hawk screeched from high over the tops of the pines, making her jump. An instant later, she heard the crunch of gravel and spun around, as a man stepped from the darkness of the pines.

Startled, she let out a cry and stumbled back, sliding in the loose dirt and dropping partway into the barrow pit.

"Sorry, didn't mean to scare you," Nettie's husband, Bob, said as he seemed to appear out of nowhere. "I was just out for my nightly walk."

Destry stumbled up out of the barrow pit, trying to still her pounding heart.

Bob looked past her to the cross. She followed his gaze. The cross, although weathered with age, seemed to glow as if it had absorbed the last of the day's light.

"I always get a little spooked when I walk past here," Bob said. "It's just such a…lonely spot."

She nodded, wondering why he walked this way if it bothered him. "I've never come out here before." She hadn't wanted to see it, hadn't wanted to think about the person who'd killed Ginny West.

"I heard the pastor's wife won't even drive down this road."

Destry felt a chill run the length of her spine. She'd forgotten the pastor's wife and Bessie Crist had found Ginny's body. Linda and Bessie Crist had been on their way to visit a sick friend when they'd seen what they'd thought was a dog that had been hit beside the road.

"Well." Bob pulled his coat around him as if suddenly chilled. "I best get back. Don't want to worry Nettie. You going to be all right?"

She nodded, realizing that was the most she'd ever heard Bob Benton say. At the store and church, Nettie did all the talking.

It had gotten dark, the temperature dropping as night fell over the valley. She told him goodbye and headed for her pickup. Even with the heater going in the truck, she couldn't shake the cold that snaked up her spine as she headed back to the ranch.

CLETE KNEW HE was driving too fast. At one point, he thought about calling Bethany and making sure she was home. But he wanted to surprise her. Or was it catch her?

The night was black, the stars and moon obscured by the low clouds. The wind had kicked up as it often did, coming down out of the Crazies in a roar. The Native Americans had been afraid of these mountains and the wind that howled out of them. Some believed they were the ones who had originally named the mountain range, believing any man who went into them was crazy.

As he neared the house, he saw that the lights were on. Bethany's SUV was parked out front. No other vehicle was in sight, but that didn't mean her lover wasn't parked around back or behind the barn or even down the back road out of sight.

Just the thought of her in their bed with another man...

Clete fought to control his temper.

"You scare me sometimes," Bethany had said after a fight early on in their marriage.

He scared himself since he knew what he was capable of and never let himself forget. He'd backed off, pulled away and had known it was part of the reason he'd become distant. If he cared too much… He knew that was crazy, but he'd seen his parents go through it. Their love had turned toxic with his father's jealousy turning to physical abuse. Clete had promised himself he would never let that happen with Bethany.

That is why he drove up in the yard and sat in his truck for a few minutes trying to calm down. After he felt a little less tense, he climbed out. With a start, he saw Bethany in the dark shadows of the porch. She must have heard him drive up and come out. He wondered how long she'd been standing there, watching him, waiting.

As he closed his truck door and walked toward her, he couldn't help remembering the first time he'd kissed her. She'd been nothing more than a kid when she'd come up to him at the Fall Harvest Festival and tried to get him to buy her a beer.

Bethany had always been gutsy. He liked that about her. *Loved* that about her. She'd told him that night on the dance floor that he was going to marry her some day.

He'd laughed because she was so young and yet so serious.

"Is everything all right?" she asked now from the darkness. She sounded worried. "You're home so early."

"Is that a problem?"

She seemed to shrink at the sharp edge in his tone.

He watched her reach for the doorknob behind her as if she just wanted to get away from him.

"I wanted to surprise you," he said, softening his tone.

"Well, you did. I'm glad you got off early. Dinner's not ready yet, though."

He realized there was only one thing he was hungry for as he followed the sweet scent of her perfume into their house.

It wasn't until later, lying next to her in the damp crumpled sheets, that he realized she must have just gotten out of the shower before he drove up. Nothing suspicious about that, right?

As DESTRY PULLED into the yard, she saw in her headlights that someone had left her a note.

The night was dark, only glimpses of the moon peeking through the clouds. It was another cold evening, the air scented with the smell of snow. As she looked toward the Crazies, she knew the peaks would be dusted with fresh snow come morning.

Getting out of the truck, she looped her purse over her shoulder, her hand slipping inside where she felt the cold metal of the gun, and its weight reassured her. Nothing moved in the trees. The wind whispered in the tops of the pines and sent fall leaves skittering across the yard, but nothing ominous came out of the darkness.

At the door, Destry pulled off the note. It felt heavy. She realized why as she saw two large house keys taped inside. She used one to open the door, turning on a light so she could read the note.

Rylan's handwriting. She recognized it even though it had been a long time since she'd last seen it. He was left-handed, so his writing was distinctive and yet completely different from her left-handed brother's.

She read: *"I hope you don't mind. I changed your*

locks. You might want to start locking your doors. Just a thought. Rylan."

Destry stared at the note and smiled. He'd changed her locks? She couldn't help being touched. As she closed and locked the door behind her, she realized she'd left the door unlocked earlier—just as it had been when her brother stopped by.

This was rural Montana, no one locked their doors. Few people, herself included, could even find the keys to their doors. She would lock her doors at night, but she'd be damned if she would during the day.

She felt the cold keys in her hand and smiled again at the thought of Rylan changing her locks. She was more than touched by his concern, she thought, her smile widening.

Maybe he hadn't changed as much as she'd thought. At least their feelings for each other hadn't. She thought again of the kiss and felt warmth rush through her veins. As irritating and stubborn as the man was, she still loved him.

If she closed her eyes, she could recall the feel of his bare skin under her fingertips just as she could the beat of his heart as they lay entwined the night they'd made love. She'd clung to that memory for eleven years, but the desire they'd shared was just as strong now as it had been then.

Dropping the keys into a dish by the door, she reminded herself not to get her hopes up. As long as Ginny's killer ran free, none of them could move on.

She started up the stairs when she saw him. A large dark figure moved past the windows beside the back door. For a just an instant, she froze, her heart lodging in her throat. But she quickly willed herself to move as she raced across the room to snatch up the shotgun.

The sky had darkened to blue velvet, but there were enough stars and the moon to see for some distance as she threw open the door and stepped out, shotgun in hand. A stiff wind whirled her stray hair around her face, reminding her of earlier today when Rylan had brushed it from her eyes.

She swatted that thought away as she lifted the shotgun and took aim. The man must have heard her coming because he was hightailing it toward the creek. She raised the shotgun toward the sky and pulled both triggers. The man stumbled as if hearing the boom and fearing he'd been shot.

"Next time I won't miss," she yelled after him, then shut the door and locked it as the man disappeared into the far woods.

NETTIE BENTON SHOT up in bed with a start. Instantly, she froze, listening. The window facing the store was cracked open where she could hear if there was any trouble down the mountain.

But as she listened, she heard only the wind in the tall pine trees outside. One of the branches scraped against the side of the house. Was that what had awakened her?

Carefully, she slipped out of bed. Clouds scudded across the midnight-blue sky, giving her only glimpses of stars and a sliver of silver moon.

When she looked through the pines toward the store on the hillside below, she could see the faint light she'd left on inside the back door but nothing else.

Nettie considered going back to bed but knew she

wouldn't be able to get a wink of sleep until she checked the store. If someone was down there trying to break in again, maybe it hadn't been a bear the first time and maybe the robber was back. She would love nothing better than to catch the thief and show that Frank Curry. Her money was on one of those wild Thompson kids.

She glanced toward the bed. Bob must have gone into the guest room to sleep again, no doubt complaining that she snored. Or more likely so she wouldn't hear him cry out from one of his nightmares. Last night she'd awakened and would have sworn he was calling out the name Ginny.

Carson coming back had everyone talking about Ginny again, she told herself. Nor was there any reason to wake Bob. She could handle this herself, she thought as she hurried to the back door, pulled on one of the down coats from the hooks, slipped on a pair of mud boots and rushed out of the house.

The wind howled around her, rocking the tops of the pines and sending dust scurrying across the narrow path in front of her. She hadn't realized it would be so dark in the trees. Too late to go back for a flashlight now, though.

Watching for any movement in the thick pines next to the store, she made her way quietly down the steep hillside toward the back of the store. She hadn't gone far when she realized she should have brought a weapon.

She was almost to the back of the store when a sound stopped her. Something grunted on the hillside off to her right. The wind picked up the hem of her nightgown, making it flutter at her ankles.

Her whole body tensed, her stomach dropping, as a huge grizzly ambled down the hillside through the pines. It stopped to overturn a dead log as it scrounged for ants.

Nettie gauged the distance back uphill to the house. She was closer to the store and it was downhill. But with growing panic, she realized that she hadn't grabbed the keys to the store when she'd left the house. Fortunately she kept a key hidden in a hollow space in one of the logs by the back door of the store.

Another grunt.

Nettie knew better than to run but covered the distance to the back door as fast as she could. The grizzly had seen her, though. She didn't doubt that for a moment. It had probably picked up her scent the moment she'd left the house. Fortunately, it must not have thought her a threat because it hadn't even looked in her direction, let alone charged her.

She frantically reached back into the log opening and felt around for the key. A limb cracked behind her, and she caught the distinct putrid smell of the grizzly bear. She could hear it moving slowly toward her, crunching the dried pine needles under its huge paws.

Her fingers trembled as she dug out the key. But before she could get it into the lock, the key slipped from her hand, dropping to the ground at her feet.

Panicked, she fell to her knees, felt around wildly, scooped it up and pulled herself to her feet. She couldn't hear the grizzly now, but she didn't dare turn to look. The scent in the air was so strong, she swore she could feel the bear's nasty breath on her neck.

Nettie fumbled the key into the lock, turned it and the doorknob at the same time, and practically threw herself into the back of the store.

As she turned to close the door, she saw the grizzly's

steering-wheel-sized head peering in at her, its nostrils flared, eyes bright in the faint starlight. She slammed the door, locked it and leaned against it as she fought to catch her breath and still her thundering heart.

She was shaking so hard her teeth were chattering. Behind the store, she could hear the bear foraging around in some empty boxes her husband hadn't taken care of yet.

Anger overcame the fear. She'd wake Bob up and get him down here, that's what she'd do. But as she picked up the receiver she heard a loud crash outside as a massive limb blew off one of the old cottonwoods along the creek.

With a curse, Nettie listened for a dial tone. The line had gone dead. She slammed down the receiver. Not only was she trapped here in the middle of the night, her husband didn't even know she was gone—let alone that she was in trouble.

The bear was still digging around in the boxes, hoping to find something to eat. What would he do when he finished? Grayson had nailed a piece of plywood over the back window. She just hoped it held in case the grizzly decided to break in. There were other windows, most too high for the bear to try to get through, though.

Sighing, Nettie padded into the main part of the store in the dark since the electricity had gone out with the phone. A little starlight lit her way down the grocery aisle to the front window.

The street was empty. The Branding Iron was dark. So were the upstairs windows of the apartment where Kate LaFond lived.

Nettie started to turn away when she saw a light bobbing along behind the café. She recognized the figure armed with a flashlight and, of all things, a shovel. Kate LaFond was heading for the ancient stone garage set off to one side behind the café.

What in the world was the woman up to at this hour? And what was she doing with a *shovel?*

Just then the store backup generator came on, along with the store's lights. Nettie was caught in the glare. How had it slipped her mind that the backup generator that kept the freezers and coolers running would come on—along with the security lights?

She ducked and turned out the lights, but soon enough that she hadn't been seen? As her eyes adjusted to the darkness again, she glanced across the street but saw nothing. Either Kate was working in the pitch dark of the old garage. Or she'd decided not to dig tonight because she knew she'd been seen.

CHAPTER SIXTEEN

EARLY THE NEXT MORNING, Destry called Rylan to thank him for changing the locks at her house. She suspected after finding Ginny's letterman jacket, he'd needed something to occupy him.

"Not sure why I bothered. Your house was unlocked when I came by to replace them."

"Which made it lot easier for you, huh," she joked. "Anyway, I don't think I'm going to be having any more problems."

"I'm afraid to ask."

"I threw some buckshot in his general direction and told him next time I would take aim."

"I hope whoever the dumb bastard is realizes you're serious."

"How are you doing?" she asked.

"Okay. It was just such a shock seeing her jacket with…"

Destry knew he was thinking about the blood. There'd been so much of it. "Anyone could have put that jacket in one of the clothing drive bins."

"But why now? Why after all these years?"

She'd been wondering the same thing. "A guilty conscience?"

"You still suspect Pastor Tom."

"The more I've thought about it, the less sure I am,"

she had to admit. "Did you see his face when you pulled out Ginny's jacket? I thought he was going to pass out. And last night I ran into Bob Benton and he reminded me that it was Tom's wife and Bessie Crist who found Ginny."

"Yeah, I remember that."

"Well, I'm thinking I might go talk to Linda and Bessie. Since they were the first people on the scene, maybe they might remember something now that didn't seem important back then—or that they didn't notice at the time."

"I want to go with you," he said.

"Are you sure?" She would imagine it would upset him to hear how his sister had been found again. "I can—"

"I'm sure."

Her phone beeped in her ear. "I'm getting another call. Can I call you back?"

He said she could and she took the other call. "Hello?"

It was her friend who worked at the lab.

Blood thundered in her ears. "You got the paternity results."

"Do you want me to mail them?"

"Can you tell me…" Destry held her breath. Although, after finding the photograph of her mother, didn't she already know what her friend was going to say?

"There's no match between your DNA and the sample you brought me."

Destry nodded. Confirmation. WT had been right. She wasn't his daughter. "Thank you," she managed to say. "I appreciate you doing this for me." Her hand shook as she replaced the phone.

So, who am I?

When the phone rang again, she thought it would be Rylan. Instead, a recorded message came on. "This is a collect call from Montana State Prison. If you will accept a call from… Jack French…press one. If you—"

Jack? She hadn't heard from him since he'd gone to prison. She pressed one.

"Sorry I had to call collect," he said.

"It's not a problem. I'm just surprised." She had a sudden mental image of Jack. The cowboy was too handsome for words and always grinning. Talk about happy-go-lucky, that was Jack French. He took nothing seriously. How else had he gotten arrested for some late-night cattle rustling that had landed him in prison?

"I heard Carson was back," Jack said now. He sounded older, possibly even more mature. She wondered if this experience had changed him. He'd been working the prison cattle ranch, and, according to people who'd heard from him during his sentence up there, it wasn't much different than working for WT Grant, except the guards treated him better.

"How did you hear that?" she asked, amazed how information traveled so quickly across a state as large as Montana—even to prison.

"We talked before he left Vegas. How is he?"

She didn't know how to answer. Fortunately, Jack didn't give her a chance.

"Listen, I've been doing a lot of thinking. Time on my hands, you know," he said with a laugh.

"About the night Ginny died."

Silence. "Yeah."

Her heart leaped to her throat. "Carson wasn't at the ranch all night, was he?" She already knew the answer, realized she'd suspected it the moment her brother had involved her in his alibi.

This time the silence was longer, so long Destry feared they'd been disconnected or, worse, that Jack had changed his mind and hung up. After all, Carson had always been his best friend.

"Jack, you have to tell me the truth, no matter how bad it is. I have to know so I can help him."

"That's why I called you. It's been hell keeping his secret. That night I tried to talk him out of following Ginny. He suspected she was meeting some married dude."

"So he did go into town." The words were as heavy as her heart.

"Yeah." Jack cleared his throat. "When he came back, oh, man, he was a total basket case. I've never seen him like that. He kept saying she was gone. There was blood on his shirt sleeve."

Destry covered her mouth with her hand for a moment, tears burning her eyes. "Did he tell you what happened?"

"All I could get out of him was that he'd seen her and that he'd blown it and she was gone."

"Jack, you don't think he…" She couldn't bring herself to finish.

"Naw, Destry. Did you know he came up here to visit me a few times and he wrote me, too? He couldn't kill her, you have to know that. He *loved* her."

She wished she could be as convinced as Jack. Carson had lied about going to town. What else had he lied about?

She thought of Rylan. He'd always suspected that Carson had lied. That he was still lying about what happened that night. Once Rylan knew that Carson had not only gone into Beartooth, but also that he'd seen Ginny that night, had gotten blood on him, he wouldn't believe anything her brother said. Destry wasn't sure she did anymore. She felt sick.

Could Carson have put Ginny's letterman jacket in that clothing bin at church? The church was open all the time. Anyone could have gone in and left it without the pastor or Linda seeing them.

After she hung up with Jack, she called Rylan, thankful to get his voice mail. She was too upset to talk to him right now. She left a message, saying she had something she needed to do but to let her know if he could go to Linda's and Bessie's later this morning.

At the big house, she saw the sheriff's car parked out front. Fear gripped her. Frank couldn't have gotten the report on the jacket this quickly.

She tried not to panic as she hurried inside the house. "What's going on?" she asked when she saw the three somber faces in the living room.

"I was just asking your brother to come down to my office for a talk," Sheriff Frank Curry said. He sounded irritated, and Destry guessed this wasn't the first time he'd tried to get Carson to his office. "We're waiting for his attorney."

Destry glanced at her brother. He appeared shaken. WT looked as if he might bust an artery, he was so furious.

"Could I talk to my brother alone for a moment?" she asked. "Don't worry, we'll be right back."

The room fell deathly silent. Destry looked to her brother. Her anxiety increased when he wouldn't hold her gaze.

"Just make sure he doesn't go out the back door," the sheriff said.

"He won't," she said and motioned for her brother to come with her. He rose slowly, clearly not wanting to talk to her any more than he did the sheriff.

As she led him down to WT's den, she told herself he couldn't have killed Ginny. Yes, he'd lied about leaving the ranch, lied about seeing Ginny that night. That's why he looked so guilty.

Carson went straight to the bar and poured himself what she guessed wasn't his first drink.

"Do you think that's a good idea?" she asked.

"At this point, it can't hurt."

"The sheriff wouldn't be here unless he'd found evidence implicating you," she said to his back. "But you swore you didn't leave the ranch that night. Jack swore it as well, and you threw me into the mix for good measure. I need to know the truth."

Carson sighed before turning around, drink in hand, to face her. He looked shamefaced. "Are you sure, Destry?"

"I know you left the ranch that night and the sheriff must, too." Her voice broke. "Tell me you didn't hurt Ginny."

He raised his gaze slowly until their eyes met, his exactly like his father's.

"Stop lying. Tell me the truth, Carson."

CARSON TOOK A gulp of his drink and then seemed to brace himself. "I *loved* Ginny." His voice broke. "It was killing me to know there was someone else."

"You never even suspected who it was?" Destry asked.

He shook his head. "But I knew he was married because there was some reason they couldn't be together except secretly."

Destry nodded and waited.

"Ginny wanted to get married, have kids. I was twenty, too young, so I put her off, telling her we'd get married after college. Then, out of the blue, she broke up with me. When I pressed her for answers, she finally told me that there was this man that she'd..." He swallowed and looked away. "That she'd slept with him."

"What did you do?" Destry asked, afraid she already knew.

"We fought. I tried to hold her. She shoved me away and fell and hurt her wrist."

Destry remembered that Rylan had been upset with her brother in the weeks before Ginny was murdered. He'd also mentioned that Carson had hurt Ginny one other time. "Oh, Carson."

"I wanted to know who he was, so I started following her. That night I followed her. She was driving one of the ranch trucks. She parked it behind the bar, then sneaked down to the old Royale theater."

"What were you planning to do?"

"Maybe I planned to confront him. I don't know." Carson put down his empty glass and scrubbed his hand over his face. "It was pitch-black inside the theater, but I knew my way around from when I was a kid."

Every kid in the county must have played on that stage, she thought, fear making her sick inside. The rumor was that a hair clip belonging to Ginny had been found in that room under the stage.

"I didn't go in right away. I guess I was afraid of what I might do if I found her with him. When I finally went in, it took me a while to find her."

"Who was she with?"

He shook his head, his Adam's apple working as he swallowed. "She was alone, a single candle burning in that room under the stage. He'd been there but he'd left. When I found her, she was crying and upset. He'd broken it off. I told her not to worry, I would take care of her. I took her in my arms and one thing led to another. But afterward…" He looked away, and she feared what was coming.

"She told you she was pregnant."

He nodded, apparently not surprised that she knew about the pregnancy.

"And you changed your mind about wanting her," she said, filling in the blanks.

"No, I just wanted her to tell me who the father was. I wanted to… I don't know what I wanted to do. Punch him in the face."

"But she wouldn't tell you?"

"No, so I stormed off. I left her lying there and headed back to the ranch. But halfway home, I realized it didn't matter who the other man was. I loved Ginny. I would love her baby, no matter whose it was. I turned around and went back."

Destry held her breath.

"She was gone, but I could see that there'd been a struggle. I lit the candle. There was blood…" He stopped and shook his head, his eyes bright with tears. "I knew something horrible had happened to her."

"Why didn't you call the sheriff? Why didn't you—"

"I couldn't. I'd just been with her. I had her blood on me. Who would believe that I hadn't been the one who'd hurt her?" His gaze implored her to understand. "I was young and stupid. I thought I saw someone at the window. I ran." His voice cracked, and she could see him fighting tears.

"Her killer must have just left with her. Maybe was even still in the building. Or maybe he was the person you saw at the window. If you'd called the sheriff…"

"Don't you think I've told myself that a million times for the past eleven years?" he snapped. "I was a punk kid, running scared. Your boyfriend had already told me that if I ever laid a hand on her again… Once he told the sheriff…" Tears welled in his eyes. "I loved Ginny. If I had called the sheriff. If I had gone looking for her. If I had just tried, I might have found her before she died. I might have saved her."

"Was her letterman jacket there?"

He looked surprised. "No, why?"

"It turned up in one of the clothing bins at the church."

Carson looked sick. She got up and went to him, putting her arms around him. She understood now the demons that had haunted him the past eleven years and the change she'd seen in him. "It isn't your fault she's dead."

"If I hadn't left her there—"

"You might both be dead."

The den door opened behind him. "Your attorney's here," Margaret said.

Destry straightened, her brother rising and turning away to wipe his tears. "We'll be right there."

Would the sheriff believe him? She'd believed him eleven years ago when he'd told her he'd been at the ranch all night, just him and Jack. Then he'd dragged her into it, making things even worse between her and Rylan. But she'd believed him because she hadn't wanted to believe he was capable of murder.

"I'm sorry I involved you," Carson said, as if reading her mind. "I wasn't sure anyone would believe Jack."

They hadn't. Nor had it helped dragging her into it. Everyone had always believed he'd killed Ginny. Carson had a temper. He'd admitted to hurting Ginny once, even though it had been an accident. He'd made love to her that night, but afterward when she refused to give him the man's name, he must have been furious.

"Jack has had some second thoughts about that night," she said. "He called me this morning."

Carson nodded. How long before Jack recanted his story to the sheriff, since clearly it had been eating away at him all these years? "I told him when we talked recently that I don't want him lying for me anymore."

"The sheriff must know that you were with her that night," Destry said.

His eyes welled with tears again. "She told me the baby was her lover's, but I knew she just wanted it to be his. I think she had this crazy idea that he was going to marry her."

LATER THAT DAY, Linda Armstrong opened the door and seemed surprised to see Destry and Rylan standing there. The parsonage was small, wood-framed and painted white like the church with a small stoop out front. Destry had never been inside. Few people had. Linda preferred to hold any gatherings down at the church, saying the parsonage was just too tiny.

"If you're looking for the pastor, he's down at the church," Linda said.

"Actually, we wanted to see you." Destry noted that Linda was dressed up as if she was going somewhere.

"I'm sorry if we caught you at a bad time. We can come back."

Linda seemed to hesitate. "I have a few minutes." She stepped back to let them enter. "What is this about?"

The house was simply furnished and sparsely decorated. In the living area there was a large cross on one wall and several plates with Bible quotes on them, nothing else on the walls.

"We need to ask you about the night you found my sister," Rylan said. "I know it's been a long time, but I was wondering if there was anything else you might have remembered."

Linda looked surprised by the question. "I have done my best to forget everything about that night. I don't understand why you would want me to relive it."

"We're trying to find Ginny's killer," Rylan said.

Linda lifted a brow, her gaze shifting to Destry. "Isn't that the sheriff's job? And anyway, I thought everyone already knew…" But she didn't finish the thought.

"If you could just tell us about that night, maybe something will come to you," Destry said, realizing the pastor must not have told his wife about what they'd found yesterday in the clothing bin.

"I told the sheriff this eleven years ago," Linda complained. "It was…awful. I saw what I thought was a dog that had been hit at the edge of the road. Bessie Crist was with me. She can tell you probably better than I can. I was so upset, I can't swear to anything. I just remember slowing down and there in my headlights…" She shuddered. "I thought she must have been hit by a car. I still wonder if that wasn't the case."

"The coroner confirmed that her injuries indicated foul play, not a hit-and-run," Destry said.

Linda sniffed. "I'm running late for an appointment."

"You didn't notice another vehicle leaving or hear anything when you got out of your car?" Destry pressed.

"I've never heard such quiet. It was completely still. There wasn't even a breath of breeze." She sighed. "I'm sorry, but I really can't add anything more and I have to go."

BESSIE CRIST WAS a tiny gray-haired woman with bright blue eyes and a ready smile. She served Destry and Rylan coffee and bite-size sugar cookies that she'd baked only the day before.

"It's almost as if I knew I was going to have company," she said as she settled into the chair across from them.

They sipped the coffee, complimented the cookies and finally got around to their reason for being there.

Destry put down her cup and said, "We hate to ask, but—"

"Linda called to tell me you'd been to her house asking about that night. She said not to let you upset me." Bessie shook her head. "Linda worries too much about other people." She reached over and placed her hand on Rylan's. "You poor child. It must be so terrible for you to lose your sister like that. What can I do to help?"

"We'd appreciate anything you can remember about that night," Destry said. "We still don't have a clear picture of what happened."

"Well," Bessie said. "It was one of those dark nights where the headlights are just a swatch of gold pointing into the darkness. I spotted her. Linda was too intent on her driving I suppose. I saw what I thought was a dog that had been hit beside the road. Linda didn't want to stop. She was afraid the dog might be rabid and bite one of us."

"So she thought the dog was still alive?" Destry asked.

Bessie blinked. "I suppose so. I told her we couldn't just leave the poor thing."

"So you saw movement?" Rylan asked, sitting forward.

Bessie frowned. "No, I don't think so, but Linda would know better than me. When she stopped, Linda told me to stay back while she went and checked. I saw her stooping down. She had her back to me so I couldn't see what it was. It wasn't until later when I saw that her arm was bleeding that she told me she'd fallen down and cut it, she'd been so upset at seeing Ginny like that."

"How was it that the two of you were on that road that night?"

"Linda had called me and said poor Mrs. Burke wasn't doing well and she needed to drive out to see her and did I want to go along. I'd always enjoyed Mrs. Burke's company, plus she makes a wonderful cup of coffee. So I readily agreed to the drive. I don't drive much myself anymore. Can't see all that well."

"So what happened then?" Destry asked.

"I got out to see if I could help, but Linda said to get her phone and call the sheriff. I dug her cell phone out of her purse but couldn't get it to work. So she came back to the car after a few minutes and punched in 911. That's when I knew, when she told the dispatcher it was Ginny. I took a blanket out of the backseat and carried it over to your sister to cover her up until the sheriff and the ambulance arrived."

The room fell silent for a few moments. "It wasn't until the next day that I heard it hadn't been an accident. *Murder*." Bessie shivered and hugged herself. "Imagine, murder here in Beartooth. I told Linda whoever killed that girl had to be a stranger," Bessie said emphatically. "A stranger passing through."

That, unfortunately was harder to imagine since Ginny's ranch pickup had been found behind the Range Rider and Ginny wouldn't have gotten into a car with someone she didn't know and trust.

Rylan was quiet on the ride back to town. They hadn't learned anything new. Instead, he'd been forced to hear the details of how his sister's body had been discovered dumped beside the road.

She felt badly for him and wished there was something she could say. But like him, she felt sick after hearing the details and could understand why Linda had been so adamant about not wanting to relive them— maybe especially if she suspected her husband had been involved with Ginny?

Destry knew she wasn't basing that suspicion on anything but the pastor's suspicious behavior when they'd asked about the Bible quotes. Certainly not any evidence. Given how upset Pastor Tom had been when Rylan had found the letterman jacket, she was less sure of him as a suspect.

Rylan dropped her at her pickup. "Thanks. I'm not sure I could have done that alone."

"Anytime," she said and climbed out. "Thanks again for changing my locks."

He nodded distractedly. She watched as he headed for the Range Rider as if he needed a drink. Or was he meeting Kimberly there?

RYLAN STEPPED INTO the Range Rider. He didn't need a beer so much as he needed a distraction from his thoughts. Hearing about his sister from the two women who'd found her had left him shaken—and furious. He hadn't wanted Destry to see him like this.

"What'll you have?" Clete asked as he came down the bar to where Rylan had taken a stool.

"Just a beer. Whatever you have on tap." The bar was quiet this time of day. A couple of regulars were at the other end watching some daytime game show on the small television.

"So, how are things going?" Clete asked as he set a frosty glass of beer down on a bar napkin in front of him.

"They're going." Rylan took a sip of the beer. It was cold and tasted wonderful on this fall day. The morning had been cold, but as the day wore on it had warmed up.

He and Clete both turned as the front door of the bar opened. Clete's wife, Bethany, came in on a gust of fall breeze that smelled as if someone was burning dried leaves. It instantly transported him to another fall when he and Destry had been in high school. Destry with flushed cheeks and bright eyes as they raced through the fallen leaves.

Rylan sipped his beer as Clete and Bethany exchanged a few words. He heard Clete ask her why she wasn't working her shift at the café and Bethany told him Kate asked her not to come in because it wasn't busy.

As Bethany started to leave, though, he caught a glimmer of light flash at her throat. Before Rylan could stop himself, he stood and grabbed her arm, turning her to him.

"Where did you get that necklace?" His tone was sharper than he'd meant it to be. He'd just been so surprised to see a locket like the one he'd found hidden in his sister's jewelry box.

Bethany froze. *"What?"* Her hand went to the heart-shaped locket at her neck. All the color seemed to wash from her face as she closed her fingers over it, balling the heart in her fist as her gaze shot to her husband behind the bar.

Clete was watching the exchange, no doubt having heard the shock and surprise in Rylan's voice.

"Sorry," Rylan said quickly, letting go of her. "It's just that I think I've seen one like it and I was wondering where you got it."

Clete leaned across the bar toward her. "Let's see it."

"It's just an old locket I had lying around," Bethany said nervously.

Rylan watched the exchange, confused. He hadn't meant to cause a problem between them, but clearly he had.

Clete motioned for his wife to remove her hand so he could see the locket. She did it with obvious reluctance. From his expression, he'd never seen the locket before and was just as curious as Rylan as to where she'd gotten it—and no doubt why she was reacting the way she was.

"Like I said, it's just some old thing I've had."

Clete nodded, but he didn't seem to believe her any more than Rylan did. The silver wasn't tarnished like Ginny's had been. The locket looked new.

He could think of only one reason Bethany would lie about it and quickly changed the subject, figuring he would catch Bethany alone and talk to her when Clete wasn't around.

As she left, he saw that Clete was upset. What the

devil was going on between the two of them? He could only guess, if he was right about the locket and her lying.

Bethany, he realized with a start, reminded him of his sister. Hell, she'd even looked like Ginny when the two of them were in school together. He remembered a time when Ginny had complained that Bethany was dressing like her, had even had her hair styled like hers.

There was a resemblance even now, he realized. The reddish-blond hair, the fair coloring, the sprinkling of freckles. Both women had that girl-next-door look about them.... Like Destry....

CHAPTER SEVENTEEN

ON HIS RETURN from the sheriff's office, Carson had gone straight to the bar in his father's den. He was still shaking, only too aware of how close he was to being arrested for Ginny's murder. Once the DNA results came back on Ginny's letterman jacket—

He turned at the sound of the door opening behind him. The last person he wanted to talk to right now was WT.

"Cherry." He should never have brought her here, knowing the kind of trouble he was in.

"Your father said you had to go down to the sheriff's office. Is everything all right?"

"I think there's a good chance I'm going to be arrested."

"For your high school girlfriend's murder. But you didn't do it."

"No, but I lied about seeing her that night. I lied about a lot of things at the time."

"You were young."

He laughed at that. He'd been lying to himself for years.

"This isn't working out, is it?" she said. "I knew you were hung up on what happened before you left Montana, but since you've been back here, I've seen the change in you."

"The thought of being arrested for murder changes a person."

"That's not it. This place means more to you than you pretend it does."

"Sorry, but when did you get your degree in psychology?" He hadn't meant the words to come out so sharp.

She merely smiled. "I know you, Carson. There's more keeping you here than your father's money."

He wanted to argue that she was wrong as he watched her take off the diamond engagement ring he'd bought at a Vegas pawn shop. That life felt a million miles away and suddenly not as glittery as it had seemed when he and Cherry had been a part of it.

"What are you doing? If you can just wait—"

She held the ring out to him.

He shook his head. "Keep it. I don't want it."

Cherry studied him for a long moment. "I do love you and I hope you get all this figured out. I understand why you feel the way you do about your father, but your sister cares for you. Don't hurt her." She turned to leave. "I'm going to pack and then you can take me to the nearest airport. It had better not be three hours away," she joked.

"An hour and a half." He was glad that they could still share a laugh together.

Carson watched her go, hating that she was right. He hadn't resolved the past. He wasn't sure he ever could.

His cell phone rang. He opened it without looking to see who was calling and instantly regretted it. The threats were getting more detailed. Time was running out, his desperation growing along with the interest on his gambling debts.

Destry would get him some money. It would hold

hem off temporarily. But then what if he still didn't
have his hands on the ranch?

A thought whizzed past. Maybe there was another
way. If he could get a stake, maybe he could win back
enough at the local poker game to keep the wolf away
from the door and stall for even more time.

With a jolt, he realized this turn of events might work
in his favor. Wouldn't WT pay to have Cherry gone? If
he played his cards right, he could make this work for
him. He could redeem himself.

At the sound of the old man's wheelchair coming
down the hallway, Carson prepared himself for battle.

Cherry didn't understand the problem was between
him and his father. Even though he'd been young when
his mother had died, he remembered only too well how
things had been between WT and her. He'd seen the way
WT had treated her. That's why he'd kept his mother's
secret and would take it to his grave.

It was also why he'd promised himself he would pay
his father back for being so horrible to his mother. That
day was almost here, he thought as WT wheeled into
the room. Maybe Destry wouldn't have to get hurt, too.

WT SAW CHERRY flounce out of the den and overheard
her say she was going to pack. He watched her head in
the direction of her room and couldn't wait to see the
woman gone.

He suspected his son felt the same way. Carson had
never planned to marry her. The bluff had been wasted
on him. Or if he had, being in Montana on the ranch
had changed both of their minds.

"You were right about Cherry," Carson said as WT
wheeled himself over to the bar.

"So, she *is* a stripper?" WT said, purposely misinterpreting what his son was saying. He saw Carson grit his teeth and fight back the anger that always simmered just under the surface. Cherry had turned out to be a lot smarter than he'd first thought. She might not have been so bad for Carson after all. But her life was in Vegas. Carson's was here.

"I can't marry her."

WT said nothing. Was he supposed to act surprised by this?

"I need to let her down easy though, especially after bringing her all the way up here and promising her a big wedding," Carson said.

WT wished Carson wasn't so transparent. And yet it made things easier often, didn't it? "I can run her off for you, or if you're feeling generous, you can drive her into Big Timber. I'll pay for the bus trip back to wherever you picked her up."

"I told you. I *love* her. I can't do that to her. If you won't help me, then maybe I should go back to Vegas and marry her, let the chips fall where they may."

Carson was bluffing again, but WT didn't call him on it. Getting rid of Cherry would be worth every penny because the woman wasn't cut out for ranch life. She would lure Carson away eventually.

"How much?" he asked, as his son started out of the room.

Carson stopped but didn't turn. "Five thousand dollars."

WT swore and put up an appropriate fight, but he would have paid twice that much to get the woman out of his son's life. "Fine," he said after a few minutes of negotiation. "I'll write you a check."

After Carson left, WT rolled over to the window. There was fresh snow on the tops of the peaks and fewer leaves on the cottonwoods and aspens every day. Winter was coming. He knew firsthand how inhospitable this country could be. He'd survived the blizzards, the howling winds that screamed down out of the Crazies, the scorching summers that baked the earth and starved the land and animals.

He'd seen the way the younger generations were leaving the land for what they considered a better life and higher wages. The mass exodus reminded him of the stories his father had told about the 1920s when thousands of farmers and ranchers had been starved out. They'd left everything, fleeing. But his family had stayed and fought, barely surviving.

He'd changed that. He'd thrived here at the base of the Crazy Mountains, and damned if he'd let anything happen to his ranch. While other ranches were being sold and divided up into twenty-acre tracts, his wasn't going to be one of them, if he had to fight until his last dying breath.

As he surveyed what he'd accomplished, he waited for that surge of pride he used to feel and frowned when it didn't come. All of this didn't feel like enough, never had. He'd hoped when his son came home, he would feel differently. He'd been waiting years for Carson to return and take over the ranch.

His fear had always been that Carson was too much like his mother. Just the thought of Lila made his stomach roil, even though she'd been gone almost thirty years now. Gone, he thought, but not forgotten since he was reminded of her every time he looked at her daughter.

Now, though, he feared Carson had taken after him—in all the worst possible ways. WT shoved away those thoughts, reminding himself how far he'd come from that old house where he'd been raised. Look where he lived now. He smiled to himself, remembering how his new house had been the talk of the county.

Just as his son had been the talk of the county, his thoughts darkening quickly again. It had been eleven years since the "trouble," as he liked to think of it. Plenty of time for the heat to die down, just as he'd assured Carson.

But the sheriff's latest visit had made him worried that his son might be headed for prison. Worse, there wasn't a damned thing he could do about it.

"You what?"

"I forgot I was wearing the locket," Bethany said into the phone. "When I stopped by the bar to see Clete… Well, it was really weird. Rylan West saw the locket and he had such a strange reaction to it."

The sigh on the other end of the line was heavy with anger. "What are you trying to do?"

"I wasn't—"

"You just happened to forget to take it off?" He sounded furious. She wished she hadn't called. Why had she told him, anyway? He probably would have never found out.

"It's not that big of a deal. I came up with a story."

"A *story?*" He didn't sound as if he had any faith in her.

"I said it was mine, that I hadn't worn it for a long time and had forgotten about it." She could hear him moving around the room. She wondered where his wife was. She must be in another part of the house because he hadn't gotten mad about her calling him at home.

"What did you do with the locket?" he asked, emphasizing each word as if she was a child.

"I hid it."

"I want you to get rid of it."

She shook her head, even though he couldn't see her. "But *you* gave it to me."

"Yes, unfortunately, and I now see that it was a huge mistake on my part."

"I won't *wear* it again."

"Bethany, clearly I can't trust you to get rid of it, so I want you to bring it to me." She heard a noise in the background like that of a door opening and closing. "I'll let you know when. Wait for my call." He hung up.

She put down the phone and looked at the small heart-shaped locket, the delicate silver chain curled around it. She'd been so touched when he'd given it to her that she'd cried.

"I never thought anyone like you would ever care about me like this."

"Why would you say that?"

"Because you're smart and successful and people look up to you. Me, I'm just…nobody."

"Bethany," he'd said lifting her chin so their eyes met. "You're special. I've never met anyone quite like you."

"I just wish we didn't have to keep this a secret." The moment the words were out of her mouth she'd seen her mistake. He'd become angry, explaining to her, as he had so many times before, that the only way they could see each other was if they kept their feelings secret.

"You have to trust me. The timing is all wrong.

Maybe someday, but for now… You do trust me, don't you, Bethany?"

She'd nodded and he'd kissed away her tears, then he'd made love to her. She'd felt cherished and…well, special.

Now she picked up the locket and chain, cradling it in the palm of her hand. It felt cool to the touch, just as it had the day he'd put it on her. She didn't want to give it back. She couldn't. After he called and she went to meet him, she'd say she'd forgotten it.

What if he really did break off the relationship like he had said? He was already upset about the notes and had said they should stop seeing each other. She'd thought he was overreacting, but now she was worried that he might really mean it. The thought sent an arrow to her heart. He was all she had to look forward to each day. Clete didn't care. He pretended to. She thought about last night. Last night she'd loved him just as she had at the beginning.

But last night he'd been jealous, worried that a man had given her the locket. Now that he thought that wasn't true…

She sighed and got up to tuck the locket in the back of her lingerie drawer. Clete would never look in there.

She closed the drawer, a mixture of dread and apprehension as she waited for her lover's call.

CHAPTER EIGHTEEN

CLETE REYNOLDS NODDED and smiled when necessary but was only half listening to the conversation at the bar.

He regretted not confronting his wife last night about the silver locket she'd been wearing yesterday. He'd suspected Bethany was up to something for some time now. He tried to pinpoint exactly when he'd become suspicious. After working in a bar, he knew the signs. It was the little telltale things.

The first time was the night he'd caught a whiff of unfamiliar aftershave when he'd walked into his house. Bethany had just been getting home. She was hanging up her coat when he'd smelled it. He hadn't been able to place it.

Bethany had seen him sniff in her direction and frowned. "What?"

"Nothin'." He'd let it go. Bethany hadn't seemed the type. She wasn't tall and leggy. Or slim, for that matter. Let's just say the woman filled out her shirts and jeans. She was more a homegrown girl, not the kind men whistled at on the street or did double takes because she was a raving beauty. Bethany was simply... cute, sweet looking.

The second time he noticed something was when he realized she'd changed clothes since she'd stopped by the bar only an hour earlier. Her hair had been different, too.

Earlier it had been styled. Now it was pulled up in a ponytail and looked damp, as if she'd just stepped out of a shower. Which was impossible since he knew for a fact she hadn't been home.

He'd taken her out behind the bar and, lighting a cigarette, casually asked her about it. She'd said she and her friend Cassie had taken a dip in the creek because it was so hot out.

Last night, he'd been determined not to do whatever it took to get the truth out of her. He didn't need a repeat performance of what he'd done at a bar in Missoula after he'd realized his girlfriend was cheating on him and he would never play football again. He didn't need another stint behind bars—even overnight—because of another unfaithful woman.

So he'd waited until he'd cooled down. Let her think she was pulling the wool over his eyes. If he bided his time, he would catch her.

But now as Clete stood listening to the same bar talk he heard every night, he wasn't sure he wanted to catch her. Maybe whatever was going on would just play itself out. Maybe it already had. He suddenly couldn't bear the thought of losing her. If he confronted her, would she choose her lover or her husband?

DESTRY NEEDED TO clear her head, and the best way she knew how was on the back of a horse. Her talk with her brother had upset her more than she wanted to admit. She feared he was facing prison, or worse, the death penalty. She shuddered at the thought.

She found their ranch foreman Russell Murdock in the tack room. The familiar scents of the barn filled her. She breathed them in, stopping to visit her horse for a moment before stepping to the doorway of the tack room. Russell was putting away a halter.

"Hey, there," he said when he saw her. He gave her a big smile, just as he had since she was a girl. Russell was a big man like WT, handsome and easygoing.

When she was a girl, she'd wished he was her father rather than WT. Russell had definitely acted more like one, that was for sure. As she studied him, she knew, until she learned the truth, she would look at every older man in the county, speculating as to whether or not he could be her father from now on.

"Going for a ride?" he asked.

She nodded.

Russell smiled and leaned back against the tack room wall as he took her in. "I know that look. Bad day?" He'd always made time for her, always had lots of patience, as well. "If you're wondering about those new stalls your father wants built, Grayson Brooks is on his way out to start working on them. He said he'd planned to put new locks on your doors today, but that you'd called him and canceled?"

"Rylan already changed my locks."

Russell lifted a brow. "That was nice of him."

She had to laugh. Russell had always known how she felt about the cowboy.

"I saw the sheriff's patrol rig in front of the house. I don't mean to pry." He shoved back the brim of his hat, his face open. Since the time she was small he'd told her if she had a problem she was always welcome to come to him. He'd been good to his word.

She felt her face heat as she recalled asking him if what she'd heard about sex was true. She'd grown up around animals all her life, so she knew about them. It was just hard to imagine people doing the same thing.

She must have been all of eight. Russell had been great
about answering her question. She was forever grateful
to have him in her life.

"Carson might be in more trouble than we thought,"
Destry said now. "I suppose you know WT isn't well."

He nodded. "Margaret told me, but I figured something was up when he got Carson home."

"He wants Carson to take over the ranch."

Russell said nothing for a moment. "What does he
want for you?"

"Marriage. To Hitch McCray."

Russell sighed, his gaze locking with hers. "Between
you and me, Sweet Pea, you aren't seriously considering that, are you?"

He hadn't called her that in years. "Not a chance,"
she said with a curse.

Russell cocked a brow at her. He'd threatened to
wash her mouth out with soap when she was seven if
she didn't quit swearing like the ranch hands. She felt
even more love for this man who'd filled in for the father she should have had. She couldn't imagine what
her life would have been like if Russell hadn't always
been around since the beginning.

"How well did you know my mother?"

Russell let out a surprised sound. "Why are you—"

"But you liked her."

"Your mother was a very special woman. Of course,
I liked her, but the only man Lila ever loved was WT."

She studied him. "No secrets between us, isn't that
what you always said? Nothing I can't ask you."

He smiled. "Nothing's changed."

"Is there any chance you might be my father?"

"You're WT's daughter," he said.

She shook her head. "You've been more of a father to me than WT, so I just thought…"

Russell glanced past her. "Looks like your brother's fiancée is leaving."

She turned to see Carson loading Cherry's suitcases into the back of the sports car.

AFTER BOB BENTON had found his wife sleeping on the office floor rug down at the store this morning, he'd stared at her, surprised that she could still astound him after all these years of marriage.

"What were you thinking, coming down here alone? What if it had been some criminal breaking into the store?" he'd demanded after waking her up and insisting to know what was going on.

"I'd take care of it the way I take care of everything else around here," Nettie had snapped as she'd stomped out the back door and headed up the mountainside to the house.

Bob had watched her until she'd reached the house, then he'd gone into the office to call the Montana Fish, Wildlife and Parks to tell them about the grizzly. Not that they could do anything. They'd already put out a trap, but clearly it wasn't working.

With that done, Bob had taken care of the boxes he'd failed to break down the day before and got ready to open the store.

The temperature had dropped again last night, and even with the sun out now, it was going to take a long time to warm up. As he unlocked the front door and put up the Open sign, he felt another panic attack coming on as he saw the sheriff's car parked across the street at the Branding Iron.

He couldn't stay here. He'd thought about going south

for the winter, but he knew Nettie would never leave
the store. Until that moment, he hadn't thought about
going alone.

Why couldn't he just pack up and leave like the rest
of the snowbirds who spent only a few weeks in this
godforsaken country each year? That could be the answer to all his problems, he realized.

He brightened, even though it meant a change of plan.
He was going to Arizona. Who knew what awaited him
down there in the sunshine? Maybe a sparkling pool and
young women lying around it in tiny swimsuits.

Nettie had already told everyone that she was going
to work in this store until she fell over dead. Someone
would find her dead one morning when she failed to
put out the Open sign. He'd always thought that *someone* would be him.

What if the sheriff got suspicious? Bob stopped in the
middle of the chip/cracker/cookie aisle waiting for the
panic attack to come again. Would people really question why he'd left without Nettie? No one who knew
her, he told himself. Not even the sheriff.

Relief washed over him. He'd spent his last winter in
this damned place. His last summer, as well, because
once he left he wouldn't be coming back—even if Nettie
would let him. He was putting this place and the nightmares behind him. Arizona would be a new beginning.

"WHAT ARE YOU so happy about?" Nettie demanded
when she returned to the store to find her husband whistling. As far as she could remember, she'd never heard
the man whistle once in his life.

"FWP is coming out to check the bear trap," Bob

said and smiled as if that was the source of this unexpected glee.

She studied him. Bob Benton was never cheerful. He hadn't been when she married him, and that certainly hadn't changed during their many years of marriage. She recalled his moody, odd behavior, all the nights he'd gone for long, late-night walks, coming back more worked up than when he'd left.

"You'll never guess what I saw last night," she said, unable to keep it to herself any longer. "Kate LaFond was digging up something in her garage in the wee hours of the morning." Or burying something, she couldn't be sure which from this distance.

Bob didn't answer, but that was nothing new.

"I told you she's hiding something."

"Kate's just messing with you, Nettie, don't you see that? She probably saw you over here watching her." He wagged his head sympathetically. "Or you just dreamed it. It's none of our business anyway. I cleaned up those boxes in back," he said as he headed for the back door. "Got the cash register ready to go for you, and now I'm going to go pack."

She'd been too angry with him for trying to brush off what she'd seen that she hadn't been listening—that was until she heard the word *pack*.

"Pack?"

He turned then to look at her. It struck her that he even appeared different somehow. Taller, as if a weight had been lifted off his shoulders.

She frowned as she considered him. What had gotten into *him?* If she didn't know him better, she would suspect he'd fallen in love as part of some delayed midlife crisis.

"I'm going south, Nettie."

"*South?*" she repeated, wondering what the devil he was talking about.

"Arizona. I'm thinking I might buy a place down there with the money my father left me."

Nettie scowled, remembering how Bob's father had left everything to Bob—making sure she was cut from his will. And that, after all the years she'd taken care of his worthless son. Her blood still boiled at the reminder.

"Did you hear me, Nettie? I'm leaving right away, before the first snowfall."

Was he serious? Apparently he thought so.

"The truth is… I'm not sure I'll be back."

She didn't know what to say. The one thing he hadn't mentioned was her going with him. Because he knew she wouldn't? Or because he didn't want her to?

"Just like that?" she finally managed to ask.

"It's been a long time coming. I think you know that." His smile was a little sad. "I never was your first choice anyway."

She couldn't argue that. She was just surprised that Bob had known.

"I hope I haven't ruined your life, Nettie." His words came out hoarse with emotion.

"What are you talking about?" she asked, feeling a tremor of worry move through her. Bob had been acting more than a little strangely lately, not to mention the nightmares. "What have you done, Bob?"

He shook his head, turned and left, closing the door behind him.

Nettie thought about going after him. Instead, she stood alone in the middle of the store waiting for the reality of his leaving to hit her. After a few moments, her eyes filled with tears, and she began to laugh and cry. Unable to settle on one or the other, she sat down in the middle of the store aisle and continued until all she felt was a huge sense of relief.

RYLAN CALLED DESTRY, but there was no answer. He left a message and waited around for a while for her to call back. When she didn't, he considered trying to find Bethany and talking to her alone about the locket. But he realized she might be more apt to tell Destry the truth than him.

So he did the only other thing he could. He saddled up and went for a ride. The West Ranch ran adjacent to the W Bar G, both connecting to forest service land and the Crazies.

He rode up through the pines but hadn't gone far when he saw her. "Great minds think alike," he said as he caught up to Destry.

She laughed, though she didn't seem all that surprised to see him. They rode along together as they climbed up through the pines to an open ridge.

Destry swung down from her horse to walk to the cliff edge.

"This always was one of your favorite spots," he said, joining her. The view was incredible. Destry had always said she felt as if she could see to the end of the planet from here. It seemed that way on a clear, cloudless day like today. The afternoon breeze stirred the stray tendrils of hair beneath her Western straw hat.

He'd been anxious to tell her about Bethany and the locket he'd seen, but now he didn't want to spoil the moment with talk of the murder or what had kept them apart all these years.

To his surprise, when he looked over at her, there were tears in her eyes. "Destry, what is it?"

She shook her head.

"I've noticed that there is something going on with you. Please, you know you can talk to me."

She glanced over at him. Her blue eyes glistened. She made an angry dash at the tears with her sleeve.

When she didn't answer, he stepped to her, took her shoulders in his hands and turned her to face him. "What is it?"

She tried to avoid his gaze, but he pulled her closer, until there was nothing she could do but meet his eyes.

"It's the ranch. I'm going to lose it."

"Lose it?" he asked in surprise. He knew that the W Bar G was doing great with Destry running it.

"WT's not my father."

"What?"

She shook her head. "Apparently my mother had a lover before I was born. WT has known about it all these years. It explains his lack of interest in me."

"How long have you known this?"

She shrugged. "I guess I've always suspected something was wrong. I just never thought… When I realized he'd gotten Carson back to take over the ranch, I confronted him and he told me."

Rylan took a moment to digest this. The ranch had become Destry's life. To lose it… "He's giving your brother the ranch? So it isn't really lost. Your brother wouldn't kick you off." The bastard better not, if he knew what was good for him, he thought.

"Carson is in trouble and plans to sell the place to pay a large debt he has."

Rylan had to bite his tongue to keep from swearing. If he could have gotten his hands on Carson at that moment—

"I don't know who my biological father is," Destry said, her voice breaking. "I don't know who *I* am."

"I do," he whispered as he drew her to him and, cupping her beautiful face in his hands, kissed her softly. "You're Destry Grant and I admire the hell out of the woman you've become. Never doubt what a strong, capable, amazing person you are. I never have."

DESTRY FELT AS if she could finally breathe as they rode through the pines and the growing twilight. It had helped to tell Rylan. She smiled to herself remembering his words.

He'd held her for a long while before he'd told her his news.

"You aren't going to believe this, but that locket I found in Ginny's things? I saw one exactly like it."

Her heart kicked up a beat. "Where?"

He explained that when he'd gone to the bar, Bethany had come in to see her husband. "She was wearing one that I swear is identical. When I said something about it, she… Well, I think she lied to me about where she'd gotten it. I think she lied to her husband, as well."

A brisk breeze leaned the grass over and ruffled the horse's mane. Destry felt goose bumps skitter across her skin. "We have to find out where she got it."

"Yeah, that's what I was thinking. I don't suppose you want to—"

"Yes."

He'd grinned over at her. "Let's see if Clete is working at the bar tonight when we get back. I definitely think we need to talk to her when he's not around."

Rylan left her partway down the mountain, saying he would ride on down to her house and wait for her there.

Destry headed toward the barn and corrals. Earlier as she'd been about to ride out, Grayson had stopped her to ask about the new stalls. Now, as she led her horse into the barn, she saw that he had finished one of them and left her a note to let him know what she thought.

He'd done a beautiful job, she thought, as she unsaddled her horse. She'd have to remember to call him and tell him.

Knowing Rylan would be at the house waiting for her, Destry finished unsaddling her horse, put away her tack and headed for her pickup. She hadn't seen her brother since he'd loaded Cherry's suitcases into his sports car. She wondered if she would see him again. It would be just like Carson to disappear again.

Right now, though, she was just anxious to get down to the house and Rylan. His news about Bethany having a locket like Ginny's felt like the first real break they'd gotten.

RYLAN RODE DOWN the mountain, his mind reeling with everything Destry had told him. As he came out of the pines and down into the valley, he breathed in the day, trying to imagine how he would feel if he didn't have his family and the ranch.

As he rode through the sun-paled grasses, he saw tracks where a vehicle had recently crossed this pasture. The tracks led to the east along the fence line. He hadn't gone far when he saw the barbed wire gate lying on the ground. There were fresh tracks into the property.

His heart began to pound. Riding through the downed gate, he galloped toward the homestead house. He couldn't see it from here because of the thick band of trees between him and the house. Reaching the edge of the trees, he looked for a vehicle but didn't see one.

Maybe the gate had been down for some time. Destry said she'd chased her stalker away, but he feared that firing her shotgun hadn't been a strong enough message. Maybe the man didn't know Destry, didn't realize that next time she wasn't kidding about not missing.

Getting off his horse, he led it into the dense trees, looking for any sign that the man had returned. He hadn't gone far when he found both fresh footprints and older tire tracks. He worked his way through the dense windbreak of pines, aspens and large old cottonwoods that grew along the creek until he saw the house in the distance.

The sun had set, leaving the sky a fiery orange. The house was dark. Destry wouldn't be home yet. Closer, something moved. A dark figure crept around the corner of the house.

Rylan tore after him, determined that this time he wasn't letting the man get away.

As Destry drove up into the yard, she saw Rylan. He had someone down on the ground. She jumped out, digging the pistol from her purse as she did, and raced toward them.

"What in the world?"

Rylan looked up. "I caught your stalker."

"No, you've got the wrong guy," Hitch McCray slurred. Destry could smell the alcohol from where she was standing. His gaze shifted to her. "Destry, you're the one who told me someone had been hanging around your house, spying on you. I was driving by when I saw a man trying to break into your house. I was only trying to catch him. I swear it."

"I've already called the sheriff," Rylan said to Destry, without letting Hitch up.

"The man took off through the trees," Hitch said to Rylan. "I would have caught him if you hadn't tackled me. I was trying to protect Destry."

"How was it again that you just happened to be driving by?" Rylan asked.

Hitch looked from her to Rylan and back again. "There's no law that says I can't come out here to see Destry."

"That's what I thought," Rylan said. "So much for you just driving by."

"This is just a misunderstanding," Hitch said, clearly drunk. "There's no reason to involve the sheriff in this."

"The dispatcher said the sheriff was in Beartooth, so he should be here soon," Rylan said. He sounded relieved, and when Destry looked at him, she could see it in his face. He'd been afraid for her, and now he'd caught her stalker red-handed. "He used a damned screwdriver to try to break into your house."

"It wasn't me, I'm telling you," Hitch said.

"Just shut up. You can tell it to the sheriff."

"I told you to call Deputy Billy Westfall," Hitch said. "He'll sort this out."

Billy Westfall? He'd see that Hitch never saw the inside of a jail cell, Destry thought, as she heard the sound of a siren in the distance.

"You're lucky I didn't shoot you the other night," she said, thinking that if she'd known it was Hitch she might have pelted him with a little buckshot.

"I don't know what you're talking about," Hitch mumbled.

By the time the sheriff arrived and took Hitch into custody, it was too late to go to Bethany's and ask about the locket.

"Are you going to be all right?" Rylan asked after everyone else had left. Hitch, it had turned out, along with trying to break into her house, had hit another vehicle when he was leaving the Range Rider bar. So it would be at least a day before he could get out on bail—that is if his mother paid it. The sheriff said that was doubtful, so Hitch would probably be spending some time behind bars, and Destry should be safe from him.

She wasn't worried, now that she knew it was Hitch. "I'll be fine," she told Rylan. Hitch had torn up the wood around the door, but he hadn't broken the lock.

"I'll feel better knowing your stalker is behind bars," Rylan said. "Once I find out what time Clete goes to work tomorrow, I'll give you a call." He stood in the doorway, hat in hand, looking at her in a way that made her melt inside.

"Thank you."

He nodded, as if trying to think of something more to say.

If he kept looking at her like that and didn't leave soon—

"Tomorrow then." He turned and walked to the back of the house where he'd left his horse.

"You sure you can find your way home in the dark?" she called after him.

He laughed, a wonderful sound that made the night feel magical. "The horse can. That's all that matters." And then he was in the saddle, tipping his hat and riding away.

CHAPTER NINETEEN

THE NEXT MORNING, Deputy Billy Westfall inspected his face in the bathroom mirror. "Damn, but you are one good-looking son of a bitch," he said and grinned at his image.

Behind him, his girlfriend, Trish, leaned against the doorjamb and rolled her eyes. "As my grandmother always said, 'that would sound a lot better coming from someone else.'"

He mugged a face at her before she turned back to whatever she'd been doing. He watched her go, a little crestfallen that it appeared the magic might have gone out of their relationship.

When they'd first gotten together, she would have laughed and agreed with him, and the two of them would have ended up in the shower lathering each other up.

Billy looked in the mirror again, his confidence lagging. It wasn't just Trish's recent indifference to him. He'd thought by this age, he would be sheriff. The fact that he was still a deputy at thirty nagged at him.

All he needed was one good case to solve by his lonesome, he thought and nodded to himself in the bathroom mirror. He'd already envisioned the headline that would appear in the local newspaper.

Billy "The Kid" Westfall Singlehandedly Solves Case of the Century. The newspaper in Big Timber would put the story on the front page, along with his picture. People would be talking about it for years. Come election time, he'd run against Frank Curry and beat him by a landslide.

And then he'd be the one sitting behind that big desk. He'd be the one who everyone tipped their hats to when they passed him. He'd be *somebody*.

His hand went to the sidearm holstered at his hip. He ran his fingers over the grip, palming it as he stared down his image in the mirror. On the count of three, he drew the .45 from the holster with lightning speed, a move he'd practiced in front of a mirror for hours.

He'd show Frank Curry, he told himself as he reholstered the .45. "Trigger-happy, my ass," he whispered, recalling how Curry had threatened to fire him for being a hothead.

All that would change once he made a name for himself. And Billy had a good feeling that time was coming soon.

"Where are you off to?" Trish asked, checking the clock on the wall. "You're not due into work for a couple of hours."

"WT Grant called and wants me to come up to his place for a little talk," Billy said puffing out his chest.

"Why would he want to talk to *you?*"

Yep, the shine had definitely come off this love affair.

"Maybe he doesn't like the way the sheriff is handling the Ginny West murder investigation."

She still looked skeptical. "Don't go getting yourself fired, Billy. Your job is hanging by a thread as it is."

Billy glanced around the apartment, sizing up how long it would take him to pack up his stuff and move out. Not long at all, he thought.

WT GRANT STUDIED the tall, lanky deputy, hoping he hadn't made a mistake.

"Have a seat," he said as he steered Billy Westfall into the expansive living room. "What can I get you to drink?"

Billy looked around the room, big-eyed, before settling his gaze on the fully stocked bar. He licked his lips as he took in all the pretty bottles filled with alcohol. WT could see the internal battle waging.

"I'm going to have to pass this time," Billy finally said. "I'm scheduled to work this afternoon."

WT nodded. "I'll just pour you a short one then." He rolled over to the bar and poured them both a shot of bourbon.

Billy settled into one of the deep leather chairs and looked pleased as WT handed him the crystal glass.

"I'm sure you were curious after my call," WT said, turning his own glass in his fingers as he studied the deputy over the rim.

Billy was trying hard not to look too eager. WT liked that. Just as he liked the good-looking deputy's cockiness and that burning ambition that shone in his dark eyes. Billy was perfect.

"I'm sure you've heard that my son, Carson, has returned to the ranch," WT said.

Billy nodded and took a sip of the bourbon. He leaned back, crossed his legs and took in the room again.

"I need to know if I can count on you if there's any trouble," WT said and held the young man's gaze.

"Yes, sir," Billy said, sitting up straighter. "There's trouble, you just call me."

"Of course, you might need some help…."

It took Billy a moment. "I know someone who could back me up."

"Another deputy?" WT asked, afraid the man wasn't getting it.

"No, sir. Is that a problem?"

WT smiled. "No, actually that was what I was hoping you would say. So we'll keep this to ourselves."

Billy nodded and smiled. "Just what I was thinking. I take it you're expecting trouble?" he asked, sounding hopeful.

"I'm always expecting trouble," WT said as he glanced out the window wondering when his son would be back from getting rid of his fiancée. Or if Carson would be back at all.

RYLAN PICKED UP Destry the next afternoon. As she slid into the passenger side of his pickup, he knew he couldn't keep being around her like this. Last night, it had been hell leaving her. As he'd ridden away, he'd glanced back to see her silhouetted in the doorway. Desire had spiked through him, hotter than a Montana summer day.

This afternoon she looked fresh from a shower. Her burnished auburn hair looked damp, her skin glowing. Not to mention she smelled citrusy and good enough to eat.

He moaned under his breath as he got the pickup going. Being with her and yet having this distance between them was killing him. He couldn't take much more of this.

She wore a pale orange cotton Western shirt with pearl snaps down the front, jeans and boots. He tried not to notice the way her jeans hugged her perfect behind.

Her hair was pulled up in a long ponytail today. He itched to free it and bury his fingers in the silky depths.

The fall breeze stirred the loose tendrils around her face. The past eleven years had made her even more desirable than she'd been at seventeen.

"Is everything all right?" she asked.

He hadn't realized he was gripping the wheel, a pained expression on his face. "Sorry, I was just…" He waved off the rest since he suspected from her small knowing smile that she knew exactly what his problem was.

It reminded him of their last year in high school. They'd been determined to wait until they were married before they were intimate. After graduation and a long, hot summer, they'd both agreed they didn't need to wait. They were ready to commit to each other.

And they had, he thought as he drove toward Bethany Reynolds's house. That long-ago commitment still had a death grip on his heart.

"I'm glad you confided in me," he said, studying her out of the corner of his eye as he drove. She seemed stronger and more determined today. Having her stalker behind bars had to have given her some peace. But, like him, she seemed more upbeat. Both of them were hoping that Bethany held the key to Ginny's murder and this would finally be over.

"I was thinking about the older men Bethany would have come in contact with through her job at the Branding Iron," Destry said. "Pastor Tom always writes his sermons down there on Fridays or Saturdays, the days Bethany works. But a lot of men hang out at the café."

Rylan didn't want to talk about Ginny's murder. He wanted to talk about them but, he reminded himself, there was no *them*. Not yet anyway, he assured himself.

"I just want to say, I'm sorry about the situation with the ranch," he said.

She nodded, smiling over at him. "I know you don't want to believe that the man is Pastor Tom," she said, changing the subject.

He realized that Destry probably regretted confiding in him, especially about her brother. Remembering what his mother had said about what she'd witnessed between Ginny and Pastor Tom, he shared it with her.

"I have to admit that since Bethany didn't attend church, I thought there probably wasn't a connection between her and the pastor. I forgot about his sermonwriting at the café where she works. By the way, I told the sheriff about your suspicions."

She gave him a look that made his heart pound. "Thank you for taking me seriously."

"I always do."

Destry laughed at that.

He studied her profile for a moment, thinking just how serious he was about this woman. They were bound by the past and by their love as much as by his sister's death.

"I broke my promise to you," he said, concentrating on his driving. Even as he said it, he knew it was a lie. He'd promised that night with Destry naked in his arms that he would love her forever. Over the years he'd felt as if that promise was a curse since he hadn't been able to forget her—no matter how hard he'd tried.

He felt, rather than saw, her turn from the window to look at him again. "I'm sorry," he said, sorry, too, for letting her think he'd ever stopped loving her.

"We were young," she said and turned away again.

"Not *that* young."

"Do we have to talk about this?" she asked.

"No. But there is something we do need to talk about." He told her about his girl-next-door theory, how Ginny and Bethany had the same coloring. "And I thought of you and thought whoever had been coming around your house was the same man."

"It's a nice theory, but Hitch didn't offer me a silver heart-shaped locket. Nor do Ginny and Bethany and I look that much alike."

"It's that fresh innocence, and maybe the freckles."

She mugged a face at him.

He regretted teasing her about them when they were kids. "I love your freckles. I always have."

After that, they rode in silence southeast through rolling pastures and hay fields, the land falling away from the Crazy Mountains toward the river. He watched the summer-dried landscape blur by with a sense of nostalgia. This country that he loved was deeply connected to Destry, and his feelings for her were rooted in them both.

Rylan liked the contrast between the rolling farmland and the pine-covered steep mountains of the Crazies. The valley was fertile and settled; the mountains were still wild and uncivilized. He'd always felt that pull between the two.

A half mile up the road, the land changed. Ravines with rock outcroppings and stands of pines and juniper sprung up. As they drove over a rise, the Reynolds's house came into view. It sat back against a small bluff surrounded by pines and tall cottonwoods. He was relieved to see that Bethany's SUV was still parked out front. He'd checked earlier, before he'd called Destry. Clete was at the bar. Bethany should be home, but that didn't mean she would talk to them, let alone tell them the truth.

"This could be a wild-goose chase," he warned Destry, not wanting her to get her hopes up. It was too late for him.

"Carson thinks the same thing we do, that Ginny's secret lover gave her the locket," Destry said, an edge to her voice that reminded him of what still stood between them—that deep perilous chasm that neither dared cross as long as the killer remained at large.

"Did he know Ginny was pregnant?" Rylan asked, hearing a catch in his voice. He was treading carefully. He didn't want to fight with her today. Just being with her like this felt nice. He didn't want to spoil it. But he had to know.

"She told him it was the other man's baby."

Stubbornly, he still didn't want to believe there *had* been another man, a man who'd made Ginny keep secrets, a man who had killed her to keep her from having what he believed was his baby.

As he pulled off the county road and dropped down a narrow dirt track to the Reynolds's house, he told himself that if there had been a secret lover, he'd seduced Bethany Reynolds into the same deadly pact, and they were about to find him.

NETTIE FELT STRANGELY free after Bob left to go pack. Free and independent, as if she could do anything she darn well pleased. It felt good, she thought, as she went to stand at the front window, considering the rest of her life.

She could see Kate over there pouring coffee and chatting away. It galled her. It was high time she proved

to the town—and Bob before he left for Arizona—
exactly what that woman was up to.

Locking the front door of the store, she sneaked out
the back and cut across the road to the empty stone shell
of the old garage off to the right and a little behind the
café. She figured if anyone had seen her, they'd think
she was headed kitty-corner across the street to the
post office.

Working her way to the opening of the garage, she
kept an eye on the street and the back of the café. Kate
LaFond was always busy with her large table of ranchers who were there every day at this same time. But
Nettie wasn't taking any chances.

When she was sure the coast was clear, she stepped
inside the garage and glanced around. The large wooden
barn-style doors that had once hung at the front of the
garage had rotted off years ago. All that was left was
the remaining three sides of the stone structure.

The same sandstone had been used to build the store.
But unlike the store, the garage had fallen into disrepair.
Claude had been sick a lot over the years and hadn't kept
things up, Nettie thought as she checked the street and
the back of the café again.

Often the cook would come out back for a smoke.
Lou Parmley had been doing that for as long as she
could remember. Claude had hired him right out of high
school, and Lou had stayed on when Kate took over the
café after Claude had died.

Once she was sure there was no one watching, Nettie moved deeper into the dim structure. It didn't take
long to find the spot where the earth along the edge of
the stone wall had been dug up. The shovel Kate had

used was still propped against the wall, soft damp dirt still stuck to the blade.

Nettie stared at the spot, wondering if Kate LaFond had dug up something—or buried something. She could hear Bob as if he was standing next to her.

"She probably buried a dead cat that got hit on the road. But if you need to dig it up, then be my guest. Serves you right for being so damned nosy."

She grabbed the shovel and told Bob's voice in her head to shut up. Digging was easy since the soil had already been turned. She kept glancing toward the street and café as she sunk the blade in the dirt and turned over several shovels full. At one point, the blade rang out, but it was only a rock she'd struck.

After she'd dug down a good six to eight inches, she hit more rocks and leaned on the shovel for a moment to catch her breath. There wasn't anything here.

"No dead cat," she said to Bob, who of course couldn't hear her. He wouldn't have listened anyway, she thought.

So Kate had dug something up. But what could have been buried there? And if something had, who buried it there? Claude? Or Kate herself?

Disappointed and yet still intrigued, she quickly shoveled the dirt back into the hole. She eyed it to make sure the soil looked as it had when she'd come into the garage, then, leaning the shovel against the wall where she'd found it, Nettie started out of the garage when she heard the back door of the café slam.

Moments later she heard the crunch of gravel. Someone was headed this way. Nettie looked around for a way out and spotted a hole in the stones at the back of the garage. She hurried to it and had just shimmied through the opening into the tall weeds growing along the back when she heard someone step into the garage.

She held her breath, which wasn't easy since she had been breathing hard moments before. She listened but heard no movement inside the garage. That didn't mean someone wasn't still there, though. Probably Kate. The woman must have eyes in the back of her head. Or maybe she'd spotted her when she'd crossed the street. Kate would have guessed where she was headed, especially if she had something to hide in this old garage.

She heard the sound of a box opening and closing. Nettie recalled seeing several wooden boxes along one wall of the garage. Tool boxes. With a shudder, she realized that Kate could be arming herself.

She waited, taking shallow breaths, her back pressed to the rough stonewall. Grasshoppers flew around her in the weeds that were almost up to her neck. If she squatted down, she was fairly sure no one would be able to see her.

In the distance, she heard the back door of the café open and slam shut. Finally she let herself breathe as she made her way around the edge of the garage. There was a pile of old junk among the weeds. She skinned her shin on an rusted car chassis and, seeing that she couldn't get through the junk, turned back. She had no choice.

She'd have to get out the way she'd gone in—through the garage. She crawled back through the hole, scraping her back on the rough stones but finally dropping into the cool darkness of the garage.

When she looked up, she saw the slim silhouette in the opening where the garage doors used to be. Nettie froze. At that moment, she half expected Kate to snatch up the shovel and come flying at her.

Instead, Kate let out a chuckle, then turned and

walked back to the café. Nettie didn't move until she heard the back door of the café slam again. Then she took off like a bullet back to the store, fearing Bob had been right.

Kate LaFond *was* fooling with her. Just as Bob had said.

BETHANY JUMPED AT the sound of a vehicle coming up the road. Her heart had been hammering since she'd come home and found another note on her door. It was the third one she'd found; the other two had been on her SUV when she'd gotten off work at the café.

At first she'd thought they were from Clete, that he knew. But they weren't in his handwriting and they sure as heck didn't sound like something he would write. The notes scared her and, worse, now that she was no longer sinning, she resented getting another one.

That's why she'd called him the moment she found the note. When a female voice answered at his end, though, she'd quickly hung up. If he'd been home, he would know it was her who'd called. It wasn't the first time she'd called and had to hang up.

Now, at the sound of the approaching vehicle, she rushed to the window, afraid it might be him coming up the road. Surely he wouldn't do something so dangerous. Clete might be watching the house even now, and if he caught him here…

At first she felt a rush of relief when she saw that it wasn't her lover's or her husband's vehicle. Then she recognized the man and woman who pulled in and got out. Her hand went to her throat, but of course she wasn't wearing the locket. It was hidden.

She let Rylan knock a couple of times before she

went to the door. By then, she told herself she was calm enough and could handle this.

"Hey," she said, pretending their stopping by was a pleasant surprise. "What are you two doing out this way?"

"We came to see you," Rylan said. "Mind if we come in?"

She couldn't really object, now, could she? "Of course not. Come on in. I'll put on some coffee. I don't think Clete ate all the chocolate chip cookies I baked. I'll check."

"We don't need coffee or cookies," Destry said. "We need to ask you about the locket, the one Rylan saw you wearing at the bar."

Bethany stopped in midstep. "The locket? I told you—"

"We need to know where you really got it," Destry said. "It's important."

"I can't see why it would be," she said and saw Rylan and Destry exchange a look.

"I found one exactly like it hidden in my sister Ginny's jewelry box," Rylan said.

Bethany frowned.

"We suspect that the man who gave it to her was someone she'd been seeing in secret," Destry said.

What were they getting at? "I thought she was dating your brother."

"She'd broken up with him. Carson believed she was seeing a married man."

"What does any of this have to do with my locket?" Bethany asked.

"If the man who gave Ginny the locket killed her, then I think you can see what we're getting at," Destry said.

"Why would you think *he* killed her?" Bethany heard her voice break.

"To keep his secret," Destry said.

"And you think the same man gave me my locket?" she asked.

"Did he?" Rylan asked.

"No, I told you. It's just a piece of jewelry I hadn't worn in a while."

"Here's the thing," Destry said. "If you are seeing someone in secret, then you need to know there is a good chance that he's done this before. Ginny ended up dead, and we think it was because he felt threatened. If he feels threatened again, he might kill again."

"That's a lot of ifs, and none of them have anything to do with me," Bethany said, getting upset. "Are you sure you aren't just trying to find someone else to blame for Ginny's murder other than your brother?"

What they were telling Bethany was making her more than uneasy, and she didn't like the feeling. They were wrong, of course, but that still didn't make her feel any better.

"I told you I don't remember where I got the locket. It isn't like it is a one-of-a-kind piece of jewelry. There must be thousands of them around." When she was being honest, she admitted it was a fairly cheap piece of silver. Its value to her wasn't in dollars and cents, though.

"Even so, doesn't it seem odd that two lockets exactly alike turn up in Beartooth?" Rylan asked. "I wonder what the odds are of that happening, unless the same man bought them?"

"We'd like to see the locket," Destry said.

Bethany felt trapped, but she had no choice. It would

be even more suspicious if she said she'd lost it or thrown it away.

She went in the bedroom and came back with the locket. Rylan held out his hand, and she dropped it into his large palm. Her own hands were shaking, so she hid them in the rear pockets of her jeans.

After a few minutes, Rylan handed the locket to Destry. "It's identical, isn't it?" Destry looked at it for a moment, then nodded.

Bethany reached for the locket, but Rylan took it back from Destry and pocketed it.

"I'm sorry," he said, "But I have to give this to the sheriff. If we're right, then your boyfriend could be a killer, in which case, you're in danger. Bethany, you need to tell us who gave you this locket."

"You're making a mistake protecting this man," Destry said.

She couldn't believe this was happening. "I already told you. It's just some old thing I've had, and I resent you suggesting that I might be cheating on Clete. If that's all, I have wash to do."

Destry looked as if she wanted to say more but changed her mind.

"Take care of yourself," Rylan said as they left. "I'm sure you'll be hearing from the sheriff."

Bethany waited until she heard them drive away before she dropped into the nearest chair. Her legs felt like water, and she was shaking all over. She thought about the age difference between herself and her lover, the secrecy, his anger when she'd told him about forgetting to take off the locket.

"You remind me of my first love." That's the first thing he'd told her the day at the café. He'd been so sweet. She'd felt his gaze on her as she'd poured him a cup of coffee so he could warm up before he had to go back out into the cold. It had been winter and snowing. The café had been empty except for the two of them. Lou had gone out back for a smoke. It had felt cozy joining him in the booth to talk. She'd basked in his gaze, feeling the heat of his desire, reveling in it.

Bethany pulled out her phone to call him but quickly changed her mind. He'd said he would call. She hated to think what his reaction would be when she told him Rylan was taking the locket to the sheriff.

She was still sitting there, trying to get her fear under control, when the phone began to ring. It rang twice, then stopped. She held her breath as it began to ring again. Their secret ring. It was him.

CHAPTER TWENTY

RYLAN COULDN'T HELP the uneasy feeling he had as he drove away from Bethany's house. "What do you think?"

"She was lying through her teeth and scared. But now I'm worried about what she will do. If we're right, then she'll be scared enough that she'll contact him so he can reassure her."

Rylan shot her a look. "She couldn't possibly believe him over us."

Destry laughed. He'd forgotten how much he loved her laugh or how it affected him. "She's in love with him. She desperately wants to believe him. But as scared as she is, it will probably take more than him just telling her to trust him. I was thinking that she'll insist on seeing him."

"You think she'll go to him."

Destry nodded.

Was it possible Bethany would lead them to Ginny's lover—and killer? Anxious, he couldn't believe they could be this close to finding out the truth.

"Or he might come to her. Either way, she's in danger."

"I'd hoped she would tell us the truth, especially with you along," he said.

Destry seemed amused by that. "Clearly you don't know how strong a secret bond like hers can be."

"Love or lying?" Love, he got. The secrets, the lying, that was all alien to him. "I know a spot where we should be able to see her house, but she won't know we're watching. You up for waiting a while and seeing what happens?"

"Definitely. I don't like leaving her alone right now."

He turned the pickup around and drove back to a side road that wound up a ravine. Shifting into four-wheel drive, he climbed up out of a ravine onto a rocky, tree-lined ridge.

Through the pines, he could make out her house below—and had a good view of her SUV. He shut off the engine to wait. The pickup cab suddenly felt too intimate. Turning the key, he put down his window. Destry did the same, as if she, too, felt the closeness.

Sitting there with her reminded him of the old days. When they were teens, she used to come deer hunting with him. They'd spent many hours driving back roads, hiking through the woods, riding horses or sometimes just sitting in a pickup together. They'd always ended up making out. Did she remember steaming up the windows on his old pickup all those nights parked on some old logging road?

A warm breeze stirred the tendrils of hair that had escaped her ponytail. The air smelled of dried leaves and golden stubble and Destry's faint, sweet scent.

"Do you remember us?" he asked before he could stop himself.

She looked over at him. "Rylan—"

"I never stopped thinking about you. I tried my damnedest, too."

"So I heard," she said with a smile.

"I missed you. So many times when I was on the

road driving late at night, I wished you were there with me." He shook his head. He knew he shouldn't be doing this. But if they found Ginny's killer, then maybe they could find their way back to each other. He was filled with hope that they still had a future. If her brother hadn't killed Ginny, if it was the mystery lover, then there was hope.

"I'm sorry I left the way I did. Destry, I'm so sorry."

DESTRY TRIED TO fight the tears that welled in her eyes at his words since these were words she'd only dreamed of hearing. Just the way he was looking at her stirred up all those feelings she'd fought for so long.

She didn't know what to say, even if she'd been able to speak. Rylan never gave her the chance. He reached for her, dragging her into his arms. She breathed him in, his masculine scent and the great outdoors. It had been so long since he'd wrapped her in his arms like this in the cab of his pickup. Her arms went around his neck as he dropped his mouth to hers.

She felt herself melt into him and the kiss. He drew her even closer. His body felt solid against hers and so familiar she ached with need for this man, the only man who'd ever made her feel like this.

"I never broke my promise, Destry," Rylan said as he drew back to meet her gaze. "I never stopping loving you."

And then he was kissing her again, deepening the kiss, their bodies molding together as the fall breeze brought the scents of the season through the open window.

Suddenly Rylan let out a curse and drew back. "Bethany, she's on the move." He hurriedly started the truck and dropped off the ridge into the ravine as they both lost sight of Bethany's SUV.

Destry was so shaken by the kiss and Rylan's words all she could do was hang on as they headed down the two-track, the tall weeds in the center brushing the bottom of the pickup.

She looked over at Rylan, saw him breathe in the scene even as he raced down the road, fulfilled by it as she was. She hadn't been wrong about him. He loved this land the way she did. And he loved her.

"Listen, tomorrow let's ride up into the high country one last time before the snow gets too deep. I need to check a few things up there at the camp. You know that place we used to go?"

She nodded.

"Come with me. Let's get away from all this. Just for a while."

The thought of Rylan in the small camp up in the mountains, the two of them sitting around the campfire or snuggled together in a sleeping bag, made her heart leap. She knew he was counting on them finding Ginny's killer and finally putting an end to this rift between them. He was that sure that if they found Ginny's secret lover that they would have found the murderer?

She knew that was what they both were counting on, for Carson to be cleared so it would clear the way for them to find again the love that had connected them for so long.

What would it hurt to be gone for a couple of days? She had Carson's check. She could drop that off, then pack for the horseback trip up in the mountains. A couple of days in the mountains with Rylan would be a dream come true.

"We need this," he said as he drove. "Come with me no matter what happens today." He reached across the seat for a moment to squeeze her hand.

She touched her tongue to her lower lip, relishing the memory of the kisses. The passion was still there. So was the love. She almost told him then how she felt and that she would go with him, follow him anywhere because she'd never stopped loving him, either.

But something held her back as he drove as fast as he could down through the ravine. Bethany had a good head start because they hadn't been paying attention. Destry could see that Rylan was worried they might have already lost her.

As they hit the county road, there was no sign of Bethany.

"She had to come this way, right?" he said.

There were only a few side roads, most of them going into the rocky foothills or rolling fields now planted with winter wheat.

He turned onto the road they'd driven in on and roared down it toward the Crossroads.

Why was Destry hesitating? She'd loved being back in his arms, loved kissing him again. She felt her heart soar at the thought of putting all the bad feelings behind them and finding their way back to each other.

As the pickup came over a rise, she saw Bethany's SUV turn east toward Highway 191. "There she is."

"I see her." He gunned the pickup, and they flew down the unpaved road, gravel pinging off the under-carriage, the engine roaring.

Destry watched the SUV getting smaller and smaller.

"I think you're right about her running to her lover," Rylan said as he kept his foot on the gas pedal.

By the time they reached the Crossroads, Bethany had disappeared again.

Rylan swore as he turned east and floored the gas. "I'm not sorry I kissed you. Just in case you're sitting over there wondering." He shot her a look but quickly went back to driving. "I'm not sorry that I told you I never quit loving you, either."

She knew what he wanted her to say. She might have, too, if they hadn't come flying over a rise and seen Bethany's SUV pulled off the side of the road ahead.

Next to it was a bright red sports car—Carson's. Bethany was sitting in the passenger seat.

Rylan started to slow but then gunned the engine, flying past them in a blur. But not before they'd both seen Bethany in her brother's arms.

Rylan didn't slow the truck until they were out of sight of the sports car. He pulled over to the side of the road and sat for a moment before he looked over at Destry, as if waiting for an explanation. As if she had one. His face was flushed with anger.

"Carson didn't give Bethany the locket," she cried. "He isn't the other man."

"Quite the coincidence since he was involved with Ginny and apparently now Bethany."

"Carson swore to me he didn't give Ginny that locket."

Rylan raised a brow. "Destry, he lied about you being at the ranch that night eleven years ago."

She couldn't argue that. She knew now why her brother had dragged her in as his second alibi—just as Rylan had always suspected.

"When are you going to see what is right in front of your eyes? Your brother is guilty as sin. He always has been."

"Carson couldn't have given that locket to Bethany. He hasn't been in town long enough to start an affair." She knew she was clutching at straws, still defending her brother out of fear that Rylan was right about him.

"How do you explain what we both just saw back there?" he demanded.

"I can't. Not right now anyway."

"You mean not until you ask your brother and believe whatever lie he tells you." He slammed the pickup into gear and made a U-turn back the way they'd come. "Your brother is taking the ranch from you. That should have told you everything you needed to know about him. It's high time we got the truth out of him."

But by the time they reached the spot where they'd seen Bethany and Carson, the red sports car was gone. Bethany's SUV was still parked beside the road. It was empty.

Destry felt confused and worried. Why did it keep coming back to Carson? Because he was guilty?

Rylan dropped her off at her house, leaving without a word. By the time she reached the big house, Carson still hadn't come back. She thought about waiting for him, but WT was in a snit and Margaret was busy cleaning, so she cleared out.

Back at her own house, she paced the floor, too stirred up to sit. She couldn't wait to speak with her brother, but like Rylan had said, she feared Carson would lie to her.

Her heart ached. She didn't want to believe Carson was guilty. But the true heartbreak was Rylan. Hadn't she warned herself not to get too close? Once they'd seen Carson with Bethany, she and Rylan were back where they'd been all these years—apart—with Ginny's murder between them.

As the poker game broke up, Carson couldn't believe he'd lost three thousand of what he'd gotten from WT and another five grand in credit before Lucky Larson cut him off.

"You're done," the ranch hand said. "Leave your IOU." Carson scribbled his name and the amount he owed. "You'd better be good for this."

"I am. I'll have the money soon, trust me."

"I don't trust you. But I know where to find your old man. Something tells me the last person you want to know about this is WT Grant."

Carson grabbed the ranch hand by his shirt collar with both hands. "You say a word to my father—"

"I won't as long as you don't take another powder. You disappeared eleven years ago. How do I know you won't again?"

Carson let the man go. "Because I'm not going anywhere until I get what I came home for."

"Just make sure you pay off your IOU soon," Lucky said. "Otherwise, maybe we'll have to talk about you putting up your sister as collateral. I haven't forgotten that Destry and your ranch manager fired me. She owes me."

"Leave my sister out of this," he said. The cowboy had never hidden his interest in Destry.

Once outside, Carson stood in the shadows of the pines a little disoriented. He could hear the creek nearby. It took him a moment to remember where he was. It was like that when he gambled. Lost time, lost money, lost memory.

The cold air seemed to bring him out of it. He'd planned to call Destry and tell her he wasn't going to need her money. That's when he'd felt lucky and thought he could make back enough that he could hold off his creditors until he got ranch money. He'd given Cherry a couple grand of the five he'd gotten from his father and left her at the Bozeman airport, three grand burning a hole in his pocket. Unfortunately when he'd called Lucky Larson, this afternoon was the soonest he could get into a game. He'd been a little late because of Bethany.

As he started toward his sports car, he heard someone call his name. A man came out of the pines, moving fast.

Carson didn't have time to react before a fist connected with his jaw.

CHAPTER TWENTY-ONE

DESTRY THOUGHT OF the certified check she had yet to give to her brother. Her hope was that it would take the pressure off, give Carson time to reconsider selling the ranch. She knew she was probably just kidding herself, but she couldn't sit back and do nothing.

But Rylan was wrong. She was no longer blind when it came to her brother.

Unable to sit still any longer, Destry headed up to the big house to wait for Carson. She was glad to see his red sports car parked out front. But when she entered the house, she found WT alone in the living room.

She had just stepped into the room and was about to ask him if he'd seen Carson when her brother stormed in. She gasped in shock. "What happened to you?"

"I ran into your boyfriend's fist," Carson said as he came into the room. He pushed past her and WT to get to the bar where he took a towel and some ice and applied it to his bruised jaw. His left eye was almost swollen shut and the color of a thunderhead. His lip was cut, his cheek red and his knuckles on both hands skinned.

"I hope you held your own," WT said.

Destry ignored him. "Rylan did this to you?" she cried. Rylan had been furious, but she'd hoped he'd taken off for the mountains instead of taking out his anger on Carson. This was Rylan's way of resolving things?

"Didn't I just say that?" Carson said, dropping into a chair with his ice pack in one hand and a drink in the other. He closed his eyes as if his pain was worse, thanks to her.

"Someone tell me what the hell is going on," WT demanded. "Last time I talked to you, Carson, you were taking Cherry to the bus station and coming right back. That was two days ago."

"You took Cherry to the bus station?" Destry asked.

"The airport." He shot WT a scowl. "I wasn't putting her on a *bus*."

"Rylan was at the airport?" WT's tone was disbelieving.

"I took her yesterday. Today I went for a ride. I stopped for a drink, all right?" Carson snapped.

"I thought you weren't going back to the Range Rider?" Destry said, unable to keep the fury out of her voice. She was just as angry with Rylan, but this wouldn't have happened if Carson had stayed on the ranch. She knew that was unreasonable, but she couldn't help feeling that her brother just asked for trouble, bringing it on himself.

"What were you doing at the Range Rider?" WT wanted to know.

"I wasn't," Carson said impatiently and took another gulp of his drink. "I was at a friend's." He shifted his gaze away from Destry's.

"A *friend's?*" Destry said. "So you have been seeing Bethany Reynolds?"

"What?" Carson cried.

"I saw you with her this afternoon. Did you give her a heart-shaped locket just like you did Ginny?"

Her brother glared at her. "I told you I didn't give

Ginny a locket. As for Bethany, I just happened to see her as I was driving by. Her car had broken down beside the road. She was upset. All I did was calm her down and give her a ride into Big Timber."

"Big Timber? Not Beartooth?"

Carson let out a curse. "That's where she wanted to go. You think I've got something going with *Bethany*?"

"Do you?" WT asked, as if he, too, didn't trust that his son was telling the truth any more than Destry did. "She's married to *Clete Reynolds*. You think Rylan can throw a punch, wait until Clete gets his hands on you."

"Are you both crazy?" Carson demanded.

She shoved the certified check at him. "Make sure that gets where it's supposed to go or you'll have to deal with me."

"Is that a check you just gave him?" WT bellowed.

"Both of you, get off my ass," Carson said, throwing down his drink and the bar towel. The half-melted ice cubes careened across the hardwood floor as he stalked out with the check gripped in his hand. A moment later they heard the rev of the sports car engine, then the sound of flying gravel as he sped away.

"What the hell was that about?" WT wanted to know as Destry started to leave, as well.

"Don't you know?" she asked him, meeting his gaze.

"Would I have asked if I knew?" he snapped.

"Maybe if you took the time to get to know your son, you'd *know* what was going on," she said and headed for the door.

"WANT TO TALK ABOUT IT?"

Rylan glanced over his shoulder as his father walked

into the barn. He continued to saddle his horse. "Not particularly."

"That's quite a shiner you got there. Run in to a door, did you?"

"I honestly tried not to get into it with Carson Grant," he said with a sigh. "I'm not proud of what I did, but it's been a long time coming."

"And Destry?"

Rylan stopped clinching the saddle for a moment, recalling the feel of her in his arms, her lips on his. "I love her, but as long as her brother is walking free, there's no hope in hell for the two of us."

Taylor West sighed. "You're that sure Carson killed Ginny?"

"I don't know and I can't stand around waiting for the sheriff to arrest someone."

"So you're heading for the hills this late in the evening?"

Rylan turned then to look at his father. "I keep messing things up. I can't stay here right now. I know you're disappointed in me."

"No, son. I'm not sure I wouldn't have done the same. I talked to the sheriff again today. He says he's making progress."

Rylan shook his head. "I'll believe it when I see it."

"You sure you want to leave now?"

"I can't face Destry right now, and I know the woman. She'll come looking for a fight of her own once her brother tells her what happened. There's enough animosity between us."

He wouldn't have left now if her stalker was still on the loose, but with Hitch behind bars for a while, Destry would be safe.

"You could hit some weather up there."

Rylan nodded. "I'm packing for snow. I just need to get my head on straight, and I can't do that here. I think best on the back of a horse. You know that."

His father chuckled. "I feel the same way. But this might not be a problem you can ride away from, son."

"I know. I'll be back in a couple of days. You can do without me that long?"

"Your mother and I are flying down to Denver. There's a bull down there I want to take a look at. Your brothers will be handling things here on the ranch. They've almost got the rest of the hay brought in for winter."

"I haven't been much help lately. I'm sorry about that. I've been worried about Destry, but after today it appears that the only person to worry about is her brother, so she should be all right. Add to that, the woman is stubborn as a damned mule and she's capable of taking care of herself."

His father placed a hand on his shoulder. "This is going to resolve itself."

"Yeah? Unfortunately it looks like it will be too late for Destry and me by the time it does."

"Be careful up there," his father said, glancing toward the mountains.

THE CALL CAME in the wee hours of the morning. Destry sat up in bed with a jolt. It took her a few moments to realize what had awakened her.

She'd come straight home after her encounter with her brother. She'd been worried but even more disgusted with Carson and his lying. While she was worried he'd get in more trouble after taking off the way he had, she'd known, though, that if she went into town looking for him, she would have been tempted to pay Rylan a visit—one that would make matters even worse.

The phone rang—and apparently not for the first time, she realized. She snatched it up, aware of the hour, fear instantly growing in her chest. No one called this time of the night unless it was bad news. Her first thought was Rylan. Then her brother. "Hello?"

"Destry, it's Margaret. Carson's been shot."

"Shot?" The words made no sense. Destry sat up and tried to catch her breath. "Is he all right?"

"The doctor said the bullet caught him in the shoulder. They're rushing him into surgery. That's all I know. WT and I are headed for the hospital now."

"I'll meet you there."

"Destry?"

She had turned on the lamp and had been looking around for clothes to wear but stopped as she heard something else in Margaret's voice.

"WT told the sheriff about Rylan beating up his son. He's convinced that Rylan shot Carson."

"No, Rylan wouldn't do that."

Thirty minutes later, after trying Rylan's number and leaving him several messages, Destry rushed into the hospital. She hurried down the hall toward the sound of raised voices, recognizing WT's and the sheriff's.

"Have you lost your mind?" Sheriff Frank Curry demanded. He was standing in the waiting room beside WT's wheelchair. There was no sign of Margaret.

"Rylan West shot my boy!" WT bellowed.

"So you decided to take the law into your own hands by offering a fifty-thousand-dollar reward for Rylan West? Dead or alive?"

Destry gasped, but neither man heard her. Nor had either looked in her direction when she'd come into the room.

"That would be against the law," WT said.

"You sent Billy Westfall after him, knowing he'd bring Rylan West in draped over his horse. Damn you, WT. You've signed that cowboy's death warrant," Frank yelled.

"It's your deputy just doing his job, something I fear you are no longer capable of doing, Frank."

"You know Billy Westfall is a hothead. Hell, WT, if word gets out about this fifty-thousand-dollar reward you've offered, every other gun-crazy son of a bitch in the county will be after Rylan. Do you have any idea what you've done?"

"I'm just trying to get justice for my son."

A nurse stuck her head into the room and cautioned them to hold down their voices.

"When have you given a damn about justice?" the sheriff asked, lowering his voice. "You sure that's what you want, WT? Because if your son lives, there is more than a good chance I'm going to arrest him for Ginny West's murder. And if those vigilantes you sent out kill Rylan West, I'll be back with a warrant for your arrest, as well."

"On what charge? You can't prove I sent anyone after him. Nothing wrong with offering a reward for the arrest of whoever shot my son."

"I'll find some charge to lock up your sorry ass," the sheriff said.

"Excuse me."

Destry turned as a doctor appeared in the doorway behind her. WT and the sheriff also turned. Both seemed surprised to find her standing there. The sheriff looked embarrassed that she'd overheard them.

"You asked me to let you know when Carson Grant was conscious?" the doctor said. "He is asking to see the sheriff."

"To tell you that Rylan West shot him," WT said.

"Actually, he said Amos Thompson shot him," the doctor said. "Apparently he and Mr. Thompson got into an altercation outside the bar in Beartooth before the shooting. But I'll let him tell you himself."

Frank arrowed WT a withering look and swore as his radio squawked. He stepped away but came back a moment later. "Bethany Reynolds is missing. Clete found her SUV abandoned beside the road."

"You just get the man who shot my son," WT ordered. "I'm sure Bethany Reynolds is fine. Carson said he gave her a ride to Big Timber earlier."

"Carson gave her a ride?" The sheriff swore. "Call your vigilantes off, WT, and pray that you aren't too late. You do remember how to pray, don't you?"

"Have you forgotten I saved your life?" WT called after him. "You wouldn't be here right now if it wasn't for me."

Frank stopped and turned. "No, WT, I haven't forgotten. You've just gone too far this time."

"Call those men you sent after Rylan right now and tell them he didn't shoot my brother," Destry demanded.

But WT only shook his head. "It's too late. Lucky saw Rylan headed into the mountains. He and Westfall have already gone after him."

CHAPTER TWENTY-TWO

THE SUN WAS just cresting the horizon when Destry reached the ranch. She glanced toward the Crazies, golden in the cold fall morning light. Rylan had gone up into the mountains just as he'd said he was going to, and now he had a bounty on his head and two men hunting him, probably more.

The only edge she had was that she knew where Rylan was headed. All she could do was pray that Billy Westfall and Lucky Larson didn't.

She was in the barn when she heard the creak of the wheelchair. She didn't turn, couldn't bear to look at WT right now.

"Where do you think you're going?" he demanded behind her.

"I'm going after Rylan before you get him killed."

"The hell you are."

She continued to saddle her horse. Life was a choice, she saw that now, and she was making hers. Since her brother's return, she'd been fighting to save him and the ranch. Now she knew that she couldn't save either. But she might be able to save Rylan.

"After everything that saddle tramp's done to hurt you, you'd risk your life for him?" WT asked.

"What about what you've done to me?" she snapped, turning on him.

WT had the good grace to lower his gaze but said in his defense, "Whatever I did, it was for your own good."

She glared at him as she turned to slap her saddlebag closed and reached for the reins. "Don't try to stop me."

"How could I?" he said, indicating the wheelchair.

"You couldn't, even if you weren't in that chair. Maybe it's time you quit using it as an excuse."

"Just like your mother," he said in disgust.

She swung around again, all her anger, frustration and pain coming out as she looked into the face of the man who, for twenty-eight years, had been her father. "You couldn't possibly understand what it's like to really love someone, to forgive them for hurting you, to be willing to give up everything for them. I love Rylan, and someone has to stop this."

"You'll get yourself killed if you go up there."

She shook her head sadly. "Then I will die trying." She led her horse out of the barn and swung up into the saddle.

"You might need this," she heard WT say behind her.

She turned, and he wheeled over to hand her the rifle and scabbard she'd overlooked in her anger.

Their eyes met for a moment. She thought she glimpsed something akin to regret in his eyes. She took the rifle, and as she spurred her horse, she heard him say, "Good luck."

WT GRANT WATCHED her ride off, surprised he was fighting back tears. She'd always been a natural on the back of a horse. Her back was straight, her head high. She'd also been as stubborn as any woman he'd ever known. Damn if she *wouldn't* die trying to save the man she loved.

"Fool woman," he muttered even as he felt a surge of pride that threatened to close his throat. Sometimes she was so much like her mother and enough like him, that she really could have been his daughter.

"She's gone after Rylan, hasn't she?" Margaret said next to him. He hadn't heard her join him. He ignored her, not wanting her to see his moment of weakness.

"I've never told you what to do," she continued.

He snorted at that, but it didn't shut her up.

"This time, though, I can't sit back and see you make the biggest mistake of your life, and for a man like you, who has made so many…"

"I tried to stop her from going," he said in his defense, although he hated defending himself to her. Probably because he knew soul deep that he had no defense for the things he'd done.

"I'm not talking about her riding off to find Rylan. I'm talking about this ranch that you've spent your life building."

"I'm doing the only thing I can."

"Oh, stop being such an old fool and treating me like one, as well," Margaret shot back. "You're leaving the ranch to that louse of a son of yours to get back at Lila for hurting you. The only way you can get even with her is by punishing her daughter, who just happens to be the only person in your life, besides me, who gives a damn about you."

He didn't answer. Couldn't since he knew what she was saying was probably true.

"Destry is *your* daughter, Waylon, in every way that matters. She's never been anyone else's. She's a hell of a lot more like you than Carson is, and she loves this ranch. She still loves you, even as difficult as you have made it. You die and leave this mess the way it is, and I will never forgive you."

"Butt out of my business, old woman."

He could feel her still standing there, but he couldn't look at her. He couldn't bear to.

"Just remember. You brought this on yourself." She dropped an envelope on his lap. With that, she turned and stormed off muttering "old man" and a few choice words he wished he hadn't heard.

He didn't need to open the envelope to know what was inside, but he did anyway. Margaret had quit him. He balled up the short note and threw it as far as he could. He'd never felt more alone sitting there in the dim light of the barn as the sun rose over the land he'd fought so hard for. Dust motes danced in the air like the remnants of failure.

The damned woman was right about one thing. He was an old fool who'd already made way too many mistakes in his life, and he feared he was about to make another one. But that had never stopped him before.

SHERIFF FRANK CURRY had his hands full. His trigger-happy deputy Billy Westfall hadn't just taken off in the mountains after Rylan and the reward. He'd left word at the office that he'd deputized Lucky Larson, one of WT's former ranch hands, to go with him.

Frank swore that no matter what pull Billy had with his grandfather, he was sacking him—if Billy lived long enough. He couldn't help worrying about Billy and Lucky armed and dangerous up there in the Crazies. Rylan had no idea what was coming after him. Frank just hoped to hell Rylan West saw them before they saw him.

His radio squawked. It had been doing that all morning with one problem to solve after another. Clete had been calling him repeatedly for updates on his missing wife. So far, Frank hadn't located her. Where he wanted to be was in the Crazies looking for Rylan West, but that wasn't possible with everything that was going on down here in the valley and him one deputy shy.

"It's Bethany Reynolds," the dispatcher said. "You want me to patch her through?"

He breathed a sigh of relief as he took her call. He'd been trying to contact her. "Bethany, where are you?"

"I need to talk to you."

He needed to talk to her as well about the locket. "Okay, just tell me where you are."

"You won't tell Clete?" she asked, sounding scared.

"Not until we talk." He took down the address. "I'm on my way."

Bethany was staying at an out-of-the-way motel in Big Timber. She'd registered under an assumed name after telling the clerk that her husband was after her and trying to kill her.

"Is that true?" Frank asked once they were settled in her motel room. He took the chair by the window, while Bethany said she was too nervous to sit.

"Clete killing me?" she asked. "It's possible once he finds out…." She started to cry. "I've done something awful."

Through tears and nose-blowing, she told the story.

"He used to come into the Branding Iron Café after the regulars had left and we would sit in a back booth and talk. He seemed so lonely. I felt sorry for him at first."

Frank heard the catch in her throat. He knew what

was coming. As impatient as he was, he didn't interrupt Bethany's story. He let her tell it the way she seemed to need to.

"I would make him laugh and smile, and he said that seeing me helped him get through the day," Bethany continued, her gaze shying away. "Then one day he came out to the house to drop something off for Clete. After that, we started meeting. At first we would just talk, and then…"

"One thing led to another?" Frank offered.

She nodded. "I knew it was wrong, but he was so sweet and he needed me and I guess I needed him. He listened. Clete doesn't listen. And Grayson does little romantic things."

"Grayson?" Frank hadn't been able to keep the shock out of his voice. "Grayson Brooks, the local contractor?"

Bethany nodded through her tears.

"He gave me the locket, the one Rylan took from me and gave to you."

Rylan had suspected the man who'd given his sister the locket was Tom Armstrong, but when Frank had talked to Tom, the pastor had denied not only having an affair with Ginny, but also giving her a locket. Not that even pastors weren't apt to lie about something like this.

"Grayson gave you the locket?" His tone must have given him away because she started to cry harder. When Frank had compared them, he'd seen that the lockets appeared to be identical.

But Grayson Brooks? He'd known Grayson all his life. The entire community wanted to make him a saint because of how he doted on his sick wife. Anytime anyone needed something done, Grayson would show up with his tools and fix whatever it was.

Frank had been in law enforcement long enough that he knew people often had secret lives. But this was one he couldn't get his head around.

"Is it true he gave a locket just like it to Ginny?" Bethany asked.

"It appears so."

She hugged herself, eyes wide with fear. "Is he going to kill me, too?"

THE COTTONWOODS ALONG the creek were like a golden thread woven into the pale fabric of the land as Destry rode into the Crazy Mountains. The land changed with the altitude, going from the rich grasslands to the stands of shimmering aspens still clinging to their leaves, to a sprinkling of pines and finally into the heavy timber. The wildflowers that had blanketed the ground all summer had dried, their heads now bobbing in the breeze as she passed.

Ahead the land rose in sheer rock bluffs. She wound her way along the granite faces and through the dark green of the pines, watching for any sign of Rylan's tracks—or the men after him. Mottled sunlight fingered its way down through the branches.

Clouds obscured the peaks, sending down a cold biting wind that moaned through the boughs of the trees and bent the buckskin-colored grasses under its will. The mountains were dark, a deep blue, the color deepening as the day wore on. The tops of the pines swayed and sighed with the wind, the cold deepening the higher she rode up the mountain.

Destry looked back only once at the ranch she loved. She'd made her choice.

She found the first fresh tracks a few miles from the ranch. One horse and rider headed back in. Rylan. With relief she saw that no one else had crossed his tracks. At least not yet. The hours passed, the October sun doing little to warm the air here in the mountains.

As she crossed the creek, the water rushing clear over the rocks, a buck came bounding out of the brush, startling her and her horse. Instinctively she reached for the rifle in her scabbard, only to relax as the deer crashed through the brush and disappeared.

Destry knew she was jumpy. Ahead, a stand of aspen blazed orange, the leaves fluttering in the wind. Over the roar of the creek and the wind in the trees, she knew she wouldn't be able to hear any other riders until she was almost on top of them—and they wouldn't be able to hear her.

She told herself that Billy Westfall didn't know where Rylan had gone. More than likely he would head for the Forest Service cabin over on the North Fork. That would cost Billy hours.

In the distance, a coyote howled. The eerie sound made her flesh crawl. She felt alone and vulnerable. It was a new feeling, one she resented. She'd never been afraid here.

But then she'd never had anything to fear other than a grizzly or bad weather. Now she had at least two men up here in the high country with her, both armed and determined to find Rylan West and collect the reward. She doubted they would let anything or anyone stop them—especially up here where there was no law. Up here, it was every man for himself.

GRAYSON BROOKS STUDIED his wife. Anna's eyes were closed, her thin lashes fluttering like tiny bird wings against her pale cheeks. Her color was fairly good today, compared to what it had been just a few days ago.

The hand he held was so thin, just skin and bones, and yet so delicate, just like Anna. He'd fallen for her the moment he'd seen her. People joked about love at first sight, but it had been exactly that.

She'd stepped into a ray of sunshine. Her strawberry blond hair had seemed to catch fire, lighting up her delicate features. Her wide blue eyes were bright as the freckles that had dusted her cheeks and nose. She'd looked so innocent, so pure, as if she'd been saving herself for only him.

Grayson looked from Anna to Dr. Flaggler, who was slowly packing up his medical bag. Neither spoke as the doctor headed for the door. Grayson watched Anna's chest rise and fall before he let go of her limp hand and followed the doctor out.

"She's better," Grayson said, practically challenging the doctor to disagree.

Dr. Flaggler nodded, his keen old eyes the palest of grays. Grayson saw compassion brimming there. "Cancer patients often seem to bounce back some during the final stages."

Grayson shook his head angrily and turned away to hide the burn of tears. "She's only forty-two." But she'd been sick for the past fifteen of those years.

"I'm sorry." The doctor had said this each time the cancer had returned. But each time, Anna had been able to fight it. Each time, though, the fight had taken a toll on her body. Now she was frail, little fight left in her.

"What about chemo or some new drug?" Grayson asked as he walked the doctor out to his car.

Dr. Flaggler shook his head as he opened his door

and tossed in his medical bag. They'd had this discussion already. He could see the finality in the doctor's expression.

"A month at the most. A couple of weeks are probably more realistic." The doctor met Grayson's gaze. "She should get her affairs in order."

With that, the doctor climbed into his car and left.

Grayson stared after him for a moment before going back to the house. Anna's *affairs?* The word ate at him the way her cancer had eaten away inside her body.

When she'd first been diagnosed, he'd told himself that it was his penance. He'd prayed for forgiveness and the cancer had gone into remission.

Each time he'd strayed, the cancer had come back. This time, it was going to kill the only woman he'd ever truly loved.

He'd never been strong. Not like Anna. Nor was he as forgiving. She knew of his needs, the hunger in him that was not unlike cancer. It ate away inside him. He'd prayed not to feel this need. He knew it had nothing to do with sex and everything to do with finding that old Anna, the one he'd lost. He'd filled that need with a young body and pretended.

But Anna had known. He'd seen the pain in her eyes each time. As careful as he'd been, she always knew. His infidelity had sickened her. It had been no surprise when it had appeared as cancer in the breast over her heart.

"Grayson?" Her voice was a whisper. She reached for his hand.

"I'm here, sweetheart."

He closed her hand in his, and she drew him closer.

He had to bend down, putting his ear practically against her lips to hear her.

As he listened, tears welled and spilled. He brushed at them with his free hand. Drawing back, he met her gaze.

"How can you forgive me?" he whispered.

She shook her head, but the movement seemed to have exhausted her. She closed her eyes, her hand went limp in his.

He gently placed it on the bed next to her. At the sound of a vehicle coming up the road, he left her, closing the door to her room.

SHERIFF FRANK CURRY sat in front of the house for a few moments before he climbed out of his patrol pickup. For too many years, he'd been the one who brought the bad news.

"I'm sorry but your son has been killed in a bar fight."

"I'm sorry but your daughter was in a car accident tonight on the way home. There was nothing the doctors could do."

He hated that part of his job. He was fine with arresting bad guys or even questioning those he suspected were guilty. But this was the first time his investigation had brought him to the door of a person he would never have suspected.

"Afternoon, Sheriff," Grayson Brooks said as he opened his front door. "Why don't we talk out here on the porch so we don't disturb Anna? She's resting."

Frank nodded and took one of the chairs at the end of the long porch. The sun slanted down to coat the floorboards in warmth. A light breeze stirred the tall pale grass in the field. In the distance, a dozen Angus cattle stood, red as blood in the sunlight.

"I think you know why I'm here," the sheriff said as Grayson took a seat and stretched out his long legs. He had a kind, open face. Today he looked older than his forty-five years. Usually he could pass for much younger. Frank could see how both Ginny and Bethany would have felt safe with this man.

"I need to ask you about Ginny West and Bethany Reynolds," Frank said.

Grayson nodded but didn't look at him.

Frank pulled a tape recorder out of his jacket pocket, set it on the porch railing, turned it on and, after the preliminaries, said, "You gave both Ginny West and Bethany Reynolds a heart-shaped locket, is that right?"

"I gave it to Anna on the day we were married."

"And you gave one to Ginny West and later Bethany?"

He nodded, tears welling in his eyes. "I gave them a locket like Anna's so they could wear it when we…" He took a deep breath and let it out. "When we were together."

"Was Ginny West carrying your baby?"

Grayson swallowed, his face a mask of pain. "Anna always wanted a baby, but she couldn't have one. How is it that often the women who so desperately want a baby can't have one and the others…"

"I have to ask you, Grayson, what happened the night Ginny West died?"

He shook his head.

"You didn't meet Ginny that night in town?"

"I met her." For a long moment, he seemed lost in the past. "She'd called upset because she'd gotten another note, a Bible quote. I didn't know what to do. It seemed so unfair that she was pregnant. I wanted a baby with Anna, not Ginny. I should never have gotten involved with her. She was so young, so…innocent."

Frank waited for him to continue.

"That night, I told her I would pay for an abortion. Or if she was determined to have the baby, I would pay her to leave town and continue to support her as long as she kept my part a secret."

Frank could well imagine how that had gone over. He thought of Ginny, how pretty and sweet she'd been. He tried to imagine what she'd seen in Grayson, who would have been thirty-four to her twenty. What Frank saw was a lonely, sad man with a sick wife. Whatever Ginny had seen that attracted her, it must have been the same thing Bethany had seen.

"We met at the Royale."

That would explain why she'd left the ranch pickup behind the bar that night. It would have been easy to walk down to her old abandoned theater without being seen. It would also explain why the hair clip was found there.

"She cried and then she got mad because she didn't want to hear that I wasn't going to leave Anna. We argued. I heard someone coming and left, promising that we would talk again when we were both calmer."

"She was alive when you left?"

He didn't answer, again seeming lost in the past. "I just left her there. I went out the back way and drove home to Anna. I told her everything." He broke down, his next words barely audible. "She forgave me. She always forgives me, no matter what I do."

Frank allowed him time to pull himself together before he asked, "Do you have any idea who left the Bible quotes for her?"

"No. Anna didn't just forgive me. She insisted that I help Ginny, that I be a father to my child." He looked as if he might break down again. Grayson Brooks had always seemed like such a strong man. Frank saw now how his weakness had been slowly eroding him over the years.

"Grayson, I have to ask you. Did you kill Ginny?"

"Kill Ginny?" He seemed shocked by the question.

"You said yourself you wanted her to either get rid of the baby or leave town. You had the most to lose."

He shook his head. "I had everything to gain. Anna and I wanted the child Ginny was carrying to be part of our lives. You should be talking to Carson. He went into the theater as I left. I thought maybe he and Ginny would get back together. I knew she still cared about him. That was until I heard she'd been murdered."

"If that's the case, then, Grayson, why didn't you come forward with this information?" Frank demanded.

"By then, it was clear that Carson had killed her. I figured it was just a matter of time before he was arrested."

"You also didn't want anyone to know about you and Ginny."

Grayson hung his head as if in shame. "It was bad enough what I'd done. I didn't see what the point was in having the whole county talking. If Ginny had lived, then it would have been different. But with her and the baby gone, I had to think of Anna." His voice broke. "I couldn't do that to her. Anyway, I had good reason to assume that Carson Grant would be arrested for what he'd done, since I wasn't the only one who saw him go into the theater that night."

"Who else saw him?"

"Bob Benton. He was coming back from one of his nightly walks and I saw him cut between the buildings and stop. There's a window where he was standing that looks down into the room where I left Ginny. I saw him glance in. He would have seen Ginny and Carson together. He might have even seen Carson kill her before getting rid of her body on the road out of town."

"What was Bob Benton doing between the buildings?"

Grayson shrugged. "He didn't come forward, either?" Frank shook his head. "I wonder why?"

Frank was wondering the same thing as he shut off the digital recorder. "Did you love Ginny?" he asked.

He looked confused by the question. "I love *Anna*. She's the only woman I've ever loved."

"Then why the affairs?"

Grayson again looked surprised. "They reminded me of Anna when Anna and I first met. They had this sweet innocence about them. For a few stolen hours I could pretend they were her—before the cancer."

CHAPTER TWENTY-THREE

A BLUE GROUSE rose from the deep grass in a thunder of wings. The mare reared, almost unseating Destry. But she hung tight as the grouse flew off into the fading light. A quiet dropped like a shroud over the mountains.

She settled the horse and fastened her gaze again on the dense timber ahead. The mare's ears prickled, and Destry thought she caught the scent of a campfire on the wind.

On the ride up, she'd crossed elk and deer tracks but no horseshoe tracks other than the single ones she'd been following. She'd stopped long enough to let the mare eat some grass and get a drink from the creek while she scanned the mountainside with her binoculars.

She ate some jerky, sniffed the air for the scent of a campfire again but found none. Nor could she see anything in the darkness of the heavy timber ahead. The sunlight was now obscured by low clouds. The day had become bleak and the wind stung. A pewter-gray sky hung over the top of the snow-capped peaks.

As she rode through a tight canyon between the peaks, she spotted a patch of burnt earth where someone had recently made a fire. Climbing down off her horse, she inspected the tracks around the small fire ring. Two men. She'd stumbled onto Billy the Kid's camp. But she wasn't the only one, she saw. Someone else had been here. Rylan? Or was someone else tracking them, hoping to collect on the reward?

The cold dampness seemed to soak through her duster all the way to her bones. She could see tiny crystallized snowflakes dancing in the air. A snowstorm was imminent. It wouldn't be hard to get snowed-in up here in the high country this time of year. She'd brought what food she could pack, but not enough if she couldn't get out of the mountains in a few days.

Destry looked toward the mountain peaks ahead of her. Rylan was up there. She could feel his presence. Just a little farther. The clouds hung heavy and damp with the promise of a snowstorm, but there was no turning back now. She couldn't leave Rylan up here with killers on the hunt.

She climbed back on her horse, urging the mare forward.

THE VALLEY WAS bathed in the warm rays of the sunset, but a bank of dark clouds had settled in the Crazies, Sheriff Frank Curry noticed as he drove toward Beartooth.

He was wondering when the first snow would blanket the lower ground and stay for the rest of the winter, when he spotted Bob Benton's pickup coming down the road toward him. He hit his siren and lights. Bob drove on past and didn't appear to be slowing down.

Flipping a U-turn in the middle of the two-lane, Frank went after him, noticing that Bob had his camper shell on the back of his truck, and it appeared to be full of boxes. After talking to Grayson Brooks, the sheriff had left Bob a message asking that he call him. He hadn't heard a word, and now Bob seemed to be leaving town.

Frank got right up behind the pickup, flashed his headlights and started to pull alongside, when Bob finally slowed and pulled over to the edge of the road. There wasn't any traffic, but then there seldom was on this stretch.

Getting out of his patrol pickup, Frank walked up to the driver's side of Bob's truck.

"I know I wasn't going over the speed limit," Bob said after rolling down his window. "I got a taillight out or somethin'?"

It was just getting dark enough that the glow of the dash lights inside the pickup cast an eerie light over Bob's face. Frank could see that the man was sweating, even though the night was cold, a chill wind blowing through the truck window.

"You didn't get my message?"

"Your message?" Bob echoed.

Frank pulled off his flashlight and shone it into the windows of the camper shell. "That's quite a load. You moving?"

Bob hesitated. "It's a private matter, Frank."

"I'm going to need to see your license, registration and proof of insurance."

"You have to be kidding." He let out an impatient sigh and began digging the documentation out with obvious irritation. "If this is about me and Nettie—"

"Actually, it's about Ginny West."

Bob froze in midmotion of pulling his registration from his glove box. When he did move, it was slowly. "Ginny West?" he repeated.

"I have a witness who saw you standing by the theater that night."

He handed Frank his license and papers. "A witness?"

"I think I'd better follow you to the sheriff's department," Frank said after giving all three pieces of information a cursory glance.

"Is that really necessary?" Bob asked. He'd paled in the pickup's dash lights.

"I need your statement. The quicker I get it, the sooner you can be on your way."

Bob started to whir up his window.

"Uh, Bob. You can't outrun me in this pickup of yours, so I hope you won't try."

Bob looked sick and scared, like a man with a horrible secret.

NETTIE DIDN'T GO up to the house until she knew Bob was gone. She'd seen his pickup go by in front of the store. He'd had the camper shell on the back but she could tell he hadn't taken all that much.

No man could pack up all his belongings in such a short period of time. And yet she knew he was gone. As he'd driven past the store, he'd turned, as if knowing she would be looking out.

She'd seen his expression and known he wouldn't be back for anything he'd left. It depressed her that the sum of his life with her could be loaded in the bed of a small pickup.

Nettie finally had to go up to the house after he'd left just to see. She opened the door and stepped in, listening. It didn't seem any different. She half expected to see Bob in his chair, asleep, a book lying open on his lap.

His chair was empty, but the book he'd just finished was on the small table next to it. She made a note to herself to get rid of the chair. Then she turned and walked back down the mountain to the store.

As she started into the back, she glanced into the woods at the bear trap the FWP had dropped off. It was still empty.

Nettie shot a look over her shoulder, the skin prickling on her neck. She'd be glad when they caught that damned grizzly.

Putting Bob and the bear out of her mind, she walked through the store to the front window. Kate LaFond was serving a table of ranchers and their wives who'd come in for dinner.

Past her, Nettie could see the old garage where she'd seen the café owner digging. Had the woman been playing with her?

Nettie shook her head. Kate LaFond was hiding something, and if it took until her last dying breath, Nettie intended to find out what it was.

"HOW ABOUT YOU start by telling me the truth?" Sheriff Frank Curry suggested.

Bob Benton sat across from him in the interrogation room, looking as nervous as a heifer in a bullpen. They'd been going at this for some time.

"Did. You. Kill. Ginny West?"

"No," Bob cried. "I told you. I had nothing to do with it." He was sweating profusely, his face red and blotchy.

"But you were there that night and you're obviously hiding something."

"Maybe I should call a lawyer."

"Do you need one?" Frank asked.

Bob swallowed.

"Listen, if you didn't kill her, but you saw something that will help in this investigation, then you have to tell me. Bob, what are you afraid of?"

"That what I tell you will incriminate me."

Frank chewed on that for a moment. "Short of murder, you have nothing to worry about. What did you see?"

Bob looked like a man in physical pain. "Can't you turn off the tape recorder?"

Hesitating only a moment, Frank shut off the recorder and waited.

"I go for walks at night." He couldn't meet Frank's gaze. The sheriff watched Bob swallow and felt his stomach roil. What secret was Bob Benton about to reveal?

"The witness saw you between the buildings by the theater," Frank prodded. "The witness said there's a window that looks down on the room where Ginny West was and that you were seen looking into it. What did you see?"

Bob began to cry in huge silent body-racking sobs. "I saw them making love."

Frank felt a chill settle deep in his bones. "You saw Ginny and *Carson* making love?"

Bob nodded but kept his head down, his body jerking with the sobs.

It was the same room where he and Lynette had both lost their virginity and probably a lot of other girls in town, Frank realized. Did Bob know that?

He suddenly felt sick to his stomach as he realized

why Bob had been beside that building that night and no doubt many other nights.

The man was a Peeping Tom. It was all Frank could do not to lose his temper and do something he would regret. He swallowed back the bitter taste in his mouth, the revulsion, the fury, and asked, "Did you see him kill her?"

"No," Bob said, wiping his face as he glanced up with red-rimmed eyes and quickly looked away. "I left."

Frank studied him for a long moment. There was more. He could feel it. "But you went back."

The room fell silent.

Bob stilled, then nodded and began to cry again. "It was horrible. The blood." He began to cough as if he was going to be sick.

Frank kicked the trash can over to him, but Bob managed to pull himself together after a moment.

"Did you see the killer?"

"Carson. He was mopping up the blood. He had blood on him."

"Did you see Ginny or the weapon in his hand?"

"No. I ran." He lowered his head further, a broken man.

Frank would have loved to have thrown Bob in a cell down the hall, but the Peeping Tom law was weak at best. In a case like this, the only thing he could hold him on was withholding information in a criminal investigation. "Where were you headed when I pulled you over?"

It took Bob a moment before he raised his head. "Arizona. Quartzite."

"I'll need you to sign a statement. You might as well get yourself a motel, because I can't let you leave town.

Not yet. And Bob, if and when you get to Arizona, get some help."

"I will. I promise."

As soon as he had Bob Benton's signed statement, the sheriff headed for the hospital to arrest Carson Grant.

IT BEGAN TO SNOW, huge flakes that whirled on the wind and pelted Destry as she rode through a narrow gap between two rock cliffs. She shivered against the cold. Her body ached from the long ride, from the fear that had settled in as painful as the snowy cold. The country opened a little, but between the trees and the snow, she couldn't see five feet in front of her face.

She climbed off the mare to walk the last part, praying Rylan hadn't changed his mind and turned back. Or worse, that Billy and Lucky had already found him. An eerie quiet blanketed the mountainside that not even the wind in the pines could chase away.

Destry suddenly felt entirely alone, as if she was the only one on this mountain. It was a strange, alien feeling because it came with a fear that this time her headstrong determination was going to get her killed, and Billy Westfall might be the least of her worries.

Being trapped in the mountains in a late fall storm was deadly. Even if she changed her mind and headed back now, she wouldn't make it. Not with the snow falling so hard, not with the temperature dropping so quickly.

Her mare needed rest. So did she. The horse stumbled, as if bringing home just how dire the situation had become.

The snow swirled around her on a gust of wind. Her head came up, her heart pounding as she caught a whiff of campfire smoke. But at the same time, the mare snorted and pulled back on the reins, ears up, sensing something on the wind.

Destry patted the horse as she drew her rifle from the scabbard. She tried to see ahead through the trees but the blowing snow was blinding. Stumbling forward, leading her horse, she followed the scent of the campfire as she cradled her rifle. She'd always been a better shot than her brother, especially with a rifle. She just hoped she wouldn't have to use it.

As she was almost out of the dense pines, she came up short. The small fire she'd smelled had burned down to only coals. She could see where someone had made a camp against the cliffs and a fallen pine, but there was no one there.

Her heart and hopes plummeted. Rylan had been here, but he was gone.

A limb snapped off to her left. She swung the rifle. A dark shape came out of the pines. Her finger trembled on the trigger for an instant before the man took shape, and she saw his face.

"Could you please lower that rifle?" Rylan said. "You're making me nervous."

CHAPTER TWENTY-FOUR

RYLAN SHOOK HIS head as if he couldn't believe she was here. His gaze locked with hers.

She lowered the rifle, but she didn't dare move, didn't dare breathe, as he took a step toward her. The look in his eyes held her motionless as he closed the distance until they were merely inches apart.

He lifted his hand slowly as if gentling a skittish horse. His fingers brushed back a tendril of her wet hair, his rough fingertips skimmed over the tender skin of her cheek, sending a shiver through her.

"I'm glad you don't try to cover your freckles," he whispered hoarsely.

His warm brown eyes were dark with a desire she knew well. His touch, the way he was looking at her, it sent her pulse into a full gallop.

His hand slipped beneath her braid to cup the nape of her neck. He slowly drew her to him. His gaze locked with hers as his mouth dropped to hers.

Her breath escaped in a rush, a soft moan that spilled from her. He drew back to look into her eyes again. "Destry." The word came out half plea, half curse. "What the hell are you doing here in the middle of a snowstorm?"

"Looking for you."

"Well, you found me," he said, his voice as rough as his fingertips.

The words tumbled out in a rush as she told him about Carson being shot, WT offering a fifty-thousand-dollar reward for Rylan, and Billy Westfall teaming up with Lucky Larson to come after him.

Rylan nodded. "I suspected *something* was up. I saw a campfire down the mountain and checked it out. I gathered Westfall and Larson were looking for me, so I gave them a couple of trails to follow. I just assumed it was over the dustup between me and your brother."

"Dustup? Is that what you call it?" She noticed that his right eye was turning a little black-and-blue and his cut lip was in the process of healing.

"It's been coming for a long time. You know that. But I never would have shot him."

"I know that. It's another reason I'm here."

"So you trust me?" His grin was crooked, but his gaze was intent.

Did she? She loved him, but she wasn't sure she could trust him with her heart. She heard his horse whinny somewhere in the distance. "You heard me coming."

He nodded and smiled. "I thought the deputy and your ranch hand might be smarter than I figured them." He sobered. "I'm sorry about your brother. Is he going to be all right?"

"The bullet missed anything of importance. Amos Thompson was the one who shot him, but by the time Carson was conscious and told the sheriff…"

"Your father had put a reward out for me. Fifty thousand?" He let out a low whistle. "I'm impressed. I didn't know I was worth that much."

"That's not funny. They're probably tracking you as we speak."

He shook his head. "They were traveling light. I'm

sure by now they have been forced to turn back. They clearly weren't as determined as you. Nor as well prepared for the weather," he said, taking in her duster.

He still had his hand cupped around the nape of her neck. His fingers gently caressing her warm skin, making it feel hot under his touch.

"Come on, let's get out of this weather. I moved the camp when the storm came in." He led her and her horse around the cliff face to where fallen rocks had made a windbreak. Rylan's camp was back under an overhang of rock that had formed a cave of sorts. "I was just about to get another fire going."

She took care of her horse, hobbling the mare with his in the pines. By the time she returned with her saddlebags, Rylan had a warm fire blazing at the edge of the entrance into the rocks. She piled her gear with his out of the falling snow back under the rocks. When she turned, she saw that he was watching her, his eyes dark again.

He shrugged out of his slicker and dropped it on a rock nearby. "You came all this way to warn me, huh? Even after I got in a fight with your brother?"

She removed her slicker, as well. Water ran from it in rivulets of melted snow. "Why does that surprise you?"

He laughed. "Everything about you continues to surprise me." Their eyes locked as the smoke from the campfire curled up and out into the falling snow. Past it, thick, lacy snowflakes fell in a silent shroud, blanketing the country below them.

Destry felt the warmth of the fire heat her face. Or was it Rylan's gaze? It was hot enough to melt away the last of her misgivings. She felt herself go liquid inside. It didn't matter what was happening down in the valley. She and Rylan couldn't change any of it. All of that would play itself out, one way or another. She had given up on saving her brother or the ranch.

But she hadn't given up on Rylan. Couldn't. She'd had to make a choice. She'd chosen the man she loved.

"I came after you because I've never stopped loving you. Never will. No matter what happens up here or below these mountains," she said. "You can either take me on those terms or not."

He grinned. "That's laying it right out there." His grin faded, his gaze smoldering coals. "It won't be easy," he said, shoving back his Stetson.

She smiled. "When has it ever been easy for us?"

His gaze blazed hotter than the fire burning behind him as he took two long strides and pulled her roughly to him. Her heart took off like a shot. This time the kiss was pure passion, his mouth taking possession of hers the way he'd taken possession of her heart years ago.

He hooked an arm around her waist and pulled her against the solid sinew of his body as his other hand brushed across her cheek, sending shivers ricocheting through her. Her chest crushed against his, and she swore she could feel the thunderous beat of his strong, resilient heart.

She slipped her arms around his neck as he swept her up and carried her over to his sleeping bag stretched out on soft earth.

"I've always wished that our first time had been in a proper bed," he said as he lowered her, his face inches from her own. "Not happening this time, either. Maybe someday, huh?"

His words ignited the fire that she'd kept banked for eleven long years as she watched him toss aside his coat.

As he leaned down to kiss her again, she grabbed each side of his Western shirt and jerked, hearing the snaps sing. Her palms pressed the warm sun-browned flesh over the hard contours of his broad chest, desperately needing to feel him pressed against her.

She traced along a familiar scar, then ran her fingers over several new ones. Her gaze lifted to his and she felt tears burn her eyes. "You've been hurt," she said in a choked whisper.

"We've both been hurt," he said as he lowered himself onto the sleeping bag beside her and took her in his arms.

RYLAN FELT HER face pressed against his bare chest, felt the hot tears and pulled her closer. "I'm so sorry, Destry, for leaving."

"All that matters is that you came back."

His lips found hers again. He pulled her on top of him, the crush of her lush rounded breasts firing a passion in him he'd never felt with any other woman.

"Destry," he breathed as she sat up and shrugged out of her coat, then her Western shirt, exposing a pretty pink bra. He could see the dark of her nipples beneath it. He felt a jolt of desire fire his body.

His gaze met hers as she unhooked the bra, releasing her full breasts. He drew her down, his mouth finding the hard tip of her nipples, his tongue caressing a moan from her lips.

Later he wouldn't remember taking off her jeans or his either. But he recalled the feel of her bare flesh against his, the heat of her skin and fire in her pale blue eyes like a flame that never died out.

He entered her, stealing her breath and his. She

arched against him, her hair fanned out across the sleeping bag. He cupped her buttock, lifting her into him until there was nothing between them, no breath of air, nothing but their passion and need and, yes, love, he thought as she shuddered against him, her face beautiful in the pleasured glow that heightened her freckles.

He loved this woman. Had never stopped loving her. He knew then that he couldn't live without her. As she'd said, whatever happened, he wasn't letting her go. Not again.

He looked into her eyes, saw to his amazement not just love but forgiveness lighting them. A moment later she let out another cry of pleasure as she arched against him. He finally let himself go, releasing all the pain, regret and guilt of the past eleven years.

Destry Grant loved him and he loved her, he thought holding her to him, their bodies glistening with sweat in the firelight as they tried to catch their breaths. Loving her was one thing, he realized as he looked into her eyes. Saving her was another. It was one thing to say she'd let go of everything. But he couldn't shake the fear that she was still dangerously involved in what was happening in the valley below these mountains—whether she wanted to be or not.

THE SHERIFF HAD called ahead. He knew Carson was being released from the hospital. He planned to be there.

"What are *you* doing here?" WT demanded when Frank walked into the hospital.

He'd hoped Margaret would be here. Unfortunately he didn't see her. "How is Carson?"

"He's going to live. They're releasing him. I'll be

taking him home." WT gave him a challenging look, daring him to say different.

Frank shook his head. "I can't let you do that. I'm going to have to take him in. Given the evidence and the eyewitness—"

WT let out a curse. "*Eyewitness?* Where the hell has this eyewitness been the past eleven years?"

The sheriff didn't answer. It would come out soon enough that Bob Benton had been there that night. Carson had admitted having intercourse with Ginny before her death.

Grayson had been her lover and met her that night at the theater. The pastor's wife had found her beside the road and had apparently attempted CPR. Because of all that, all of their DNA had been found on Ginny West's body or at the murder scene.

With Bob's testimony about seeing Carson with Ginny and later seeing blood on Carson, Frank thought he had a case that would stand up in court.

"I suspect you've seen this coming for eleven years," Frank said when WT quit swearing long enough for him to interrupt. "I don't think you would have sent Carson away unless you knew he was the one who'd killed that girl."

WT shook his head, but a lot of the fight seemed to have gone out of him. "He's my son. I was just protecting him." Beads of sweat had broken out on his forehead. He wiped at them with a shaky hand. "He has to take over the ranch. I've been waiting for that since the day he was born."

"I'm sorry."

"Are you?" WT looked pale and small in the wheelchair. "You think Carson is like me." He let out a humorless laugh. "But you're wrong. He's just like his mother. And Destry...."

Frank held his gaze. "Destry is just like you."

WT scoffed at that. "I suspect you know better than that."

"Lila and I were just friends. Never anything more. She loved you till her dying day."

WT swore again. "I know you think I killed her," WT said. "I wanted to, true enough. But I couldn't have hurt her..." His voice broke and he looked away. "Now you're going to put my son in prison to get back at me."

"That's not true, WT."

"Lila's horse spooked." He shook his head. "I know I should have left her where she fell. I knew you would never believe me. But I couldn't leave her there. I carried her down to the house and called you."

That had been WT's story, and there had been no way to prove otherwise, although Frank had always suspected there was more to it.

"This isn't about Lila," the sherrif said quietly.

"The hell is isn't." WT met his gaze with anger burning like a bonfire. "You think you were the only man to fall for my wife? Everyone loved Lila. *Everyone*," he said with a sneer.

"You're wrong about Lila, just as you're wrong about me." There was only one woman Frank had ever loved. Lynette.

WT shook his head, still fuming with a fury that encompassed the world around him. There was no reasoning with him.

"The best way you can help Carson is to get him a good lawyer," Frank said. "It will be up to a jury to decide if he's guilty. Everything else is in the past. Dragging it out won't stop your son from being arrested."

"Like hell. You do what I say or—" He broke off and grabbed his chest.

At first Frank thought he might be faking it. But all the color had drained from WT's face. An instant later, he slumped over in the wheelchair.

"WT? Nurse! Nurse!" Frank called until he saw one running toward them. "My friend. I think he's having a heart attack."

"Does WT know where you are?" Rylan asked as they lay together in the sleeping bag listening to the crackle of the fire. The flames licked with tongues of hot orange at the wood, shooting sparks up into the night like fireflies that drifted on the wind with snowflakes.

"We said our goodbyes in the barn," she said.

Rylan chuckled. "Let me guess. He wasn't happy about you riding up into the mountains to warn me."

She smiled. "You could say that."

"I'm sorry."

"Don't be. As people say about WT, it's complicated. He was my father for all these years, good or bad. Everyone said I was like him in temperament and like my mother in looks."

"You have never been like WT in temperament," Rylan said with a chuckle as he slowly ran his hand from her waist down the curve of her hip. "You said you didn't know who you were. But you do now, don't you?"

She looked into his eyes and smiled. "Destry Grant."

He laughed. "Well, Destry Grant, I hope to change that. How do you like the sound of Destry West?"

She blinked.

"I didn't mean to do it this way. But nothing about our relationship has been what you'd call usual. The thing is, I don't want to wait another day to make you my wife. Say yes, woman."

She laughed, tears pooling in her beautiful blue eyes. "Yes."

"Someday our children are going to ask us where we were when daddy proposed," he warned her. "What are you going to tell them?"

Destry laughed. "That we were in the Crazies in a snowstorm beside a crackling fire, and that it was the most romantic moment your father could have ever chosen."

SOMETIME DURING THE NIGHT, the storm broke. Destry woke to see blue sky and sunshine. The snow glittered like billions of diamonds, so bright that it hurt her eyes.

Rylan stirred beside her. They lay in each other's arms like that for a long while. As she stared out at the beautiful day, she wished they could stay here forever. The snow had turned everything a silken virginal white. It was dazzling.

Just as being here in Rylan's arms felt amazing. But she knew they couldn't stay here forever. They would have to go back, and she feared what was waiting for them.

"There's something I need to tell you," she said, her words coming out on a white cloud in the cold morning air. "WT's not well." She could tell Rylan didn't know what to say. "He apparently doesn't have much time left."

"Like you said, he's your father, the only one you've ever had."

She nodded. "I can't help the way I feel, no matter how he's behaved toward me or what he's done."

Rylan hugged her. "You have to go back."

She nodded against him. "I do."

"We'll go together."

Just then, she heard the *whomp whomp* of helicopter blades. The horses whinnied, and Rylan was out of the sleeping bag and pulling on his jeans and boots as he rushed to the opening of the rocks.

Destry wasn't far behind him. She watched the helicopter hover over the open snowfield twenty yards away, then slowly set down in a shower of snow. It wasn't until she saw Sheriff Frank Curry waving to her that she knew that the fear she'd awakened with this morning was real.

"It's WT," the sheriff said when he'd made his way through eight inches of fresh powder to reach them. "He's had a heart attack. He wanted me to find you."

She nodded. "I need to see him."

"We'll have to hurry," Frank said.

Rylan promised to bring her horse out as soon as he could break camp. "I'll see you at the hospital later." He hugged her tightly before letting her go. She clung to him for a moment. Frank assured her that Billy Westfall and Lucky Larson were no longer a problem. They had come out of the mountains last night, both suffering from hypothermia and half dead. WT had retracted his reward for Rylan.

She hurried to the helicopter, telling herself it didn't matter that she and WT didn't share the same blood. They'd shared their love for the ranch and Montana. WT was her father and he was dying.

Rylan waved, standing in the snow in front of the

rock cliff. As the chopper lifted and turned toward Big
Timber, she lost sight of him. Out the window, the day
shone like a jewel as they flew along the edge of the
mountains, Crazy Peak rising over eleven thousand feet
in a cone of crystal white.

When they dropped out of the mountains, the land
below bare and dry, Destry saw the W Bar G spread before her and began to cry. She wasn't going to make it in
time. She felt it heart deep. Just as she'd told Rylan, she
and WT had said their goodbyes yesterday in the barn.

CARSON PUSHED OPEN the door to his father's hospital
room with his free hand. His left arm was still in a
sling, his shoulder where the doctor had dug out the
bullet was bandaged and hurting like hell.

Getting shot had more than wounded him. He'd lain
in the front seat of the sports car unable to move, praying that someone would come along and help him. He'd
had a lot of time to think as he'd lain there on the verge
of bleeding to death. Fortunately a rancher had come
along and, it being Montana where everyone stopped
to help when they saw a vehicle beside the road, he'd
been saved in more ways than one.

He'd heard about people seeing a white light right
before they died. That they glimpsed their entire lives
passing in front of their eyes. Neither had happened.
In fact he couldn't be sure what had happened to him
was even real. No doubt it was nothing more than loss
of blood that made him think Ginny had come to him.

"Only a few minutes," the nurse warned as she looked
up from the end of WT's bed when Carson stepped into
the room. Putting back his father's chart, she left.

Carson went to his father's bedside. WT Grant had

shrunk down to the pale old man lying there. Carson thought of how much of his life he'd spent being afraid of his father, the rest hating him. All that anger seemed to have bled out of him after being shot.

WT opened his eyes. "Son." He looked surprised to see him.

Carson pulled up a chair and sat down. When his father reached for his hand, he clasped it, startled that there was still a lot of strength there.

When WT spoke, his voice was a whisper. "There's so much I need to say."

"Don't try to talk. Let me." He cleared his throat.

"You don't have to say anything. I know you hate me."

Carson couldn't deny that he had for years. He'd blamed everything on his father. "I want you to know. She loved you. Mother. I used to hear her crying herself to sleep at night. There wasn't anyone else until you moved out of her room, until you stopped being her husband."

WT's old eyes filled. He shook his head. "I don't want to talk about her. The ranch. I had to—"

"I only wanted the ranch for the money, but a part of me wanted to destroy the ranch to get back at you for hurting my mother." His father didn't look surprised. "I'm sorry I'm not the son you wanted."

WT squeezed his hand and tried to say something, but Carson interrupted him, needing to get this out. "I didn't kill Ginny." WT didn't seem to be listening. "Dad, I'm telling you the truth. I know you think I did, but I didn't. I could never have done that to her. I *loved* her." But WT had closed his eyes. His hand suddenly went slack.

Carson saw that he was gone even before he heard the monitors go off. He felt the change in air pressure in the room, heard a nurse rush in. A moment later, the sheriff and his sister burst through the door.

He didn't realize he was crying until his sister knelt down beside him. He leaned into her, her arm around him, and they both cried for their father, the meanest man in Sweetgrass County, as Nettie Benton was fond of saying.

DESTRY FELT NUMB as they gathered in the hall outside WT's room a while later. Margaret, who'd been waiting in the hall for them, put her arm around her.

"I'm sorry," Sheriff Frank Curry said. "But I have to take Carson in. I only let him come say goodbye to his father."

"It's all right," her brother said before Destry could argue. "Get me a good lawyer, will you?"

She nodded as the sheriff led him away.

"Come on, I'll take you home," Margaret said. "Why don't you come stay in one of the bedrooms up at the house with me?"

Destry shook her head. "Rylan is bringing down my horse later. I need to go home."

"I understand."

"Will *you* be all right?" Destry asked. Margaret was dry-eyed when they'd found her waiting in the hall, but it was clear she'd already done her share of crying for WT.

"I'll be fine," the older woman assured her. "Do you mind if I make the arrangements for the funeral? WT and I discussed it earlier."

Destry was relieved and said as much. "I wish I could have gotten here before… The sheriff said he was asking for me?"

"Yes, but you mustn't feel badly about that. He said

the two of you had already said your goodbyes before you rode up into the mountains."

She smiled at that, remembering that she'd thought that same thing in the helicopter.

"He *did* love you," Margaret said. "Against his stubborn will."

Destry nodded, her throat constricting with emotion. "I know how you felt about him. I'm sorry."

"Don't be. I'm thankful I was able to spend all these years with him."

"But you deserved so much more."

Margaret shook her head. "I always knew that the only woman he would ever love was your mother. Waylon and I, well, we understood each other. He cared about me. I was the only woman in his life other than your mother. That was enough."

They drove in silence for the rest of the way home. Destry had never been so happy to see the homestead house.

"We'll talk later," Margaret said as she pulled up in front. "But there's something I have for you." She reached into her purse and drew out a small buckskin bag. "It's a few of your mother's things I was able to save for you. I didn't want to give them to you until—"

"Until he was gone."

"I knew how much it would hurt him if he saw you wearing anything of hers."

Destry nodded as she took the bag but didn't open it. "Thank you." She put it into her jacket pocket, gave Margaret a quick hug and climbed out before she began to cry again.

"Let me know if you need anything. I'll be at the house for now."

"I'll be fine," Destry said. "Rylan will be here soon. He's asked me to marry him."

"About time," Margaret said and smiled. "I knew the two of you would find your way back to each other."

Once in the house, Destry stood under the hot shower letting the heat seep into her. She felt chilled as if in shock. WT was gone. Carson was in jail facing a murder conviction.

She thought of Rylan and hugged herself, praying he would make it safely out of the Crazies. The sheriff had assured her that word was out that Rylan hadn't shot her brother, and WT had canceled the reward.

She knew by now that news of WT's death would be making the grapevine rounds—as well as Carson's arrest. She thought of the check she'd given him to pay his gambling debts. He'd need more money for a good lawyer.

As she came out of the shower and dressed, she remembered the small buckskin pouch Margaret had given her. She dug it out of her jacket pocket and, taking it over to the bed, carefully poured out its contents.

Her breath caught. There were diamond earrings, an agate ring, a turquoise necklace and several silver bracelets. But that wasn't what had stolen her breath and had her pulse pounding.

Lying on the bed was a thin silver chain with a misshapen heart locket—exactly like the one Bethany had showed them yesterday. Exactly like the one Rylan's sister had hidden in her jewelry box. Like it, this one was also tarnished.

CHAPTER TWENTY-FIVE

AFTER THE SHERIFF took Carson to county lockup, he drove to Beartooth to check on Nettie. He'd been worried about her for years. But now with Bob gone, he had to make sure she was going to be all right.

As he pushed open the door to the Beartooth General Store, the bell tinkled. He noticed that it was almost closing time. After the day he'd had, he'd lost track of the time.

"Lynette?" he called.

She came out of the back. He studied her as she moved behind the counter, trying to discern how she was taking Bob leaving her.

Good riddance, he'd thought, but he needed to make sure Lynette wasn't hurting from it.

"What?" she said as he made his way to the counter.

"Just needed a bottle of orange soda," he said, walking past her to the cooler. He could feel her gaze on him. Was he that transparent? Probably.

"I'm fine," she said.

"Who said you weren't?" he asked as he set the soda on the counter and dug out his cash.

"I don't need you checking up on me."

"Is that what you think I'm doing?"

"I know you're here for more than a bottle of orange

soda," she said, hands going to her hips. "If this is about Bob leaving—"

"It isn't. But if you need anything…"

She mugged a face at him but then seemed to have a thought. "There is something you can do for me that you should have already done," she said. "I need you to find out everything you can about Kate LaFond."

He wondered if every man felt this way about his first love. Grayson Brooks apparently had. He'd kept trying to find his Anna in other women.

For years Frank had been forced to hide the way he felt. But no more. He was still crazy about this woman, he thought, as he opened the soda and took a drink. The years hadn't diminished it in the least. Lynette was still that redheaded, feisty woman who'd made his blood run geyser hot.

"Kate LaFond's hiding something," Lynette continued. "I saw her digging in that old garage of hers in the middle of the night. Bob said she's just messing with me because she knows I've been watching her. But she couldn't have known I was watching that night. Nope. It's more than that." She took a breath. "Frank?"

He nodded and smiled.

"Have you even heard a word I've said?"

"Yep. I'll see what I can find out about Kate LaFond. I trust your instincts, Lynette."

She opened her mouth to argue but quickly snapped it shut. "Seriously, you'd do that for me?"

"I'd do anything for you, Lynette. Don't you know that?"

"You're not just doing it to appease me? Or because you think I'm an addled old woman or that you feel sorry for me?"

He grinned. "You can't be sure, can you?"

She started to stomp off mad, but he touched her arm and stopped her.

"Feel sorry for you?" he said. "Why would I do that? I think you are the strongest, most determined and, by far, the most interesting woman I've ever met, and you've only improved with age. Addled? Not hardly. Sure, you're a terrible gossip, but," he said, quickly raising a hand to keep her from flying off the handle, "that's only because you have a keen sense of people and you like to share it and because we're all flawed and you find that interesting, the same way I find watching crows interesting."

She cocked a brow at him. "Is this your idea of sweet talk?"

"Is it working?"

She scoffed at that but gave him a weak smile. "This is because Bob left me, isn't it?"

"Nope, I've been wanting to say this to you for years. I'm not sorry to see Bob go. I've been hoping he would." Bob would have to testify but the Peeping Tom aspect wouldn't come out if Frank could help it. Not to protect the bastard but to protect Lynette. "With him gone, there is nothing stopping you from becoming the woman you've always wanted to be."

"And who exactly do you think that woman is?"

He shrugged. "I have no idea. But I can't wait to get to know her."

She smiled. He hadn't seen that particular smile in a very long time. It held no sarcasm, no sharp edges, no cynicism, and it lit up her eyes with a light that burned bright. For a moment, in the last of the sunlight coming through the front window of the store, she was seventeen again, back when the two of them were crazy about each other. Back before they'd both tried to find happiness with someone else, no matter how fleeting.

DESTRY JUMPED AT the sound of a vehicle pulling up outside, and moments later there was a loud knock at the front door. She was too shocked over what she'd found in her mother's jewelry to move at first.

Peering out finally, she saw Grayson Brooks. She stared down, confused. What was he doing here? If this was about the barn stalls—

She wasn't up to company right now, but Grayson's knock was insistent.

Leaving the jewelry on the bed, she hurried downstairs to open the door. "Grayson? If this is about the barn stalls—"

"I heard about your father and also about your brother being arrested," he said. "I just stopped by to tell you how sorry I am."

"Thank you. I appreciate that." She was distracted, her mind still racing after seeing the silver locket. It had to be just a coincidence, and yet she knew better. She thought about what Rylan had said about the women the man had given the lockets to all resembling each other—and she was the spitting image of her mother, wasn't she?

"Do you mind if I come in for a few minutes?" Grayson asked, his Western hat in his hand. "I don't want to bother you at a time like this."

She did mind. But Montana ranching hospitality was legendary. Most households always had a pot of coffee on. "No, of course not, come in. I could put on some coffee…" She was glad when he shook his head.

"I just wanted to apologize. I feel responsible."

"Responsible?" What was he talking about?

"The sheriff didn't tell you?"

"We only spoke for a minute at the hospital."

Grayson looked around the room nervously. "My timing leaves something to be desired." His gaze settled on Destry and he smiled. "Has anyone told you that you look just like your mother?"

"Yes, as a matter of fact." He was making her uncomfortable the way he was staring at her. Why would he feel responsible? Certainly not for WT's death, but for Carson being arrested?

"Your mother and I... Well, I always admired her. Used to see her in church all the time. What a beautiful woman she was. She was a bit older than me, but didn't look it. I was seventeen when she died." He moved farther into the room, smiling as he looked around. "You haven't changed a thing in this room."

She stared at his back, realizing two things simultaneously. He'd known her mother and had been in this house.

"She was so young and innocent-looking," Grayson said, turning to face her again. "Just like you are now."

Destry fought to make sense of what he was saying. She couldn't help the shudder that moved through her. Or the fear.

"Anna and I married young. She was seventeen. She'd just had another miscarriage and had gone up to Great Falls to spend some time with her folks, when I happened to run into your mother at the post office. She reminded me of Anna. I used to watch her in church. But I guess I already told you that."

Destry tried to take a breath, her heart a drum in

her chest. He'd watched her mother? Is that what he was saying? Or was he trying to tell her— Her stomach dropped.

It hadn't been Hitch. Just like he'd argued. There'd been someone else sneaking around her place.

"Everyone loved your mother. We were all devastated when she died and in such a freak accident," Grayson said as he moved around the room.

"Horseback riding can be dangerous," Destry said, edging toward the back door and the loaded shotgun. He was making her nervous. She wished he would just leave. She didn't want to use the shotgun. She prayed he wouldn't make her.

She was almost to the shotgun when he said, "But I didn't come out here to talk about your mother. I have something for you." She turned to see he was holding up a silver locket. "I gave one to your mother years ago. I bought this one for you."

SINCE HE WAS already in town, Frank walked down to the small, hole-in-the-wall post office to pick up his mail after he left Lynette. There'd been talk of closing these small post offices lately, but townsfolk like those in Beartooth had fought it.

"The post office is what makes us a town," Lynette had argued. "It's where everyone comes to get more than their mail. They stop and visit. You take it away and you take away the heart of these small communities."

Frank could hear faint music playing in the back of the post office and the voices of several locals visiting with the postmistress, asking her about her new grandbaby.

Lynette was right, of course. It would be a real shame if post offices like this were to close. But that didn't mean she was going to be able to save this one or the others on the chopping block. It would come down to money, he thought, with no small regret.

He dug out the stack of mail, realizing that he hadn't been in for a few days. As he was sorting through the bills and junk mail, he saw that one of the letters had been returned because it needed more postage, but it had been put in the wrong box by mistake.

As he started to take it to the window to give it to the postmistress, he realized there was something familiar about the handwriting. For a moment, he couldn't put his finger on it. When he did, he stumbled to a stop, heart racing.

The handwriting. It was the same hurried scrawl as that of the notes Ginny West had received before she'd been murdered.

DESTRY'S BLOOD TURNED to ice. She was only inches from the shotgun. *"You and my mother?"* She thought of the chain and locket lying on the bed upstairs. "Are you telling me you had an affair with my mother?"

Grayson quickly shook his head. "It wasn't like that. I'm not sure she ever even wore the locket. At least never when I saw her. But she was nice enough to take it and thank me. I could tell she thought I was too young for her and she was in love with someone else."

Destry felt a moment of relief. Then Grayson took a step toward her, holding out the silver locket. "I don't want that," she said.

He frowned and stopped. "But I bought it for you. I thought… Well, it doesn't matter what I thought. Everything has changed. I'm going to lose my Anna soon." Sadness filled his eyes. "Once that happens, I won't have anything left." He looked at the silver chain, the locket dangling from his thick fingers. "I won't need this or want it."

"You're the one who's been watching me from the woods," Destry said, backing up until she could feel the cold steel of the shotgun.

Grayson nodded. "I wanted to know everything about you before I gave you this."

A jolt of fear shot like a lightning bolt through her.

"You reminded me so much of your mother. But like your mother, you're in love with someone else, aren't you? I'd hoped you might like me."

She snatched up the shotgun and pointed both barrels at him.

He took a step back. "Please, I don't mean to scare you. I just had to—" He raised a hand and took another step back. "That's not necessary."

She moved toward the phone. "We'll see what the sheriff has to say about that."

"The sheriff already knows," Grayson said. "I told him everything. Except for how I felt about you. I'm sorry. I didn't mean to upset you." He moved toward the door.

"You're not going anywhere until the sheriff—"

Grayson stopped and smiled. "You won't shoot me. You could have the other night and you didn't. Don't worry, I won't bother you again."

She was tapping in 911 when she heard another vehicle approaching. Grayson turned and left quickly, leaving the front door open. He was right. She couldn't very well force him to stay since they both knew she wasn't going to shoot him.

Destry put the phone back and hurried to the door, the shotgun in hand, as a vehicle she didn't recognize pulled into the drive. As Grayson sped away, Linda Armstrong stepped out of the other vehicle.

Destry never thought she'd be glad to see the pastor's wife. Her hands were shaking as she leaned the shotgun against the wall by the front door and said, "I can't tell you how glad I am to see *you*."

Linda frowned. "Was there a problem?" she asked, looking after Grayson's pickup as he sped away.

"Not now," Destry said with a shake of her head.

"I came out to give you my condolences," Linda said. She'd brought a box of candy from the general store. Destry recognized the brand Nettie carried. There appeared to be a card taped to the top of the box.

Destry was just thankful for the company right now. She still felt shaken by what Grayson had told her. "Come in. I'll put on a pot of coffee. Please make yourself at home. I just need to make a quick call."

She hurried upstairs and called the sheriff's department. The sheriff was on a call, so she left a message for him to return her call as soon as possible.

"Was that Grayson Brooks who just left here in such a hurry?" Linda asked as Destry came back downstairs.

"He dropped by to give his condolences," Destry said as she went into the kitchen to make coffee. No way was she telling Linda what Grayson had said, since the pastor's wife was good friends with Grayson's wife, Anna.

"You have some wonderful artwork," Linda called from the living room. "I was just admiring it."

Destry had the coffee going before Linda finally appeared in the kitchen doorway. "It should be just a minute. Have a seat," she said as she dug out some cookies Margaret had baked a few days earlier.

"Doesn't it get lonely out here by yourself?" Linda asked as Destry put a plate of cookies and two cups on the table. "It's more remote than the parsonage. At least I can walk down to the store or the café."

"I like peace and quiet," Destry said as she noticed the card the pastor's wife had brought. It was addressed as if she'd planned to mail it and had changed her mind.

"I miss the ocean," Linda said and took a bite of cookie. She'd never made her feelings about Montana a secret, which hadn't exactly enamored the locals over the years. Fortunately, everyone liked Pastor Tom.

Destry felt for her, being forced to live somewhere she didn't like. Wasn't that what WT had been trying to do with Carson?

"It gets dark here so early in the day, especially in the winter." Linda shivered, even though it was quite warm in the house.

Destry didn't know what to say. Fortunately, she heard the coffeepot shut off and hurried to get them each a cup. When she turned back, Linda was staring at her. Even when Destry poured the woman her coffee, she didn't stop staring.

Destry felt uneasy, still spooked from Grayson's visit. "Do you like sugar or cream in your coffee, Mrs. Armstrong? I'm sorry, I should have asked."

"Please call me Linda. Mrs. Armstrong makes me sound so old," she said. "Black is fine." She picked up her coffee cup, but was watching Destry over the rim as she took a sip and put it down. "I remember the first time I really noticed you. You were wearing a yellow dress. Tom commented on how lovely you looked in it. Every time you wear it, Tom always says how pretty you look in it."

Destry smiled uncomfortably. "He says that to everyone in church."

"Does he? I guess I haven't noticed."

She felt goose bumps skitter across her flesh at the look Linda was giving her.

"I saw you and Tom with your heads together after church," the woman said. "Your discussion looked rather intense."

Like Linda's discussion with Grayson, Destry thought with a sudden chill. Did Linda know about the lockets? About Grayson's relationship, not only with Bethany, but with Ginny?

"Mrs. Armstrong, I have no interest in your husband," Destry said, getting to her feet under the pretense of refilling both their cups. Neither of them had hardly touched their coffee.

She topped off Linda's cup and her own, then returned the pot but didn't sit back down. "The few times we've even talked, Tom was merely offering his help if I needed any," she said, leaning against the kitchen counter.

"That's the way it always begins, isn't it with men? Tom used to offer your mother help and that West girl when she came to him crying because she was carrying his baby—"

"Ginny?" Destry didn't realize she'd let the word out until she saw Linda's expression.

"Yes, Ginny. Sunday you asked my husband about the notes, didn't you? You said a friend of yours had gotten one. You made that up."

"No, I—"

"Don't lie to me," Linda snapped.

The card Linda had brought her suddenly caught her eye again. It lay on top of the box of chocolates on the table. Even from where she stood, she could see the familiar scrawl of the angry handwriting—

With a start, Destry knew where she'd seen it before. Linda had written the threatening notes to Ginny before she was murdered, and now Destry knew why.

SHERIFF FRANK CURRY stepped into the church and removed his hat as he headed for the office. The door stood open. "Where is your wife?" he asked the moment he saw the pastor behind his desk.

"Linda? She'd running some errands."

"I need to ask you if you've seen this before." He took the bagged copies of the notes Ginny had received and laid them on the desk.

Tom Armstrong's reaction was immediate.

"That's your wife's handwriting, isn't it?"

"Yes." He looked sick. "She promised me she would stop. I'm sorry. Who was it this time?"

"Ginny West."

All the color drained from the pastor's face.

"Ginny West confided in you, didn't she? Did you tell your wife?"

"No, of course not," he cried. "She overheard and misunderstood."

"She thought Ginny was pregnant with *your* baby?"

Tom nodded. "Yes, but once I explained…"

"You're sure she believed you?"

The pastor looked away, and Frank sighed as he

picked up the evidence from the pastor's desk. "I need to talk to your wife."

"It's not her fault. It's mine. I broke our vows years ago, and she has never been able to forgive me. She gets insanely jealous sometimes if she even sees me talking to a woman."

Frank felt his heart drop. "Who is your wife jealous of now?"

Tom frowned, then his eyes widened in alarm. *"Who?"*

"She's been talking about Destry Grant after seeing us together at church Sunday. That was one of the stops she was going to make today. But she wouldn't hurt Destry." Tom wrung his hands, fear making him sweat. "No, she wouldn't hurt Destry."

"What aren't you telling me?" Frank demanded.

"The guilt must have been killing her. I've seen it eating away at her, but I didn't understand what was causing it until I found the jacket. Don't you see? She's been doing penance all these years. Why else would she have kept Ginny's letterman jacket other than to remind her of what she did?"

"What *she* did?" That stopped Frank in his tracks. "*You* put the letterman jacket in the church clothing bin?" He let out a curse. "You're afraid she'll do it again."

THE PHONE RANG, making Destry jump. She snatched up the receiver from the kitchen wall. "Hello." Her brain was racing. Linda had written the notes. Linda thought the baby Ginny had been carrying was Tom's. And now Ginny's letterman jacket had been found in an old clothing bin at the church.

"Destry, it's Sheriff Curry. Don't say anything. But if Linda Armstrong is there—"

"Yes."

"She is?"

"That's right," Destry said, turning her back to Linda.

"Tom and I are on our way. Are you going to be all right until we get there?"

"I'll certainly try." She hung up the phone, pulse pounding in her ears. She glanced toward the back door, belatedly remembering that she'd left the shotgun by the front door. When she turned back to the kitchen, she saw that Linda had gotten up from the table.

"Who was that?" Linda asked.

"Just a friend of mine."

"Liar. That was Tom, wasn't it?"

"No, it wasn't Tom."

Linda let out a laugh as sharp as barbed wire. "What is it about Tom? Women just can't seem to resist him. I heard Ginny crying and telling my husband that she didn't know what she was going to do if he didn't leave his wife and marry her. I thought Ginny was determined to have him and that's why she got herself pregnant. When she caught me putting another warning note on her car, she threatened to tell Tom. I promised to stop, but I knew I couldn't trust her. I thought she was lying about the baby not being Tom's."

Destry took a step back. "Did Tom tell you Ginny was carrying his baby?"

"Of course not, I knew he would lie, too, just like he always has," Linda said, moving slowly toward her. "Ironic, isn't it?" Her laugh died on her lips. "Grayson thought the baby was *his*."

In a flash, Destry recalled Sunday and the intense conversation Linda had been having with the contractor. "Grayson confided in you."

"His wife is my best friend," Linda said indignantly. "He confessed everything, even how he felt about your mother—and now you."

Linda took another step toward her. Destry noticed that the woman had one hand behind her back. Destry's gaze shifted to the kitchen counter behind the pastor's wife. With heart-stopping fear, she saw that one of the knives was missing from the wooden block where she kept them.

Her pulse began to pound as she backed out of the kitchen. "Is Grayson the one who hurt Ginny?" Destry asked. She could hear the sound of a siren in the distance. The sheriff would be here soon. Grayson and his silly lockets, his romantic gestures. He hadn't killed Ginny. Who was she kidding?

Linda's eyes glittered with hatred. "Ginny cried and swore on her Bible that Tom wasn't the baby's father. I didn't know it was Grayson fooling around with her. Even when she swore it wasn't Tom…" Her voice died off into a low moan. "I didn't mean to kill her. I just wanted to talk to her, to tell her she wasn't having Tom. I knew about that sinful place in the old theater. I wasn't surprised to find her there after your brother left, her smelling of sex." She made a disgusted face. "She grabbed up a piece of old pipe that was lying on the floor and threatened me. I… I tried to take it away from her." Linda touched the underside of her left wrist.

Destry saw the thin, white line of a scar and remembered what Bessie had said about Linda's arm bleeding.

Not, though, from a fall later beside the road, but at the old theater during a struggle with Ginny.

"Ginny was telling the truth," Destry said. "It wasn't Tom's baby. It was Carson's. That's who she'd been with just moments before you found her in the theater. You killed her for nothing. Tom had never been involved with her and Grayson had broken it off."

Linda didn't seem to hear her. "I panicked. At first I thought she was dead. I knew I couldn't leave her there. It would lead the sheriff to Grayson. I had to protect him for Anna's sake. Ginny's letterman jacket was lying there. I wrapped her in it and carried her out the back way to my SUV. She wasn't all that heavy. Just a child." Her voice caught. "Then I realized she was still alive."

A chill snaked up Destry's spine. She didn't want to hear any more of this, but she didn't dare stop her from talking. The sheriff and Tom would be here any moment.

"I realized what I had to do. I would take her to the hospital," Linda was saying, a dazed look in her eyes. "I never planned to kill her. I hadn't gone far when she woke up. I'd put her in the passenger seat so I could keep an eye on her. I told her not to be afraid, I was taking her to the hospital. But when she looked out the window, she realized I wasn't on the right road. I hadn't realized I'd taken a wrong turn until that moment. She started screaming, thinking I was taking her out in the woods to kill her. She..." Her voice broke with emotion.

"It was an accident," Destry said.

"She opened the door, and before I could stop her, she threw herself out." Linda stopped moving, stopped talking. When she spoke again, her voice was low, controlled. "I saw it in the side mirror. I was shocked. I started to stop, but she wasn't moving. She was just lying there. I panicked."

"But you went back," Destry said. "You went back with Bessie."

Linda nodded. "Yes."

Destry saw her worst horror in the woman's eyes. "Ginny wasn't dead."

"She would have told the sheriff. No one would believe me that it had been an accident. I had no choice. I put my hand over her mouth and nose as I pretended to give her CPR."

Destry couldn't help the gasp that escaped her lips.

Linda's gaze seemed to clear. "I know that was Tom on the phone a few minutes ago. He found Ginny's letterman jacket where I'd hidden it. I couldn't get rid of it. I needed to keep it where I could look at it. I needed to beg for forgiveness every day for what I did."

"Tom knew?" Destry asked, shocked.

"Tom?" Linda shook her head with a smirk. "I wanted to bare my soul to him, but I knew he wouldn't keep my secret. I knew I couldn't trust him. And I was right. When I found the jacket missing, I knew what he would do with it. He would betray me and now he has."

She took another step, and as she did, she brought her hand out from behind her back. The blade of the knife flashed in the light coming through the kitchen window. "I'm already going to spend the rest of my life in prison, so *I* have nothing to lose. I won't let you have Tom. Or Grayson."

Destry broke then and ran to the shotgun, grabbed it up and swung around to point it at the woman's heart. "Put down the knife. I don't want to shoot you."

"Grayson told me you fired a shotgun at him the last

time he was out here. He said he'd seen it by the back door when he'd looked in your window. He is enchanted by you. That's why he came out here, wasn't it? To tell you. I saw the silver locket he left on the shelf by your front door."

Destry hadn't realized Grayson had dropped it there before he left. "I have no interest in Grayson or Tom."

Linda took another step toward her. "He'll still want you, though. He can't help himself. Your type are like nectar to bees for men like Tom and Grayson."

"Please don't make me pull this trigger," Destry said, remembering that she'd replaced the buckshot with heavy load steel. At this distance, even buckshot would kill the woman.

Linda took another step. "Tom will blame himself for your death, just as I'm sure he blames himself for Ginny's. Let him live with that guilt. He deserves it. Him and his holier-than-thou attitude. I saw the sheriff's car down at the church. I knew he'd given him Ginny's jacket. Which meant it was just a matter of time before my blood was found on it. My husband has committed the ultimate betrayal, don't you see?"

Destry knew she had no choice. As Linda took another step toward her, she pulled one trigger and flinched. The gun made only a dull click.

Linda smiled.

Destry pulled the second trigger, but even before she heard the empty click, she knew. While she had been making coffee, Linda had emptied the shotgun.

AFTER RYLAN PUT Destry's horse in the barn and hung up her tack, he rode toward her house, anxious to get to the hospital. He feared he would be too late. He just hoped Destry hadn't been too late.

But as he rode past her place, he heard a siren in the distance. The sound seemed to grow as if headed this way. A bad feeling settled in his belly. He'd seen Russell when he returned Destry's horse. Russell had told him that WT had died and Margaret had taken Destry home. As he neared her old homestead house now, he saw that the fence was still down from the other day when he'd caught Hitch McCray sneaking around her house. Was it possible Hitch was out of jail already?

Thinking he was probably on a fool's errand, he rode through the open gate and galloped toward Destry's house. He couldn't shake the feeling that she was alone and in trouble.

He had just crossed the creek, when he heard the scream. He swung down from his horse, dropping the reins as he raced across the grass to her back door.

It wasn't until he was almost there that he heard a loud sermonizing female voice. The loud chant of words sent his pulse racing.

"I will rescue you from a forbidden woman, from a stranger with her flattering talk, who abandons the companion of her youth and forgets the covenant of her God; for her house sinks down to death and her ways to the land of the departed spirits."

By then he'd reached the back door, and what he saw through the window made his heart drop. Linda Armstrong had a knife in her hand and Destry backed into a corner.

Destry had the shotgun in her hands, but the barrel wasn't pointed at Linda. He didn't have time to make sense of that when the blade of Linda's knife caught the light as she lunged forward, righteous fury blazing on her lips. Destry swung the shotgun.

The gun stock grazed the pastor's wife's head, but she didn't go down. She stumbled back, readying herself to charge again. As she swung the knife, the blade missed Destry's shoulder by a hairbreadth.

It happened in the instant Rylan was reaching for the doorknob. He grabbed it, expecting to find the door locked. He should have known better. It was still daylight. Destry was determined not to spend her life locked in.

The door swung open with him right behind it. Linda heard him and turned, brandishing the knife. He held up both hands. "I don't know what's going on, but you don't want to use that," he said to her.

As Linda charged him, her scream pierced the air.

He dodged to the side as she thrust the knife at him. She turned back, quicker than he'd expected, though. He saw the blade, felt it burn as it cut through his shirt and into his arm.

Linda came at him again, the knife blade gleaming in her hand, blind fury blazing in her eyes. Like a startled grizzly, she charged him.

Linda was almost on him.

He tried to step away, but Linda was too close.

A loud crack filled the air as the stock of the shotgun connected with Linda's head. She stood for a moment looking stunned, the knife still gripped in her fist. Then her eyes rolled back in her head, and she crumpled to the floor at his feet.

Rylan kicked the knife away and, stepping past her, dragged Destry into his arms. They both stared down at Linda unconscious on the floor as the sound of a siren filled the air.

EPILOGUE

It RAINED THE day of WT Grant's funeral, but quickly turned to snow before the service was over. To Destry's astonishment, the whole county turned out to pay their respects.

Carson had been released from jail and cleared of all charges after Linda Armstrong finally confessed to the murder of Ginny West eleven years ago and the attempted murder of Destry Grant and Rylan West. The crime lab found Linda's blood on Ginny's letterman jacket, just as she'd feared.

Carson stood next to Destry at the gravesite as Russell Murdock, her father's long-time ranch foreman, said a few words over the coffin before it was lowered into the ground. Russell had been surprised when Destry and Margaret had asked him.

"You knew WT as well as anyone," Margaret had said. "We all know how he felt about religion. He would have wanted you to say something over his grave."

"I'm not sure I'm the right person to do this," he'd said.

"You might be one of the few people around who can think of something good to say about him," Destry had told him.

Russell had chuckled at that. "In that case, I'd be honored."

The service broke up with everyone invited back to the big house. They came with casseroles and condolences. Margaret played hostess from the kitchen while Destry moved through the throng of people, thanking them for coming. There was a crowd because few of them had ever seen the inside of WT's folly.

Carson disappeared shortly after they arrived at the house. At one point, Destry saw him outside, standing at the edge of the pool, looking off toward the Yellowstone River as if surveying his kingdom—much like WT used to do when he was alive.

"How are you holding up?" Rylan asked, as the crowd began to thin.

"Okay," she said. "I appreciate your family coming."

"I don't know what happened between WT and my father years ago, but at one time they'd been friends. I know that my mother and father think the world of you." He grinned. "And my brothers are jealous as all get out."

She couldn't help but smile.

"Can I see you later?"

"You know where I live."

"Still going to stay at the homestead until our wedding?"

"Until Carson makes me move."

Rylan's jaw tightened, and she regretted her words. Rylan and Carson had given each other wide berths all day.

Russell was one of the last to leave. Now he seemed downright shy as he approached Destry, hat in hand. He kneaded the brim of his hat and studied his boots.

"I can't tell you how sorry I am about everything," he said, not for the first time.

"I'm just glad Ginny's killer has been caught."

"And that it wasn't your brother," he said.

"I saw you talking to the sheriff. Did he mention what will happen to Linda?"

"Frank said the state will require a mental evaluation to see if she's competent to stand trial." He shrugged. "Either way, she'll be locked up for a long time."

"I wonder how Tom is doing."

"I'm sure he blames himself."

She nodded. "Linda was counting on that. It's too bad. He isn't leaving, is he?"

"Everyone is trying to convince him to stay. I think he will."

"Destry, there's something I need to tell you." Russell looked down at his boots for a moment, before he met her gaze again. "I know about the paternity test. Your brother told me, but I knew already. WT wasn't your birth father. I am. I would have told you sooner—"

"But you knew how WT would take it."

He nodded and studied her for a moment. "You knew?"

"I found a photograph of you and my mother." She couldn't hide her relief as she looked at the big man and smiled.

"It wasn't an affair. Your mother was having her issues with WT. We just happened to be in the same place, so to speak. It was only once. We both regretted it. Your mother loved WT." He smiled shyly. "I was hoping that maybe you and I could get to know each other better. That is, if—"

"I'd like that and I suspect my mother would have liked it, too."

He smiled then. "I know she would have."

CARSON STOOD AT the edge of his father's swimming pool and looked out across the W Bar G. What was it about land that drew some people as if they felt a need to take root like a tree and grow there? He'd never understood it, still didn't.

He let his thoughts drift on the breeze. They took him back to something that had been nagging at him. At his father's funeral a few weeks ago, he'd seen a woman who'd looked familiar, but he hadn't been able to place her. He couldn't shake it because he felt that remembering her was somehow important.

Hearing a door open behind him, he turned, figuring it would be Destry. The two of them hadn't said much to each other since he'd gotten out of jail. He'd never forget that she was the only one who'd believed him innocent. But even she had begun to doubt him. Not that he could blame her. He'd certainly given her reason. He thought about what she'd done, trying to help him, and felt so much love for her that it nearly dropped him to his knees.

"WT's lawyer is here. It's about his will," she said, joining him at the edge of the pool.

"Remember when we were kids and I taught you to swim?" he asked. "I think about those days a lot." He took a breath and let it out. "Here. It's the check you gave me. I don't need it now. The casino wrote me off as a bad debt when they realized I was probably going to prison. I suspect Cherry had something to do with it."

Destry took the check and folded it before putting it into her pocket, then she turned, and he followed her back into the house. "Once they hear that you were cleared—"

"I'll make sure they get paid, don't worry."

The lawyer was waiting for them in WT's den. "If you'd both like to take a seat."

"I think I'll stand," Carson said. "Can I offer you a drink?" he asked the lawyer, who shook his head. "Well, if you don't mind, I think I'll have one. Destry?" She, too, shook her head as she sat down, her hands clasped in her lap.

He poured himself a drink, the lawyer waiting patiently. Carson watched his sister's face as WT's will was read. He smiled when he saw her astonished expression and heard her gasp. Her gaze flew to him.

"It's pretty cut-and-dried," the lawyer was saying as he handed Destry the papers to sign. "Your father made provisions for Margaret and for Carson but left the ranch to you as sole owner," he said to Destry.

"Carson, was this your doing?" she asked him.

He had to laugh. "In a roundabout way. I'd say it was more my bad behavior and the fact that, ultimately, he knew you were the one who loved this place and would see that his legacy lived on."

"You knew he'd changed his will?"

"I'd hoped he did the right thing, but I couldn't be sure. I think he was trying to tell me at the end, but I didn't let him."

"He can't have left everything to me," she said. "It's not right." Destry ignored the lawyer to go to her brother. "I can't agree to this."

"He only left you the ranch," Carson said. "As his attorney said, WT made a provision for me. He knew you would never live in this house, so he left it to me. Of course he knew me well enough that unless I live in the house and get a paying job, it reverts to charity if Margaret doesn't want it."

"He was trying to control you right till the end."

"Or maybe he just didn't want Margaret to live here

alone," Carson said. "I can walk away and make a life for myself. Maybe I will. I don't know yet. Now that Ginny can finally rest in peace…"

"Carson—"

"I love you, little sis." He pulled her to him and gave her an awkward hug. He'd be glad when his shoulder healed, but he knew some wounds never would. "Dad did the right thing in the end. Be happy. *I'm* happy for you. I really wouldn't have wanted it any other way."

As he started to leave the room, he remembered the woman he'd seen at the cemetery. "Hey, I saw a woman at the funeral." He described her to his sister. "You know who she is?"

Destry smiled as if she thought he was going to be all right if he was already interested in some woman he'd seen at the funeral. "Sounds like Kate LaFond. She recently bought the Branding Iron Café in Beartooth."

"Kate LaFond?" He nodded, thinking how strange it was because he knew that that hadn't been her name when he'd crossed paths with her years back.

RYLAN WEST AND DESTRY Grant's engagement party was held just before Christmas at the community center. There was a country band and lots of food and dancing.

Everyone was there, including friends and family. Destry's best friend, Lisa Anne Clausen, was finally back from Wyoming where she'd been taking care of her young nieces and nephews while her sister recovered from a car accident.

"I am so glad you're here," Destry said, hugging her. "I can't tell you how much I've missed you."

"Nothing ever happens around here and then I leave and all hell breaks loose," Lisa Anne complained. "It will give those women on the grapevine enough fodder to last till spring." Her gaze went to Carson, who was standing over by the door. "I'm going to have to go dance with your brother. He looks so alone over there."

Lisa Anne had always had a crush on Carson, dreaming that he'd come back one day, sweep her off her feet and they'd get married and have a bunch of kids who'd grow up with Destry's bunch of kids here in the shadow of the Crazies.

Destry had once dreamed the same thing, all of them getting together for Sunday barbecues, their children playing together in the creek just as they had as kids.

She shoved away the thought since it wasn't going to happen. Carson had made it perfectly clear this life wasn't for him. After WT's affairs were all wrapped up, she figured he'd pull up stakes and be gone any day.

But he was still here, she thought, as she watched Lisa Anne go over to him and strike up a conversation. A few moments later, she was dragging him out onto the dance floor as the band broke into a slow country song.

Bethany and Clete Reynolds joined them. Destry watched, glad to see they seemed to be working out their problems. And there was Hitch McCray doing his best to get one of the Hamilton girls to dance with him. His mother had gotten him out of jail and paid his fines. Some things never changed.

Destry's gaze settled on an older couple on the dance floor, and she had to smile as the sheriff twirled Nettie Benton around, both of them laughing.

Russell smiled at her from across the room. It was good to talk to him, to learn about her mother from a man who had loved Lila and loved talking about her.

"I've been looking all over for you," Rylan said, coming up behind her. He nuzzled her neck as he looped his arms around her. "I think they're playing our song," he said, turning her to face him.

She looked into his eyes and felt that wonderful tug at her heartstrings. She loved this man, would always love him and couldn't wait to become his wife. There was nothing standing between them, and, as problems arose, which they were bound to, they would face them together. Their love for each other was the lasting kind.

She smiled at her future husband. "Wait a minute. We have a song?"

He laughed and, taking her hand, led her out on the dance floor. "We do now."

* * * * *

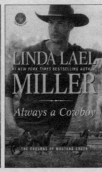

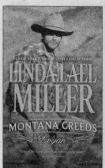
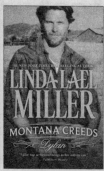
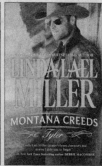

**Trouble comes to town for the
Cahill Siblings of Gilt Edge, Montana,
in this captivating new series from
New York Times bestselling author**

B.J. DANIELS

In the nine years since Trask Beaumont left Gilt Edge, Lillian Cahill has convinced herself she is over him. But when the rugged cowboy suddenly walks into her bar, there's a pang in her heart that argues the attraction never faded. And that's dangerous, because Trask has returned on a mission to clear his name—and win Lillie back.

When a body is recovered from a burning house, everyone suspects Trask…especially Lillie's brother Hawk, the town marshal. Will Lillie give Trask a second chance, even if it leaves her torn between her family and the man she never stopped loving?

Available February 28!

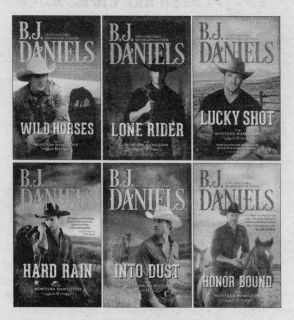

REQUEST YOUR FREE BOOKS!

2 FREE NOVELS
FROM THE ROMANCE COLLECTION,
PLUS 2 FREE GIFTS!

YES! Please send me 2 FREE novels from the Romance Collection and my 2 FREE gifts (gifts are worth about $10). After receiving them, if I don't wish to receive any more books, I can return the shipping statement marked "cancel." If I don't cancel, I will receive 4 brand-new novels every month and be billed just $6.49 per book in the U.S. or $6.99 per book in Canada. That's a savings of at least 18% off the cover price. It's quite a bargain! Shipping and handling is just 50¢ per book in the U.S. and 75¢ per book in Canada.* I understand that accepting the 2 free books and gifts places me under no obligation to buy anything. I can always return a shipment and cancel at any time. Even if I never buy another book, the two free books and gifts are mine to keep forever.

194/394 MDN GH4D

Name	(PLEASE PRINT)
Address	Apt. #
City	State/Prov.	Zip/Postal Code

Signature (if under 18, a parent or guardian must sign)

Mail to the **Reader Service:**
IN U.S.A.: P.O. Box 1867, Buffalo, NY 14240-1867
IN CANADA: P.O. Box 609, Fort Erie, Ontario L2A 5X3

Want to try 2 free books from another line?
Call 1-800-873-8635 or visit www.ReaderService.com.

*Terms and prices subject to change without notice. Prices do not include applicable taxes. Sales tax applicable in N.Y. Canadian residents will be charged applicable taxes. Offer not valid in Quebec. This offer is limited to one order per household. Not valid for current subscribers to the Romance Collection or the Romance/Suspense Collection. All orders subject to credit approval. Credit or debit balances in a customer's account(s) may be offset by any other outstanding balance owed by or to the customer. Please allow 4 to 6 weeks for delivery. Offer available while quantities last.

Your Privacy—The Reader Service is committed to protecting your privacy. Our Privacy Policy is available online at www.ReaderService.com or upon request from the Reader Service.

We make a portion of our mailing list available to reputable third parties that offer products we believe may interest you. If you prefer that we not exchange your name with third parties, or if you wish to clarify or modify your communication preferences, please visit us at www.ReaderService.com/consumerschoice or write to us at Reader Service Preference Service, P.O. Box 9062, Buffalo, NY 14240-9062. Include your complete name and address.

Turn your love of reading into
rewards you'll love with
Harlequin My Rewards

**Join for FREE today at
www.HarlequinMyRewards.com**

Earn **FREE BOOKS** of your choice.

Experience **EXCLUSIVE OFFERS** and contests.

Enjoy **BOOK RECOMMENDATIONS**
selected just for you.

PLUS! Sign up now
and get **500** points
right away!

Earn
FREE
REWARDS
Join
Today!
HarlequinMyRewards.com

MYR16R